IN A MAGNIFICENT SAGA THAT CAN BE
CALLED AN AUSTRALIAN *GONE WITH THE WIND*,
A GIFTED STORYTELLER WRITES POWERFULLY
AND MOVINGLY OF AN INDOMITABLE WOMAN,
AN UNFORGETTABLE LAND, AND THE
FORCES THAT BIND THEM TOGETHER.

South Lies
The Valley

VERONICA GEOGHEGAN
SWEENEY

author of The Emancipist

South Lies
The Valley

BANTAM BOOKS
NEW YORK · TORONTO · LONDON · SYDNEY · AUCKLAND

SOUTH LIES THE VALLEY

A Bantam Book / August 1990

Library of Congress Cataloging-in-Publication Data

Sweeney, Veronica Geoghegan.
    South lies the valley / Veronica Geoghegan Sweeney.
        p.   cm.
    ISBN 0-553-34917-1
    I. Title.
PR9619.3.S838S6   1990
823—dc20   89-18442
                                                  CIP

Published simultaneously in the United States and Canada

PRINTED IN THE UNITED STATES OF AMERICA

RRH   0 9 8 7 6 5 4 3 2 1

TO MY HUSBAND

There was a man sent from God,
Whose name was John

Acknowledgments

Although this book is a work of fiction and the characters within it (bar some renowned Fenians who are only mentioned) are not based on any persons, the places mentioned *do* exist, but as a background for the action only.

I found John Griffith's book, *A History of Kangaroo Valley* of great value, and would also like to thank the people of Kangaroo Valley for their help in my research of the area.

My thanks to Jill Hickson and Carol Serventy, my literary agents, and to all those at Transworld Publishers who made this novel such a joy to write.

Special thanks must go to Susan Bray Bollinger, and to Judith Curr for her sensitive editorial help, her faith and her encouragement.

One

"Why am I in Ireland? I'll tell you. When the war between the States ended, last year, most of us men was caught unprepared. Hell, peace is fine for most folks, but you try spending four years shooting Confederates an' waiting to be shot in your turn and it makes you a mite *unsettled*. Hard to take to civilian life after all that. Some buddies of mine volunteered to go West. Make war on the injuns where they were making war on Johnny Reb a few months earlier. That ain't my style. My daddy had said to me, 'Emmet,'—I was named after Robert Emmet, your great Irish leader—'Emmet,' he says on his deathbed, 'don't you ever forget that you was conceived in County Kerry, and it's only by the Grace of God you was born in Massachusetts.'"

He shifted a little and swore under his breath as another drop of rainwater struck him on the back of the head and rolled down into the collar of his shirt. He glanced at the man beside him.

Brendan Kelehan, a dark hat pulled low over his hair, did not seem to be aware of the discomfort of this vigil. Maybe because he was Irish, and had been a farmer before he was a lawyer, and used to Ireland's weather and primitive conditions. You couldn't get much more primitive than this stable loft in the narrow dinginess of this lane off Weaver's Square, Dublin. Perhaps they should not be talking, but the curve in the cobbled alleyway gave a clear view of the mist-hung mouth of the street, and the gaslight on the corner would show any figure, even a dog, that moved in the fog towards them. And they had been here for more than three hours.

Besides, better to keep the younger man talking. Keep his mind busy. Kelehan did not seem nervous, was surprisingly calm for a man setting off on a perilous and shady undertaking such as this. But Emmet Ginnane had seen men calmer and tougher than Kelehan break under fire before now, and he would watch the Irishman carefully.

"You sure you're a crack shot with that revolver?"

The deep, lazy voice with its well-educated, almost English tones, murmured, "I never said that. Pat McNally told you that. Success with firearms and success with women share that in common, don't you think? They're always best left for others to boast about on one's behalf."

Emmet thought about this, then, "I remember McNally saying you were an expert with a handgun and with a rifle. He and a few of the others—Daniel Hutton, I think it was, and Devoy himself, once—told me about that time you caught two burglars in your house—they'd killed one of your servants—struck him on the skull too hard, and . . ."

"That was a long time ago." For the first time in those long hours there was an edge to the voice, and Emmet Ginnane welcomed it. He was still unsure whether he liked this confident Irishman with the well-tailored clothes and the silver-grey hair. That was the reason for the hat, to cover the telltale colour of the man's hair, at odds with the face, for he was only about thirty years old. The straight silver hair gave him something of the look of the grey foxes Ginnane had seen in Canada. He could admire those foxes, but by God, he wouldn't trust one. He wondered, not for the first time, how much he could trust Brendan Kelehan.

"It *was* a long time ago," Ginnane drawled, "that's what worries me."

Kelehan, lying face down in the rotting hay beside him, turned slowly to study Ginnane. "You asked Devoy for my presence; I didn't volunteer for this."

"I asked for a tough man, a man who could use a gun, and who *would* use one, should the need arise . . ."

"Should the need arise." Kelehan repeated the words for emphasis, and Ginnane detected, or thought he detected, insolence in the man's tone. He kept himself in check, however, turned back to the view of the twisted, dripping alleyway, lit feebly by the lights in the brick tenements. No one, nothing stirred . . .

He must be careful. It was always like this, waiting in ambush. The nerves frayed easily; you *knew* what was going to happen, you dreaded what was going to happen—and yet your nerves strained towards the moment. From the look of Kelehan, he had never known the feeling. Did not want to.

Ginnane once more began to wonder if Kelehan had been the right man for this job. True, he was highly recommended as a man who could keep his head in a crisis—but Ginnane was beginning to think that Kelehan was the kind of man who had to have trouble thrust upon him before he would react. Maybe he was a man who fought like a demon with his back to the wall—if this was so, he could be a liability to Ginnane on this night.

"I want to know," he persisted, "are you with me in this? For if you aren't, Kelehan, I'd prefer you to get your ass out of this loft and run back to your safe little lawyer's office."

"Don't goad me, Ginnane, you'll gain nothing by it. I'm here because Devoy wants the man questioned . . ."

Ginnane snorted, and noted that Kelehan stiffened immediately.

"I mean it, Ginnane—I'm following orders . . ."

"We're to question a possible—no, a *probable* informer. An informer is a spy, Kelehan. A traitor."

"I know that." Still the voice was reluctant.

Ginnane pressed his point, "In the army—in *any* army—they shoot spies and informers. But maybe this ain't a war to you. Maybe it's a game. Maybe it don't matter to you that hundreds of our best men are in prison, waiting to go on trial for treason—Irish patriots just like you and me. And these men might hang, Kelehan—because dogs like this Ned Costin are getting paid by the British to hand over lists of names!"

"Do you think I don't know that? And after last night, at Pilsworth's . . ."

"Yeah—you remember that. Even if you're right, and Devoy wanted us going up to Costin all friendly—don't you think something's changed after last night? Devoy's in prison, and St Clair, O'Kelly, O'Neill and Curry—I'd need all night to count their names to you. And who gave their names to the police, Kelehan? Who?"

They were still speaking in whispers, and only once in a while did they dare glance away from the lane's entrance to look at each other. Ginnane glared at the Irishman now, but the large-boned, aristocratic face remained intent on the entrance to the Square. He did not answer.

Ginnane was silent also for some minutes, then: "I came over here to do what I saw as my duty. Hundreds of Irish-Americans have done the same—thousands are waiting the signal, back in the States, and they'll come. You can't breed the Irish out of a race, you just can't. And Fenianism was born in America, don't you forget that . . ."

"Ginnane, this is not the time nor the place to lecture me on the American contribution to . . ."

"If you fellers over here had listened, called the revolution for the month or two after the war back home . . ."

Kelehan turned to him hotly. "I have relatives in Boston—I was there until the Civil War broke out—I know a fair amount about the Fenian movement—in Boston and New York. Sure, I know the Fenian Brotherhood owes its birth to O'Mahony and Doheny in New York, for they couldn't come home after their part in the rising of '48. But we here in Ireland know when it's time to take arms—Ireland owes no allegiance to a governing body setting itself up in New York any more than she owes her loyalty to the one in Whitehall . . ." And, as Ginnane was about to speak, "The Brotherhood in America is already split, with General Sweeny urging an attempt to annex Canada. That might cause Her Majesty's government some inconvenience, but it's not going to benefit Ireland."

"I can't talk for General Sweeny—maybe he knows what he's doing. I'm here doing what I know how to do, *fight*. If this man is an informer, he'll be dangerous, Kelehan, and I don't want you turning yeller on me."

"I don't want you murdering some innocent Irishman. You say you're a soldier, Ginnane, then for Christ's sake, follow the orders we were given—or I'll begin wondering whose side you're on—Ireland's—or your own."

Ginnane made a sudden move, and Kelehan tensed. But no. This was foolishness, and they both knew it. Kelehan began to speak, but Ginnane, with his keener senses, suddenly clapped his hand over his mouth.

"Someone's coming," he hissed.

It was true. Footsteps were approaching, crossing the Square it seemed, and then, slowly, the dark shape of a man became discernible from the surrounding, all-pervading fog. He walked with a jaunty step, and half-whistled beneath his breath. As the two in the stable watched, he gave a small skip, as much from reaction to the cold as from an exuberance of energy.

Kelehan frowned, for it was an oddly youthful, high-spirited action for a man such as Ned Costin. And this thought had barely formed in his mind before a door in one of the grim-faced, frowning facades of gabled tenement buildings was flung open. Someone who knew that light-hearted footstep, who waited each night in the ground floor apartment overlooking the street, now thrust a shining, fair head around the door and ran the few paces to be caught up in the man's arms. Hair in one long blonde plait that fell past her hips, face turned to nestle against the collar of her man's overcoat, she walked with him, beneath his arm, murmuring her welcome all the while, until the door closed, and the candle-lit hall, the warmth of the poor rooms within, were closed off from the dripping street and the two cold and silent watchers in the straw.

Neither spoke for a long moment. Emmet Ginnane sucked his teeth, shook his head. The scene seemed to have disturbed something within the hardened soldier. "Touching, ain't it? Let him leave home for three months and it'll be a new feller she'll be welcoming. One thing the War taught me, Kelehan—you can't leave a woman for no time at all before she's warming her bed with some other man. So leave 'em alone altogether, that's what I say. You married?"

The abrupt question brought Kelehan's gaze from the windows of those ground floor rooms, and he glanced once at Ginnane before returning to his watch on the street. "No," he said.

The way the woman had run, lightly, her slender figure leaning towards the man she knew would catch her, hold her to him—something of the woman reminded him of Katherine. Of course, the woman's hair was blonde and straight, and Katherine's was a thick cloud of curls the colour of newly polished cedar . . . But in such a way Katherine used to run to meet Oliver, in the early days of their marriage, when Kelehan had watched them with an aching fascination and a bitter, rancorous envy of his friend.

Katherine doesn't run to Oliver in that way any more . . .

No. Well, of course, they had been married five years now, and Katherine was—what? Twenty-eight?—and there was young Chris, as lively and devilish and exhausting as a four-year-old can be. The realities of marriage had changed Katherine, yes. But if Oliver was sent to war . . .? No, Kelehan thought drily, his bitterness tempered even then with pride in Katherine, she would not turn to another man. Not even to him. Such was her loyalty, and her strength of character. Such was the woman with whom he had compared all other women, all these years, and found the others wanting.

Ginnane was saying, his voice low with his memories, "I was married. I married late, after roaming all over the States and Canada— trapping, mostly, though I tried my luck with the rest of them at the diggings in California, and later, up at Frazer River. Settled down, finally, back in Nebraska, on the place my daddy and me had carved out of nuthin'—got me a girl from Omaha, married her and had me two kids by the time my Daddy died. A week later, they fired on Fort Sumter . . ."

Kelehan kept his eyes on the gas-lit swirls of fog about the entrance to the Square, but he could hear the bitterness in Ginnane's voice.

"Never answered my letters. Not one of 'em—and she had no excuse, she could read and write. Came home from the War to find the place deserted. My mother had died, and that bitch had buried her, sold all the stock and run off with a travelling doctor feller. Hadn't even written me to say she was leaving me, let alone that my mother had died . . ."

Kelehan, who had been called back to Ireland from Boston with the news of his mother's death, only six weeks before the secession of the southern states, still found that he could feel some sympathy for Ginnane's wife. How many women, all over America, had been left to look after farms and families during the years their men were away fighting? It must have been a hard and lonely life . . .

He thought of Katherine, and felt again the chill of fear that had come with the news that Devoy, the Fenian leader, and most of his lieutenants had been arrested the night before. If Devoy, O'Neill, St Clair and the others were being taken into custody, then Oliver Carron, he, Brendan Kelehan, and those other men whose writings were enraging the British Government would not remain at liberty for long. Perhaps McNally could care for Katherine—but Pat McNally had a wife and children of his own. Daniel Hutton? No, there was a softness, almost a femininity about Daniel that made it hard to believe he could cope with a woman and child entrusted to him; despite his intellectual and literary brilliance, Daniel was not a practical man.

Why hadn't the Brotherhood made their move earlier? For, in his heart, he knew his American comrade was right. 1865 had been the time.

He became aware that the normally taciturn Ginnane was, somehow, expecting an acknowledgement of his story. Kelehan asked, "Did you try to find your wife?"

Ginnane snorted. "America ain't the size of Ireland, boy. Sure,

I tried, but it was as if she disappeared off the face of the earth, her and my two little girls. I sold the place afterwards—didn't have the heart to farm it, after all that, and I tried to find my wife— but it weren't no good. I ended up in New York—that's where I heard that men were needed over here, that the revolution was happening at last."

"So you came here, because you had nothing to lose."

A pause. "Yeah," Ginnane said. "That, and because I remembered what my daddy had said. There didn't . . ."

He stopped, and both men heard the footsteps this time.

A figure materialized slowly through the heavy mists. Though the shoulders were hunched, Kelehan recognized the light frame, the distinctive head, betrayed as the man moved slightly to the left and was silhouetted against the bluish and ghostly orb of the street lamp.

Kelehan had met Ned Costin on only a few occasions. A narrow-shouldered man with a head unfortunately constructed like an inverted triangle, a broad, high forehead tapering to a pointed, elongated chin. His fine, dark hair was always worn the same, swept from above the right ear across the head to fall in a ragged, greasy fringe over the left ear. This alone would have given Costin an other-worldly appearance, but his watchful eyes and probing questions, his desire to be privy to every plan and conversation, while holding his own counsel and several lingering grudges, had finally led to him being watched by members of the Brotherhood, and the results were disturbing. He had been seen drinking in a respectable tavern in Baggot Street with two recognized policemen in plainclothes, and another member had sworn that Costin was a regular customer at a well-known, high-class brothel off Rutland Square. And it was difficult to imagine how he could afford these frequent indulgences of the flesh following, as he did, an erratic career loading barges down on the quays.

Such was the fuel of suspicious circumstances that led to this night.

The man had a hundred yards or more to walk, and there was time enough for Ginnane and Kelehan to climb stealthily down the ladder from the loft. As Ginnane, last to descend, was about to turn, Kelehan placed a hand on his arm. 'Remember, no violence. We report back to headquarters and we let our superiors take it from there.'

"We ain't got no superiors, for all you know . . .!"

"Someone will have taken Devoy's place. No violence, Ginnane, promise me!"

"Alright—now shut your trap . . .!"

They waited by the half-open door, through which, hidden by the shadowy darkness, they could watch the street.

They had agreed on what was to happen. As the figure, bundled in a long black overcoat, passed the doorway, they moved silently after him.

It took Costin three paces to sense a presence behind him, one and a half paces in which to turn—and by then they had him crowded against the side of the stables. Rain dripped from the rotting eaves, upon them and about them, but the three men were aware only of each other.

"We want to talk to you, Costin. The Brotherhood has some questions for you."

Ginnane's voice was calm, businesslike; perhaps, Kelehan thought, even more frightening in its lack of aggression or veiled threat.

"I . . . of course! You startled me, begod, you did! Creeping up on a man like that—all you have to do is ask—anything I can do as a loyal member of the Brotherhood, anything! Come out of the rain, lads, come home to my place and I'll fix us a drop of the stoff and we'll talk."

He began to lead the way down the narrow street, towards his own home. The two men walked very close to him, almost abreast, yet apart from showing the natural nervousness of a man who had been jumped in a blind alley by two men who might yet be assassins, Costin seemed in control; was apologizing in advance for the state of his rooms.

The end of the alley curved abruptly, ending in a small space where four workmen's cottages were strung together, behind four pitiful patches of garden that did not seem to grow anything. Ned paused at the second house, felt in his pocket for the key, muttering about the lock being damaged and difficult to work.

Kelehan glanced at Ginnane who distrustfully had manouevred his heavy-shouldered frame to stand over Costin, in case he bolted inside.

What if the man is innocent? What if his ugliness and his bitter malevolence have made him enough enemies to wish to damn him? If he denies the allegations, will Ginnane listen? Costin wouldn't be the first . . .

It happened too fast. Ned whirled and seemed to bring his fist up hard into Ginnane's chest, at the same time stepping behind the man, pulling him around so that Ginnane's bent, gasping body was between Kelehan and himself. And it seemed in that brief, nightmare moment, that Costin was helping Ginnane, struggling to support the heavy frame, even while Kelehan was moving around Ginnane's bulk . . .

Ginnane fell against Kelehan, the full weight of the man, and he was as tall as Kelehan and a good twenty-five pounds heavier, catching him off-balance. When Kelehan touched him, his hand came away warm and wet, and the knuckles of one hand had struck the hard metal that protruded from Ginnane's chest.

"Don't move . . . Don't move! It's his own gun I have, and I'll kill you!" Costin was backing away—it was difficult to see the object in his hands, but the sharp *click* of the hammer mechanism told Kelehan that the final contact between Costin and Ginnane had been for the killer to take the Colt revolver from the man's belt.

"You are an informer . . .' Kelehan managed.

"I know you, lad—keep your distance, and don't follow me, and I'll say nothing to the police . . . Don't move . . .!" He was stumbling backwards, along the lane; another minute and he'd be out of sight.

Kelehan moved, enraged beyond thought, and Costin, who had begun to run, turned in time to see Kelehan rush forward, sensed that he, too, had a gun . . .

He fired the heavy Colt, almost at the same time as Kelehan, on one knee on the wet pathway, his own revolver in two hands to steady it, had fired, accurately, fatally.

Neither man saw the effect of his shot. Ever afterwards, Brendan Kelehan would wonder who fired first, for the two shots made one long explosion, and he himself knew only the force that struck his left shoulder and knocked him sideways, numbing him, shocking him into immobility, leaving him feeling as if half his body had been blown away, staring sightlessly, without pain, as yet, but with the knowledge that something was wrong, *wrong*, and he tasted the fear in his mouth along with the rain that began to fall, more heavily now, on his face as he lay on the path.

"Kelehan . . ."

He knew it was Ginnane. The voice filled him with panic. Remembrance came flooding back with that voice, laboured as the breath that came from the man lying a short distance from him. Kelehan crawled towards him.

"Kelehan . . ."

"I'm here."

"I pulled it out."

"What?' Bemused, then—the knife. He did not mean the knife . . .

"I pulled out the knife . . ."

"You fool!"

"Maybe it's done for me. I been done for a thousand times, Kelehan. You face it . . . that many times . . . and you lose the fear. Had to pull it out, boy . . . I don't want nobody finding me looking like some stuck pig . . . don't you see? Costin . . . you shoot him?"

"Yes."

"Dead?"

Kelehan glanced up. Costin lay like a dark patch of crumpled refuse in the gutter. There was nothing about the shape that betrayed life, or that it was human.

"I think so. Yes, he's dead."

Ginnane sighed. "I was right. Admit . . . I was right. He was a traitor . . ."

"Yes, Ginnane. I was wrong."

He had been too trusting, had talked even the more experienced Ginnane into lowering his guard. If he hadn't, if he had trusted the older man's intuition . . .

Doors were opening in the little cul-de-sac. Voices murmured, lamps became visible in windows and doorways. Footsteps approached, cautious, wary.

"Run, Kelehan! Before someone sees you and can identify you . . ."

Only a second's pause. "No."

"You useless pile of shit! Who'll report back if you don't get . . ." A rattling gasp for breath. Around them, the lamps, the figures, came closer. Some paused by the body of Costin, and bent over it, and murmured, "Dead . . .", "He's dead . . ."

"Kelehan . . .?" Only a breath. Kelehan bent over the man. Ginnane managed, "Some earth . . . Any earth around . . .? Soil . . . in my hand . . ."

A full three seconds elapsed before Kelehan, pain beginning to claim his body each time he moved, each time he breathed, began to understand.

There was soil nearby, against one of the low walls that divided the dingy gardens from the street. He took a handful of muddy earth and opened Ginnane's hand, pressing the wet, black soil into it. The fingers closed upon it.

"Better this way. Never felt right . . . between you and me— the War, back home. They was Americans, just like me—even though they tried . . . denying it. This . . . is different . . .' He raised his hand a little, looked at his fist and its small burden. "Better to die for this. Ireland . . . ruled by Irishmen . . . freedom. Something real, that. Something right . . .'

The words fluttered through the crowd like tattered leaves before a wind. "Fenians . . .", "Fenians . . .", "They're Fenians . . ."

"You'd best go." A man stood over Kelehan, holding a lamp that threw weird shadows on a face made grim by hardship. "We knew the likes of Costin, this is no surprise, sure." And through the murmurs of agreement around him, "We don't know what your argument was with him, and we don't care—but you'd best be gone. Your friend's dead, and the police will be along soon."

He had been waiting for Ginnane to speak, but the man was right, the drooping eyelids covered lifeless eyes. Kelehan closed them. He looked around at the faces of the poor, the inhabitants of these tenement slums, united against the English presence, the English laws, and nodded. He rose, and a young man stepped forward.

"Y'r arm's bleeding—they'll be able to see—they'll know you've been shot." He was pulling off his coat. It was then, as the fair-haired woman moved to stand beside him and spoke, that Kelehan recognized the young married man who had come home to such a joyous welcome, not an hour before.

"Michael," she said, "not your good coat!" The pleading in her voice. But Michael was already bullying and pushing an almost incapacitated Kelehan into the warm coat. "It fits—sure it's lucky we're of a size."

Kelehan pulled money from his jacket pocket, for it was a good coat, something the couple had saved for, something the young man had worn with pride.

"Arra, no!" He stared at the money Kelehan had pressed into his hand. "I'd be buying four overcoats for this . . .!"

"Take it. It's my life you're saving."

"Get you gone—get you gone, boy!' the older man with the lamp urged. "Without you, it's clear what happened." And he placed Ginnane's gun, which someone had taken from Costin, near Ginnane's left hand. They could not place it in his right hand.

Before Kelehan turned and made off swiftly down the street, he glanced back, once, at Ginnane's face, and then at his right hand, fallen back, lifeless, the fingers slightly uncurled, to show the handful of Irish soil, moulded to the shape of his grasp.

Two

He was awakened by his own hoarse cry from a dream in which they were amputating his arm. Then came the pain, for in starting awake, he lurched sideways against the wall of the park shelter, and the pain in reality was almost as agonizing as that of his nightmare.

But that, at least, was over. He managed a grim smile, rocked his body a little, nursing his forearm gingerly and staring out into the drizzling darkness of wet parkland, waiting for the pain to subside.

Even through the heavy overcoat he could feel the swelling of his upper arm. The bullet was still in his shoulder, lodged in muscle no doubt—even with his limited knowledge of anatomy he imagined that was what had happened. And the bone broken, perhaps . . . He realized he was breathing too quickly, shallowly, and concentrated then on taking slow, deep breaths.

"Where to go . . . Where to go . . ." The sound of his own voice brought him a kind of comfort, for he knew, in his heart, that—in Dublin, at least—he was truly alone. It came to him with a kind of clarity that he had been very remiss in not including some dull, respectable acquaintances whose reputations were beyond reproach amongst his many forward-thinking, Republican comrades. All his friends, on this twenty-third day of February, 1866, were as much at risk as he himself.

Brendan moved his hand on the slatted wooden seat. It was moist, and sticky—something dripped from his fingers and fell with a faint sound upon the dusty floor of the shelter. The bleeding had not stopped, then . . .

"Where to go . . ."

He must not go to Katherine. Oliver was known to be a Fenian, and the fact that Brendan had not spoken to any of the Brotherhood but Ginnane since that morning, meant that it was even possible that Oliver Carron had been arrested earlier in the day. There had been no way of knowing—in times such as this they could not risk visiting each other's houses. To throw suspicion upon Oliver would be to involve Katherine—and there was the child to think of. Young Christopher was ill, had been for weeks—if Oliver *was* at home, and safe, the last thing he and his family needed was their friend

Kelehan lurching through the door, dripping his dangerous, patriotic blood upon the carpet.

So there was nowhere to go, no place safer than this gothic-looking gazebo that had risen before him as he had run across this strange expanse of parkland. But he must move on. The decision was not even made from fear, by now; it was a disembodied voice within him that warned him, calmly, that he was bleeding to death. Calmly, too, came the acknowledgement that he did not want to die. He grasped the back of the bench and rose to his feet.

The park was silent, empty. He was able to walk without difficulty along the deserted paths between the lawns and shrubs to the large, wrought-iron gates.

He paused. There were houses, comfortable, four-storied terraces rearing their heads to gaze critically down upon him from the opposite side of the road. He wondered what street he was in, had just turned towards the nearest corner when the roll of carriage wheels, the clop of a heavy horse's feet behind him made him glance around.

He stopped at the same time as the hopeful cabbie. The great grey horse, a ghastly shade in the blue glow from the street lamps, pulled up readily enough and turned blinkered, incurious eyes towards Brendan.

The cabbie said, "Cab, sir?" encouragingly.

Brendan hesitated, placed his bloodied hand out of sight within the overcoat pocket—and found a handkerchief there. He held to it gratefully, feeling it already dampening within his grasp. It would see him home, or . . .

"Yes," he said, and opened the cab door with his right hand.

"Sir? Where to, y'r honour?"

And the address came to his lips before he could prevent it, "Seventeen, Chatham Row."

It was foolish, it was reckless and unforgivable, but he had to see her. Oliver would be all right. He was of well-born Protestant stock, and he had many friends in high places, despite his known Republican ideals. Yes, surely Oliver would be at home, reading a book before a comfortable fire, Katherine in a chair beside him . . .

"Sir?"

Brendan started awake to see the broad face of the cabbie peering in at the door. "We're here, sir." And a frown, a thrusting forward of the head, "You all right, sir?"

"Yes, of course." He had drifted into unconsciousness, for how long he had no idea; the handkerchief was a sodden ball within his left hand.

The man helped him down, and Brendan turned away a little as he fumbled within his jacket for the money for the fare.

It was raining a little harder; Brendan stood on the pavement and watched the cab disappear up the narrow street, swallowed by the darkness and the steady rain, appearing once, silhouetted against a street lamp, the cabbie's shoulders hunched beneath his oilskin cloak and battered bowler hat pulled low.

There were three bells by the doors, one for Markoski's, the small exclusive gallery that fronted the street, another for the gallery owner's residence at the rear, and another for Oliver Carron's apartment on the upper floor. Brendan rang the correct bell from long familiarity and leaned against the doorway, made himself, once more, take slow breaths, deep breaths . . . Let him be there, let him be safe, let Katherine be safe, let Katherine be there . . .

Through the glass panel in the door, he saw the light grow dim as some hand turned down the gas lamp on the stairs. His heart began to thump in warning—he had taken a step backwards and turned . . .

"Who's there?"

Light, feminine voice, a frightened whisper. Katherine.

"It's Brendan Kelehan, Mrs Carron—I've . . ."

He had no idea what to say, but even as he paused, the bolts were being drawn back, and the door swung open.

"Mr Kelehan . . . Come in. Quickly, please—come inside."

And he found himself standing in the darkened hall, so close to her that he could smell the perfume of her hair. The relief of seeing her was so great that despite the years of their friendship—and he had guarded himself so well that he had never allowed himself even to use her first name—he longed to pull her to him, hold her. She was standing so damnably close, and looking up at him as if she wished to study every line of his face. *She was worried for me.* The thought came with that strange clarity that comes when all of one's senses are alert, aware of any subtle differences. And here was something different. It even seemed—and it must be his crazed mind, the pain in his shoulder—that she leaned towards him slightly.

"It's Oliver, isn't it? Something's happened . . ."

"Yes . . ." And she had recovered, was looking away, glancing up the stairs, touching the white broderie anglais of the collar of her dark blue gown. He cursed himself then, for it was only when he had broken the spell that he knew he had not been mistaken.

He reached out, touched her shoulder—and instead of pulling away, she took his hand, and held it. Her eyes filled with sudden tears.

"I am *so* glad you're safe—I thought . . ." Again she withdrew the intensity of her green eyes from his face, glanced down the hall to where Mr Markoski had his own apartment. "We must go upstairs—Mr Markoski has had enough of a fright today."

She led the way up the narrow stairs to the four-roomed apartment. Usually bright and warm, the living room was chill and in half-darkness; no lamp burnt, and the fire in the grate was mostly embers.

As soon as the door was shut behind them, he turned to her. "I'm afraid I may be placing you in danger, but I didn't know where else to go, and I had something to tell Oliver; information that must be passed on . . ."

She had a strong, humorous face, but the past several hours had taken something from her. Her face was pale beneath the faint freckles on her cheeks and nose, and her mouth was held as if she controlled a great deal of pain within. He took her hand in his.

"Tell me what's happened."

"Just a moment . . ." She moved towards Christopher's bedroom, and they both paused to look in. There had been a fire in the tiny grate here also, and the meagre light played on the features of the small boy lying asleep in his bed.

Brendan moved forward, gazed down at the four-year-old Christopher. The dark hair, inherited from his father, fell in curls onto his forehead and the thick black lashes threw long shadows on cheeks that still held the rounded curves of infancy. Beside him, the small, misshapen head sharing the pillow, was a blue felt rabbit Brendan had given the boy on his first birthday; now, minus one ear and one eye, the little toy remained his constant companion.

Brendan looked at Katherine, smiled—and stopped, seeing the tired way she leaned in the doorway, that the look she gave her son, still discernible in the limited light from the grate, seemed to go beyond the boy to some private world of her own.

"Mrs Carron . . ."

"I wanted to check if the ringing of the bell had woken him." Even as Brendan approached her, her eyes, dark-shadowed, did not move from their fixed gaze upon her son. "He's been sleeping so fitfully these past few nights, with the coughing, you see."

She looked up at Brendan as if suddenly seeing him, and her voice lost some of its other-worldly quality. "I'm sorry. You look tired, ill. Come into the living room, by the fire—I . . . I've let it die down, sitting there thinking."

At the living room hearth she bent to place more twigs and small logs on the fire. Brendan, who would normally have helped, made his way gratefully to the largest armchair and sat down.

"Oliver—where is he?" he asked, but he knew, of course. He already knew the answer.

"He was arrested this morning, with most of our friends." The voice was clear; not Irish, not anglicized, but something in between, and still retaining a touch of the flat vowels of her Australian homeland. She seemed to speak without emotion, but Brendan could tell she was beyond it.

"I heard the shouting from here—ran downstairs. There were about a dozen policemen—several of them were dragging Oliver—they must have been waiting for him—they pulled him towards a carriage, he was shouting and trying to beat them off . . . then he saw me, and told me to stay back, to stay out of it. But I screamed for him—they had struck him, were dragging him into the carriage. Some of the men pushed me back, took my arms and dragged me up the stairs . . .

"They flung things about a little, looking in cupboards, beneath beds . . . When Christopher began crying, they left. They were almost sheepish . . ."

She had ceased her work at the hearth, but still had her back to him. Now she raised her head and looked about vaguely, "I tidied the rooms . . ."

"And Oliver?"

"Daniel Hutton's sister, Bridey, came to me with news about midday. The police had arrested Daniel early this morning—Pat McNally has been taken, too, and Tim Gleason. They're all in Kilmainham Gaol—the . . . the charge is treason."

Her head drooped; Brendan stood, and using his right hand, helped her to rise and led her to her chair. As he was about to straighten, she gripped his sleeve. "Your left arm—you haven't moved it— why are you hiding it?" She pulled his hand from the coat pocket, unaware, in her horror at the blood, of the agony she caused him. Her eyes came up to his.

He smiled, with as much conviction as he could muster. "I was hurt, a little. A quarrel within the Brotherhood . . ."

"Someone has tried to kill you. Don't lie to me. Did the police do this? What is it—a bullet wound?"

She had released his sleeve and he straightened, moved back, slowly, very slowly, to his own chair, all under the hard gaze from those green eyes.

"You bloody fool."

He stared at her. Always outspoken, he had, nevertheless, never heard such language from her.

"Mrs Carron, it's not as bad as it seems—I simply . . . bleed a lot. It's a very small wound . . ."

"Most bullet holes are."

"It wasn't the police. Look, I have to go—I just wanted to see . . ."

He was struggling to stand, but it was much more difficult than it should be. And suddenly she was there, before him, and her arms came out and she had embraced him. He saw her face, so lovely, so close to his own, after all these years of longing . . . He felt her breath on his cheek as she spoke, but her words . . . her words meant nothing. He thought, looking down at her, "I'm going to drown in your eyes . . ." and he was afraid, then, that he might have spoken the words aloud. What would she think of him? Here she was in his arms at last and he could barely see her, she seemed to be fading from him, like a dream.

He found, of a sudden, that he was slumped sideways in the large, winged chair. It was Oliver's favourite chair, he knew . . . Katherine was bending over him, her face held concern, her hand was against his cheek . . . His first thought was a prayer that his bloody arm would leave no marks on her cushion covers . . .

"Foolish . . . Foolish . . ."

She was gone from him, then she was there again. A bowl steamed on a small table before the fire, and she was taking hold of him, encouraging him, bullying him to stand, to remove the overcoat, his jacket . . .

He was seated once more, and he started as the cold steel of her scissors touched his flesh as she snipped away at his bloodied shirt.

"Sorry . . . Bit of a mess, I'm afraid," he mumbled. "Sorry . . . Nowhere else to go. Everyone in a scrape . . ."

He had a picture in his mind, before he lost consciousness, of the green eyes raised to him in silent disapprobation and hurt.

A scrape. The wrong phrase to use. She saw him as foolish. She saw all of them as foolish, this day.

And he suddenly saw, all over Dublin, all over Ireland, the women who would be wearing just the look that Katherine Carron wore now. The women who loved their country and desired its freedom just as much as their husbands, fathers, sons; women whose menfolk now crowded in dark cells, who might never come home, tonight, or ever again.

Three

He awoke, stiff with cramped muscles, to find that he still lay in the large armchair before the fire. He was wearing a soft shirt of Oliver's, and a rug was drawn up to his chin. His feet rested on a footstool and pillows supported his back and head.

He straightened himself painfully, lowered his feet to the floor and looked about him.

In the dim light of the pre-dawn, he could see Katherine, lying asleep upon the settee against the further wall, her head on a pillow and two rugs over her. Brendan walked over to her, stood looking down at her.

It was only then that he realized what had awakened him, for it seemed that Katherine was in the grip of some nightmare. The bright chestnut hair, drawn back loosely in a band at the back of her neck, was escaping to fall in strands about her face and across the pillow as she turned her head restlessly, back and forth. Brendan, concerned, heard her whimper, like a child, a murmur of pure terror, and he sat down on the edge of the settee beside her, took her shoulders and awakened her gently. "Katherine . . . Katherine . . ." and it was natural, right, that she should reach for him, that he should hold her, feeling her heart beating against his chest, his eyes closed, his fingers in the tangle of her hair.

She was sobbing, drily, still confused, her body stiff within his arms; her hand, unknowingly gripping his left arm, sent a stab of pain through his shoulder, but he barely noticed it. "Katherine . . . Katherine, it's all right . . . It's all right . . ."

A sharp intake of breath—she seemed to realize where she was, what had happened, and yet, oddly enough, she did not move away hurriedly, but raised her head slowly to look up at him. A strand of hair had fallen across her eyes, and he lifted his right hand and brushed it back, aware that he trembled slightly, cursed himself, did not wish for anything to frighten her into pushing him away, withdrawing from him.

"I . . . I was dreaming." She leaned her forehead against his right shoulder, and with relief he realized she did not yet wish to move. "It's a dream I've had ever since I can remember . . . I'm in a dark place, and I'm frightened, but I can't run—I try to move, but I can't. And I know that . . . It's hard to explain, but there is something I'm *missing*. Some . . . warmth—some *safety*. Oh, it's very confusing, but in the dream I'm reaching out, and crying for . . . whatever it is." She lifted her eyes to his. "It's ridiculous, isn't it?" She looked about a little, and he saw with sadness that she was beginning to realize her position, and its unsuitability. She let go his left arm.

"Your shoulder . . . I must have hurt it . . ."

"No, nct at all." Perhaps he should move first, it was undoubtedly the gentlemanly thing to do, but he knew, also, that it took more self-denial than he possessed to relinquish her of his own free will.

He found he was gazing into her eyes, that she herself had been studying him, and the seconds had gone on . . .

It was Katherine who moved, at last, and Brendan stood abruptly, unwilling to have her think that he would hold her against her wishes. She moved briskly to the fireplace, and he had several seconds to think of what he must do, for the clock on the mantelpiece said seven o'clock, and he knew he must soon leave, for he was placing her in danger with each minute he remained. He had often planned, with his other Fenian friends, where they should go, when—and if—they found the police were hunting them. He watched Katherine, bent to the fire, and his heart grieved. "I must go soon," he said.

The fire needed very little tending; she placed another log in the grate and turned to him. "But where will you go? You can't return to your own house—the police may have your name, as well as Oliver's."

He did not answer, and she was silent a moment, sensing his thoughts, his need to plan. He stood there, gazing into the fire, still holding the rug about his shoulders, and tried to think of what alternatives, if any, he had.

She said, "I'll make us tea—and a good breakfast for you. You must be hungry."

With her words he realized that he was indeed hungry. He murmured his thanks and sat down once more by the fire. By the time the meal was ready and they were seated on either side of the small table, eating porridge and bacon and eggs, he knew what he was going to do.

"If Devoy and St Clair and Oliver were arrested, then I'm sure I'm a wanted man. Therefore," he said unwillingly, "I can't see that I can do anything further, here in Ireland. I could, perhaps, help raise funds in America—I have an uncle, Vincent Kelehan, who's very active in the Fenian Brotherhood in Boston . . ."

"Yes, I've often heard Oliver mention him. You could stay with him?"

"I worked in a law firm in Boston for two years, until just before the Civil War in '61." To Katherine his voice seemed to sober suddenly, but he continued, "I wanted to stay and fight, but Uncle Vincent said that Ireland needed all her sons—besides, the whole concept of American against American was repugnant to him. He was an Abolitionist, of course, but the South has so many Catholics—it went against his grain, and his faith."

"So you're fairly close to him? He'd understand what's happened?"

"I'm certain he would. It was his influence that gained me the position in the Boston law firm—though he'd much rather I joined his own exporting company. He and Aunt Rose have no children."

She nodded, "You'll be safe then, as they're obviously fond of you. But you can't leave yet, you know that. Your shoulder—I think the bullet is still there . . ."

"It is. I know a doctor who can be trusted to keep his mouth shut."

"Where? I can take a cab and fetch him . . ."

"He's in Cork."

She stared at him, and he grinned. "Yes, I'm afraid so. But you must see that I have to leave Dublin immediately . . ."

"Your shoulder may become infected . . ."

"The train journey is only several hours at the most, given the usual delays of our Irish railways. From the feel of it," he touched his left shoulder gingerly, "you did a grand job of bandaging. I don't think it'll begin bleeding again. No, I can make it to Cork without difficulty. I have several friends in the city, and often visit them. There's a train about ten in the morning, I believe."

"But . . . if you're recognized . . ."

"Perhaps my name isn't on the list. Unlike Oliver, I never made speeches, and my writings have always been more concerned with the economics and constitutional problems of setting up an Irish Republic, rather than the means of gaining it." She caught a note of irony in his voice as he said, "I've played it very safe, looking back on it. Oliver always said I was a moderate, didn't he?"

"You weren't very moderate yesterday evening."

He looked up at her sharply. "No. No, I suppose even Oliver would be surprised at yesterday's recklessness. I'd always planned to fight, but I never . . ." He almost said, *I never thought it would be Irish against Irish.*

He brought his right hand down hard upon the arm of his chair.

"Damn Stephens and his caution! We shouldn't have waited! The civilian leaders are disappearing into prison, and those regiments who've sworn the Fenian oath are being transferred overseas . . ."

Katherine was gazing into the fire. "Oliver and Daniel were speaking only two days ago of the threat of informers . . ."

"That's it, I'm afraid. Informers within the army, informers in civilian life—did you say that Patrick Foley was arrested with Devoy and the others? I never trusted Foley, but I've obviously done him an injustice."

"So it's over . . ." Her voice was soft; when she turned to face him her eyes were large with something like disbelief. "It's over, isn't it, Mr Kelehan?" She looked into the fire, and he hated to see the faint twist of bitterness to the normally smiling mouth. "The Irish Republican Brotherhood . . . the great hope for Ireland's future. A rebirth of the Fianna—only a myth, a dream, after all."

"The Fianna weren't a myth," he was stung to reply. "A legend, yes—and many legends have their basis in fact. You've studied your Greek history—if ancient Sparta had a standing army, the nation dedicated to the encouragement of a first-rate fighting force—then why not ancient Ireland? Doheny's dream, in the fifties, wasn't an impossibility—but in the years that it took for 'Fianna' to become 'Fenian' I'd had hopes that the movement would have been more widely accepted, and better organized . . ."

"It's over," she repeated. "All the hopes we had, all the plans . . . everything Oliver believed in, gave his life to. Over." Her voice a breath of despair.

He was reluctant to admit, even now, that she might be right. "I know it seems as if the English have spies everywhere—the constant betrayals and arrests are demoralizing the people. If the movement in America would only concentrate its energy and support, give over this idea of marching on Canada . . ."

"Canada! How will that help Ireland?"

Brendan shook his head. "An attempt to break British power overseas. I agree with you, but there's nothing to be done. England is a strong and clever little country. Its people have been carving themselves helpings of this island for so long that they think we're being unreasonable in wanting it back. Like a wealthy woman with a jewel case filled to the brim, she's not going to part with one string of emeralds—even if she gained them by theft in the first place."

"Mister Kelehan, I know you're bitter, but you forget, sometimes, that my background is English . . ."

"But your family have been Australian for three generations, have they not?"

"Still, I'd appreciate it if you were not quite so acrimonious. We don't have all that much time, and there are other problems to be discussed."

"Such as?" He took his cup and saucer and leaned back carefully in his chair.

"Such as what I am to do with the two thousand pounds."

He sat up slowly, immediately. "What's this? What two thousand?"

"Oliver brought it home yesterday—it's mostly from American sources—sent to John Devoy, but Oliver was to look after it. I gather it's to purchase firearms."

"Yes," Brendan said consideringly. "So it arrived, did it? Bravo."

"Well?" she said when he did not continue. "What am I to do with it?"

He grinned wryly. "For a start, I suppose I must borrow two hundred pounds of it, to take myself to Cork and Boston. I don't dare risk going to my bank for funds. I shall leave you my note for it, and send you the money as soon as I get to Boston." He scowled thoughtfully. "As for the rest, you and Oliver will have to look after it."

"But—that's absurd! Oliver's in prison!"

"So are Devoy, St Clair—and any of the others who could tell you what to do with it."

"You take it," she said suddenly. "Take it back to Boston with you!"

"My dear Mrs Carron, what good would that do? It only just came from there. Anything could happen over the next few days or weeks. The Americans wouldn't want their money back so soon. Just think if I handed it back to them—and my uncle had a great deal to do with the collecting and sending of it—and the revolution went off after all? They'd probably be bitterly disappointed that they weren't included."

Katherine was silent, seated straightbacked in her chair, gazing at him coldly. "Your American friends wouldn't be amused by your flippancy, Mister Kelehan, and neither, at the moment, am I." She shook her head, sighed. "I've known you for five years—you're an almost constant visitor to the house, and yet . . . I don't really know you."

"You do . . .!" For the thought of this upset him.

She smiled, shook her head. "No, Brendan. Do you mind if I call you that? I think I can, after all this time. No, you're a complete mystery. To everyone who knows you, I think, not just to me."

"Perhaps," he said, with an unsuccessful attempt at lightness, "it's because I'm a mystery to myself."

She smiled gently. "That idea has occurred to me, also."

He scowled into the fire. "May I have a brandy, do you think?" he asked abruptly.

"Brandy? With breakfast? I . . . I suppose so." She fetched the brandy, a good French type that was Oliver's favourite, and a glass, and brought them back to the table.

"Won't you drink a glass with me?"

"Really—at seven in the morning . . ."

"A toast to my voyage. Who knows when I shall be able to return to Dublin?"

She gazed at him for some seconds, then turned and fetched another glass from the cabinet.

Over the remains of their breakfast, Brendan raised his glass to hers. "To Boston—and to a speedy homecoming. For us all."

He had needed brandy for the pain—it was returning, and he had to keep it at bay, somehow, for the long journey ahead.

But he almost forgot the gnawing at his arm and shoulder for, with the first glass of brandy, Katherine began to talk. It was stress, fatigue, and the unaccustomed alcohol, he knew, but it did not matter; with only the slightest of verbal leads from him, she was speaking to him as a friend—a friend of *hers*. And that was enough.

She spoke of Christopher, of her worry over his health, how she wished she and Oliver could take him to Australia to grow up in a climate that would improve his persistent coughs and colds. She spoke of Oliver, of his dreams for the Republican movement, of her fears for his life now that those dreams were in danger of being shattered.

And then, suddenly, so suddenly that he found he had stiffened, withdrawn his gaze from her, she was speaking of her marriage to Oliver. They had not discussed that time, five years ago, had never dared discuss it, for they had become friends in the intervening years, and this topic threatened both of them, striking at the very roots of their relationship.

"Did you . . . did you ever regret your actions, at the time of my marriage to Oliver?" she asked.

"I . . ." he stammered, "yes, of course. You're happy—you have Christopher . . ."

She gave him no help; when he could not go on, she simply regarded him quietly. Then, "It took me a long time to forgive you," she said.

"I know." And suddenly he welcomed the chance to speak. Perhaps this mad night had some positive side after all, if he had the chance to explain a little of what had haunted him for years.

"Oliver makes excuses for me—that with the death of my mother, and my father so soon after, I became a trifle unhinged." He smiled bitterly. "But that wasn't it. I came up from Wicklow feeling depressed—I was grieving, and it was natural. But I think I'd have made the same decision if I hadn't been mourning for my parents. To come to the house of one of my best friends, and to find a party in progress, to have him introduce me to a lovely girl from Australia, whom he had only known for a week and a half—who had only been in the country for little over two weeks—and to hear him say that he was eloping in three days' time . . . It just seemed a monumentally foolish thing for you both to do."

He felt uncomfortable, tapped his foot, drummed his fingers on the arm of his chair; but still she did not speak, and he would not look at her, for he knew she would be waiting, with her quiet eyes, determined to hear everything he had to say. "I knew—because Oliver told me—that your family was here as part of a world tour, and he told me that your father had refused his permission for you both to marry . . . I saw a lot of you in those three days—we spent the entire Tuesday in the park together, the three of us, remember? I . . . Forgive me, but I felt you were both making a terrible mistake. Oh, I knew you were in love—Oliver is like a young Adonis, to hear some young ladies speak—and you . . . you're lovely, and brave, and amusing and clever—it's no wonder Oliver fell madly in love with you.

"But neither of you were children, and you were behaving like children. I had a feeling—with both of you—that you were trying to run away from something; you each thought the other could . . . rescue you, in some way. Am I speaking nonsense? It's what I felt, anyway, at the time.

"I think I lived a lifetime in those three days. Truly, I think I did. I met your family at the dinner Oliver organized on the Thursday, remember? I almost spoke to your father then, for I liked him very much. Oliver had spoken to me privately—I can tell you this now—as if your father was a cross between Attila the Hun and Mister Barrett of Wimpole Street. He *was* a little grim, in his suspicion of Oliver, but to me he seemed a fair man, not likely to be unjust—simply very protective of his family."

He turned to face Katherine, knowing that this speech was long overdue. "I waited . . . I thought you and Oliver would realize how foolish you were, in your plan. I waited until the morning you were to leave, and I came to Oliver to try to talk him out of it. He wouldn't listen. He left to meet you, to drive north with you—and I spent a wretched hour walking the streets, before I finally decided I couldn't allow you to make such a devastating mistake. Oliver is married to his work, to his Republican writings, to his poetry . . . he's coped very well with marriage, and . . . and I gather you've both been happy—but then—*then*—I couldn't foresee anything ahead of you but misery. And after only three days in your company, I cared enough for you to want more than that for you."

His shoulder was hurting a great deal, and he paused, careful not to betray any discomfort upon his face. He drank a little brandy, and waited for her to speak.

Her voice was soft, measured. "It took me a long time to forgive what you tried to do. Father was furious when he found he was too late to prevent the marriage; so furious—and you wouldn't know this—that he's never written to me, in all these years."

She smiled a little, a smile for his benefit, but it bore the effect of the years of her hurt. "I was something of my father's favourite, you know. It's been very hard. All these years. No word from him. My mother and my sisters, Edwina and Laura, and my brother Joe—they write letters to me, of course . . . but I hurt my father deeply. It wasn't so much my disobedience, for as you say, I was no girl—but it was the fact that I'd deceived him and my mother. He seemed to become almost insane with the thought of the lies I had told them, in order to run off with Oliver. And then, of course, there was the most important factor— Father loathed Oliver. He distrusted his good looks, his talent as a poet, and especially his political beliefs. My father became . . . a man I didn't know. A stranger; all humour, all understanding —and he always had a great deal of both qualities—gone from him."

"You miss your family a great deal, don't you?" he asked gently.

"Yes," wistfully. "Oliver has often said that we'll go to Australia one day, and that Father will melt when he sees Christopher—I'm certain that he will, too, you know." And her smile, for the first time that night, was genuine, and held all her normal warmth. "But while Oliver devotes all his time, and any spare money we have, towards the Movement, I can't imagine when I'll see Kangaroo Valley again."

"Kangaroo Valley . . ." Brendan repeated the name of the place;

it had always appealed to him. "I imagine a valley with herds of kangaroos bounding across the prairie."

"Stop using those American words! We don't have 'prairies', I told you, we have plains. And Kangaroo Valley looks more like parts of England or Ireland, because it's in the chain of mountains that runs down the east coast. I've told you lots of times, it's not the outback . . ."

He was grinning at her.

"Oh, you're teasing me again . . ." almost crossly.

"You told me there's not many kangaroos left, I remember that— I think that's dreadful, and I wish you hadn't told me. I much prefer my vision of a sea of leaping brown furry creatures. Did the settlers shoot them for food?"

She nodded. "But the Valley is mostly farmland, now. There are still a few families of cedar-getters living in the hills around the Valley—they live off the land. It's sad to imagine them killing kangaroos, wallabies and koalas for food, but they do."

She stopped, sighed, looked a little awkward. "Yes, I must be homesick. I do talk about home a lot, don't I?"

But he was skilful at drawing people out, partly from his legal training, but mostly from a genuine liking for people, and for this woman in particular. Both here in Oliver's apartment, and on their frequent visits to Brendan's country home, Avonwood, in County Wicklow, Katherine had spoken to him of her family home, Barrengarry, on the other side of the world, yet never far from her thoughts.

As she spoke now, he felt he knew the family he had met only briefly, five years before. She spoke of her impatient, inexhaustible father, Marcus, her beloved mother, Suzanna, her two younger sisters, and of her good-natured but fiery-tempered brother, Joe. And she told him of her home, back in Australia, painted a picture for him of a green and pleasant valley hidden within a range of inhospitable, scrub-covered mountains; of a two-storey, red-brick homestead amongst pine trees, and all around, the escarpment walls holding back the brooding bush, mile on mile.

He would have listened under any circumstances, just to hear her voice, to watch her face. But now that face was alight with love and the fondness of her memories—and she was a good storyteller— the house in its valley, and the people, seemed to come alive for him as she spoke.

Finally, and his attention began to be marred by something like dread, she approached once more the time of her family coming to Dublin, five years ago.

"That was a strange time, wasn't it? My father had always dreamed of taking us to Europe." Her voice was reflective. "And yet I visited only England, before coming here. We were to tour Ireland for a few weeks only—and then we were to sail for France." Her voice faded.

Brendan was holding rather too tightly to his glass. "But you met Oliver," he stated.

"Yes . . ." rather abstractedly.

The brandy bottle was within an inch of being empty. The firelight flickered in rich reflections in the curved amber glass. Brendan had lost his fatigue, was beyond it. Even the pain meant little. Katherine had never, in the five years he had known her, spoken to him in this relaxed, almost intimate, manner. Even given her emotional state, and the effects of the brandy, she would not, if she did not feel comfortable, safe with him, reach for the bottle, as she now did, and refill her empty glass.

She was scowling now into the liquid, turning the glass, tilting it to and fro, gently.

"What's the matter?" he prompted, and was rewarded with an immediate, if sharp, glance.

"I won't see you again, after tonight, will I?"

He was taken aback, as much by the coolness of her tone as the words themselves. "I don't know," he admitted, "after some time in Boston . . ."

"It would take years before it was safe for you to return. And if Oliver is released—*when* he is released—I'll make sure we leave Ireland."

"Will you?" He smiled and leaned forward a little. His arm began to pump, painfully, but he ignored it. "Would Oliver ever leave Ireland, Katherine?" He loved the newfound feel of her name on his tongue and repeated it, "Would he, Katherine? I doubt it."

"Of course, you know him better than I do." She seemed to relax in her chair, but did not take that cool gaze from his face. "Exactly how well *do* you know Oliver?"

Brendan was perplexed by the change in her tone from the warm friendliness of a few moments before. "I've known him since we were at university together . . ."

"Ah, yes. First-born sons, packed off to Trinity. Jolly friends on the same cricket team. So you'd have known Oliver more than ten years."

"Yes . . ."

"What was the real reason behind your opposition to our marriage?"

He stiffened, but had not had time to speak, before she went on, "Don't let that closed look come down over your face, Brendan."

"Because I thought you were both making a mistake! Oliver had no right to—" And he stopped himself in time.

"Ah . . ." almost a sigh from her. "So you were acting purely from altruistic motives."

"Katherine." He could not understand this sudden concern with the past. "Katherine, it was five years ago. Your marriage has been a happy one—I was wrong . . ."

"You took too much upon yourself, Brendan."

"Perhaps it was because of the regard in which I held both of you . . ."

"You should have come to me!" Her hands clenched, and the one holding the brandy shook the liquid about in the glass.

Brendan began, "I begged you both to wait . . ."

"You know what I mean!" She leaned forward. "I'll talk about this now, because, as I said, I have the feeling I'll never see you again—and I want you to know, Brendan, how bitterly I resent you . . ."

"For attempting to . . ."

"For not telling me the truth. For hiding from me the fact that Oliver much prefers the company of men to that of women. And that he prefers Daniel Hutton above anyone."

He had no memory of moving, but he was there, by the window, with the only thought in his head that he wished himself a million miles away. And yet he had known, he *had known*, deep inside himself.

He leaned his head against the window frame; his head buzzed, and he did not want to clear it but tried to follow the relentless ringing in his ears, draw it around him like a heavy curtain that would block out her words. But they were said. She had waited her moment, all these years, and now gave him this burden to take with him when he left her. And why not? There was justice in it, after all.

"I thought . . ." he said finally, finding the words with difficulty, "that he had changed, or . . . No, not even that, because I didn't believe that he had given in to . . . whatever drove him. It . . . wasn't pronounced at Trinity—or he kept it from me. He was simply shy with women, many fellows are."

"But when you heard we were to marry . . ."

"I knew—or at least suspected—what a struggle he was having.

He never spoke to me about it, of course, perhaps because he felt I wouldn't understand. I don't," he added ruefully, "but my respect for his intellect, his wisdom and . . . his *generosity of spirit* . . . I couldn't turn against him, even if I had known."

Katherine murmured, "Those are the very reasons why I love him."

He stared at her, full of pity for her, and tried not to think of the young Oliver, agonizing to him about whether he should marry or not, "A man should, *a man should* . . ." and Brendan's own amused indifference until, at that dinner at Oliver's bachelor apartment, he had met Katherine Prescott.

"What could I have told you?" he asked her now. "Even if I had any real proof—" He stopped. "And do you?" he challenged.

For a long moment she did not speak. Her face was turned away from him, and he wondered if she had heard. Then, "I went to find him—at Daniel's apartment—the night that Pagan O'Leary was arrested . . . two years ago. I wanted to tell them, you see. I didn't bother to knock . . . I came into the parlour, and was about to call them . . ."

She stopped, and the words hung in the silence. Finally she said, "They didn't know I'd been there, they didn't see me. I went home to Christopher."

Brendan said harshly, "Daniel should have stayed in England— he'd have been more use there and done less harm."

"What difference would it have made? Oliver would have found someone else. It's . . . the way he is." The tone in her voice, of quiet and utter despair, made him turn slowly.

Across the room, across the gulf between them, she looked up, caught his glance, and smiled a little. "I like Daniel so much. Odd, isn't it? I live like a sister to Oliver now; he doesn't seem to notice. To him, everything is as it always was. And we had good times— the best times of my life. Remember how inseparable the three of us were in those early years? Some of that closeness still remains, for I know Daniel is very fond of me. It was he who convinced me to learn something of Irish history, who made me aware of the social and political problems in this country . . ."

"Katherine . . ." He moved back to his chair, cursing the table that lay between them. He wanted to take her hand—more, to pull her to him . . . "Katherine," he spoke almost tersely from his armchair, "I did everything I could to protect you, before the marriage and after it. All these years, you knew you could rely on me, could come to me if . . ."

"Mama?"

They both started.

Christopher stood in the doorway of his room, rubbing the sleep from his eyes with his fists. Then he focussed on Brendan.

"Uncle Brendan!" He ran over, tripping on his nightshirt just as he reached Brendan, and came up with a jolt against the arm of the chair.

Brendan winced, inhaled sharply as the pain tore through him, and when he opened his eyes it was to find that Katherine had quickly scooped up the boy, and was seated with him on her lap.

"Want to sit on Uncle Brendan's lap! Want to play horse!"

"Hush, darling . . ."

"Katherine, you must understand that I didn't have anything definite to tell you—my own misgivings weren't enough! Yet even they drove me to see your father . . ."

She shook her head, glanced down at the boy. "Not now . . ."

"Katherine, I must tell you—I can't go away from you knowing that you resent me for . . ."

"Later, Brendan, please!"

"There is no later."

In the silence a log settled with a rush of sparks.

"Ooh . . ." Christopher watched, impressed, then turned back to look between his mother and her guest. "Don't be cross with Uncle Brendan, Mama."

Katherine scowled across the table but, meeting Brendan's suitably injured look, she laughed, softly.

"Well . . . Mama is not cross any longer. But we won't quarrel about this, will we?"

"There is no quarrel. Nor will there ever be."

They smiled at each other, and Brendan knew that this fragile truce was all that he could hope for at this moment.

But she must come to trust what he had said; the truth lay in the fact that if he had had proof of Oliver's past, it would have been the very first subject to be broached with Katherine's father. And if he had known such a thing, Marcus Prescott would not have allowed the marriage to continue. He would not have stopped until there had been an annulment.

No, Katherine believed him, would forgive him. But he would not, to the end of his days, forgive himself.

"Brendan?" It was the second time she had spoken his name. He looked up. "Brendan, I've decided something. When you're ready to leave for the train, Christopher and I will come to the station with you."

"That's madness . . .!"

"No. If they're looking for you, they'll be looking for a man alone, not a father being sent off on a business trip by his family. You'd be much safer."

She looked down at Christopher. "And you'd like to see the trains, wouldn't you, darling?"

Christopher, much confined to the apartment due to his weak chest, opened his dark eyes with delight, nodded furiously.

Katherine looked up to Brendan. "There, it's settled."

So it was that at eight-thirty, with the small boy breakfasted and dressed in layers of warm clothing, the three walked as calmly as possible out into Chatham Row, and caught the first available cab to the station.

They arrived with twenty minutes to spare, and were forced to sit in a corner of the small refreshment room, Brendan with a copy of the *Irish Times* held before him.

Twice, policemen strolled past, and another wandered over to stand by the ticket barrier just as they were entering the platform, but he, like his predecessors, did not appear to be searching for any man in particular.

The ticket collector waved Katherine and the boy through so that they could bid goodbye to Brendan. And suddenly, with the great black engine wheezing close by them, with so few minutes left and the future yawning uncertainly before him, he found five years of emotions within him and no time and no words to express them.

"I'll come back," he promised, "I know we'll meet again."

But what kind of words are these? He was ashamed, ruffled Christopher's dark curls to cover his discomfort, said "Oliver will be all right." The words came out rather awkwardly.

"We'll find a good lawyer—I can't see that they'll hold him for long." But her eyes did not hold the confidence that her words did.

"Oliver will be *all right*," he repeated, his hand on her shoulder, willing her some hope for the years ahead.

"Yes." She nodded, but did not look at him. She bent and picked up Christopher, held him in her arms.

"Katherine . . ."

The whistle blew.

"Katherine—I wish it had been different. I wish you'd met me, first."

She smiled gently, reached up and touched his face. "Then it would have been you they dragged away yesterday, perhaps. And I . . ." She stopped, and her gaze left his face, taking her smile with it. After a brief pause, she said, "I wonder if anything would have been really different. For both you and Oliver, Ireland came first. And I wouldn't have it any other way,' as he began to speak. "I'm proud of both of you."

The whistle blew once more.

He caught her in his arms awkwardly, ignoring the pain. Christopher hugged him delightedly, and, not comprehending, crowed his goodbyes over the warning hisses and grunts of the engine. Brendan leapt for the door as the train began to move.

"I love you . . ." he said, as he looked back, but in the noise and rush he had no idea if she heard him.

They grew smaller and smaller as the train pulled out, the slim figure of the woman, with the child in her arms, their pale faces turned towards him, hands raised in farewell, slowly dissolving in the trails of escaping steam and smoke as he was carried further and further away.

Four

It was a pity that there was not a vacant compartment available, for he would have preferred to be alone on this journey. But there seemed to be families or groups of voluble friends in every section of the carriage he passed through. He settled, finally, in a window seat opposite a soberly dressed couple, both in their fifties, each apparently preoccupied with private thoughts. They gave him one glance as he seated himself, and returned their gaze to the grey and crowded buildings of Dublin as they fled past the window.

Neither had returned his smile, and that, too, relieved him. His shoulder and arm had begun to throb once more, and even his left hand felt hot, looked swollen. He felt warm all over, in fact, and knew that a fever was possibly developing for it was cold enough in the carriage. The last thing he wished, feeling as he did, was to have to converse with his grim-faced fellow travellers.

Nevertheless, Brendan's gaze was drawn back to them fairly frequently. There was something about the man, seated by the window, directly opposite, that reminded Brendan, unwillingly, of his father. Yes—that same long, squared jawline, the thin, hooked nose—features that, softened by his mother's more classical features, Brendan had inherited. The man's face did not hold the humour which, even in quiescence, was obvious in James Kelehan. The strange hard lines of bad temper or suffering or both were etched deeply down the side of nose and mouth, and the eyes were deep-set, dark and unreadable. James Kelehan was always readable—the clear blue eyes flashing intelligence.

Brendan sighed. It was not the time to think of his father, nor of his mother, honey-haired, gentle, yet fond of subtle skirmishes with her husband—necessary rebellions, Brendan admitted, in order to curb James's enthusiastic projects which ranged from commercial hot-air ballooning to a plan to join a hunting expedition to Africa.

Brendan found himself smiling at the fleeting maze of cobbled streets. He saw none of it, was back, instead, at Avonwood, listening quietly to his father's friends tell of strange places, successful scientific experiments, archaeological finds, the latest mystical star found by some astronomer at a far-flung observatory.

James Kelehan admired the intellectual, the trailblazer, the pioneer. Brendan always believed his father would have become one himself, had he not fallen in love with Kathleen Nihill of Kilcoole and sired a son and seven daughters.

So with love and responsibility, James Kelehan was moored to the family home at Avonwood, and instead of going out into the world as his brother Vincent did, he brought the world to Avonwood.

The house, in the shadow of the Sugarloaf Mountain in County Wicklow, saw many carriages come rolling up the drive. A prodigious and gifted writer, James's articles and his correspondence with the great minds of his day brought many a world traveller to anchor temporarily in the still waters that Avonwood provided. There were balls and soirées and shooting parties—and always the talk, talk, of great quests and adventures, with names that thrilled like strange spices on the tongue.

Brendan would grow up to be an explorer, a scientist, an archaeologist, an astronomer . . . "That's grand! That's my boy!" James would swing the lad about in squealing delight, and a few days later books on the subject would appear, a miniature laboratory, a telescope. James's disappointment when Brendan lost interest in one career after another was sometimes intense, but there was always something new to take its place. He'd be a general, an admiral, a sheep farmer in New Zealand, a diamond mine owner in Africa . . .

In the meantime there was school, navy blue uniform and classrooms and rough and tumble play which was a way of marking time until the Adventures began. And then there was Trinity and the fierce competition and the knowledge, for the first time, that to be Catholic meant one had to be cleverer, faster, stronger than the others. Adversity was excellent training, James used to tell his son and his friends, Oliver Carron among them. For what was an Adventure without adversity?

And America—travelling with Uncle Vincent through several states, by coach and rail. Cotton plantations in the south, factories in the north, ranches in the west. Trading a hunting knife of British steel for a bow and arrow from a young Indian in Arizona. And the talk, talk, talk, of Abolition, states rights . . .

Brendan had almost convinced Uncle Vincent that to wear the blue uniform of a Union officer was a great Adventure, when the letter arrived from Dublin.

His mother had died of the mysterious growth in her lungs, a few days before he returned. James wandered about the halls and rooms of Avonwood, and smiled gently at the plans Kitty, his youngest, was making for her approaching marriage. Three of his daughters married, three with vocations and happily ensconced in a teaching order in Dublin, his youngest and favourite daughter to be married to a strapping young Delgany farmer, and his only son home again from America—but Kathleen was gone, and now that no impediment stood in the way of great Adventures, it seemed that the adventure had gone from James Kelehan. Suggestions of trips to England, Europe, the South Seas, met with good-natured disapproval. He had neglected the estate all these years, he said, there was too much to do, and the winter was setting in.

These last months of James's life were the only time when Brendan and his father quarrelled. He could not stop the older man from long rambles in blistering cold winds to view the stock, the ploughing; nor from riding off on chilly mornings to visit distant tenants and walk about their holdings, sometimes in icy rain showers. James shrugged away offers of help and any expression of concern from son and daughters; he refused invitations to Dublin and politely put off prospective visitors. He lived long enough to escort Kitty down the aisle, but within three months Brendan had to visit Ann, Mary and Ellen at St Canice's in Dublin to tell them the news, and his four married sisters, Sally, Margaret, Elizabeth and the newly-married Kitty were wearing mourning.

"I'm sorry . . .?" He started awake, having heard the man opposite addressing him.

But the stranger was scowling at him. "I didn't speak, sir. You were dreaming, I think." The pleasant rise and fall of a Cork accent. Yet the man, and even the narrow-faced little woman, with her deep-set black eyes beneath the brown woollen bonnet, were gazing at him suspiciously.

It was hot . . . he felt so hot . . . If he could only take off the coat, a new and expensive one of Oliver's that Katherine insisted he have for his journey. But no—the pain in his shoulder was tearing at his arm, at his very insides—what if it had begun to bleed again? What if these two saw it?

The train chugged and rattled its way south, and, as familiar as he was with the territory over which he travelled, it seemed to Brendan that they must be taking new lines, different turnings onto strange tracks through even stranger country. He would grow panicky, seeing a mountain, a river, a hamlet that he could not remember, and wonder if he had missed a connection, was even now being carried away, far to the west, and further from his goal. But then a familiar station slid by and he would relax, only to doze and wake, equally fearful, as the nightmare journey went on and on.

At one stage he thought—he may have dreamed—that the man and woman were eating, had a cloth spread out over their knees, a wicker basket between them. The woman nibbled at a piece of bread and meat, turning it round and about in her hands like a small, black-eyed mouse consuming a crumb. But when he woke next and looked, there they were, as stiffly demure as ever, hands in laps, watching the scenery and, every once in a while, allowing their eyes to slide sideways to fix on him with that same unblinking, conjecturing stare.

He tried to control his thoughts, to think of Katherine, of Boston, but he was beginning to worry. What if Tom Delaney in Cork, a more vocal rebel than even Oliver since the days when all three were at university, had been arrested also? What if the police had returned to Oliver's apartment, and threatened Katherine until she had broken, told them his destination? Had he mentioned Tom Delaney by name? But Katherine would not betray him, she would not.

I want you to know how bitterly I resent you . . .

But she would not betray him, she had too much loyalty, too much integrity. It was this that he loved so much in her.

A ticket inspector yanked the door open, hailed them all three in a hearty manner, and Brendan only just controlled his involuntary start, managed a smile at the man as he checked his ticket.

And then he would not go. Taking the polite answers of the three for interested encouragement, he launched into a mostly one-sided discussion on the arrests of the previous day. There was no telling if he were Royalist or Republican; he did not take sides, kept to the role of impartial reviewer, and despite the murmured and noncommittal responses, stayed for a good ten minutes regaling them with all the facts and his own thoughts on the outcome of the inevitable trials.

"Can't hang them, of course—too much sympathy, and it's not as though it's a bloody massacre that's been going on. No, nipped in the bud, it's been, like in '48. And just like then, transportation it'll be, you mark my words—off to Van Diemen's Land, or . . . where is it they send 'em these days?"

"Fremantle." The word came from Brendan's lips almost automatically.

"Aye, that's the place. But 'tis a funny thing about Australia, many a man has come back from there better off than when he started out."

Finally, his news and his philosophy at an end, and half the train yet to be enlightened, he rolled to the door and with a final wink and "A good journey to you," he was gone.

Brendan avoided looking at his companions; even shared exasperation can lead to a conversation, and he had no wish for it.

When sleep began to beckon he welcomed it, but it soon became apparent that he was to have no easy rest. He dozed fitfully, starting awake with half-formed replies on his lips to answer Katherine, Oliver, even his father and mother, who seemed, each for an instant, to be here with him, demanding of him, pleading with him.

Every time he awoke he felt the eyes of his companions upon him in curious study, and he tried to stay awake, unable to bear the thought that the very real ghosts who kept him company with the clacking wheels of the train would lead him into some burbled reply that yet made sense enough to betray him.

The woman was gazing at him now, with earnest appraisal. Her little eyes glittered like chips of jet in a pointed face of alabaster.

He looked away, and it was then she moved her head a little

towards her husband, and "Fenian . . ." the word rustled from the rest of her murmured phrase like a rat out of old papers. It invaded their neat world and threatened them—it was obvious from the suppressed horror and consternation with which they gazed at each other.

When they turned to him it was they who avoided his eyes, they sat bolt upright in their new and dangerous knowledge and pretended not to see him. And all the while they were planning, planning— and he knew it. Could see the worry in the man's face; he dare not fetch the guard and leave his wife alone with this cornered and desperate traitor . . .

Brendan attempted to rouse himself, but his limbs were stiff and lethargic, they refused to obey him. Even his thoughts were mutinous and still fled to and fro from Katherine's presence to the scuffling, shouting panic of yesterday's skirmish in the streets, to the safety of Avonwood and his parents.

You've been a fool, boy! Playing soldiers—what about your responsibilities?

"I've—!" He started awake. It had seemed so real—but no, it was not his father haranguing him; there had been no words at all, simply the grim figure of the stranger opposite, already recovering from the start Brendan had given him with his half-formed exclamation.

There was nothing to be said, no point in attempting to explain. He leaned towards the window; the glass felt cool and hard against his forehead; if only the train rode more smoothly he could rest here like this. There shouldn't be too many more miles to Cork. Beyond the rain-streaked pane he could see the soft, green countryside, blurred already by the rain, now dissolving further with the dusk.

He had no knowledge of how long he slept, whether it was a few seconds or more than an hour, but the soft slurring of taffeta awoke him, and with terror he watched the woman who, having risen smartly from her seat, was already marching determinedly out the compartment door.

The whistle blew once, twice; Brendan had a last glimpse of the man's face, hardened, a look almost of challenge upon it—and the train ran shrieking into a tunnel, burrowing into the blackness with confident familiarity, not checking its headlong speed.

"Oh, God . . ." Was it his own voice? He rose, and in the utter darkness, groped for the door.

Hands were upon him, he cried out in agony as a large fist closed around his upper arm—a blur of faces, the smell of dust, the wedge of the seat above him as he struggled to rise from the floor. The guard was there, among other men in dark uniform; he grinned, delighted at finding himself in the middle of one of the topical dramas that so fascinated him. His lips moved, but with the rush of blood in Brendan's ears, he could barely discern the abusive, triumphant phrases.

He had a vague sensation of being lifted, of a great hubbub all about him; jerking movement as he was carried, rolling, lurching back and forth—and lights, lamp lights, piercing his eyes through the darkness.

The woman's face was there, floating above him, her mouth a pinched line, the light throwing severe shadows on the sharp planes of her face. Her black eyes were lost in blacker, deeper hollows; it was as if he were being perused by a disapproving skull.

A man's voice, "Take him away—where's the carriage?"

The woman disappeared, all was dancing, myriad lights in the dark, and then only the dark.

The room in which he found himself was small, with a high ceiling and wallpaper covered with rather malevolent dark flowers on a muddy-coloured background. The window, like the room, was narrow and tall, but the curtains were of light gauze and through them he could see a patch of blue sky upon which a few clouds remained fixed as if they, like the tortuously twined blossoms on the wallpaper, were printed on a backdrop.

There should have been bars on the windows.

The realization had him rising to a sitting position, his heart beginning to hammer with the memory of that train journey. He was not in gaol. Then where was he?

A quiet voice from the corner of the room, "It's all right, Mister Kelehan. You're with friends."

Even as he turned, the woman, that same, dark-eyed little mouse of a woman who had studied him for the long hours of the journey south, was rising from her chair by the small grate and was approaching him. She placed her knitting, at which she had obviously been busy while waiting for him to waken, on the bed, and adjusted the pillows behind him so that he could lean back comfortably.

"Just a moment." She interrupted him as he was about to question her, and turned towards the door.

"But I need to know . . .!"

She was gone, leaving the door ajar behind her.

There was a murmuring outside, and in the minute or so that Brendan was left alone he had a chance to further study the room and his own person, noting that he wore a clean linen nightshirt and, feeling his shoulder carefully, discovering that, painful though it was, the swelling had subsided.

"Yes, the bullet's gone, y' fool. And great trouble you caused us, ranting and raving until the doctor thought he'd have to near drown you in the chloroform to shut you up!"

"Tom!"

The sturdy, sandy-haired figure in the doorway swaggered forward, stood gazing down at the patient with mock disapproval before hoisting up the trouser legs of his dark brown suit and plumping down upon the bed.

The two men gazed at each other, Brendan with relieved delight and Tom still with the severe look upon his face.

"Brendan, Brendan, what were you doing? What in God's name were you trying to prove? Getting involved with a street skirmish— when you knew that the police force is nervous enough and ready to shoot at anything suspicious."

"It wasn't the police, Tom . . ."

"And don't I know that? A message came through from Paddy Kennedy in Dublin—and of course the newspapers are full of the details of a sordid double murder in a Dublin back street. How could it happen? Ginnane was an experienced man—and you knew the suspect—didn't you know that he could be dangerous?"

Tom stopped then, for he saw the look that passed across Kelehan's face. Of course, the man would feel badly enough without being attacked the minute he opened his eyes. "I'm sorry," Tom continued. "I've been waiting without for hours for you to wake, and worried out of my mind for days whether you'd live or die—it's in my nature to abuse the people I care about." He took a deep breath, grinned, and said, "Let's begin again—would you be after telling me what happened, in your own words, if you please, sir?"

So Brendan told him; of Devoy's lieutenant approaching himself and Emmet Ginnane towards the end of a meeting of the Republican Brotherhood, of the order to find Ned Costin and question him— and he told, with his clinical lawyer's ability to record facts, the cool details of that night that had changed his life forever.

Tom shook his head at the end of the story, and his own voice was heavy. "So many good men, good officers, betrayed into English hands. What will James Stephens say to this, I wonder . . ."

"I'm hoping he'll call a revolution," Brendan said drily, "while there's still an Irish patriot left outside prison walls."

"Stephens has problems enough in America . . ."

"For God's sake, Tom! They're not gaoling Fenians in America! The people are suffering here, now! And why? Because we live in an occupied country, and we're speaking out for independence. Don't talk to me about the problems of the Movement in America—they don't have problems—they just argue as if they do."

Tom screwed up his face as if to protest, then heaved a sigh. He shifted his not inconsiderable bulk on the bed, and grunted, reluctantly, in agreement. "I wish Stephens would send us word— with every day that passes we lose men, good men, into English hands. And those regiments loyal to the Irish cause are being sent to the four corners of the earth . . ."

"It makes me wonder," Brendan murmured, "what it's all been for."

"Ah, now don't go losing faith now, not you, lad! But it seems that your contributions to the ideals of the Republic are over, for a while, at least. I asked Paddy Kennedy if there was a warrant for your arrest, but he hasn't been able to find out. He did say— and I agree with him—that you'd best be gone out of Ireland at the earliest opportunity."

"Oh?" For the thought struck him like a cold shower of rain. To leave Ireland . . .

" 'Oh' indeed. So what are your plans now, my young wild goose? To which foreign clime will you fly this winter? England? America? France?"

Brendan scowled at Tom's levity, then sighed. "America it will have to be. I can stay with my uncle in Boston—as you know, my family have business ties in the United States. I have a good farm steward at Avonwood, who's been prepared for this type of emergency for years, and I have most of my assets from American sources, anyway. I'll be able to stay there indefinitely—not that I wish to leave at all."

"You must, you know that. I can call at Avonwood for you occasionally and look after your affairs in Dublin. And it won't be long before you're back—you'll be able to return with the American Fenians when the time comes. America will send thousands to Ireland's aid—all good men and seasoned soldiers. Why, half America is Irish born or of Irish blood—there are ex-soldiers—Union and Confederate—who only await the call and the Atlantic will be alive with an armada that will have them quaking in Whitehall!"

The fire in Tom's words left Brendan strangely unmoved, and this disturbed him. But it was only because he was tired, that was all. He had been ill, and was lacking in his usual strength. When he was stronger the old energy, the old optimism, would return. But now the plans, the dreams, were difficult to listen to; in the light of what he had seen in Dublin they were difficult to relate to. Tom spent his time helping his father and uncles run a business based on ownership of several ships that went forth from Cork Harbour to all points of the globe—so far, Tom had been untouched by the sound of angry, starving people prepared to face guns and death in their rage for justice.

Brendan said, as much to divert Tom's theories of warfare as to relieve his own curiosity, "The little dark woman—is this her house?"

"Aye. Hers and her husband Michael's. And lucky you were to come across them."

"But they informed upon me. The woman—she called the guard—I was under arrest, or . . ." as he saw the bewildered look on Tom's face, "I *thought* I was . . . There were many people shouting—and the guards . . ."

Delaney was shaking his head. "You were mad with the fever, boy—do you realize how bad that shoulder was? The Sherrys—that's their name—Michael and Bridget Sherry—they could see you getting worse and worse as the journey went on. Talking to yourself, you were, at the end, and it was a good thing you passed out when you did or you'd have given the entire game away."

"What do you mean?" He felt sick at the thought of what might have happened, what he might have muttered in his delirium.

"Mrs Sherry had left the carriage," Tom lowered his voice, "to go to the convenience, I believe—and no sooner had she gone than you started up with a yell that could wake the dead. It was just as the train passed through a tunnel, and think of the fright you gave Michael Sherry, for you tripped over his feet and fell half-across him, still bellowing like a bull, and when he tried to stand, you both rolled onto the floor, where after damning all police and all Englishmen, you passed out, praise be to God. 'Twas as he checked your heartbeat that Michael Sherry found you were hurt. Only a few miles from Cork, it was, and it was only as the train pulled in that Mrs Sherry informed the guard. Most solicitous, he was—as was everyone concerned, who helped the Sherrys load you unconscious into their carriage. Their servant, Martin, drove you all here to their house. He's of a medical bent, is Michael Sherry, y'see—has a little pharmacy shop just along St Patrick's Street."

"But how did you . . ."

"Ah, you've been raving for a day and a half with the fever—

muttering my name, amongst others . . ." He drawled the last word, looked long and keenly into Brendan's face.

"Oh, God . . ."

"Think nothing of it—they're good people, the Sherrys. They'd been in Dublin a week, visiting relatives—heard about the number of Fenian arrests—and put two and two together. Michael being a chemist, he found a good doctor for you. By the time their groom, Martin, had visited half the Thomas Delaneys in Cork and found me, you were asleep like a babby and already beginning to mend. You've been here for two days now."

"Two . . . Good Lord. How kind they are. Tom—Tom, I thought they'd discovered me, had betrayed me—I felt sure I was being taken to prison. And I wake up here."

He looked about him. The narrow little room, the dark-patterned wallpaper, looked much less threatening, much more comfortable and homelike. And, as if on cue, there was a brief tap at the door and both his hosts entered the room and came, smiling, to stand by the foot of the bed.

The looks that they exchanged with Tom Delaney already bespoke a kind of friendship, and seeing them now Brendan wondered how he could ever have been so ill and confused as to think badly of them. Michael Sherry was the same dark-clothed, grey-haired, hawk-faced individual, but his words of concern for Brendan were genuine and kindly. Bridget Sherry said little, but came to him and fussed gently with his pillows and the coverlet in a way that was totally out of keeping with the mean-spirited woman he had, on the train journey, believed her to be.

She did not allow the men to speak for long, but, once the pleasantries of introductions, relief and gratitude were over with, she shooed Tom and her husband from the room and admonished Brendan that he must rest. Brendan would have protested, for there was much that he wanted to know, but felt he owed the woman obedience in this, at least. As it was, despite his speculations, all concerned with his friends in Dublin, he drifted in and out of sleep throughout that afternoon, awoke to Bridget Sherry about to feed him a bowl of soup in the evening and, despite his determination to plan his actions for the next few days, fell afterwards into a deep and dreamless sleep.

Tom Delaney was a regular visitor to the house in the days that followed and, always welcomed by the Sherrys, never ceased to tease Brendan with his luck at finding the couple. Michael Sherry was gruff, to be sure, but his words, and as Brendan was to discover in the following days, his nature, were tolerant and worldly. He had been in the army himself when younger, had travelled widely and none of the strange sights or experiences had failed to impress themselves upon him and broaden his outlook; this and the scientist's ability to carefully study all sides of a question made him a broadminded, intellectual man with whom Brendan had many long discussions in the evenings.

His wife, Bridget, had had no such opportunity to travel in her youth, spending this time in Cork with, after her marriage, only occasional forays to west coast resorts or to Dublin. But her narrow little face and small features belied the generosity of the character within. Childless, she had suffered from ill-health for years, and pain had helped mar features that nature, it was true, had not been overly magnanimous with in the first place. Yet the handicaps of a childless house and a delicate constitution had served to draw her closer to her husband, and in the evenings when the three would sit together in Brendan's room or, later, when he felt more recovered, in the sitting room, he enjoyed the fond banter that went back and forth between the couple.

"You're both so kind," Brendan said, on the day that marked one week since he had arrived in their house. "I feel as if I've known you both for years, not merely a matter of days. But I must, tomorrow, make arrangements for my passage to Boston. Tom has been to the shipping company, and . . ."

The "Nonsense!" from Bridget came swift on the heels of a growled "Rubbish, boy!" from Michael.

Brendan shook his head, "I'm undoubtedly a wanted man, don't you see? With every day I stay with you I'm endangering both of you as well."

"You're still very weak, Brendan—you couldn't face the unhealthy atmosphere and poor food of a long sea voyage." Bridget's face had screwed itself into a mask of disapproval, the knitting needles in her little hands chattered like a scolding squirrel, and Brendan had to smile, for at that moment she looked rather like one.

"But you've done far too much for me already," he began, before Michael burst out, "What in the name of all that's holy are you talking about? We've lived a contented, quiet life in this house for thirty-four years—Bridget was saying only two days ago that you've brought the only bit of excitement into our lives that we've ever experienced. I was a bit surly at that thought, at first, but within a few minutes I saw that she was right. I don't know if this dream of an Irish Republic is ever going to be a reality, but if we've played our own small part in helping you and Tom and all the other boys like you, then I'm well content.

"Besides," he added, puffing on his pipe and glaring into the fireplace, "it's not often I get to sit up until two in the morning, arguing law and politics with someone as astute as yourself. You're a clever young man. Your father would have been proud of you. But take my advice—and not only mine, but Bridget's, for she's as worried about you as I am—start thinking beyond this coming rebellion, to what you want out of life for yourself. You've given enough for the Fenian Brotherhood, I'm thinking. Stay clear of trouble when you get to Boston, you hear? And *don't*, as Bridget will tell you, be thinking that you're fit to travel for at least another two weeks."

It was impossible to argue with them that night, and Brendan finally had to withdraw his troops in defeat, to regroup for an assault the following day, hopefully with Tom as support detachment.

He dreamed that night, and not for the first time in that week, of Katherine. But whereas the other dreams had been vague, evanescent illusions that fled away even as he grasped to hold their memory on waking, this dream was vivid. It woke him and had him staring upwards at the deep shadows of the high-ceilinged little room.

He had been walking with her, through the Dublin streets; it was snowing, and it must have been close to Christmas, for their arms were filled with packages that Brendan was certain, in the dream, contained presents for their friends. This was the dream; nothing untoward, nothing unusual, it contained no passion nor intimacy. But there was a feeling of *togetherness* between them, a sense of loving propriety in the way they walked, arm-in-arm, that meant that, in the dream at least, they belonged to each other. It was a husband and wife who laughingly juggled their Christmas gifts along the familiar streets, for their open affection was too proud, too courageous for lovers.

The following morning, Bridget came upon him writing a letter to Katherine at the small desk in his room.

"To a friend," he said, feeling that some explanation was necessary. "The same that you saw farewelling me on the platform in Dublin. I have to know how her husband and my other friends fare."

Bridget smiled, nodded, collected the linen that she had come for, and left him again.

Michael, when he returned from the shop for his midday meal, took the letter with him to post. And all that day and for the four days that followed, Brendan read in his mind the letter's contents, over and over.

My Dear Mrs Carron,

(He had glared long and resentfully at this necessary return to formality.)

I am well and recovering at the house of friends in this city.

I wish that I might be in Dublin, in order to offer whatever support I can to you and young Christopher at this time. My thoughts are constantly with you, as I know they shall be during my long voyage and the months of my exile.

If you can, without danger or inconvenience to yourself, write to me care of the General Post Office, Cork, as close as possible to a return post, as I must leave very soon, and inform me of Oliver's health and what the future seems to hold for him and for our other friends, I would be eternally grateful.

Even more than this, I would wish that you write to me of your own situation; if you need me, you have only to say and I will return to Dublin. Our last conversation affected me deeply; I do not exaggerate when I say that I dread every mile that carries me further away from you, knowing that our discussion—of matters of such importance and of so many years' standing— was interrupted at such a time by my leaving Dublin. We must talk further— to sail from Ireland believing that you still harboured bitterness towards me would tear me in two. I have acted honourably, though perhaps not wisely; always the way, it seems, when loyalty and personal interests and feelings are in conflict.

Remember the long years of my devotion and weigh them, if some rancour against me still remains, against that unwitting sin I committed all those years ago. Whatever, I beg you, do not let me leave—and I do not wish to leave without seeing you once again—without knowing that you forgive me and will think kindly, in the future, of

Your Devoted Friend,

Brendan Kelehan.

He had made no second draft of the letter, and worried, constantly, once it was well away from him, that she would be frightened into not replying. What began as a formal and polite letter, he observed to himself bitterly, descended halfway into an impassioned plea that would do credit to a lovesick schoolboy. But it was done now, and there was no calling it back.

Mindful of the danger his friends were in on his account, he determined, on the fourth day of waiting, to check the post office for a reply, and his stubborn insistence caused another quarrel with his hosts, who claimed even the short distance of three city blocks was far too great for Brendan to manage. After more than an hour's wrangling, a compromise was reached; their coachman, Martin, was charged to drive him to a point close to, but at a safe distance from the building. That way Brendan felt he was in some measure protecting the Sherrys' identity.

But in the end the precaution proved unnecessary. Not only was there no policeman waiting for him, but no letter, either.

It was absurd, he thought, that night before the fire, the newspaper spread unread upon his lap, murmuring replies to Michael and Bridget's conversation, to be so cast down. Four days was not long— perhaps Katherine was busy; she would be busy, surely, with visiting Oliver and looking after Christopher.

But the next day passed, with its visit to the post office proving once more to be fruitless, and the next day, and the next came with the same result. The clerks grew to know him, glanced at him with bored smiles of recognition, and shook their heads.

"Brendan?" Bridget had begun clearing the table after luncheon that day and paused, seated herself once more, and to his dismay, folded her hands together in a relaxed yet business-like manner that made it clear she was ready to hold a serious discussion. Brendan could only feel relieved that she had waited until Michael had returned to his shop before beginning.

"Brendan, I don't want it to appear that I'm an interfering old woman—I am," she smiled, "but I have the added voices of Michael and your friend Tom behind me when I speak to you like this. Are you expecting some important news from Dublin?"

After a hesitation, "No," he said. "Simply some word as to the health and welfare of my friends—and that's important enough."

"Of course." Bridget smiled, cowled the clever black eyes by lowering them to the tablecloth for a moment, and then, as if addressing the dish of butter, "It's nothing, I hope, that will convince you to return to Dublin."

He did not answer immediately, being reluctant to lie to her and not knowing how else to answer. She said finally, "Tom, Michael and myself have seen you fretting for an answer to your letter. It was, I believe, addressed to the lady with the young son who saw you to the Dublin train."

"Yes. She's all alone now, you see, with the sick child, and her husband in prison . . ."

"And you're worried about them, naturally. But you know, you can't help them by returning to Dublin. Tom says all your associates have been arrested, and those few who have escaped have sent messages for you to stay in hiding for several months at least. The best thing for you to do would be to stay here for another month or so, until you're quite strong, and then leave for Boston, as you'd planned."

It was not until now, hearing her calm, sensible words, that Brendan realized he did not wish for this at all. And it was not only Katherine that held him to Ireland, that tugged his emotions remorselessly back towards the capital.

"There are other matters, you know," he said, toying with his napkin ring. "I leave behind a junior partnership in a law firm and a fairly sizeable estate in County Wicklow, as well as properties in Bray and Dublin itself that require managing."

"You're quite a businessman," Bridget smiled.

"Not I, my grandfather, and my father after him, aided by my Uncle Vincent, who sent money and sound advice back from Boston. I have most of my assets in America, actually; I don't need to stay in Ireland for financial reasons, but . . ."

"I know," she nodded sympathetically, "You feel a sense of responsibility."

He grinned, rather deprecatingly, "I must sound foolish in the extreme, Mrs Sherry, but I never saw myself as a rebel as such, certainly not as a man important or dangerous enough to have a price on his head. My involvement with the Republican Brotherhood grew gradually from my father's dreams of an Ireland possessed of her own government, her own laws. At university my friends were fired by the same dream. I was no leader—I'm a conservatively minded Catholic landowner to whom it all seemed the one real, worthwhile thing, the one adventure—" and he nearly winced at the word, "that I've indulged in, in my rather safe, boring life. I have no wife, no children, nor any hopes in the matter in the near future; my parents are dead, my law practice, my very lifestyle, is safe and predictable . . ."

"I suppose, you foolish man, that you thought life held no further surprises for you?"

"Well, yes. Though it embarrasses me to admit it."

"I can understand it, for didn't Michael and I think exactly the same thing until you boarded that train in Dublin. But you have less cause—why, you're only thirty-two years old—you don't seem like a confirmed bachelor. Why haven't you married? Have you never been in love with a girl? Never?"

He wished there was some way to excuse himself from this interrogation, but unless he was determined to be rude there did not seem to be any way of escape. He sat there, feeling more uncomfortable by the second.

She said gently, "Brendan, do you ever talk to anyone? Any of your friends?"

He looked up, surprised. "Why, I talk to Tom, to you and Mr Sherry for hours on . . ."

"You *converse* with us, Brendan. Your background has given you wit, and charm and manners that could take you to the Queen's court in England, I'm thinking. But even Tom, who's known you all these years, speaks of you as a 'dark horse'—a loyal friend, and generous, but never, in the years since you graduated together, have you talked to him of anything but the plans for Ireland's future."

It was true. The aims of universal suffrage, the return of land ownership from English to Irish hands once more, even the—for some—alarming thought of completely separating church and state in the new order—these had occupied much of Brendan's conversations, not only with Tom, but with all his friends.

"I've kept busy," he murmured, "and I've been happy. A man who's miserable with his life, why, he'll talk and talk of his problems to all who'll listen. But what excitement is there in a contented life? And who wants to hear a man describing the joys of his existence? Happiness is a boring topic of conversation, haven't you noticed? Those who have it are embarrassed by it, those who don't are resentful."

"What's the name of your friend in Dublin?"

The question caught him unawares, as he suspected she had meant it to. "Katherine. Katherine Carron."

She nodded slowly. "I realize that you wish to reassure yourself that your friends are safe, but to return to Dublin yourself is madness. Before you leave for Boston you must give us Katherine's address, and Michael and I—or Tom— can call and visit her when we're in Dublin, and help her in any way we can. *You*, my dear, must leave Ireland—not only for your sake, but for hers."

"I think you have the wrong . . ."

"I've lived a long time, and my impressions are generally correct. Michael and I passed you at the station—we didn't know who you were, any of you, but the poignancy of your parting was very moving. I turned back in the carriage doorway and saw the three of you embrace—the little boy obviously adores you—I thought, at the time, that he was your son. And I saw the look on your face as you held Katherine. She may not be your wife, but you wish she were."

He was silent, drank a mouthful of his cold tea for something to do, and waited.

"Let her go, Brendan. Let her find her own life with her husband and her boy. You have no part in it."

"You don't understand." He could hold back no longer. "There has never been anything dishonourable between Katherine and myself. I have remained close to the family, it's true, but more to help them than anything else. Oliver is my friend, but he's not . . . practical. You know the type; English background, English money arriving regularly—without any real need to work at all. Oliver is the finest chap—the kindest heart imaginable—but quite spoilt by a childhood with his overindulgent Mama and several aunts. I often wondered how Oliver would have turned out if his businessman father had lived. He made his money in cloth, wool in Yorkshire, linen in Belfast—a man of granite, I believe. He died young and left Oliver to spend the profits—half-heartedly and unhappily, most of the time. He has a law degree, but doesn't practise, spends his time writing ferocious poetry and even more ferocious articles in the *Irish People*. Katherine was the best thing to happen to him." And he could not keep the trace of bitterness from his voice, had to consciously hold back the emotion that almost had him admitting *the best thing to happen to me also*.

Bridget watched him quietly. "You know," she said finally, "your friend Oliver isn't the only one who's spoilt."

"I haven't been . . ."

"You just listen to me now. All your life you've had whatever you wanted. You've never gone hungry nor barefoot, there was always someone to look after you—and amongst beautiful surroundings, if Avonwood is as fine an estate as Tom tells me it is.

"Now your parents are dead, and your sisters are moved away—and you're lonely, Brendan. No, don't deny it. That's what drove you into your commitment to the Fenians. And I think it was the reason you've stayed so close—like a fond older brother—to Oliver and his family. You've told yourself all these years that they need you—when, in fact, *you* it is who need *them*.

"Go to Boston, Brendan. Find a nice Irish girl over there—I believe the place is thick with 'em! Or, if not, come home in a year or two, when things have settled down, and I'll find you a Cork girl who'll make you a grand wife! Just don't, *don't*, my dear, keep breaking your heart over a woman who made her choice years ago—and chose another, not you. Fine woman Katherine may be—but if she's as fine as you believe she'll choose duty and honour above any feeling she has for you."

He said, in a low voice, "Katherine has no feelings for me, beyond my being Oliver's friend."

A silence followed his words, and there was no way of knowing what Bridget might have answered to this, for they were interrupted by a tapping on the door. Martin stood there, holding his hat and woollen scarf in his hands.

"Pardon, Ma'am, Mr Kelehan—I was to have the carriage ready after luncheon . . ."

"Sure and run along, then." Bridget stood, and began once more to gather up the remains of the meal. She held Brendan's gaze. "And remember all I've said."

And Brendan did, despite his discomfort at her reading him so clearly. In future years he would look back and wonder if the two singular happenings on that day, that made him doubt himself and his feelings so much, were not to be the catalyst that changed his ideas of himself and his existence.

For the letter from Katherine was waiting at the Post Office, and, reading it afterwards in his room, he spent a good two hours gazing at the view of the winter-bare garden from his window; and Bridget's words, and Katherine's words, went round and about within his head.

Katherine had written;

My Dear Mr Kelehan,

Thank you for your letter and your fond concern; I have only just returned from Kilmainham, and have told Oliver of your news and of your kind offer of help to us. He sends you his fondest regards, and wishes me to convey to you his sense of thankfulness that you are almost recovered and are in no danger.

(Brendan had smiled rather grimly at this line; what Katherine meant was that he had, thankfully, avoided arrest.)

We wish you all the best on your overseas trip; it is a pity that you cannot return to Dublin and visit us, but we are both most concerned that you take this voyage for the sake of your health, and will, thereby, return to us as your old self once more.

Oliver's situation is not serious; he is well and in good spirits. We have had several conversations in the past week, and I am pleased to write that Oliver had decided that, as soon as circumstances permit, he, Christopher and myself will also be taking a sea voyage. Dublin weather is affecting Christopher, as you know, and Oliver, too, will benefit from a warmer climate. We have decided to spend several years in Italy, just the three of us. Oliver is most excited at the prospect; some good, it seems, has come from our present predicament.

I am so happy with these plans, as you, my dear friend, can imagine. This will be a new chance, a new life. I can bear all that fortune will cast in my path in the next few months, just knowing that there is, at this moment, somewhere on the Italian coast, a little villa on a sundrenched hillside where my darling Christopher will grow strong and well again.

Write to us when you are settled in Boston; Oliver will be craving to hear news from you.

You are in our thoughts and prayers always,

Your Friend,

Katherine Carron

Brendan remained in his room for some time, and had no idea of how dark it had become until, with a brief knock upon the door, Tom Delaney entered.

"What're you like, sitting here in the dark? Where's the lamp?" He fumbled in his pocket for matches and lit the solid, china lamp on the desk.

"Tom?" Brendan's voice came quietly to his friend's ears. He still had not moved from his seat by the window.

"Aye?"

"You'd said you'd heard of a ship leaving for Boston on Wednesday?"

"Aye, but that's only three days away. You haven't had a reply to your letter to your uncle yet, have you? You'll not be leaving so soon, surely."

Brendan rose from his chair and pulled the heavy russet-coloured drapes shut with a flourish of a curtain coming down on the final scene of a play. When he turned to face his friend it was, to Tom's delight, with the bright and careless smile of the Brendan he had always known; gone was the wan stranger of the past few weeks.

"The time has come for further adventures," he grinned. "Perhaps James Stephens needs a bit of a jog to get this rebellion on its unsteady feet."

Tom snorted. "As if James Stephens and the American Brotherhood would listen to the likes of you—upstart Wicklow sheep farmer . . ."

"Wounded in action . . ."

"Oh, I've no argument with your going to Boston—you'll be able to speak firsthand to the American Fenians of how things are over here. But, lad, no one knows you're here in Cork—you can stay here for as long as you like—with the Sherrys or with me and my family—and go to Boston in a few months. Maybe you won't need to go at all—the call to arms might come at any time, and Boston is too far away."

Not far enough, Brendan thought. Bridget had been right; he had been trapped, all these years, through his own need, not because of Katherine, nor Oliver. Oliver who, now he was faced with adversity, was showing all the courage and tenacity that those closest to him had always sensed he possessed.

"I have plans to make," Brendan murmured. "I need that distance, Tom. Frightening though it is for me to contemplate, I must decide what I'm to do with the rest of my life."

Five

The house of Vincent Kelehan on Chestnut Street, Beacon Hill was, like its owner, of large, stolid, somewhat portentous exterior and possessed of a wayward, almost eccentric charm within. His friends—and his enemies, too, for he was successful and had, as he was wont to boast, only as few enemies as fair-dealing success could bring a man—blamed it on his Irishness. But the adornment of his home was as idiosyncratic as the rest of Vincent's character; there was not another Irishman born who could have devised a house like the one Vincent and Rose Kelehan resided in.

Brendan had a private belief that Vincent was the reincarnation of a Greek despot—only this could explain the preponderance of pale marble, the feeling of uncluttered space, so completely out of tune with the times; the desire for pastel shades and large windows that seemed to bring the outdoors into the huge old house and leave one with the feeling that it was open to the sky.

In all weathers, Brendan thought, on the day that he returned to Boston, as he handed his damp coat and hat to the manservant and strode into the main hall. The rain made a fearful racket upon the glass dome above the curved double staircase; it threw patterns on the wall that made it seem as if the marble, too, were weeping with damp. It was deceptive; two great fireplaces filled with blazing logs warmed the hall, but nevertheless Brendan shivered pleasurably. The pale grey marble of the hall, the matching dove grey of the window drapes and the steady, streaming rain overhead gave him the illusion that he had walked through a doorway only to find himself in the open air once more. In a Roman ruin—a temple, perhaps, or the house of a wealthy senator. Brendan knew, in this period of dark rooms, much plush and braid and clutter of furniture and bric-a-brac, that the house of Vincent Kelehan was regarded as a white elephant of grotesque proportions.

Yet Brendan loved it, loved the very airiness and sense of space that others found bare to the point of impoverishment. He smiled at this, standing in the centre of the great hall, gazing about at the few excellent paintings and the carefully-placed statuary that lined the hall and marched, at eye-pleasing intervals, up the walls of the staircase.

The manservant, new to the house since Brendan's last visit in 1861, had retired with coat and hat when Brendan had insisted on announcing himself. Mister Kelehan, he had been told, was in the library. Brendan, after his few moments alone, feeling the great house welcoming him once more, was about to turn to the library door when a voice from above him called, "Are you lost?"

He looked up, but there did not appear to be anyone there. The two wings of staircase met at the landing and continued upwards, empty, towards the first floor.

"Are you? Are you lost?"

Allowing his eyes to travel down the right-hand side of the staircase, Brendan found his interrogator. A small face peered out at him from between the carved marble balusters. Features could not be discerned, but the light from above shone on fair hair, and the eyes looked dark and unblinkingly solemn.

"No, I'm not lost." He moved forward. The face pulled back, disappeared, then reappeared abruptly over the balustrade between two small hands. The chin had to be raised to look over. Short, straight gold hair and very dark eyes.

"I used to get lost. I don't now. I used to fall down the stairs." This alarming news was spoken with the utmost satisfaction. "I hurt my head," he continued, placing a small hand to his temple, "but it got better."

"I'm very glad to hear that."

A second's pause, in which Brendan's tone was studied, his face perused, and a general assessment was made, then only the top of the gold head was visible as the careful tap, tap, of small shoes, cautious after an early career fraught with incident, came down the curve of the stairs towards him.

The boy paused on the last step, and Brendan, who had moved

to the newel post, stood regarding the child with the same open curiosity with which the child regarded him.

"What's your name?" the boy asked.

"Brendan Kelehan. What's yours?"

"Damian O'Boyle. I'm four. How old are you?"

"Oh, I'm quite old. I'm . . ."

"Damian?"

Brendan heard the rustle of skirts that accompanied the calling of the child's name, but by the time he looked up the girl had paused at the top of the stairs and was staring down at him.

Even at this distance she gave the impression of being quite tall and unusually slender. The skirts of her pale blue dress were of the latest fashion, the full gathers pulled back over the crinoline into many folds behind. He saw both views of her in quick succession, for one hand was raised quickly, in an embarrassed effort to push back the long fair hair that fell loose about her, then she had whirled and fled off into the upstairs hall before he could speak. From somewhere in the recesses of the house a door shut.

"I'm here!" Damian called, belatedly. He was too small to see over the curve of the upper banister.

"Who was that?"

Brendan had muttered the word half to himself, but Damian volunteered immediately, "Mary Rose. She'll be cross. I got up when I shouldn't. I wasn't sleepy. I'm four. I'm too big for naps. Nich'las has naps. He's a baby. Can you button my boots?"

One small foot was held up to Brendan and he saw, in truth, that the small boots were unfastened. The two sat down on the steps together and, as Brendan struggled with the miniature buttons, he was wondering at the vision of Mary Rose.

He had seen her only two or three times during his visit to America in '61, when her parents had brought her with them on a visit to Boston. For the rest of the time, the O'Boyles lived in a small town in Illinois, some miles from Chicago. Brendan had a vague memory of a coltish, pale child with thick gold braids, who seemed to shrink within herself whenever someone addressed her. She had been tall for her age even then, at eleven or twelve years old, and had been rather round-shouldered, he remembered, as if she was somehow attempting to contract herself, make herself inconspicuous in a hostile world.

Yet her parents, Rose's sister Bernadette, and her husband Patrick O'Boyle, adored the child, and insisted despairingly that the shyness was a stage she was going through. Brendan remembered that he used to tease her, gently, almost flirting with her, and she had, on some rare occasions, shown him a smile of such radiance that, he had declared later to her parents, he had no doubt but that Mary Rose would one day soon blossom like the flower for which she had been named.

It had been a young man's amusement, the words typical of a young man's condescension. But he had been right. Somewhere in the five years since he had left the United States, the child Mary Rose had grown into a woman.

He shook his head, smiled a little over the small boot in his hand. Neither Vincent nor Rose Kelehan had been regular correspondents, but one of their letters, about a year ago, had told him that to everyone's surprise, Bernadette and Patrick had had a son late in life, followed, only a few months prior to the date of their letter, by a second boy. This must be the O'Boyle heir then, and 'Nich'las' the latest addition to the family.

He found himself looking forward to seeing the parents. Bernadette was several years younger than Aunt Rose, and she and her husband were an outgoing, laughing couple, interested in the arts, especially music. Although related to them only by marriage, Brendan identified with Bernadette and Patrick even more than with his own uncle and aunt; this visit, as with the others in the past, he anticipated many evenings spent at concerts and the theatre, events that the older Kelehans tried to avoid as much as possible.

"Are your mama and papa in the library?" he asked Damian.

"No . . ." rather carefully from the child, the word a little elongated. "Papa and Mama are in heaven now."

His tone was matter-of-fact, the inflection that of the kindly adults who had instilled this euphemism within him. Brendan could only stare; having finished fastening the last little shoe, he lowered it to the steps.

"I have to see Uncle Vincent, Damian. Don't you think you should go upstairs and tell Mary Rose where you are?"

Brendan had stood, and the child rose also, but it soon became apparent that he had no intention of trading the company of this interesting stranger for that of Mary Rose and Nicholas. He slipped his hand confidently within Brendan's and trotted beside him, sometimes pulling a little ahead of him, towards the double doors that led to the library.

The first knock upon the door proved to be inadequate; it was a large room, and Vincent and Rose would undoubtedly be seated at the opposite end, beside the fireplace. Brendan knocked a second time, quite loudly, and when no answer was forthcoming, he opened the door and walked in, the width of the doorway and the narrowness of his companion enabling them both to pass the threshold at the same time.

Despite the heavy knuckling on the door panels and the footsteps across the parquet floor, they neither of them immediately looked up; they were absorbed in their conversation.

"She was a brainless, irresponsible girl when she was in her father's charge, and she's a brainless, irresponsible woman now she's in her husband's charge." This from Aunt Rose.

"Her father is my friend," patiently from Vincent.

"Is she or is she not—"

"And he's my business associate . . ."

"Is she or is she—"

"And I don't believe in antagonizing . . ."

"Is she or is she not a complete fool and a bad influence upon Mary Rose?"

"Yes!" Vincent's fist came down hard on the arm of his chair. Aunt and Uncle glared at each other across a table spread with the remains of afternoon tea, the sight of which was the cause of Damian running forward and interrupting what promised to be an interesting conversation.

"Darling boy!" Damian ran straight to Aunt Rose, who lifted the little boy into her ample lap. Damian snuggled down into the folds of the black alpaca gown and lifted one hand to point—so it was Rose who, following his arm, first saw Brendan standing there.

Her eyes grew wide in the plump face, and "Darling boy!" she repeated with, if possible, more excitement, and Damian found himself evicted from her lap as quickly as he had taken possession of it. Sweeping around the table, she rushed forward towards her eldest nephew.

Vincent, too, had stood. "Brendan? Brendan, lad! I thought you were Eben!" Tall, robust, his powerful neck straining at the snowy, starched confines of his collar, Vincent marched across the floor to pump Brendan's hand, thump him on the back. "Never even looked up," he told Rose who was clinging, moist-eyed, to Brendan's other arm, "Thought he was Eben, come to take the tea things. Brendan, lad! Only just received your letter telling us you were coming ...!" There was a pause, and husband and wife glanced at each other. Then, with one accord, they both turned on Damian.

"Damian, go upstairs to Mary Rose . . ."

"Take a bun and run along, there's a lad . . ."

Damian had already helped himself to a bun. He hastily obeyed his uncle and took another, before retreating out the library door, content with his spoils.

Vincent rang for more tea and they settled down beside the cavernous fireplace with its frieze of chariots and horses that seemed to move with the flickering of the flames.

"An accident on the lake," Aunt Rose's voice was low, as she explained the events of the past few months. "They loved boating, both of them. This time the children had colds, so they left them with the governess and went out for the day with another two couples . . .

"One of the men, a strong swimmer, managed to get to shore—all the other five were lost. It was a severe and sudden storm, last July. I can't help but think that if they *had* had the children with them, they wouldn't have sailed so far, taken such a risk . . ."

"No point in that now, my dear, no point. The children are safe, as they may not have been had they gone with Patrick and Bernadette." There was tenderness in the way Vincent spoke; it was apparent, too, in the way he reached out and held his wife's hand.

Brendan looked at both of them: Rose had a broad, good-tempered face beneath fair hair that was streaked now with silver. Vincent had only the faintest resemblance, in the hooked nose and the deep-set eyes, to his brother James. He was a bigger man, a hard-headed and astute businessman who cared for little outside his work and his home—it was as if, early in life, he had decided to leave all interest in intellectualism to his more percipient older brother. Yet there were similarities; both were good men and fair, both had made good marriages to splendid women. To watch Vincent and Rose was to be reminded, strongly, at this moment of James and Kathleen Kelehan. Brendan felt at the same time bereft and yet warmed by his memories.

"And Mary Rose and the little boys?"

Vincent turned to him. "Bernadette and Rose were always close, as you know. We're godparents to all three of the children and Patrick had requested that we act as their guardians should anything ever happen to himself and Bernadette."

"When the accident occurred," Aunt Rose continued, "there was no question about what was to be done. We travelled to Crystal Lake and, when all the details were taken care of, we brought the children home with us. You must have left Ireland before receiving our reply to your letter, my dear—we told you to come, by all means, and explained that we now have three children."

And Rose, despite her grief, could not but allow some of her newfound contentment to shine through. Brendan had always thought it was a tragedy that the couple had not been blessed with children of their own; now, through another tragedy, the great deal of love and warmth that Rose had to offer had an outlet at last.

"So, I have three cousins now." Brendan leaned back in his chair. "I've met Damian, but I've yet to meet Nicholas, and I saw only a brief glimpse of Mary Rose . . ."

"Ah, Brendan, hasn't she grown to be a beauty? She was named after my Rose, you know. We have a steady stream of young men calling at the house, all with various sisters and female cousins in tow, of course, for propriety's sake." Vincent chuckled, it was obvious that he was enjoying himself immensely.

"It must have made great changes in your life," Brendan smiled at Aunt Rose.

She leaned forward in her chair, "This house has come alive, my dear. Oh, in the first days it was a scramble," she laughed at her husband, "as we discovered to our cost that the objects and furnishings of this house were not the most suitable surroundings for two little boys galloping loose about the place. But with the smaller pieces placed at higher points, and a playroom furnished by trial and error, we've settled in together very well. Mary Rose has been wonderful, of course, though it has been hard for her, a girl of her age, to have the little ones so dependent upon her. For the first few months they wouldn't let her out of their sight, and she was so patient with them. It helped her get over her grieving though, much sooner than she would normally have done. I had her out of mourning dress sooner than most people would approve, I think, but I don't believe a young girl like that should be spending the happiest years of her life in crows' colours."

The door opened at this point, after a brief tapping, to admit the young manservant, Eben, with the tea things and, following him, Mary Rose with Damian trotting beside her and a chubby, lively baby in her arms.

The girl came first to stand by Brendan's chair and, having stood, with Vincent, when she entered the room, he could see that she was a good few inches taller than average height and so slim, so narrow of frame, that she reminded him of the fables of nymphs or dryads, an evanescent creature of such ethereal grace that she was not really human at all.

The hair was now drawn demurely back into a beaded net at the back of her head, and her smile was certainly human and warm.

"Cousin Brendan," the blue eyes sparked mischief, "what terrible things have been happening to you in Ireland that you're so changed?"

"I . . ." He was puzzled, even discomfited by her words, glanced at his uncle and aunt—and then remembered. They had not spoken of it but, in the five years since he had been absent, his hair had prematurely and progressively turned from the dark brown that she would remember to a steely silver. He himself had become grudgingly accustomed to it, though he liked it none the more for that. His hand now came up to brush the straight fringe that had fallen onto his forehead, with something like irritation, but he smiled. "Hard work, I fear, Cousin Mary Rose, no more glamorous pastime than that."

To his consternation he heard a slight "Hmph!" of disapproval from Aunt Rose, and caught the look of warning that Vincent threw her. Brendan had told them the truth in his letter, but they had obviously not told Mary Rose, and he was grateful for that.

Mary Rose was still smiling at him, and the eyes—surely this was not the same shy child he would often find in this very room, hiding from company behind a book, who begged him not to disclose her whereabouts to her relatives and other visitors—the eyes were pure devilment. Lord, she was lovely, perhaps the most beautiful girl he had ever seen. It was going to be most enjoyable to see the stir that she was obviously making upon Boston society.

"And this is Nicholas." She held him forward a little. "He's fourteen months old now. Will you say hello, Nicholas?"

Nicholas, who had been studying Brendan from beneath furrowed brows, decided to forgo the pleasantries and, grinning, simply threw himself into his older cousin's arms, crowing his welcome in cheerful though unintelligible babble.

Brendan's sorrow at the tragic deaths of Bernadette and Patrick was to weigh heavily upon him in the next few days, but here, in the bright, warm room, in the company of the three children, he was able to postpone his grieving for two people he had liked and respected very much. He was helped by seeing the changes that the children's presence had made in the lives of Vincent and Rose Kelehan. Both seemed younger, more lively and expressive, had lost the air of sedate formality that, with their wealth and their years, had begun to settle upon them. The whole house, it seemed, had a sense of busyness, of lively anticipation; there were several more servants now, to cater for the children's needs, and they were a happy, cheerful group who were gathered to be introduced to Brendan on that afternoon.

The Kelehans' coachman had been dispatched to the shipping office to collect Brendan's luggage, and by the time Brendan climbed the stairs to bathe and change for dinner, he found all his clothes unpacked and the suit he would need pressed and laid out for him.

Vincent had said that he wished Brendan to have a week at home before returning to Masterton and O'Dea, the firm of attorneys with whom he had spent several busy and happy months in the winter and spring of 1861. It had all been arranged when Vincent had received Brendan's letter from Cork, and though the firm were delighted to find a place for him once more, Vincent insisted that Brendan see some of the city and enjoy himself before taking up his career once more.

Besides, it was obvious Vincent wanted to talk in depth of what was happening in Ireland.

Brendan considered all this while he was dressing, and during the few brief moments of silence over dinner. Only he, Rose, Vincent and Mary Rose dined beneath the large chandelier in the formal dining room, the two boys having had their supper in the nursery.

He could not deny he was enjoying, already, the luxury of the lifestyle here on Chestnut Street; it was a far cry from his untidy though spacious rooms on St Stephens Green, and even from the casual comfort of the big house of Avonwood, where the furnishings were precious but tattered from age and generations of well-loved cats and dogs, and where the servants, fond and condescending and having known one since one was in nappies, often objected, like relatives, if they felt one was making the wrong decision.

But for all the seductiveness of a life of ease in this great house, Brendan knew, even on this first day, that as soon as he was settled he would find rooms of his own in Boston. To stay would be to be one more burden that his aunt and uncle should not have to bear; and besides, he would be busy and his home would be busy, with men planning the insurrection in Ireland which would surely come within the next few weeks.

His arm, almost as if on cue, gave him a sudden stab of pain and his mind was suddenly crowded with images of those last few days in Dublin—the last time he had visited Pilsworth's tavern, the familiar faces of O'Kelly, Devoy, St Clair, Daniel Hutton, Oliver Carron. He was attending the factory workers' meeting, was caught up with Daniel in the insurgence as police moved in to make arrests, and he was in the dark of that alleyway with Ginnane and saw once more the frenzied face of Ned Costin, the gun . . .

His knife fell from his numbed hand with a clatter—". . . and I told her that it was nothing unusual for a child of Damian's age—" The noise stopped Aunt Rose halfway through her sentence. Then they were calling for Emily, the maid, to fetch another knife for Mister Brendan, and Brendan himself, relieved to have his own unpleasant thoughts interrupted, looked up—and met the eyes of young Mary Rose, seated directly across the table from him.

She watched him with a faint smile on her lips and a conspiratorial look in the steady blue eyes. She was saying to him, *I know you dropped that knife because you were lost in your past and had forgotten us. I know, and I want you to see I know.*

He smiled at her, and she returned his smile, but still that knowing look lingered on her face. He had seen it, this feminine, mock-innocent expression, on faces of varying degrees of attractiveness in drawing rooms and ballrooms ever since he turned eighteen and began to move in society. Through several brief liaisons and the years of his devotion to Katherine, he had taken the look for granted; it was something to do with the illusion women had that he was attractive, and his twenty thousand pounds a year, both combining to make him Eligible; the label as obvious upon him as if it had been sewn to the back of his dinner jackets. He had ignored it, nearly all his adult life.

Now, he watched his young cousin lower her thick-lashed lids, then raise her eyes to his once more—and with the beauty of that face the smile she gave him was radiant, breathtaking. And the look in her eyes held that same knowing challenge.

"Don't let's go home immediately," Mary Rose said, as they came through the church gate onto the sidewalk the following Sunday after Mass. "Let's walk along the river for a while—it's such a lovely day."

The weather was still chill and cold, but, like a gift in the midst of weeks of bad sleet and rain, the sky was a soft, clear blue today, and the sun, when one faced where it rode low in the sky, actually warmed one's face.

She was pleased when Brendan smiled at her suggestion, and taking this for consent, she grinned, and turned back to find Vincent and Rose.

She was less pleased to find that Damian wished to accompany her, and, having her aunt and uncle's blessing, she returned to Brendan wearing a slightly discontented scowl with a cheerfully unconcerned Damian marching behind her.

"I'm coming for a walk, too," he announced breathlessly, then turned and shot off through the gates before pausing to look back at Brendan. "Which way?"

Brendan pointed, and Damian ran off ahead. Mary Rose watched him go with a sudden fondness; it appeared he would be no diversion after all.

There was a small park along the embankment, and Damian was soon plunging back and forth on a swing, declaring to Mary Rose in a loud voice that he was going to fly over the River Charles, over the world, over the moon. She found that an occasional interjection of "Will you?" and "That's grand, Damian!" kept the soul of the small explorer satisfied. She found she could speak with Brendan quite freely, and once more, as on several occasions over the past few days, the conversation turned to his future plans.

"But there's nothing for you in Ireland. Why, people are leaving Ireland in droves—and probably always will. They don't call this the New World for nothing, Brendan. Look at my father—and Uncle Vincent—you could make a fortune here!"

"I have a tidy little fortune," he laughed, "quite enough to keep me for the rest of my life."

Mary Rose was relentless. 'Well, in America you can *keep* it. What are the business opportunities in Ireland, or anywhere in Europe, I should like to know? Maximum loss, minimum profit, that's how it'll be—until you have to live off your capital, and . . .'"

She looked up in time to see him turning away to hid a grin, and ran around him to catch the look, took him by his arms in her mock anger and tried to shake him. "What's so funny? Why are you laughing? Why, any fool could tell you I'm speaking the truth. Ask any banker or stockbroker—Uncle Vincent's friend Mister Crossley at . . ."

"Mary Rose, Mary Rose . . ." He placed his hands on her shoulders and she stopped, suddenly, gazing up at him. "Do you ever consider, my dear, that there are more important things in life than profit and loss . . ."

"Yes. Love," she said, taking him aback with her promptness.

"Well . . . security and love are equally important, I suppose. But, Mary Rose, I can be of some *use* in Ireland, don't you see? I'd been planning for some time to give up my rather safe law practice and work in some poor area—in tenancy cases, perhaps. Even if I'm rarely paid by my clients, I'd like to help those less fortunate than myself."

"But you can do that here. There are thousands of poor people in Boston . . ."

"I'm an Irishman, Mary Rose. Ireland is home."

"There are thousands of poor Irish in Boston . . ."

"Ireland is *home.*" His hands were heavy on her shoulders with the words. The emphasis was clear. *I am not at home here.*

Something indefinable and heavy settled in her chest. She found herself looking at the top button of his waistcoat. And then, to her horror, she heard her own voice ask, "You're in love with a woman back in Dublin, aren't you?"

If he had answered straight away. A little laugh, and a "No, not at all." But he was silent, and the seconds passed.

When, finally, she looked up at him, he was gazing across the Charles, his eyes fixed not on the further shore, but on his past, she knew. Even the hands upon her shoulders were now an insult, for they remained there only because he had forgotten her.

"Well? I'm right, aren't I?"

He looked down at her, gripped her shoulders in a friendly manner and let her go, offering his arm once more as they continued along the embankment. She was worried that she had gone too far, but he spoke, finally, and there was no sense of irritation in his voice.

"There was someone. But it's over now." Then, suddenly, "No—it had never really begun, if I'm honest with myself. I loved her, but she wasn't in love with me."

"A woman would be a fool not to love you. How could she refuse a man like you?"

"She didn't. I never spoke to her of my feelings—when I met her she was already committed to one of my best friends."

He looked rather unsure of himself for a moment, and she hastily said, "Go on, please."

And he did, scowling at the path before him as they walked. They turned then, and walked back the way they had come, keeping close to the little playground where Damian was now in conversation with another small boy and his nanny.

Mary Rose had the feeling that he was not a man who often spoke of his emotions; that he was telling *her* made her content, however painful his words were. There was a strength about him, for he was a man of great self-reliance—yet he was possessed also of a vulnerability that drew him to her with each new day she was with him.

"They'd known each other barely two weeks," he was saying

now. "And yet, despite that, they decided to elope. It was ridiculous, of course . . ."

"Why?"

"What?"

"Why was it ridiculous? She loved your friend, didn't she?"

"Mary Rose, even at your tender age, you'd know that it takes more than two weeks to come to know someone . . ."

"Not if it were true love—if they were the two God had chosen for each other . . ."

"Well, it wasn't, and He didn't." He was cross now. Mary Rose lowered her eyes demurely as they walked on and let him continue. "They married, anyway. And she never knew how I felt."

"Ah . . ." Mary Rose sighed, forgot her own interest for a moment, for it was a tragic and charming story. "And you never saw each other again . . ."

"Of course we did—at least four or five times a week—her husband was one of my friends, remember."

"Oh." The story was not particularly charming, after all. She went on, "And there was no one else besides . . . her?"

"No."

"Not in—how many years since she married your friend?"

"Five years. No, there's been no one else." He looked at her with that infuriating amusement. "Has no one ever told you that you're rather a forward young lady?"

"No," she said, "but they do tell me I'm far too outspoken. Five years . . ." she lamented, "how sad, Brendan. That's truly sad." And because she felt she had to have more details, "How old was she when she met you?"

"About twenty-three, I think."

"Twenty-three! Why she was quite an old maid. No wonder she leapt at your friend when he proposed! Though I do believe that both men and women in Ireland marry later than people in other countries."

"She wasn't Irish, she was born overseas, in the colonies." She looked up in interest, and, as if feeling he had spoken too much, he glanced at his watch. "I think we'd best be heading for home, don't you? We'll be late for dinner."

She fell into step beside him as they turned, and waited quietly while he called young Damian to them. Then, when they had turned up Mt Vernon Street, and Damian once more had toddled ahead, she prompted, "The colonies—how interesting! India? Was she brought up in India?"

"No," he said.

"Africa, then. How exciting!"

"No," he laughed, "actually, she was born in Australia."

"Oh." And she was unable to keep the disappointment from her voice. Brendan remarked on this, and she admitted, "Well, yes. There's not really much in Australia, is there? Just a lot of desert and several peculiar species of animal. So," she added with bright consideration, "I can't really blame your friend for being unmarried at such a late age. It would have taken her all that time, given her background, to acquire some amount of sophistication in order to take her place in the world, would it not?"

"Miss O'Boyle, I do believe that you are something of a snob."

Fortunately his eyes were twinkling, and she ventured, "Certainly not, I'm simply interested in studying human nature. If I'd been a man, I'd certainly have become an anthropologist." She was silent a moment, then continued, "I suppose her family became wealthy in those goldrushes of the past ten years or so. I hear they've brought quite a fortune to many poor ranchers."

"Well, for a start, they don't call them 'ranchers' in Australia. Apparently they didn't have the Spanish influence there that they had in this country. They're called farmers, and their land would be farms, or properties. The really large holdings, many of them bigger than some American states, are called stations."

"Stations? How odd. And what would your friend call a corral, or a prairie?"

"A yard, and a plain. And they don't have cowboys, either, the men who tend the stock are called just that, stockmen."

"My," Mary Rose murmured with a smile, "you have remembered every word of what she told you." And that was a mistake, for his face closed, and he looked ahead of them with the trace of a scowl. She went on quickly, "I like that word, 'stockman', much better than 'cowboy'. It sounds more . . . more . . ."

"Mature?"

"Yes—" and she looked up, sharply, hearing him give a sudden, soft laugh.

"I don't see what's so amusing, Cousin Brendan. I'm sure I'm not to blame if I appear ignorant. I *am* ignorant, but I'm not afraid to own it, and I want to learn!"

He had stopped walking, and turning to her, stood for a moment gazing down at her face. "What is it you want to learn, Mary Rose?"

"Everything," she said without hesitation. "Life. I want to know about life."

They were standing very close, studying each other's faces. Mary

Rose found that she was barely breathing when he turned away, suddenly, and walked on. As they rounded the corner into Chestnut Street, she heard him mutter, "I think anthropology would be safer."

"It would be perfect," Mary Rose sighed, "were it not for the fact that he has an overriding social conscience and . . . and some kind of loyalty to a lost love that's now absolutely out of his reach."

"Absolutely?" Myra Gorham leaned back against the cushions of the chaise longue and watched her friend pacing up and down the small space between the furniture.

It was a spacious room, but Myra's pride was that it was filled with objets d'art, "in scattered, deceptively informal style with a studied mixture of periods", was how she had described her new home to a wincing Vincent and Rose a few months before. They had hoped that Myra's marriage to a wealthy and unimaginative young banker would remove her from Mary Rose's acquaintance, but, if anything, young Mrs Gorham, Mary Rose's first friend on coming to Boston, showed an even greater interest in her welfare than when she herself was single. Rose Kelehan suspected that, with the excitement of the betrothal and the wedding plans finally over and her object attained, Myra found matrimony generally, and her husband in particular, to be rather tiresome. But whatever her reasons, Mary Rose was a constant visitor to the tall, narrow house on Beacon Street.

"Yes, thank goodness, she's married. So there's nothing, really, in the way—except that he might need a little—a very little—push."

"Your little push, Mary Rose, sounds more like proposed coercion."

"Coercion?" Mary Rose whirled on her friend with such force that her broad skirt caught a spindly-legged table and brought it over with a bump onto the carpet, spilling a tassled doily and several ornaments with it.

"Oh, look what you've done!"

Myra stood with a furious rustle of petticoats, pushed her skirts as closely to her sides as she could, and sailed like an attacking barquentine up the narrow fjord between the piano, two Louis XV chairs and an escritoire of inlaid walnut.

"Nothing's broken—the carpet's very thick." Mary Rose was down on her knees on the richly-patterned pile, already adjusting the table's contents to their former positions. "It's your own fault, Myra, for having your parlour so cluttered with furniture."

"It is not cluttered," Myra bent over to adjust the doily, her glossy, fair curls falling forward on either side of the handsome face with its patrician nose and rather heavy, rounded, jawline. Several admirers had often remarked, to her secret delight, that she had the look of the Venus of Milo. Now the small mouth was pursed with irritation, the broad, pale brow creased with a less than divine scowl. "It is not cluttered, it is *arranged*. You know very well that this house is the talk of Boston society . . ."

"I know, I'm sorry . . ."

"I've worked very hard to have things just so."

"And they are." Mary Rose hugged her friend, who looked slightly happier and returned, mollified, to the chaise longue.

"Tell me more," she said, arranging her shawl as she leaned back again, "about this handsome cousin of yours."

"Well, really, he isn't my cousin, though I call him that. My Aunt Rose married *his* Uncle Vincent, so while we share an uncle and aunt, we aren't related by blood at all."

"That's convenient. If it becomes serious," Myra pronounced. Her eight-week-old marriage to Ralph Gorham lent her, both she and Mary Rose felt, a greater experience of life that merely added to her other advantages over her friend. Mary Rose had always been impressed by Myra; she was a full twenty years old, had lived in Paris, Rome and Madrid with her diplomat father, and she secretly smoked cigars—once her parent's, now her husband's. And she could swear volubly in four languages.

"It will become serious." Mary Rose gave up her marching and came to sit in an uncomfortable red plush armchair close to her friend. "I've adored him for years, you see. He was always so handsome, with his dark hair and grey eyes—and now—oh, the shock when I saw him! His hair has turned a kind of dark silver and it falls onto his forehead in such a . . . a . . . disarming way. I came out of my room, that first day he arrived, and there he stood at the foot of the staircase, looking up at me. I felt . . ." The emotion that the memory engendered was too much for her and she stood once more and began her perambulations amongst the furniture.

"Do sit down, Mary Rose," Myra watched the dangerous, sweeping skirts with trepidation.

"I felt . . . as if a hand had touched my heart—oh, I know it sounds silly, but that's truly how it felt. I shall never, never feel like that with anyone again! He was the first man I ever loved, when I was a naive little schoolgirl—and now I'm a woman, and I *know* he's the right man for me!"

"That could be true," Myra said, consideringly, "but how does he feel on the matter?"

"Him?"

"Yes, you needn't look so blank. Does *he* feel you're the right woman for *him*?"

"Really, Myra, he only arrived four days ago . . ."

"But you should have some idea . . ."

"He gave me a very . . . secret smile over dinner."

"Perhaps he had indigestion."

"Stop it! It was a very *intimate* look, as if we shared the same thoughts. As if he wanted to look into my soul."

"How very intense. How old is your cousin?"

"Thirty-two."

"That's quite old, dear. When a single man of thirty-two is intense in a young lady's company, it's fair to say that his ambitions may not always be matrimonial."

"I don't care what he's thinking about *now*. What I want is your advice on how to make him think as *I* do."

"And you want to marry this Brendan Kelehan . . ."

"Yes."

And there was no doubting Mary Rose's sincerity or determination. The little chin was up, the blue eyes directed nowhere but towards a future she was certain she could forge to her own ends.

"Well," Myra sighed. "I shall have to see him first. If he is as splendid a specimen as you say he is, I shall support you in any way I can. I shall hold parties every week to which you will both be invited . . . No, no, don't crush me—you can show your gratitude by ringing for tea."

"You know," she said reflectively, as Mary Rose trotted dutifully to the bellpull, "it's almost a pity we can't tell men what terrific trouble we go to in order to enhance their lives with our presence."

Brendan, looking back upon that time in years to come, often wondered at how quickly those months in Boston passed. He was busy at the office of Masterton and O'Dea, it was true, and, despite Vincent's and Rose's protests, he found himself a sunny, comfortable house on Charles Street and moved in only three weeks after his arrival in Boston.

Still, he was very often at the house in Chestnut Street, and since Mary Rose had inherited her parents' love of theatre, opera and ballet, he frequently found himself accompanying her.

Much of his father's fortune had been made on the American stock market, due to Vincent's advice, and Brendan was able, after visiting his Boston bank, to send the equivalent of five hundred pounds to Katherine. He had borrowed only two hundred and fifty, but said in his letter to her that he wished her to use the remainder to help Oliver's legal costs.

He received a gracious, though brief letter in reply, touching in its gratitude. It appeared that the case against Oliver and all those Fenians within Irish gaols was to be pursued with heavy and swift retribution. There were rumours that the Crown would press for the death penalty. Brendan, worried, wrote further letters to her, asking for news of Oliver and her and Christopher's progress, but no answer came.

And in the meantime, there was Mary Rose.

When was it he had given up the effort to remain detached, amused, condescending? He found himself talking to her, of his family background, of his sisters who, having heard the truth at last from letters sent from Boston, now wrote furious, fond demands and admonitions by almost every ship that sailed from Dublin; of the events of his final night in that city, and of his first, fortuitous meeting with the Sherrys of Cork City.

He found he did not speak of Katherine, never mentioned her again, and Mary Rose, it seemed, to his relief, had lost interest in the topic of his strange lost love from the Antipodes.

At the ballet, the theatre, at soirées and dinner dances, he was immensely proud of Mary Rose; her youth, her untarnished optimism and self-confidence healed an ache within him that, slow in its progress, had coloured his personality and outlook without his being aware of it until, with her presence, he was free of it. And the strange thing, the unbelievable thing, was that this delightful creature seemed to adore him. He did not, as the weeks went by, any longer doubt or worry about this; he allowed matters to evolve as they would.

And Uncle Vincent and Aunt Rose, whom he half-expected to frown upon what was seemingly developing under their roof, appeared, on the contrary, to delight in the thought that Mary Rose and Brendan were constantly in each other's company.

So time passed, pleasurably and without seeming to pass; when he found himself alone with Mary Rose in the Gorhams' garden during a musical evening, he kissed her with no thought in his head of the future or the repercussions. When, two days later, Vincent asked him if he were "serious about Mary Rose", it was logical to answer that he was, as if he had given the state of his emotions a great deal of thought. And when Vincent asked for a possible date for the wedding, it seemed perfect sense to suggest that it should be as soon as possible.

He had, of course, a serious discussion on the subject with Mary Rose—if they married, it would mean an eventual return to Ireland, not, he agreed, to his dreamed-of practice in the inner city, but to a comfortable country lifestyle at Avonwood.

Mary Rose readily agreed; she loved the country—had she not been brought up in Crystal Lake, Illinois? She would not miss the city one bit—and returning to Ireland was merely a return to the roots that had been transplanted to American soil only one generation before.

If time passed pleasantly and smoothly before this decision was made, once the plans for the marriage were under way the weeks became a frenzied blur of activity. Brendan was content with the thought that he would possess, for always, the woman who had made him forget all that had hitherto occurred in his life; the years of loneliness, of study and work, and bitter disappointment in his country's inability to pull free from the yoke of foreign subjugation, and most of all, perhaps, he felt that Mary Rose would be the one who could make him forget Katherine Prescott Carron. He scolded himself, still, for spending time wondering how he could phrase the news of his marriage in a letter to her and to Oliver, and for wondering how she would feel when she read it. It should not matter; in only a short time it would not matter; he would be too busy here, with raising more money for the rebellion, and, later, with Mary Rose in Ireland, raising a family of their own within the solid walls of Avonwood.

"I know that you have your future planned, and that you're looking forward to the way of life you foresee for yourself and your wife— but Brendan, my dear—are you certain Mary Rose is the right wife for you?"

Brendan looked up at his aunt in surprise. They had been discussing wedding plans, for as the nearest relatives of bride as well as groom, Vincent and Rose were taking keen delight in these preparations. The question, after a thoughtful pause in the conversation which could have been for something as innocent as the choice of flowers for the church, caught Brendan completely unawares.

"Of course," he said. Then, with a faint worried frown, "Why, do you think she would be unhappy with me?"

"No! Oh, no! My dear, there isn't another man in the world in whom I have greater trust to look after Mary Rose. You will be the best husband the girl could possibly have—and I hope the child is aware of how fortunate she is. It's simply . . ." She chewed her lower lip, hesitant, as if aware of how delicate the topic was, caught between her loyalties to the man she looked upon as a son, and the girl she looked upon as a daughter. "Though I have no doubts that you are the best husband for Mary Rose, I wonder if Mary Rose—as much as I love her—would be the best wife for you. You're a complicated man, Brendan, with a complicated life. You have many responsibilities." She had lowered her eyes, and he wondered just how much she knew of his involvement with the Republican Brotherhood. "Perhaps you would be happier with a more mature woman—someone who understands that you may be preoccupied sometimes, or working long hours, or late for dinner . . ."

He said with a smile, "Surely you believe Mary Rose is mature enough to understand . . ."

"I wonder. I . . . I cannot help but wonder, my dear. Mary Rose was always a delicate child; she was much indulged by her parents. That, and being protected from the rough-and-tumble that a child with brothers and sisters must suffer as a matter of course, has meant that she has . . . a low tolerance for life's problems. It took her a great deal of time, I believe, to adjust to the presence of her two little brothers, though now, as you've seen, she's devoted to them. But still, her nervous system is extremely delicate . . ."

"Aunt Rose," with mock severity, "you're frightening me."

"Am I, dear?" She looked even more concerned. "I don't mean to. I simply wish to make you aware. This marriage is taking place with a little too much haste—I should have been firmer a lot earlier—for I feel that you and Mary Rose need to know each other better."

Brendan came to his aunt's chair and kissed her forehead. "Aunt Rose, I am a bachelor of thirty-two years of age—more than that, I'm the elder brother of seven volatile and energetic sisters. I know enough of the feminine mind to see Mary Rose quite clearly. I can see that she's young, and spoilt—I can also see that she had a kind heart, an endearing nature, and a very clever brain. I love the girl. And I assure you, whatever little tricks she has learnt in the past for turning events to suit her purpose, I'm more than capable of dealing with."

"But . . . should you have to? Wouldn't a relationship built on mutuality and honest respect be better? Brendan, to Mary Rose, I'm afraid this marriage is a mere romantic idyll—she has no idea . . ."

"I need her, Aunt Rose." And the solemn, for once unguarded

look in his grey eyes made her pause. "I promise you, I'll do all in my power to make Mary Rose happy."

She knew he was sincere, and she nodded, smiling gently at her nephew, patting his hand where it still lay on her shoulder. But her mind was not truly comforted, and her thoughts remained unquiet.

To Mary Rose the smell of orange blossom always brought back to her that heady, intoxicating time before the wedding. She and Myra decided to make the headdresses and bouquets themselves with sprigs of orange blossom from the small orchard behind Myra's house. They wore old silk gloves as they experimented, twisting the foliage this way and that, and chatting all the while.

"Will you *really* go back to Ireland?" Myra asked the day before the wedding. She had never before had the gratification of someone as utterly beneath her spell as Mary Rose, and the thought of losing her, even if it were months or years away, was beginning, to Myra's surprise, to be an inconvenient one.

Mary Rose, who had been waxing poetical on the subject of Ireland for weeks, even having bought several books on such subjects as Irish history and culture, had, in the past few days, fallen strangely silent on the matter of the new home waiting for her across the Atlantic, and, when she now paused and scowled across the fragrant blossoms in her hands, Myra lowered her own work and waited avidly for something that promised to be of interest.

"I know I *said* I would," Mary Rose began hesitantly, "but I've been thinking, these past few days. I miss Mama and Papa very much— but I have to admit that my life here in Boston is so much more interesting than it was in Crystal Lake. I love the city, Myra—I love Boston. And Brendan's doing so well, here. I've been meaning to speak to him about this . . ."

"What? Are you *mad*?" Myra rose from her chair, dumping her bouquet unceremoniously onto the seat, and came to sit close to Mary Rose on the chaise longue. "Look, Mary Rose, the last few days before a wedding are always fraught with horror for a young man—they'd be sheer hell for a confirmed bachelor with the success of Mr Kelehan. The last thing he needs is a deep discussion on the matter of you finding the thought of his ancestral home to be boring you to tears before you've even seen the place."

"But . . ." Mary Rose bit her lip, broke off a dead leaf and tore it into little pieces as she spoke, "I have to discuss it with him— it's only fair, isn't it?"

"No—it's cruel—he's miserable enough, right now, thinking of the ordeal he's about to go through. If he can give up his career as an Irish rebel and become respectable for you—not to mention all the *other things* a gentleman gives up on marriage . . ."

Mary Rose blushed. Myra had had to explain Everything to her some weeks before, and she still winced at the thought of her own ignorance on such matters all these years.

"The least you can do," Myra finished sternly, "is to keep quiet on a matter which he would not thank you for bringing up."

"You think I should wait until *after* we're married?"

"Of course. When you're betrothed—agree to anything. Afterwards—well, one's head is clear and one can put one's case so much better."

"Oh. Well, all right. Anyway," Mary Rose brightened, "perhaps the political situation in Ireland will remain difficult for some time. Perhaps we won't ever be able to go back there. Although," she considered, "I wouldn't mind going there for a visit."

"That's right," Myra agreed readily. "Those big old Irish houses are just full of antiques that'd be worth a fortune over here."

Mary Rose said nothing, but it was one of the few times that she almost did not like Myra. She wished her friend possessed a little more sensitivity in some matters and a little less cleverness. But then, Mary Rose sighed over the orange blossom, it was unreasonable to expect too much of people.

It was early April, and the morning gave a gift of clear sunshine for the marriage of Mary Rose and Brendan.

When Mary Rose walked up the aisle on Vincent Kelehan's arm in a dress from Paris made of creamy white satin in four tiers and a train four yards long, it was agreed that the simple bouquets of orange blossom carried by the bride and three bridesmaids were the most understated things about what was regarded as the wedding of the season. Vincent had spared no expense in this, the marriage of his beloved niece and nephew, and everything, from the pale rose satin of the bridemaids' gowns, to the food served beneath a canopy in the garden of the house on Chestnut Street, was of the finest available on the eastern seaboard.

The honeymoon was spent in New York, the weather still not too warm for that city, and Brendan took delight in showing Mary Rose what he knew of the city, and in learning to explore it together.

It was here, accompanying his young wife on shopping trips to furnish the house in Charles Street, that he noticed Mary Rose's avidity and strong sense of competition, for almost everything she saw she had to compare with items of similar practicality and worth in her friends' houses, especially—to Brendan's horror—the house of Mrs Gorham.

It seemed as if Mary Rose were driven by desire to have pieces of comparable style but of greater and, preferably, more obvious expense, and since Brendan disagreed, being most at home in the uncluttered space of Vincent and Rose's home, these shopping trips were the cause of their first quarrels.

And in this, too, Brendan learnt a great deal about his young wife, for it became patently obvious that Mary Rose had never before been faced with someone who told her "No."

With part of his mind, during the tempers and tears and bitter reproaches which twice had the hotel manager knocking on their door to request a lowering of volume, Brendan studied the problem and came to the conclusion that married life was going to be very much the same as growing up in the presence of his seven younger fiery-tempered sisters. In fact, and he took courage from this memory, the very worst-behaved as children and young girls, Ann, Mary and Ellen, were the very ones who, on maturity, had learnt such self-knowledge and control that they had joined the teaching order in Dublin and were very content.

He would watch Mary Rose stamping her little foot, declaring him a monster for not seeing that all her friends would laugh at her if she should have to settle for an eight-piece dining setting instead of twelve. Brendan's calm observation that the dining room would not hold the twelve-piece setting and that three guests would have to sit outside the window and two on the chandelier brought renewed tears and an accusation that he was mocking her.

With clothing and personal apparel, however, he indulged her completely, and it was a vastly different Mary Rose who came back from a dressmaker or a milliner during those weeks. They happily bought gifts for Vincent and Rose, Damian and Nicholas also. A great many for the latter two, as Mary Rose was missing the younger children. She would very much have liked to have them at her own new home, but agreed reluctantly with her husband and aunt and uncle that the boys were better left in the familiar surroundings of the house in Chestnut Street, and that she and Brendan should begin their married life alone together.

He told himself he was being churlish, yet it had worried Brendan that his young wife seemed to want to fill the house with other

people, and even on their honeymoon was making plans for parties
to be held on their return.

"My most precious moments are those I spend alone with you,"
he murmured to her, interrupting her talk of guest lists and who
should be seated with whom. The fact that they lay in bed in their
hotel suite, arms about each other, made Mary Rose's deliberations
seem all the more puzzling to her husband. "You do like being alone
with me, don't you?"

"Yes, of course, but . . ."

"We couldn't be doing *this* . . . if we were surrounded by . . ."

"Don't, Brendan, I was talking. You mustn't do that while I'm
trying to have a discussion . . ."

One heavy arm imprisoned her. "I want to talk about us, my
dear. About *you*."

He kissed her, demanding a response from lips already forming
an argument against intimacy. When he released her mouth, moving
his lips downwards along her stiff little jaw, he thought he heard,
imagined he felt, a sigh.

But her arms came about his body, and he forgot everything in
the possession of her. It was only afterwards, lying in that sweet
weakness that comes with giving one's body to one's beloved, that
Mary Rose's voice came softly; "If you really loved me, you'd want
everyone to see how happy we are together. All our friends are
expecting us to entertain them—what will they think if we ignore
them?"

He did not answer.

"Brendan?" Her fingers traced his hairline, the ridge of his
eyebrow. He realized that during lovemaking she never touched him
like this, as if she wanted him . . .

"I want everyone to see how wonderful you are, how lovely our
home is—you won't spoil everything for me, will you, my darling?"
The little fingers stroked his cheek, did not seem to feel or sense
the tightened sinews.

When he said, "I'll spoil nothing for you, my love. You have
my word on that," she nestled down against him with a little sigh
of contentment.

Later, when she slept, Brendan rose and moved barefooted across
the thick carpet to pull back the drapes and stand at the window,
looking down onto the city.

It was raining, and tonight even Manhattan lay silent, the imposing
buildings blue-grey and lonely in the gaslight, and the faint shimmers
of lit windows reflected on the wet and empty sidewalk and street.

Katherine.

First the word, then the pain, and only then the thought of her, the vision of her before him.

I must not. I must not . . .

His fists beat lightly upon the broad window sill, as if he could as easily knead away the impression that had come so swiftly, carved itself so deeply into his mind.

But it was there. He could pretend otherwise—and he would, he must—but there was no escaping from the fact that Mary Rose had not been able to dispel his longing for Katherine Carron.

"What's to become of us?" he murmured. But there was only the quiet breathing behind him, the chill of the room, and the steady, gentle rain on the great city beyond the glass. And there was no answer for him.

When they returned to Boston a month later, it was to find the box-room of their new home filled with the things they had bought, and they were not finished unpacking two days later when a note arrived from Vincent, asking Brendan to attend a meeting at his house that night.

"Such short notice," Mary Rose murmured. They had been visited by the Kelehans and the two boys only the day before; she had the feeling that this appointment had something to do with this secret Fenian Brotherhood—which to her did not seem so secret since all her Irish-American friends boasted that they supported it or had fathers, brothers or husbands who had taken oaths of allegiance to it. She knew that while they were in New York Brendan had visited someone important at the Metropolitan Hotel and had come back muttering about Canada. He had been cross all evening and did not even wish to see the new travelling suit and fur she had bought.

She had hoped that once they were settled back in Boston he would forget the nonsense of secret meetings and plots of rebellion against the British—who seemed to be managing Ireland as well as they were managing most of the other countries of the world. Her father had been a peaceful man, a gentleman farmer whose allegiance was to Illinois, not to the land his father had left as a boy. She could not understand Brendan's preoccupation with the fate of Ireland's politics, and when she lay with him at night and felt the deep, puckering scar on his left shoulder, she hated Ireland and she hated the Irish who still called on him, and men like him, to place their bodies before the guns of English soldiers and risk being blown away for the sake of a dream.

Brendan seemed to sense her displeasure that he was leaving her on this, the second night in their own home, but he knew also that the meeting was to be of some importance, since Vincent, a sensitive man when it came to Mary Rose's feelings, would be as aware of this as her husband.

Brendan had found American Fenian meetings to be exciting affairs; there was always much shouting and disagreement and a great many wonderful speeches and declarations—usually including personal reminiscences of the Ireland the members had left behind. Now, in their new, comfortable and often well-insulated lives, they did not quite know how to take Brendan Kelehan. His deep, well-spoken voice which could—and often did—have him mistaken for an Englishman, made them uneasy, as did his disapproval of the idea of marching on Canada to discredit England by its annexation. He talked of Ireland in a calm, knowledgeable way, it was true, but his demands for men and arms and money to be sent *now* were too precipitous. After the first few meetings, when he realized that things in Boston could not be hurried by an outsider, he became almost too silent at meetings, and made people uneasy with his habit of sitting or standing off to one side and watching everything with a faint smile. Countering this, and responsible for his continued acceptance in the group was his strong blood tie with Vincent Kelehan, one of the driving forces in the Boston Movement, and his own part in a brush with a murderous informer, proudly, though privately, related by Vincent when he had first received Brendan's letter from Cork.

On this night there was much discussion on the Fenian march on Canada under the command of Brigadier General Sweeny, the wisdom of it, and its possible effects and outcome.

Brendan leaned back in his chair and only half-listened to the voices raised in disagreement. It was some time later, when he was lost in conjectures of what must, by this time, be happening to those of his friends still in prison in Dublin, that he realized the voices had quietened considerably; in fact the men were listening with barely an interpolated word to John Walsh, the senior partner in an accountancy firm in the city. The word "Dublin" was mentioned, and Brendan sat up and began to pay attention.

"It was delivered to another member, for safe keeping, and that was the last that was heard of it."

"But he must have placed it in a bank vault somewhere . . ." A big, sandy-haired, blunt-featured man called Brophy interrupted.

"Hush and I'll be telling you. Devoy felt he could trust this young man—a lawyer he was, of good family," he checked a paper he was holding, "name of Oliver Carron. Carron was subsequently arrested himself, you see, and he died in prison in March . . ."

Many voices were speaking, calling out questions, suggestions— and then the room was silent, waiting, and Brendan realized he had been on his feet for some seconds, that his shout of "No!" had been loud enough to carry across all their voices and silence them.

"Brendan, lad?" It was Vincent. "Brendan, is that your friend Carron?"

"Yes," Brendan sank slowly onto his chair, aware now of the stares of pity and confused sympathy on the faces all about him.

There was a brief pause while the men gazed at each other, at Brendan, and back to John Walsh.

Walsh cleared his throat, looked down at the tightly written pages in his hand and continued, without looking at Brendan, "Well, as I said, there's been no trace of the two thousand pounds."

"Carron's hidden it."

Brendan whirled on the speaker, the bullet-headed Brophy. The man had been a high-ranking official in the police force for years, but had retired early to join his family in running a chain of butcher shops throughout Boston and its smaller, surrounding towns. His voice was still as definite and ponderous as if he continued to walk the streets with a truncheon. "Carron hid it, or he gave it to someone else for safekeeping."

The last sentence robbed Brendan of a reply.

"His wife? Kennedy here—" Walsh tapped the letter, "he says the wife left Dublin for a town called San Cristofero in Southern Italy, just after her husband's death. Took her little boy with her and just . . . left. Kennedy had to bribe a cleaning lady to get any address for the woman."

"Sounds very suspicious," Brophy muttered.

"Don't be a fool," Brendan rounded on the man, "the child was ill—it was natural she'd take him overseas for his health . . ."

"Kennedy says he's certain Carron didn't hand the money to anyone else," Walsh continued. He looked over at Brendan and sighed, said awkwardly, "The lads in Dublin are loath to let the matter drop. Two thousand pounds would buy arms for hundreds of men . . ."

"And it's our money!" A voice from the midst of the men, and there were loud growls of agreement from his fellows.

"I vote we write back to Paddy Kennedy and have someone sent after the woman—maybe there's someone in Paris who can go—

enough of the Brotherhood have to be hiding on the continent these days. Someone should go and question the woman . . ."

Again there was assent from all over the room.

Brophy said, as the noise subsided, "I plan to go to Europe this summer anyway. I'll go to this place, Saint Christopher, or whatever it's called—and I'll see this Carron woman. If she's got the money, or knows where Carron hid it, I'll get the information from her."

There was only the vaguest murmur at this. Scowling faces considered Brophy for a moment; he was not popular, and there were rumours, which many of the members believed, that his retirement from the police force was because of a misuse of his power—and a violent one at that.

"I don't know . . ." Walsh began.

Brophy's voice grated him into silence. "It was bad enough with our envoys being betrayed into English hands and the money going into English coffers. It's hard enough that the leaders of the Brotherhood in Ireland, and those leaders within the British Army who could have raised the country, are being betrayed, *by Irishmen.* But if this money has been stolen, and stolen by an Irishman, or even an Irishwoman, then we must make it seen that we'll not have it." Brophy's large, flat features were suffused with colour. "If one person can get away with stealing from the Brotherhood, then other poor, weak-hearted creatures will try it—and the whole movement will be at risk, rotting from the inside out! Stop it now, I say. That was our hard-earned money—sent to aid Ireland, not line the purse of some unscrupulous little opportunist!"

He had them; they followed his thoughts with enraged fervour, roared their approval.

And once again Brendan found himself speaking, and the room was listening in respectful silence to words that seemed to come as concisely and logically as if he had actually known what he was doing, had hours, days, to plan this speech.

And it was done; he had a brief glimpse of Vincent's face, worried, apprehensive, but the room was already abuzz with the news, and those at the back or who were hard of hearing were having the words repeated to them.

"Brendan Kelehan knows the woman. Brendan Kelehan is going to Italy immediately. He's going to bring back the money . . . the absconded money . . . the stolen money. He's going to Italy to see the Carron woman and bring it back."

"You're going . . . alone?"

Brendan looked up from his plate, paused with his spoonful of vichyssoise halfway to his mouth and replaced it, carefully, in the bowl, stirring the delicious contents and hoping he would be able to finish his meal. Mary Rose, seated straight-backed in her chair opposite him at the dining table, was dangerously pale.

"My love, I must . . ."

"It's business, you say—but you've never mentioned any business interests in Italy . . ."

"I'm telling you now."

"Then why can't I go with you? I've never been to Europe . . ."

"I want to take you to Europe—but I'll be returning from Italy immediately. There'll be no time for sightseeing—when you accompany me to Europe, I hope the trip will take us several months . . . Perhaps next spring."

"You're going to leave me here, while you go—to . . . to Rome, and Florence, and . . ." her voice was rising. "Oh, you're selfish! Just so selfish! You know how I'd love to go . . .!"

"It's for a few weeks only . . ."

"Even a few weeks . . ."

"No, Mary Rose. In the spring, I'll take you to Italy, France, Switzerland . . ."

"And what am I to do while you're away? Stay here in this cold house . . ."

"This house isn't cold . . ."

"All alone, for weeks, maybe months!"

"You have friends to visit," he said mildly, "and your shopping trips—I don't see that your routine is going to be disrupted at all. Even when I'm here, you prefer to attend the theatre with Myra and her husband nearly every night of the week . . ."

"That's not true! Two or three at the most—and that's only because you won't take me! You're always at your meetings with your Irish felons . . ."

His mouth twitched despite himself. "The word is Fenians, my dear, though some of us do have rather unsavoury pasts, I must admit . . ."

"And when you *are* at home you're poring over work from the office or simply too tired to go out. What am I to do? Give up all my amusements?"

"Heaven forbid." Quietly. He returned to his soup.

"And what does that mean?" After a pause, the tone was low and ominous.

He looked up at her, dabbed his mouth with his napkin, put aside his bowl and all thoughts of a peaceful evening. "I simply made a comment. I don't expect you to give up your amusements, Mary Rose. I would hate to think of you staying at home, wasted behind a book or a piece of embroidery, when the gaslight and greasepaint beckons."

"I hate it when you speak so sarcastically. It does you no honour at all, amusing yourself so viciously at my expense."

"Mary Rose . . ."

"I wish I'd never married you! You're not at all what you pretended to be! I hate living here, and I hate my days spent shopping and . . . and *amusing* myself . . . and . . . and I hate you, most of all!"

"For God's sake, Mary Rose—do you want the servants . . ."

"I don't care if they hear me! I don't care what anyone says or thinks about us! I've tried so hard to keep everything as it was between us—and it's not! It's boring! Boring! Boring!"

She stood, and Brendan rose from his seat also, coming around the table to her, but she backed away.

"Stay away from me! Go to Italy! Go to . . . go to hell! I don't want to live with you any more! I don't want to share a house with you! And I don't want you . . . *touching* me—not ever again!"

He stopped, as if she had struck him, stared at her, as pale as she was herself. "Is that part of it?" his voice low. "Answer me. Is it? I thought you were beginning to . . . to feel some kind of response . . . My God—have you hated our nights together? All of them? When I thought . . ."

He could not continue, but Mary Rose, it seemed, could, and did. "Myra said I have to put up with it—Aunt Rose said I'll come to like it . . ."

"You will, my dear, if you'll only be patient. I've tried, Mary Rose—I care more for your pleasure than my own, for it's such a part of what a marriage should . . . Dear Lord—this is no conversation for the dinner table! Mary Rose . . ."

"I don't want to talk about it! I hate it, and I hate you, and I don't want to be married any more."

"What will you do, you stupid girl? Do you want to go back to Vincent and Rose . . .?"

"I wanted to," she said sullenly, "but Aunt Rose said I must give the marriage a chance . . ."

He stared at her, unbelieving. "You went to Aunt Rose, and told her you wanted to end our marriage? And just what did Aunt Rose say to that?"

"She said . . . I was being immature. That . . . that I had . . . unreasonable expectations . . ."

"Bravo, Aunt. And now?"

"I don't care any more. I know they'll take me back at Chestnut Street, and I don't care about the scandal. I don't want to live here any more, and I don't want to have children, and I don't want to go to Ireland . . . Oh!"

He held her by both wrists, and pulled her to him sharply, his face set with rage. "And have you only just made those decisions, Mary Rose? Or are they something you've been discussing with Aunt Rose and Myra Gorham ever since we returned from our honeymoon?"

"I just . . . I . . . No, I didn't just think of them!" she burst out, defiantly. "I never wanted children! You were the one who kept talking about them—filling your wretched boggy Irish home with them! I don't want to be a mother! I hate the idea, and I always have! And I never would have gone back to Ireland with you, so there! I hate the idea of going to Ireland! I want to stay in Boston, and if you'd insisted, then you'd have gone back to Dublin on your own! You've no right to make all the decisions—my feelings matter, too! We do everything your way, and you don't care what I'm feeling! You're the most selfish man I've ever met, and . . . and I wish I *hadn't* met you! I wish I'd never set eyes on you! I want to go home to Vincent and Rose and Damian and Nicholas . . ."

She was sobbing violently, and Brendan, equally shaken within himself but outwardly calm, let her go and stepped back.

"Is this the truth? You agreed with me, when I spoke of the children, and yet you never wanted them?"

"No . . . !"

"And you married me, with that lie between us . . . among others . . ." the words spoken almost to himself.

Mary Rose seemed not to have heard. She was half-collapsed over the table, weeping loudly.

He gazed at her for a long and wretched moment, but Mary Rose did not see the pain on his face. He said, finally, "I shall have your things moved back to Chestnut Street tomorrow. I'll be taking ship the following morning, so no one will wonder that you're going; it will seem that you wish, quite naturally, to stay with your close relatives while I'm away. So you see, Mary Rose, everything has worked out splendidly. I shall sleep in my study for tonight. Goodnight, my dear."

He kissed the top of her head, and ignored her as he felt her fingers clutch for him, heard the voice that began to rise inexorably upwards to a wailing scream.

He set his jaw and tightened his stomach muscles as he climbed the stairs, but could not block out the sound of shattering glass and china that still reached his unwilling ears.

Bianca Azzopardi had been born and raised in San Cristofero, had married a local farmer, had raised his children and supported them by housekeeping when he had died at thirty-one. Her especial responsibility, for five years now, had been cleaning and caring for the three cottages on the D'Unnunzio estate.

She had not had much experience of the world outside San Cristofero, except for the foreign people, mostly *inglesi*, who rented the small villas for varying periods. She was proud that she had learnt to speak English, that she had made friends among these people, who often returned year after year. She grew accustomed to the strange ways of these people from the far north, with their flat, drawling language. They amused her, often, but could rarely surprise her.

And then, in March, the woman with the child had come, and that spring of 1866 had been disturbed, saddened. She watched her own six children more carefully, prayed for them more often. The family grew closer together, for the appearance of the woman and the child.

She had not forgotten them, would not, even if the Irishman had not come. He arrived in May, and well-bred and courteous as he was, his questions had disturbed her further.

He had stayed at the inn in the village at first, but had then moved to the house in the orange grove that the woman and boy had shared. Bianca had told him everything. She had to—he was the kind of man who demanded the truth from one—yet the kind of man also who made one regret the harshness of that truth, the pain that it would cause.

She had added, quickly, "He is with Saint Christopher, Signore. His *patrono* has taken him to heaven where Our Lady will care for him, as his own mother she would care for him . . ."

But the strong face beneath that straight, thick hair the colour of new silver had remained set, nothing had changed, no words she could say could make it change from that icy disbelief that had come with her first words. "The boy? Oh, Signore, he was ill even when they arrived—he seemed to get better, would run about with my Nino, but . . . only two months . . . maybe less—

and . . . he is dead, Signore. It happened ten—eleven—days ago . . ."

She answered the remainder of his questions, as well as she could. The mother had left after the funeral, she said she was going home.

He had missed Katherine by just one week.

The man was intimate with the family—secretly, Bianca suspected that he was the little Cristofero's father, though the woman had said that he was dead . . . Still, this grey-haired stranger with the young face and grey eyes—he knew the woman, grieved for the child as if it had been his own. Why, then, had he not known where "home" was? Why the endless questions, each time she came to the house, of all that the Signora Carron had said in those last few days?

And when the questions, fruitless as they were, were done, he would lapse into silence, would sit there at the table with his gaze on the green branches and creamy blossoms of the orange trees outside the window, or he would leave, abruptly, whether it was fine weather or no, and go out to walk on the hills. He unpacked no books or papers from his luggage, refused to see any of the curious, friendly *inglesi* in the district who called to pay their respects, choosing instead to remain alone, brooding about the cottage and its environs.

After more than a week of this, Bianca reluctantly confided in her eldest daughter that she was afraid—may the Holy Virgin and all the saints prove her mistaken—that the handsome *irlandese* was losing his wits.

Brendan had found his way to the little cemetery two days after his arrival. There was a small, fenced section for Protestants, mute witness to the many foreigners who came here, suffering from ill health, most of them elderly, to spend their last years in the healing sunshine.

The headstone was much newer than any of the others, but it was not this that first drew his attention. Unlike its plainer fellows, the very height of the monument drew the eye to it immediately. A winged angel stood poised, wings and arms outstretched over the little grave, on the square block that stated,

CHRISTOPHER JOSIAH CARRON
Died 4th May 1866
Aged four years and four months

And, beneath that, Christ's words,

"Suffer the little children to come unto me"

Brendan walked to the graveside often, after that first day. He saw few people on the way and spoke to no one. He found himself holding silent conversations with the boy, and wondered, sometimes, if he was losing his mind. He could not have saved Oliver, could not have saved Christopher . . . Could he?

"Uncle Brendan!" The boy would run to him, clasp him about the legs, look up at him as if he were the strongest man in the world, and—yes! "Uncle Brendan can do *anything!*" he had claimed once, making the adults laugh.

Oliver had said—and not once, but often—"If anything should happen to me . . ." *And it did, it did and where was I? I promised you. I promised.* "Look after Katherine and Christopher . . ." *I promised . . . I promised.*

Oliver's body had been released to his relatives. He would have been buried in the family vault in Dublin. But Christopher . . . Brendan moved to one of the stolid and unpretentious English headstones and sat down. If Katherine had returned to Dublin . . .

"Signore . . .?"

If Katherine had meant Dublin when she had said "home", and had returned there, surely she would have taken Christopher's body back with her, to be buried beside his father.

But Christopher was buried here, in Italy, with a stone angel bent over him, as if guarding the place, as if keeping the boy company . . .

Katherine would have seen the piece of statuary when she had visited the stonemason to order a tombstone. She had chosen the angel to stay with Christopher . . . because she herself was going away. Far, far away, perhaps—nearly ten thousand miles . . .

Suddenly he no longer had doubts; the angel he had gazed at for a week or more, had told him all he wanted to know. Katherine did not take Christopher back to Dublin because she herself did not return to Dublin. She had, indeed, gone home. To a hidden valley at the end of the world.

"Signore . . .?"

The voice broke through his thoughts at last. "Bianca?" He smiled at her. "I think I know where Mrs Carron has gone."

Bianca returned his smile; she was glad to see the change in him. Now there would be no more agonizing, Australia or Ireland, Ireland or Australia—which had she hinted at, which had she most spoken of . . .?

"This is good news, Signore. Where does the Signora go, do you think?"

"Home to Australia—to her family." He was about to tell her

his thoughts on the matter, for he knew her to be a good woman, one who had cared for Katherine, who had helped nurse Christopher, at the end, with a tenderness born of her affection for the little boy and the natural pity of a good heart.

But Bianca was holding a small cardboard box in her hands, and looked hesitant, uncomfortable.

"Signore, I see you grieve, day on day, now. I have here something for you. Maybe you will be more sad, but I think it was meant that you should have this. The Signora, she gives it to my Nino—he was the friend of little Cristofero—but two years older, Signore—Nino, he feels too old for such a thing. I put it away in this box—but now I give it to you. The Signora and her little one—they would like you to have it."

He took the box from her, remained standing, gazing at it. When he looked up, her short, sturdy figure in black dress and shawl and boots had already turned away, and she was moving silently across the green grass, down the hill towards the village.

Brendan opened the box. In it lay a small blue felt rabbit, minus one ear, minus one eye.

He lifted it out of the box and seated himself on the square headstone. He held the worn little toy in his hands for a long time, and was thankful that Bianca Azzopardi had left him to his solitude.

Six

The road to the Valley was blanketed with snow on that early August day that Katherine Carron returned to Barrengarry. The ice-encased leaves of the sturdy eucalypts dripped, a multitude of stalactites, and pock-marked the banks of snow the wind had gathered and pressed about the trunks. But nothing, no imprint of hoof or carriage wheel, nor fall of melted ice, had sullied the snow that lay upon the track, and it seemed to Katherine that the dray in which she rode was the first, the very first vehicle, to climb to that high gap between the trees where the road seemed to hover over nothingness, a deep, pale blue space where the world ended and Kangaroo Valley began.

She smiled a little at the thought. It would be comforting if it were as simple as that; to return to Barrengarry with all the past obliterated gently, inexorably, and an unimpeded future before her, as clean and unmarked as the snow that crunched and squeaked beneath the patient hoofs of the four bullocks.

The dray slid a little, the wheels finding ice beneath the snow, and Katherine clung tighter to the edge of her seat.

"Nearly went, Father."

Katherine turned to see the two children regaining their precarious seats on her luggage; the thin, freckled faces grinned shyly at her. Beside her, in the driver's seat, their father, Amos, merely grunted.

Katherine sighed with some satisfaction; despite this unprecedented cold weather she would soon be among her own family. It had been fortunate indeed that old Amos Murphy had been in Wollongong the day she arrived. It had been an uncomfortable trip, and the small inns along the track to the high country were primitive in the extreme, but she was saved from questioning by her driver at least. Of all the settlers who lived in the Valley or on farms perched on the escarpment surrounding it, Amos was the most taciturn, the least curious.

In the twenty-seven-hour journey from the coastal town of Wollongong he had given only monosyllabic replies to Katherine's or his children's remarks about the countryside, and had shown not the slightest tendency to wonder what she had been doing for the past five years, or why she had now returned. She guessed that his children, a boy and girl about twelve years old, much impressed by her fur-trimmed cloak, stylish travelling costume and the exotic labels on her luggage, would dearly love to have quizzed her, but, awed as they were by "Missus Carron", they were more in awe of their father. Amos sat, his seamed face like weathered sandstone, around which the grizzled growth of his beard clung like old lichen. The eyes, narrowed permanently by decades of squinting into the sun or against the force of wind and rain, gazed between the horns of the leading bullock, and the children were left to speculate between themselves in whispers like dry grass that crackled occasionally into stifled laughter.

They were silent, now. Amos jumped down and went to the head of the lead bullock, walking it up the last treacherous steps. So it was that they came to the crest; and first the snow-tipped trees on the far ridges became visible, then the dark green of the trees on the slopes, then the still-green grass of the Valley, untouched by snow, lay before them.

Katherine heard an "Aah" from the young girl, and smiled. Yes, it was beautiful, all the more so in this freak winter, with the unaccustomed snow on the hills. Katherine's heart contracted a little as they moved forward, and more and more familiar landmarks became visible. There was the roof of the Brodys' first homestead, perched on its small rise, the rickety fences and grazing cows looking like children's toys from this distance. Smoke, rising into the cold air from among the wooded areas of the Valley floor, marked the other, more distant homesteads, as yet hidden in their cleared alluvial plots by the banks of the many creeks. That pillar of smoke would be the Brodys' new homestead, Cambewarra; that to the south would be the Huckstables' Bendeela . . . and the grey roof was Murchisons' place . . .

A sharp cry from one of the children cut across her thoughts and she turned first to see what had startled the child. Amos had already stopped, and the beasts had halted with him: Katherine, seeing both children staring with mute horror over her head, only then turned to gaze at the road before them.

He must have stumbled out of the tangled vines and ferns at the edge of the track, for the road had been clear before them when Katherine had last looked. But he was here now, lurching up the rutted path, feet splashing in the runnels of melted snow, clothes muddied, hair matted and face streaked with dirt and . . .

"Blood! He's got blood all over 'im!" It was the boy who spoke. The dray jounced a little as he sprang down from it and began running down the road towards the apparition.

Katherine glanced at Amos, who seemed transfixed where he stood, gazing in open-mouthed shock. "Mister Murphy . . ." Katherine prompted.

She was rewarded with a startled look from him before he, too, began to run forward. "Molly, hold the team!" he called back to his daughter, and Molly, thin pigtails bouncing, jumped down from the dray to run to the bullocks' heads. She began immediately to lead them to a tree growing close to the track, and by the time Katherine, hampered by her trailing skirts, had reached the injured man, young Molly was already close to her heels.

The stranger had fallen, and Amos and the boy were bent over him. As Katherine drew closer she could see that he was in his fifties, with thinning grey hair and a long, fine-featured face. He seemed to be struggling to remain conscious; his eyes would focus on the faces about him, only to roll upwards as the lids closed upon them.

"Mister? Mister, what happened to you?" Amos placed one gnarled hand beneath the man's head and raised it a little. The heavy lids flickered and opened, and for a moment he stared at Amos' broad, honest face.

"Horse . . ." he murmured, then swallowed. "My horse . . . he took . . . my horse . . ."

Amos glanced up at Katherine, down at the man again. The boy, beside Katherine, muttered "He's been robbed," and, in a sudden, hushed tone, "*Bushrangers.*"

"Quiet, Billy." Amos scowled up at his children. "You two, run on down the hill to Mister Brody—tell him someone's been hurt and we're bringing him down. Go!" The two children fled, running on brown legs as sturdy and sure-footed as mountain ponies', down the muddy track into the Valley. Amos returned his worried gaze to the man. "Mister? What's your name? Where do you come from?"

The man's eyes had closed once more, and Katherine spoke before she realized quite what she was doing. He was so pale, there was ice on his jacket. . . "Sir, you must have a family—your wife, perhaps, will be worried about you. We must know your name, where you come from, so we can notify your family."

His eyes opened, fixed on Katherine. "Barton . . . Gilbert Barton . . . of Campbelltown." He took a deep breath, then murmured, "Water . . . please . . ."

Katherine turned to Amos. "Do you have any?"

"No, but there's a bottle of spirits in the brown leather bag. Fetch that, if you please, Missus."

Katherine ran back to the dray, where the animals, exhausted after their climb, stood patiently waiting, the heads with the broad horns drooping, moisture pouring in warm clouds from their nostrils.

She found the leather bag, containing what seemed to be part of Amos' own supplies purchased in Wollongong. The bottle of alcohol was buried beneath tins of tobacco, tea and baking soda. The label had been all but obliterated by frequent handling, and Katherine smiled as she pulled it from the bag. She knew it would not contain rum made in Sydney or Melbourne, but would be a sample of the locally produced illicit brew made by several of the Valley dwellers. Even Amos Murphy, she thought, tripping over her skirts as she ran back to the two men, was not averse to buying locally for his strictly medicinal "spirits".

"It . . . won't be too strong for him, will it?" she suggested as she handed it to Amos.

He scowled at her. "I water it down, Missus," he growled. "You don't think I'd drink this evil stuff unless it was an emergency, do you?"

"No, of course." Katherine lowered her eyes.

The man, Barton, lay pale and unconscious. Amos held the liquor to his lips, forced it into his mouth, but none seemed to be swallowed.

"Ah, Missus, . . ." Amos sat back on his heels, raised his eyes to Katherine, "I think he's gorn, Missus."

"Gone?" She stared at the man. "You mean dead? He can't be . . ." She felt chilled, an inner cold that had little to do with the biting mountain air. "Feel for a pulse, Mister Murphy, isn't that what . . ." But Amos was gazing at her uncomprehendingly. Katherine reached down and took Barton's hand, almost recoiling at the icy touch, but she held the wrist, her fingers pressed against the flesh. It fluttered slightly within her grasp as if the spirit were struggling to be free.

"Help me lift him, Mister Murphy, he's not dead at all."

"Help *you*, Missus? Little thing that you are? Just stand back . . ."

As she rose, Amos pushed her off a little, bent, and picked up the injured man. Katherine stared, amazed at Murphy's strength, as he carried his burden back towards the dray. Grunting a little, lurching once or twice when his foot rolled on a stone, Amos nevertheless belied his own meagre frame and the fact that he was almost the same age as the man he carried.

They settled Gilbert Barton as comfortably as they could among the rugs in the dray, but he lay still and did not stir all the seemingly interminable miles down into the Valley. The original Brody homestead, a slab-built affair with a broad verandah at the front, re-roofed in recent years with corrugated iron to replace the original wooden shingles, lay to the right of the road. It was the first of the Valley dwellings they would pass, and though Katherine knew that there was much resentment between old Mikey Brody and her family, she could not risk Barton's life by taking him the further five miles to the Huckstables' place.

She was unprepared, however, to find old Mikey planted square in the middle of his drive, the Murphy children hopping from one foot to the other in the grass to either side of him. The man's very stance bespoke aggression, and not for the first time Katherine was irritated at the long-running family feud. Should it matter, forty-eight years later, that Mikey and Katherine's grandfather, Josiah Prescott, had quarrelled over water rights? Admittedly, there had been fisticuffs amongst the two camps of farm workers; there had been fences cut and stock let loose; both sides had indulged in such tactics.

Finally, Josiah Prescott had applied, in secret, to his friend Lachlan Macquarie, then Governor of New South Wales. An enquiry was held, and the mistake whereby the Brody family had had grants of land that had monopolized the water of the Valley was rectified. It had been fair, not only to Josiah Prescott, but to the other three settlers who were then struggling to raise crops and stock in the Valley. But the re-delineation of boundaries lost the Brodys much of the rich alluvial soil as well as the creeks and rivers themselves. They still held four thousand acres, much the same area as they had been given initially, but their five brief years of glory as rulers of the Valley had gone forever. Though the Brodys still owned the finest land, Josiah Prescott and after him his son Marcus had cleared more slopes, planted more crops, improved more fences and stock and were, in this year of 1866, undoubtedly the wealthiest settlers in the Valley. So Joe had written, rather smugly, to Katherine only a few months earlier. Katherine, knowing her own family, did not doubt it, and now, seeing the look of unremitting dislike upon the face of Mikey Brody, she knew that nothing in the past had been forgotten.

She was gathering herself to greet the old man, when he strode forward abruptly to meet the dray. "Another one," he stated, staring down at the unconscious Barton.

Amos, in the driver's seat, nodded grimly. "Seems so."

Brody glanced for only a second at Katherine before addressing Amos. "First one found near one of *their* properties in Robertson. Now the girl brings another one home. Bad luck, these Prescotts."

Amos had the good grace not to reply, but began clambering down from the dray. Katherine bit back a sharp retort, watched, instead, as Mikey placed a hand on Amos' arm, began whining, 'Don't rightly think your man's best served here. Doctor's at McEgan's—there's a birth expected—been there since last night. Take 'im to McEgans'.''

"Well. . ." Amos drawled, and shifted from foot to foot, scratching his head reflectively.

Katherine broke in impatiently, "The man's half-frozen, Mister Brody—as a Christian, you must let him rest here. We can send for the doctor!"

Brody had turned away a little, scowling off at something along the road as Amos suggested, "Could fetch the doctor here. Long way to McEgans—lower Valley and all—a good ten miles."

"Don't want the house full of visiting Prescotts," Brody glared.

Amos shrugged, "Your land. They can't trespass. Christian thing, though, to take the man in." He jerked his head. "You got a horse in the house yard—my boy can ride fast—can have the doctor here soon, if he'll come."

Brody hesitated. Katherine thought, *I said all that. It's as if they didn't hear me.* Brody was scowling down at Barton, then, "Yairs . . ." he looked up. "Get going, boy—bridle and saddle on the verandah there."

Billy needed no further urging but shot off to do as he was bidden, and Mikey turned back to Amos. "Can't have him dying on my doorstep, I guess," he muttered, almost reluctantly, "I'll help you in with him."

This time Katherine did not attempt to help, nor did either man glance in her direction as they carried Barton into the house, followed by a wide-eyed, silent Molly. Katherine watched Billy ride off down the drive, then walked over to wait by the dray, resting one hand on the back of one of the oxen, grateful for the warmth that came through her thin gloves, and for the comfort of the nearness of a living creature.

The hostility of the old man had her trembling. Ridiculous, but it seemed suddenly as if she had never left this valley, had never known the world outside and the bright, fine dreams that had lived in her Ireland.

My Ireland, she said to herself for the first time, acknowledging with a stinging of sudden tears that her Ireland has perished with the hopes of the Fenian Brotherhood, that the liberty and equality to which they had pledged themselves had faded from the horizon like a mirage; in its place lay death, or a life in chains in the Western Australian prison colony. It was as if Oliver had never existed, nor Christopher . . . She was left with nothing, except perhaps her memories, and they were tainted with bitterness.

So. It was wrong to come home to Kangaroo Valley, for nothing had changed here—as nothing would have changed, she told herself drily, once she reached Barrengarry homestead itself. Why, she admitted to herself, she had not written nor telegraphed her arrival, so unsure was she of the welcome she would receive from her father. Her presence may very well cause problems for her mother, Joe, Laura and Edwina, should they defend her. What kind of future was that? Better the life of a retiring widow in an English seaside resort, or a *pension* in Paris—or even the dry shell of her life in Dublin . . . anything but to try to go *back* for solace. One could never go back.

"Miss Prescott?"

A male voice from behind her, and she turned, surprised to see a broad-shouldered, fair-haired man in his early thirties seated on a tall bay. He had ridden up the drive unheard, unnoticed by her. Stephen Brody. And she realized what old Mikey had been watching approach along the driveway, and why he had given in then, rather than risk a family altercation and certain defeat before the strangers. Mikey was tough, but when faced with his equally strong-willed grandson, there was no doubting the outcome. And Stephen, Katherine knew, would not hesitate to offer shelter to any man or woman in need—even a Prescott, should the occasion ever arise. Katherine smiled upwards at the familiar, friendly face, watched it cope with pleasure mixed with embarrassment. "I mean . . . Mrs . . . I'm sorry—they did tell me your married name . . ."

"Carron." She walked towards him, and he moved his horse forward and dismounted to take her hand. "After growing up together, I'm surprised to find you so formal, Stephen—have I changed so much?"

"No," the blue eyes smiled into her face, "not at all. But I had my doubts, at first—as to if it really was you, and then . . . yes, I wondered if you'd changed. Europe is a long way away—and it's been five years. Welcome home, Katherine."

Again she felt the prickling of tears. It was absurd how easily her emotions, kept so strictly under control all these months, were stirred this morning; but she was realizing now just how much this homecoming meant to her. To hide her feelings at this, the first sign of kindness, she turned towards the house. "Your grandfather will see us," she cautioned with a smile, for Stephen still held her hand, "I'm sure he won't—"

"Approve? Of course not. But I'm rather too tall now for him to whip me for being seen with one of 'those Prescotts'. Do you remember the tree house Joe and I built beside the creek. You and Laura and Edwina forced your way in by sheer numbers one day. I'm awfully sorry, Katherine, about . . ."

Katherine was laughing at the memory. "Oh, Stephen, I've missed them all so much—I can't wait to see them again. Is everything well with them?"

A shadow fled across Stephen's face, and seemed to take with it his smile. He at last let go of her hand. "Well," and it was as if he spoke with reticence, there was a conscious effort to recover himself, "I haven't seen them for . . ."

Footsteps on the wooden verandah boards, and Mikey, Amos and young Molly returned. Mikey stood glowering between Stephen and Katherine and made no move to come down the verandah steps. Katherine began a question, but Amos shook his head. "No change, Missus."

"No point in you waiting around here." Mikey glared at her from the steps, "Better push off."

"What's happened?" Stephen asked, and Katherine told him, briefly, of the man Barton. All the while, Mikey scuffled and huffed and scowled from the verandah. Stephen nodded, at the end of the tale, and smiled an engaging smile at his grandfather. "You're right, Grandad, Mrs Carron should be safe at home—particularly after such a shock as she's been subjected to. I might borrow your buggy and drive her home to Barrengarry . . ."

"If you think for a minute, boy . . ."

"I haven't driven the bay gelding since I bought him for you— I'd like to try out his paces." He smiled. "I think Mrs Carron would have a more comfortable journey in the buggy than on the dray— no offence meant, Mister Murphy."

"Alright with me—I got my pay for the trip."

Stephen's reminder of the gelding's background silenced Mikey, and he watched in dour silence as the buggy was brought from the shed, the gelding was caught and harnessed, and the bags were transferred from dray to carriage. Then a grim farewell from Amos, a shy wave from Molly, and Stephen and Katherine were headed away down the drive; a telling silence from the old man on the verandah following them like cold rain at their backs until the homestead was out of sight.

"Stephen," Katherine began as the road, now mercifully flat and gently meandering through forest and cleared meadow, rolled out before them, "what were you going to say to me, before the men interrupted us?"

"I . . . that I was sorry . . ." Stephen looked uncomfortable, spoke haltingly, "to hear the news of your tragedy. Laura—Miss Prescott—told me. It's been . . . Well, I should imagine it's been a terrible time for you. To lose your husband, then your little boy . . ."

He had caught Katherine's glance, and stopped. She realized that, with his words, her hands had clenched in her lap, and she made herself relax them, told herself that she must face these questions, this kindness, the well-meant, ignorant pity . . .

Stephen continued, "I hope you don't mind, that Laura—Miss Prescott mentioned the matter to me. I've asked about you frequently

over the years—and she was so upset . . . It was a double tragedy
for you, the deaths so close together . . ."

"Two months . . ." Katherine murmured, without realizing that
she had spoken until the words were out.

"Yes," Stephen said heavily. "I trust . . . I hope they didn't suffer
too greatly."

It was not a question, but she nevertheless felt the silence that
lay expectantly beyond his words. The silence yawned like a chasm
awaiting her good manners to bridge it, and she forced out her reply.
"My husband, Oliver, died of pneumonia. He was not ill for long.
Christopher . . . Christopher's consumption had developed slowly,
since the autumn before his father's death. We were not . . . able
to take him abroad for a cure at that time. After Oliver's death,
I sailed with Christopher for Italy . . . We were there for six weeks
. . ." She fell silent for several seconds, then continued, "He *seemed*
to improve—then began to fail, very quickly. Six weeks. It was
over in six short weeks. It was already too late, you see."

Her voice had faded. She made an effort to collect herself, draw
herself back from the sickroom, with its view of the orange trees
and the blue of the bay beyond, the small white face on the pillow,
the little fist clutching the much-loved felt rabbit—the church bells
from the village—they sounded so often and so loudly—the orange
blossom that mingled its perfume with the ocean breeze and the
sickly-sweet smell of that little room, that little, final prison . . .

"Miss Prescott—indeed, all your family—were so distressed for
you. Laura—Miss Prescott—hoped you would come home—but she
told me you preferred to remain in Europe."

"I changed my mind."

Her voice was polite, but the tone was rather heavy and final.
It clanged in the cold air like a door in his face, and Stephen knew
it. After a pause, he said, in a subdued voice, "Your family will
be very happy to have you home again. We all are."

She flashed him a grateful smile, and was silent. But her brain
had begun to be teased by one thing, and she considered it as she
drove; Stephen had obviously become quite friendly with Laura,
though he tried to hide this by reverting to the more formal "Miss
Prescott". Perhaps she had been unwise, in her pleasure at seeing
a familiar and friendly face, in recalling their childhood use of
Christian names. She could not answer for Laura, who would now,
strange as it was to believe, be a grown woman of twenty-two.
But she herself needed distance from people for some time, she knew
this, and she could see just as clearly that Stephen wanted no such

distance. It had been obvious in the expression on his face when she had first turned to him, in his holding her hand for a fraction too long, even for childhood friends such as they were. And the memory rose unwillingly to her mind that when her family had left Kangaroo Valley for their European tour, one of the reasons she had been glad to distance herself from the place was that it was becoming increasingly clear that Stephen Brody was regarding her with more than fondness. She had not been tempted beyond the natural feelings of flattery at his attentions, for he was charming, handsome and had been well-educated at one of Sydney's finest colleges.

Perhaps she simply knew Stephen too well. Five years ago she had left longing for new surroundings, new people; and faced, as she had been in Dublin, with an eventual return to the Valley and its genteel boredom—she had chosen escape. Through the numbing pain of the past six months, she confronted the realization for the first time on that road to Barrengarry that she was not sorry. No, not for anything. There were no regrets.

Seven

They were silent for the remainder of the drive; it was as if Stephen finally sensed that her mind was filled with her own thoughts, and he did not intrude further. The three miles to Barrengarry passed, and all along the road Katherine noted changes. The scrub was being gradually pushed back; here was a field ploughed and ready for sowing, there was a young orchard, bare, dark branches like crooked fingers begging alms from the parsimonious August sun. Yet it was the same, it was home; the folds in the hills that led up to the escarpment were becoming more and more familiar, and there, at last, was the dark green of the pines that surrounded the homestead of Barrengarry.

"Five years is a long time," Stephen said, and Katherine felt a slight irritation with him that, silent for the past few miles, he chose to speak now and intrude upon the communion that existed between herself and her home. He continued almost carefully, "I want you to know that, no matter what ill-feeling exists between our families, I was and will always remain your friend."

Katherine had been gazing at him, but now averted her eyes back to the rooftops of Barrengarry, visible now between the pines, smoke rising cheerfully from the great chimneys. She thought, he said almost the same words to me five years ago. Why do they seem as empty now as they did then?

Stephen had never been as outgoing, as spontaneous as his friend, Katherine's brother Joe. Stephen's reticence, his caution, Katherine told herself rather severely, should not be a reason for suspicion now any more than five years ago. But she could not deny the fact that Stephen's words made her uneasy. Perhaps the fault lay with her: five years ago she had been chary of any threat to her freedom; perhaps she had grown too cold, too suspicious, after all that had happened. And she felt a further resentment of Stephen for demanding this—even if it were simply an offer of loyalty and friendship—*now*, after finding that poor soul on the roadway; Katherine did not want to think, to consider anything beyond the fact that she was home . . . home.

"Thank you, Stephen." She hoped her voice held the correct amount of gratitude, of dispassionate graciousness.

"I've called at Barrengarry once or twice, in the company of the Huckstables. Emilia is a friend of L . . .—your sister's." There it was again. Katherine remained silent. "I hope I may call again, with Emilia and Rafe, in the not-too-distant future."

"You mean, when my father is away on business?" She could not help it, but tempered her words with a smile.

Stephen first looked taken aback, then smiled in return. "Your Mama is a woman of great discernment. She doesn't hold it against me that your grandfather and mine quarrelled with each other nearly fifty years ago."

"Of course she doesn't. And quite rightly."

There—a gap between the pines, and the great oak front doors beneath the broad verandah . . . Mother's chair, to the left of the door, just as it had always been . . .

The buggy turned up the drive, rattled over the little bridge that Edwin Prescott and his convict labourers had built, forty-three years before. The house now faced them directly, and such was the welling up within her of joyous memories of safety, laughter, warmth, that Katherine did not hear Stephen's words until he had repeated them,

"I would do anything to see the rift between our families repaired."

Katherine merely smiled quickly in his direction, and only later did she feel that she had been insensitive. But then, so close to the house and her past, now the centre of her future, the complications that Stephen represented were resented and pushed to the back of her mind.

She was thankful that he refused to come in. Both expected the door to be opened suddenly from within, but the house remained silent, and one by one, two by two, the travelling bags were deposited on the verandah, and Stephen, taking Katherine's hand once more, left with a final, long look as the buggy rolled off down the drive.

Katherine did not immediately knock on the door. She touched her mother's chair, gazed at the faded cushions—once crimson, now a dusky pink—the same cushions that had lined the chair since Katherine had helped make them, at twelve years old. She walked along the verandah, past the table against the house wall where they would often dine in the long summer evenings, and the heavy, wrought iron bench on which she, Joe, Laura and Edwina would scuffle for vantage at the table. There was no chair here for Marcus—he was not often home, and when he joined the family for these summer feasts it was a much more subdued affair, and a chair was brought for him from the dining room.

Katherine stood at the corner of the verandah, gazed over the bare bushes and shrubs of the garden, between the great pine trees, to the horses, dull-coloured in their shaggy winter coats, grazing in the fields. The wind that had brought the snow to the high country all about the Valley roared through the pines, but the sound was no frightening thing; as a child she had revelled in it, heard in the sound all the power of nature, along with its promise, a whispering of its secrets. Standing there now before a frost-blighted garden, in her costume of widow's black, she could almost travel back to that world of promise, forgetting the existence of the twenty-eight-year-old woman she had become, who had, in the past five months, buried a husband and a son.

Such was the power of childhood memories. She saw Joe, leading a charge of policemen against a gang of cut-throat bushrangers who had hidden squealing in the rhododendrons; Joe leaping up and down, the straight, pale hair bouncing like heavy silk fringe, exhorting Katherine to jump from the lower branches of a pine tree, declaring that Mother's parasol would act as a type of balloon and carry her off across the paddocks; she saw the riding parties coming home in the dusk, the darkly handsome Rafe Huckstable, his thin and acerbically clever sister, Emilia, and Luke Murchison, who flirted with Katherine, her sisters and any of the other young ladies present . . . and Joe, leading them in song, or telling a joke, or gently teasing one of the girls who always seemed to surround him.

"Let them be happy." She said the prayer aloud, standing in the final moments of her strangeness, of her ignorance of her family's fortunes. "Let the years have been good to them all."

And she turned her back upon the garden and walked to the front door. She knocked and waited. No sound from within. Where was Peggy, or Carl? Still no answering footfall from beyond the door, and she had her hand upon the knocker once more when she decided, no, this was her home, after all . . .

She turned the large brass doorknob and pushed—one side of the heavy twin doors swung inwards. The large hall lay before her, the broad semi-circular sweep of mahogany staircase rising from it to the floor above. It was the same, all the same, yet as Katherine entered the house she became aware of a sense of wrongness over this very matter.

She had left Barrengarry five and a half years ago, and the house had been redecorated five years before that; the rugs, the wallpaper, the furnishings were all the same, but worn now, faded. There was an air of sad neglect to the hall that struck her with surprise, almost shock.

She stepped over the threshold and closed the doors behind her. The heavy rosewood grandfather clock ticked ponderously, at the foot of the stairs. It was as if it were trying to say that nothing had changed, nothing had changed . . .

But she knew, now, that something had. Her excitement at being home, and Stephen's presence, had overridden her impressions of the house's exterior; now she admitted to herself that the outside of the house betrayed the same signs of deterioration; the white paint on the verandah posts had been peeling, the fences beyond the pines were leaning a little drunkenly compared to former times when they had marched across the property in upright and military precision.

Surely, she thought, as she walked into the hall, her skirt trailing through sun-dapples filtered through the coloured glass of the fanlight, surely there were no financial problems. Joe's letters had not mentioned any reversals in the family's fortunes; Mama would have kept these things from her, and Laura . . . Edwina's letters had been few, but even Edwina would, like Joe, have grumbled about economising should they have had to do so.

And it was just as she was beginning to wonder, with a sinking heart, if the family had not moved from the homestead, were living with Grandfather Gordon in Moss Vale or, worse, in the town house in Sydney, that she heard voices overhead.

Female voices, beginning to overlap and rise in agitation, it seemed; and as Katherine moved to the stairs, began to climb, a door opened somewhere in the upper corridor, and the voices were louder, one at least growing more shrill and intense by the second.

The owner of the voice had paused at the door of Suzanna Prescott's sitting room, where she and her daughters often spent the afternoon with their books or their sewing; she had paused and turned violently back to address the occupants of the room, so suddenly that the dark brown, almost black ringlets still bounced on her shoulders. Edwina. Stiff of back, square of jaw, fury bristling from her like a cross kitten.

"I can't! I won't! And if you weren't so afraid of him you wouldn't expect me to! You always take his side! You took his side against Katey, too! And Joe! And if I . . ." There came a murmur of reproof from within the room and, victim of the storm within her, Edwina suddenly burst into tears. "I'm not! I didn't! Oh, what's the use of trying to—!"

She had broken off, turned and fled along the corridor towards her room, and Katherine.

When they collided it was with such force that, although Katherine put out her hands to steady her sister, Edwina bounced back a few steps, coming up against the wall with a bump.

And they were staring at each other, mute with their shock. Katherine had time to note that the pretty child she had last seen in Dublin had gone; at nineteen, Edwina had matured into a beautiful young woman, despite all the distortion that anxiety, anger and tears had at this moment inflicted on her features.

"Teddi . . ." Katherine said, unconsciously giving the pet name first coined by the three-year-old Laura when she had first attempted her new-born sister's name.

"Katey . . .?" And the green eyes had flown wide, and she launched herself into Katherine's arms. Katherine found herself almost smothered in the strong young grip, but had no time to gasp, to speak, before Edwina had whirled away from her, fled to the doorway of the sitting room and was standing with all the portentousness of a sibyl and proclaiming, "Katey's here! Katey's home!"

Katherine moved to the door, and Edwina, her despair commuted to ebullience, took her by the arm and hustled her into the room.

"Katherine . . ." Her mother was standing before her, and

Katherine almost faltered, such was her shock at the changes in that beloved form. Paler, somehow smaller, as if diminished from the *inside*; the bright chestnut hair, once so like Katherine's, was streaked with grey, and the face—how changed . . . Only the eyes, those intense green eyes that she had passed on to all her children, only these were the same, now filled with sudden tears.

"Mama . . . Oh, Mama . . .!"

How thin she had become; Katherine could feel the bones beneath the heavy gown and shawl. Where was the figure that had been called Junoesque, the tall, well-rounded and graceful frame of the woman who, even in her forties and the mother of four children, had been called the most beautiful in the colony? Yet the beauty was still there, though it shone like a faint flame through thick glass. Illness and fatigue had, quite obviously, distorted it; the light now only flickered that had burnt so brightly, so consistently upon them all.

The familiar perfume of lavender enveloped Katherine with her mother's embrace, and for a moment she shut her eyes and, as on the verandah a few minutes before, she forgot everything, could allow time to stand still. But only for a second, then she was pulling back, glancing about the room to see, standing quite close, her arms already outstretched, Laura.

As they were hugging, she said, "Katey," quietly, "Katey, you've come home after all—I prayed so hard that you would." Katherine's cheek was wet with Laura's tears, and she pulled back a little to gaze at her younger sister.

Like Edwina, Laura had matured and grown lovelier, the blonde curls demurely pinned close to the nape of her long neck, and her fact lit up with surprise and delight. Yes, Laura had been happy in the intervening years, it showed in the colour in her rounded cheeks, the unspoilt curve of her lips.

"*I* knew Katey would come home! I never doubted it for an instant!" Edwina, changeable, irrepressible, was blowing her nose on a lace-trimmed handkerchief, and the next moment was ushering Katey inexorably to the chaise longue, arranging her mother beside her, and seating herself on the footstool, declaring, "Oh, Katey, you couldn't have come at a better time—it's been so . . ."

Laura was asking, "How did you get here? We heard no carriage."

"Stephen Brody drove me, I met him at his grandfather's house."

This was greeted with surprise by all about her, and Katherine had to explain once again the grisly apparition on the Cambewarra road. Amid the murmurs of pity and concern, Laura said, "And

Stephen didn't stay? I would have thought . . ." All eyes had switched to her, and she lowered her fair head suddenly. "But of course, he'd know we'd have so much to say to you . . ."

Suzanna put in quickly, her hand clasped over Katherine's, "My dear, what a tragic year this has been—" her eyes filled once more with sudden tears, "and for you, most of all."

Katherine squeezed her mother's hand in return. "I'm home among you once again—I think I can cope now. I only hope Father will welcome me. If I'd received one letter from him all these years— only one—then I'd feel more sure of myself. I didn't write of my coming because, to tell the truth—"

She was not allowed to complete her sentence; there were cries of protest from all three; Marcus knew her place was here, especially now, in a time of grief . . . And Katherine, looking at her mother and sisters, all three dressed in black as she was, to mourn the loss of a man they hardly knew, and a child they had never seen, felt a wave of gratitude and warmth. Among these good women she only now realized how alone she had been, how lonely she had felt.

"Oh, Katey, don't cry! If you do, we shall all dissolve into tears!" Edwina had sprung up from her seat and was now marching to the window. "I shall call Peggy to make us tea—she and Carl are in the buttery." She flung wide the window and screeched, "Peggy-y-y!" into the cold air.

Suzanna winced, but accustomed to Edwina's excesses, merely sighed, "I think you should go down, dear."

"Well, don't say anything interesting until I come back." And Edwina flashed a grin before running out of the room, dark curls dancing, with a swish of black taffeta petticoats.

There was a silence while the three remaining woman gazed at each other, then Suzanna said, "We're glad to have you home, my darling, but . . . tell me, it wasn't Joe that brought you home before you were ready to come?"

"Joe? I've had no letter from Joe for months. I sailed immediately after Christopher's funeral." The word was difficult to say even now, even here. She went on, seeing the look on their faces, both frozen of a sudden, expressionless. "Is Joe in trouble of some sort? He hasn't been gambling? Has he quarrelled with Father and run off?" It was possible, in fact probable; they had come close to this on so many occasions over the years.

"Katey . . ." Her mother's voice sounded strained, her grip on Katherine's hand hurt, their rings bit into each other's flesh. "Katey, dear—Joe died in May. Only four days, my dear, after your little Christopher. We wrote to you . . ."

"I'd already sailed . . ." Katherine spoke through stiff lips. It wasn't true. It was a joke. One of Joe's pranks . . .

Laura said, "It was a race—he and some friends from Moss Vale organised races regularly at a property near Glenquarrie . . . That Saturday, Joe's horse went down with him, and the horses behind couldn't . . ." Laura stopped.

"He didn't suffer, it was very quick. He was gone, Rafe said, by the time the onlookers reached him," Suzanna continued. "Rafe . . . brought him home to us."

"Joe." Katherine murmured the name almost as a reproach, as if he stood before her, as he had done so many times, attempting to look apologetic and abashed over some scrape or another. But the humour and energy always warred with the contrition on that sunburnt, handsome face. One always forgave Joe; even Father, who tried very hard, could not long remain angry with his son.

And now? This hurt he had inflicted would not fade away. To all of them, Joe's leaving was a kind of betrayal in the senseless, wasteful manner of it.

She gazed at her mother and sister, realizing now that their gowns of mourning were not merely for Oliver and Christopher. *Death comes in threes*—wasn't that the saying? And she shivered.

"Father . . ." This would destroy Father . . .

There was the briefest of exchanged glances between Laura and Suzanna. "Your father is well—as well as can be expected," her mother added. "You can imagine how difficult this has been for him."

"Is he here? Can I see him now?"

Suzanna's reassuring smile did not entirely succeed. "He spends much of his time in Sydney lately. The company takes up much of his energies, and his philanthropic works . . ."

The door opened behind them, just as Katherine was noting to herself that there was no trace of bitterness or even dryness in her mother's tone. Marcus Prescott's reputation as a forward-thinking and benign entrepreneur had not, however, been earned without some sacrifice on the part of his wife and his children.

Edwina's voice from the door cut across her thoughts. "Peggy is bringing tea up to us—you should have seen her face, Katey, when I told her you were home."

She smiled in answer to Edwina's bubbling enthusiasm, but her mind was still on her father. "He should be here with you, Mama.

Let someone else mind his affairs in Sydney—what does he have partners for? Even his social reforms can evolve by themselves for a while, surely. When does he come home next?"

It was Edwina who, as usual, stepped recklessly into the ensuing silence. "We're all wondering if he's coming home at all—there's no need to glare at me, Mama, Katey had to know sometime."

She turned fully to her eldest sister. "Father left for Sydney just after Joe's funeral. In all these three months or more, he hasn't been home at all."

Eight

Later, in her room, Katherine prowled up and down the familiar, well-worn carpet, and tried to cope with the feelings engendered by that first meeting. Suzanna, Laura and Edwina believed her to have retired because she was tired from the journey; this might have been true, she admitted, but she felt it would be a long time before she would ever feel rested and content again.

Joe is dead. Joe is dead . . . The words, repeated within her head, though her heart ached for him, brought no real acceptance, not even reality. Joe had been twenty-seven, only a year younger than Katherine; they had grown up together with the communion and mutual toleration of identical twins. It was Joe who had defied his father in supporting Katherine's marriage to Oliver, Joe who had helped them elope, who later wrote regular, fond, amusing letters describing the doings in the Valley; her son had been named Christopher Josiah . . .

Perhaps it was her rage against her father that kept her from weeping, from throwing herself on the bed and tearing the coverlet in her grief as she would like to, as she felt, somehow, that she should. But she could not help remembering the three pale faces about her, the calm, genteel, feminine strength that her mother and sisters displayed. Yet the strain was written there, in the occasional, unguarded glance of the eyes. They were worried, and they were frightened.

She caught herself up in her thoughts of what she could do to help, with a sudden sense of wonder at her own strength. Oliver, who had done all he could to protect her from unpleasantness and hardship, would be amazed, she told herself, to see the woman she had become. For there could be no giving in to emotion now. For all that had happened in Ireland, and Christopher's death, the solace she had sought here would not, she knew, be found. The last thing her mother needed was a further emotional burden; rather she should have some of the responsibilities removed from her shoulders. *And if I keep busy, I can keep my sanity. I won't remember what's happened. I won't.*

Standing at the window, gazing out over frostbitten fields to the high, green slopes of the escarpment, grey-laced with snow on the highest rise, she told herself that tomorrow she would drive to visit Joe's grave. Perhaps it would be real then. Perhaps she could cry then.

And the following day, when she was rested, she would return to Sydney. No matter what her mother or sisters might say to attempt to dissuade her, she would return to Sydney, and confront her father.

When, in the early hours of the morning, her old nightmare claimed her, she was not really surprised. In the dream she was lost, lonely, groping with her hands for a presence that meant safety, warmth, and which was just out of reach. She whimpered, waking, and lay, as reality returned, gazing at the loved and comforting shapes of her old room.

Joe . . . Her sense of loss was overwhelming. She lay until the dawn, watching the little room come to life in its soft colours of rose-patterned wallpaper and bright rag rugs. She was home . . . yet without Joe the old house seemed tired, sad. Perhaps this was what she had sensed on entering the house the day before. She had not realized, all her life, how much of Barrengarry's warmth and life had come from Joe's presence.

That morning she had Carl harness the carriage horse to the light, two-seater sulky and, accompanied by Laura, who insisted on driving, she made the reluctant journey to the Valley cemetery.

It was no larger than half an acre, and surrounded by an incongruous picket fence weathered to a grey that made it almost indistinguishable from the bush that it held back. It was silent here, but for bird calls and far distant ringing of axe on timber, where some settler prepared more firewood.

But today there was a wagon and horses at the edge of the roadway, and through the thin trees Katherine and Laura could see a group of several people standing about one of the graves.

"Oh," Laura murmured with sympathy, "it's Mr O'Mara and his children."

Katherine glanced at Laura, then turned in concern to study the family in the clearing. Jim O'Mara straightened from where he must have been adjusting something on the grave, or perhaps setting flowers in place, and he now towered over the band of young people, all steps-and-stairs, clustered about their father.

"One of the children . . ." Katherine began.

"No, his wife, Eileen, unfortunately. Childbirth with the youngest, about seven months ago. I should have told you before, as you knew her quite well, didn't you? With so much happening, though, I forgot. Mr O'Mara was in a terrible state, at first; Joe and Father spent a lot of time with him—it eased his grief, to talk to them. And Mama helped teach the eldest girl how to look after the baby . . . somehow he survived—a lovely little thing—and they seem to be coping. Such a tragedy! They're good people, and I liked Mrs O'Mara—very much like Mama—same red hair and gentle disposition . . ."

"And clever," Katherine put in, for she remembered how she used to discuss the idea of a Valley school with Eileen, who had been only five or six years older than Katherine. She had taught all her children to read and write, and grouped other settlers' children together on the makeshift verandah of their slab homestead where she and Katherine had done their best to teach the little ones to write their names, at least.

Katherine felt a pang of guilt, remembering how little she herself had done, how the trips to Sydney and the house at Balmain always seemed to interrupt Valley plans, promising, seductively, the theatre, parties and shopping outings that she—and her younger sisters, apparently—could never quite resist.

We have been spoilt, she thought, by possessing both worlds. And she looked around her, for the first time, at the rise of her beloved escarpment, and wondered that she had not thought of it before— to some people this Valley was a prison from which, due to the subsistence level of their farming lives, they would never escape.

Jim O'Mara was one, however, who loved the Valley. Though

his life was a hard one his children were growing up at last, and there were two of the boys who looked, to Katherine, to be almost as tall as their big-boned, sturdy father, and the girl who held an infant in her arms seemed mature, older than her years.

They were all introduced to Katherine, the boys smiling shyly, holding their hats in their hands, and the girls ducking their heads beneath their bonnets while still trying to take in as much as they could of the exotic costume of the lady who had returned at last from the mythical place called Europe.

"I am so sorry," Katherine held Jim's great calloused hand in hers as they said their farewells, "I shall miss Eileen very much."

"Yairs . . ." in the deep and resonant drawl. The tortured blue eyes in the creased, tanned skin rolled unwillingly over to the narrow, grassy little hillock with its simple white cross. "But I bin thinking— she left a lot to all of us. More than most folks do, I reckon. Sophie an' Annie, they keep reading to us, just like their Mama did, and— it's funny, but I can see her in all of them—and how what was *her* will go on to *their* kids. If you know what I mean." The brow was creased, he turned to Katherine and Laura a little anxiously, as if worried that he was not very clear.

But he was, of course. Katherine swallowed the constriction in her throat, and Laura did not bother to try to stop the tears welling.

They stood and waved goodbye to the family as it drove off in the creaking, solid wagon, children hanging from every edge, lifting their hands in farewell.

Eileen's grave was closest, and the two women walked to it, bent their heads in prayer for a few minutes, before turning to find their brother's grave.

It was there, quite close to their grandparents, Josiah and Laurissa Prescott, and placed between two shadowing eucalypts. To Katherine's surprise it was no mound of recently turned soil. Somehow she had expected a sign of rawness in the earth, like the wound within her. Instead, the headstone and the rectangle of white bricks that marked the boundaries of Joe's last resting place had a settled look to them; the flat surface of the grave itself was spread with white marble chips. It seemed to have been there for years.

Laura stood silently, holding the bunch of winter blooms she had gathered from the garden to place on the grave. Katherine sensed her sister wanted to speak, to offer her words of comfort, but was hesitant to intrude on Katherine's thoughts.

The little plot was neat, for Suzanna or her daughters, in their sequestered life here, had found time each week to visit and pluck any weed that had the temerity to raise its head from amongst the marble pebbles. The only chore needing to be done now was the filling of the low stone vase with the water from the bottle they had brought with them, and the arranging of the holly and winter jasmine. Even this was done without words between them.

That completed, they stood back and surveyed their work. Laura said hesitantly, "It looks pretty, doesn't it? I mean, the red and green and white . . . against the marble . . ." Her small voice trailed away.

It's Joe's grave—and it's hideous.

But she turned to her sister and managed to smile. "Yes," she said.

They stood there for some minutes, gazing at the neat white bed of stone and listening to the wind soughing in the young windbreak of pines, and the birds that carolled overhead.

He isn't here. The thought prevented any real communion with the memory of Joe. Katherine glanced sideways at Laura, but her face was lowered, her gaze fixed on the vase of brightly-coloured flowers that seemed to Katherine merely to mock their errand. Joe was not here; she knew already that she would return to this place only when her mother requested it, or on Joe's birthday each year.

Without looking up, Laura said, "I almost envy you, not being here when he died—although, of course, I wouldn't part with these past five years I've had with Joe here . . . still, it would be good to remember him as you must remember him. It must be hard for you to connect this grave with Joe, the Joe you knew."

"Yes," Katherine repeated, "it's the finality that's missing. No matter how old I become I shall always half expect Joe to come careering up the drive on his horse, or to hear his voice singing in some part of the house . . ."

"Oh . . .! Joe's terrible voice . . .!" Laura giggled.

"And he'd sing all the louder . . . !"

"Father once threatened to lock him in the cellar—whenever some new piece of music would arrive, Joe would sing it over and over for three days . . . !"

They were laughing, each holding the other's hand, and Laura's eyes were filled with tears as she laughed. "Oh, Katey! God must have wanted him, don't you think? He made us all laugh—he was gifted in making people happy—was that why God wanted him?"

"I don't know, dear—I don't know!" She placed her hand under Laura's elbow, and guided the younger woman back towards their carriage.

Laura and Katherine might have missed seeing the two women quietly watching them from the other side of the road, for they made no sound, simply waited. Laura had her hand on the edge of the carriage, her head lowered, about to lift her skirt a little to climb into the vehicle; it was Katherine who saw them first, and her sister's sudden stillness made Laura, too, look up.

It had been five years, but Katherine knew them; bare black legs beneath tattered dresses, possum and wallaby skins wrapped about their shoulders. Myeela and Tigoora, black eyes watchful, openly curious.

She crossed the road to them, only just aware that Laura was following her. As she approached, the dark faces of the two women broke into slow smiles of pleasure.

"Miss Kate—you home from walkabout . . ." It was not a question. Tigoora, at twenty-five, two years older than her smaller, round-faced friend Myeela, reached out a hand to Katherine. They held to each other firmly, smiling into each other's faces.

"Yes, Tigoora, I'm home. Myeela . . ." Myeela was laughing, the familiar throaty, infectious laugh that Katherine remembered from her childhood. Little fat Myeela, always tagging after Tigoora— all of them playing together in those early days before the Valley began to fill with people, before they began to grow, before Suzanna and Marcus hired a governess and the golden days were over forever.

"You bin gone too long. Happy you come back." And the large black eyes sobered, swung over to the graveyard. "Mister Joe gone. You father gone. You gone. Missus Suzanna not like old times. Maybe better now. Happy you back. You got man, now?"

Katherine was long accustomed to the directness, but still it surprised her, pleased her: here were two people who had not changed, who would not change. Their tribe, the Woddi Woddi, was part of this land, part of her memories.

"I did have." She told them. "He died."

The two women lowered their eyes to the ground, neither spoke for a moment, then, "I had a girl child—she die," Myeela murmured.

"I'm sorry . . ." So even the laughing Myeela had been touched by tragedy.

"Got four baby, now. Tigoora got five—and new one coming." Myeela looked sideways at her friend.

Tigoora smiled, the mother's pride lighting the wonderful eyes, the fine white teeth flashing. She patted her stomach unselfconsciously. "Soon, now." she said. Then, looking between Katherine and Laura, "you misses—find man, have babies. Bad thinking, you crying too much tears for Mister Joe."

"White women do things different," Myeela put in.

Katherine shook her head, "Tigoora is not wrong. Too much grieving is a bad thing." She sensed, rather than saw the disapproving, almost shocked, look that Laura gave her.

Tigoora shifted from one dusty foot to the other. She carried in one hand a bag of woven plant fibres filled with some kind of bulbous roots about which the earth still clung. These, undoubtedly part of the evening meal, she changed to the other hand, uncomfortably, then began, "Miss Kate, you father come home?"

"I . . . Yes, of course."

"Good thing he come back soon, eh? You tell him, Gurral says he come back. Walkabout too long."

Before Katherine could speak, Myeela had put in, "Where he gone, you father? Big water?" She gestured towards the east, towards the escarpment that divided the Valley from the alluvial coastal flats of the Shoalhaven district, and the Pacific coast. It was the way the Woddi Woddi would go on their journey through the territory that was theirs, following the fish, the game, the vegetation in season. Never staying too long in one place, never depleting Nature's store. Moving on to allow time to replenish—the eternal, necessary "walkabout" of the black people of Australia.

"No, my father four times as far—that way!" She pointed to the north. "Big town, many people, many houses. Sydney."

"Why?" Myeela asked.

Katherine and Laura looked at each other. "Well—working . . ."

"He have more cows there?"

"No, he . . ."

"He have too many cows. Too many horses. Too much work. He go, his women stay. No good, that. Black fella, he take his women, look after them good. No leave them. Gurral says, Boss come home. You tell your father Gurral says that, 'ey?"

The two Woddi women had turned away.

"Tigoora, Myeela!" Katherine called. "Is there any trouble? Is everything all right with the tribe?"

For the first time, the highly expressive eyes gave nothing away. Tigoora and Myeela gazed without emotion upon Katherine, before Myeela repeated, "Gurral says, Boss come home."

Katherine took a step forward, but the women were already moving away, between the trees. Laura's hand was on her arm. "No, Katey, they won't tell us anything more. It's between old Gurral and Father."

Gurral. Seated beside Laura on the drive back to Barrengarry, Katherine thought of the ancient black man. Why, he had been "old Gurral" for as long as Katherine could remember. Patriarch of the tribe, striated with ceremonial scars and forgotten wounds from long-ago battles, his white hair drawn back and tied round about with a length of red rag—he liked the colour red, requested a new piece of scarlet cloth from Suzanna every year or so—sleepy lids over eyes that had watched the nightmare of the white man's coming—and had learnt to live within that nightmare. To guide his people through a world where the barbed wire and post-and-rail fences spread further each year, even as the game that was their staple diet grew more and more scarce.

And Gurral wanted Marcus Prescott to come home.

"I'm wearing two pairs of gloves," Laura grimaced, "and I'm still cold." She changed the reins back and forth as she flexed first one hand, then the other.

"I'm sorry, how thoughtless of me." Katherine, concerned, placed her hand over Laura's. "Let me drive . . ."

"No, no . . ."

"Come, stop the sulky, Laura. Let me take the reins."

They haggled for a little, but Katherine prevailed and took the reins from her protesting sister. Laura, vanquished, settled down into the warmth of the rug and Katherine's muff with a happy sigh, and for a mile or so no word was exchanged. Then:

"Katey," rather carefully, "you're not planning on . . . confronting Father, are you?"

Bother, Katherine thought. "Confronting?" she murmured, her eyes on the road before them. "I'll tell him of Gurral's message . . ."

"You were planning on a campaign to bring Father home long before Myeela mentioned Gurral. You're worried, as Teddi and I are worried, about Mama, aren't you?"

Katherine tried to keep the grimness from her voice. "Even Myeela noticed it—Father's failed all of you."

"That's harsh, Katey. He was brokenhearted . . ."

"He was self-indulgent. And callous."

"Katey!"

Katherine glanced at her sister. Laura's look of horror was almost comical. "Why are you so surprised? You know I'm speaking the truth. I always have spoken my mind—*to* Father, and about him."

"Yes," Laura nodded consideringly. "Yes, I remember you always did—and caused fearful rows. It's just strange, after all these years, to hear someone standing up to him—none of us ever learnt to do that."

"Not even Joe?" And there was pain in the asking.

"No," the wistful voice beside her. "Not even Joe. He'd smile and agree, and go his own way—in most things."

"Perhaps that was best," Katherine sighed. "I simply couldn't stop myself from telling Father when I thought he was wrong."

"You and Father are too much alike. Mama always says that."

Katherine herself remembered her mother saying it, heard the patient sigh in the voice. And it had irritated her. She did not like the thought that she was like her father.

"I've written to him several times, asking when he's coming home," Laura was saying. "So has Mama, of course. Edwina is cross with him, so she hasn't written at all, despite all Mama can do to persuade her."

And Katherine remembered then the scene of the previous day, when she had climbed the stairs to the sound of Edwina's shrill and protesting voice.

"Edwina is in love, and Father doesn't approve of her choice, is that it?" She could tell by the look on Laura's face that this was the truth. "Who is it, Laura?"

Laura sighed. "Rafe Huckstable."

Katherine's hands on the reins did not slacken, nor did she turn to look at her sister. Laura could not possibly have known the effect of her words, and went on, unwittingly. "Oh, I know he's far too old for her, and he's as much of a scallywag as he always was— but he began to notice her after the Cummings' ball a year ago, and of course Edwina succumbed to his charms immediately."

Katherine's face must have betrayed something of her emotions in the quick glance that she shot at Laura, for her sister laughed a little. "One can't blame the poor young thing—Katey, he's even more handsome than when you left! Every girl in the Southern Highlands has fallen in love with Rafe Huckstable at one stage or another. Except you, of course, cool thing that you are. I remember how you used to laugh at Arabella Murchison and the Cummings girls for losing their hearts to him." She looked away for a minute, and Katherine saw her chewing her lip; then she had turned abruptly to say, "To tell the truth—and you mustn't laugh, Katey—I was feeling so very depressed after we all returned from Europe without you that even I was silly enough to believe Rafe's gallantries. Only for a few weeks—he began paying attention to a girl over in Burrawang after that."

There was a short silence while Laura watched Katherine's face with some anxiety.

"Ah," Katherine said. "I see."

"Oh, don't be cross with me, Katey; I behaved with the utmost decorum, I assure you. Mama wasn't upset, and even Father was sympathetic."

"*Father* was sympathetic?"

"Well, almost. He said he was glad that I was sensible enough not to lose my head over a young villain like Rafe, and that the experience had probably been good for me. It was, too," Laura said, with a wry smile.

Katherine said, "I'm glad you weren't hurt. Father was right to be proud of your common sense. Not every girl Rafe courts is wise enough to see that he's merely amusing himself."

"I know," Laura murmured. "Remember Daisy Cummings? Her Mama had to take her to Sydney for three months—the poor girl almost went into a decline. None of the Cummings girls are married, by the way. They're still the same—as pale and wan-looking as ever."

"Not still in a decline over Rafe?"

"Oh, no! They spend their time in good works, baking pies and knitting shawls for the elderly—and agitating for a church here in the Valley. They actually managed to see the Archbishop while on a visit to Sydney two years ago—the poor man made the mistake of saying he'd look into the matter personally—since then Daisy, Marietta and Bessie have been writing to him every week. One letter *each*—can you imagine the poor, besieged man? I hope they succeed— I don't mean to sound as if I'm mocking them, they do a great deal of good. But it does seem as if they're settling down into spinsterhood—it wouldn't be so bad if they didn't do it so . . . *collectively.*"

Katherine had to smile, but Laura was immediately serious once more. "It's Teddi I worry about, Katey. She's met polite, presentable young men when we've been staying in Sydney or visiting Grandmama and Grandpapa at Moss Vale, but here in the Valley there are so *few*. And Father didn't seem to see that there was a danger in allowing Teddi to grow up in the Valley . . ."

"You and I did—it was a wonderful childhood."

"Yes, but you and I were always more steady than Joe and Teddi. They were both alike in that they shared a romantic, reckless streak."

This was true. And it had already destroyed Joe. Katherine turned to Laura, worried now. "How serious is it between Edwina and Rafe? I can imagine that Teddi has convinced herself that this is the great love affair of the nineteenth century, but what about Rafe?"

"That's the odd thing. I really do believe he's genuinely fond of

Teddi. Who knows how far it would have gone, had Father not forbidden them to see each other?"

"He did that? Rather strange, wasn't it, in view of the fact that he let Rafe flirt with you . . ."

"Katey," gently, "Father could see that nothing serious was meant. With Teddi, Rafe is different—she's grown to be a beauty, as you know—and she's lively and funny and independent—Rafe is fascinated with her. Perhaps he needs a woman with a strong personality. Edwina certainly has that. And they look wonderful together—they're both very much alike, physically and emotionally."

"Sometimes that's not a good thing," Katherine stated.

"I know," uneasily from Laura. "Father seemed to think so, anyway. About four months ago he prohibited them from seeing each other, as I said. Teddi cried and fumed for weeks, but Rafe stayed away from the house, to give him credit. Then Joe . . . died. And Father left for Sydney, and . . . Katey, Teddi's seeing Rafe again. And not only secretly, either. He's called to the house to visit Mama and she allows Teddi to be present. She's too soft-hearted. Then, yesterday, Carl was on his way to mend a fence down by the creek and found Teddi and Rafe there, *embracing*. He was as cross as Father would have been, and reported it straight to Mama. She's decided to be firm now, and—well, you saw the result when you arrived yesterday. Katey, will you talk to Teddi?"

"I will if you like, but my dear, I'm the last person to be lecturing her—a runaway myself who eloped with a young Irish lawyer and poet after knowing him a fortnight? I, who have been disinherited, struck from the family Bible?"

Laura laughed. "What nonsense!"

"Have I?" Suddenly it was important to know. "He said he would, Laura. Did he strike my name out?"

"Katey, I read from that Bible every Sunday—we all do. You're there, safe and sound. As if Father would do that! But he's a nasty man, all the same," she scowled, "for threatening to."

Laura seemed to sense with this knowledge the depth of the bitterness that had existed between Katherine and their father, for she said, carefully, "Katey, you will be tactful, talking to Father, won't you? We all want so much for you to be reconciled—Mama, of course, most of all. These past five years without you have been very hard on her. It would please her so much to have the family united again."

"I'll try," Katherine promised. "But a great deal depends on Father, you know that."

They were passing Radley's Store—not that that edifice deserved the title marked in fading letters above the door. The bark-shingled hut with its small, calico-covered windows and sloping earth floor sold liquor, flour, sugar and tea—and the quality of these staples was often as questionable as the heavy-shouldered, bearded proprietor, clad in greasy apron, now standing before the door.

A women was with him, having just preceded him from the building, and two children followed, ragged, unkempt boys of about seven and five. The woman herself, on hearing the sound of the carriage approaching, turned her faded brown bonnet towards the sound. The small face beneath the rather shapeless brim suddenly lost its frown and became alert, watching the horse and sulky draw near.

They were never really part of the Prescotts' world, the cedar-getters, although the woman, who was Katherine's age, had been known to her, along with her many brothers and sisters, all her life. Born a Mosley, she had married into the Crolin family; they, like the Tallons, Mosleys and Greens worked the hills surrounding the Valley, and sometimes within the Valley itself, keeping to themselves, their camps moving from one isolated slope to another. And their children, too, kept to themselves, more suspicious, more shy of the settlers than the Woddi Woddi had ever been.

To Katherine it had always seemed a miserable, lonely existence, particularly for the women and children. The men were brown, wiry creatures, looking out from behind long, often luxuriant beards with a proud, sullen mistrust. The women and children always seemed too thin, as if they were ill-nourished, and this was probably true, as the cedar-getters rarely left the Valley area unless to deliver timber to Moss Vale, Bowral or Mittagong, and their camps moved too frequently for their families to benefit from planting crops or vegetable gardens. The men shot what game they could, and the woman's baskets, which she now lowered to the ground, bore a sample of the remainder of their diet: flour for damper and thickening the meat stews, tea and sugar. The liquor, everyone in the Valley knew, was something the cedar-getters made for themselves. Radley's store was used as an occasional meeting place—and the local belief was that half the "rum" sold by Radley in bottles bearing Sydney and Melbourne labels was brewed no more than a few miles away, in some ferny glade close to the Valley walls, yet far from prying eyes.

"Miss Prescott . . .?"

The woman was walking forward. Katherine drew the reins and the horse halted, the woman walking even closer. "Miss Prescott, the baby's just fine, now—I thought you'd like to know . . ."

Laura smiled. "I'm so glad, Mrs Crolin . . ."

"The boys didn't get sick, 'cause I bedded them down separate—and the girls are real well now. I can't thank you enough—you're better'n any doctor, I reckon." The face was thin; fine bones over which the brown, freckled skin was stretched taut. The eyes, rather prominent hazel eyes, ringed with tiny, premature lines, skittered to Katherine. "I . . . I remember your sister—bin away . . ."

"Yes, this is my sister, Katherine Carron . . ." Laura began.

"I remember you, Mrs Crolin, how do you do?" Katherine smiled. "Your boys have certainly grown."

And with part of her mind she was thinking, the woman is my age—and she looks fifty. What sort of life does she lead? What is this country doing to her?

Essie Crolin contemplated the two boys, hanging back shyly at some distance. "Yes, they've growed. All my family has growed. One for every year I bin married. Can't grow more'n that—unless I start havin' twins, God forbid."

Katherine willed herself not to look at Laura, but could see in her peripheral vision how her sister ducked her head a little, and she could imagine the blush creeping up Laura's throat.

"Miss Laura helped my fambly—real good, she was. Influenza fair near killed half my kids." Mrs Crolin was explaining. She turned to Laura once more, lowered her voice a little. "Charlie—my husband—he's real sorry now, about the way he behaved when you was up our place." She paused to run her tongue across straitened lips. "You know what men're like when they've had one too many. He'd been up at—He'd bin drinkin' with friends all afternoon. And he's a real proud man, Miss Prescott—won't take no charity from no one. He didn't mean that, what he said to you—an' when I explained to him after, he said he was real sorry. I hope there ain't no ill-will . . . I'd feel so bad, after all you done . . ."

"That's quite all right, Mrs Crolin," Laura said, with, Katherine noted, much of Suzanna's gentle courtesy, "I quite understand. And I am glad that the children are all well and recovering."

"I'm glad to see you again, Mrs Crolin—goodbye." Katherine had read Laura's signals from a lifetime of sibling intimacy; it was time they were leaving.

"Good day!" the woman called. "Give my regards to your mama . . . Oh, and if you could, tell your father . . ."

Two things happened at that moment. The smaller boy wailed something to his mother, and the sulky hit a series of ruts in the road that Radley, in the interest of good customer service, had so stirred himself as to half-fill with rocks. The little carriage bounced and swayed and squeaked. Laura and Katherine had both looked back to wave at the woman standing watching them, one hand raised in farewell. Now the sisters glanced at each other. Katherine asked, "What did she say about Father?"

"I didn't hear. Shall we call . . ."

"Oh, no, let's not pull up and start all over again." She glanced upwards at the clouded sky. "It looks like rain, and besides, I can't go to Father with messages from everyone in the Valley."

"You're so impatient, Katey," Laura admonished tolerantly. Then, after glancing behind them, "Did you see the way Mr Radley glared at us before he disappeared? I nodded to him, too—out of good manners—and he merely scowled and turned his back and walked inside. What a boorish man . . ."

"I've never even nodded to him since he blackened Joe's eye all those years ago," Katherine said grimly.

"*He* said he was trying to break up a fight . . ."

"He didn't have to strike Joe—he was only twenty at the time, and Bert Radley would have made two of him."

"Joe shouldn't have been in that place—Father said it served him right."

Katherine was silent. *Father said.*

There was still so much resentment within her. All these years of his silence; no reply to letters that told of Christopher's birth, Oliver's death—and although she had left Italy before any letter from home could have reached her, somehow she knew that her father had not written to her when he had received her letter telling him that Christopher, his only grandchild, was dead. And it irritated her to come home and find that not only the family but the entire Valley seemed so dependent upon him.

As they drove home a light, chill mist began to fall. They passed several small landholdings, smoke rising from rough-built chimneys, but they saw no sign of life in all that time, and travelled in silence for some while before Laura said, "I don't know if this is the right time to tell you—you've had so many burdens to bear these past few months . . . It's just that you're going to Sydney tomorrow and I may not have another opportunity to talk to you for some time."

Katherine was watching Laura closely. She was right, there had been so much information—mostly unpleasant—forced upon her that she was dreading any further revelations. But this, surely, would be the news of her growing friendship with Stephen Brody.

"Did . . . did Stephen Brody mention me when he drove you home yesterday?"

"Only in passing," Katherine smiled, "but he passed that subject very often." Laura was blushing a little. "Really, Laura, Father must be in despair with us—all three involved in forbidden relationships—he'll think we're all conspiring to flaunt his authority."

"Oh, I never meant to do that! And I'm not, at the moment, for Father doesn't know that Stephen and I are . . . well, are fond of each other.

"I have a favour to ask you, Katey. I don't want you to *tell* Father about Stephen—but could you *talk* about him? Tell him how Stephen helped you home yesterday and was so kind to you after your dreadful shock—*you* know how to do it! Just find out if he really resents Stephen so much . . ."

She petered out, and the same idea was occurring to them both. Stephen Brody had been resented bitterly by Marcus Prescott, five years before, and for this very reason—his tenacious and ardent pursuit of one of Marcus's daughters.

"Katey . . ." Laura's little face looked pale beneath the thick, fair hair, the green eyes were large in their unconscious pleading. "Katey, did you love Stephen?"

Katherine had no need to consider, to hesitate. She placed one gloved hand over her sister's, hidden within the muff. "No, Laura. If I had, could I have left the Valley to go overseas? Would I have married Oliver? No, until Oliver I'd never . . ." Now, this was awkward. What had she felt for Rafe Huckstable? She had never faced up to what had happened, to her own uncharacteristic behaviour and her consequent sense of shame. She could not do it now. She said, "I'd never known real love until I met Oliver."

And this was true. Through everything, all that had happened, his regretful lies and unwilling deceits, she had loved him, and she knew that Oliver, tortured within his mind as he was, had loved her. Towards the end, when prison had robbed him of the family he had taken for granted, he had loved her more than ever. She knew that had he lived to be released, she need never doubt his loyalty again, for they had in adversity recaptured the strength of emotion that had first drawn them together.

"That's the way I feel about Stephen," Laura was saying softly. "He told me that what he'd felt for you had been infatuation," (*Hmmph*, thought Katherine) "—and I believe him—but it's good to hear you say that, it sets my mind at rest. It wouldn't upset you, then, if Stephen and I should marry, eventually?"

"Oh, Laura, of course not!" and Katherine gave her sister a hug. Even then, however, her gaze went unseeingly over Laura's head, and she had a mental picture of her father's face in reaction to the match. No, Katherine wished the couple well. Marcus Prescott, however, would need a great deal of convincing.

They found their mother in the downstairs parlour when they returned, seated nervously on the edge of her chair, across a tea table from a young police officer.

He sprang to his feet as soon as Laura and Katherine entered the room, and bowed over their hands with a confident and easy manner.

Katherine, disturbed at suddenly discovering an official of the law within her home, had to consciously relax and remind herself that this was not Ireland, and her family were not involved in anything illegal.

Suzanna was explaining that Stephen Brody had ridden to Moss Vale the day before to report the attack on Gilbert Barton. The doctor and Sergeant Lloyd had returned with him.

He was tall and very neatly dressed, Katherine noted, a man who seemed proud of his uniform and what it represented. Yet there was little formality to the man's approach; Thomas Lloyd had an honesty and a natural, almost boyish ease that made him, even in the dark uniform and shining, spurred boots, appear at home in the, albeit faded, formality of Barrengarry's parlour.

He had, he confided, the job of investigating the death of another man only three weeks before, in scrub country out of Burrawang. It seemed the incidents might have been connected, but Gilbert Barton had not yet regained consciousness and could not, therefore, be questioned. Could Mrs Carron tell him exactly what had happened on the road from Wollongong yesterday?

Katherine told him all she could, though it was little enough. She could see he was disappointed, that he had hoped for some clue that would give him a possible direction to take. He did not have an enviable job, Katherine thought, feeling rather sorry for him in his obvious frustration.

It was a deceptive face, she considered, broad, stubborn, with a humorous mouth and expressive eyes, capped with a thatch of tight, light brown curls, now darkened and stiffened with some type of hair dressing in a vain effort to straighten it into what—he obviously thought—was a more suitable style for a serious member of the Force. There would be those who presumed him to be naive, who would mistake his artlessness for gullibility. But there was something in the blue eyes, in the incisiveness of his questions and the manner of his speech that told her it would be foolish to take this man too lightly.

After the questioning, Suzanna asked him to stay to lunch and he grinned, nodding as eagerly as a schoolboy.

"He's so *young*," Suzanna murmured, as Carl led their guest to the bathroom to wash the travel dust from himself. "Isn't that a sign of growing old, when policemen begin to look young? But he'd be about twenty seven . . . no, it's still too young," she decided. "I can't help but wish, pleasant young man though he is, that this dreadful matter could be in the hands of some mature officer."

"I think he's very capable, Mama," Katherine submitted. "He gives me the impression of a man so suited to his job that he needn't pretend officiousness. He must be competent, or his superiors wouldn't send him on such a difficult assignment."

"I hope Mr Barton will be all right," Laura murmured from the window seat, from where she had watched the interview. "Poor Katey—what a terrible welcome home you've had! It's a pity . . ." She stopped.

"What's a pity, dear?" Suzanna encouraged.

"Oh, Mama—it's a pity we had to be here at all! Why didn't you insist that we go to Sydney with Father, after the funeral? It's not fair on Katey to have to run back and forth between you and Father like this—we should all be together, like a real family."

In the brief silence, Katherine noted that the words affected her mother deeply, she sat stiffly, her hands having come together in her lap, and she gazed at her beloved Laura as if she were something threatening and not quite pleasant, like a drift of ectoplasm that had no right to manifest itself out of the cedar panelling.

But, "You must trust your father's judgement, dear," she said. "And until this unfortunate accident of Mr Barton's, we've been coping very well here by ourselves; I've been proud of both my girls. Now Katey's with us again, and it's a sign that everything will soon sort itself out very nicely." She smiled rather wickedly at Laura. "Besides, there have been some consolations to being here in the Valley all these months, have there not? By staying, I'm sure we've saved the Post Office services from being hopelessly inundated with letters going back and forth between Kangaroo Valley and Balmain."

"But . . ."

"Hush . . ." Suzanna frowned, and a few seconds later, the young sergeant returned.

Edwina, who had been schooling her new filly in the horse paddock all that morning, breezed into the room only a short time afterwards, pink-cheeked and obviously pleased and impressed with their handsome visitor. Her animated conversation, about horses and hunting and the news from Moss Vale, occupied most of luncheon, and Katherine was pleased to find the atmosphere of the house lightened due to the presence of their guest.

Even so, in odd moments, she would see a fleeting look of wistful introspection on her mother's face, and she remembered Laura's uncharacteristic outburst, *We should all be together, like a real family.*

Nine

Katherine was in her room, changing for dinner, when there was a tap at the door. Peggy bustled in, her round face, always damp with exertion for she was never still, alight with the thought of a possible drama.

"Mister Huckstable's arrived, Miss Katey. The Missus is talking to him in the parlour now. *Usually* he'd stay to dinner but after the shenanigans between him and Miss Edwina, he might be sent off with a flea in his ear . . ."

"Peggy, I think this is between . . ."

"Miss Edwina—I was just called into her room—and she says, could you go down and give your respects in case your Mama needs any assistance."

"Really, Peggy, I don't think . . ."

But Suzanna's voice was heard then, calling for Peggy from the foot of the stairs. Peggy stood still, her fat little mouth pursed, the white-blonde eyebrows raised, then, "Uh-huh—that's her polite, *warm* voice—I knew he'd get around her. He'll be staying for dinner."

She had turned away and Katherine, laughing despite herself, had to ask, "How can you tell that? Mama simply called your name . . ."

"She has a *tone*, y'know. Yous kids always knew, but you forget.

Yous always used to be able to tell whether she was cross or not, by how she called your name . . . a warm tone or a cold tone, is how I describe it . . .''

Katherine smiled, had she ever been so perspicacious? She shook her head, "I don't remember . . ."

"You bin away too long," Peggy said briskly, and made for the door. "You wait—Mister Rafe Huckstable will be at dinner."

"Peggy . . ."

Peggy stopped. Katherine sat down on her bed. "I was going to ring for you, actually . . . I *was* changing for dinner but I'm so very tired after all the travelling—and thinking of the journey to Sydney tomorrow . . ."

"Poor lamb, of course . . ." and nothing more needing to be said, Peggy helped her into her nightdress and robe, put more wood on the fire, and left promising to pass on her regrets to her Mama, and that an especially tasty supper would be brought up on a tray.

Katherine, left alone, settled down into her fireside chair, and drew up her knees beneath her robe. The fire was quite fierce, but its mountains, crags and valleys mesmerized her and she remained oblivious to the possible effects of the heat upon her complexion.

She would have to face Rafe Huckstable at some stage—and she would carry it off with charm and dignity. But she would not meet him tonight.

For Peggy had been correct in her reading of Suzanna—her tone of voice and her susceptibility. When Peggy returned, half an hour later, with a light vegetable broth and a small, golden-crusted chicken pie, it was to announce that Mister Huckstable was dining with Miss Laura, Miss Edwina and the Missus. Edwina was "sparkling like a fizzy pink firecracker, Miss Katey—there'll be trouble when your father hears about this . . . but it's wonderful to see her so bright-eyed and happy all the same, even if it is doomed to disaster."

With which Cassandra-like observation, Peggy retreated to her realm on the ground floor.

After her meal Katherine left the tray and its remains outside her door, and turned out the light. If someone chanced to open the door they would believe her to be asleep and would not intrude.

But Katherine returned to her chair by the fire, curling up within its depths once more, and for the first time, of necessity, relived all that had passed between herself and Rafe Huckstable.

It was true that she had treated the pangs of Arabella Murchison and Daisy, Bessie and Marietta Cummings with great amusement. For she had been very safe herself, at that stage.

Safe, not because she could look with casual indifference upon Raphael Winton Huckstable, for no one, man or woman, could ignore the physical perfection of the man; one simply wanted to stare at him, stare and stare for the sheer pleasure of it. No, she was safe because he had not, in all the years of their growing up together, ever singled her out.

It was gratifying—if anything about the affair could be said to be gratifying—that when it happened, it was not in the Valley, where there were, at most, only three or four families who had daughters of enough sophistication to interest him. Instead, she had been shopping in Market Street in Sydney, having been staying with her father for a few weeks at the town house in Balmain, when a voice behind her had spoken her name—and looking up from the window display she had been perusing, she saw herself, and Rafe Huckstable standing behind her, his top hat already being doffed with one elegant hand. When she turned, his eyes, soft brown and merry, were shining into her own, and he was looking *only* at her.

His family's town house was in Drummoyne, and like the Prescotts', set amid large gardens running down to the harbour. The houses were close enough so that meetings in the town or out riding were easily arranged.

She told herself that he was an old family friend, that he was an escort on whom she could depend, and an interesting, safe companion, of whom, since he was a close friend of Joe's, her father would not have disapproved.

But her father never knew. And Rafe sensed she was not speaking of their meetings to her father and did not mention it. It became a kind of unspoken game between them. She had many friends in the little harbourside community of Balmain, all within riding distance, and Marcus, busy about his work or serving late on committees and attending meetings, left her much to her own devices. He had trusted her in those days. "Kate is the level-headed one," she often heard him say in describing her, and "why can't you be more like your older sister?" he would tell one of her mutinous siblings. When she had eloped with Oliver, Marcus had called her "deceitful". And this hurt more than all his angry words—and there were many of them. It hurt because she knew it to be true.

Her father had not been at the Balmain house for her to inform him where she was going, late on that particular afternoon. She told her father's manservant, Tobias, that she was visiting the home of one of her friends, Gloria Patterson—and she had.

But two hours after her arrival at the Patterson home found her riding through the gathering dusk along the broad, busy road that led from Balmain, through the little township of Rozelle, to Drummoyne, and down towards the harbour.

There was a curious suspension to her reasoning at that time, and no amount of hindsight could find any logic in her behaviour—what seemed natural, even *right* at the time, became totally reprehensible to her later self. Was it the one time her instinctive impulses had controlled her and had that propulsion, frightening her in its very intensity, made her run towards the future that held Oliver—gentle, logical Oliver—and a seemingly safe life?

Standing with Rafe at the foot of the garden in the dusk, watching the flying foxes blacken the sky over the water as they left their shaded trees and flew—north to south—to feed in the cool night. Watching the storm clouds over the harbour, and the tall ships moored in the river's mouth, the lightning above them all, threatening, threatening, coming closer with a fretful muttering that grew to a clamouring roar. And laughing, standing on the slippery rocks, the water soughing about them, leaning back in Rafe's arms against Rafe's chest and laughing at the rage of the heavens.

Turning her about in his arms to face him he had kissed her for the first time, a deep demanding kiss that had drawn forth from her a keen pleasure, a rush of desire of such acute and sudden intensity that the cataclysm of the skies above the harbour seemed merely part of all she was feeling.

When they pulled back to gaze at each other, when she looked up into that face—the smooth brown skin, the perfect, strongly moulded bones of brow and cheek and jaw—when she gazed into shadowed dark eyes it was with a sense of wonder. She had known Rafe Huckstable all their lives—and yet nothing in their growing friendship had prepared her for this. The extent and intensity of emotion made her feel bemused, shaken.

And the outburst of sound that occurred then, the erupting, unbearable, multisonorous convulsion of the heavens, caught her completely unaware. She turned sharply with a half scream, throwing up her hands towards her ears—and even as she felt her balance go, felt Rafe grab for her, she saw the sparks flying from the mast of the ship lying at anchor a few hundred yards offshore, saw the flames shoot upwards and the mast begin to topple even as she herself fell heavily, the two small steps that she took to regain her balance taking her off the rocks and down . . .

"My God, Katherine! Katherine, are you all right?"

She began to laugh. Standing in icy sea water that lapped about her knees, her long skirts billowing on the faint pull of the tide, she laughed and laughed—and all the harder for Rafe's worried tone, his attempts to pull her up to him, his agitated concern as he changed from foot to foot, attempting to haul on her weak arms, on fingers that were useless from laughter.

"Katherine—I'm sorry—I tried to catch you—hold on to me, my darling . . . Katherine, this is serious . . . there are sharks in these waters . . . come closer—grip my hands . . . ! My God, you're hysterical—don't panic—don't faint! *Grip my hands* . . . Katherine!"

He had pulled her out finally, and he stood rocking her in his arms as she tried to convince him that she was unhurt and not even frightened. They laughed together, then kissed once more, and turned to watch the rain blow in, over the furthest shore, across the harbour and the broad mouth of the Parramatta River. They saw it fall on the still smoking, shattered mast of the tall ship, saw the lights springing up on the deck and in nearby vessels.

They gazed at each other, and then turned without another word, his arm beneath hers, for she was hampered by her riding dress, the heavy trailing skirts saturated now.

No servants were in the house—she had not, and never did ask about their absence. He led her himself to his sister Emilia's room, and, left alone, she changed by lamplight into one of Emilia's cotton housedresses, borrowing a shawl to cover the too-large neckline, for Emilia was taller, more broad-shouldered than Katherine.

She felt giddy, drunk with a kind of madness that night. Just to turn and look at herself in the ample cream and blue floral gown, its only concession to frivolity a row of pintucks across the broad flat bodice, made her laugh. She could almost visualise Emilia's rage at her clothing being borrowed; and she would like it even less, knowing whose ample bosom was filling the shapeless moderation of her gown.

Emilia Huckstable, two years older than Katherine, had inherited the same features from her parents as had her brother Rafe. Unfortunately, the long, handsome visage, square jaw and high intelligent forehead that so marked her brother with distinctive good looks appeared in a most unattractive light on a woman. What was more, Emilia was tall, touching six feet in height and broad shouldered.

Perhaps the most unfortunate aspect for her, physically, was that she did not have the warm, expressive dark eyes that Rafe possessed. Emilia's were blue—the palest blue eyes that Katherine had ever seen—and yet it was not their colour but their expression which made one uncomfortable; as if Emilia disapproved of whatever she saw. The mouth, too, was an unfortunate, unrelenting line.

Emilia had been a bully when they were younger. Bigger than all the other children, she had wielded her power as if she were a queen of a small feudal state. Fiercely proud and independent, always rebellious, Emilia was passionately attached to one other human being. For "Raphael" or "my baby brother", she was ferocious in defence, using her quick intelligence, incisive wit or physical superiority, whichever was called for. This continued until it was finally drummed into her that she was a Lady, and therefore above running about the countryside like a hoyden, whereupon the quick intelligence, the independent spirit were kept at home, learning the feminine running of a large household. And the wit became sharper still, with constant use.

And here was Katherine, in Emilia's gown, sailing down the staircase as if on her way to a ball, with her small smile of revenge still hovering about her face; the wickedness in the green eyes that boldly confronted Rafe in the parlour intoxicated him.

The fire was blazing in the large marble fireplace and its glow on the fine objects around the room would have given a peaceful feeling, had it not been for the storm that roared and raged above them.

In the end, it was the storm that saved her. To sit with Rafe on the settee, find oneself in his arms—her thoughts went no further. The feelings engendered by his embrace were robbing her of any power to pull away, take his hands from her, move from him . . .

And lightning had struck again, quite close—both had started, stared at each other, smiled, and withdrawn once more into a world in which nothing existed but the uncharted continent of their two bodies . . .

Someone was hammering at the door. Someone was shouting loudly, panic in the voice, and hammering at the great front door.

The fright they received made them conscious. Rafe had kicked off his shoes, his shirt was unfastened, its tails out of his trousers, The bodice and hem of the boring little housegown were, Katherine noted in sudden horror, much too close together for any pretence to modesty. She hiked the former up and pulled the latter down as she sat up, her gaze fixed on Rafe's face.

He was tucking in his shirt, fastening buttons incorrectly, pulling on his shoes. "Dash upstairs, there's a good girl—I may have to bring him in—it sounds like Mitford-Wells from next door."

Katherine snatched up her shawl and did as she was told, taking the damp riding dress with her from where it lay drying on a chair before the fire.

From the top landing she could hear the voices, Rafe's murmuring, Mitford-Wells's excited, urgent. Then the door shut. She could hear Rafe coming up the stairs two at a time.

He stopped on seeing her there, smiled at her, seated as she was like a small girl on the step, her dress pulled over her knees.

"I have to go," he said gently, seating himself beside her, "wait downstairs, I won't be long. It seems a tree has fallen on part of the stables next door—the horses seem to be unhurt but the tree is blocking the doors. Will you be all right?"

"Of course."

"I'll just go up and change." He kissed the top of her head, and was gone along the corridor to his room.

Katherine had not moved when he returned and he drew her up with him, led her downstairs and saw that she was comfortably settled with a few back copies of *The Illustrated News of the World* before he left. Again, a kiss on the top of the head, and he was gone, promising to return as soon as he could.

But she would not be there.

She rearranged her riding clothes, sat with the magazines on her lap, unopened, and gazed into the fire.

Her foolishness amazed her. She had walked open-eyed and consenting to the very brink of social ruin. And why?

These past two weeks had been a magical time—the happiest she had ever known. Yet she had known also that it would end, must end. She did not love Rafe Huckstable—and he certainly did not love her. There could have been no future for this relationship and, having come so far, it might have spoilt a tolerant friendship between herself and one of Joe's closest friends. How could she greet him in the future—and why hadn't she thought of this?

The only thing she had learned from this, she thought, as she changed into her own clothes, still damp and sea-smelling, was that she knew herself so little . . .

She replaced the shawl and gown in Emilia's large and aseptic bedroom, and went out of the house by the back door. Mitford-Wells's property was some hundred yards away, across lawns and rockeries and high dividing hedges, so no one from next door saw her saddle her own horse and lead him out into the rain-clean night, although she heard the sound of voices and axes above the faint, fading rumbles of the retreating storm.

Only Tobias and Libby, the cook-cum-housekeeper, were at home when she arrived, and she laughingly told them of having a fall, of staying with Gloria until the weather cleared and her costume had been sponged and partly dried.

Libby was suspicious, but she was a silent, excellent woman, up from the infamous Rocks area with a convict parent background and a rigid and tenacious ambition to rise above it. She kept those family secrets that fell across her path with a close guardianship born of a desire that life should run as smoothly as possible—for all the household. Now, in the little slope-roofed bedroom under the eaves, she took the proferred clothes that must have smelled like some creature dredged up from the harbour bottom, raised her calm blue eyes to Katherine's face for only a second, and was gone with a "these'll be ready for you the day after tomorrow, I reckon, Miss Katherine."

"Thank you, Libby," she said gratefully.

In the morning she had remained in bed with a cold—stayed there even when Libby tapped on the door and came in, telling her in puzzled tones that Mister Rafe Huckstable was downstairs.

Her father came in later that day, having spent the night at his club in Castlereagh Street. Her cold had improved to the extent where she was able to return on the train to Picton and wait at the family's regular little inn for a message to be sent to Carl to come and fetch her in the buggy.

Rafe had stayed in town. She saw him again in the spring, at a dance held at the Cummings' homestead. The conversation, stiltedly drawn forth from them during the enforced intimacy of a progressive dance, was brief. Rafe said, "Why, Katherine? Without any word, even a note . . ."

"I . . . I couldn't find anything to say."

"Even 'goodbye' would have been something. And we're to leave it at this?"

"Yes. Of course."

"It was foolish? A whim? We won't mention it again—is that how it's to be?"

"Rafe . . . I'm sorry."

He had looked at her, but she could not find anything further to say, wanted the music to move faster, faster . . . And it released her at last. She whirled free of him, and found herself swung about in Joe's giddy embrace, and another girl moved into Rafe's arms.

Now five years had somehow passed. Rafe was seated downstairs, gazing at the picture that Edwina must surely make in the candlelight.

Was she running away from him? No, for the distant accord which had been their relationship before those two mad weeks in Sydney had returned in something like its old ways in the six months before the family had left for Europe. Stephen Brody, lurking with an eager smile whenever she had chanced to ride out from Barrengarry even before that visit to Sydney, now, in those six months, made every excuse to be with Katherine. He was gentle and cultured and easy to be with, and she walked a narrow line between detached fondness and actually encouraging him.

Suzanna was secretly pleased; Marcus was furious. He took to inviting Luke Murchison, a big, bluff, solid and wealthy landowner from the eastern side of the Valley, to dinner each Saturday night, began regaling Katherine with Luke's manifest and noble qualities while muttering dark imprecations against all upstart Irishmen with the name of Brody.

Suzanna, in desperation, had been the one to suggest Europe; Marcus and Katherine, for their vastly diverging reasons, quickly agreed. And Joe, Edwina and Laura, as always, were eager for any chance that would take them away from the Valley and into the world.

The voyage itself had filled a need in Katherine—she saw this only years later. Now, seated by the fire in her bedroom, Rafe sipping port in the dining room below, his very invisible presence stirring old ghosts from the past, she saw the events of those two weeks in 1861 very clearly. A need for adventure, for something *new*— a feeling that at twenty-three, life was passing her by. Rafe had been *there*; attractive, challenging, dangerous.

She smiled at the thought of the woman she had been. If she had but known; life would unfold all the drama that she wanted or needed, without any prompting from her.

There was a tentative tapping at the door. She lowered her feet to the floor and called, "Come in."

Somehow she had expected Peggy, not content with the message that the empty tray signified, calling to see if she was all right, to offer a hot cup of cocoa and a description of the dinner and its guests. But it was her mother who entered; the tray was gone, Peggy obviously having respected Katherine's desire to be alone.

"May I come in for a while, dear?"

"Of course, Mama." Katherine smiled, padded over to pull another chair closer to the fire.

When they were seated, her mother said, "My darling, it grieves me to see so much unhappiness in your young life. And this evening . . ." Here a reluctance crept into Suzanna's manner. Katherine found herself tensing. But Suzanna continued, "I hesitate to tell you this now, but I need to discuss the matter with you.

I've been too long alone, I think—the girls rely on me—and yet there's been no one to whom . . ."

Katherine reached across and took her mother's hand. "Oh, Mama—this has been a dreadful time for you." And she was thinking, *Father, you should be here, why aren't you here?*

Suzanna made an effort to smile. "Katey, dear—Rafe broke the news to us after dinner. The man that you and Amos Murphy discovered on the road yesterday . . . he died this afternoon, without regaining consciousness. I didn't want to tell you before you went to bed—I wanted you to have as sound a sleep as possible—but if I told you tomorrow morning you might have decided not to go to Sydney. And with poor Mister Barton's death I really have come to the end of my courage."

The pale, thin hands trembled beneath Katherine's. Never in her life had she seen her mother break down completely. She watched in fright and dismay as the thin shoulders in the black velvet gown attempted to stay square, trembling with the effort that her mother made. "Katherine, tell your father to come home." The voice choked, broke on the last words. "Tell your father he must come home."

Ten

The railway that would one day link Sydney with Melbourne had progressed little further than the small valley town of Picton, sixty miles north of Kangaroo Valley. Katherine decided to travel this route, through the Southern Highlands, rather than the coastal route through Wollongong by which she had returned to Barrengarry. It meant that she could visit overnight with her grandparents, Suzanna's mother and father, Edwin and Angela Gordon, at their spacious home on the outskirts of Moss Vale.

It had been a difficult journey, though the snow had melted and now ran in gushing waterfalls that cascaded with bruising force amongst the ferns all along the track from the Valley. It was all but overgrown in places, having been built by cedar-getters early in the century, and had not, as yet, received the government attention that the road to Wollongong had.

She rode on Dryad, a delicately built, sure-footed Galloway mare, mountain-bred in the south of the state, one of several of her type that Marcus was using for breeding at Barrengarry as they were the best type of horse for a journey such as this, when a cob or thoroughbred might easily fall and break its own or its rider's neck.

Carl accompanied her on a bay gelding, taller and broader in the chest than the pretty Dryad, and he led another horse, a placid old mare long proved in the Highlands, with Katherine's belongings in two valises strapped to the horse's back. Katherine looked back, during their perilous climb, at the wall of hills that ringed the Valley, separating it from the high plateau of the Berrima district and the green, alluvial slopes of the Illawarra on the coast. What had made men and women like her father's parents choose to settle, with all the land they owned in other, more civilized parts of New South Wales, in an inaccessible spot so far removed from the world?

Perhaps that was it. Hadn't the seclusion, the safety, the feeling of being set apart, untouched by all that sped by outside, been the very reason that she had returned here from Europe? The Valley would always be there, change would come slowly. It was safe— as safe as any place on earth could be.

And then the thought of Gilbert Barton came to her. For him there had been no safety in the Valley, only death. And it had already thrown a shadow over the place. Rafe had been subdued at dinner, Suzanna had said, and his father, Rupert Huckstable, was meeting the Cummings and Murchison families in the morning to discuss the visit of the next-of-kin, if any, and the Anglican minister, Mr Dodds.

Even at Dovewood, her grandparents' home, set in the midst of ten acres of gardens and as comfortable and welcoming as ever she had remembered it from her childhood, the spectre of what had happened in the Valley did not leave her. She spent the evening in the warmth of the library, talking with Edwin and Angela about Ireland, about Oliver and Christopher, carefully tending to the truth so that she would not worry them with the details of treason, pain and heartbreak. Even so, they seemed to sense her distress, and for the latter part of the evening they talked of local matters, discussed the latest books and music, and she went up to bed with an easier mind and an exhaustion from the long ride that somehow allowed her to sleep, for the first time in many weeks, without nightmares or restlessness.

She left them, tall, slim figures, standing at the front door of Dovewood and drove on to Picton in her grandparents' brougham.

"Carl?" she asked as, with the miles from Dovewood, her worries about her mother and sisters returned.

"*Ja*, what?" he answered through gritted teeth biting possessively down upon his pipe stem. He turned his brown, wrinkled benevolent face, the face of a kindly and absent-minded wood gnome towards her and blinked his dark green eyes.

"Carl, you will be careful at Barrengarry, won't you? I know it's early for the ploughing, but perhaps you could send for a few of the lads from Burrawang to stay on the property . . ."

"I can take care of Barrengarry."

"I know, but I worry about you all—to have some more men on the place . . ."

"You take care of yourself, Miss. I bin with Barrengarry since your grandfather came to Valley—near fifty years—never had no trouble so far. My Peggy is silly girl in some ways, perhaps, but she is like a shadow to your mama. We got dogs, we got guns. You don't worry. Just have good time in the big smoke and get your papa back here."

Katherine lapsed into silence. She began to wonder whether she would be welcome back in the Valley if she failed to bring Marcus with her. Perhaps she could drug his wine and shanghai him—once they were on the train to Picton it would be too late for him to shout and bellow. She found herself smiling.

The train was late; her nerves keyed up, she could not refrain from once more reminding Carl to be alert to danger—and then was forced to listen to his acerbic declarations that he knew his job and his responsibilities, and so did his wife. Miss Katey must not *nag*—a nagging woman was bad for a man's digestion.

Yet it was sad to see the gnarled little gumnut of a man standing in his flapping dark greatcoat, watching her carefully until the last, as the train pulled out. "Talk to no strangers—do not drink the city water without first boiling . . . !" were the last words that floated up to her over the gathering hiss and wheeze of the engine. The station disappeared, the houses flew past, and then there were only the stubbly yellow fields, and the bush, as they climbed higher, closed around them as the train chugged north.

She was half-dozing when they pulled into the main Sydney station in the outer suburb of Redfern. There were still miles to go, she thought, disgruntled, handing in her ticket and jostling through the crowds on the station. She wondered when the promised Sydney Central was going to be built, closer to the heart of the city. Politicians and their promises . . .

A woman pushing a baby carriage ran one wheel into the back of her shoe, tripping her, and she turned, crossly . . .

The woman was apologizing, but Katherine did not hear.

For a man was walking obliquely across in front of her, at a distance of some twenty yards. As Katherine stared, he turned into one of the platform entrances, showing his ticket to the attendant and disappearing, walking smartly, along the platform by a waiting train.

"Father . . . ?"

Katherine ran forward. A family of seven or eight small children were suddenly in front of her, eyes everywhere but where they were going, and when bumped and herded by what they saw as a militant young woman with two heavy valises, they took fright and ran this way and that in front of her, looking for their parents and cheeping like frightened chicks.

"Father!"

The conductor's whistle trilled, the train whistle shrieked, and the train began to pull out, just as Katherine pushed past the entrance.

"Oy! Ticket, Miss?"

"I don't want to catch the train, I must stop someone . . ."

But it was gathering speed, pulling away from her. My God, what if he were returning to Picton, then on to the Valley . . .

"You missed it, Miss, sorry."

"Can't you stop it? It's my father! I haven't seen him for five years . . . !" She broke off abruptly, realizing that one or two passers-by were staring.

The station attendant grinned. "Can't see how a bloke'd abandon a daughter like you, love. No offence meant!" he added quickly, seeing the affronted fury in the green eyes turned suddenly on him.

"Where's the nearest telegraph office?" she asked curtly. "I have to send a message to arrive before the train reaches Picton."

"Picton? Your dad hasn't gone to Picton, miss—that train's only goin' a few miles down the track, to Rookwood."

"*Rookwood* . . . ?"

She realized she had been standing there for several seconds, her gaze unseeingly on the last carriage as it swayed off into the distance.

"Thank you . . ." she murmured, and headed towards the cab stand, not hearing the "No trouble at all, Miss" that followed appreciatively after her.

She gave directions to the cabbie, and seated in the creaking, dusty carriage that smelled unpleasantly of cigar smoke and mouldy leather, she began the five mile journey from Redfern to the house in Balmain.

Rookwood.

What would her father—and it was her father, there was no mistaking the solid figure, the set of his shoulders or that jawline beneath the top hat—what would he be doing, going to Rookwood? They did not know any families there, it was miles out of the city, a boring little town surrounded by a great deal of bush . . .

And a cemetery. The largest cemetery in Australia. This was Rookwood's only claim to renown.

The ringing of the doorbell echoed through Tobias' dream, made it fragment, dissolve. It had been a pleasant dream, and he struggled to remain within its cocoon, but reality was already thrusting him out into consciousness.

Even before he opened his eyes he knew that he was sitting uncomfortably slumped sideways in his armchair, the fire had gone out, and the doorbell was scolding with a peremptory shrillness. He rose to his feet, swore silently at the newspaper that, forgotten in his lap, now cascaded, its pages separating, onto the floor. He left them there and made his way, in his down-at-heel bedroom slippers, through to the front of the house. stopped at the hall mirror to brush back the grey hair from his forehead and opened the door.

He stood there for some seconds, staring at the woman in black cloak and fashionable hat who waited on the verandah.

Katherine would, under other circumstances, have been amused at the expression on the face of her father's manservant; she had rather hoped, arriving unexpectedly as she had, to catch Tobias and Libby and enjoy their excitement, for no matter what her father's feelings were, she knew they would welcome her home.

But the sight of Tobias robbed her of any speech, not to say enjoyment. The grey stubble on the narrow face, the bleariness in the brown eyes now, like the loose mouth, almost circular with shock, and the creased suit, dingy shirt and what appeared to be food stains down the waistcoat . . . She slapped him up and down with her eyes and gazed at him in horrified disbelief.

"Oh, Miss Katherine . . ." The heaviness in the tone preceded a flush that crept from the loose, greyish collar to fade into the receding hairline. The reddened eyes were lowered and he stood back, after a momentary hesitation in which, she felt, he would have dearly loved to shut the door and plead with her, from behind it, to return at another time.

The master wasn't home, he said, closing the door behind her, juggling the two valises and preceding her along the hall. He had left more than an hour ago—no, he didn't know Mr Prescott's destination, but had been told not to expect him back until late.

Katherine had barely spoken more than a stiff greeting, and now marched into the parlour. Tobias, a few steps on towards the stairs when he noticed her absence behind him, dithered a little in the offending carpet slippers, then placed the bags down at the foot of the stairs and peeped around the corner into the room.

Katherine was at the window, drawing back the heavy curtains that darkened the room, then whirling to yank dust sheets—truly worthy of that name—from the furniture.

Tobias bustled in, ringing his hands. "No, Miss Katherine—there's really no . . . You shouldn't be doing that, Miss Katherine—I'll do it . . ."

"You! What's happened here, Tobias? Where's Libby? How could you allow the house to look like this?"

He began to stammer a reply, but she was off, charging out of the parlour and inspecting each room with the thoroughness of a colonel inspecting troops and a tone of voice like a pistol shot. Tobias could only follow her about the house, standing in the hall in terror when she stamped into the kitchen—only to mutter "disgusting" and turn on her heel and leave. He raised a silent prayer of gratitude that she did not inspect his own room in the servants' quarters, but her reaction at the sight of the kitchen and, later, upstairs, Mr Prescott's rooms, was quite frightening enough.

He gained a short respite in rushing upstairs to her room in the attic with the valises, and stayed to put a match to the kindling and timber in the fireplace, his hands trembling. He could hear doors slamming on the lower floors as if a whirlwind were assaulting the house—as it seemed, indeed, Miss Katherine was proving.

A corner of a newspaper beneath the dry sticks in the fireplace, yellowed and soot-stained, lifted itself in its death throes. The date in the corner of the page caught Tobias' gaze: *3rd February, 1861.* Five years ago.

He had not counted the years, and now sat back on his heels in some surprise to realize how long it had been. This fire had not been lit because Miss Katherine had not been here since Libby would have set it last. *Five years ago.*

He was overwhelmed by his sense of shame, wished he could lock the door, clamber down the drainpipe and disappear into the narrow, steep Balmain streets. Sixteen years he had been coming back and forth from Barrengarry to the town house; now it was possibly all over. He put his face into his hands—and then froze in horror.

Could Miss Katherine have smelled the whiskey on his breath? He panted into his cupped hands, sniffed quickly, then repeated the test: pant-sniff, pant-sniff, pant-sniff . . . He sat down on the carpet, his head buzzing. Well, it *seemed* only faint, but it was difficult to tell, he walked round in a fog of fumes these days . . .

"Tobias!" the clear, sharp voice from below.

He replaced the fireguard and ran to the stairs. She called, "Meet me in the parlour," and he heard the tap of her heels descending to the ground floor.

Tobias essayed the attic stairs with some care, then took the outside staircase from the first floor to the ground, risking his neck by taking two at a time. He hurtled through the kitchen door, emptied half a handful of cloves from the floral canisters, chewed them furiously and flung himself out the door again to spit the remains into the bushes.

Katherine waited in her armchair in the parlour, leaning back, watching the dust motes dance in the winter light that came through the high, narrow windows. They were so dirty one could barely see the garden, let alone the street. She concentrated on the sunbeam . . .

Mama used to say that the tiny objects they could see in the light were house fairies—there were few enough of them, in those days, with Libby and two housemaids. She and Joe used to follow the tiny specks about a room, sure that if they could only get close enough, they'd see a tiny pair of iridescent wings, lissome little limbs in gauze, and golden hair . . .

It was a large sunbeam, lighting up the carpet, part of one charry corner of the uncleaned grate, one end of the mantelpiece, and the lower right hand side of the portrait that hung over the fireplace.

Within the frame, one of Katherine's small black shoes was lit up with brightness, and two of the legs of the ornate stool upon which she sat. The rest of the painting was harder to make out, with the beam of light cutting across her vision. She moved slightly in her chair, and the faces appeared: it was this very room, some twenty-six years ago. Marcus, slim, broad-shouldered in his dark suit, looked down tenderly at his—then—small family. Suzanna, seated on a chair, gazing off to the right with that same sad, gentle smile that was so much a part of her character; and the baby Josiah on her lap, fair-haired, his face alight with inquisitive joy, leaning a little out of his mother's arms, as if he could not wait to grow, to meet the world.

Joe . . . Why aren't you here? her heart grieved. *How can you be gone, Joe, without a goodbye, and so soon . . . too soon?*

It was almost as if she heard his voice, as he had so often lamented to her after some scrape: *I've let you down, haven't I Katey? You won't tell Father, will you? It won't happen again. I didn't mean it to happen. I wish I was like you . . .* Yes, he had often said that, *I wish I was like you—you're the strong one . . .*

The face of the girl-child in the portrait, leaning from her seat on the stool against her mother's arm—was it a strong face? Katherine peered at the family portrait; no, that small Katherine, caught forever in doe-eyed innocence, showed no hint of the woman she would become. Rather, she looked a little wary of the world—or perhaps, Katherine thought more practically, she did not like the artist. She had a vague memory of a rather irascible man with a heavy blonde beard, who constantly tried to keep the small dog, Charmian, out of the portrait, until Marcus, relenting to Katherine's demands, had let the faithful little black-and-tan terrier be included. The artist had grumbled, but Charmian, allowed at last to remain with her small mistress, had sat obediently by the leg of the stool—and yes, the sun was moving, and the small canine face with the bright eyes, luminous and lively, was seen, leaning against one childish foot.

Katherine returned to study her parents. Were they happy, then? They went on to create Laura and Edwina from their union—they must have been born in love, there must have been *something* that had brought these two people to share nearly thirty years of their lives—and having shared it, how could they throw it away?

The door opened, after a faint knock, and there was a gentle and politic clearing of a throat.

"Yes, Miss Katherine. I'm here."

She turned to look at Tobias. He had somehow found time to comb his hair, and there were shoes upon his feet.

"Where's Libby, Tobias?"

"Libby . . . She . . . she left us, Miss. Wasn't long after we come up from the Valley that last time, after Master Joe—" He stopped. "I can't tell you, Miss Katherine, how sorry I am . . ."

"I know, Tobias. Please go on. Libby."

"Libby became a bit . . . upset with the master, Miss Katherine. That's all I should say, really, except that she left us of her own accord, and Mr Prescott wrote her a grand reference."

Katherine studied him for moment. Then, "My father is drinking heavily, isn't he? When did it start? No," as she answered her own question, "there's no need to ask; it was Joe's death, wasn't it?"

"It . . . He . . . Yes, miss, it started then. Before we left the Valley, really. He hasn't let up since, hardly."

"And you, Tobias? When did you start drinking?"

Tobias' mouth popped several times as he opened and shut it. The pointed chin trembled, and to Katherine's discomfort, the brown eyes filled with tears.

"Oh, Miss Katherine. It was years ago—when my wife died— nearly twenty years ago, Miss Katherine. I was a drinking man, I admit it, and I lost my first position because of it. Mister Prescott took me on, Miss—I told him the truth and he took me on and gave me a chance—and I never took a drop, Miss Katherine, not for sixteen years . . . An' then the master come back from visiting his club and he offered me a drink with him . . ."

Tobias was choking on the words. Katherine cut in, "Very well, go and tidy yourself, I won't need you for a while."

But as he turned, gratefully, to leave, she asked, "Do you know where Libby is?"

"Yes, Miss—a doctor's family, on the Victoria Road."

"Can you send a message to her? Tell her that I'm home, and wish to see her."

Tobias stared at her. She read the dazed hope in his eyes; perhaps things might be all right, perhaps things could be the way they were before . . . "Miss Katherine—if you could . . . I saw Libby cry as she was leaving."

"I shall do my best, Tobias. Go, now. Make yourself a cup of tea—and I'll have one in my room, with bread and butter, please, in two hours," and she wondered if even this order would be stretching his culinary capabilities.

A tremulous smile, a bow, and he was gone, the footsteps almost back to their former briskness as he pattered down the hall.

It was two o'clock in the morning when Marcus Prescott arrived home.

Katherine had fallen asleep in her armchair, having spent the evening unpacking her clothes and sorting through those stored at the house, folded away by Suzanna and Libby and packed, amongst lavender and cloves, in two cedar chests in her room. Tobias, shaven and clean-clothed, had surprised himself as much as Katherine by managing to present a simple yet delicious supper in the dining room, and she was gentle with him, noting his pallor and the shaking of his hands.

At midnight he had awakened her from her doze before the parlour fire, and suggested that she retire. "Mr Prescott is sometimes very late, Miss Katherine. And sometimes . . . Well, he doesn't come home until morning, staying the night at his club."

She was exhausted, and agreed that it would be best to see her father in the morning.

Yet when the front door slammed and she heard his voice, loud enough to carry up two floors to her little room, she found herself wide awake, her heart hammering. She lay there, listening to the indiscernible words, the barely audible murmur of Tobias' replies.

Then there was silence. Katherine lay back against the pillows and waited for the footsteps to ascend to the bedrooms on the first floor.

But her father was obviously not prepared to retire, for no footsteps were heard. The house waited, and Katherine waited, wide awake, now, and considering. She would not sleep again tonight, not so close to seeing him, with so much having happened in the long years.

She rose and dressed, unbraiding her hair and pinning it back loosely with a pair of combs. A shawl about her shoulders and she was prepared—as prepared, she told herself, heading for the steep little attic stairs, as she would ever be.

Voices again as she reached the first floor, the head of the main staircase. She came down slowly, pausing to listen.

"I looked in the cabinet and it's not there—now fetch it or I'll get it myself and you'll be the worse for it!"

"Sir . . . You've had enough for tonight, don't you think? Tomorrow . . ."

"Tobias, have you gone mad? Spring cleaning the bloody parlour as if you were Libby—and telling me what to drink and when to drink . . ."

"Sir, it's just that . . . Tomorrow we can talk, and I can explain . . ."

"Explain *what*?"

They were there below her, as she reached the turn in the staircase. Poor Tobias in his nightshirt and robe, pinned beneath Marcus Prescott's gaze like a rabbit before a snake. "I . . . well . . . today . . . I tidied the house because . . ."

"Because I came home today. Good evening, Father. Or should I say, good morning?"

The face that was raised to hers was older than she remembered, but worse were the ravages of months of overwork, bad nutrition and alcohol. His colour was not good, there were deep lines about his mouth, and the eyes, so dark a hazel that they were invariably described as being brown, had discernible pouches of flesh beneath them. Worst of all, and still more frightening, was the sudden, startled alarm on Marcus's face—and it did not change. He could only stare, it seemed, as she moved down the steps towards him, pausing at the foot, uncertain. She had been braced for coldness, anger, had hoped for a welcome, an acceptance—but there was neither. Nothing but this haunted look. Katherine was overwhelmed by the fear that nothing had changed, that he meant those last, cruel words that he had flung at her as he had left her, in Oliver's apartment in Dublin. He had denied, for the future, that she was his daughter, and the look of bitter betrayal had been the last she had seen of him, until this moment.

"Father?"

His lips moved; she barely caught the murmured, "My God . . ."

She walked towards him and, suddenly determined that he was not to distance himself with those cold eyes, she held out her hand to him. He did not take it, stared down at it, then up into her face.

"Oh, God . . ." he repeated, and his voice broke on the words, his face constricted as if a tremor of pain had suddenly claimed him. "Katherine . . ." And his face crumbled, his arms reached for her, and she was held tight against the broad chest. "Katey . . . Katey . . ." he spoke her name over and over, and her forehead was damp with his tears.

Eleven

Katherine could not speak, and was only barely aware of Tobias moving past them into the parlour, preparing to resurrect the fire in the grate.

"Stupid of me . . . foolish . . ." Marcus was ducking his head, half-turned from her, feeling for his handkerchief and blowing his nose. "I'm very drunk, you see, and you're not seeing me at my best. Come in here . . ."

He guided her into the parlour, but stopped, turned to her with a sudden look of disbelief, touched her face with his hand. "Perhaps God is good, after all. You know, I'd . . . begun to doubt Him."

It was Katherine's turn to stare dazedly. This man seemed a stranger, a hesitant shadow of the energetic, warm but overpowering figure who had controlled her life—who, even in absence, still controlled the lives of so many people in the Valley.

They sat down in chairs to either side of the fire, and a nervous and excited Tobias backed out of the room, stammering about tea and hot toast.

Father and daughter sat taking in the changes in each other. Marcus was the first to move, drawing a hand across his face as if he could change himself, the world or both, and seemed bewildered at still finding the difficulties and not the words to deal with them.

"I want to say so much . . . Oliver—Good Lord, can you ever forgive me? And the boy—I wrote to you, did you receive my letter? I'd have written after Oliver's death, but . . . your letter was addressed to your mother . . . I was mentioned, yes, I know—but it was clear that it was meant for her eyes—your hurt, your homesickness. After all I'd done, all I'd said—the years of neglect—My God, if I could only have swallowed my pride years earlier—I could have written to you, advised you, sent you money, if you needed it . . . I had a letter started—couldn't put the words down, felt I had no right . . . Heavens, I wish I wasn't so drunk . . ." A harsh and rueful burst of laughter. He ran his fingers through the greying brown hair. "Tonight, of all nights, you arrive to find me inebriated and incoherent. I might make a better job of this if I were sober . . . But I did write to you after we received the letter from Italy— I didn't tell your mother that I'd written. Did you get my letter?"

"No, nor Mama's. I left Italy—immediately after the funeral," she finished.

He nodded. "It's just as well, you'll be happier here in Australia. You won't know your sisters, though," the smile was natural, fond. "I should like to travel down with you, but I'm needed here . . ."

"I've been home to Barrengarry."

He blinked, the eyes confused. "You've been to the Valley?"

"I stayed only two days. I came back to Sydney to see you."

"Then . . . you know about Joe . . ."

"Yes," she said softly. "Mama told me. She's taking it very hard, Father."

He rose to his feet and moved off towards the curtained windows, then turned back again. The conversation was sobering him, fast. He said, grimly, "It was so . . . unexpected. A vile joke on the part of the Almighty. No man should live longer than his son. No man, nor woman should have to live longer than their children— it takes the heart out of you."

He spoke softly enough, but the words twisted inside Katherine. She could sense his pain, but he did not see her as a mother, did not think, in his own grief, of the dark-haired, dark-eyed four-year-old boy who would never grow to manhood, who lay alone on a windswept hillside in southern Italy. She pushed the thought of her own hurt aside and considered Suzanna. He could not possibly think that Suzanna's agony was less than his own— then why were they not together, drawing support from each other?

"Will you come back to Barrengarry with me, Father?"

"Eh? Yes, of course. But I can't go just yet, as I said. Laurence has been ill during the past few weeks, and Robin and I have been running things—nice lad, Robin, but doesn't have the business sense that his father has—and even Robin has to have time off—the boy is always catching chills—he looks consumptive . . ."

"Father . . ."

"You won't mind staying for a week or so, would you? I'll be ready to go back then, as Laurence is coming home from a few weeks in the mountains. It'll do you good to stay in the city for a while, see how things have changed." He went on, nervously describing the city, its spread to north and south and west, incorporating so many small towns. Katherine listened, realizing that he needed to talk to gain time to adjust to her presence, to all that had happened.

Tobias arrived with tea, coffee, toast and cold roast beef sandwiches.

Father and daughter ate in silence for some time, smiling occasionally over their tea cups, neither of them hungry or even thirsty, but it seemed to cement their accord, this supper, a re-enactment of many suppers they had had together in former years.

"Your mother and the girls—they're well?"

She lifted her eyes to his. Why did she receive the impression that he asked this question carefully, almost reluctantly? Perhaps he did not want to hear her answer, and now, just for now, perhaps she should lie and tell him tomorrow how things were . . . But the hesitation lasted only a second. To think of them brought her sense of injustice to the fore. "They miss you a great deal. Mama is under a lot of strain—she takes on more and more decisions, now Carl is getting older. Her health is not good. Laura and Teddi are coping well with the isolation of their lives, but still, it's hardly fair on them, or good for them at their age, to be so removed from civilization and society. I worry about them turning out like the Cummings girls . . ."

She had been right, he did not want to hear this. He sat holding his tea cup and saucer, looking down into the depths of the liquid with a flat incuriosity, as a man fishing for long hours fixes his gaze on the water.

He said, "I doubt if that is likely. I receive letters from them, remember. They want me home, of course, but certainly don't seem eager to leave the Valley lately. Teddi's letters, particularly, are almost too contented to be true. Is she still seeing Rafe Huckstable?"

"As a friend only. He visits the house . . ." and, as her father made an impatient gesture, "but it's as well he does, as Mother and the girls are severely cut off from social contact. Mama looks really unwell—I was concerned to see how much she's altered—she doesn't leave the house very much to go visiting. The girls would, if they could come to Sydney more often, enlarge their circle of friends." She left the thought in the air, but Marcus was silent and did not seem to follow her inference. Katherine looked down at her hands, clasped loosely in her lap, and found a wave of anger rising within her. He did not want his life ruffled with thoughts of Suzanna and the girls being unhappy. Yet their only means of action, of change, must come through him. Here she, Katherine, sat, like an advocate on her family's behalf, pleading in tactful, measured tones, for some clemency, some understanding of their situation. He ought to know. He ought to have cared enough to find out, long since.

He said, "In a few months I may be able to take them to Melbourne for a few weeks. No doubt they do need a change. Would they like that, do you think?''

There it was again. A second chance for her to agree and make things comfortable between them. How easily she had forgotten the old games.

"Father," she said quietly, replacing her tea cup on the table and facing him, "is this the beginning of a permanent separation between you and Mama?"

He looked up, but the surprise and amused concern on his face came a fraction too late, and in his blusterings of protestation he did not often meet her gaze. "Good heavens, no! Really, Katey, you have the most astonishing ideas! Many men have to be away from their families for periods of time; it's necessary in order to provide for them." He stopped abruptly, rose to his feet once more and moved about the room restlessly. "Has your mother said something to you about a separation?"

"No, no! It's my own assumption—and I'm glad to find I'm wrong. It's just that you've been so long away from the Valley—more than three months, Father."

"*Three months*?" He stared at her. "Has it been three months?" He leaned his elbow on the mantelpiece, put his head down until his mouth rested reflectively against his fist. He tapped the knuckle of his thumb against his teeth, and Katherine watched him, recognizing the gesture as one he often made when deep concentration was needed, when he was confronted with a sudden and confounding problem.

She felt a rush of affection for him, dishevelled, bemused man; changed as he was, the stance of him brought back the father she had known. There was a sudden biting of tears within her that she had to force down; it was as if she were looking at his portrait, and he, the real man, were . . . dead. No, far away, or lost, or . . . The thought, unbidden, had frightened her. She tried not to look at him with the rising fear and panic she felt. Had they crossed five years of bitterness only to find that the man she remembered, and had missed so much, no longer existed?

"Father, what is it? Is it your grief over Joe? Or is it something more? Have you . . . have you met someone else, here in Sydney? Are you in love with another woman?"

The hand stilled its gentle tattoo against the firm mouth. The eyes, capable of extraordinary softness in their usually watchful depths, now turned upon her with a steely, clinical enquiry that made her wish she had not spoken. But only a second later, a laugh had burst from him, an unconscious, explosive laugh, and he came back to his chair and sat down, studying her with a smile.

"I've had to consciously remind myself for years that my children are grown up—and still I can be surprised." He shook his head. "I can't imagine you asking me a question like that five years ago— even if you suspected me with a lot more evidence than you have now. And to answer your question," he continued, "no, there's no woman come between your mother and myself. It's as you say, Joe's death," he finished in a low tone, as if the very phrase hurt him.

"I know what it's like to lose a child," she said softly. "I wish you could have seen Christopher; you'd have been so proud of him. Oliver's sensitivity and intelligence, yet a fearlessness, a restless sort of curiosity that reminded me of you." Again, the heavy welling of grief within her, a yearning that was so strong that she almost brought the child back, just out of her reach, so close did he seem, yet so achingly far away. She stared at the table before her, willed her emotions under control. "I came home," she continued when she was able, "because I wanted to see you all, to be with you. No one cares so much for one as one's own family. I've found that out in three short days. Let us help you too, Father. Don't shut us out."

He had turned his gaze towards the fire. "Soon, yes. It's just that . . . not everyone can grieve in the same way, Katey. I've had . . . questions . . . to ask myself. About the way Joe died, the kind of life he was leading, what I could have done to steer him better . . ."

"No one 'steered' Joe, Father . . ."

"I could have been firmer with him."

"This is madness, it's useless!" She spoke quickly, decisively, to still his words and the unwilling realization within herself that he was right. "It's past, now, Father. You did all you could for him. We all know that."

It tore her apart to see him like this; better the good-natured, self-opinionated, bullying man of her memories.

"What have you been doing, all these months?" she asked.

"Working hard—drinking hard, too, there's no denying it. I don't know how it got out of hand, but it has. I shall stop, I think. You've sobered me a great deal already." He glanced over at her with a wry frown. "I suppose you've been all over the house, and seen my rooms . . ."

"Yes."

He sighed. "I thought so. The realization went through my head almost at the same time I saw you. I saw myself through your eyes . . . Yes. Things will be more organized, now. You will stay for a week or so?"

"Yes," she smiled, "of course."

"I'm glad," Marcus said, "I need time to get to know you all over again. Is that three o'clock striking? We'd best retire." They stood as the last notes of the grandfather clock in the hall were still echoing through the house. Marcus was saying as they headed for the door, "Your room is all right? You're sure it's warm enough? Good. I may not be here when you awaken—some business today was unfinished and I have to return to it tomorrow . . ."

"In Rookwood?" The words came out unbidden. She smiled in the face of his sudden, wary look. "I saw you at Redfern, hurrying for your train. I did call to you . . ."

"Oh. I was paying my respects . . . a business associate—well, a friend, almost—died suddenly. I missed the funeral—too busy. So I went out today. Very depressing. It's one of the reasons you find me like this. Many of my associates and friends have passed on in the last year or so—I find it harder to take, all the time."

He seemed somehow abashed, ashamed of his emotion. Katherine thought, *he's feeling his own mortality.* Could this be the reason he was becoming more flexible in his thinking, daring to talk about his weaknesses, his fears, in a way he never had before? Even now, he was gazing at her with a look that seemed to ask her understanding. She stood on tiptoe and kissed his cheek before turning to precede him up the stairs.

When they separated on the first floor, Marcus said, "That young man—the friend of Oliver's who was so violently opposed to your marriage—whatever became of him?"

"Brendan Kelehan?" Katherine paused, one hand on the newel post, the other holding her shawl about her.

"That's the fellow—hair going prematurely grey at the temples, as if he worried a lot. He certainly worried about you."

She said stiffly, "Brendan left Ireland to live in America. Boston, I believe." Marcus nodded, turned away. "Why? What made you ask about him?"

Her father looked thoughtful. "I rather liked him, liked his style. Your marriage was obviously happy—I'm glad I was wrong in my fears about that . . ." He stopped awkwardly, then, "I was wrong," he murmured, "so it doesn't matter now."

"What were you going to say? Tell me." She made her voice sound bright, mildly curious.

"I thought—and these were intuitive decisions, made on meeting both young men only two or three times—that I'd have preferred you to have chosen young Kelehan. When he came to me, hat beneath his arm, all nervous dignity—almost more English than Irish, wasn't he?—he was obviously torn between loyalty to Oliver and his belief that the marriage would be a mistake. It wasn't difficult for me to see that he was in love with you himself. But he wasn't spiteful—he simply wished me to speak to you, ask you to wait. I was impressed with him, as I had been when I'd met him on other occasions. Even your Oliver seemed to look up to him—he was a responsible sort of chap. You've mentioned him once or twice in your letters."

She felt herself growing more and more agitated, the feeling exacerbated by the fact that there was no reason to feel upset, surely . . .

But her father was looking at her with an unquiet expression in the dark eyes. "*Were* you happy, Katherine? Was it really what you wanted? Tell me I was wrong, all those years ago. Tell me you've been happy."

She smiled. "Yes, Father. I have no regrets about marrying Oliver—and many happy memories. So you can rest assured that you were wrong," she laughed gently, "you and Brendan Kelehan."

She wondered, lying in bed that night, what her father would have said to the news that Oliver Carron had died in Kilmainham gaol, for her letter to her family had mentioned only his death, of consumption, after a long illness. She decided that she would never speak of the real facts—they would not understand her pride in Oliver; they would not understand Oliver himself, political agitators being far removed from their experience.

Yet Marcus had always been passionately interested in social reform, and had lent his not inconsiderable reputation and support to many efforts at forming protective legislation and unions to combat the exploitation of workers in the filthy, ill-lit and dangerous factories of Sydney. If Marcus had only stayed in Ireland a month, two months, and come to know Oliver . . .

I'd have preferred you to choose young Kelehan . . .

Her thoughts alighted on this disturbing confession and then fled, like a bird sensing danger in a movement of shadows. Brendan had been her friend—a good friend, she admitted it—but there was no point in thinking of him now. He was part of the turmoil of those last months in Dublin, a disturbing spirit in this safe world to which she had returned, bringing memories that she need not face, would not face.

I am a different person now. Not the girl I was when I left Australia, not even the woman I left behind in Dublin. I'm someone new. I've had to be. Just as my world here is not the same, I have to be different, too; I must fit into it, somehow.

It was her last conscious thought before sleep claimed her; she would not remember it, but the realization never left her. It became the core of her survival in the shifting world through which she would move.

During the following weeks she found that her father was true to his word. She watched him slowly and laboriously regaining himself, reorganizing the frightening downward spiral of his life alone except for the impressionable Tobias and reclaiming some of the dignity the household in Balmain had always possessed.

Libby came to tea, huge shoulders stooped within the demure black coat, the flat, shapeless black hat, adorned with four incongruous purple feathers, screwed severely onto the coils of straw-coloured hair. She marched past Tobias's hopeful and welcoming smile with downcast eyes. She greeted Marcus with downcast eyes. She looked fully, once, at Katherine, finding her in the parlour, and sat before Marcus, holding a cup of rapidly cooling tea in her large hands, and listened as her former master, with all his old eloquence, pleaded that she return to them. At twice her former salary. Katherine, too, enjoined her to stay.

Libby, who had hitherto not flinched, now sighed, and raised her pale, quiet eyes, first to Katherine, then to fix themselves upon Marcus.

"The money don't count," she said. "But I'll take it, not being one to pass up an honest opportunity. But it ain't that, properly, Mr Prescott—it's that Miss Katherine's home, and Tobias is cleaned up and is himself again." She looked at Marcus, hard and tellingly, until Katherine was forced to cough into her hand to cover the beginnings of her smile. Libby said nothing to her captive employer, however, but a simple, "It's a decent household again, I believe, and I'll come home as soon as I can."

Somehow, until Libby worked out her notice, Tobias and Katherine managed with the housework and cooking divided between them. Her father was concerned; having been born to money and raised to regard it with the same presumption as he regarded his hands or feet, he could not imagine a life without servants. One simply did not *do* for oneself. Katherine, whose household help in Dublin had come and gone with Oliver's financial fluctuations, had been accustomed to coping alone for months at a time. Now, she took a fierce delight in going through the house, taking curtains down and washing them, polishing the brasswork, glassware and silverware. Coming home to find her aproned and pink-faced, her hair caught up in a scarf, waxing the balustrade of the staircase, Marcus remarked that it was as if she were the housekeeper and Libby the returning mistress.

She was dressed in the same outdated housedress and apron, her hair in an old silk shawl, the dust and wax-coated crystals of the chandelier in a myriad pile on the sheet-covered dining room table, when Robin Mitchell came to call.

"Your father left these papers at the office—he was going on to a meeting of the museum committee, and he should have taken these with him to look over tonight—they have to be signed and away in tomorrow's post . . ."

The large brown paper folder, tied with red tape, was held out to her. She had to wipe her hands on her apron, flushing furiously, before she could take it, aware that the young man had been speaking at such a rate to hide his embarrassment at finding her in this state.

"I . . . I'm sorry I've disturbed you . . ." he added politely.

She smiled at him. "Please come in, Mr Mitchell."

She did not think that he actually would, so had to leave him alone in the parlour while she raced to the kitchen where the unfortunate Tobias was on hands and knees, scrubbing the stone flags of what would be, in only twelve days' time, once more the domain of the redoubtable Libby.

"Quick! Tea! Cake! For two, please!" she hissed at Tobias, before running out of the room, back to the hall and up the stairs to her room for a hasty toilette.

And in the end she was glad that the unwelcome visitor decided to stay. She had seen remarkably little of Robin Mitchell, considering their fathers Marcus and Laurence had inherited the empire bannered Prescott, Mitchell and Co.; but the two families tended not to mix very much socially, and it was only recently, Marcus had told Katherine, that Robin had come home from Paris, where he had spent years painting very bad portraits of middle-class merchants who usually refused to pay once the paintings were finished.

He had, much to his fond and patient father's delight, volunteered to join Prescott, Mitchell and Co., and for his first eight months had created havoc with his well-meaning but inexperienced zeal. Old Laurence's illness had been viewed with alarm not only by the firm but by all who had to deal with it; yet the added pressure of having so much at stake seemed to instil the erstwhile prodigal with a capable confidence, as if the eight months had been a practice period for him. All agreed that difficult though it had been, the end results were worth it. Robin was articulate, amusing, hard-working; now he was shown to be sensible, astute, a clever negotiator and fair-minded administrator.

Yet the strain of his new-found career was telling on him. Katherine sat across the tea table from him, watched the blue eyes, bright with intelligence in a face marred only by its thinness and pallor. He looked like an exceptionally handsome man—only a year or two older than herself, Katherine remembered—who was driving himself much too hard. *He looks consumptive*—those were her father's words, and they could be true.

"I never thought I'd adjust to living back here in Australia," Robin was saying, "but there's something to be said for accepting one's responsibilities. I feel I'm at last able to do something for my parents, after all they did for me . . . and perhaps Charles Darwin is right in his views on heredity—I have the odd sensation sometimes that I'm doing what I was born to do—as if the gift for good business practice has been handed down through the generations." He smiled suddenly. "And the odd thing is, even my painting has improved. Now my very existence doesn't depend on selling my canvases, I only paint what I like, when I like—and for some reason my own taste must be better than my illustrious teachers' in Paris, as I've sold more paintings of Sydney beaches and sun-bleached hills since I've been back than I ever sold when I was trying to copy the French masters."

Katherine laughed with him. She found herself feeling very pleased that Marcus had such a man working with him; for all his self-deprecating humour, Robin would not, she was sure, allow her father to be carried away by any too-outreaching philanthropic ambitions. Laurence Mitchell had had to almost forcibly check Marcus on several occasions during their long association; Marcus, unlike Robin, having inherited very little of his forebears' business acumen. Marcus was a caretaker—and sometimes a careless one—rather than an accumulator, such as old Josiah had been.

"I'm very glad," Robin was saying, now, brushing a strand of dark hair from his forehead rather nervously, "that you've returned from Ireland, Mrs Carron. I think you'll have noticed that your father has been . . . drifting—if you know what I mean. Joe's death was very hard for him to accept . . ."

"I know," Katherine said softly, "but he seems to be adjusting now, don't you think?"

"Oh, yes! He's almost his old self. Having you home again has been the turning point, I believe. You will stay in Sydney for a while, won't you?"

"I'm afraid I can't. You see, our property in Kangaroo Valley is being run by our elderly overseer with no other help, and . . ."

"But surely that's simply a matter of hiring a younger man for the job, and perhaps more farmworkers. You must see that the city businesses are central to your family's fortune—they support the country property—it doesn't support them."

For some reason this rankled. "Barrengarry, I think you'll find, Mr Mitchell, *is* central to our family. No one feels this more strongly than my father. It's as if Barrengarry *is* the Prescotts."

He smiled gently. "It obviously is for you, Mrs Carron. But," he continued, "your father is needed here. In earlier years, yes, it was possible to spend a great deal of time in the Valley—but the business was structured differently then, and there was much less competition. Now, the company needs your father's experience and expertise. I do hope he'll be staying."

There was a question implied, if not heard, in his words. Katherine was studying Robin, marvelling at the different facets to the man. She was almost beginning to decide she did not like him quite as much as she had a few minutes before. But he had been watching her almost as intently, and his expression now softened. "I don't want to worry you, Katherine—may I call you, Katherine? I was used to doing so as we were all growing up . . . Things have not been so well for the company in the past few years. We've lost several experienced men from the board, and my father's recurring illness had affected business; though your father has done his best, he's often been running things single handed, and with a company importing and exporting the quantities that we do, something has to suffer." Again the concentrated scrutiny of his gaze. "Do you understand? It would be best for everyone if Marcus would concentrate—for the next year at least, on the business . . ."

"I'm sure my father knows where his responsibilities lie, Robin." Yes, it was easier to return to the guarded familiarity of childhood names. One could say one's mind much better, without formality of manners in between.

Robin smiled. It was curious, but he had a smile of great sweetness. Katherine was reminded suddenly, with a nostalgic little pang, of Brendan Kelehan. "Katherine," Robin was saying gently, "your father feels his responsibilities are everywhere. He's an energetic, dedicated, truly Christian man—he should, I've sometimes felt, have gone into politics—but he'd insist on doing everything himself, as he does now. There are too many causes in his life. He must cut down on some of these committees he keeps forming and attending; he must stop selling his assets to build orphanages, or to pay legal costs for men he believes are innocent; he must not go back to the country—not now, until we have Prescott, Mitchell and Co. back on its feet. If he doesn't, my dear, then . . . to be cruelly blunt, I can foresee your family's fortune being drained away until there is nothing left."

Katherine stared at him. Could her father be so foolish as to do these things? Orphanages are all very well, and necessary, but Barrengarry needed new fences . . .

"There's no need," Robin continued, "to worry your mama and sisters about this, do you think? Being so far away, I expect they have enough problems . . ." And he sounded concerned. "They are well, I trust."

"Yes," Katherine murmured, her mind full. "Yes, they are. I have hopes that they might soon be able to spend some time here in the city . . ."

Robin's face came alight; there was an eagerness there that denoted more than concern. "Why, that's wonderful! I . . . I would like to call to see them, if they do return to Balmain. Give them my best regards, won't you? I'd . . ."

He paused to cough a little, having in his excitement (*Over Edwina or Laura?* a highly amused Katherine wondered) spoken too quickly, inhaled carelessly. Katherine waited, but the mild clearing of his throat had become a coughing spasm, and she finally began to become concerned. Robin was scarlet, bent over in his chair, holding his handkerchief to his mouth. The blue eyes, fringed with the thick black lashes, were filled with panic as he struggled against the paroxyms that possessed his body.

"I'll fetch you some water," she said, and ran from the room to the kitchen, returning with the drink. He was calming now, the gasping struggle for breath having been won, and he was leaning back in his chair, breathing deeply, shakily. "Thank you," he murmured, as he accepted the glass of water.

They spoke of other things for the remainder of his visit, the theatre and concerts in Sydney, and she talked of Barrengarry and her hopes for the property.

When he had gone, after suggesting that he would like to call again in the future, Katherine relaxed back into her armchair and stayed there, deep in thought, for some time.

She was afraid for Robin Mitchell; afraid, too, for the firm of Prescott, Mitchell and Co. Marcus would never involve himself entirely in business affairs and forget the work on behalf of the city's underprivileged, nor would he forget Barrengarry; it was simply not in the man's makeup.

And could the company depend on the new presence and driving energy of Robin Mitchell? Yes, Katherine thought, but for how long?

Her hands knotted together in her lap. She might be wrong, please God, let her be wrong . . .

She had not dared to look directly at Mitchell as she had come back into the room, did not want to see, even by accident, the white linen handkerchief that he held to his mouth. It would have been like something out of a dreadful novel if there had been specks of blood on the white cloth. So she did not know.

But she did know. All the way along the hall, as she ran to fetch water for him, the sound of his cough, that unmistakable, consumptive cough, had followed her. It was part of all her final memories of Oliver, of Christopher. The unmistakable protest of lungs so diseased that they could barely function. She was suddenly overcome with a feeling of helpless pity. Robin Mitchell, like Oliver Carron, seemed to be a man driven by the strength of his own indomitable spirit.

She wondered whether to speak to her father about the matter that Robin had raised—but in the end she handed over the papers as she had been bidden and said nothing of the young man's apprehensions. Her father knew what he was doing, she told herself, and besides, there was Barrengarry to think about. Marcus had already promised to see about new fences when he returned, and the house must be painted and the carpets replaced . . . No, there was no point in stirring up trouble where none existed, for she knew that Marcus would not take kindly to her interfering in his business life, let alone the officious young Mitchell.

Contrary to her father's suggestion, she did not see very much of Sydney on that visit. The activity in organizing the Balmain house and her projected plans for Barrengarry kept her occupied and happy. She drove out occasionally with her father, mostly on Sundays after church, and Tobias drove her into Sydney on weekdays when she needed to shop; but she found herself postponing visits to Gloria Patterson, who had recently married, and her other old friends; soon they realized they must come to her, and they did. Katherine entertained them with a warm, well-mannered interest in all that had happened to them, and her guests chatted happily to her—only realizing, halfway home, that their hostess had actually said very little about her own life.

It became a rumour among the Prescotts' acquaintances that Katherine was paler, more withdrawn; always quietly confident in herself, she was now more self-contained than before. Those of her friends, Gloria among them, who wanted the details of five years in the ancient city of Dublin, beginning with a scandalous elopement, came away dissatisfied. Katherine did not notice; she had more important matters on her mind.

For it was becoming increasingly clear as the days passed that Marcus was most unwilling to return to Kangaroo Valley.

Katherine's letters to Suzanna and the girls had at first mentioned five days' time . . . When that period was up, Katherine wrote that she hoped they'd be home in another week. A week later the message was the same.

It was more than Robin Mitchell's influence; when, three weeks after her arrival at Balmain she confronted her father and asked, if he would not return, that he send for Mama and the girls, he refused. He did not want the house filled with people—she knew herself how late he worked; he drew her into his study and urged her to read his correspondence files, letters and reports from various committees and investigative sources concerning housing standards, industrial injuries; not to mention the work he brought home with him each evening from Prescott, Mitchell and Co.

Katherine pleaded their need for him in the Valley, repeated the various messages designated for him, begged him to consider that his first commitment was to his family. In the middle of a sentence, Marcus, turning from her in exasperation, muttered, "You sound just like Suzanna!"

She was struck into silence as abruptly as if he had slapped her. Then, quietly, "You say that as if it were an insult."

"It wasn't meant that way . . ."

"Mama has a right to complain—though I, for one, have never heard her!"

"She simply doesn't understand, and never has understood, about the importance of what I'm attempting to do!"

"She does! I'm sure she does! But your philanthropic work is so demanding, Father! It takes so much of your time, your energy, of *you*, that there's so little left over—not enough to be a husband for her. There just isn't enough of you to go around—can't you see that she'd be hurt, knowing that she's the last of your priorities?''

She thought that he would explode with loud denials, commands for her to mind her own business—but though his temper seemed on the very point of detonation, the pause went on, and gradually Marcus began to relax, the tension left his face and body, and he leaned back against the edge of his desk.

"There are things I can't explain to you, Katherine . . . The business needs me . . .''

"I realize that—then why can't Mama and the girls come . . .''

"Your mother and I are better off apart. Joe's death only affirmed something we knew for many years—that there was very little besides you children that kept us together.''

"That's up to you, isn't it?'' Katherine struck back, to cover her shock at hearing such words. "Perhaps you haven't looked very hard. It's easier to give up and shirk your responsibilities.''

"Look, young woman . . . !''

"I have a personal motto for you, Father. Thank goodness it doesn't apply to the rest of the family—but you should emblazon it above your office door: *I love humanity—it's people I can't abide.*''

She was heading for the door.

"Katherine!''

She stopped and turned in the doorway. "I'll be returning to Barrengarry in the morning . . .

"I told you—only another week or so and I'll be free to return with you . . .''

"No, Father, don't rush your affairs. They've managed without you for so long in the Valley that you'll probably find, very soon, that you're not missed.''

She climbed the stairs, ignoring him calling her name, the demands for her to return.

Twelve

The meeting between father and daughter over breakfast the following morning was a cool one. Marcus made no effort to persuade Katherine to stay, nor did he mention again that he would be free to travel home in a week's time. He did hand Katherine three small boxes; gifts, he said, that he had purchased for Suzanna and the girls some weeks before, and a similar-shaped box for herself.

"Open it with the others, when you're home," he said. She kissed his cheek in well-mannered and restrained gratitude, and had Libby place the little packages with her luggage. When she left in the carriage with Tobias, who was to drive her to the railway, her father stood at the gate, straight-backed, one hand raised rather stiffly in farewell.

Katherine, though she left the Balmain house in Libby's capable hands, fretted crossly all the way to Picton in the train, unable to shake the feeling that the visit had not been a success, that somehow she had failed all of those who had been depending upon her.

But what was it they had wanted? What was it, exactly, that Marcus Prescott was expected to achieve in the Valley? His own family missing him she could understand, but the Valley seemed to look to Marcus as a pivotal part of its life; without his presence the inhabitants were, it seemed, floundering.

But that should not be so; it had always been a place filled with rugged, individualistic people, a cross-section of nationalities and religions who all seemed to survive together in mutual respect—perhaps because of their very isolation. They served the land, were as tough, yet adaptable, as the land demanded them to be.

But the Valley population was growing, she had seen that herself in the number of new settlers' huts since '61—perhaps, with the shrinking distances between the homesteads, the growing familiarity between the settlers, had come the desire for something tangible, some sign that they were standing together in the wilderness. They were, at last, becoming a community. And they would need leadership, a spokesman.

She wondered about this uneasily all the way south; she was glad that no one was expecting her, and was thus able to take the coach

from Picton to Moss Vale, and a hired carriage the few brief miles
to Dovewood. Edwin himself rode home with her, and stayed for
three days at Barrengarry; Katherine was pleased, as her grandfather's
presence made the fact that Marcus had not returned much easier
for the family to bear.

And there were other matters, it appeared, that had been keeping
Suzanna and the girls busy during the weeks that Katherine had
been away.

She and Edwin had met Carl at the main gate to Barrengarry,
bent over the little rustic bridge, muttering imprecations against it
as he hammered new boards into place. He had greeted them, and
they had ridden on towards the house. Later, Katherine took Carl
to task for not warning her, but he shrugged and said, "Should you
ask what is happening and who is at Barrengarry, I tell you. You
don't ask—still you find out. The driveway is not a long one."

Edwin had insisted on taking the horses to the barn, and Katherine
was alone as she ran up the stairs into the comforting, shabby
familiarity of the house.

"Mama?" she called, then, seeing the parlour door open, "Laura?
Teddi . . .? Oh, you've . . . !"

She had been about to say, "You've changed your hair," for the
figure seated on the settee, turned towards the window so that the
light fell on her tapestry-work, was Teddi's size, wore Teddi's dress—
only the ringlets were pulled back more sleekly, more demurely than
Edwina's thick curls would usually allow.

The fine neck and its crown of dark ringlets swung up and about
to face Katherine, then she had stood, the sewing falling from unnerved
fingers. "Oh! You must be Katherine . . ."

Katherine walked into the room slowly, found herself staring at
the apparition, the changeling that was not Edwina, as if she had
just appeared by walking through a wall. "Yes, I'm Katherine
Carron." She recovered herself. "And you're . . ."

The young woman—she looked, Katherine judged, to be twenty-
three or four—ducked her head and bent to recover the fallen tapestry.
"Flybutton . . ." she murmured, or a word that sounded very like it.

Katherine blinked. "I'm sorry . . . ?"

The face was lifted to Katherine; a thin face, pale, with a scattering
of freckles, rather prominent grey eyes with short dark lashes;
frightened eyes. Katherine had the discomfiting feeling that she had
disturbed a sleeping owl. The young woman took a deep breath. "Fleur
Barton. It's a silly name, isn't it, Fleur . . . My . . . my father was
killed here in the Valley some weeks ago, and my mother and I . . ."

"Oh . . ." The poor man she had found had had a wife and a daughter—it struck Katherine with some surprise, as she had begun to think of Gilbert Barton as merely a name; a tragic figure who now had little bearing on the reality of her life. Yet here the reality was.

She was saying, ". . . and your mama insisted we stay here when we arrived after hearing the news . . ."

"Do sit down, Miss Barton."

Both women seated themselves on the settee. Fleur's nervous little fingers plucked at the edges of her rather ugly tapestry, a pair of myopic and imbecilic pug dogs on a background the colour of a mustard plaster. "We came only to make arrangements for the funeral, you see. Mr Dodd, your minister, came from Sutton Forest—he was so very kind . . ." She lowered her head for a moment. "The problem was . . . money, you see. We . . . we don't have a great deal, my mother and I. It would have been very difficult for us to have Papa's remains brought home to Campbelltown, so . . ."

"Your father was buried here in the Valley?" Katherine suggested when Fleur paused.

"Yes. And Mama was so upset—she has a bad heart, you know— that your mama simply insisted that we stay here for a few days . . ."

The last words hung in the air, both women reluctant to approach the fact that the funeral had been more than two weeks ago.

"Your family has been so good to us," Fleur went on, "I had no mourning clothes and Edwina kindly gave me this one of hers. We have all become great friends—I shall miss them all so much when we return to Campbelltown, in a day or so," she added.

"Your mama has recovered, then?" *This is typical of Suzanna*, Katherine thought, her kind heart and good manners were always dragging her commonsense far behind.

"Oh, yes. We'll be leaving very soon. We've imposed on you enough."

Katherine smiled, murmured some polite reply and excused herself, hearing Edwin entering the hall.

They found Suzanna upstairs in her sitting room, seated with a small, almost completely round little woman, with a soft, pretty face and those same large, frightened eyes that she had passed on to her daughter.

She took Katherine's hand in both hers on being introduced— to Katherine it was like being thrust into a padded velvet muff— and squeezed.

"So this is your eldest girl. Such lovely hair—she has your hair—

but facially she must look more like your husband, does she? The
younger girls look much more like you . . ." And with that she
turned her attention to Edwin, and did not see the gentle look that
Suzanna gave her stunned daughter, nor hear her speak.

"Katherine looks just like herself—and very welcome she is . . .
Hello, darling . . ." Suzanna embraced her daughter, then her father,
and Katherine could not help but note how her gaze went between
them, anxiously, towards the door. "Your father . . . he didn't come
back with you?"

"No, Mama." It hurt to meet those vulnerable green eyes. "There
were business matters . . . he said he should be free by the end of
the week . . ."

"Good! We'll plan something special to welcome him back."
Suzanna rallied quickly, Katherine saw, aware of the smiling but
curious gaze of their visitor.

Suzanna rang for tea and the four sat down, Edwin, his
granddaughter was sure, suffering with composure the imposition
of the unexpected female company. Mrs Viola Barton, however,
chattered and twinkled in a way rather at odds with a woman newly
widowed. She gave the illusion of enjoying herself immensely, yet
Katherine was still left with the impression of a highly nervous woman;
the mother, unlike the daughter, had simply found a way of
camouflaging her fears. Katherine watched her as she praised Suzanna,
Laura and Edwina, the fat little hands gesturing as she told the story
of the past two-and-a-half weeks; fingers pressed to her temple in
occasional concentration, clasped to the heavy swelling of her bosom
when describing the anguish she had suffered.

Sometime during this account, Fleur entered the room, edging
around the wall timidly to seat herself in a corner and listen in
silence to her mama.

Katherine found that she pitied the women, educated and genteel
as they obviously were; they had, neither of them, been privy to
Gilbert Barton's business affairs and were completely incapable in
his absence, of taking up the reins of their own destinies. Katherine
could not see how Suzanna could have done otherwise than give
them this respite in which to reassess themselves and to help them
decide what to do.

"And I shall see Gilbert's lawyer immediately we return to
Campbelltown—I'm hoping we at least own our little house, and
perhaps have a little left in the bank. If not, having talked it over
with your mama, I shall take in boarders and should, with careful
management, make ends meet."

Viola finished on a triumphant note, and Katherine smiled and glanced at Fleur, expecting, somehow, a look of agreement or encouragement in the daughter's eyes.

Fleur, however, appeared to be chewing the nail of her right thumb, and the grey eyes were directed without favour or interest on the pattern in the rug near her mother's feet. She might not even have been listening.

That night Edwina called by Katherine's room for a chat, sat curled on the foot of the bed and began immediately on the subject of Fleur.

"She's a strange one, don't you think? *Almost* pretty—I mean, all the features are there, but the expression on her face is so *tortured*—she's always flinching at something. And she works her mouth all the time, as if she's stopping herself from screaming aloud only with the greatest of efforts at self-control."

Katherine was sitting up in bed, braiding her hair. She gazed at Edwina, then laughed, "Really, Teddi, you sound like a novelist."

"I *could* be a novelist, too; I'm a great student of human nature. I could write a wonderful book one day, equally as good as . . . as . . ."

"*Wuthering Heights*?" Katherine suggested.

"Oh, well, no. Not as good as *Wuthering Heights* . . ." Teddi paused, catching the steady look in her elder sister's eyes rather than the note of irony that had marked her suggestion. "Why *Wuthering Heights*?" Edwina asked, then her head came up a little, and her eyes grew round. "Ooh, forbidden alliances with black-haired rogues . . . That was almost too deep a reference even for me, Katey. You know about Rafe, don't you? Who told you? Laura, I suppose. And you just felt you *had* to tell Father."

"I did not—but he already knew the Heathcliff-like Mr Huckstable is brooding round the place—and it's your own fault for not continuing to berate him with letters demanding to be taken to Sydney."

"Is *that* how he knew? Oh, I was so stupid!" She flung herself across the bed.

"You're not as discerning a student of human nature as Father is, that's for certain."

"He's *always* a step ahead of us," she lamented. She looked up at Katherine sharply. "Well? What did he say?"

"Nothing."

"*Nothing*?"

"He was very non-committal. My guess is, he's waiting for the romance to run its course, or . . ."

"It'll *never* run its course," Edwina promised darkly.

". . . Or he'll come back here and thrash the pair of you."

The green eyes were round. "He *wouldn't*."

"Behave with propriety," Katherine lectured severely, "with no more of this sneaking away to the scrub for your little trysts; act like adults and prove the strength of the affection you have for each other, then, in time . . ."

Edwina had launched herself into Katherine's arms. "You talked to him, didn't you? I can tell. Oh, Katey—and to think Rafe was beginning to say that we should stop meeting each other for a while, until Father sees reason . . . ! We won't need to now, will we? Oh, Katey, would he really allow me to marry Rafe?"

How hard it was to look into that beautiful, open face! And yet, once she had looked, had seen the love, the hope, the trust that was written there, she could not look away. Katherine, with her grave misgivings and all her experience, stared at Edwina and her unshaken, unwavering young confidence, and felt a hundred years removed from her.

"I think," she said carefully, "that Father needs to be convinced that Rafe has stability and good sense."

"Oh, everything will work out well then, for he has. And you'll have helped us too, indirectly. You and Oliver were so happy together—*you* knew when you found the right man for you—and Father was completely wrong in his objections to your marriage. The experience will count in Rafe's and my favour, don't you think?"

When Katherine came down to breakfast the next morning it was to find Edwin, Suzanna and Laura talking excitedly.

"Katey—just think," her mother enthused, when good mornings had been exchanged, "your grandfather wants us all to go to stay at Dovewood for a few weeks . . ."

"Wouldn't it be wonderful, Katey?" Laura put in. "And Grandpapa said we'll hold a ball—didn't you, Grandpapa?"

Laura's almost childlike enthusiasm was quickly squelched by her elders.

"Don't call it a ball, dear," Suzanna lowered her voice as if a critical Society could hear the very word. "We're in mourning, remember. Joe, Oliver, little Christopher . . ."

"Joe, Oliver and even Christopher would want us to enjoy ourselves, Mama," Katherine said briskly. "They did. And Joe and Oliver, I know, were always very critical of long periods of mourning where families shut themselves away from their friends . . ."

"What I suggested," Edwin rumbled, glaring at the women from beneath thick grey brows, "was a dinner party—a Very Large Dinner Party. No one in this family will be breaking any rules of good taste—bothersome though they are. We will simply bend the rules to suit ourselves. Dovewood always was a world of its own, anyway. People who want to come and drink my champagne and dine on Armand's *cuisine* can either come uncomplainingly, or stay at home." This rather militant speech, to his astonishment, brought hugs all round. Even Suzanna seemed mollified, gazing at her beloved father with glistening eyes. As an only child now, after the deaths of several brothers and sisters in infancy and childhood, she was extremely close to Edwin and Angela Gordon and delighted at any opportunity to visit her old family home.

Katherine, who had had an interview with her mother the previous evening, where she had been forced to juggle the truth about her father like a conjuror so as not to upset Suzanna, now felt a wave of relief and elation at her grandfather's timeliness. Two weeks at Dovewood! And who knows, perhaps from there she could persuade her mother to return to Sydney with the girls, for she had her doubts whether Marcus would be coming home to the Valley within months . . .

A bustling and a rustling on the stairs, and Katherine turned, expecting Edwina—but that young miss, after lying awake for many hours planning her marriage to Rafe Huckstable, was still sound asleep in her feather bed. The noisy harbinger of rustling taffeta preceded Viola Barton, whom Katherine, in the excitement of Edwin's news, had forgotten.

And behind Viola, flowing silently in her wake like a convent novice, was Fleur. She seated herself and tried hard to disappear as her mother clutched hungrily at the conversation and had soon embroiled herself in plans for the trip to Moss Vale as if her name had been mentioned in the invitation. She had been told *so* much about Suzanna's mama—it would be so nice if they could meet before the return to Campbelltown. Katherine watched with growing horror as her mother and grandfather were manipulated. How could good manners so betray one? This move to Moss Vale was the perfect time to put the Bartons on the coach for Picton, where they would take the train northwards to Campbelltown . . .

"I'm sure my wife would love to meet you, Mrs Barton . . ." Edwin began.

"Would she really? Well, of course, we have gardening in common—I believe you have fine gardens at Dovewood—though my little plot at the front and rear of our house doesn't give me much room for *imaginative* horticulture—Well, I am delighted! Isn't it wonderful, Fleur? Thank you so much, Mr Gordon!"

"We must go home, Mama."

The voice was small, but finely honed. It cut across Mrs Barton and brought her nodding, smiling little head to an abrupt stillness. She stared at her daughter.

"We must go home," Fleur said. "We mustn't impose any longer."

"But . . . Mr Gordon was so kind as to . . ." The fearful desperation was almost childlike.

"We have things to do. We're simply avoiding facing the facts. Papa is gone and we must go home and begin to make a life for ourselves."

Viola Barton's mouth was a perfect O. The prominent grey eyes could not have held more amazement if the young woman had just risen from her chair to the ceiling and back again. In the passing seconds, when it was clear that the bemused Mrs Barton could not gather her wits, Katherine realized that this, undoubtedly, was the longest and most positive statement that Fleur Barton had ever made in her life.

"Fleur . . ." her mother said, in a little voice that almost squeaked with discomposure and reproach.

Fleur, under the amazed scrutiny of the entire table, was already looking unsure, her gaze began to waver, her lips to tremble.

Laura, reaching across to touch the white hands tightly knotted together on the tablecloth, said, "And you will make a new life, I know it. But given the circumstances, since you have to pass through Moss Vale anyway, there's no reason why you both can't stay, is there, Grandpa? There are plenty of rooms at Dovewood."

And Edwin, amused despite himself and touched by Laura's natural kindness and grace, was saying, of course, there was always room at Dovewood for their friends.

Suzanna began making plans, and Laura met Katherine's gaze, lingering a little challengingly as she saw that her older sister did not approve.

Bother you, Katherine told Laura silently, but Laura was already turning to the protesting Fleur, offering to help her dye one of her own ballgowns, and trying to interest the confused young woman in choosing between jet beads or a few demure pearls as an ornament.

Marcus's gifts to his wife and daughters had been necklaces, simple
in design, and yet far too expensive for any one of them not to see
the uncomfortable conscience behind the gifts. No one mentioned that,
however, and Suzanna, considering her own necklace in her room
during one of the rare moments she was now able to have alone with
her daughters, made the pronouncement that she would wear the gift
to what was now consistently referred to as the Very Large Dinner
Party. They would all be wearing black gowns, of course, though
décolleté enough to call for some adornment. Suzanna's necklace had
been of jet and diamonds; Katherine's, emeralds; Laura's, the most
ornate setting, of garnets, and Edwina's, a single pearl drop in a
diamond setting. The girls had, on opening the boxes, looked at each
other and decided to wear the gifts.

In the days of preparation they felt a reckless excitement in knowing
that there were many people who would regard their behaviour as
highly improper. What was worse was that they were encouraging
the Barton women, whose bereavement was even more recent, to fly
in the face of convention. But for all of them, bar, perhaps, Katherine
and her perambulations around the world, their lives had been
characterised by loneliness and isolation for many months at a time.
So when propriety seemed about to assert itself, Katherine went about
from one weakening will to another, and convinced them that this
jaunt was harmless, and of no one's concern but their own. When,
in answer to a letter from Suzanna, a reply came from Marcus saying
he was glad that the girls were to stay at Dovewood, everyone relaxed
visibly—only Katherine had to hide her irritation. *Father says* . . .

She was amazed, in this time, that Laura was so prepared to leave
Barrengarry for, sensitive to the feud and his son-in-law's feelings,
Edwin had never mixed with the Brodys, and the girls knew that
Stephen would not be on the guest list that Edwin was sending out
to friends in the Valley and the other towns in the Highlands. Laura
took it in good part, however, after an afternoon when she rode
out alone and came back, pink-cheeked and smiling, having, she later
admitted to Katherine, met Stephen and arranged to meet in Moss
Vale in a week's time.

The Huckstables, Rupert, the steely-grey patriarch, his cheerful
little wife, Martha, and Rafe and Emilia, would be invited. The
thought added a fillip to Edwina's enthusiasm, which would have
been exhausting to live with even without the thought of Rafe waltzing
with her.

"And you? Do you ever feel lonely, darling?" Suzanna asked Katherine as she helped pack her daughter's clothes in the large travelling chest.

"Lonely?" Katherine looked at her mother in surprise. "Mama, how can I possible be lonely, surrounded as I am with people all day?"

"It wasn't family and friends I was meaning, dear," Suzanna said patiently. She studied her eldest daughter for a moment, then seated herself on the edge of the bed. "Despite Marcus's objections—which will be numerous and forceful—I have no doubt that Edwina and Laura will eventually have their way regarding their young men. They're both in love at the moment, and it's very hard to ignore the blissful atmosphere of the house—it might, I thought, be disconcerting to be confronted with starry-eyed young women at every turn; to be their confidante, as I know they would elect you, to every downturn and hopeful nuance in the relationships. Does it make you feel . . . left out?"

She smiled at her mother. "I'm too busy to think of that, Mama— and too pleased for the girls—though I do wish sometimes that they had made their tasks a great deal easier and chosen young men of whom Father would approve."

Suzanna shook her head, smiling. "There are so few in the district— as a matter of fact . . ." She hesitated. "I know that Stephen, before you left . . ."

"No, no, that was only friendship—on my part, at least. Laura and I have talked about it. Please don't worry, Mama."

"How I wish you were all settled with nice young men. You, too, Katey. You shouldn't remain a widow."

Katherine was amused by her mother's wistfulness. "I'm happy with my own company, Mama—I think I shall quite enjoy being an elderly aunt who brings gifts for the girls' children. You mustn't matchmake for me, Mama," as Suzanna made a gesture of impatience, "I expressly forbid it."

Suzanna looked affronted. "As if I would do that! But if you did meet some young man who truly loved you—no, don't roll your eyes like that—I hope you'll give the relationship a chance to develop, Katey. You were always independent, but now you seem so self-reliant you frighten me. It's not good for a woman not to need someone, darling. Half the joy of life is to share it with someone you love." She stopped, suddenly discomforted. "But how insensitive of me—you know that."

Katherine kept packing, placing piles of fine lawn underclothes, camisoles, pantaloons, petticoats, in the trunk.

Suzanna said, perhaps in an effort to lighten the atmosphere, "But if you do marry again, please find someone a little closer to the Valley than Dublin."

They laughed together, and Katherine turned to gaze out the window, still smiling, but with the thought of Brendan Kelehan suddenly before her. More unsuitable, even more dangerous, than Oliver. And yet . . .

"Why did that make you look so thoughtful, Katey?" her mother asked gently.

Katherine sighed, without turning from the view of the pine trees, the winter-faded fields. "There was a man—in Dublin. You would have met him once or twice, he was a good friend of Oliver's— Brendan Kelehan."

"I remember him. Very direct gaze, and greying hair—quite distinguished. He was a lawyer, wasn't he—his parents had just passed away." Suzanna paused, then asked. "Are you missing him? Are you fond of him, Katey?"

"Oh, yes." She turned to her mother, then spoke quickly as she saw the distress in her eyes. "Oh, no, Mama, not in that way. But Brendan has always been very kind to us. Actually," the thoughts came unbidden to her consciousness even as she spoke, "he was always kind. The most *caring* man. Oliver relied on him a great deal. And I treated him very badly. I . . . I blamed him for something that wasn't his fault; I was cruel—one can be, when one feels trapped, and frightened."

"Darling, what . . ."

"Oh, it's nothing—I don't want to talk about it now—it's over. But . . . I've not been able to forget about Brendan. I don't know where he is, or what has happened to him. I made myself *not care*. I was selfish, and mean, and . . . dishonest. It bothers me that he cared for us and I treated him so callously."

"Darling . . ." Suzanna was on her feet, had crossed to Katherine and held her daughter in her arms. "You mustn't talk of yourself like this. I know you better than anyone in the entire world—you're not capable of conscious cruelty. I'm sorry for Brendan—I remember him very well—a nice boy, but very intense—though perhaps that was because he was so unhappy about your marriage. It was quite obvious that he wished he had been the one to discover you, not Oliver!" She smiled, then sobered a little. "We don't mean to hurt those who love us, Katey. It happens too easily, for to love is to make a decision to be vulnerable—to risk great joy one risks emotional wounds. Do you understand? It's just so tragically easy to hurt someone who loves you. But think of this—Brendan was a mature young man; he understood and accepted your decision when you married Oliver. And I'm certain he understands your reasons for your decision now, whatever the circumstances."

Suzanna was wise enough and loving enough, Katherine saw, to refrain from asking any further questions. She felt a great wave of love and gratitude as she gazed at her mother. But still she wondered about the ghost of Brendan Kelehan, of all those ghosts of those years in Dublin, and wondered if she would ever free herself from the doubts and regrets.

Thirteen

Her grandmother was there to welcome them, standing on the verandah of Dovewood, the mellow stone house that Edwin had built in 1827.

Through the excited greetings, the introducing of Viola and Fleur, Katherine gazed between her grandmother and grandfather, a warmth growing in her heart; for she knew that these two had not changed in all the five years of her absence. Edwin, as straight-backed and military-looking as ever, relaxing visibly now he was back within the walls of his beloved house and with his wife beside him. And that wife, Angela, her tall figure as slim and flexible as that of a woman half her age, still held the remnants of her great beauty in her clear grey eyes, the fineness of her bone structure and the gloss on her luxuriant hair, auburn shot with silver now, but dressed fashionably and effectively.

Katherine hugged her grandmother, looked into those fearless eyes and prayed that somehow she might still inherit the woman's strength and character.

It was difficult to have more than a few words with her grandparents that day. Both Edwin and Angela were concerned for Suzanna, how tired and drawn she looked, and there were Viola and Fleur to be entertained, along with the other guests who were arriving constantly from all over the Southern Highlands.

Dovewood was a spacious house of twelve bedrooms, having been built for entertaining and for the large family that Angela and Edwin had planned to have. Nine children had been born to them, at their first home in Wollongong, and at Dovewood, but of those nine children, only Suzanna had survived. Two of the girls had died of illnesses as young adults, the rest, four boys and two girls, had succumbed to various childhood illnesses or infections and had not lived more than a few years.

But Dovewood, oddly enough, did not become a sombre house of ghosts, of unfulfilled potential. Suzanna had married Marcus Prescott when she was seventeen and he nineteen; Katherine, named after one of her deceased aunts, was born that same year, and Joe the year after. In those early days the family often stayed at Dovewood on the way back and forth from the Valley to the townhouse in Sydney, and there were always other guests of their grandparents, business friends of Edwin's, who brought their families down from Sydney, up from Melbourne—attractive men, beautiful women, bright as butterflies: Dovewood was always alive, a place of happy memories for Katherine.

She wondered if the playhouse was still there, having had no time to explore the gardens on her previous fleeting visit. This little sanctuary, buried deep in a corner of the gardens that was now wilderness, had been built for the three eldest girls, Suzanna and her sisters, more than thirty years ago. After luncheon, when the family was resting, Katherine pulled on her cloak and a sturdy pair of shoes and went downstairs, planning to search the large grounds for what remained of the little building.

She reached no further than the gun room, for she heard voices and stopped, as anyone would, hearing an excited voice exclaim, "I tell you, a clever person could make an absolute fortune!"

There appeared to be no rejoinder to this piece of fascinating news, but, as Katherine moved closer, she could detect the well-modulated accents of her grandfather's voice murmuring a reply. Katherine moved still closer to the door.

The gun room was Edwin's particular sanctuary; he had no interest in actually killing things—indeed, rode to hounds only when it was one of those civilized, well-managed affairs, where some intrepid horseman rose before dawn and galloped over timber dragging the remains of a fish or rabbit dinner on a string. The hounds, let loose in the morning, were unaware of the difference, and everyone scrambled happily through the scrub, being scraped off on trees, falling into creeks and arriving back, nicely exhausted, at a prearranged spot in some homestead's house paddock in time for luncheon.

Edwin loved guns, however. His collection was one of the finest in New South Wales, and his interest and avidity had secured him a position of respect that made up for his distaste for "firing bits of lead at harmless creatures that can't shoot back".

The atmosphere of the gun room, Katherine knew, would be thick with cigar and pipe smoke; the smell came through the fine cracks around the door and made her wrinkle her nose. There were three or four men within the room, all talking excitedly, however, and she did not move away.

Land at Moss Vale was being subdivided, a whole town was being laid out—but it was the railway . . . something about the railway. And "His Excellency" was mentioned—that would be the Governor, wouldn't it? "His Excellency's influence . . ." twice she heard the phrase, but it rose above the mutter of voices only to be submerged immediately by loud rejoinders.

Bother. Katherine pressed her ear to the door—but it was then that strong hands took her shoulders, very close to her neck, and she found herself pulled back, spun about and propped up against the wall, a few feet from the door.

The hands remained on her shoulders, the thumbs pressing her chin upwards to gaze into Rafe Huckstable's face.

She began to speak, to say something, anything, her heart beating with the shock of being so unceremoniously treated, and harder still on seeing who it was who held her. "I . . . I don't think that's the way to greet an old friend, do you? Leaping out of the woodwork like that . . ."

He smiled, slowly. And with sadness she saw that the past five years had not been kind to him. There were shadows now, beneath the dark eyes, and the face was thinner, the jaw stiffly thrust through the flesh, barely covered by the taut brown skin. It was the face of an ascetic, the dark depths of the eyes holding darker, deeper shadows that Katherine could not guess at.

He, in turn, was studying her face, and pulled back a little, the better to take her all in, tilting his head on one side. He murmured, "I'd forgotten how it felt—watching you, the endearing little efforts to pull your dignity about you—it's like a stab from an old wound. Six years, and you can still rob me of my reasoning, with your damnable unconscious posturings. I ought to break your little skull like a walnut." The thumbs pressed her head up and back against the wall.

She wanted to touch him, to reach out and hold that broad, spare frame. It had been so long, so long since a man had held her, since she had seen that naked want in a man's eyes. And she knew now, as an awakened woman, what she had foolishly tried to ignore for nearly six years or more. She wanted Rafe Huckstable. Despite logic, despite good breeding and high morals—and family loyalty . . . ?

She watched him, her eyes narrowed a little, feeling the desire, thankfully, draining from her. She smiled. "Raphael Huckstable, you could almost have me believing that you meant that."

It was enough, her bantering tone, her smiling disbelief. Rafe had no choice; the black depths were veiled, and after a second's pause, he let her go, took a step backwards, and bowed elaborately.

"The rake's progress thwarted, yet again." His soft tone unreadable. He glanced at the door, from behind which the growl of voices had continued without a check. "May I accompany you on a stroll in the gardens? Or do you wish to risk crumpling your pretty ear for enlightenment?"

"I wasn't spying! It's just . . ."

"Come outside."

He took her arm, a little forcefully, for she was cross now, and they left the house by one of the side doors, out onto the verandah and down into the gardens.

"I can assure you," Rafe said helpfully, "that there was nothing of importance or even mild interest being said in that room. I left it only for a few minutes and was returning most reluctantly."

"Someone was saying something about a fortune to be made in Moss Vale."

"Ah, yes, they were starting on that subject when I left."

"What is it? I wasn't aware of anything unusual at Moss Vale. Have they discovered gold, or . . ."

"You really are excited, aren't you? Why this sudden avaricious interest, Katherine? Are you thinking of making some investments?"

"Not at all." She lowered her eyes, away from the probing glance, wished too that there was some way of politely removing her arm from his; it lay against her ribs, and even with the encagement of her stays, she felt her heart thudding, too close to his forearm, she felt, for him not to notice.

"The railway is expected to be through to Moss Vale next year," Rafe was saying. "From being a one-horse town miles from civilization, it'll be a one-horse town with a railway station. There are town allotments, of course, but no one—until now, at least—has shown any interest in building a city there. Mittagong is only ten miles to the north, and that has the iron mine and steel works—though it's been closed since April. If someone starts mining and smelting again, it would seem natural to build a city at Mittagong, not Moss Vale."

"What about the governor?"

"What *about* the governor?" He looked at her with wicked interest. "Was a scandal being discussed within that smoke-filled den? Perhaps I shouldn't have left."

She had to laugh. "No scandal, not even any gossip. It's just that His Excellency has been showing some interest in the district, and I was wondering why, that was all."

"The air, Katherine, the altitude of the Highlands is very salubrious, they say. His Excellency has been known to visit the area, drink at the spa on the Bong Bong Road, and to stay with various friends in the Highlands."

So this was all. Katherine felt oddly disappointed. Still, she would find an opportunity later to speak with her grandfather alone. He would tell her . . .

Rafe had turned to her, had taken both her hands in his, and only now did Katherine glance back and realize that their walk had taken them behind a hedge of gardenia and out of view of the house.

"I wanted to tell you—I'm so sorry, Katey." Rafe's voice was low, gentle. "I thought of Oliver Carron as the luckiest man in the world . . ." He scowled down at their locked hands. "I still think he was lucky. To have you for five years . . ." He stopped. "He must have been a very special man."

"He was, Rafe."

Rafe nodded slowly, not lifting his eyes. "And your boy . . . Life's been very hard for you, Katey."

"I'll cope."

He looked up, taken aback by the abruptness of her reply. "Yes. Of course you will. But you shouldn't have had to suffer as much as you have. If you'd only stayed . . ."

"I couldn't have stayed! I don't have any regrets, Rafe. Yes, I've returned to the Valley—alone—just as I left it. But Oliver and Christopher enriched my life beyond anything I'd ever known or believed. To have had them share my life, to be able to have loved them, was worth every bit of pain I suffered at their loss. I'd do it again, if I could only bring them back—if anything could bring them back!"

He did not speak, but instead pulled her into his arms, and the suddenness and force of his embrace caught her unawares. *He pities me*, she thought, wildly, and it angered her, the irritation directed as much at herself as at Rafe. Did I sound pitiful? Was I mewling and looking pathetic and lost?

She grasped his arms to push him back from her—but the voice, from off to Katherine's left, made them both start, half-turn towards the sound.

"A most disgusting and disturbing display."

Emilia Huckstable stood on a patch of the lawn—with one part of her mind, Katherine noticed that it was a dry patch, frost-bitten, and Emilia stood in the centre of it, as if the cold fury that emanated from her was enough to freeze the very ground on which she walked.

She was dressed in a coat and matching hat of a dark mulberry, both fashionable yet understated, her dark hair pulled back from a central parting above the strong-boned, heavy-browed face, so much like her brother's. She clutched an elegant umbrella in both hands, almost as if she were about to ward off an assailant.

"I would have visited Barrengarry earlier to pay my . . . respects, Katherine." The voice seemed to crackle on the winter air, "but I honestly thought that it was too soon, that after all you'd been through you would be too distressed, for some time, to receive visitors."

"Emilia . . ." Katherine began.

"But I have obviously underestimated your *receptiveness*."

"That's enough!" Rafe said sharply. He released Katherine slowly from his embrace and she was grateful for this, that he betrayed no sign of shame or embarrassment. "You don't understand, Emilia . . ."

"I don't think there is very much I wish to understand about the very accessible Mrs Carron." In that second that they stood transfixed by her venom, she turned her gaze to Rafe. "How could you be such a fool?" she said, her voice low. "Young Edwina is worth ten of her!"

"By God, I'll . . . !"

Rafe strode forward, but Katherine took his tensed arm and held to it. She watched Emilia turn and sail across the lawn, disappearing behind the greenhouse, in the direction of the back verandah, half-expecting the grass to wither as she passed.

"Let her go, Rafe," Katherine said heavily. "Any explanations we might give will only make it worse."

He fumed silently, then turned to look at her. The well-remembered, half-quizzical smile played suddenly across his mouth. "The first embrace I've ever given a woman, born out of sheer empathy and compassion, and it's made a spectacle of the worst order of debauchery."

"Perhaps you're not intended to escape from your reputation." Katherine could not help smiling. "The rake progresses—despite himself."

"No," he said.

She frowned, unwilling to believe all that seemed restrained behind that word.

"No," he said again.

A currawong called, loudly, harshly, in a pine tree close by them. It was answered by another *currah, currah, currawah!* from a distant corner of the garden. A frog cleared its throat beneath the roots of the gardenia hedge and a cricket, having paused mid-bar at the currawong's call, now tentatively began his song once more.

Katherine said, in an effort to break the mood that held them, "You'd better return to the house, Rafe. Grandpapa might be looking for you."

"You'll come, too . . ."

"No, I'd like to walk by myself for a little while . . ."

"Katherine . . ." He took her elbows in his hands.

"No, Rafe. Please."

He stood gazing down at her as if he would argue further, then turned abruptly and walked away towards the house without looking back.

The whole scene had made her furious; she could not imagine Emilia spreading gossip, for the woman had her own sense of honour that was as rigid as her bearing. But it rankled within Katherine that the old jealousy and disapproval should find such ample fuel to feed on. She had matured beyond worrying what Emilia Huckstable might think of her, but still, she had wanted this return to the Highlands to be a new beginning—and somehow it seemed that the old problems, the old animosities, had not changed; it was beginning to seem as if there were merely new problems, added to the old.

She turned her back resolutely on the vanishing Rafe, gazed about the garden, gaining her bearings . . .

There. To the right, where the bleached wooden teeth of an ancient picket fence once held back the old orchard from the rest of the property. Through the quiet avenues between the trees, one would come upon a stand of silver birch, planted by Angela, soon after the homestead was built. In the centre of the little forest of imported trees would be the playhouse.

Yet Katherine paused at the picket fence, her feelings disturbed, her curiosity about this very important part of her childhood spoilt somehow by the scene she had just taken part in. She had wanted the time for herself, she had wanted a free mind when she found the playhouse again; it was private, it belonged to no one but herself.

She had felt this as a child, when Joe had shown no interest in it, regarding it as a "girls' hideout", and, years later, Laura and Edwina had somehow aligned themselves with Suzanna's feelings of sadness about the place. Laura used to say it was depressing; Edwina declared flatly that it was haunted. As children, the two girls had preferred the sun-dappled sand by the creek at the opposite side of the property or a favourite space of lawn near the rose arbour. No one, it seemed, had any interest in the playhouse but Katherine, who found the wistful shades of the three little girls for whom it was built, Suzanna and the long-dead Aunt Katherine and Aunt Lucy, to be acquiescing and undemanding company.

But now the mood had been spoilt—she would not bring the memory of Rafe's demanding embrace and Emilia's bitter disapproval to her childhood sanctuary. At the picket fence, she turned back towards the house. As she passed the place where Rafe had paused and taken her into his arms, she remembered something, something she had pushed to the back of her mind.

Something in his look of sympathy, the warmth that she had never really seen before in Rafe, had reminded her of Brendan Kelehan. It had been just as Rafe pulled her into his arms—it had lasted only a second—it was enough, however, to rob her of any conscious thought. She had had no time to take pleasure in Rafe's embrace.

Brendan. It was as if he was not about to allow himself to be forgotten, pushed into her past. She had been thinking about him, despite herself, in the days since she had tried to tell Suzanna about him. No matter how she rationalized it to herself, she had betrayed all the respect and trust that Brendan had had for her.

She would write to him, she thought, there couldn't be too many Kelehans who were lawyers in Boston. She would write to him and explain everything that had happened. He had always listened, always understood. He would understand now, she was sure of it.

At a distance, near the rose garden, she saw Emilia walking between her parents, Rupert and Martha Huckstable, and for a moment Katherine felt a slight panic that the woman would be confiding in her parents the story of what she had witnessed between Katherine and Rafe. But no—Emilia caught such power—she would see it as power—to herself, it swelled the empty store of her life and filled her days, this study of other people's weaknesses. She would not share this morning's triumph even with her parents.

Katherine's footsteps faltered a little as she suddenly remembered Emilia's words, *You fool—young Edwina is worth ten of her!* It was odd that such a deliberate barb should hurt her, but it made her feel, once more, the heavy disappointment that this homecoming had brought. She would write to Brendan about that, too. Perhaps . . . and her footsteps slowed almost to stillness, she should have gone to Brendan in Boston instead of coming home. But would her own confusion have been made any clearer by being close to a man who had always disturbed her, who would, she knew, demand even more of her if he knew her to be free?

She had to put the questions from her, but she knew, at least, why she had turned back at the gate to the old orchard, why she did not want to find the little house in the birch wood. It would be very crowded; the three little ghosts, Katherine herself, and Rafe, Emilia, and Brendan Kelehan.

It was that evening, helping Suzanna brush out her hair before retiring, that Katherine put the idea to her mother that she should return to Sydney.

"But . . . though I'd love to go, Katey, your father said he'd be returning to Barrengarry in only a matter of weeks . . ."

"We can't be sure of that, Mama. You know how Father has been prevaricating lately. And, anyway, let him come home to Barrengarry if he wishes—you haven't been to Sydney for more than a year—it's *your* turn to visit the city and enjoy yourself."

Suzanna seemed oddly pale, agitated at the thought. Katherine was about to ask her if there was anything the matter, anything preventing her from going, when her mother rose from the dressing table and walked restlessly about the room for a moment before seating herself on the edge of the bed. She looked up at Katherine with something like defiance and there was, at last, some touch of colour in her cheeks. "I *can* go. There's no reason why I can't. And . . . and I have shopping to do—I need new gowns—and there's the theatres, and my old friends . . ." Her eyes were flashing. "You're right, Katey. I will go!"

"Then it's settled." Katherine was delighted. "I shall arrange everything as soon as we return to Barrengarry."

"But the girls . . ." Suzanna looked suddenly thoughtful.

"Laura and Edwina will come too, of course. It will be equally as good for them as for you. Promise you'll come, Mama! Don't find excuses!"

"I promise." The large green eyes, soft and vulnerable, came around to face Katherine directly and she smiled, so that Katherine saw, for the first time since she arrived home, the mother she had always known. "I shall go, and I shall enjoy myself immensely. Marcus can make of it what he will."

It was a strangely challenging statement, but Katherine was so pleased at her mother's decision that she let the opportunity for a query pass by her. The months of Marcus's absence had hurt Suzanna deeply; Katherine's very failure to snap him out of his mood of grim introspection had finally awakened Suzanna to the fact that only she could change her own circumstances, and Katherine was delighted to see that she meant to do just that.

The coup kept Katherine elated for most of the following day; the house guests—and there were many—went for a picnic to Fitzroy Falls, as it was a clear day, suddenly and surprisingly warm after the cold of the previous weeks. But with September only a week away, spring would officially begin. Soon, Katherine thought, looking back from the buggy at the still dormant gardens of Dovewood, the country she loved would awake with the scent and colour of an Australian springtime.

Katherine stayed aloof from Rafe, though several times she found him gazing at her. At the picnic site, Emilia singled out Edwina and had her eat the packed luncheon with the Huckstable family. Suzanna and Laura seemed happy with this; Katherine's mind was divided on the matter. Rafe was a consummate philanderer; that he had flirted with her and meant nothing by it, she could accept. But whatever he said to Teddi—let him mean that. She was so young, but she would be a loving, cheerful, fiercely loyal wife—she did not deserve to be betrayed. She would not be. When there was time, Katherine decided to speak to Rafe again—or, better still, make Suzanna confront him, and ask him his true feelings for Edwina.

Luke Murchison and his sister, the garrulous and dimpled Arabella, and Bessie, Daisy and Marietta Cummings sat with Suzanna, Katherine and Laura on rugs on the dry winter grass. Luke, too, seemed to share something of Katherine's uneasiness at Rafe's interest in Edwina, possibly because he had seen his younger sister, like the Cummings girls and most other young females in the Valley, fall beneath Rafe's spell, only to suffer the heartache that came with his waning interest.

"Do you think it's wise, Miss Katherine? Miss Edwina is so

young . . ." He spoke softly, while none of the others were listening.

"I know. Yet she has a great deal of common sense, Luke."

His broad face, sunburnt and freckled in those areas not covered by his thick brown beard, was creased into a worried frown. "Miss Emilia would look after her, I'm sure. She's very fond of Miss Edwina, she'd advise her correctly."

Katherine paused with a forkful of ham halfway to her mouth. Luke was still gazing over at the Huckstable party. Katherine tried in vain to work out his faith in Emilia; was it to advise Edwina should she decide to become Rafe's wife—or to help her avoid the threat of dishonour at her dangerous brother's hands?

And where did Luke's interest lie? At thirty-four, he had never married. The blue eyes, rather soft, childlike eyes because of their very thick, long, black lashes, were fixed, still, on Edwina. It was amusing for Katherine to remember that this was the young man whom her father had always preferred as a marriage prospect for herself in the days before the fateful trip to Europe. But no, it seemed that Edwina had yet another hopeful suitor in the stolid and successful young farmer by her side. Unless—and she had to lower her head to cover her smile—Luke was staring dreamy-eyed not at Edwina but the woman beside her. It filled Katherine with hopeful amusement to consider that Luke saw in his visions of perfect womanhood the stiffly rectitudinous form of Emilia Huckstable.

"Tell me about Moss Vale."

"What about Moss Vale? This land business?"

"Yes." Katherine leaned forward in her chair. Her grandfather, on the other side of the hearth, had just lit his pipe and now relaxed back into the depths of the ancient wing-backed armchair and was puffing contentedly.

"It's been talked about before, in all the towns along the route of the railway. Buy up land, sell to those who want to move out from the city . . ."

"Will it work, this time?"

The room was dark, lit only by a lamp on the nearby desk, and the fire in the hearth. Edwin's old beagle bitch, Cassie, snored softly on the rug at their feet.

"Yes," Edwin said, after some consideration. "Yes, I think it will work with Moss Vale. It's becoming fashionable, y'see, to have a country house. Lots of people in this colony, up from nothing, feel they've got to have some visible sign of their wealth—a house is

permanent, stable—and it sounds very grand, does it not?—'Leaving
on Saturday for a few days at our summer place in the Southern
Highlands.' Very impressive. His Excellency's patronage began it—
and now it's rumoured he's considering buying a summer residence.
Lots of men want to be seen where the governor is seen—in a few
years, who knows? Certainly the inns and guesthouses are thriving
with visiting 'Pure Merinos' from Sydney, even now."

Katherine was thinking hard. "And there are some good blocks
of land available? Acreages, with streams, like Dovewood—land
suitable for landscaping, just as you have with Dovewood?"

"Yes, I believe so. The land is richer here, than further
north . . . Katey, my dear, why this sudden interest in real estate?"

She smiled. "I have to have some interest, Grandpapa, I never
was very good at needlework or piano . . ."

"What about your painting?" His gaze direct, with almost a
reproof.

"I haven't had time to indulge myself in painting since I left . . ."

"And your interest in botany? You used to know the name of
every plant and tree in the Valley . . ."

It *would* be her grandfather who reminded her of this, one of the
great regrets of those years in Dublin; her longing for the Australian
bush, the joy she had once taken in her collecting and sketching of
the specimens of flora . . . It hurt even now, the years of neglect.
"That's all it was—an interest," she said flatly. "Seriously, Grandpapa,
I must make some kind of provision for my future. I don't want to
become the obligatory maiden aunt—steady, dependable Aunt Katey,
passionately interested in everyone's affairs, because she has none of
her own. I'm in danger of that already—I have a feeling I'm going
to end up meddling in the affairs of my entire family . . ."

"A good thing someone will," Edwin growled. "Should be Marcus,
though. Self-indulgent fool . . ."

"I care about them all so desperately, Grandpapa; I hate to see
them unhappy. I'm glad if I can help them in any way I can . . .
But . . . there's been no focus for my own life—do you see? I'm drifting
from day to day, fulfilling whatever need I see about me. I can't
build my life around Barrengarry, like Mama has, and I can't regard
marriage in the same way that Laura and Edwina do, as if it's a play
they're rehearsing for and quite soon the curtain will go up and they'll
be centre stage, involved in some magical experience . . . It's not
like that.

"I suppose . . ." She leaned back in her chair, "I'm afraid I have
nothing to look forward to. I become worried, sometimes, because

there isn't really anything that I want any more. And that's not normal, surely."

The old man was studying her through the curls of pipe smoke. His eyes, beneath the thin grey wisps of hair, were rheumy and tired and wise. "Speaking for myself," he said, "if I were in your position, I'd be feeling afraid."

"Afraid?" She straightened, not liking to hear if there were any further reasons for her to be disquietened.

"You've had more than your share of tragedy, my girl—and it's come on you suddenly and ruthlessly. The life you built for yourself back in Dublin was destroyed by the deaths of your loved ones, and one couldn't blame you if you were unwilling to trust anything any more. It could make you afraid to want anything, to *need* anything—in case it were taken away from you."

"That's . . . illogical."

"Human beings aren't always logical. And I'm telling you how *I* would feel. I have been through something similar, you know. We lost nearly all our little ones, Angela and myself—but it was worse, back in '37, '38—losing Katherine . . . then Lucy, when the diphtheria struck. I do know a little of what you're going through, my dear." The normally strong voice broke a little, and he covered it with a cough, leaning over to tip the contents of his pipe into the hearth, tapping the bowl against the tiles. The noise startled Cassie and she raised her head to gaze wildly about her with a flopping of soft brown ears. Finding no intruders, she cast Edwin one look of reproach, sighed, and lay down again, the greying muzzle across Katherine's foot.

"Don't try to be too strong, Katey. You are strong, you're more like Angela than Suzanna is—but you're not a machine, my dear. Don't sit back too far from life, organizing your loved ones with dispassionate regard—and don't puff up like a pouter pigeon. You were telling me just the same thing yourself—I'm simply agreeing with you. And I believe you're right—running your own affairs is a much more satisfying pastime—always believed a woman should taken an interest in these things. What are your feelings about the Moss Vale business?"

"If you think it's a worthwhile venture, I'd like to buy some blocks of land. Could you come with me, to help me choose them?"

"Town blocks?"

"No—just out of town. Blocks with ten acres or more. You see, I plan to advertise the land rather like some of the goods in the ladies' journals—I've always thought that a clever advertisement can convinice someone that they actually *need*—practically anything. This is going to be my experiment to see if my theory works," she grinned. "I'll choose the blocks with views of hills or water, and I'll describe it all in very glowing terms, telling the discerning buyer why his family needs a country house, and why I have the best blocks. But," she added, "they must be very suitable—or buyers will come to Moss Vale only to be lured to other vendors, you see."

"I see." He looked at her appreciatively. "You do understand that the advertising costs will raise the price of your investment considerably?"

"Yes, but I'm planning to charge a great deal for the land. But as I said, it will be the best, and if you're right in what you say about the direction this district is taking, as a resort area, then there must be people paying a fortune each year staying at inns who would be only too delighted to build their own, permanent homes."

Edwin nodded. "You're right, you know—I meet them all the time. Up from Sydney every month or so—money to burn, full of praise for the area but no time, most of them, to hunt for a suitable place. So many people have wanted something like Dovewood but don't know where to start."

"That's what I'll be doing. Telling them how easy it is. We can say in the advertisement that we can suggest experienced architects and landscapers—you know many, don't you?"

"So . . ." Edwin said thoughtfully, stirring Cassie with his foot, smiling as she rolled over to have her underbelly rubbed, "you provide everything already organized, for men with the need, plenty of money, but no time . . ."

"It will work, then?"

"My dear, fortunes have been made on just that formula."

Katherine stood up, kissed her grandfather's cheek. "I'll be back in a moment."

The rest of the house was asleep. It took her a few minutes, upstairs in the room she shared with her mother, to find the small velvet case inside her larger inlaid jewellery box, without benefit of lamplight in case she woke the sleeping Suzanna.

She carried the small burden downstairs and into the silent gun room. Edwin and Cassie raised their heads to gaze at her, the little beagle clambering to her feet to check the contents of the box for edibles as Katherine sat down—but she found only twinkling, shiny, cold pebbles and, checking the box further, with a deep inhaling sniff, only dust, which made her sneeze. The look of reproof she gave the two humans for thus raising her hopes was lost upon them.

Both were staring at the cascade of diamonds that Katherine lifted from the case and held in her hands.

"Good Lord . . . Did Oliver give you this?" He reached out and took the necklace almost reverently, then groped for his spectacles on the table beside him. Hooking the wires over his ears, he bent to examine the jewels.

"It's the most valuable of my pieces," Katherine was saying, "but it wasn't given to me as part of the family heirlooms—I sent those back to Oliver's eldest sister, when Christopher died."

"Good girl." He balanced the necklace in his hands, peered again at one or two of the individual stones. "My father used to collect and sell trinkets like this—just as an interest, but a profitable one. Angela had her jewels valued only last month—I take it you want me to see to the sale of this, for your capital?"

"Yes." Katherine took a deep breath. "Yes," she repeated. "I'm fond of the piece, but this way is more practical."

Edwin nodded. "All right. I'm going up to Sydney next week— I'll take this beauty with me." He gazed at the necklace and up at Katherine regretfully. "It *is* a pity—you'd look marvellous in it."

"Yes," Katherine said, with a sigh.

It was done. The necklace was securely locked away in Edwin's safe, and they had already made plans for Katherine to stay at Dovewood for a few days and make excursions to Moss Vale with Edwin to see possible sites for her investment.

She slept well that night, and awoke to greet the day of the Very Large Dinner Party with a lighter heart than she had known for many weeks. Sixty people were invited that evening, and she pattered about the house with her sisters and the silent but ubiquitous Fleur, hanging holly around the walls, arranging winter jasmine and roses from the greenhouses in vases on the long tables.

"Holly in August . . ." She shook her head. It was still strange, after five years in the northern hemisphere, to remember that Christmas would bring a riot of every flower imaginable, blossoming in the warmth of a southern summer. It was only now, in the colder months between June and August, that the earth slept briefly, and those winter berries, holly and hawthorn, lovingly planted by homesick Britons, reddened in gardens and hedgerows.

As she ran about the house, following orders from Angela, Katherine was already composing in her mind the advertisements that would appear in the better-class Sydney periodicals during the next few months:

ACREAGE
Superbly Suited to Landscaping
for
Gentleman's Country Residence

She found she was looking forward to the future—with her mother settled in the house in Balmain for the badly needed city holiday and her own future taken care of, she would stay, she decided, at Barrengarry for most of the next twelve months. Edwin was right—she had enjoyed her painting, and her interest in the wildlife and native flora of the Valley had given her, in years past, many contented hours. She would renew her correspondence with Professor Argyle in Sydney and search out, in the boxes stored beneath her bed at Barrengarry, the many delicate sketches she had made of leaf and blossom; an ambitious effort begun years before as a complete guide to the trees and shrubs of Kangaroo Valley.

She would fill her life with her hobby, her friends, her family— and even, perhaps, travel to Europe once more, in a few years' time. Despite all she had said to her grandfather, she knew that her role in the household was already written. She held the memories of Oliver and Christopher too close to ever consider remarriage; she would, therefore, be a loving onlooker to the lives that Laura and Teddi would make for themselves; theirs the expanding out into the world to find mates, to bear children and form new and growing networks of relatives. Katherine's life, she told herself, bathing that evening before changing into the black lace ball gown, could do nothing now but contract upon itself. But, by heaven she promised— placing Marcus's emerald necklet at her throat—it would contract comfortably.

It was a wonderful evening; the sense of progress, of movement in her life that had come with handing the necklace over to Edwin, remained with her. She took delight in seeing how pretty Edwina and Laura looked, how relaxed and lovely Suzanna appeared in the high choker of jet and diamonds, the copper of her hair in thick coils at the back of her head.

When the dancing began in the ballroom after dinner, Edwin asked his daughter to waltz. A few fans were fluttered disapprovingly, heads bent together, for the handsome woman in black satin should, according to some people, be home by the hearth with her daguerrotypes of her dead loved ones.

Katherine glanced over at Angela. Her grandmother stood tall, watching the fine figure of her husband sweeping the glowing Suzanna about the floor. Something glistened in Angela's eyes, reflecting the light from the enormous chandelier above them. Katherine felt a warm pricking behind her own lids and turned to watch her mother and grandfather, the affection in their gaze that seemed to warm all the room, include all the friends gathered there.

We'll survive, she thought. *We're made of the stuff that can survive anything. Even Mama. Her strength is deceptive, not obvious on the surface, to grate against people as I know mine does; but it's there, all the same.*

A dark dinner jacket moved in front of her, obscuring the view of the dancers who were beginning to join Edwin and Suzanna on the floor.

"May I have the pleasure of this dance, Mrs Carron?"

She looked up into the dark eyes. "Oh, Rafe . . ." she murmured, her gaze unconsciously seeking for Teddi against the few black-gowned figures on the dance floor.

"Miss Edwina is dancing with Luke Murchison," Rafe said, and Katherine saw that this was true. Edwina was laughing at something Luke was saying . . .

"Come."

She was drawn inexorably onto the floor.

It had been so long since she had waltzed—a ball at Brendan Kelehan's country place, Avonwood, in County Wicklow, more than a year before. Oliver had disappeared early in the evening, to discuss politics with Daniel Hutton and several Wicklow Fenians. Brendan had rescued Katherine from a heavy-footed Church of Ireland minister from Greystones and had danced most of the evening with her . . .

"Katey, I want to see you, alone—and very soon. Can you meet me later . . . ?"

"Rafe, this is absurd . . ." She lowered her voice as another couple swirled past them. "Do you have *any* feelings for Edwina? What would she say to this persistent flirtation of yours?"

The dark eyes appeared, suddenly, to turn black.

"An excellent description, if you wish to demean what I'm feeling. 'A persistent flirtation . . .' "

"What else am I to think . . . ?"

His voice came tightly. "Nearly six years, Katey—no mere flirtation can be so persistent . . ."

"You have my little sister trusting you, believing that you're a mature man whom she can rely on, build her life around. And I come back to the Southern Highlands and you're murmuring inferences that I've blighted your life, and hinting that you'd switch allegiances if I gave you the slightest encouragement. Look at your reputation, Rafe—there's not a woman or girl in this room between fifteen and forty that you haven't tried to seduce. What reason do I have for believing you? And why should I want to?''

Rafe was silent, gazing over her head as they danced; only the slight pressure on her hand and her back betraying his effort at control.

Katherine's voice had been low, but now, in the silence, she was furious with herself. She should have laughed at him, made him laugh at himself . . . But no. There was Edwina to think of. Better to face him now, let him know that she had no need for this kind of amusement.

For he had spoilt everything. A slight, friendly bantering would have been permissable; she could not deny that she was flattered by his attentions. But he had demanded too much; the delicate code of behaviour between sister- and brother-in-law—should it come to that—was in danger.

Katherine's gaze sought Teddi's, who smiled at her over the ample biceps of Luke Murchison. A conspiratorial smile, *Isn't Rafe wonderful? Aren't I lucky? Please approve of him!* All these messages were written on the lovely young face.

Oh, Teddi. Katherine felt a great sadness suddenly weighing her down. *He's going to break your heart. Now—or for the rest of your life, should you marry him.*

"There's nothing I can say, is there?" Rafe said quietly. "Nothing I can say or do . . .''

She was saved from making a rejoinder by the music gliding into a silence, brief, and ending abruptly with the polite clapping from the dancers.

Katherine turned towards her chair, but found no hand beneath her elbow. Rafe had not moved, but was gazing with interest at the large double doors leading to the hall.

A crowd of people had gathered there, and before Katherine could discover what had happened, Edwina had given a cry of excitement, had fled across the room.

The group of neighbours and friends parted, and Marcus Prescott, in his evening dress and looking as fit and urbane as he ever had, was scooping up his youngest daughter into an embrace.

Katherine was one of the few people who turned immediately to see Suzanna's reaction, and for that Katherine was glad. Her mother's face was a white mask of unforgiving animosity. It almost frightened Katherine, but even as she gazed, Edwin took his daughter's arm and Angela moved across the floor to flank her daughter. The three exchanged a look—Katherine could not read it, but it disturbed her greatly. Something was very wrong . . .

But Suzanna was moving forward and on her face, on the faces of her parents, smiles born of generations of good breeding were firmly in place.

As Katherine watched, Marcus, better prepared than his wife, stepped forward, kissed her on the cheek, stood holding her hands— and they gazed into each other's eyes with that communion of spirits that only a husband and wife can share, wordless, yet pregnant with emotion and feeling known only to themselves.

Marcus turned to take Angela's hand, then Edwin's, and it was seeing this guarded welcome from her grandfather that drove all family tensions immediately from her mind.

Of all the times for her father to come. Edwin would talk to him. Marcus would ask questions, demand, command, take control. Katherine all but stamped her foot in annoyance that all her plans for her land investment might be pirated, lovingly, by her father. For he was back with, she could tell, all the old confidence, authority, the benevolent enthusiasm of a despot returning from exile.

She had half-turned away. She would have to fight him, that was all. Argue and defend her right to her independence, her right to make her own mistakes . . . How could a day that had begun so well deteriorate so . . .

The commotion at the door had held her attention, and she had no idea that her father had not been alone. Now, with a shock that robbed her almost of the will to keep standing, she had turned to find, only three couples away and gazing directly at her, a tall figure in an expensive and fashionably-tailored evening suit, the black cloth setting off the bright silver of his hair. Her brain denied it. It had to be a mistake. But it was not. Here was her father, touching Brendan Kelehan lightly on the shoulder, leading him forward to meet her.

Fourteen

'An old friend to see you, Katey." Her father was ignorantly, inordinately pleased with himself, her look of what must have been blank and utter disbelief would be gratifying.

"Suzanna . . ." Gratefully she watched her father turn and introduce "a close friend of Katherine and her late husband—Brendan Kelehan." The very sound of the words on her father's tongue made her wince. She could not look up, gazed in the spaces between them all, hearing the pleased murmurs of greetings going on and on all about her.

"Katherine . . ." her father's voice, "are you feeling well?"

"Of course, Father." A bright voice issuing from her throat of its own volition. "How nice to see you again, Mr Kelehan. Please forgive me—the room is very close . . ."

"It is very warm . . ." Brendan's voice. Deep and rich and with that faint softening of the vowels that she would never have noticed were they not outside Ireland. Yet a cultured voice, its timbre distinct, and the laughter there beneath its surface, hidden from everyone around them but herself who was, after all, the cause of the secret mirth.

"Mrs Carron," the deep-set grey eyes were solicitous, "perhaps you might like some fresh air . . ."

Oh, the kindly tone. And there was nothing she could do—except perhaps cling to Rafe Huckstable's arm. He might protect her; he was gazing at Brendan Kelehan with a look of brooding suspicion.

But of course she did nothing of the sort. Brendan's hand was beneath her arm, he was murmuring, "It's so wonderful to see you again . . . Dublin—wasn't it? Just before my last business trip to Boston . . ."

Smiling groups of people were parting for them, glances, admiring and curious, followed the tall man beside her as they moved to one of the french doors.

Katherine almost fled out the doors onto the verandah, groped along the wall and sat down in one of the large cane chairs. There were some seconds' pause, then the french doors closed, and leisurely footsteps approached.

The cane squeaked behind her as he leaned his forearms on the high, rounded back of the chair. He sighed. From here, on the first floor, one could see the lights that bordered the long driveway—it was a pretty sight.

But the seconds passed into minutes, and though she tried, all rational thought had deserted her. Had she really been thinking, only seconds before she saw him, that the evening had been spoilt? It had been nothing, *nothing*, compared to this.

"You *are* quite well?" The voice came gently from the shadows behind her.

"Yes. Thank you." She took a deep breath, it shook a little, and she hoped he did not notice. "It was such a shock—seeing you here. I was going to write to you in the next few days . . ."

"Were you?"

"Yes. I thought you were in Boston . . ."

"No. I've been in Italy."

"Oh? When? I mean . . ."

"I left about two weeks after you. We had good winds, once we crossed the equator, and made excellent time."

The voice was well-modulated; she realised that it gave nothing away, had never given anything away.

"Why were you in Italy? It almost seems . . ." and she stopped.

"It almost seems," he said, "as if I were following you."

"Yes," she said, her voice small.

A silence. It was cold here on the verandah, but she knew they could not leave, not yet.

There was a soft thump, as of a fist coming down hard on the back of the chair, and she started. "Why didn't you write to tell me about Christopher? Why didn't you tell me about Oliver? Dear God, Katherine—I'd have come, no matter what . . ."

"I didn't think!" She was disturbed by the sudden passion in his voice. "I ran!" The word came from her before she could stop it, and she cursed herself. "I . . . didn't know where I was going, but I couldn't go *back*."

"You couldn't go back—yet you came here."

She wished he would move, come to stand in front of her, let her see her adversary, for that was what he had become. A spectre from a past she wanted to put from her forever; yet this was Brendan, whom she had trusted, who knew her better than anyone now Oliver was gone. It was hard to be cruel, hard even to defend herself.

"I had to come home. I thought I could find some sort of healing here. To find out who I am, by seeing . . . where I came from, I suppose, the woman I was."

He made no answer.

"Brendan? Why did you come here? How did you know where to find me?"

"I remembered your father's name. It wasn't difficult to make enquiries and find Prescott, Mitchell and Co. Your father was almost as surprised to see me as you were—but a little more pleased, I think. He said he was going back to Kangaroo Valley in a few days, but put the journey forward, knowing we could catch up with you all here."

He sighed. "And why did I come? I've asked myself that many times. To be blunt, the main reason was to save your pretty little neck."

As she began to turn in her chair he stepped out from behind it, sauntered over to the verandah rail, leaning back against it, arms folded.

"How could you be such a little fool?" he asked.

She straightened in her chair. "Did you come halfway around the world to insult me?"

"Stop it, Kate. Hasn't there been enough pretence between us? I want to help you now, but I can't if you're going to be wilfully obtuse."

She stared at the still figure, and felt some indefinable difference in the relationship. There was a tension to the man that she had never known before, a sharpness of tone that he had never used with her in the past.

"I'm not being obtuse," she said crossly. It hurt her, somehow, this underlying estrangement between them, this cool vigilance in Brendan that she had never seen before. "I'm sorry if I was taken aback when I saw you—it was shock, that's all. It brought a lot of sudden memories back—the last time I saw you, your wounded arm—it was the day Oliver was arrested . . ."

"The day you told me that you had two thousand pounds of Fenian funds."

She stared at him. "Two . . . The money? The money left with Oliver . . . You're here because of *that*?"

And still he did not move. He leaned almost negligently against the wooden balustrade, his eyes in shadow.

"Is that *all*?" she persisted. "But I don't have it. I put it into a strongbox at Lloyds in Dublin just before I left, and I gave the key to Daniel Hutton's sister."

Brendan took a deep breath and exhaled it slowly. "You gave the key of the safety deposit box to Daniel Hutton's sister," he repeated reflectively.

"Yes, she said she'd find some way of asking Daniel who should have it. It was too difficult for me, by then to know who had been arrested and who hadn't—and I never knew just who might be an informer . . ."

"But you trusted Bridie Hutton . . ."

"I had to trust someone. You were gone—I had no one to turn to." She stopped, looked up at the stony figure at the railing. She said softly, "You believe me, don't you?"

"No," he said quietly, "I'm afraid I don't."

She stood up, took two steps forward until she faced him. "It's the truth. Write to Bridie . . ."

"I don't have to. I shall write to our contact in Dublin and he can question her. I think she'll disclaim any knowledge of a key to a Lloyds strongbox."

She could not believe that it could hurt so much. His callous aloofness was bad enough, but that he could doubt her, after all they had shared together . . . "Do the years of friendship mean nothing to you, Brendan? Your kindness to Christopher and myself when Oliver was . . . busy, distracted . . . Can you visit my house with the freedom of . . . of my brother for five years, and then not know me?"

He reached out and took her by her upper arms; the grip hurt, although the voice seemed as relaxed and negligent as before.

"I think, Mrs Carron, that you are an extremely beautiful thief. And, I'm sad to say, in your efforts to keep your ill-gotten gains, you've turned into a first-class, albeit charming, liar as well."

Her hand had come up to his face before she could stop it—would have stopped it if she could, for it only seemed a childish, futile gesture. He had not changed his expression as he caught her four fingers in a grip that brought an unconscious cry to her lips.

"Don't you understand . . ."

"Let me go . . ."

His other hand was at her back, drawing her in towards him as she tried to pull away. He was very close to her as he said, "Don't you understand the men you're dealing with? You've heard Oliver and myself talk often enough of what happened to known informers, to those couriers who tried to disappear with papers or money belonging to the Brotherhood. Do you think that you're far enough away to be safe, Kate? You're not. You're known in Dublin and

you're known in Boston and New York. I haven't had a chance
to make contact with any of the movement in Sydney, yet, but when
I do, you can rest assured they already know about you, too. They
want their money back. If they can get it back, I might, just might,
be able to convince them that they don't need the unfavourable press
that will come if they kill you."

She was shaken, tried to turn away, to collect her thoughts, but
he still held her fast. "Brendan . . ."

When he kissed her she was completely taken aback; there was
a threat there, in the set face and shadowy eyes, but she had no
idea that he would act like this. And what surprised her further
was her reaction to that kiss. Her body still pressed against his, she
had no balance, no leverage with which to pull sharply away, and
with the sudden rush of desire that filled her, she could not have
pulled back had she wished to.

It was madness; she was frightened; *he* was frightening her, and
she knew, with all her knowledge of him, that he spoke the truth
and she was in danger. It was a paradox that the unheralded threat
was relayed to her in the person of the man she trusted perhaps
more than any other man on earth.

And how, in the midst of telling her that there were dangerous
men bent on harming her, could they suddenly find themselves in
such an embrace?

The opening of the door to the ballroom startled them; when
Rafe, followed by Edwina and Fleur Barton, stepped out onto the
verandah, Katherine and Brendan were standing a few feet apart,
gazing over the garden.

"Are you all right, Katey?" Edwina trotted up to her.

"Yes, of course," Katherine smiled. "Mr Kelehan and I were talking
about old friends in Dublin. Were we missed? There, Mr Kelehan,
not ten minutes in the room and you're the centre of supposition
already."

It was odd, this feeling of gaiety that suddenly claimed her; she
would not worry about the future—she must simply struggle to hold
onto the present. That would be difficult enough.

They returned to the ballroom and there were no further
opportunities to be alone that evening. Brendan danced twice with
her, but they talked only of her family, Joe's death and Katherine's
hope that her mother and the girls could return soon to Sydney.

He danced once with Suzanna, and obviously charmed her; once
with Laura, and three times with Fleur Barton.

"She and Mr Kelehan make a fine couple . . ." a voice behind her. Katherine had been thinking just that, for Brendan's natural ability to set people at their ease had brought a smile to Fleur's face, and the dancing had added a touch of warmth to the normally pale cheeks.

Katherine turned towards the voice. Viola Barton tapped her on the arm with her fan. "I hope you don't mind, Mrs Carron, I was just saying to your Mama that my Fleur and your Mr Kelehan make a fine couple."

"Why should I mind, Mrs Barton? Your daughter is very attractive and anyone would admit Mr Kelehan is a handsome man." She made herself smile.

What would she do with him? she wondered, turning back to the dancers. He must be sent packing as soon as possible, back to Sydney and off to Boston as soon as she could convince him that he was wasting his time. And yet . . .

Her heart ached a little as she watched him. They had always been close friends—as close as Katherine ever allowed herself to be with anyone outside her immediate family. And, married as she had been, it had sometimes still been hard to see him with other women. She had felt guilty when the few relationships he had indulged in over the years had come to their natural conclusion—guilty because she had been pleased, relieved. He was a distant but luminous satellite to her life, but she had always known her life would have been darker had he changed orbit—made a new path away from her. For she had always felt safe with him; closer to her than anyone over the past few years, with the exception of her husband and son, it was, now, as if he brought with him something of those comfortable, relaxed days in Dublin. She had forgiven him a great deal; counterbalanced against his behaviour at the time of her wedding were the many years of his kindness and support. Now, frightened and grieving over the happenings of the last few months, she was beginning to feel more and more pleased to see him by the minute. This misunderstanding about the money would all be settled very soon. Brendan could cope with any of the threats from the Fenian Brotherhood. And it was with a strange thrill of the realization of her power that the thought came to her that she could cope with Brendan.

But he must leave. Her life had been organized, she had plans, it had all been decided . . . *he has no place here.*

And yet here he was. Perhaps the question of the missing two thousand pounds was an excuse . . . it had to be. There were Fenian sympathizers in Sydney who would, had the order come, have found her out and questioned her. If they were convinced she possessed this money—and it was a fortune—then they had not chosen the best man for the job. Whoever was planning on harming her, it was not Brendan Kelehan.

No, she smiled. He had come because he wished to come. And watching the handsome head bent politely to catch the shyly murmured words of Fleur Barton, Katherine knew she was not sorry. Plans were made to be changed, adapted, she thought, and then pulled herself up abruptly. What was she thinking of? This was Brendan . . . Brendan . . .

He looked up then. The grey eyes flicked over the crowd, and found hers, and lit up with amusement and fondness and . . .

She swallowed, hard. Mrs Barton, beside her, was speaking, but she heard no words. Brendan held her gaze, and she could not look away from him, nor deny any longer what the years and the thousands of miles could not suppress. *I love him*, she thought. *Brendan. Brendan. I always have loved him.* There was simply no room for it, no place it could grow and be recognized, where it would not be improper, sordid. Until now.

She slept alone that night; while the dancing had been in progress Angela had ordered the servants to move Katherine's things to one of the smaller guest rooms at the back of the house, so that Marcus and Suzanna could have the larger room to themselves.

Brendan had the guest room next to hers.

And Katherine could not sleep.

Love had come twice in her life—or she had thought so at the time. Yet her feelings for Rafe Huckstable during those giddy weeks in Balmain could only be described, now, as infatuation. And Oliver? More than physical attraction—but there was no denying that had she known of his secret before marrying him, there would have been no love, no marriage. As it was, she had loved him until she had found out the truth—and had then continued loving him, despite the disillusionment, the hurt.

This was different again. A comfortable thing—for she knew this man extremely well—but exciting, for all that. Dangerous. It was . . . thrilling. She laughed aloud, and put her hand to her mouth, suddenly remembering Viola Barton in the room to one side of her, and the very man concerned, in the other. She rolled over, feeling as young and foolish as a girl, and smothering her sudden laughter in her pillow.

The childish joy, the unaccustomed sense of wonder, could not last—she knew this. The following day she rose early and went out into the gardens, telling herself it could not last. The frost on the grass sent myriad colours shooting back at her from the sun, wistful reminders of the necklace she had given up. Cobwebs, miracles of symmetry strung between the bare branches, were hung with dew and so fragile, so wondrously perfect, that she stopped at each one to study it before going on.

There was no-one else about. No-one disturbed her meanderings through the old gardens, down to the birch wood.

The playhouse was built like a miniature Dovewood in shape, with a verandah around three sides of the single room, the wrought-iron lace work of its trim identical to that of the main house. The stone-coloured walls, the dark green of the trim, had cracked and peeled long ago, and the roof of corrugated iron, once grey-painted to mimic the slate of Dovewood, had become earth-coloured, streaked through with rust.

Katherine loved it; walking about the little building she saw with a kind of fierce pleasure how the crocuses and snowdrops the three sisters had planted long ago were even now thrusting upwards amongst the hardy, native grasses about the brick foundations. There would be poppies and marigolds in the summer—and at the back of the playhouse, a climbing rose that now all but covered that part of the roof would burst into creamy sweet-smelling blossoms.

The door was unlocked, as always. Katherine, knowing where each small object belonged, moved in the dimness to one of the windows and opened its dusty casement to let in the air and the light.

The bare branches of the silver birches outside made moving shadows in the shafts of sunshine that poured into the little room. Dust lay everywhere, swirling upwards where her trailing skirts had disturbed the quiet years of neglect. There were four little wooden stools, and Katherine seated herself on one of them precariously; her voluminous skirts made it hard to find the tiny surface, and the state of the Lilliputian furnishings, due to woodworm and damp, made confident movement a risky business. But the little stool held.

Nothing had changed, she thought, gazing about her. There was the table, covered with oilcloth that had once been painted pale blue, she was sure, but there was no indication of this in the streaky grey surface that now confronted her. A tiny vase of cranberry glass, very dirty with the mummified remains of some long dead bouquet, was placed in the table's centre, and to one side lay a blue enamel candle-holder with its stub of yellow tallow.

There was a small dresser, no more than three feet high, against the wall, and amongst the cobwebs she could see the blue floral tea-set, made of porcelain, brought by Edwin from France for the eldest girl, Katherine, when she had been born. All the girls had played with it; there had been forty-two pieces to it, Suzanna was fond of remembering, but it was sadly depleted now, such was the carelessness of the little occupants' housekeeping. In the corner an imitation fireplace had been built of timber, cunningly painted to resemble bricks, with a small stove made with some pride by Edwin himself, from scraps of tin, and painted black, complete with tiny mock wood box and oven.

There were framed samplers on the walls—simple alphabets, as the girls' best work had been kept in the house; and a picture of a dark friendly shape, barely discernible as being a dog, a portrait by a youthful Lucy, entitled simply and mysteriously, "Muffy."

Katherine's favourite place had always been the bookshelf; here several old picture books were kept, each frontispieced by childish printing: *Lucinda May Gordon*—that had been Aunt Lucy, who had died of appendicitis at sixteen; *Katherine Ann Gordon*—Aunt Katherine, killed in a carriage accident when she was nineteen; *Suzanna Angelina Gordon*—Mama. Katherine traced the writing, smaller, neater than her sisters' though she had been the youngest, and smiled, trying to imagine the little girl her mother must have been.

There was a magic about this place, as if something of the three children remained here, where they had spent so many happy hours. Undoubtedly Laura and Edwina had sensed it as children, but the feeling of other-worldliness bothered them in a way that had never affected Katherine. "Haunted . . ." the younger girls would shiver and go off to play among the shrubs or on the broad expanses of the sunny lawn. "Haunted" for Katherine brought no feelings of terror. "Peopled" she would have said, "visited". Their laughter seemed to ring just beyond her hearing, their chatter and the patter of small shoes on the verandahs seemed to have just ceased as she recognized it. She used to bring her own books to read here, away from Joe's boisterousness and the girls' clamouring, and would find herself looking up from her book, straining to hear or regain an echo, already fading, already gone.

She had brought her problems here also, over the years. It was her own place, her secret from the time she could clamber, one step at a time, up to the verandah. This time she did not expect any easy answer to her quandary, it was too complex; but she stayed, seated on the little stool, knees drawn up, gazing at the decaying, well-loved objects and sneezing occasionally from the disturbed dust.

There was no room in her life for Brendan. He brought with him too many memories. And yet . . . his kindness and dependable strength had been her mainstay all through the past five difficult years; the newly acknowledged attraction to him, repressed for so long, was a wondrous thing that warmed a heart that she had begun to believe was past feeling, past caring for a man.

I've grown cold, she thought with some surprise. The realization did not please her. No, perhaps she was not cold; perhaps she had had too high expectations of men all her life, and not caring to come to know any of them really well, had become an easy victim of her own delusions on meeting Oliver.

He tried hard to make me love him. He tried hard to love me. It seemed perfect, because Oliver made it perfect. I was his one chance for normality, a dispassionate decision born of the loneliness and desperation of a sensitive man running from himself. She put her head down on her arms, resting on her knees. It was hard to bear these thoughts, coming so clearly to her now, as if her very life had been confined to a small room of miniatures such as this and she had suddenly thrown open a grimy window and gained perspective. It was frightening, confronting her own mistakes, her early aloofness from young men of her own age and background, the ill-fated flirtation with Rafe, the flight from her own country to the fabled exoticism of the Old World, culminating in the naive passion for the man Oliver so wished himself to be.

If she did marry Brendan . . . if she did, there could be more children—another son . . . a daughter . . . She was holding her stomach tightly, holding the tears, with her longing, deep within her.

A memory, vivid, came suddenly to her, of moving about the little rooms in Chatham Row, her body swollen with the unknown stranger that would be Christopher, smiling and chatting to a visiting Brendan, conscious—yes, conscious even then—of the solicitous tenderness in his glance that followed her like a hand upon her shoulder. It had begun then, she thought with a shock, the unwilling, painful realisation that to this man, her husband's friend, she was beautiful even in her final stage of life-giving; while her husband, though he tried his best to hide it and was as courteous and thoughtful as ever, made her feel, with his every avoided glance, as if she was flawed, distorted.

She had begun, then, to shut Brendan out, closed her mind to him even as he tried harder after the birth, to be all that Oliver could need, to bring him back to her. She had told herself, for a long time, that she had been successful. To fail, to confront his forced kindness juxtaposed with Brendan's loyal caring, would have been more than she could bear.

And now?

Now, if she wished to drive herself insane, she could sit here and imagine what might have happened if she had obeyed her father and waited a few months before marrying Oliver.

No. It was too late. Her restlessness made her stand, for the little room had become confining. She looked about it, almost in apology, before shutting the door and heading back to the lawn between the silver-grey trunks of birch and the little overgrown orchard.

The birds were awake now, the magpies carolling from the eucalypts and pine trees that edged the acres of gardens. She slowed her pace as she clambered over the fallen picket fence and came out on to one of the paths, breathing more deeply, her mind still in turmoil but a decision made, the only decision possible.

Brendan belonged to her past. For her own peace of mind, here in this place of relative safety, she could not allow him to intrude upon the life she had begun to build for herself, the plans she had begun to make.

"You look very militant."

She whirled, startled, then relaxed. Her father strolled towards her, having appeared around a turn in the path after she had come onto it.

She studied his face as he approached; she had not been mistaken last night in the flattering candlelight. He looked so much healthier than he had all those weeks ago, when she had arrived at the townhouse. His face was a better colour and he had lost the puffy, fleshy look about the eyes and jowls. The dark grey coat and waistcoat contrasted with the cream trousers and complimented the traces of silver in his hair.

"And you look very distinguished," she said honestly.

He could never look abashed, but a trace of wryness was evident in his speech and his tone of voice. "Much better than the day you arrived, eh? Well, you always had a salubrious effect on those around you. You seem to have organized your mother and the girls very well."

And you don't know the half of it, she thought, as they fell into step together.

She was pleased to have him with her; it would be much better if he could volunteer the information she wanted to hear, that he was returning to the Valley indefinitely. But Marcus' mind was obviously pursuing a different tack.

"So the young man's come to find you." Marcus scowled beneath his hat brim towards the house, as if he could see the enigmatic Brendan through the wall. "Had you thought this might occur?"

"No," she answered candidly, "I was extremely shocked to see him here."

"So was I, when Robin Mitchell announced his arrival in the office on Thursday. Katey," and he looked worried, genuinely concerned when he turned to her, "has there been anything between you? I'll make no moral judgements nor lectures, if you're honest with me."

Katherine was completely taken aback. "I shall be honest with you. I was loyal to Oliver; even to his memory. I never encouraged Brendan Kelehan in any way whatever, at any time."

Marcus nodded, the keen hazel eyes scanning her face. "I thought I'd better ask—though I knew it would be out of character for you to form such an alliance."

She pondered this. "Why?" she asked finally.

"You're too honest," he said flatly. "So this *tendresse* has been simmering in young Kelehan all these years, has it?" He gave a silent whistle, and his air of quiet amusement irritated Katherine. Before she could comment, he said, "What are you going to do about it?"

"Do?" she blinked, "I shan't do anything at all. He's only visiting Australia. When he's seen enough gum trees, kangaroos and koalas, he'll go home to Boston."

"Boston? He tells me home is County Wicklow."

"Well, yes. But he's been in Boston for some months."

"Why is that?" Marcus's footsteps were slowing, he was interested.

"Didn't he say? I expect it's business—and he has relatives in Boston."

"Nothing to do with the troubles in Ireland, is it? I took him to my club while we were in Sydney and old Hargreaves—he was a magistrate in Belfast for years—started haranguing him on Ireland's politics the minute I introduced them. Kelehan amazed me, tied the old bigot in verbal knots—knew far too much for a bookish lawyer-cum-country squire. What was most interesting was his anger. Not obvious to just anyone—but I always like to study the men I'm dealing with, and inside, Kelehan was raging. It was as if there was much more at stake than a simple discussion with a snobbish old windbag. What he was talking about had touched his own experience. What was it?"

Yes, Marcus was returning to his old self. Katherine smiled bitterly; the period of his dark introspection after Joe's death was obviously

over. What the effect of her sudden arrival and housewifely ways
had begun, the puzzle of Brendan had continued. Marcus was
intrigued, he had a new interest. It was this, as much as a re-awakening
of family responsibilities that had brought him back to the Highlands.
She had been right to be wary of him, he would be as manipulative
an influence in her life as he had ever been. But she was not, at
the moment at least, resentful. It was enough to see his intellect
sparking—whatever the cause—and to see him here, back with
Suzanna, where he belonged.

"Well?" he prompted.

"I don't know if I should talk about Brendan. Perhaps you should
ask him about his politics . . ."

"I know all about his politics," Marcus said impatiently. "He's
an anarchist. Or would be, if he were given power in Ireland. I
presume he's a member of this Fenian Brotherhood you read so much
about these days. What I was wondering was, is it purely intellectual
or is he capable of getting out there with a green flag in one hand
and a pistol in the other?"

Katherine hesitated, and Marcus noted it.

"Ah," he said. "I thought so. Needn't have asked, really. You
can see it in him, some turbulence just below the surface . . ."

"Nonsense," she said, "I've never seen that in all the years I've
known him."

Marcus shot her a strange look. "No," he said carefully, "but
he's a man who prides himself on his restraint. He regards himself
as very conservative, I daresay. But I still feel that the well-educated
exterior masks an extremely forceful individual."

"Do you mean violent?"

Marcus looked thoughful. "If he were pressed, yes."

Katherine had always had faith in her father's judgement of
people—barring her wilfulness over Oliver—and despite her own
knowledge of Brendan, she felt an odd prickling of apprehension.
He had, after all, cared enough for the Fenian Brotherhood to place
himself in physical danger on that rainy night in Dublin. What length
would he go to if he believed that she possessed the missing Fenian
funds?

Suddenly the romantic notions she had held since the previous
evening seemed hollow and foolish in the extreme. He had made
no declaration to her, had been, in fact, remarkably cool, considering
the amount of trouble he had taken to find her.

"What's the matter, Katey?" Her father's voice was serious, his
gaze probing. "What's between you and Brendan Kelehan?"

"Really, Father—he was Oliver's friend, that's all. I told you, I'm as surprised to see him here as you are . . ."

"And now?"

"What do you mean?"

"Are you going to encourage him or not? For it's plain to me, if it isn't to you, that he's come all this way for one reason. He's not about to give up easily . . . What's the matter?" he asked abruptly.

"Nothing . . . I simply had not expected . . ."

"It's more than that, you're genuinely frightened, you looked at me just then as if you'd seen a ghost . . ."

She took a deep breath. "I'm disturbed to think you may be right—how tragic if Mister Kelehan has a *tendresse* for me, and has come halfway round the world to ask me to marry him . . . why, father, it's ridiculous! And yet I *am* very fond of him—he's a dear, loyal friend of many years standing, and I'd hate to see him hurt . . ." She looked at her father suddenly, "do you think perhaps you should speak to him—delicately, of course."

"Well," her father pondered, "it may come down to that—but don't send him packing too soon, mind—as I told you a few weeks ago—prophetic, wasn't I?—I rather like the man. Let him stay for a few months, to realize that you're far too stubborn and independent and insolent to suit him. Not that I think it would do any good," he lamented mildly, as she was about to protest, "or I'd be trying to convert his interest towards Laura or Teddi. I'd almost prefer an Irish Catholic for a son-in-law to Rafe Huckstable or Stephen Brody. But there you are—willy-nilly, you have a suitor, Kate. And after three days in his company, I don't think Petruchio came better armed or more determined."

Her father was grinning, enjoying this development immensely. Katherine, trying to talk seriously to him through his humour, was interrupted by the bell for breakfast. They turned towards the house, Marcus whistling irritatingly all the way.

To excuse herself from breakfast would have looked strange and heightened her father's interest and curiosity. Katherine felt secure, beneath her exasperation, for she knew that Marcus did not believe for an instant that she would accept more than friendship from Brendan Kelehan. No, that did not bother her. It was her father's innocently chosen words, *he's come all this way for one reason—and he's not about to give up easily.*

And, violent?

If he were pressed.

Fifteen

It was best not to think about it. Live for the moment, gazing about at the relatives and friends peering beneath the silver dish-covers at the sideboards, or sitting sleepily subdued over their bacon and eggs, muffins or toast, delicately dissecting the events of the previous evening as they dissected their baked tomatoes and kippers.

She loved them all, she thought, with the feelings of one who realizes he is under threat of some sort. Yet—and here Brendan Kelehan entered the room as if on cue and her heart lurched, pulling her gaze down to her own plate—yet she loved him also, the very cause of her indecision and distress.

He had not yet seen her, was answering a "Good morning" from Edwin and Angela, and was being asked to join them at their end of the table. Katherine concentrated on Laura and Edwina's chatter and did not look up again until Brendan's voice, beside her, startled her.

"Good morning, Mrs Carron . . . Mrs Prescott . . . Sir . . ." and, nodding, smiling his charming smile, he addressed all the family— and moved on.

"Such a nice young man . . ." Suzanna murmured, and Katherine refused to look up at her mother, knowing that the wise green eyes on the opposite side of the table were eloquent with unspoken dialogue, and almost as much teasing mischief as her husband had displayed only a few minutes earlier in the garden. She cut savagely into a sausage that she did not want and thought crossly that her parents had undoubtedly stayed awake talking last night, Suzanna questioning Marcus closely about the Irishman. Suzanna would delight in this. Brendan's very familiarity with her life these past five years would make Suzanna feel safe, would prove his stability in her eyes, even as it made Katherine uncomfortable and apprehensive.

She stole a glance at him. Having charmed Marcus and Suzanna, Brendan, with his quiet ability to listen effectively, was gazing upon Edwin's face, watchful, absorbent as a sponge.

"Oh, Katey, I'm so happy for you."

She turned with a withering look upon Edwina, who, seeing it, continued hurriedly, "Oh, I know it's too early, but . . . Laura and

I think it's just *wonderful*. How devoted he must be to you. It must be so gratifying to know already that he's so loyal." Her gaze flickered over to the Huckstables' end of the table. "I wish . . ." she stopped on this rather wistful note, and when Katherine, still gazing at her with the same fixed, icy stare, did not respond, Edwina lowered her gaze and her attention to her scrambled eggs.

Brendan and Edwin had been joined by Mrs Barton and Fleur, and as the men stood to seat the women, Katherine could not help but notice the smile, the slight flush upon Fleur's face as Brendan pushed her chair in for her. For a moment, despite the sombre clothing, she was almost beautiful, and it came to Katherine that Fleur had had that same look of happiness, of radiant expectation, the night before. She thought hard; had it been there before Brendan arrived, or did it materialize as suddenly and mysteriously as the Irishman within their midst? The evening had become a blur for Katherine, she had been too concerned with her own feelings to notice any of the other guests. One thing was certain; whatever had lit Fleur Barton last night, this morning it was Brendan Kelehan.

Katherine sighed, dragging her eyes from the sight of Fleur gazing tremulously at Brendan. He was answering some question put to him by Edwin Gordon. Fleur seemed to study every pore of Brendan's face, and—foolish girl!—when Brendan glanced at her, the wrapt, dewy look did not heave her features as she returned his smile. How naive, Katherine sniffed, to make herself so obvious. Really, it was painful to watch. Her mother should speak to her.

It was not easy after breakfast to escape from the good-natured crowd of relatives and friends, but she managed, when several of the ladies asked Angela to show them the garden, to find a retreat in one of the deep window seats in the library. She found a copy of Gould's *Handbook of the Birds of Australia*, published only the year before, and turned sideways, leaned back against one wall, put her feet up on the seat before her, and flicked unseeingly through the pages of illustrations.

She did not care what he did. Only that he should leave as soon as possible. How fortunate that she had *not* been foolish enough to choose him, all those years ago. "His devotion . . . his loyalty . . ." Teddi had cooed. He who believed her to be a thief, who chased her halfway round the world on the request of some faceless dealers in guns and violence, who accused her of stealing two thousand pounds.

She found she was gripping the book hard; how much worse it would be if he knew about the necklace. If he doubted her word now, after all they had been through over the years, after she had risked her life and Christopher's to see him onto that train to Cork City and to freedom . . . If he doubted her now—what would he say to the coincidence of her grandfather attempting to sell, on her behalf, a necklace worth precisely—for she had the receipt from the jeweller—two thousand and fifteen English pounds, three shillings and eleven pence.

She could only hope that Edwin would not broadcast her plans— and only last night, a few seconds before Brendan had entered her life, she had worried about opposition from her father! No, this was worse, she thought, drawing up her knees to hug them, scowling out the window, past the wrought-iron lace work of the verandahs to the clear, cold morning. It mattered that Brendan did not believe her. It mattered that he doubted her word.

She sighed. She would have to see him again, as soon as possible, to try to convince him of her innocence . . .

Voices cut across her thoughts, men's voices, and the heavy tread of several pairs of feet approaching along the verandah. There were chairs out there, she knew. She heard the creak of wickerwork, the scuffling of settling feet, a pause in conversation as bodies relaxed, and vision strayed about the surroundings. Pipes were lit, she could hear the soft inhaled *peh, peh, peh*, as the little bowls of fire were sucked into life.

The conversation which must have begun over breakfast continued. Rafe Huckstable was making a comment concerning a Rugby game he had seen recently, and someone, who had recently returned from Melbourne, was trying to convince him of the superiority of a new game, the ground rules even now being laid down in the southern city. "In a pub, you can bet!" Rafe chuckled. The adherent of the new sport, something called Australian Rules, was having a hard time cutting through the laughter to discuss the merits of the game.

She heard her grandfather's voice, bringing up a recent speech by Premier Martin regarding trade levies, and two other men—one sounded like Rupert Huckstable, Rafe's father—talking about the rumours from the north of a further division of territories—northern Queensland wanted separation from the southern part of the state and its capital of Brisbane. "Rough-heads up there," someone murmured. "Let them try it once and they'll be forming little republics all over the north—an intractable lot, Queenslanders. Don't like being organized . . ."

And then, just as she found herself dozing off to sleep, her head on her knees, she heard Kangaroo Valley being mentioned, and came awake, realizing that there was a change in the atmosphere. Only one voice was speaking, that of a newcomer, and all the men were listening.

". . . I don't *know* any more details than that! It's rather a garbled chain of communication, I'm afraid—someone rode for Dr Lang and when he was halfway to the Valley some chap—rough-looking, unkempt—met him on a shaggy pony and told him his services wouldn't be needed—it was just a flesh wound—result of an accident. I ran into Dr Lang in Moss Vale and he told me. No names were given, apparently."

"Sounds like cedar-getters." For the first time, Katherine heard her father's deep, distinctive voice. Though he spoke quietly, meditatively, the other Valley dwellers were more excited.

"Shot . . ." marvelled Rafe, "I must admit I've often thought of taking my gun after them—they're indiscriminate in the way they kill game, and I've seen the erosion in the hills where they've been through and taken every tree—whole hillsides sliding into the creeks—no groundcover can hold the soil and the animals are frightened off—those they haven't shot for their pelts."

His father, a tall, ascetic-looking man with fine features and steely grey hair retreating over a high forehead, murmured, "Koala pelts . . . It's a sad business. I can remember eating koala—native bear, my father called it—when I was a boy. Wouldn't do it now—harmless, good-natured creatures."

"Those were the days when it was necessary to hunt to survive," Marcus put in. "Now we have cattle, sheep, chickens—unlike the cedar-getters. They won't plant crops and, unlike the Woddi Woddi, they'll hunt the game in the Valley until it's gone for good. *Then* they'll move on."

There were unhappy murmurs of agreement from all the men.

"And no name given?" She recognized Luke Murchison's voice now. "Though it does sound like cedar-getters, doesn't it, from the description. They have a tendency to solve their disagreements their own way. I wonder who shot whom?"

"Katherine?"

She turned, the book sliding from benumbed fingers to the carpeted floor with a bump.

"I'm sorry . . . I'm so sorry . . ." Fleur Barton stood there, quite close, misery written in every line of her small frame; she seemed, in her wretched embarrassment, ready to shrivel away and disappear beneath the nearest low-built piece of furniture.

"It's all right, Fleur—it's just that you startled me." Katherine reached for the book just as Fleur bobbed for it. She straightened, stood wringing her hands.

"My father used to say that—he used to say I sneaked about . . . it's just that I move quietly—the carpet is so thick here . . ." She seemed to study the carpet, then raised large grey eyes to Katherine. "I didn't mean to suggest that *you* thought I was sneaking—it's just that—all I meant to say was that I tend to startle people. Sometimes. I move quietly."

There was a pause, Katherine smiled. "Did you wish to speak to me, Fleur?"

"Well . . . yes . . ."

Katherine stood. "Let's go over by the fire, shall we? I was just about to, as the men discussing politics outside were beginning to disturb me."

How easily I lie these days, she thought, leading the way to where a fire burned in the ornate iron and tile fireplace. *I lie quite unconsciously, without thinking. Is it all those years of making excuses for Oliver, to Christopher, to friends, to myself?*

She knelt to place a new log on the fire, and found herself overbalancing dangerously when Fleur tried to help and almost pulled the heavy offcut of eucalyptus log out of her arms.

"I'm sorry . . ."

Katherine placed the log in the grate amid a flurry of sparks, while Fleur danced from one foot to the other.

"Sit down, Fleur—I'm all right, really. It was kind of you to help."

And they were both seated, Katherine studying the woman with a look of polite interest she hoped would disguise her pity and— yes, exasperation. What had the men been discussing? If it concerned the Valley, it concerned her . . . Never mind, she would question her father about this afterwards.

"I . . . I don't know how to begin." Fleur looked miserable, twisting her fingers together in her lap. Katherine, watching them, saw with surprise what beautiful hands they were, long of palm and fingers, pale and unmarked and tapering to shapely, elongated nails. But then, Katherine thought, Fleur was like that; it was as if her self-loathing drew a dark screen about her, hiding her in the shadows that the world, too thoughtless, too busy, could not be bothered to penetrate. And beyond the starting, frightened eyes, the nervously working mouth, was an extremely pretty woman.

"I . . . I'll probably never see him again, but I just might, as we seem to have made so many friends in this area, Mama and I, and we may be back on visits. So . . . I felt I should come to see you, as you've been very kind to Mama and me, and from what everyone is saying, they seem to think that you and he . . . that he's especially . . . I don't want to . . . Oh, dear!"

"Fleur," Katherine said gently, "what are you trying to say?"

Fleur straightened in the high-backed chair; there was an instant's pause, and she said, "I would very much like to know if you have any special affection for Mr Kelehan. I . . . don't mean fondness, you know, I mean the kind of affection that leads one to hope for . . . marriage."

In the silence, a voice, Rafe's? Luke's? separated itself from the low rumblings outside the window, to say loudly, "At a *tavern*? Why didn't you say so? That'd be Radley's—only one tavern in Kangaroo Valley."

Katherine, in her discomfort, her desire to be back, alone, listening in the window seat, found her own fingers knotting together, mirroring Fleur's frantic, nervous twisting. Katherine placed her hands casually on the arms of her chair, made them stay there, in an attitude of calm. "Fleur, this is very strange . . ."

"I know, and in normal cases it wouldn't be any of my business, but, you see, Mr Kelehan asked me for three dances last night, and this morning he asked me to go walking with him in the garden— oh, it was only for a few minutes, but it made me consider . . ."

She lowered her eyes, chewed her lip, made several fresh starts at conversation, while Katherine, mesmerized, could not bring herself to interrupt. Finally, "I am twenty-six years old, Katherine. I have never been married. No one has ever asked me. I've never been out of our home very much in order to meet people, and Papa never allowed Mama or me to entertain. I've never had any friends—until Papa died, in such a terrible, terrible way, so far from home, and everyone in the Valley—and here—has been so kind! This—on top of all the lovely things that have been happening—is almost too much happiness to be borne. Have you ever felt that way? No, I don't expect you have—you're beautiful and a lady, and you've been surrounded with so much love—I don't think you've ever known what it's like to be poor and trapped, and . . . used." The word hung in the air. Fleur was, for once, totally still. Even the pale, working hands were clasped tightly together upon the folds of her black skirt.

"I was always . . . needed. Mama couldn't manage the heavy housework, you see, and she doesn't like crowds, so it's always been up to me to do the shopping, pay the accounts . . . there was never any opportunity to do what *I* wanted to do. I read a great deal. We belong to a circulating library. The lives of the people I read about—that was the only means I had of seeing how other people lived in the outside world. Perhaps it's given me a distorted view— everyone seems . . . so happy. I didn't realise until Father died and we came here, how I resented him—oh, it's wicked to say it, I know, but it's the truth!—I resented him for keeping me away from a normal life, normal friendships."

"Oh, Fleur . . ." Katherine almost rose to go to the young woman, but hesitated, not wishing to appear pitying, and this was a person unused, as yet, to displays of natural affection between friends. She said, instead, "How sad that you didn't have some understanding relatives to stay with—and even sadder that you couldn't simply *talk* to your parents about your needs."

"Oh, but I did. I was quite rebellious as a child. One couldn't win against my father, though." The oval of her face looked pale, pinched, of a sudden. She had been gazing into the hearth, but the eyes seemed to darken and look through the fire, rather than at it.

Into the pause, Katherine said, "Fleur, you weren't misused in any physical way, were you? I mean, your parents didn't beat you?"

"Oh, Mama wouldn't, she's far too good-natured for that. Father . . . he used to say I deserved it. I was wilful and stubborn." She looked up at Katherine. "I always thought I must be. And then I came here and saw how you and your sisters treat your parents— and they you—as if you're equals—loved, and respected . . . and *listened* to. Not treated like some misguided child . . . who's mentally defective in some way.

"So you see . . . everything is new to me. I feel as if I've been released from prison—isn't that a wicked thing to say, only a few weeks after my father's death? But it's true! And I . . . I don't want to make mistakes—I don't want to hurt people, or make enemies. That's . . . that's why I had to ask you that question, before events went any further."

Presumption! The word came tumbling uncontrollably ahead of Katherine's more charitable thoughts. She said, carefully, "There is an old saying, you know, about all being fair in love and war. If I *was* in love with Mr Kelehan—would you then step back and be all coolness, out of loyalty to me?"

Fleur gulped. Put bluntly like this, it was hard to face. "I would try," she answered, "I would do my very best to repel his advances."

The laughter burst from Katherine without warning. She placed her hand over her mouth, turned sideways in her chair and rocked with laughter. It was a good minute before she looked up, and made an instant effort to control herself, seeing the stricken look on Fleur's face.

"Oh, dear . . . oh, Fleur, I *am* sorry . . . but I've known Mr Kelehan for so long, and the thought of us all being involved in a triangle like a dreadful romantic novel is so comical! No, my dear," she grew as serious as her twitching lips would allow, "Should Mr Kelehan fall in love with you, you may respond with whatever degree of enthusiasm you wish. You have my blessing."

There was a second of watchfulness, and Katherine became, in that instant, aware that Fleur's naivete should not be confused with lack of intelligence or perception. The grey eyes told Katherine that Fleur knew she was being mocked. But she smiled, letting the moment pass.

"I am silly, I suppose, and unsophisticated . . . a woman even as much as ten years younger than I would have said nothing . . . but it's as I said, you and your family have been so kind . . ."

"Think no more of it—it's a pleasure for us to have you as our guest. And I hope the future is as bright as you wish it to be." Katherine paused then, feeling she should say something further on the matter. "If nothing eventuates between you and Mr Kelehan, Fleur, you won't be too disappointed, will you? You're a very attractive woman—now you're moving into society at last, I'm sure you'll find a young man with whom to share your life, if that's what you want. In the meantime, make a life for yourself, away from your Mama. A woman owes it to herself to be as self-reliant and independent as she can . . ."

Fleur had stood, and Katherine followed her to the door. She appeared to be listening to Katherine's words, but at the library door, as she crossed the threshold, she paused and looked back, looked Katherine directly in the face, and smiled.

"Oh, I have plans for my life—I shan't go on as I have, don't worry. But neither do I intend to be 'disappointed' as you call it. I think Mr Kelehan has made his feelings clear already, and when he asks me, I intend to marry him."

And she was gone. Katherine could hear the neat little heels and the slur of black taffeta petticoats as she walked. It made Katherine realise that Fleur had always sounded like that when she walked; despite the demure aspect, the little feet had always beat a positive, brisk tattoo on the parquet floors of Barrengarry. Katherine shut the door and walked slowly back to her chair to stare into the fire, uncomfortable with the dawning thought that she might have just been played for a complete fool.

She was still chafing, her head filled with possible rejoinders, *post facto* and useless, when Edwin knocked and entered the library to tell her that he would take her to Moss Vale in an hour's time.

"Everyone's going to a picnic at Bundanoon—not interested in that, are you? Seen it all before, haven't you? Seen one valley, see 'em all. We'll take the brougham in case it rains. Charles'll drive, no sense in all of us getting wet. Wear sensible shoes." And with that statement he shut the door abruptly after himself.

Katherine was glad of her grandfather's timing, although when she met her mother and grandmother on the stairs, they were less pleased, seeing Edwin's decision to take Katherine for company on the business trip as an old man's wilful disregard for Katherine's wishes; but when she had convinced them that she would truly like to see Moss Vale once more, they subsided worriedly into murmurs of what-the-other-guests-would-say.

"By which they mean young Kelehan," Edwin chortled as they set off, warmly tucked beneath travelling rugs, in the comfortable but ancient brougham.

Katherine, conscious of her grandfather's coachman, Charles, close above them, lowered her voice, and hoped her grandfather would do likewise. "Please, Grandpapa, don't be starting . . ."

"Oh, I'm not starting anything—the rest of the household is muttering that you'll be remarried within the year—but I'll want to hear it from you." He turned to her, eyebrows raised.

"Why are you looking like that?" she asked.

"I'm waiting to hear it from you."

"Grandpapa! Stop it! I have no intention of remarrying—not Mr Kelehan, nor anyone else."

"Well, miss, you'd better make sure of that, for if you turn him down there's many a young woman at that party last night who'll be after him like an echidna after ants!"

Katherine wasn't amused. "You mean Miss Barton, in particular . . ."

"I meant all of 'em. You were too busy staring at him yourself last night to see how he made every female head in the place turn round like so many clockwork dolls. But yes, now you mention it, that deceptively prim Miss Barton is making her interest abundantly clear. The excitement is making her pretty—best watch her, m'dear."

Katherine felt besieged. Why must life be so complicated, *now*, when all she wanted was a quiet place to grieve, to heal, to build a new life for herself where she could be independent, free of any emotional tie or encumbrance? To care was to be hurt—and Brendan was already part, albeit as an observer, of long years of fear, shame and emotional agony. To escape from him, however, was one thing. To watch another woman succeed to the position she had denied herself was, it was steadily appearing, a different matter.

"Mr Kelehan must make his own choice," she muttered, aware of the surly note in her voice, but unable to give her tone a suitable lightness. "One thing I will tell you, Grandpapa—Brendan is no fool—he's escaped matrimony all these years—he's not about to rush into any liaison with some green young woman who doesn't share his background. Whoever marries Brendan Kelehan must be prepared to live the rest of her life in County Wicklow. I could not. All through my marriage there wasn't a day that passed that I didn't think of these hills—ugly, scrubby country to Irish eyes, I suppose— but home to me. I couldn't live out my life far away from them again. No, not for the greatest love in the world."

Her grandfather turned, at the end of this speech, and lowered the carriage window. There was a fresh smell on the wind, eucalypt-laden, but something more. Spring, Katherine realized, gratefully. She was about to point it out to her grandfather, this warm taste of growing things that permeated the breeze through the bush— but Edwin was saying, his eyes out the window, "You're like me, you know. Of all of them—even Joe, God rest him!—you're most like me."

He turned to her. "Family—family matters. And independence— perhaps most important of all. Only with the strength of money behind you can you feel totally secure in this world. Your other grandfather, God rest him!—old Josiah Prescott—now he was a man after my own heart—generous, a kindly man—but a *builder*, one who understood wealth as a . . . a *defence*. Your father . . ." Edwin sighed, "a strange mixture. He should have been a Catholic, should have been a saint. He sees and feels too much of the world's sufferings. Doing his small share isn't enough. He'll sacrifice everything. What I'm worried about . . . what I'm afraid of . . ." and his voice dropped to a murmur as he turned away a little, "is that he'll sacrifice everything along with him."

Katherine gazed at the back of her grandfather's head, the sleek silver-grey locks that curled a little over his collar. I know what he means, she thought, her stomach contracting a little. I know what he means. And she wished for all the world that she did not.

The little hamlet that would become known as Moss Vale suffered, as did several of the villages in the relentless path of the railroad, from an indecision by its few residents and the government alike as to what to call it. The surrounding area had been known as Sutton Forest and this would be the first choice for a name for the railway station that would be complete and operating in December of the following year. But there were those, Edwin among them, who had known Jemmy Moss, whose hut had stood in the vicinity of the townlands, and whose name had already been accepted by many settlers, as well as the Post Office, as the true title for the district. Sutton Forest, Edwin argued, as the brougham bounced along, was a tiny hamlet some three miles to the south, named after a politician in 1820. It was ridiculous to have the post office called Moss Vale, and the railway station something entirely different . . .

They were driving past the railway works, and Edwin was raising his voice over the clamour and ring of metal on metal, the pounding of the hammers, when the carriage drew to a halt unexpectedly.

"What's this . . . ?" Edwin thrust his head out the window. "Charles!" he roared, then, in a different voice, "Oh, young Brody! How are you, sir!"

Stephen! Katherine was pleased, wanted to push her grandfather back and poke her own head out the window. But she was forced instead to fidget on the seat beside Edwin, while a good-natured conversation went on, shouted above the cacophony of their surroundings, all still, unfortunately, unintelligible to Katherine's ears.

She finally plucked at her grandfather's sleeve. "Grandpapa? *Grandpapa*! Do let's meet Mr Brody for lunch—Father isn't about, you know."

"Eh?" The grizzled whiskers twitched, then he nodded abruptly and thrust his head out the window once more. ". . . At the Rose and Garters! I say, we'll meet you at the Rose and Garters! Garters! *Garters*, man! At the inn!"

Katherine cringed back, smothering her laughter in her furred muff. An ill-timed silence had descended on the railroad workers just as Edwin was trying to convey the name of their meeting place, and forty begrimed workers were now staring at the sight of the elderly man, who looked for all the world like a visiting statesman, bellowing, "Garters! Garters!" at a fair-haired young man on horseback.

It was good to see Stephen again. In the neat but unpretentious dining room of the nefariously titled inn, Katherine took his hand with real pleasure. The unforgotten warmth and kindness of his personality beamed at her, and she felt the trip to Moss Vale had been worthwhile for this, if for no other reason. Laura would be pleased to know that she had seen him.

The three enjoyed their lunch together; there was no need for apologies on Edwin's part concerning the lack of an invitation to Dovewood; Stephen and his married sisters and their husbands were welcome there at any time, but were, to Edwin's disgust, as stubborn as Marcus Prescott in this one regard—neither would set foot within a gateway if there was a possibility the other would be there. They talked amicably about the evening before, however, and Katherine assured him that Laura had looked beautiful indeed. The news that Marcus had arrived halfway through the proceedings, swept the smile from Stephen's face, however, though he recovered, remembering his manners.

Edwin, always to the point, brought his fingertips down on the table top smartly. "All this sneaking about—rubbish, that's what it is. Ride straight up to Barrengarry, tell him you're in love with his daughter. The man won't horsewhip you!"

"I'll do that, sir," Stephen blushed uncomfortably and Katherine felt sorry for him in his distress, "but I haven't saved as much as I wish to, sir. After my father's heart attack, it's been difficult overseeing the Sydney businesses and running Cambewarra single-handed—he and my mother depend on me a lot, these days. My brothers-in-law help as much as they can, but they have their own properties, and families to support. My grandfather keeps offering to run the place for me," he grinned, "But you know what he's like—he can't accept that we're living in the age of steam, he tends to try to undo any improvements I make, insisting the old ways are best. I . . . I want the house to be comfortable and attractive before I bring a wife back to it—at the moment, Cambewarra looks almost as rundown as my grandfather's homestead."

"Shouldn't matter," Edwin pronounced, and would have gone on to argue the beneficial effects of a woman at Cambewarra but for Katherine placing a hand upon his arm.

"You mustn't push Stephen, Grandpapa. It will all happen at the right time."

"Hmph . . ." Edwin muttered, and lowered his head over his roast lamb, while Stephen threw Katherine a look of gratitude.

She considered quietly for a moment, and asked, "When did you come from the Valley, Stephen? Have you heard any news of a shooting there?"

Stephen placed his knife and fork down upon his plate, the better to speak. "I was one of the first at the scene—only because I happened to be passing that way. I was the one who came to Moss Vale to fetch Doctor Lang, and I saw him head off towards the Valley— but that was yesterday evening, and this morning I've heard that someone met him on the way, told him he wasn't needed, and to turn back."

"Was it cedar-getters?" Katherine asked, interested.

Stephen frowned. "Yes and no. You know how they're finding it harder and harder to discover good stands of timber that haven't been worked out . . . Well—and Mr Gordon would know this but perhaps you wouldn't, having been away—some of the more unscrupulous cedar-getters have moved off their licenced grounds and they're taking timber from private property."

"I've heard tales of this," Edwin said grimly. "No complaints were made through legal channels, though—as far as I know, nothing's reached the magistrates, or I would have heard."

"And I can tell you why," Stephen volunteered.

"I heard the gunshot as I was riding back from checking on my grandfather—I know he hadn't wanted Gilbert Barton in the house, Katey, but he's an old man, and sudden surprises like that are hard for him to cope with. He helped my sisters nurse him—and when Barton died—despite himself, Grandad took it very badly. Since then he's become very crusty and withdrawn—even less sociable than he was before. So I ride over to check on him a bit more often— and annoy him to boiling point by doing so.

"Anyway, I was riding home when I heard a shot—from the direction of Radley's, from what I could judge, so I changed my mind and headed in that direction, arriving there within . . . oh, about five minutes of the gun going off, I think.

"There were horses outside—none that I recognized, but when I came into the building I found I knew several of the people there. Some of them were strangers, sitting stricken, not daring to move. Charlie Crolin was seated on the floor, leaning back against the bar where he'd fallen—or where Bert Radley had propped him, for he was down on one knee by Charlie, who was gazing wild-eyed at every face around him and repeating all the while, "He shot me . . . He shot me . . . You all saw it, didn't you? He shot me . . . !" As if anyone could have been in that single, sleazy room and somehow missed the gun going off.

"No one answered him, except Radley, murmuring for him to be still as he tried to look at the wound. It was hard to tell where it was, or what damage had been done, for the blood had spread quickly, all over the front of Crolin's shirt, and he kept brushing Radley's hands away, as if he didn't trust the man. And I hardly blamed him—Radley wore that greasy apron that I'm sure he sleeps in, and his hands were filthy . . .

"And Amos Murphy was standing not far away, just as he had been standing almost since the gun went off, I'm certain, simply holding the pistol loosely, the muzzle pointing down. It was an ancient weapon—almost interesting in its antiquity, now I think about it, but of course there was no chance to note all that at the time. All I could do was stand in the doorway and stare."

He gazed between Katherine and Edwin, rather abashed. "I daresay I would have done something, if some action had been called for, but—we all know old Amos—solid as a rock—most unlike him to go off his head like that. Though he was behaving a bit strangely, standing there muttering about one's hand offending one, and good servants and bad servants, and vengeance belonging to the Lord— you know all the references I mean, though it was hard to connect them with what had just taken place. I think maybe old Amos was just as frightened by his actions as everyone else, and was riffling through all the Biblical quotes he could think of to find one that might excuse what he'd done.

"I managed to stammer out, 'What's happened, here?' and felt like a bad actor making an entrance in a bad play. All eyes turned to stare at me.

"Someone sidled up to me in the dimness and took my arm— I jumped, startled—but it was Frank Crolin, Charlie's brother, who seemed delighted to have an audience and wanted to grab me before any of the other witnesses. He said, 'An attempted murder, it is. That's what. By *him*.' And he thrust a finger out towards Amos. 'And him a relative, and all. Of sorts.'

"And he was right, you know. I remembered then that Amos's family had been cedar-getters. His mother—or his grandmother— had been a Crolin, too."

"I didn't know that," Katherine said, glancing at Edwin.

Edwin nodded, heavily. "They have a complicated inbred society in those logging camps. I remember the incident when I was a young man—Amos Murphy's parents and relations were killed in a bushfire in the Meryla Pass area—he was taken, as a boy, to stay with some minister and his wife in Berry, and raised by them. His other relatives didn't object to him going, didn't bother trying to claim him. But he never felt part of the family in Berry—I think his own background must have been Catholic, but the minister—I *think* he was a minister, he was a highly religious man—was very low-church indeed—and I'm speaking as a Presbyterian. Amos returned to Kangaroo Valley when he was in his thirties, and went to work on the Brummells' little selection. He married the eldest daughter and in time inherited the place."

"The cedar-getters resent him, I think," Stephen put in. "He's become fairly successful, too, making deliveries to and from the Valley, and running a good-sized beef herd. His very ambition would make the cedar-getters resent him."

Katherine was becoming impatient. "But what happened at Radleys?"

"Well, there I was, with Frank clawing at me, accusing Amos of being a homicidal maniac, when Radley, who seemed almost to have given up trying to help the struggling Charlie, looked up and growled, 'Don't believe it, Brody—self-defence, it was. Charlie pulled a knife.' And with that, Radley reached under a nearby table and skidded a short-bladed hunting knife across the floor towards me.

"Frank dived on it, but I put my foot out and clamped down, hard, pinning it to the floor—and pinching Frank's fingers at the same time, unfortunately. While he was howling—and with his brother clutching his shoulder and moaning that he had been murdered, it was hard to get one's thoughts together—I picked up the knife and held it firmly, as I had the feeling that if Frank got hold of it first he might have been tempted to even up the score with Amos. They all carry knives, of course, but there was something about that moment, and Charlie's weapon spinning invitingly across the floor, that was the dangerous time. Frank glared down at his own knife, but then looked at me—and seemed to think better of it. If it had been Davey, who's as sneaky as they come, or Charlie, who isn't really bright enough to consider consequences, it might have been a different story, but Frank, although as mean as any of them, at least had the intelligence to realize that more violence would gain him nothing.

"I said, 'I think we'd better notify the authorities.' Now that, perhaps, was the worst thing to say, for as if they were all worked with the one string, every man in the place started to rise to his feet, eyes on the door—even the injured Charlie. So I amended it and said quickly, 'I should ride to Moss Vale for Doctor Lang.' And they all relaxed into a nervous silence.

"Radley said, 'Yes, you do that.' He'd at last managed to check on Charlie's wound, for he said, as he stood, 'Only through the fleshy part of the shoulder—nowhere near the heart—but a doctor should clean out the wound, I guess.''

" 'I'll die!' Charlie was groaning, 'I'll die and yous don't care! That murdering . . .' " Here Stephen looked tellingly at Katherine, so that she guessed the missing word, " '. . . has done for me, and yous don't care!'

" 'Shut up!' Radley said, then sauntered over to me, with a horrible kind of familiarity that almost made me step back, 'Mr Brody, this is really a family matter. It appears Charlie and Frank here made a mistake with the boundary line of their timber ground—they took a few trees from Mrs Halstrop's place . . .''

" 'I aint sayin' we did that!' Charlie stopped moaning long enough to add.

"Amos said 'You did,' his voice heavy, not taking his eyes from Charlie, who shrank back a little. 'You took advantage of a widder with no men on the place to stop you, and you took her timber . . .'

" 'I tell you we didn't know it was her land—thought it was guv'mint land! An' she should thank us, anyways,' Charlie screamed, 'clearing off her paddocks for 'er!'

" 'You never asked her,' Amos said, heavy as fate. I tell you, I wouldn't have liked to face him, not in that mood.''

"Who's Mrs Halstrop?" Katherine asked.

"She *was* a Brummel," Stephen said, "only lately returned to the Valley. She's a midwife, I believe. Related to Amos by marriage . . . Not as helpless a woman as one might think." His eyes met Edwin's for one of those infuriating glances men give each other, full of understanding, concerning matters their womenfolk are too delicate to hear.

Stephen went on, "Amos's sense of family responsibility made him feel obligated to defend her land against encroachment. I gather this confrontation between him and the Crolins wasn't the first—he'd repeatedly told them to move off the property. Radley told me this as I walked back to my horse to ride for the doctor. Bert was most emphatic that Amos coming from a cedar-getter family should make this a cedar-getters' matter, and asked me not to involve the police.

"Well, I rode for Doctor Lang, and you know the rest—someone rode out from the Valley to meet Doctor Lang and told him there was no need for his services.''

"But Charlie could be . . ." Katherine began.

"Dead? I doubt it. No, I think he's recovering himself and wants to save doctors' bills and any further questioning from Doctor Lang or the police. Doctor Lang said he was going to inform Sergeant

Lloyd, but if it's anything like other incidents, the Sergeant will ride to the Valley only to be met by a wall of silence: 'Shooting? What shooting? Just a friendly disagreement, officer. No need to have troubled yourself.' Even Lloyd knows that there's little you can do with the cedar-getters, they have their own way of solving their own problems.''

There was a silence. Stephen remembered his plate of food and took up his knife and fork to eat the now-cold roast lamb and vegetables.

Edwin was thinking deeply. "I don't like this. Nothing so serious has ever happened in the Valley before. I must admit, Katey, I'm glad your father is home. I hope he'll stay, now.''

"Yes,'' Katherine murmured, without much faith in this hope of her grandfather's.

Edwin sighed. "Still, with all the violence in the district, perhaps it would have been better if Suzanna and you girls had gone to Sydney to be with him, at least until things settle, 'til this bushranger is caught, and some changes come to the Valley.''

"Changes?'' Katherine's head came up. "What do you mean, 'changes'?''

"Katey, the resources of Kangaroo Valley aren't limitless. Only the Woddi Woddi know how to preserve them—their 'walkabout' means that they never stay long enough in any one part of their tribal lands to seriously deplete the animals they hunt or the vegetation they gather. Now, with the Woddi, the settlers and the cedar-getters, there's no room any more. Each faction will have to pit itself against the others in order to survive. It's happened already, in that nasty scene that Stephen witnessed. The Valley needs civilization: schools, a regular police force—however small—churches, meeting places— the people have to begin to stand together and to discuss the difficulties. Change must come to the Valley . . .''

"No.'' She was unsure why she, who had been urging for a school for some years before she had left the Valley, should have said the word, and with such finality. The men were staring at her. She tried to collect her thoughts. "Matters probably reached a head yesterday between the Crolins and Amos. The cedar-getters have had a fright, and they might even move now, further west—they've been threatening to for years . . .'' And when Edwin and Stephen looked doubtful, "There must be somewhere else for them to cut their timber! There won't be any trouble in the Valley—there's no need to talk of 'change' coming. I don't want the Valley to change. Not if it means the Woddi will leave, driven out by men like the

Crolins. Sometimes civilization just isn't worth it—not if people are going to be hurt."

Neither man knew how to deal with this outburst. They did not look at each other, conscious of the fact that it would have the appearance of patronization, a male statement on her lack of logic.

Stephen said gently, "Katey, the Woddi Woddi and the cedar-getters will have to adapt—that's the way of things. Nothing stays the same forever."

Something in his tone made her look up at him, and there stirred some emotion in the blue eyes that drew her and spoke, she was unnerved to see, more than his words. He kept the contact of their gaze, and she could not, for a moment, drag her eyes from his, wondering at what he meant.

Then her grandfather was saying, "Stephen's right. Whether you like it or not, Katey, the world is going to discover the Valley, either invited in, or being forced to step in, with all the complexities of law and government and civilization in its wake. I just hope it's a smooth transition, for all our sakes."

And this grim philosophizing, Katherine thought blankly, came about because of a couple of quick-tempered Valley-dwellers flaring up over timber rights?

No, there was something more than that, something they weren't able to put into words.

Am I holding on to the past? Katherine wondered, and realized that she was, holding on as if it were the last lifeline she possessed. *It's all I have*, she thought.

It was with some regret that they parted company from Stephen, after luncheon was over, but it was just as well; she wanted no one, besides her grandfather, to know of her speculation in the real estate market. She mentioned this to him when they were in the carriage once more and heading southwest, out of the little township. Edwin growled that of course he was going to keep silent about this.

"Your mama would think it a slight against your father that you didn't trust him to handle your business affairs—and if you did, your father would be donating three-quarters of your fortune to an orphanage. No, girl—I understand well enough. And I approve of what you're doing. Some of the most astute business brains I know belong to women. Some have had to be—they're single women, or widows, or married to dissolute, useless husbands. All seem remarkably successful—probably because they're more cautious, and because they're better judges of character. Men are too trusting. Many a business deal has foundered on the erroneous assumption that someone who went to your old school or who belongs to your club must be as reliable as you are yourself. No, women are more suspicious and more careful, where money is concerned . . . Ah—here we are!"

The landscape was all that she had hoped it would be, sloping on either side of the road so that views were possible of the low hills to the west. The only nearby properties were two large stone edifices, country houses of the kind Katherine had in mind for her buyers and belonging, Edwin told her, to a successful Sydney real estate baron and a leading shipping owner, respectively.

They talked of details on the return trip, and Edwin was pleased, once more, at Katherine's intuitive grasp of the principles of advertising. "Twelve months or so—perhaps sooner," he prophesied, as they entered the gates of Dovewood through a light, drizzling rain, "and you'll have at least three hundred per cent return on your investment. Maybe even more than that."

Katherine was content with these figures. Edwin was a shrewd businessman, as cautious as he was honest. She knew her investment was safe, and was considering already how best to invest her profits— more land, or stocks and bonds?—as they entered the house.

Something of importance, some emergency, was even now being enacted, for servants, wide-eyed, whispering, hurried back and forth from the parlour, and from within that room came the sound of many excited voices. Katherine and Edwin glanced at each other before divesting themselves of their cloaks and hats, handing them to a preoccupied maid, and hurrying into the parlour.

The centre of attention, to Katherine's surprise, was Viola Barton. She was half-reclining on the settee, her little, stocky legs thrust out and resting on an embroidered satin footstool. At Katherine's query of concern, Laura, Edwina, Bessie, Daisy and Marietta Cummings—even the normally reserved Emilia Huckstable— gathered about, each breathlessly determined to relate the story.

"Only just after you left . . ."

"He's gone, now—such a nice young man . . ."

". . . Youngest son of the founder of the company—family lawyers for some years . . ."

". . . Had no idea where to find Mrs Barton and Fleur—it took all this time . . ."

"My dear, a *fortune*!"

"Fleur fainted—she's upstairs with Mama and Grandmama . . ."

"Sole beneficiaries . . ."

"Thirty thousand pounds a year . . . !"

". . . Properties all over Camden and Campbelltown and several farms in the Valley . . ."

"No one knew! He . . ."

"He never told me!" A wail from Mrs Barton. The round, soft face looked white and stricken, Katherine, who had had to reprimand herself several times during the past week for becoming easily irritated with her foolishness, now felt genuinely sorry for the woman, who looked truly ill.

"Never told me when we were married—and all these years, scrimping and saving—not even enough to launch our Fleur into Society . . . Oh, the pity of it! To find all this out now! *Now*! Twenty-eight properties—shops and farms and houses—all his! All his, all these years, buying them up, bit by bit, and never telling his own wife!"

Katherine was almost as overcome as the others, managed to stammer her replies of amazement, concern, but poor Mrs Barton scarcely noticed; her little head beneath its white lace and ribbon was bent over an already damp handkerchief, and she sobbed bitterly.

Katherine turned and met her grandfather's gaze. It was one of the few occasions that she had ever seen Edwin Gordon totally nonplussed. But there were further surprises.

As they left the room together, they came upon Fleur, pale but composed, moving across the broad hall from the stairs. She smiled, fielded the tentative congratulations and expressions of concern, and said at once, "Mama will be returning almost immediately to Campbelltown, as Mr Digby, the lawyer who brought the news, will stay in Moss Vale and accompany her home to attend to the considerable financial arrangements."

She took a deep breath and turned directly to Edwin. "Mrs Gordon, sir, has been most kind to me—she made this offer before knowing of my . . . my good fortune. And despite the news, welcome though it is, I would, pending your approval, like to accept."

"Yes, my dear?" Kindly, from a mystified Edwin.

"Mrs Gordon and I have become firm friends, and she has asked me if, since for the most part she's isolated from female companionship here, I would remain, as her companion. If you approve, sir, I would very much like to remain at Dovewood, and call it my home."

Sixteen

There was no reason to dislike Fleur Barton. Katherine tried to tell herself that she should be glad that Angela would have some feminine company at Dovewood.

But *Fleur*, her indignant brain kept repeating. Why not bring Edwina to live at the house, or Laura? No, they were tied to the Valley by their heartstrings, Katherine admitted crossly, neither would wish to put yet more miles between themselves and Stephen Brody and Rafe Huckstable.

But how clever of Fleur—now it was accomplished no one, it appeared, was surprised, as Fleur had struck up a friendship with the much older woman almost immediately.

"They're both talented pianists . . ." Suzanna pointed out to Katherine, "and they've spent a great deal of time in the garden—apparently Fleur is a very keen gardener. Didn't you notice them wandering in and out of the glasshouses, little shears in their hands?"

"No," Katherine tried to keep the scowl from her face, the rancour from her voice. "It seems Fleur has been very busy."

They were seated by the fire in the library after lunch, alone except for Cassie, the beagle bitch, her head resting on Suzanna's foot. The copies of the *Illustrated Sydney News* lay forgotten on the women's laps. Suzanna leaned back with a little sigh. "I must say, I have to remind myself to be charitable. One couldn't blame poor little Fleur, even if there *were* some trace of . . . of . . ."

"Calculation?"

"Yes—isn't it awful?—*calculation* to her staying here. Try to see Dovewood through a stranger's eyes, dear. It may not be a very large house, but it is quite lovely. To a girl like Fleur, kept imprisoned in poverty all her life—well, the events and surroundings of the past few weeks have been heady, indeed."

"I understand that, but she's not a girl, Mama, she's a grown woman, and highly intelligent. I just hope that Grandmama and Grandpapa know what they're doing."

And Suzanna nodded, her brow clouded a little.

There! Even her mother was suspicious. Katherine rustled the pages of her magazine restlessly, looked at the illustrations without actually seeing them. I wish I'd known what Fleur was planning, Katherine thought—I'd have spoken to Grandpapa about it. As it is, now it's too late—Fleur will be treated as one of the family and be with us for years, I can tell, unless some man can be found to marry her.

Her fingers stilled on the pages and she was forced to confront a petty, irrational thought that had been rattling its sabre at the back of her mind for days. It was foolish to worry about it—and she did not want to marry Brendan herself so it should not matter, but . . . Fleur, it seemed, had already made it plain that she desired the state of matrimony. And she had decided that Brendan Kelehan would provide her with it.

"Katherine . . ." something in her mother's voice made her look up. "I want to thank you, darling, for whatever you said to your father . . ."

"But I didn't speak to him very much when I was in Sydney—although we did have a few rows," she admitted with a frown. "Do you think my quarrelling with him did any good? Somehow I doubt it. No, Mama," Katherine smiled and reached across to take her mother's hand, "Father came home because he knows his place is with you. It just took a little time for him to realize it, that's all."

"Katey—dear, you mustn't expect too much." The earnest look was still upon Suzanna's face, "I mean of your father and myself. There's . . . a great deal of bitterness there. I want us to be together again, just as it used to be," she said hastily, seeing that Katherine was about to question her, "but it may take time. Forgiveness . . . doesn't always come easy, not for your father, nor for me."

Katherine murmured, "I understand, Mama, of course."

But really, she did not. Why can't everything remain the same? she asked, not for the first time since she returned; why is it that everything is flawed, threatened, in a way that was impossible when I was young? Did I come all the way home, cope with the years of longing and homesickness before I *could* come home—only to find that nothing will ever be the same? Or . . . and this was, perhaps, more frightening still—was I simply too young and too selfish, growing up in such safety here, to see very far? Is this the legacy of my years with Oliver, to see the subtleties of people's needs as I saw his, and feel, always, the same sense of helplessness, that I can do so very little for them?

And what did Brendan want? The ludicrous story of the Fenian money—and her fingers curled at the thought that he suspected her of actual *theft*—could this be the only thing that had brought him all this way?

There was no opportunity that day to see him, to ask him of his plans. Edwin, Marcus and several of the male guests, including Brendan, had set off to visit a neighbour's property and view its stable of blood horses. It was the evening before she had a chance to speak with Brendan.

Most of the guests were grouped about the piano listening as Laura played and sang, and several others were playing checkers or chess around the room; when a chess table fell vacant, Brendan asked Katherine to join him. It was a quiet corner near the heavily draped windows, a little chilly, for it was the furthest from the fire, but Katherine was pleased that they had a certain amount of privacy.

They concentrated on the game for some minutes, then Katherine asked carefully, "You seem to be enjoying your stay—will you remain long in New South Wales, or are you planning on seeing Melbourne before you leave?"

He raised his head to gaze at her. "I've been asked to stay at Barrengarry. Didn't your father tell you?"

She faltered, such was her surprise, and felt herself flush a little, aware that he was gazing at her keenly. "No! No, I haven't spoken to Father this evening. You won't stay, will you? I mean, with the state of affairs in Ireland you'll be needed back there, and . . ."

"Are you so keen to see me face a row of British cannon? I always thought there was something Spartan about you, Kate. You'd make a fine wife for a Spartan warrior. What was that they used to tell their husbands . . . ? 'Come back with your shield, or on it'."

"I didn't mean that! You're making fun of me . . ."

"On the contrary, I'm serious. And while I'd love to please you by leading an Irish battalion into battle, I'm afraid you're bound for disappointment. There are no leaders, Kate." And the voice had lost its bantering tone and was deep with seriousness and a kind of grief. "Every few months there are more trials. They've built gaols in Western Australia . . ."

"I've read of it—Fremantle."

"Yes, and all those who could have led Ireland are to be sent to rot there—or at home in Kilmainham, which is almost worse. Oh, the talk in Boston and New York is very fine, and their hearts beat with the right kind of courage and fervour . . . but in Ireland itself, the English know what we're planning within a few hours of the decisions being made—too many men are using the information for their own gains, and there are others who act out of fear—for themselves or their families." He toyed with one of his pieces, turning it round about within its square. "No," and the voice was heavy, his head bowed so that the thick brows shadowed his eyes, "no, our chance went with those members of the Brotherhood who had military experience; we should have struck immediately the peace was declared in America. Irishmen from North and South would have thronged the harbours to get to Ireland—and the Irish in the British Army would have followed. But O'Mahony hesitated and Stephens seems all talk and little action. There've been too many arrests, Ireland is frightened—even America can't do much if Ireland herself is too cowed and apathetic."

He caught her gaze, held it for a monent, then smiled grimly. "You're disappointed in me," he stated, rather than suggested.

"I've never heard you speak like this before. We were so caught up in it all, for so many years. The living room rang with the differing opinions, the plans, of how best to succeed. You were one of the most articulate and . . . it's just strange to find you so . . . so . . ."

"Cowed and apathetic?" he suggested.

"No, Brendan!" She glanced at the group about the piano, for her disclaimer had been more vehement than she had meant it to be. No head turned; only Rafe Huckstable, playing chess by the fire with Edwin, looked up, his dark eyes intent on Katherine's face. Katherine lowered her gaze, addressed her concentration to the board for the moment and made a move hastily, taking one of Brendan's pawns with her knight. "You sound . . . disillusioned. It saddens me."

"Does it?"

And in the pause, she had no option but to raise her eyes to his.

To look at him was to look within him, and there was a shock at such intensity of contact. It was—and she shrank from the thought—as if their souls and their bodies, naked to each other, were drawn to each other, and touched. There was nowhere to recoil to, no escape. No words, no defence.

It was Brendan who broke the spell, and even for him it was an effort, she could tell, for whatever had possessed her had possessed him as utterly. "Dear God," he breathed, and there was no blasphemy intended, for it sounded like the prayer of a man in despair, "I didn't want this to happen. You don't know how hard I've hoped that I could look at you again and feel nothing."

Her mind was blank; she heard his words but could not respond to them. Despite all her rationalizations the force of what lay between them robbed her of thought. She only knew that she was frightened, as if he possessed a power over her that he only now thought to exercise, and all the more frightening for the years of courteous familiarity that lay between them.

"I don't . . ." she searched about for words, for his gaze, his intensity, seemed to be asking them of her, "I don't know what you want of me, Brendan. To find you suddenly back in my life again . . ."

"Took you completely by surprise," he suggested. "I'm sure it did. You were settling down nicely, weren't you? What an inconvenience to have this disillusioned Fenian arrive on your doorstep and take away your trousseau money. No wonder you turned such a charming shade of green when you saw me last night."

Her mind was struggling to follow him through the image of his repressed, unaccustomed bitterness. "Why do you say 'trousseau money?' I haven't got your wretched Fenian money, if that's what you mean. And if you're suggesting I'm planning on marrying again, I don't know how you could imagine that. I have no intention of remarrying."

His gaze, guarded yet calculating, had not left her face. "How do you explain the fact that Rafe Huckstable is even at this moment using my back as an invisible dartboard? It's exactly like walking into the pages of *Wuthering Heights*."

She dragged her eyes from his long enough to glance across the room. Brendan was right—although Rafe was attempting to concentrate on his game, the sight of Katherine with the mysterious Irishman seemed to have some terrible fascination for him. And the glances he cast them made his already sombre dark looks appear threatening indeed.

Katherine tried not to smile. "He *would* make a good Heathcliff," she admitted, "but you're mistaken. He's courting my sister, Edwina . . ."

"I know. I know nearly all your family gossip—by the end of the week, I plan to know all of it. But something no one seems to notice—even yourself, for some mysterious reason—is that, while Mr Huckstable is courting your sister Edwina, it's plain to anyone with any observation that he's in love with you. Stop tapping your foot and looking about so wildly, Mr Huckstable will think I'm beginning to bore you, and will leave your grandfather to come to your rescue. And I want you to myself, if only for this short while."

"Why?" she asked crossly, "you only seem to want to insult me. You've been in the house less than twenty-four hours, and you've accused me of being a thief and a liar, and now a flirt who steals my own sister's beaux. Any other woman would have slapped your face by now."

"But you're not any other woman."

Only Brendan Kelehan's voice could make that rejoinder both a compliment and a promise.

He said, "You're tapping your foot again."

She glared at him. "Brendan, go away. You're the sort of Irishman who should never travel. You're an extremely bad ambassador. Go home to Avonwood, and breed hunters and setters."

He leaned back in his chair and smiled at her. "I'm in no hurry to return. I have a job to do, remember?"

"But . . . My God, Brendan, what do I have to do to convince you? I don't have the Fenian money! What little I have is my own—and I've had to sell what I can of my jewellery—the few pieces that Oliver gave me . . ."

His wooden, unchanging gaze seemed impervious to any reasoning—and suddenly she longed to reach across the table and actually slap him, strike him, anything to break that mask of dispassionate speculation with which he regarded her.

"Are you trying to tell me," she asked finally, "that you're planning on staying in the Southern Highlands until I give you two thousand pounds to go away?"

"I think it would be best," he admitted. "If I left it to the lads . . ." he let the sentence hang.

"Stop trying to threaten me. Very well," with some degree of triumph, "we shall just see how long this game of yours will last. However long it is, you're going to end up looking extremely foolish. Have you written to your friends in Dublin, asking them to check at Lloyds?"

He bowed his head a little. "I have, if only to show you how very willing and optimistic I am about being wrong. I dearly hope that our contacts will tell us that there *is* a safety deposit box in your name. But it is, I must warn you, the action of a man allowing his heart to rule his head."

She contemplated the familiar features of the man before her. "Has your heart ever ruled your head, Brendan? I doubt it."

"If you think that, my dear, then it only shows how little you know me."

"Oh, I admit that. The man who arrived last night and began

immediately to fling accusations at me bears no resemblance to the man I thought I knew."

There. There was a slight flicker, a shifting of the light behind the grey eyes. She smiled a little, "And why should it bother you that Rafe Huckstable might be pursuing me? Why should it bother you if I do decide to remarry?"

"It won't," smoothly. "I shall be very glad. I hope there is some man in the Highlands with a strong will, and a healthy bank balance who's capable of keeping you under control."

She stood up from her chair, but his voice, soft, controlled, forced her to pause.

"You've made a very bad mistake."

She looked down at him.

His head lowered, his hand moved his knight with a neat little flourish, to the square adjacent to her queen.

Brendan looked up. "Checkmate," he grinned.

Laura was radiantly happy. That afternoon she had managed to slip away and ride into Moss Vale, where she met and talked to Stephen for two and a half hours. She came into Katherine's room late that night and sat on the foot of the bed to tell Katherine of her afternoon, having a great deal to do with what Stephen thought, and what Stephen said, and how fair his hair looked in the sunlight.

"No wonder you were playing so many love songs tonight. Mooning over the keys, staring into space."

"Oh, Katey, I wasn't! Was I?" she asked, unsure.

"No," Katherine laughed. "Or, I daresay you were, but you looked so pretty that no one would have looked beyond the picture that you made. What a pity Stephen couldn't be here this evening! When are you going to speak to Father, Laura?"

"Oh, I'd like to see him straight away, but Stephen says to wait." She sighed. "Mother agrees with him—she says it's best to let Father settle back into Valley ways for a few months, and let him see how steady Stephen is, and how fond he is of me . . . but it's hard, Katey. I'm filled to the brim with happiness, and I want to sing Stephen's praises from the mountain tops, really I do! And I have to creep about and not mention his name, and say nothing when Father mutters 'Those Brodys'—I'm as bad as everyone else in our family, stubborn and proud through four generations—and I think the whole feud is so silly!"

Katherine nodded sympathetically and stifled a yawn. She loved

Laura dearly, and was as keen to see an end to the foolish bickering between the families as Laura herself, but she was tired from lack of sleep the night before, and Laura's little chats seemed to be the same minor victories and defeats over and over again, in different settings. Perhaps, she thought, it's because I'm not in love that I find it all a little . . . well, *tedious.*

There were so many other things to think of. The shooting in the Valley, the message from Gurral that her father should return—would she be allowed to accompany him when Marcus met the tribal elder? And the land, the advertisements she had to compose to appeal to the city dwellers . . .

"And Brendan Kelehan!"

Katherine started.

"Oh, really, Katey—did you think I wouldn't notice? I had an excellent view from beneath the top of the grand piano—you and Brendan were beautifully framed. Speaking intimately with your heads together one minute, then quarrelling—and whole minutes spent gazing silently into each other's eyes . . ."

"You're beginning to sound like Teddi," she said crossly. "Really, Laura—I hope you're not speaking to anyone else like this. Mr Kelehan isn't the slightest bit interested in me . . ."

"Oh, no . . . ?"

"No. In fact . . ." Why did a picture of Fleur Barton come suddenly to her mind? "He's virtually spoken for. He had a fiancée—in Ireland—and for all I know, they may be married by now."

"Don't you *know*?"

"I didn't ask him."

"But if he's such a good friend . . ."

"It's still not the sort of thing one *asks*. It doesn't matter. He knew Father all those years ago, and he's now Father's guest . . ."

"Yes, Father said he's coming back to Barrengarry with us. I think he's interested in the fact that Mr Kelehan owns an estate in Ireland. We all walked up from the stables together this afternoon, you see, so I know. Father was talking of what an invaluable experience it would be for Mr Kelehan to look after an Australian estate. I might be wrong, but I *think* Father is looking for a farm manager—an overseer, or whatever one calls them!"

"He's not! He wouldn't say anything of the sort . . ."

Laura looked surprised, then a little piqued at having her veracity questioned. "You weren't *there*, Katey. Father actually said—and these are his *exact words*—'I need some capable man to look after things, I have commitments in the city that will keep me there for a great deal of time over the next several months.' "

"He *didn't* say that!"

"He did, Katey! Go and ask him! He and Mama were discussing it over dinner—didn't you notice how quiet she became? He doesn't plan on staying very long at Barrengarry. He really wants to go back to Sydney!"

There was no time nor opportunity to talk with her father; the following morning was spent in packing and farewells, and Katherine realized that she would have to wait until they were home before she could face him with what Laura had surmised.

But she did speak with Angela. Her grandmother drew her aside as the family was gathering in the hall, the horses and carriages waiting in the drive. "Dear," her grandmother said, the fine, intelligent eyes studying her face, "I want to know something, and I trust you, Katherine, to tell me the truth. Does your mother resent me for inviting Fleur to stay with me at Dovewood?"

Oh, dear. Katherine's glance unwittingly sought her mother, over near the doors, even now shaking hands with Fleur Barton, as gentle and courteous as ever. "Grandmama, don't think that—perhaps . . . she's been worried about the girls . . . I think she would have liked them to stay sometimes—it's so *quiet* in the Valley, and she feels they need to meet more people . . ."

"I understand." Angela nodded firmly. "How stupid of me, not to see that . . . And how foolish of Suzanna not to ask; all yesterday I kept finding her looking at me with those tragic eyes of hers." She looked hard at Katherine. "Families tend to think each member is a mind-reader, you know, and it's not true. If only I'd known . . . Still, it's not too late, for this house can fit in everyone I love and never be crowded. Tell that silly, proud daughter of mine that I *asked* if Teddi and Laura would come to stay—for a month, or six months, if you like.

"Really . . ." she said, almost crossly, staring at the unsuspecting Suzanna, "your mother must think I care more for hostessing silly politicians and their wives than I do for my own family. Katherine, a word of advice. Always treat your family as strangers—I mean, with the same thought and courtesy you'd employ when dealing with strangers. While familiarity doesn't always breed contempt, it very often breeds misunderstandings. Tell her to send the girls to me, there's a dear."

Katherine hugged her, and as her father, from the steps, was calling her, ushering his brood of women into the carriage, she had to hurry off. There was time only for the briefest of farewells to Fleur, "Goodbye, Miss Barton—I know you'll be very happy here . . ." and it was sincerely meant, for everyone was happy at Dovewood.

"I shall be, Mrs Carron." And Katherine was in the carriage and halfway down the drive before she realized what it was about Fleur's reply that so irritated her. The slight emphasis on the "shall," "I *shall* be, Mrs Carron," and the smile that did not reach those soft, grey eyes. There was a subtle message of defiance, even of challenge there.

Then she shrugged it off. Her mother was right, she must be charitable. And Fleur's harmless passion would soon spend itself. The object of it had mounted his horse, and was even now cantering off down the drive, to draw level with Marcus's solid chestnut cob. Brendan would not be visiting Dovewood often enough for even Fleur to believe a romance was possible.

Katherine smiled a little—she must remember to tell Brendan that she had invented a fiancée for him. It was a clever idea and should, at least, stop the endless, wistful talk amongst her parents and sisters. She settled back in the seat, after one last, fond glance back at the mellow walls and roofs of Dovewood, almost invisible now, behind the trees.

Normally, they would have travelled with the Huckstables, but they, like the few other Valley families, had opted to stay in Moss Vale to see relatives not often visited, given the distance and difficulty of terrain between the Valley and the outside world.

Brendan Kelehan wondered, as he rode, at the circumstances that found him heading towards Kangaroo Valley. He ought not to be here. Not in Australia, and especially not on this road, winding through scrubby forest, bearing him further and further from his responsibilities—and nearer to Katherine's home, and an even closer involvement in her life.

The two thousand pounds of Fenian money—and he did not doubt for a minute that she had taken it—had been the excuse to bring him after her—but he was honest enough with himself to know that he would have come, without this reason or any other, on hearing of Oliver's death.

I love her too much, he thought, and while he knew the words would not excuse his behaviour in the eyes of the world, or even himself, they were nevertheless the sum of his reasoning, his motives, his actions, and so much a part of him that he no longer bothered with rationalisations.

He could not tell Katherine about his marriage. He would leave eventually, cured of his obsession, or he would return to Boston only to make it possible for Mary Rose to divorce him. If Katherine would have him, after his confession of what he had foolishly done, then he meant to marry her. His feelings for Mary Rose were a combination of guilt and shame—doubly so for the lack of any real warmth when he remembered her. He knew his parents, his sisters, Katherine herself, would despise him—he despised himself, but less for his abandonment of the girl than for his using her, for marrying her under the pretence he had forgotten Katherine.

"I am as guilty as Oliver," he thought suddenly. "Both of us married for the wrong reasons, basing those vows on lies that we hoped and prayed would somehow become truth."

But there was no turning back, not yet. Having found Katherine again, he could not, would not leave her. Not now.

He did not know what the future would bring, but the present had them travelling with their faces turned southwards, towards the valley that had become almost mythical for him. This was the country that had formed Katherine, made her what she was. He would see it and, for a while, be part of it. And she would be near. He could ask nothing more.

So the little cavalcade wound on its way, the elderly but still smart family carriage, Tobias driving the wagon loaded with boxes and trunks, and Brendan and Marcus on horseback.

They stayed the night with friends, in a sprawling timber homestead on the edge of the escarpment, and in the mist of the dawn's light they began the tortuous journey, round and about the shoulders of the hills, down, down, into the fertile green basin below.

Katherine, for the length of the journey, tried to ignore Brendan— or, rather, she tried not to appear to notice him, but this was impossible. He would stare and stare at some landmark, and turn to Marcus or herself and make some comment, unthinking in his pleasure at being here, that struck only Katherine and her father as strange. After a late luncheon, Laura volunteered to take Brendan to see the stables and the horses, and Katherine declined to accompany them, saying she had to speak to her father.

But once in the office, for the first few minutes, it was Marcus who did the speaking, much to her discomfort.

"Did you see the man?" Marcus almost crowed, sitting back in his chair in the study and swinging back on its swivelled base like a boy with a new toy. "Did you see his face? What did you do, Katey—paint pictures of Barrengarry and the Valley for him? He knew we were coming in down Meryla Pass—he knew Yarranga Creek—and Barrengarry Mountain. He stared at the homestead until I thought one of the chimneys was on fire."

"I . . . I used to talk of it a great deal. Of the house and the Valley—and all of you, of course. I suppose," she finished lamely, "it's his lawyer's mind, trained for detail."

Marcus was still, watching her keenly, then he nodded, slowly. "I see. And you can't give me a better reason than that for Mister Kelehan's unusual susceptibilities?"

She didn't answer him, shifted restlessly on her chair, and began on a different note.

"Father, I don't think it was wise to bring Mr Kelehan here— I wish you would have asked me first. He's . . . he's a part of a past that isn't . . . that's not very . . . I thought it was all behind me!" she burst out finally. "I came home to build something for myself, to put down roots here in the Valley." She stood and walked about on the fine, well-worn carpet, scowling at the pattern and treading firmly, as if she could crush the past as easily as the pile beneath her feet. "I don't want him here, reminding me of those years! I don't want any quarrels, any bitterness—I've had enough of it! I want some peace, Father, and I can't have it while that man is in the house!"

Marcus stared at her. "Good God, Katey, you haven't come home to die, girl! What in Heaven's name are you talking about? Peace? You're too young to have peace, even if you think you want it— and you don't. And you don't want quarrels, or bitterness? You'll get that wherever you are, whoever you're with—even the closest of families have their battles. Who on earth do you think you are— and what on earth did you expect of the Valley, to come home with such eccentric ideas?"

"You don't understand . . ."

"Damn right I don't!"

"Father, stop swearing . . ."

"You'd drive any man to swearing . . ." He stopped abruptly, and narrowed his eyes. "Ah," he said, "I *think* I do understand. A little, anyway. You haven't told me the truth, have you, Katey? You've misled all of us. Oh, don't worry, I'll keep silent—it would only upset your mother further and make her worry about you. But there was no need to lie to me. You were miserable with Oliver Carron, weren't you? I'd hoped, for your sake, I'd been wrong all those years ago, but I wasn't."

She was tired, and the sharp mind, the observant hazel eyes before her gave no opportunity to gather herself for a denial. "Yes," she said.

Expecting a series of probing questions, she stood there, waiting. But Marcus, leaning back in his chair, his feet thrust forward in his still dusty boots, made no effort to query her single response. He gazed meditatively upon her, and it soon became apparent that he was intent upon his own mental processes; that it concerned herself she had no doubt, but it was as if he needed nothing further from her in order to reach his own conclusions.

He said, "I'm no fool, Katey. I didn't bring Brendan Kelehan to Barrengarry to throw him in your path—the last thing I want is for you to disappear back to Ireland, married to a Catholic. But I do need the man here. He's trustworthy and I think he'll fit in well in the Valley. Coming from a small farming community in Ireland, he'll understand the ways of people cut off, as we are. He's helpful, yet he keeps his own counsel. I've been interviewing men in Sydney for some time—just now and then, as someone is referred by friends . . . it wasn't until Kelehan walked into my office that I finally found the man I was looking for. Someone to whom I could trust Barrengarry for several months while . . ."

"No!" She had not really believed Laura, she realized now. "How could you, Father? Haven't I helped you for years? Joe and I often ran the farm while you were away for months. I can hire the lads from Burrawang for the mustering—did it never occur to you that I could run this place?"

"It needs a man, Katherine . . ."

"But I can do it! I've done it before! You know as well as I do, that Joe was never—" she stopped, but it was too late. On a lower note she said, "Joe was never . . . very much help. He . . . he just didn't have the patience, or the ability at bookkeeping . . ."

"He would have learned."

"Yes. Yes, of course. But I meant that . . ."

"You did a great deal to help Joe—he admitted that on several occasions. But it would be different if you were here by yourself with only Carl to help with the heavy work. Those stockmen and shearers—all seasonal workers—they're a wild mob, Katey. No matter how much of the organization you did—they *knew* that Joe was here, that he was in control. Alone, just a household of women—no, I don't like it. I don't like it and it never occurred to me that we'd have it."

It was hard to speak, it meant too much to her, and voicing her plea in the face of his determination was like trying to stand in the face of an onrushing tide. "I want . . . to . . . *contribute* something. I want to be *useful*. I came home because I wanted to do something to *help* . . ."

"You can help Brendan, just as you used to help Joe. And there are other matters, too. Have you thought of visiting the settlers' wives, perhaps organizing a school—not to teach it yourself, of course, I don't want anyone to say that one of my daughters had to work for a living—but you could set it up, organize everything."

"It's not . . . what I had in mind."

"What did you have in mind?" He looked grim of a sudden. "You didn't . . . you hadn't letters from Joe, telling you of that foolish scheme of his, had you? You didn't come home believing that Joe would leave here and *you* would . . ."

"It wasn't a foolish scheme. It made sense. He wrote to me that he was planning to go north, to Queensland . . ."

"All boys have dreams like that—he'd never have gone. What would he have done? Played at being an adventurer, dreaming of some fortune in the tropics . . ."

"Many a man has become an adventurer and made a fortune in the tropics . . ."

"Joe wouldn't have gone. It was a dream. He didn't have enough initiative, and—he wouldn't have left us, that's all—this is his home . . ."

"He wanted to be independent, Father . . ."

"He wouldn't have gone! He didn't go! He died! He's dead! You won't do a better job of running this place that he would have done! It's a man's job, and you're a woman, Katherine—stay with women's things and leave this decision to me!"

He had raised his voice; it seemed to ring in the air about them, making Katherine's heart pound, as it always had; the fear of him, the child's awe of his power that, it seemed, she had never quite lost.

"And you'd leave Barrengarry in a stranger's hands?" She flung the question at him.

"Don't be dramatic—your high opinion of him was one of the things that made me trust him."

"How much *can* you trust him?"

"What do you mean?"

She paused on the brink of disclosure, the words banked up against her teeth until she could almost taste them in her rage. *He's a traitor. A man who's given his life—and almost lost it—to the goal of overthrowing Her Majesty's authority in Ireland. A man of violence who, I believe, is also a murderer. You're willing to leave Barrengarry in the hands of a traitor and a murderer . . .*

Oh, he would be aghast to hear that. First-generation Australian that he was, the blood of a hundred generations of English yeomanry coursed almost unadulterated through his veins. Those few sentences would have their effect. Brendan would be gone from Barrengarry within the hour.

But how terrible would her own position be? She knew, looking into the stubborn features before her, that Brendan's past reflected just as badly upon herself. And upon Oliver's memory.

"You don't know how capable he is. Farming in County Wicklow is a far tamer affair than here in the bush. Brendan wouldn't know a dingo from a wildcat—nor how much damage they can do to stock . . ."

"He'll learn. You'll have several weeks to teach him. Now, if you don't mind, Katey, I have months of work to catch up on . . ."

"Father, what do you mean, several weeks? Why . . ."

"I've already discussed it with your mother. You three girls will come back to the house in Balmain with me for a few months. Your mother will stay here."

She stared at him.

"It's decided, Katey—you didn't think I'd allow these flirtations with young Brody and Huckstable to continue, did you? Totally unsuitable matches. Six months in Sydney society and Laura and Teddi will have forgotten all about them. I'll rely on you to chaperone them, I think you'll do a better job than your mother has, here in the Valley . . ."

"Mama did a wonderful job! How could you! You're not dealing with two children—Laura and Edwina are grown women, now, they made their own choices . . ."

"As you did."

And you were wrong. Marcus's unfinished words hung in the air.

There was nothing she could say, nothing she could trust herself to say. And besides, to refuse to be packed off to Sydney would mean staying on in the Valley, sharing the house with the unwelcome presence of Brendan Kelehan.

"I think we should discuss this later," she said tightly.

"Whenever you like," he said politely, and pulled his chair closer to his desk.

It had been years, years, since she had known such a feeling of black, hopeless anger. She walked from the room having to concentrate on not slamming the door, and turning towards the stairs, she ran full-force into Brendan, bouncing back and finding, to her further fury, his hands on her elbows to steady her.

She glared up into his face, careless of the spite that must be written on her own features. "Stay out of my way," she hissed, and had the satisfaction of seeing him almost recoil in the face of her rage. Still the hands held her, and she pulled her arms out of his reach. "Stay out of my way while you're here, or I swear you'll regret it . . ."

And she ran to the stairs, blocking out his voice calling her name.

Seventeen

The worst of her father's suggestion about organizing a school for the Valley was that it had long been a dream of hers, for many years before she had left Australia. It irritated her that it had been flung to her, like table scraps to a hopeful dog, she thought, only in compensation for not managing Barrengarry.

As if, she brooded bitterly, as she stayed indoors and watched Marcus and Brendan ride out each day in all weathers to view the farm and the various tenant blocks, it was in Marcus's power to bequeath the organization of the school to her. She had thought of it herself—that, and a church, and a proper store . . . But even if she did manage to gain the settlers' interest in financing the building of the school, her father would always be reminding her, with that boyish sense of superiority that was often endearing and just as often irritating, that *he* had suggested it.

She brooded around the homestead for almost a week, thankful that the weather was so bad that it precluded much activity, and the threat of any or all of them catching Edwina's cold was enough

to bring Peggy fluttering from her various roosts about the house
to forbid them from walking or riding in the rain. Katherine spent
a good deal of her time with the pink-nosed Edwina, reading to
her from favourite novels and books of poetry, and trying not to
think that she had, it seemed, come home to be as much under her
father's domination as she had been before.

The little empty sandalwood box was kept beside her bed. She
liked to see it first thing on waking, last thing at night as she blew
out the lamp. Its very emptiness was a promise that somewhere,
her grandfather was turning the necklace of diamonds into cash,
and that, soon, into land. *Her land.*

She would look at her father sometimes, at the dinner table,
and say *I'll have my land soon—my own land*, over to herself as
a child will repeat a defiant phrase. For it was her only hope.
The necklace, the land, the profits from that land. So the little
sandalwood box came to be a symbol of financial independence.
And there can be no other kind of independence without firstly,
she thought bitterly, the end of the tyranny of living on another's
charity.

Yet her father had always been generous. Suzanna and all her
daughters had had, really, all they had ever wished for.

"It's not that I'm *greedy*," Katherine would remind herself, "it's
just that I want to do things for *myself*." The feast-and-famine of
her years with Oliver—and so many times, though he tried to hide
it, it had been Brendan who had helped Oliver out of financial
difficulties—had left their mark on her. She would look at her mother
and think, I do not want to grow old asking for money from a
man. "Pin money"—even the phrase irritated her. A feminine
allowance with which to buy ribbons and trimmings. Even if a woman
was an heiress her husband had control of her money, to mete it
out as he saw fit—or to withhold it.

No, she would not grow old and be dependent on her father,
then upon the husband of one of her sisters. Who? Stephen? Rafe?
God forbid!

Preoccupied with her own thoughts, it was some days before she
realized that the initial accord between her father and mother on
being united at Dovewood had steadily eroded. Undoubtedly because
of his decision to leave her here and return to Sydney, Katherine
thought, and though she was reluctant to interfere between her
parents, she willed her mother to defend her own wishes, to demand

to be able to accompany them to Balmain, or—even better—for them all to remain at Barrengarry.

The depth of her love for the place was almost a physical thing. She rode out alone on the fifth day of their return, when the weather seduced her from her gloom; the only cloud was a bank of cumulus that sat high and arrogant on the southern escarpment and merely posed there, against a sky of deep, clear blue. The wind was slight, though chill, and one could ignore it, such was the warmth in the sun.

She had packed in the leather satchel attached to her saddle a few sheets of heavy white paper, a bottle of black ink, and two or three pens snatched up hastily as she left her room from the lower drawer in her desk where they had waited untouched for more than five years.

She had seated herself on a blackened tree trunk, felled by lightning or some ancient fire, having stopped for a few minutes only, to sketch, in this sunny clearing, the first, timorous wild flower, the deep golden bottlebrush shape of a hairpin banksia amongst its sparse and spiky leaves. Her horse, the sturdy little Dryad, stirred, and shuffled her neat little hooves in the grass. Katherine shivered, only then realizing the wind was more chill, the high, dense cloud had moved with ponderous state across the sky and had obscured the sun.

And the sun itself was far lower on the horizon than when she had set out. Somehow the hours had passed, and she had filled, she realised with a shock, four of the five sheets of paper, forgetting luncheon, her family, Brendan, everything but what was before her. The flower—odd though it was to describe the bent styles, just like metal wire, as a flower—occupied one page; a group of leaves, another. A view of the escarpment and Barrengarry Mountain another—and, seated on the ground, she had just begun to work on a sketch of a small, silver-grey moth, wings folded meticulously as a fine silk fan in miniature, alighted on a long, bent frond of grass.

She did not know why it was, but there was a satisfying contentment in the feel of pen on paper, the various strokes uncannily precise and in scale, bringing forth from the void of whiteness the twin of her subject, in firm, monochromatic detail. She loved to see it slowly evolve beneath her hand as she gazed between the fragile, evanescent creature and the permanent reflection of it, a tangible memorial long after the silver moth and this day had faded forever.

Five years ago, she thought, soberly studying her work, she would have known the species of moth—but she had forgotten. The hairpin banksia was easier; she hastily scrawled *Banksia spinulosa* in the lower righthand corner of the drawings of branch and blossom, blew upon it several times to dry the ink completely, and tucked them away carefully within the saddle bags.

Her interest in botany, especially the rich and hardy varieties of flora found in the Valley and on its surrounding slopes, had been an almost consuming passion in her early years. She had, on solitary meanderings here in the Valley and, once in the gullies about Dovewood, discovered variations of small native shrubs, and had written, in her twentieth year, to the *Australian Botanical Journal*, describing them. To her own amazement the letter had been published as an article, and the mail had included a cheque for five guineas. But best of all, perhaps, had been the letters that came over the weeks following publication, from several well-known botanists in Sydney and Melbourne, and her desk was still crowded with tied-up bundles of letters she had received in the three years of correspondence, until the time of the family's exodus to Europe.

Her father was right—once again, she thought unwillingly—it was an interest that she could and should continue. Perhaps she could travel more, collect more specimens and even, perhaps, if her drawings were attractive and technically correct enough, collect them into a book—for her own satisfaction if not a publisher's . . .

"What are you doing out here?"

She had been preparing to mount and both she and Dryad started at the voice. Katherine, standing on the fallen tree trunk, lost her balance as the horse pulled away, and only just managed to keep her feet as she jumped down.

She whirled about to face the old man, his rusty distinctive voice having betrayed his identity before she had seen him.

"Mr Brody, why did you have to do that? Were you trying to make me fall?"

He did not answer. Stood at some distance, holding an ancient breech-loading rifle in one hand, sucking on his tongue, she noted, as he did, often, when he could not be bothered replying to a question, civil or otherwise.

"Never much of a horsewoman, were you? Take after your mother—too timid. Only one of yez who can ride is that youngest with the black hair. And your brother—though much good it did him at the end . . ."

Katherine led Dryad forward to the log once more. She would not answer the taunts, was angry despite herself at the years—all her living memory—when members of the Brody clan would throw verbal mud at any Prescott in hearing range.

"That father of yours had better mind his family—you tell him that. Don't look after you lot any better than his property. You shouldn't be riding out here by yourself—though you always were a bold one in that way. Nasty types around—*you* ought to know that, bringing that poor devil Barton to me. And that sister of yours don't have any sense. The blonde one who's out to trap our Stephen— you tell your father to keep her at home . . ."

"*You* go home, Mr Brody—this is Crown Land, as I remember, and I have as much right to be here as I wish. And don't even speak to me about my sister and Stephen. You're a wicked-minded old man and if you can't be courteous *to* people and *about* them then I'd suggest you barricade yourself in your house and talk to no one but yourself."

She scrambled onto the log and onto Dryad's back, cursing the awkwardness of trailing skirts and side-saddles. She glanced once more at Mikey Brody, who stood rolling his tongue about behind cheeks covered in untidy white bristles.

"Tell that father of yours that setting his girl at Stephen won't do any good. No marriage'll come of it. He'll be wiped by the family if he even considers it—and he won't. He's not that stupid, our Stephen, he sees how things are . . ."

Katherine was heading Dryad through the scrub, back onto one of the main tracks. Brody raised his voice, flung it at her back, "Don't go thinking that marriage with a Brody will save yez! We'll laugh when Barrengarry comes under the hammer—we'll laugh while we're bidding for it! You tell your father that! You tell him . . . !"

He was mad. The stupid old man was mad. There was no logic in his words, no basis of fact in his taunts.

But Katherine rode home with her hands gripped on the reins as if she could as easily control her rage, and the gusting wind that began to blow only added to her discomfort; the day that had begun so well was spoilt—what other tales would Mikey Brody spread about the Valley? It was intolerable that he was repeating such stories to others. Surely he had some reticence—some sense of fair play and dignity . . .

She gave Dryad her head on the last mile or so despite all training to the contrary. Her impatience to be home drove her, and she only hoped that her father would not be in the vicinity of the stables to see the lathered state in which the tough little mountain horse arrived home.

The yards, the barn and stables were deserted, however, and she had ample time to walk Dryad about until she had cooled, before giving her water and feed and grooming her.

The house seemed unusually quiet. A stew bubbled on the stove, but Peggy was elsewhere in the house or had taken a brief respite in her own quarters before dinner.

Katherine merely glanced into the downstairs parlour, and finding it empty was about to head for the stars when she paused, seeing a strangely-shaped brown paper parcel sitting on top of the piano.

It was not sealed, although a length of rather grubby string lay beneath the packet. It unwrapped easily, and Katherine found herself holding several pieces of needlework. A beautifully embroidered tea-cloth; a nightcap trimmed with fine, hand-crocheted lace, four or five collars and sets of cuffs, each of the finest lawn, graced with delicate stitches of a standard and design approaching artistry.

"Wonderful work, isn't it?"

She turned as her mother entered the room. "Is this Peggy's work? With all due respect, Mama, none of *us* could have produced this," Katherine said with a laugh.

Suzanna smiled; her daughters' impatience and consequent ineptness at all but the most basic of sewing had always been a keen disappointment to her, as she was a competent though not overly imaginative needlewoman. "This work . . ." she took a pintucked, lace-trimmed collar from Katherine and seated herself on the settee to study it in the afternoon light, "was done by Essie Crolin."

The little thin-faced logger's wife with the tragic dark eyes. The dowdy, impoverished figure with the heavy shopping basket who had greeted Laura and Katherine as they had returned from the visit to Joe's grave.

"But how did it come here? It looks like part of a trousseau . . ." Katherine raised her eyes to her mother's and seated herself on a chair. "Oh, Mama—she hasn't been forced to sell it, has she?"

"No, no . . . she came calling yesterday while you were out and left us these to study as examples only. She wants work, Katey." Suzanna fingered the artfully made collar, smoothed it upon her knees as if she could sense the hours of close concentration that had gone into its creation. "She's never had to before—this is simply . . . a kind of gift she possesses, passed down from mother to daughter through several generations. But Charlie, her husband, is slow in recovering from his accident . . ." Suzanna paused on the word, her gaze hesitating equally as long and as tellingly upon Katherine.

"Oh," Katherine said, "so he was more seriously wounded than Stephen and Doctor Lang were led to believe." She scowled. "They're so independent, these cedar-getters. What if Charlie had died of gangrene poisoning—where would that leave Essie and that brood of children?"

"I asked her why the doctor had been sent away. She said, 'Charlie don't have no use for doctors. Ain't never yet been touched by a doctor.' As if to seek a consultation meant some admission of failure for them.

"But he's not able to work—not that I believe he ever was an enthusiastic worker. But the children are suffering. That's what bothers me. You've been up there at their camp, Katey, you know what they're like."

"Six years ago. Have they made no improvements?"

"They're on the move—every year, sometimes twice a year. Some of the cedar-getters are settling in one place—not the Tallons, nor the Crolin families. They're like tinkers, always shifting camp from valley to valley. Each camp more primitive than the last—or so it seems to me."

"What are you going to do, Mama? Do we really need work as fine as this? We have the machine now." Katherine's eyes went to the corner by the window where, in some pride of place, the new sewing machine, made in England and recently imported to New South Wales, stood—black metal wheel and fine woodwork gleaming.

Suzanna frowned consideringly at the collar in her hands, and said gently, "I don't see how we can refuse. Living the life she does, I don't know where she'll find the time to work at her embroidery, but this is a plea for help, Katey, don't you think? They won't take charity—they're fiercely proud, but . . . this just may be the only way we can help the family."

Katherine nodded, "You're right, I suppose. When she returns, ask her if she'll make a collar such as that for me, will you? We'll have to provide the materials—she'll never have the opportunity to purchase them—I think we have enough embroidery thread."

She considered for a moment, it was as good an opportunity as she would find—"Mama, I've always been proud of the concern you and father have shown towards less fortunate people—here and in Sydney—I've lost count of all the committees that Father serves upon. I haven't bothered to ask him, but I've wondered . . . have the Sydney businesses been paying well, these past few years?"

How much more comforting it would have been if her mother had laughed a little and said, "Of course, the warehouses and the importing business were thriving, the residential properties made a good return . . ."

Suzanna said all this—but not immediately. With Katherine's question the unguarded, mobile face betrayed, for a few seconds, shock and concern. Then, pulled into place by will, came the smile, the little laugh, the reassuring assessment of the family's business concerns.

But in those few seconds of hesitation, Suzanna's vulnerability had betrayed her; her own fears were there upon her face for her daughter to see and recognize.

Katherine heard, but did not follow, her mother's words. She was thinking of her father, only now pulling himself out of a severe depression that had lasted months—had it been caused only by Joe's death, or was there more to Marcus's anguish than that?

And Barrengarry—the beautiful but shabby carpets and drapes, the exterior woodwork dry, neglected, and the fences, some forty years old, all in need of more restoration than Carl could manage.

And the fact that Suzanna and the girls had dyed all their dresses, they had not bought new mourning. And their very presence here in the country instead of in town where the social scene would involve inevitable expense for the various entertainments . . .

Suzanna was regarding her quietly and apprehension lay only half hidden in her gaze. "Why, Katey? What's troubling you? Has your father said something . . ."

"No, Mama, not at all." Katherine took the fragile lace from her mother's hands and returned it to its fellows. "I simply wondered how the businesses were faring—to tell the truth I'd like to see father put a little more money into this place—you must admit he's neglected Barrengarry."

"He's been very busy and preoccupied in Sydney . . ." But Suzanna did not lift her eyes to Katherine's, and her voice trailed away. She turned her head and gazed out through the net curtains to the muted view of the garden and the pines outside.

Katherine waited a few moments, debating whether to press the matter, but decided it would be neither kind or fruitful. She walked upstairs to change, feeling more troubled than before. It was obvious that what little her mother knew, she did not want to know.

About the same time that Katherine was being frightened off her log by Mikey Brody, Marcus and Brendan were approached by four members of the Woddi Woddi—Gurral, the tribal leader, and three of his grown sons. They were on a hunting expedition and, pleased with the wallaby they had killed, a delicacy in the Valley in these days, Marcus and Brendan were invited back to the camp to eat with them.

Katherine heard about the visit when they returned home. Until then she had been determined to avoid Brendan, but was forced to hastily reconsider her strategy, and she asked him to walk in the garden before supper, the better to find out what had happened. Marcus seemed troubled and did not volunteer any information except that food had been scarce for the Woddi that winter and many families had already left to head towards the coast.

Brendan, shortening his stride to stroll beside Katherine, could not tell her very much more, though he was impressed by the old tribal leader, his dignity and his humour.

"But they—Gurral and your father—spoke half English and half some kind of Aboriginal language—it was hard to follow what they were saying. Gurral kept pointing to the hills, perhaps telling your father how scarce the game is becoming. Marcus listened and nodded—but he did mention the Crolins, I remember that.

"Gurral and his sons seem to know exactly how squeamish a stomach white people have. When we'd arrived in camp they invited us to eat some fat yellow grubs—and while your father did—and pantomimed great enjoyment, too—I couldn't. I picked one up, but I *couldn't* bring myself to put the repulsive thing in my mouth. Stop smiling, Kate," he growled. "I feel as if I've failed in an important diplomatic mission."

Katherine tried to look serious. "I'm sure the Woddi weren't upset."

"No, they weren't, that was just it. They *expected* me to turn faint-hearted, and enjoyed the sight hugely. One of them kept bringing the grubs back—from a little bark tray affair—and offering it to me with all the aplomb of an English butler, but I could tell that they all thought it was a wonderful joke."

Katherine laughed despite herself, and Brendan smiled. "This country is like nothing else on earth," he said, "the people—the Woddi, they're like God's children—so happy, with so little . . . and the height and the depth of the sky, the vegetation—I even like the colour of the trees—you always said it was drab. It's not drab when you look carefully, and there's much to be said even for greyish-coloured forests when you know that they stay that colour always, even when it snows, I believe . . . and thousands of square miles of desert . . ." he said reflectively. "Impossible for an Irishman to imagine on the sort of scale you have here. And most of the time you have glorious weather—for about nine months of the year! I wish . . ." he stopped.

After a pause when he did not continue, she said, "Yes?" with a smile, enjoying the sight of Brendan so enthusiastic about a place she loved.

"No, nothing. I was raving." He was scowling at the path before him, and it was as if someone had changed the picture in a lantern slide, so abrupt was his shift in mood.

"Brendan? What's the matter?"

From perusing the ground he threw up his head to scan the sky and laughed a little, as if he knew quite well the futility of looking for answers anywhere about him.

"Fate," he said, "is an amusing thing. If one can stand back and watch the poses it makes us strike. Do you ever feel like a character in a play that has no beginning and no end—but you're conscious that you must be performing for someone, somewhere? Playwrights have a word for it—dramatic irony . . ."

He was disturbing her with this unguarded, almost uncontrolled stream of images. Had the happenings in Ireland done this to him, the disappointment in the Fenian Brotherhood, or . . .

Or was it something to do with herself?

He was gazing at her, she found, with just the same watchful studious glance that she turned upon him. She smiled, shook her head a little. "I don't understand what you're saying," she told him, "but I do know that there is something like a game of charades going on between us."

"You know that?" his voice mild, unreadable.

"Yes. You know it too. Brendan . . ." and she placed one hand on his arm. It made him cease walking and he turned fully to her; it was only then that she realized the difficulty in what she had to say. "Brendan, I hope I haven't disappointed you in some way. I'm free now, it's true. And so are you . . . No, please don't interrupt—" for he had taken her arms, had begun to speak, and she placed a hand on his chest and silenced him. "Please let me finish . . .

"I realize now—I had begun to realize it before you arrived, but seeing you again made me sure, for my heart betrayed me on seeing you and I think you noticed it . . ." She stopped, breathlessly, "I know I love you, Brendan, and have for a long time. Too long . . ." her voice low, she looked away a little, "for it not to bother me a great deal. Though we behaved very well, didn't we, you and I?"

She glanced up at him, once, and felt again that sense of possession and of being possessed, of drowning in those grey eyes, and she looked away once more. "I don't need you to tell me that you love me—I've known it for years, although I convinced myself otherwise. Now you're here—and so am I . . . it's too late, Brendan. There's something in me that won't allow myself to take chances any more. Not with my life, for that's what loving means. I don't want to give over my life into someone else's hands. I can't . . . *trust* any more."

His voice was low but firm. "I'm not Oliver."

"I know that, but . . . Oliver took something from me—call it my love, my heart, whatever romantic phrase one will—I gave it willingly, but it seemed . . . *it was never enough.*"

"It's only to be expected that you feel like that . . ."

"Then you can understand if I tell you that if you're staying here in the Valley in the hope that I'll feel . . . *more* towards you, that I may consider returning to Ireland with you, then you must give up, *now*. For I won't do it, Brendan. My life is here. Your life is in Dublin, or at Avonwood . . ."

"Yes . . ."

"And you must, if you marry, choose a woman who'll return there with you . . ."

"Yes, I know. Katherine, that was the only . . ."

"Then won't you consider going now? I can't help but feel that if you stay we may begin to hurt each other. I don't know how or why, but I'm afraid that we'll lose the close accord that we have. Don't you see that it may happen?"

"No," he said, and he sounded convinced in his own mind, "I don't believe anything between us will change or deteriorate, no matter what happens."

"I . . . I might change my mind in time—perhaps, if it's not asking too much, we could write to each other, but . . ."

"I'm not leaving the Valley, Kate, not for some months. I promised your father to manage Barrengarry in his absence, and I'll keep to that arrangement."

Their gazes locked and the warmth of a few seconds previously was glazed with watchful speculation.

"You'll stay. For six months, if he asks you to," she stated flatly.

"Yes. I like it here. And I need the opportunity to think and consider my life."

"Can't you do that in Boston?"

"No. Certainly not in Boston." Barely audible.

The conversation had begun so well, and it had deteriorated yet again. It was her fault, she realized, she was pressing him and he was never a man to be pressed. At least he had stopped using the dreadful excuse of the Fenian money . . .

"I need this time, Kate. Please don't ask me for too many details, but as you can imagine I can't go home to Ireland for some time, anyway. And there are decisions—difficult decisions—to be made before I can return to Boston. I've made a mess of my life in more ways than one—"

"Will it help to talk about it?"

"No. No, I don't want to involve you. I'm sorry if my presence is making things awkward for you, but I'm here now, and I'd appreciate it if you could try to understand my need to stay."

"Yes . . ." unwillingly, then, "Oh . . . I was being questioned by Laura and Edwina and to save myself—and you—from embarrassment, I told them that you have a serious relationship in Ireland—an engagement actually," she said, with some awkwardness. "I hope you don't mind, but you must realize that if I hadn't, there'd be no end to the speculation about us."

The coolness had not left the grey eyes. It was obvious that he was not pleased, but, "I don't mind," he said, "it's just as well."

"Thank you," she said, and it was odd but there was not, as they turned back towards the house, the sense of relief that she had expected. Rather a kind of hollow inside her. Matters were settled, were they not? They understood each other, did they not? Then why did she have this ridiculous desire, as they walked back along the darkening paths in silence, to approach the subject once more, to find some tangential way back into the conversation that, leaving it as they had, had her feeling oddly lost . . . even bereft?

The following morning, early, Edwina and Katherine rode out to the Woddi camp with gifts of flour and tea and presented them to the tribe.

Gurral had greeted them, but stayed at a little distance. Tucker such as tea and flour was, it appeared, static foodstuff, under the same heading as roots and berries. Therefore it was women's business, and two or three women accepted the gifts. A sheep or lamb would, however, have come from Marcus and being game—even game kept in fields behind fences—Gurral would have politely accepted it himself. But part of the conversation the previous day had been a suggestion by Marcus that the tribe take a sheep from Barrengarry; so Gurral, planning to go that afternoon with his sons to take one of the smelly woollen ones with the fish eyes, sons to take one of the smelly woollen ones with the fish eyes, was content to stay under his humpy of bark and doze.

"You come. Tigoora say, you two come." The old woman spoke to Katherine and Edwina as the two women headed to where their horses were tied. They looked at each other. Edwina asked the old woman, in Woddi, where Tigoora and Myeela were, but Katherine could not follow the description the woman gave, though her hand on Katherine's arm was eloquent enough.

"This is Gurral's first wife," Edwina informed Katherine. "That makes her senior to Tigoora, of course. Had you wondered why there were so few women about? Tigoora is having her child." Edwina's eyes were alight with excitement and yet a kind of dread. "We've been invited to visit her. Shall we go, Katey? Father wouldn't like me to, I know . . ."

Katherine looked back at the older woman. She was grinning broadly, gesturing, encouraging the two white women to come, and suddenly Katherine made up her mind. "Yes," she nodded, but paused to glare at Edwina. "If you faint, Teddi, I'll be cross. They'll think we're very weak stock indeed."

"Compared to them, I think we are," Edwina murmured, as they followed the senior Mrs Gurral through the heavy scrub and ferny undergrowth.

Tigoora, when they reached the birthing place, seemed to be showing no signs of discomfort. She looked up from where she squatted over a shallow depression in the soil, and called in a friendly fashion to Edwina and Katherine in the Woddi tongue. It was the only flaw in a morning that would always remain with her, that in their excitement the Aboriginal women did not often remember that she did not speak their language, and though Teddi talked and laughed with them, taking her turn to support the mother in her strange position over the birthing place, Katherine herself could do little and could understand very few of the words spoken.

A small fire was lit in the depression where Tigoora crouched, women came and went from the surrounding bush, with handfuls of special leaves, collected with care, undoubtedly for some kind of medicinal or even anaesthetic properties, and these were fed to the faint, smouldering heap beneath the woman's body, kept, naturally, low enough to offer warmth and comfort without the possibility of burning. When it seemed the child was coming—

in low wails that might be pain, encouragement, prayers, or all three—eager, helping hands scooped the baby out, as the mother was tilted back in her friends' arms to lie on the grass.

Katherine kept watching young Edwina for signs of greenness, but the girl seemed too vitally interested to feel any queasiness as the umbilical cord was tied twice with strong grasses, severed, and the child placed to the mother's breast. A boy! Great good fortune! A son for Gurral! This much of the conversation Katherine could follow, watching as the proud mother crooned to her child, looking up at Katherine to say, in English, "A strong one, this one, 'ey? A great hunter, great chief, like his father, yes?"

Another fire was smouldering close by, earth packed around it. When the afterbirth came, the birthing depression was further excavated and Tigoora, her body close packed with leaves and healing ash, sat in the depression, while the warm earth was piled all about her, up to her chest.

Edwina asked a question of Myeela, who crouched, beaming, close by, and Katherine watched as Myeela answered, pointing an arc in the sky, squinting against the sun.

"What did she say?" Katherine asked.

"I asked how long Tigoora would stay here like this and Myeela said, until nightfall at least. The leaves and the ash against her body will help with healing, and the earth will help, too, apparently, it stays warm for hours and hours. Do you want to go?"

Katherine herself glanced up at the sun, it was well across the sky. "Yes," she said, "we'd better." The black women called goodbye, but were already talking loudly, happily amongst themselves, as the two exhausted women walked back towards their mounts.

On the way home they marvelled at what they had been privileged to witness. "Over a hole in the earth, Katey! Just imagine it— pop the baby in a bark coolamon when it arrives, and the following day break camp and go walkabout again, carrying the baby on your back in a fold of your fur cloak. Not a problem in the world! And we whites go to bed for weeks beforehand, and stay in bed for weeks afterwards, and die in childbirth or lose our children just the same . . ."

"Some Aboriginal women must die in childbirth . . ."

"Not often. I've talked with them a great deal. It's very unusual. No, it's 'white man's sickness' that kills them, Katey. By that they mean any of the terrible diseases we brought to them—influenza, cholera, measles, diphtheria . . ."

Was it right, Katherine wondered, that Edwina should know

all these things? She was sure, if she asked her, that Teddi could tell her what intimate things went on between men and women. She was bright and observant, and living on a farm and with much of her time spent, whenever they were in the Valley, with the Woddi, Katherine was certain that there were few of the facts of life the outspoken Edwina did not know.

"Teddi—I hope you don't talk about these things in front of other people, do you?"

"What things?"

"Birth and . . . things like that."

"Oh. Sexual matters."

"Teddi, really! You'll offend Mama and anyone else who heard you talking like . . ."

"I'm teasing you, Katey—honestly, I wouldn't prattle on like that in front of strangers! I don't want it to get back to Rafe that I'm knowing and shameless. I'll wait until we're married— and let him find out for himself!" The wicked green eyes looked sideways at Katherine then Edwina had burst out laughing.

Katherine never knew what her reaction to this would have been. For the bright carillon of Teddi's amusement brought a creaking and cawing and scolding of black shadows over the sun, and both of them ducked a little as their horses danced sideways, away from the rising, clamorous flock of crows that flapped oily, reluctant wings up into a high eucalypt. There were at least ten of them, and they eyed the two mounted figures balefully and hopped up and down impatiently on their branches.

"Something's dead," Katherine said, rather unnecessarily. The wind brought a faint but repulsive stench to them; even the horses snorted, shook their heads, pattered sideways in the dust, eager to be away.

Edwina was slightly closer to the edge of the scrub. She said, "Something's shining—over there by the big tree, where they rose."

"Teddi . . ."

"Really, Katey. Come here and see—something very bright like metal—"

She should have told Edwina to remain mounted. Or, if they needed to walk forward together on foot she should have made Edwina walk behind. Or she should have remembered the death of Gilbert Barton and ridden home to tell Marcus . . .

But it was Edwina who led the way, because Katherine hated to see dead wallabies or wombats or even sheep—and that's all it would be. Edwina had a stronger stomach, would turn back any second . . .

She was running to Katherine, running *at* Katherine, her arms around Katherine's neck, the little body rigid, "Oh, Katey, don't look . . . don't look! He's been dead a long time . . . oh, Katey, let's go home—take me home . . . !"

And she who hated to see dead wallabies had, then, to be strong, she had to see, leaving Edwina sobbing, her hands to her face, voice rising in waves towards hysteria. Yet Katherine must check—for she would be the one Father would ask, "Did *you* see it, Katherine?"

And Katherine did.

Eighteen

Brendan found her seated on a milking stool near the stable door, late that afternoon. The body had been taken to, of all places, Radley's store, as he had a large shed away from any habitation, and somehow the consensus of Sergeant Lloyd, Marcus, Brendan and Rupert Huckstable, whose homestead was the closest to the spot where the body was found, was that the store, unsalubrious though its reputation was, still had a communal and non-partisan ambience to it. Besides this, no one wanted the grisly remains on their property, while Bert Radley let it be known, on being approached by Tom Lloyd, that for a certain remunerative sum he would allow his community spirit to override his sensitivities.

For the body was not that of a Valley man. The hair colour and pathetic remains of his suit, greatly affected by the weather, were the only means of attempting an identification. So no one came forward to claim him and his first night after discovery was spent lying beneath an old oilskin cloth among the barrels, rusting harness and worm-eaten furniture in Bert Radley's storage shed.

Tom Lloyd, who had been fetched from Moss Vale, was staying the night at Barrengarry, having chosen that homestead over the Huckstables' equally comfortable Bendeela; more, Marcus remarked drily to Katherine, because of his proximity to three attractive and eligible young women than for any reasons of comfort or convenience.

Young Sergeant Lloyd, irrepressible, it seemed, despite the horrors and rigours of his vocation, was able to make himself at home anywhere, and on being offered a bath before dinner, had retired to his room for that purpose and could be heard, such was his power of revival, singing in a gruff but tuneful bass as he splashed about in the tub.

Brendan had kept his distance during the long and detailed questioning sessions, leaving Marcus to attend while Sergeant Lloyd made Edwina and Katherine, separately, relive their grim discovery.

"I couldn't tell him much," Katherine told Brendan, without preamble, as he pulled up a little three-legged stool beside hers and began, with that way of his that she had taken for granted for so many years, to fill her aloneness with the quiet support of his presence. "What could I tell him? Something silver shone in the sunlight . . . I walked closer—and it was a hipflask. Not silver, but some cheaper metal, lying there beside . . . him." She looked at Brendan, "I had to consciously say 'him', for I nearly said, 'it'. Just a shape in a dark brown suit—there was something inhuman about the poor man. Death does that, I know. The soul has gone, so I suppose I'd be right to say 'it' . . .

"His face was turned towards me. That was the worst thing— Poor Teddi, she can't stop crying—at least I was prepared, it was worse for her. He had *no eyes*. . ."

She bent forward suddenly, feeling ill, but Brendan's hands had reached for her, one arm about her shoulders, gripped her firmly, and the strength from him helped somehow. While the bile did not rise, the tears suddenly did; she felt the heaviness in her chest welling, bit her lip and turned to press her face against his shoulder.

There is safety here. Her heart told her this without words, unbidden, but she was still frightened, and it made no lasting impression. The horror and the misery built upon each other and she felt close to weeping. She took a deep breath, expecting the release of tears, for they would come now, surely . . .

But no.

She stayed, like a child, being rocked in Brendan's arms, feeling the weight of her grief dammed up within her.

"I'm not . . . crying, you know," she informed him shakily, after a pause. She lifted her face to his. "See? Tears come, but they flow backwards again, somehow. I cried when Oliver died. They released his body to me, for he hadn't lived to stand trial. Your money, that you sent from Boston, which had helped prepare his defence also helped to bury him . . . as a gentleman should be buried. At the undertakers, I had them change the hideous oblong crate for a decent coffin. Only then, when he was dressed in his best suit, his hair combed, lying in the walnut coffin with its pleated satin lining . . . I looked at him . . .

"Three weeks he had been in Kilmainham—and he looked like an old man, although he was only thirty-one. Kilmainham killed him. Even his hands had withered, there was no flesh on him—it was as if his bones were made of porcelain, his skin of parchment. I'd visited him only four days before he died; I'd noticed, then, the white strands in his hair and how translucent his skin had become. But he was able to stand, to walk. Thinking about it now, it was his spirit I saw. His spirit was so strong it kept his body alive.

"The prison doctor said Oliver died in his sleep. The pneumonia, and a weakened heart. I looked at Oliver in his coffin and I thought of the handsome boy—he was like a boy, wasn't he?—I thought of the young and vital Oliver we had known. And I cried—oh, I cried for a long time . . .

"Alice, Oliver's sister arrived—you remember her, don't you?—and she took me home. She barely looked in the coffin—you know how grim she was, wearing her rectitude like a banner. Being Low Church, as she was, Oliver had been past redemption for years in Alice's eyes, his friends numbering Catholics and revolutionaries—and some who were both at the same time."

Katherine paused and smiled tentatively. They smiled at each other, for both knew Brendan would be among them.

She looked away, towards the sun; it was resting on the western escarpment like a child's orange ball, neglected on a shelf. She said, "I'm sorry I'm talking so much. I haven't spoken to anyone else. No one here knows all this, you see. Anyway . . . that was the last time I cried. I was already sick with fear for Christopher's health. I took him to Italy, and yet only six weeks later . . . he was dead. And I couldn't cry. The pointlessness of it. The injustice of it. It went beyond tears. Does that make sense? Since then . . ." and her soft laughter mocked herself, "everything has gone wrong—but I've forgotten how to cry. Perhaps," she added, "it's a good thing."

She felt him sigh, and for a second his arms tightened about her. He said, his mouth against her hair, "Beware of your strength, Kate," as gently as if he were warning a child not to touch a strange dog, not to play near a roadway.

His words rankled a little. She became aware that they were out of sight of the house, sitting in the gathering dusk, in a close embrace. "It's good to be strong," she said. "It's so often necessary in this world."

"That's true," he murmured, "but I don't want to see you making a religion out of it. Offering up the gentle and the affectionate in your nature in the hope of a dubious kind of sanctuary—a strength that can barricade you away, not only from hurt, but from human warmth and intimacy."

She thought about this, still from the safety of his arms. She said, "Perhaps I won't miss human warmth and intimacy." She looked up into his face, and, as she thought, her words had troubled him deeply. "You're Catholic," she continued, "a Catholic family would be proud of a son who joined the priesthood, a daughter who entered a convent." She remembered suddenly, "Why, three of your own sisters have chosen to live without human warmth and intimacy . . ."

"Nonsense," he said gruffly, "you're choosing to believe that I meant only physical closeness. Ann, Mary and Ellen laugh, cry, worry over and triumph with the people they care for. It's possible to involve oneself completely with humanity and forgo a sexual union—in the same way as it's possible to perform sexual acts with many different people—and care about no one."

She had started to stiffen. How did the conversation manage to turn itself to such very earthy matters?

"I don't see that I fit into either category," she said primly, and would have liked to further distance herself by pushing back from him, out of his grasp—but it was hard to do that, a lethargy had seized her and it was warm in his arms, while the wind was chill; it was a kind of sanctuary in itself, this embrace, while they talked in detached terms of her capacity or incapacity for closeness.

And yet it was Brendan who pulled back a little, to gaze consideringly into her face before saying, gently, "Do you trust me, Kate?"

"Of course I do," she stammered, feeling herself close, too close to him for such tender scrutiny.

"If you were worried, or frightened, would you tell me?" he continued.

"I *am* worried and frightened," she said, "there's a maniac prowling these hills murdering people—I found a body not three miles from my front door—I have no reticence whatsoever in saying I am both worried and frightened."

"Of course, anyone would be," he soothed, and stroked her hair, her cheek; she only just controlled herself from pressing her face against his hand, eyes closed, like a cat, giving herself up to the agreeable pleasure of his touch. He continued, "Aside from your experience this morning; I'm speaking generally—is there anything else? Do you have any financial problems?" Her eyes opened wider, and he spoke more quickly and firmly. "I could help you—whatever it takes—I'm not poor, as you know, and . . ."

"I have enough to get by." And her voice sounded cool, aloof, even to her own ears, not the sort of voice one should use when an old and dear friend offered unlimited financial aid.

"I'm serious." He rocked her a little, but it was also a mild shaking, and the look in his eyes held a touch of impatience. "If you'd only tell me what's happened, what's led you to this . . ."

"To what?"

"Stop playing, Kate. I've tried to be patient. I'm telling you I'll fix everything—"

"I don't want anything 'fixed'—"

"What is it you want? A house of your own? Or . . . were there more debts than you told me about, back in Dublin? If it's anything at all that I can help with . . ."

Their arms had dropped from each other during this exchange, and now she stood up, rather ruining the gesture by tripping a little, as his stool was on the edge of her skirt. He stood, and, free now, she turned on him fiercely. "What is it I want?" she fumed, "it's to be left alone to remember the good, the best days in Dublin, not to be reminded of the senseless, bitter ending to it all—all the fine plans and dreams, drained away slowly, like Oliver's life, like Christopher's, before its time! And don't come to me now with your gracious gestures and your charity!"

Her terror and her horror of that morning, unable to be released in tears, found vent in her anger. "You helped us so much in Ireland—and I'll always be grateful to you—but we fulfilled a need for you, too, didn't we, Brendan? You're a lonely man—because you've never let anyone really close to you. Instead, you helped them, cared for them, and gained a sense of pleasure—of *closeness*—" she added evilly, "by feeding people's need of you. You're doing it still—you're doing it now. Are you incapable of saying simply, 'I love you, Katherine, marry me?' Not that I would, but I'd like to hear you offering *yourself* for once, only yourself."

"And you'd say no." His face cold, set.

"I . . . yes. But you wouldn't say it. It's not intimacy *you* want, either."

"You have no right to make that kind of judgement, Kate. And why should I drop to one knee and declare myself, pray, when you've just announced that you'd laugh in my face?"

"I didn't! I didn't . . . say I'd laugh in your face. I wouldn't. I'd . . . it's just . . ."

The tension radiated from him in waves, and it was more frightening than even the passion that earlier had called to something hidden and forgotten within her. There was a constrained violence to him as he stood close to her, their bodies not touching. "I've learnt something from this, at least," he said, and his measured tones did nothing to dispel her feeling that he was more angry with her than he had ever been in all the years they had known each other.

"What?" she asked flatly, unwilling to betray the curiosity she felt, but finding his silence intolerable.

"That all these years you've noticed these things about me, when I believed that very few of the thoughts behind that calm facade of yours ever concerned myself. I'd have spoken sooner, had I known my reticence bothered you."

"It didn't! I didn't notice anything . . ."

"But you just said you did."

"I simply wonder at why you . . ."

"Why I'm 'incapable' of asking you to marry me?"

"No! I don't want you to!"

"The reason I don't should be perfectly clear. I don't ask you to marry me, because I don't want to marry you. But I find I'm rather appalled at your forwardness—are all Australian women so outspoken? An Irishwoman—a well-bred one, at least—would never dream of asking a man why he doesn't propose."

She stepped back from him, feeling her hand clench, every muscle and nerve in her arm constricting with the effort not to lay the palm of her hand across his cheek with all the rage and shame he had awakened in her.

But she did not. By the time the seconds had passed, her feet had taken her away from him, back towards the house, almost of their own volition, and she was not to know, did not even consider, that he might have been left feeling more angry, more foolish and regretful than she did herself.

Tom Lloyd stayed three days at Barrengarry, questioning settlers, cedar-getters and even, with Marcus as interpreter, old Gurral and his sons. All interviews proved fruitless, until news came from Berry, on the eastern slopes of the Highlands, that a man had been missing for some weeks from his home, and Tom rode off to investigate.

Edwina, to the family's concern, showed no sign of recovering from her hysteria until the second visit Rafe Huckstable made to the house. Despite Marcus's coolness—and, Katherine noticed, Brendan's—Rafe accepted Suzanna's hospitality and Peggy's lemon teacake, and seemed determined on preserving his visitation rights to the house.

Marcus, finding his ill-mannered silences and broad-sided sarcasms ignored with stubborn courtesy, left the unwelcome guest to Suzanna. His wife, however, whose health had once again begun to deline into headaches and lethargy since returning from Dovewood, turned to her daughters to entertain him. Laura, perhaps remembering with discomfort the exquisite torment of her brief *tendresse* for Rafe, kept excusing herself in order to write copious letters to Stephen Brody, which she would hand to him in a large paper packet, receiving a like parcel, on the few occasions that they could meet. Besides, as she would hiss to Katherine in the hall before disappearing, it was *too* bad that that scoundrel Rafe, with his dreadful reputation, should be allowed tea and cake in the parlour while poor Stephen had to walk his horse up and down beside the broken tree on Murchisons' place, sometimes in the rain, while waiting for her to creep out to meet him.

Katherine, therefore, was left on both occasions to entertain Rafe herself. He was polite, amusing, and never stepped across the boundaries of good manners, but the dark eyes held, in the frequent and lengthy pauses, a conversation all their own.

Thus it was that halfway through the second visit, Katherine excused herself, declaring, with a smile, that—yes, she *thought* she heard Edwina, now . . . And leaving the parlour she had hurried up the stairs, flung herself into Edwina's room and pulled the girl bodily from her bed, announcing that four days of the vapours were quite enough, and if she did not wash and dress and come downstairs to Rafe Huckstable *instantly*, she, Katherine, would box her ears.

Fifteen minutes later, Edwina, rather pale, and with a few curling tendrils escaping from her hasty chignon, joined the world once more, beginning with tea and lemon-cake with Rafe Huckstable and, later that evening, eating a hearty meal of steak and kidney pie without, it seemed, much ill-effect remaining from her ordeal.

Edwina spent the following Saturday at the Huckstables', on an invitation that Rafe delivered from his mother and sister. Marcus and Brendan were off visiting some far-flung corner of the Valley that was Prescott land, deciding whether to clear it and lease it, sell it, or run scrub cattle, as many settlers did. Laura and her mother were discussing the embroidery patterns they wished Essie Crolin to work on, as she was expected to visit that morning. So it was Katherine, sketching the first primroses to appear in the garden, in the shadows of the pine windbreak, who first saw Sergeant Lloyd riding up the drive.

She walked forward to meet him, and he dismounted, removing his cap with a grin and smoothing the unruly brown curls. "I have some news, Mrs Carron—is your father about?"

"He won't be back until midday at least, sergeant—you must stay to lunch. And tell me what you've found—please!"

He tied his horse to the verandah rail and they walked in the garden. She was glad to find him first, alone, as he was the type of courteous young man who would hold back unsavoury details before a group of ladies. Now, faced with Katherine's direct gaze and equally direct questions, he found himself telling the complete story, without being conscious that he need patronize or protect her.

"His name was Edgar Penman—he was a rent collector, representing owners who live on the coast, in the Nowra area. Normally, all his business affairs are involved in Nowra and the Illawarra district, but in the past six months or so, he's travelled to the Yarrawa Brush—it seems there are farmers there who're falling into arrears on their properties."

Katherine nodded soberly. There were hundreds of small landowners in the Yarrawa Brush who had purchased plots averaging two hundred and fifty acres when the Robertson Land Acts had opened up the country to subdivision. In the five years since the Act had been passed, the wealthy squatters, some of whom had lost a great deal of the Crown land once under their control, were able, surreptitiously, to buy it back, as the inexperienced, the incompetent or the plain unlucky failed in their agricultural attempts. "There are mortgages on some of the propertics that are held by wealthy people on the coast?" Katherine asked.

"That's right. Well, Mr Penman was returning from Burrawang and he called in to see one of the Valley settlers, Jim O'Mara—you know him?"

The tall, sandy-haired farmer, surrounded by his many children, standing over his wife's grave in the little Valley cemetery. "Yes," Katherine said, concerned already, by some sixth sense, at what Lloyd was about to say.

"I'd questioned O'Mara, along with most of the settlers, before

I left for Nowra. He claimed, like all the others, that he had no idea of the identity of the body. But turns out he did, as I confronted him with the truth only this morning. Thing is, I believe his story, myself—he seems a good man, if a bit . . . slow, if you know what I mean. He didn't connect the description of the dead man with Mr Penman—two neighbours of his had already viewed the body, and rumour had got back to O'Mara that the body was that of a big man, and of course, he wasn't." Tom caught Katherine's gaze and looked uncomfortable. "Bodies . . . swell, Mrs Carron—gases, so the doctor tells me. I brought Doctor Hickman back with me from Nowra—he knew Mr Penman and was able to identify the remains. He also told me that Penman died of blows to the head— two or three. Much in the same way as Gilbert Barton and Roger Harcourt."

"Harcourt? Who's he? Oh, I see, the man who was killed just out of Burrawang, a few weeks before I arrived home from Europe. So you believe the three murders are connected in some way?"

"I do. They were all rent collectors, you see. And three of them— too many to be the work of dissatisfied tenants."

Katherine relaxed a little. "Then that would mean the murderer knew all the men. No one in the Valley travels much, especially not a hard-working farmer like Jim O'Mara. He has his work cut out for him running his selection and raising fourteen children alone."

"Like I said, I don't like to think it was him, either. But you can't tell in these cases. He was late in his mortgage payment— that's why Penman was asked to call in to see him on the way back to Nowra. As it turns out, though, O'Mara had paid the money to the Moss Vale agent a few days before Penman arrived. I'll be checking, but I've no doubt that O'Mara is telling the truth—he has a receipt, which he showed Penman. He left O'Mara's place satisfied, apparently—but he never left the Valley alive."

Taking Katherine's silence for apprehensive concern, he lowered his voice and said kindly, "It'll soon be over, Mrs Carron; the doctor and I will take Penman's body back to Nowra for burial. I'll question O'Mara again—and tomorrow or the day after a police inspector from Sydney is arriving—these murders are beginning to receive a lot of publicity, and people are concerned."

"Of course," Katherine murmured, "but it won't be over until the murderer is caught, Sergeant Lloyd. And I'm sure that you and the inspector will be wasting your time by harrassing a man like Jim O'Mara. He wasn't in trouble with his mortgage payments, so there was no reason for him to quarrel with Mr Penman, let alone . . .'"

she let the sentence remain unfinished, withdrawing from the very thought of Jim O'Mara committing an act of such horrendous brutality.

"The fact is," Tom pondered, "he was the last person to see Penman alive—and it would have looked better for him if he'd have remembered the man himself, rather than me having to confront him after speaking to Penman's employers and getting lists of tenants and mortgagees. Hello—here they are . . ."

Katherine looked up, following his gaze. Her father and Brendan Kelehan were just appearing, riding up the drive. She found herself feeling relieved; the gruesome subject matter upset her more than she had expected. When *would* it be over, she wondered, and could they ever forget?

She turned towards the verandah. "I'll leave you to tell them," she said, "and I'll notify my mother and Peggy that you'll be staying for lunch. Will the doctor be with you?"

"No, Doctor Hickman is at Huckstables', and I'll be staying the night there, also—I feel I've imposed upon your family enough."

She began to say that this was not so, but he had glanced off towards the approaching riders and his words cut across hers. "There is something else I'd like to ask, if you don't mind . . ."

Katherine stopped and the young policeman looked, suddenly, as if he wished she had not. A flush crept up from the tight collar of his uniform and a hand moved to it briefly before being lowered to clutch at the hat in his other hand, and to help its companion turn the cap round and round. His embarrassment made him look boyish, and this was amusing in a man of at least, Katherine judged, twenty-eight or nine.

"I wondered how Miss Barton was," Tom stated. "Since she's staying with your grandparents, I thought you may have heard. From them. Or her." He tried, in his scarlet intensity, to look mildly concerned. Katherine was staring at him, fascinated. *Fleur?*

"Why, no, Sergeant, we've heard nothing from Miss Barton or my grandparents, but I will expect a letter will come soon. In the meantime, I'm sure Miss Barton would like to hear from you—I believe she told me that she would miss the friends that she made during her stay in the Valley."

"Oh, yes," he scowled, "but I doubt that she'd mean *me*. I mean, the circumstances of our meeting weren't ideal. At her father's deathbed, and all. She'd connect me with some pretty unpleasant memories, I reckon."

"On the contrary, Sergeant, from all I've heard, your kindness and competence probably helped make that difficult and tragic time much easier to bear. The address is simply *Dovewood, via Moss Vale*. Do write to her—I'm sure she'd love to hear from you."

She smiled at him and left him there, beaming at her, inarticulate with gratitude, and headed for the house, eager to be gone before Marcus and Brendan drew close.

It was amazing, she thought, walking through the house towards the kitchen, that everyone she knew seemed to be obsessed with the problems of forming or keeping relationships. For five or six seconds she was graced with a feeling of disinterested amusement, and then, looking further into her own euphoria, she found that it was not without a certain sense of relief. Fleur's hungry little soul might just find satisfaction with the esteem in which Tom Lloyd obviously held her. Despite his bashfulness and an emotional naivete, Tom Lloyd was no green boy, and Katherine had the feeling that his interest in Fleur Barton was neither light nor fleeting. She wished him well and hoped, with the effects of the new security in which both Mrs Barton and her daughter found themselves, that Fleur would lose, if she had not already lost, the rancorous bitterness that told Katherine, despite her strong sense of logic, that something beneath Fleur's passive personality was unstable.

She had thought to find Peggy in the kitchen—and so she did, but that pink-faced and cheerful personage was moving about preparing luncheon in the presence of Suzanna, Laura and Essie Crolin, these three seated at the kitchen table, an ancient behemoth of pine, scrubbed white by years of soapstone and Peggy's energy. The parcel of Essie's embroidery lay on the table, along with a separate bundle of the materials and sketches she would need for the work the Prescott women had commissioned. Essie smiled timidly at Katherine, who greeted her politely before notifying the others of the Sergeant's presence and Marcus's and Brendan's return.

The women had been finishing a cup of tea, but now Essie stood nervously and reached for her bundles. "You'll be busy, and I've stayed too long already . . ."

Katherine joined the others in urging her to stay, but she was already edging towards the door, the bundles clutched in her thin arms and even the moderate size of the packages dwarfing her. Katherine realized how far she had to walk, not merely along the valley roads, but up the half-invisible mountain tracks towards the camp. "I'll take the buggy and drive you, Mrs Crolin . . ."

"No, no! Reelly, there's no need! It ain't far—I'm used to it . . ."

"But . . ." Katherine had made a move towards her and Mrs Crolin almost fled down the verandah stairs. "No, I won't have you going to the bother, Miss Pres . . . Mrs Carron. No, I'm right—reelly an' truly . . ." And even as she spoke she was bustling on her way, like a burdened little brown ant, across the stable yard, through the sliprails by the barn, and across the fields, some shortcut of her own knowing that would take her home.

Katherine stood at the door and watched her go, feeling a strong sense of pity for the woman. She was surprised to hear her thoughts put into words in a rough voice from the kitchen.

"Poor woman," Peggy muttered, "did you see her? Wouldn't wait for you in the parlour, perched here at the table as nervous as a possum until I fetched yez. Only your kindness put her at her ease, Missus—all we could do," she turned from Suzanna to Katherine, "to get the woman to have a cup of tea, and her having walked six miles—and another six miles home. Thin as a broom handle— don't think she eats, half the time . . . You should have seen her, Miss Katey, before yous all come in, looking about this room like it was a church or something. 'A pump *inside*,' she says, and comes to stand beside me and peer at all the ewe-tensils, counting them, I think. An' stared so hard at *that* thing that I thought she was going to burst out crying." Peggy gestured to the modern black grotesque of a stove, cast-iron legs shaped like dragon's claws, standing square in the huge chimney as if it were defending its lair, and snarling with its grate, where one could see the fires in its belly through the gaping jaws.

Peggy finished quietly, "Would give a year of her life for one of them, I reckon."

Suzanna came to stand beside Katherine at the door, and they watched as the slight figure reached the scrub and disappeared into its shadows.

Unlike her room in Balmain, Katherine's bedroom at Barrengarry was situated closest to the stairs. Her fireplace shared a common chimney with that of the parlour directly below. So it was that she heard the quarrel that night between her parents.

She woke dreaming that it was she and Oliver shouting at each other, the bitterness of years finding expression at last; and what awakened her was as much the growing volume of the voices as the growing realization that she and Oliver had never really quarrelled. Their disappointment had always been kept well in check by their courtesy and their respect. No, she and Oliver had never spoken to each other like this.

"You never cared about us! You left us here and went off to Sydney to flagellate your own conscience . . . !"

"I had no need to! I did everything I could for Joe . . . !"

"You never listened to him! To what *he* wanted! All his life you used to talk of how you wanted a son to inherit Barrengarry—and when we came back from Europe you imprisoned him here—when he asked you time and again to allow him to work in Sydney, or to travel to Queensland . . . !"

"Someone had to stay here! If I'd taken him off to Sydney with me or let him go north, you'd have been the first one to moan that you'd been left here unprotected. And this was the best place for Joe to be, until he learnt some sense of responsibility . . ."

"He'd never have found it doing something he hated! He was no more cut out to be a farmer than you were, Marcus—we'd have been better off selling Barrengarry and all moving to Balmain . . ."

"This land was a gift to my grandfather from Governor Macquarie! You don't *sell* something like that! You hand it down to your sons—"

There was a terrible pause, the silence almost unbearable, palpable as it was with the depth of her father's grief and despair.

And her mother's voice came, almost sullenly, as if driven by her own bitterness. "Joe never wanted it."

"Joe never knew what he wanted!"

"He wanted a life of his own, away from this valley, away from your shadow . . . !"

"He couldn't have handled it! He was a spendthrift . . . !"

"He was bored, Marcus—he was *bored*! That's why he gambled, why he took such reckless chances—he was bored! If he had work to do that he could take pleasure in, he wouldn't have been racing with those young men, he wouldn't have fallen . . . !"

"Are you saying it's my fault? Are you telling me I could have done something to save him?"

"He shouldn't have been here! You should have listened to him!"

Suzanna's last words were cut off by a scream—there was a thump as of something heavy, and a crash of glass.

Katherine sat up in bed, her nerves splintering with the sound. She was pulling on a robe and running out the door before she thought clearly.

Down the stairs, and she paused at the parlour door, hesitant, realizing that she would be intruding on a very personal scene between husband and wife, and that neither would welcome her presence. But their words came through the door to her.

". . . And drawing Katey into it—that's the worst part . . . !"

"I didn't!"

"You talked to her! You complained about me!"

"I didn't have to! She has eyes, Marcus! She came home to find her brother dead and her father a hundred miles from his family. She felt that you should be with the girls and myself . . ."

"She lectured me like a little schoolma'am. And I had half a mind to tell her everything . . . !"

"Katherine has her own sense of values—of which you had fallen very short, at that time!"

"You bitch, Suzanna! How dare you judge me . . . !"

"Stop it, Marcus!"

"How dare you preach to *me* of values . . . !"

"Stop it!"

"*Both of you, stop it!*"

She stood in the doorway, knowing she should not be there, knowing she should not have spoken; but to stand still any longer was tearing her apart. She could not bear it that the scene should go on, to who knew what end. Her parents gazed at her in shock, then their faces closed and they glanced at each other, and she knew she was the interloper, as she had feared, and was resented by both.

"Katey, this doesn't concern you." Kindly but firmly from her mother.

And, at the same time, her father said, "Leave us, Katherine."

"All right! But don't use me as part of your quarrel! I don't know what it's about, but I've never taken sides, and I'm not about to now. I love you both—I want you to be happy. Can't you . . . can't you find some consideration for each other's feelings, some remnants of fondness between you? After thirty years of marriage there must be *something*—some good times that held you together. Can't you use that and remember it and talk like friends—or . . . or, if not, then with the good manners of strangers? Even your worst enemies wouldn't scream in your faces as you're doing to each other!"

A silence followed her words. Marcus and Suzanna were facing each other, their glances unreadable. Then, "She has a point," Marcus said quietly. "We don't even have that, 'the good manners of strangers'. A sobering thought. We've come a long way, Suzanna. Into the depths, unfortunately. Did you consider, my dear, that it would end like this?"

Suzanna was regarding her husband warily, disturbed by the new, cool voice. She shook her head a little, whether to say she had not thought so, or to stop the detached voice from further pressing her, one could not tell.

In the pause, Katherine had time to see that it had been a lamp, fortunately unlit, that had been knocked, or swept, from a tabletop to the floor.

Suzanna followed her gaze, and bemused still, went to bend to pick up the pieces.

"Oh, for God's sake, Suzanna! Can't you stop being the excellent housewife for a minute!"

The harshness of Marcus's voice made them both turn to him, startled. He became aware of it, looked discomfited, then said stiffly, "I think this discussion should be concluded for the present moment, don't you? I'll see to the fire. You two go on up to bed."

Katherine paused, but realized that, for the time being, the situation had been diffused, and there was nothing further to be gained by staying. She murmured her goodnights; the words sounded ridiculous, floating on the oppressive air of the room. Both parents gave tight little smiles for her benefit, as they replied, then she left, and they were both still surveying each other silently.

There was no further sound from the parlour below her as she removed her robe and climbed into bed once more. She lay dry-eyed, her heart aching for them both, staring at the ceiling, questioning Joe, foolish, warm, generous and irresponsible Joe, asking why he had to die, couldn't he see what it was doing to them all?

She did not realize that she had been asleep until she woke from the nightmare of reliving the grisly find of that morning. The only difference being that the body was immediately recognizable—it was Joe's. And she was running for help, running down the streets of Dublin, finding the stately facade of the building in Fitzwilliam Street where Brendan had his rooms, and running, breathless, up the staircase to hammer at his door. He would not come, he would not answer . . .

"Miss Katey . . ." Someone touched her arm, and she started with terror, fearing—what? She awoke, and there was Peggy bending over her, a small lamp held in her hand. "I tried knocking, but you didn't stir," she whispered. "Couldn't knock too loud, or I'd wake everyone."

"What's the matter?" Katherine was already clambering from her bed.

"You haven't been asleep long—don't panic, Miss Katey. It's just your mama—she'd like to speak to you."

For the second time that night Katherine pulled on her robe and left her room, after lighting her own lamp to guide her way. As

Peggy was about to head down the stairs and out to the small apartment above the barn that she shared with her elderly husband, she hesitated.

"Miss Katey, your mama is in her sitting room. She has a little bed made up in there, has for almost a week, now. Don't tell the rest of the house, she don't want anyone else to know."

And with that, she descended into the dark of the staircase, leaving Katherine standing, puzzled and concerned, to digest this new piece of information.

How much of our affairs does Peggy know? Katherine wondered, watching the flickering shadows fade below. Whatever it was of this night's happenings, Peggy had appeared a little flushed beneath the flat cheekbones, and her eyes were lowered; she had looked upset and unhappy.

Along the corridor to the little sitting room. She had trodden this hall many times when, as a child, she had been frightened by a nightmare or stricken with various childhood aches and pains. But it had been to the large main bedroom that her slippered feet had taken her, to bleat imploringly at the heavy cedar door. Now she stood, tapping softly, at the door to the sitting room. It didn't feel right. When Suzanna was displaced, it was as if everything was displaced.

"Come in, dear."

Something was definitely wrong. She could sense it even before she noted the pillow and sheets and blankets arranged on the narrow settee. It was something in the way her mother sat in her chair, toying with a small china bell, ornamental only, that usually lay on the inlaid table beside her. The droop of the shoulders, the vulnerable bend to the neck, worried Katherine and added to her apprehension.

"Mama . . . ?"

"Come in, dear," she repeated, without looking up. "Sit down . . ." Katherine closed the door after her and seated herself in the suggested chair, almost facing her mother, across the little table. Only then did Suzanna look up.

"Katey, was it true, what your father said this evening? Did you criticize him for staying away from the Valley?"

"Yes," she admitted, "once or twice, while I was staying in Balmain . . ."

"Oh, Katey, you shouldn't . . ." tiredly. It was the hopeless resignation to the voice that made Katherine cross.

"Why shouldn't I? I wasn't about to let him go on as he was—" she stopped, for she did not want to tell her mother how she had found

Marcus, and the house in Balmain. She merely said, "You can't let him treat you this way, Mama. After thirty years of loyalty and devotion, and he's . . ."

"Katey, stop!" It was not the words that silenced Katherine but the fierce control that Suzanna used—and even then the tears were there, audible in her voice.

"My dear," when she had spent a few seconds regaining her sense of calm, "you really must not interfere in matters you know nothing about. Hard as it may be for you to understand, your father and I know what we are doing . . ."

Katherine murmured a protest, throwing herself back impatiently into the depths of her chair.

Suzanna, still speaking, stopped in mid-sentence and for a moment looked keenly at her eldest daughter. Then, in a different voice, she said, "I keep forgetting that you're a grown woman, and weak excuses will no longer do." She permitted herself a small smile. "Actually, you're probably a great deal more experienced and sophisticated than I am. In my heart, you see, I still think of you as a child; the funny, solemn little thing that you were. We were close, you and I. I loved Joe and the girls very much, loved you all equally, but . . . you were my friend, looking after the smaller children, listening so seriously when there were problems, following me about, helping me, making me laugh . . ."

There was another, strange silence, while Katherine felt her mother studying her, almost summing her up.

Finally, "You are a woman now," she said quietly, "and I hope you're my friend still. The fact that you're my daughter is no guarantee of that, but I'm relying on the woman I believe you to be. I need a friend now, Katey. For I quite truthfully don't know where to turn."

Her gaze was lowered to the surface of the table, where she proceeded to trace the pattern of inlaid mother-of-pearl with the porcelain bell, moving it round and about with an occasional *tink* as the miniscule tongue struck the sides.

"When your father left Barrengarry, just after Joe died . . . it wasn't a sudden decision. We'd talked of a separation for weeks before that. It was only when the accident happened, and we couldn't come to terms with . . . *why*. It shouldn't have happened—it was senseless, futile . . ." Her hands had made fists, unconsciously, and the little bell was knocked over with a sharp tinkling that seemed to startle Suzanna. She stared at it, set it upright and looked over at Katherine.

"Your father and I could find no solace in each other. There was only distrust there between us. You see . . ." she held the little bell in her lap, twisting it about, her eyes lowered, scowling at it, "two months before Joe's death, your father discovered that I had a lover."

She paused, raised her eyes to look directly at Katherine, almost fearfully, anxious to see the reaction to her words.

All Katherine could do was to murmur, "*You*", in order to make sure that the incomprehensible words had been said, and had actually pertained to her mother.

"Yes, Katey." Suzanna gave a long, rather shuddery sigh. "I never thought I would tell a soul, not willingly. It was hard enough to admit it to your father when he found out, and waved the proof beneath my nose."

"Proof?" numbly.

"A letter." Suzanna scowled, shook her head a little. "A note my . . . my friend, for he *is* my friend . . . It was a note that he sent me from Moss Vale. Unsigned, of course, but he shouldn't have sent it."

"And . . . Father found it?"

"Yes." Flatly. She stared at Katherine hard. "Say something, Katey," she begged.

Katherine's mouth felt stiff. "What is there to say, Mama?"

Suzanna's eyes were dark with hurt, her voice low. "Do you despise me, Katey?"

"Oh, Mama, no, no! but . . . what is it you want me to say? That I understand? I don't. Even that I approve. How can I? I've . . . I've been so bitter with Father—I've blamed him for being cold and withdrawn and selfish . . ."

"And now things are different?" Suzanna flared a little. "Your perspective has changed, has it, and now I'm the villain and your father the innocent party . . ."

"No! it's just . . ."

"I don't know how to explain it to you—but now I feel I must. No, Katey, don't get up—I want you to stay and listen."

Katherine stayed, but could not help gazing at her mother with a mixture of pity and resentment. She did not want to know, she did not . . .

"I was very much in love with your father when we married. It took me three years—not really very long—to realize that he didn't love me as much as I did him. I found out in the most unpleasant way possible, through discovering his affair with another woman. It was . . . a small infatuation on his part—the woman was a widow, well-bred and predatory—Marcus soon got over her, and nothing like it has happened since, I'm almost sure.

"But I realized then, and I was never able to forget, that it was I who loved your father, while . . . I don't really believe," she said, a puzzled wonderment in her voice even now, "that he ever truly loved me."

"Oh, Mama—he married you . . ."

"Don't be a fool, Katey—men marry for all sorts of reasons; security, loneliness, the desire for children . . . as many reasons as women have. You see that?"

"Yes," dully.

"I tried for years—I did everything I could to be all Marcus wanted. He was fond of me. I know he respected me. But *he doesn't love me.*"

"But . . . you never quarrelled—I didn't think you were unhappy. Are you saying you were—all those years? *All those years*, you were miserable together?"

Suzanna placed the little bell on the table, but continued to turn it round about. "It's so hard to put all those years into one sentence, or two, dear. The deceit—on both our parts—was necessary for the secure family life we wanted you children to have. You were what we lived for. You children were—*are*—a great bond between Marcus and myself. A great blessing." She smiled, her gentle, sad smile, and Katherine thought her heart would break. She was disturbed to realize that now, only now, for the first time, was she seeing her mother as a woman, an individual with her own desires.

Katherine stood, moved up and down the little room, that small, safe sanctuary that had always seemed the very heart of the house. When she paused at last, it was to see that the smile had left her mother's face and Suzanna was gazing up at her from haunted eyes. "You think I'm asking too much, don't you? You think I should have adapted to a life ruled by a sense of duty and respect, learnt to live without love and affection."

"No, Mama. How could I say that? I know . . . I think I know what you went through. Father has always been preoccupied with his committees and his philanthropic plans. We were always so proud of him . . .

"Oh, Mama, why did you have to tell me this? Does it matter, now? You and Father must talk to each other—perhaps what happened might even make him aware of the way he's been neglecting you. It might!" She was aware that she was speaking with some desperation, willing some response, some positive, hopeful light, back into her mother's face.

"Katey . . . I told you because of your obvious resentment towards your father. I knew it was unfair, and I also knew that he wouldn't defend himself by telling you the cause of our dissension. I couldn't bear for you to misunderstand him . . ."

"Then you must care for him . . ." Katherine stepped towards her mother, who rose and met her, grasping her hands in her own, a tight grip.

"I do care for your father—I *do*. But—how can I tell you this? *Try* to understand, Katey—it's *not over*. I've received letters from . . . the man concerned. He still loves me, and I know I'll have to see him again. Your father knows this—and that's what he can't forgive. And I can't blame him."

"You'll still see him . . ." She stared at her mother, unable to comprehend the situation, for it affected everyone, everything. "Mama, *why*?"

"How can you ask me *why*?" Suzanna burst out, her eyes filling with sudden tears. "I love him, Katey. He's made me believe in myself once more, made me *feel* again, when I've spent years in a half-life, a bare existence, like an unthinking animal. He's brought me back to life, and he needs me. I'm important to him—*as a woman*—in a way I was never important to your father."

"Who is he?" Katherine asked coolly. "Do I know him? Does Father know him?"

"Yes."

She lowered herself into her chair, avoiding Katherine's eyes, "He's . . . he's younger than I am, Katey. Your father didn't suspect his identity—he wrote the letter to me during a visit to Moss Vale, and your father thought he came from there, or even from the Valley. I never told Marcus who he was until tonight. That's . . . what began the quarrel. Did . . . you hear us talking of him?"

"No, I heard only the shouting." Her heart sank. "So Father knows, now."

Suzanna nodded slowly, her gaze still on the floor. "It's Robin Mitchell, Katey."

Katherine's mind was blank. The only Mitchell she knew was her father's big, bluff business partner, who was sixty if a day. But . . . his son. The pleasant, pale young man who had delivered papers to the house in Balmain . . .

"Mama—he's about thirty years old—if that!"

"He's twenty-nine." Her voice flat.

Katherine had no memory of moving back to her chair, groping backwards to lower itself into it.

Suzanna was speaking quickly, now, as if afraid of interruptions. "We met years ago—in Sydney, of course. And last year, when your father and Joe were going backwards and forwards to Barrengarry, Robin was very kind, escorting the girls and me to various entertainments . . .

"We didn't mean anything to happen—indeed, I thought for a long time that he was interested in Laura or Teddi," softly. "But it was me. He liked *me*. He truly cares—for *me*."

She raised her eyes to Katherine. "And I can't say goodbye to him, and mean it. I know I'm a soft, useless kind of woman—but I've at last found something to be strong about. Robin's love has given me that kind of strength. Oh, I tried to break it off—last year, when we returned to Barrengarry. That's when he came to Moss Vale—and I *had* to see him again. When he was leaving, he wrote the letter, the one your father found. Now it's all out in the open—your father even knows I receive letters from him regularly. And I write back to him. I don't know when I shall see him, but I do know that I *can't say goodbye to him again*," she repeated, almost fiercely.

"Yet Father was willing to leave you here in the Valley, and take only myself and the girls to Sydney . . ." Katherine remarked, numbly.

"Yes. Well. You know why, now, I suppose."

Katherine did not.

Her mother smiled gently, trying to mitigate the effects of her words. "Marcus doesn't care if my lover is here in the Valley. He wants only that there be a distance between us. He wants a permanent separation, Katey."

Nineteen

Barrengarry had become an uneasy place in which to be; Katherine, in the following days, found herself avoiding her father, avoiding Brendan, and even avoiding her mother, so difficult was it to confront all that her mother had disclosed.

She went with Edwina, who had a particular relationship with the Woddi Woddi, and helped dispense medicines to the elderly who were suffering, as they always did, from influenza and colds in the cooler months. Diseases unheard of, Edwina remarked grimly, before Europeans came. They brought blankets, also, and tea and sugar and flour for Myeela and Tigoora.

Katherine, as on other occasions, found that she envied young Edwina, who had a gift for languages that she had inherited from Marcus, and who had taught herself to converse almost fluently in the Woddi Woddi tongue. She, Tigoora and the other wives, Myeela and two young girls of about thirteen, as yet unmarried, chattered away in the rather guttural native tongue, laughing frequently together, and leaving Katherine to play with the baby, whose name was Mamoa. He seemed to remember Katherine—or so she told Edwina and the women—for the language barrier did not bother him, at least, and he was quite happy to lie in her lap where she sat on the grass, cooing and gurgling, and gazing up into her face with eyes like black crystal, luminous with humour and intelligence.

It was quite a large gathering of the Woddi, for spring had come, and the fish would soon be returning for breeding in the mouth of the Shoalhaven. They were waiting, Myeela told Katherine and Edwina, for more of their people to come from the northwest, and they would travel down to the sea together.

At dinner that night, Edwina was still talking of the walkabout. "They'll travel down to the coast and meet at Lake Illawarra. Woddi Woddi from hundreds of miles around. They know just where to be at any time of the year, for the fishing, or the hunting—it's so sensible, don't you think, Father? If only we were all nomads and could share our belongings and our food as the Woddi do. They'll have corroborees and the two girls we met today, Katey, are going to be given in marriage to men from a tribe near Bega. Fancy, all that way!

"Father, I've been thinking—you and I speak Woddi Woddi quite well—don't you think it would be a good idea if we wrote it down? Like a kind of dictionary?"

They had much to answer for, all of them, Katherine would think, in later years. For not one of them spoke up, thought beyond the moment. Marcus—and only Katherine and Suzanna knew what lay behind his tension, his intolerance—had snapped, "For heaven's sake, Edwina, what possible use would there be for a dictionary of some obscure Australian Aboriginal dialect? Do you have nothing better to do with your time?"

Edwina was crushed. The silence about the table was less because of Marcus's words than for his tone of voice; no one really thought, in that year of 1866, that there would be any value, any future interest in such an assignment. The tragedy, as Katherine would sometimes discuss with Edwina in long years hence, when she had forgotten all but a few words of the Woddi Woddi tongue, was that, had he been himself, had he had time to reflect, it was the sort of mission that Marcus Prescott would have approved of, even encouraged.

But everything to do with Barrengarry seemed to irritate him; he rode out every day, visited the people in the Valley, his own tenants, other settlers, the Woddi in their temporary home by Barrengarry Creek; yet there was an impatience to his actions that no one in his family had ever seen before, and it became clear, even to Laura, Edwina and Brendan, that he could not bear to be in the same room as his wife.

Two weeks after he had brought them all home from Dovewood, Marcus announced that he was returning to Balmain. Brendan would remain at Barrengarry as overseer, and the girls, he said, could make up their own minds; whether to come to Sydney with him, stay here in the Valley, or even, if they wished, approach Edwin and Angela about staying some months at Dovewood.

They were all seated in the parlour; dinner had passed in the same taut silence as had all the mealtimes over the past few weeks. This announcement, it seemed to all of them, had brought matters to a head. There was a sense of relaxed tension to Marcus, as if, with this decision, some incubus had been dispelled.

Katherine, Edwina and Laura studied everyone else in the room; they met each other's looks blankly, but saw that Brendan was studying Marcus quietly, and Suzanna was gazing at her hands, clasped tightly in her lap.

"What about Mama?" It was Laura who spoke. "What are you going to do, Mama?"

Whatever Katherine had expected, it was not the reply that Suzanna gave, her eyes on her husband's face. They gazed at each other coolly, and it was clear that they had discussed this matter. Suzanna said quietly, "I'm going to Sydney with your father."

For Katherine, there was no question of what she would do; despite the disturbing presence of Brendan Kelehan, she loved the Valley too much to spend weeks, perhaps months, in Sydney. She was made uncomfortable by the thought that her staying would be seen as an unwillingness to detach herself from Brendan's proximity, but she would survive that.

The reactions of Laura and Edwina surprised her, however.

"What does he mean by it?" Laura prowled up and down the verandah the following morning; they had found a sheltered corner where the spring sunshine fell warmly, and with only light cashmere shawls over their dresses, the three sisters had brought their sewing with them, to sit in the old cane chairs—and then to ignore their work. "He's taking himself and Mama off to Sydney and doesn't seem to care in the least what we do."

"Of course he does," Katherine countered. "Really, Laura, at last you have a little independence—and about time at twenty-two years old—you don't want Father to make all your decisions for you, do you?"

"What about me?" Edwina scowled from where she sat, elbows resting on the closed lid of her sewing basket, chin on her fists. "I'm only nineteen—I could run off with Rafe as soon as Father disappeared over the escarpment, and he wouldn't care."

"That's just it," Laura turned to Katherine. "He doesn't care, Katey. I'm glad, truly I am, that we have a choice at last in what we do—but it's Father that I'm worried about. It's so unlike him not to want to *manage* everything—and everyone."

"It was Joe," Edwina said quietly, "he just hasn't been the same since Joe died. He doesn't care about anything any more."

The two older girls turned to her, but the words of rebuttal did not come. There was too much possible truth in Teddi's words.

"I told him this morning that I want to stay." Laura said. "He simply nodded. I had to volunteer that I would behave in a ladylike manner and not cause any gossip to circulate about Stephen and myself. He murmured, 'I'm glad,' and that was all. He *didn't* prohibit me from seeing Stephen. So of course I will see him, and frequently. But it feels very strange, after more than a year of secrecy and defiance, to be told that I'm now responsible for my own actions."

Katherine smiled. Edwina folded her arms on her sewing box. "I told him this morning, also. He said he'd prefer it if I came to Sydney, or went to Dovewood, but I reminded him that you'd undoubtedly be staying, Katey, so he agreed that I could stay, too. I think," she said meekly, "that you're to be chaperone."

"Thank you, no," Katherine said icily. It irritated her, their assumption that she would stay. "If I do decide to remain in the Valley, you must make the same promise as Laura—the first whiff of scandal, Teddi, and you'll be packed off to Balmain so fast Rafe won't even know you've left. You'll make an effort to conduct your relationship with all the restraint that society dictates, or I'll tell Father to take you off with him now. I don't have the time or the inclination to play gooseberry in what you see as a frivolous lark."

"My relationship with Rafe is nothing of the sort."

"Prove it," Katherine defied.

"All right, I will." The little chin was raised defiantly. "I promise I shall behave in a ladylike manner in all things, and do all I can to help you look after Barrengarry, and I won't bring you any problems or grief at all. There!"

Laura was giggling, and Katherine, still pinned by the ferocious look in Edwina's green eyes, had to make an effort not to join her.

"Very well," she said soberly. "I believe you mean it. I think we'll manage very well together."

Though it was a pity, she thought, that she couldn't be as sure that her mother was making the right decision for herself. The gaze she had exchanged with their father the night before had held no warmth, no promise of understanding, let alone forgiveness. The presence of Edwina in the Balmain house might just alleviate the tension that existed between husband and wife . . .

"Missus Carron?"

Katherine looked around, as did both her sisters. At the bottom of the garden, on the other side of the picket fence that separated it from the paddocks beyond, a slender, almost childlike figure, in brown dress and bonnet, stood looking at the group on the verandah, from Katherine to Laura, to Edwina, and back to Katherine. "Missus Carron?"

Katherine stood, jumped down the low drop from the edge of the verandah to the path and walked towards the figure. Only on coming close did she recognise the girl.

She had not seen Molly Murphy since the day they crossed the mountains together, Katherine, Molly, her brother Billy and their

father, Amos Murphy. It had been the day that they found the
unfortunate Gilbert Barton.

Even in the intervening month or so, it seemed that Molly had
changed; she was at that age, about fourteen, when a child turns
very swiftly into a young woman. The face seemed more mature
than Katherine remembered it, and though she could not possibly
have been taller, she certainly gave the impression of a new, coltish
length to her limbs, evident in the rather short skirt and the sleeves
of her faded, sienna-coloured gown.

"Hello, Molly . . ."

"Oh, Missus Carron—I'm real sorry to interfere like this—I was
real glad to see you and the misses on the verandah, as I was near
dying of fright at the thought of knocking on the front door." She
took a deep breath. "Can I talk to you for a bit? I remember, you
see, that you were so nice, not a bit stuck up, when we travelled
all the ways from Wollongong, and I don't know anyone else who
could help me, you see . . ."

"Of course . . ." Katherine turned to her sisters, gazing curiously
at the two by the picket fence. "I won't be a moment!" she called,
and walked off along the path that followed the fence to an almost
over-grown gate that led out into the pasture.

They walked up and down the fence as they talked, staying out
of sight of the two on the verandah, for Katherine could tell that
the child was frightened and agitated.

"What my problem is—and I don't want you to feel I'm asking
you—" the pinched, freckled little face gazed up into Katherine's,
"is that I want to go into service. I . . . I know I don't look nothing—
anything," she corrected, gazing down at the faded dress she wore,
"but I'm good at housework, and needlework and anything like that,
and I'm real keen to learn—even to speak prop'ly, and how to set
tables and things. What I don't know is how to start an' I thought
you might tell me." Again the gaze came up imploringly to
Katherine's.

"Well, perhaps when your parents next take you to
Wollongong . . ."

"I haven't got any parents any more," Molly said. "You wouldn't
know, cause Father hasn't told hardly anybody, but Ma died five
months ago, while she was staying with my aunt in Berry. So there's
only Father, me and Billy at the farm, now. And Billy's different,
he don't mind Father like I do. Or maybe, being a boy, Father don't
worry about Billy like he does me—but the truth is, he's fearful
hard on me, Missus Carron. It's not the work," she added hastily,

"I don't mind doing the cleaning and washing and cooking and milking—I helped Ma do all that, and I'm very strong—stronger than you'd think to look at me, truly. But he's forever talking about how God is watching me, and reading out bits from the Bible about the harlots bringing shame on their fathers, and he questions me all the time about what I do all day, when all he has to do is look round that hut an' see I been busy from dawn 'til midnight."

"Have you spoken to him about . . ."

"He won't hear of me leavin' the Valley. Talks about the Prodigal Son—and I've tried, but I can't see no connection between that and my gettin' a nice clean job as a downstairs maid in some big house. I mean, all I'll be taking with me is the clothes I got on and my mother's best bonnet."

"Perhaps he knows he can't do without your help on the selection, Molly. With your father and Billy out in the fields all day, or making deliveries in the dray . . ."

"Oh, he'll manage." She nodded sagely. "That Mrs Halstrop, that married out of the Valley, she's widowed now and living on her father's old homestead, though it's close to falling down, despite the work she's done on it. Well, she makes every excuse she can to call in at our place, 'cos it's on the way down from their hut up the top of the slopes near Tallowa. She's not like other Valley women—this one's real sharp—says she's a midwife, but there'd be no way I'd have her anywhere near me if I was in the family way." She threw a startled look at Katherine, before plunging on. "Excuse the way I'm talking. I'm scared, you see, what Father'd do if he knew what I was planning. He *won't* miss me when I'm gone, Missus Carron, really, 'cause Mrs Halstrop will move in on him quicker'n a redbelly snake on a dozing frog. He'll be all right."

Katherine nodded reflectively. "How old are you, Molly?"

"Fourteen-and-a-half last week."

"Well, I can't promise you anything, but I'll definitely make inquiries on your behalf—the only thing is—" as she held up her hand to stem the rush of gratitude from the girl, "that I must have your father's permission. Ask him to call to see me in three days' time. By then I'll know more. And don't worry, I think I can persuade your father."

She spoke to the family at lunchtime, and received a general approval of the idea of bringing Molly into the house to help Peggy with the chores involved in running Barrengarry. They had often talked of hiring extra help, and Molly, whose family, devout, standoffish, proud, was known to all the Prescotts as being honest and hard-working, seemed the ideal recruit. Even Peggy and Carl approved of the idea, and Peggy began at once to tidy out one of the small rooms at the back of the house for the girl to use as her own.

"We'll manage just fine here," Katherine told her mother, when they were alone for a few minutes in the little sitting room upstairs. "I don't want you to worry, Mama."

"I shall," Suzanna smiled, "I shall always worry about my girls— particularly when there's so much danger about." She shuddered. "Don't ride out alone, will you, Katey? And don't let either of the other girls take any chances either. I simply won't rest until that dreadful person is caught and safely behind bars."

"We'll be careful, Mama, don't worry." She hesitated. "Mama— are things better—between yourself and Father? He . . . he doesn't seem . . . I mean . . ." She did not know how to ask.

Suzanna said gently, "Katey—I'll tell you this—you're not to tell the other girls. Your father has been very good about this, as determined as I have been to avoid scandal at all costs." She paused and Katherine, who had almost begun to relax and feel that the time alone together in Sydney might help her parents' fragile relationship, now began to brace herself for something unwanted, unpleasant.

"Your father received a letter from Laurence Mitchell a few days ago. The man is not in the best of health himself, and he was forced to write and ask if your father could come back to help with the business. Robin is ill, Katey. And to give your father credit, he didn't hold the facts back from me, but let me read Laurence's letter. The doctors fear that unless he leaves Sydney and goes to some rest home, away from any worries and pressure, Robin won't live more than a few months. One doctor told the poor old man that Robin would be dead within the year."

"Oh, Mama . . ."

"We'll conduct the details with as much secrecy as we can, and your father has agreed to help me. I'm to go to the Blue Mountains— a cottage in Springwood—and I'm going to stay there, and nurse Robin."

"His father will know! His family . . . !"

"Yes." Simply. "But it doesn't matter. If your father can face up to the consequences of my decision, then I imagine the Mitchells will also. Robin writes to me constantly, he needs me—and I will go, Katey, no matter what the Mitchells—or the rest of the world, for that matter—will say."

There was, in part of her heart, a deep admiration for her mother—and, yes—even a kind of envy. It was a wicked, self-indulgent, sacreligious union. Society would, to protect itself and the family values it upheld, feel justified in shunning the perpetrators, demanding that friends and even family—to avoid the taint of the inferior, the unacceptable—thrust them out and dismiss them.

And this, Suzanna Gordon Prescott, wife and daughter of two of the most highly respected men in the colony, was about to face. All for the inexplicable human emotion called love.

There was a shadow over the house for several days after Marcus and Suzanna left. The younger girls missed their parents, and Katherine, while she shared this, had the added burden of knowing that they would undoubtedly never see their parents together again, for the rest of their lives.

Brendan seemed to recognize her distress, but she would not speak with him of anything but the most mundane of business concerning the property. In her grief for Suzanna and Marcus—and even for Robin Mitchell—she seemed to find more and more resentments within her when she realized that Brendan sensed her anguish. How could she believe that she could cope, that everything was running normally, if she saw pity and empathy every time she looked into the knowing grey eyes? She avoided him as she avoided the recognition of her own fear and unhappiness.

Amos Murphy did not come to Barrengarry. Katherine, after waiting a week, decided to ride up the Valley to the remote eighty acres that he farmed.

Brendan rode with her, one of the few times they were alone together; and even then, only because of the long miles of the journey that would take them through much thick scrub; lonely, unsettled country, as yet unclaimed and uncleared.

The hut and its environs, however, were deserted except for a noisy yellow dog who loped round and round the horses' legs, baying and howling. The three-room dwelling, made of vertical slabs of timber, the roof of the same and capped with tin along the ridge, was crudely built but neat, both inside and out. Brendan opened the single door and called out, but there was no reply except from the yellow dog who bellowed the louder at the intrusion.

The bullocks were grazing in a paddock nearby, but there was no sign of the rough old horse nor Amos' wagon. Only the dray lay in the open-sided barn, and the dog took refuge under this at the end, and serenaded their departure from between the spokes of one of the huge wheels.

"Can we ride on up to Crolins'?" Katherine asked, "There's a Mrs Halstrop staying there who may know where Amos is."

Brendan agreed, and they rode on in silence for the most part, except when they noted something about the vegetation or a shy bush bird or animal glimpsed as they passed.

She still did not trust him, felt a waiting quality about him that unnerved her, yet perhaps it was her imagination as the man seemed the very embodiment of patience. He had said nothing further about the mysterious two thousand pounds, nor had he made any effort to discuss anything personal concerning either of them. He must, she thought, have better things to do in the world than bury himself in a remote Valley community in the Highlands of New South Wales; and yet he had stayed, running Barrengarry competently these past three weeks, and seeming to be quite content with his new life. It was strange and disturbing, but she said nothing, fearing that in asking questions she would find out more than she wanted to know.

They climbed further and further up the Valley, having to dismount, as the hills became steeper, and lead their horses. Katherine had been this way only once or twice in her life and, the cedar-getters moving about as they did, she had only her intrinsic knowledge of the Valley and of its people's ways to guide her. She found a logger's hut, by a stream that rushed gurgling loudly over rocks in an almost sylvan setting, for the vegetation was almost tropical here and the sunlight was falling, green-tinted, through the leaves overhead.

But it was the wrong hut. Brendan stood smiling, one foot resting on the chopping block, talking with a crowd of grubby children, too many to be from just one family, who crowded about them. Katherine was feeling more exhausted than she was willing to admit, and sank gratefully onto a fallen tree trunk, the dead limbs of which were being used as a makeshift clothes line; shirts and underclothes and baby linen were draped amongst the dry branches, so it seemed that a huge dead hand held the burden of fluttering laundry.

"We're Greens," a boy of about eleven volunteered, "that is, him, an' him, an' her, an' her . . . and thems the Crolins, him, an' him, an' her, an' . . ."

Brendan grinned over at Katherine, saw her hot and rather impatient face and grinned the more. "Can you tell me where we'd find Amos Murphy?" he asked the boy.

"I'll ask Ma, she might know . . ." He had taken a few steps towards the house, but stopped and turned to one of his sisters. "Lizzie, you go."

Lizzie ran into the house, and the boy turned apologetically to

Brendan. "Best if Lizzie goes. I'm not allowed inside just now."

"Oh?" Brendan raised an eyebrow, "are you in disgrace?"

A low howl filled the air, sobbed, and rose in pitch, rose higher and louder, higher and louder, until it became a scream that filled the little clearing. Several of the smaller children covered their ears, and, overhead, several parrots took fright with a squawking and beating of wings. The boy said calmly, the voice raised in proportion as he spoke, in order to be heard over the terrifying sounds from the hut, "Ma's havin' a baby in there. I got to keep the little ones quiet."

Brendan and Katherine looked at each other.

"Is there something we can do?" Katherine asked. "Should we ride for the doctor?"

"Oh, no." It was one of the girls who spoke. "Angel Regnier is here." Her approximation of the French name came out *Rennyah.*

"Ah." Katherine relaxed immediately and Brendan, curious, looked over at her. "I'd like to wait for a while, if you don't mind, I haven't seen her—except from a distance—since I've been back."

"I don't mind at all," Brendan checked his watch. "It's only just after two. But don't these . . . Well, these things sometimes take time, I believe."

Lizzie had come back, and had heard. She was a sharp-faced, precocious-looking child of about ten. "Oh, no," she informed Brendan, "Ma never takes longer'n five hours. She says we pop out like peas. Mrs Larsson says Mr Murphy an' Billy have gone to Wollongong."

It was two hours later when the periodic screams ceased at last, and the thin, guttural wail of the child was heard. All the children ran for the house, hoping to catch the first view of the baby as it was brought out to them, and hoping, too, for some food, for none of the women within had remembered to feed them.

It was some time after this that Brendan first met Angel Regnier. The very name had him intrigued, but he had not expected the large black woman who came from the hut, wiping her hands on a clean cloth, brushing a piece of thick black hair back towards the neat chignon at the nape of her neck.

She was enormous; Brendan, at six feet two, looked directly into the confident, astute dark eyes; and her shoulders were as broad as his, her arms thicker, as, unfortunately, were her hips and legs. She walked tiredly, and smiling at both Brendan and Katherine, made her way to the chopping block Brendan had vacated on seeing her. She plumped down amid the yards of grey linsey-woolsey skirts.

The collar of her dress was fine white lawn, as freshly pressed and clean as the cuffs she now rolled down over her massive arms. "It's good to see you back, Miss Katherine," she smiled, and, turning to Brendan, as Katherine was about to introduce them, "I've seen Mister Kelehan about the Valley. People speak well of you already, sir. You seem to adjust to our ways. Not many strangers manage so well."

It was odd that a compliment from her should mean so much, but such was the power that seemed to come with the woman that Brendan felt the truth of the words and was gratified, even moved. "I'm liking it very well here, Mrs Regnier," he said.

She glanced up at the hovering Lizzie. "Child, run back and fetch my coat for me—I've said my goodbyes, and I'll be leaving now." As the girl ran back to the house, Angel Regnier turned to Katherine. "I shall ride back with you, if I may. Mr Regnier worries if I'm out too late."

Katherine returned her amused smile; Angel's husband Emile was many years her senior, a frail figure with a surprisingly thick shock of steel-grey hair. Educated, highly intelligent, and possessed of one of the deepest, most pleasant-sounding speaking voices—still tinged with his native Normandy accent—that Katherine had ever heard, he was, nevertheless, his wife's physical inferior in height, width and strength. Together they had raised a family of tall, golden-skinned, athletic-looking children, who all helped to work the successful dairy farm that Emile was establishing on the two hundred acres of lush pasture that bordered the other side of Barrengarry Creek.

Brendan helped Angel to mount the sturdy chestnut gelding that the boy led from the shed, and the three were about to ride off, surrounded by the farewell party of children, when two women came out of the hut onto the narrow porch.

"Missus Regnier . . . ! Missus Carron!"

The riders paused, turned back, and the women came forward to meet them. Mrs Mosley had very fair hair, almost white-blonde, for she had been a Larsson before her marriage, and all that clan had the fair colouring of their Nordic background. Her sister-in-law Meg Larsson had brown hair—but there all dissimilarity seemed to end. They were small, narrow-shouldered, sunburnt women, their faces betraying the bitter wretchedness of their existence.

Life was hard for all the settlers' wives, but for these women it was worse. Looking at them, Katherine was reminded of Essie Crolin; there was the same undernourished frame, the grim mouth held in a line against the thought of defeat, the whole demeanour one of visible determination that the frail body could take all that it was subjected to—could, and would—and survive. They were all of a mould, the cedar-getters' women; their lives shaped them, diminished them without favour or exception, to the humourless little shapes in ragged clothes that now stood before her. She was filled with a pity and a rage on their behalf, and also a kind of admiration for their pride, for each pointed little chin was raised, the sharp eyes gazing from face to face of each of the riders.

"We'd appreciate it if you didn't mention your comin' here," Mrs Mosley said to Angel Regnier. "Mrs Green asked us to ask you. An' you too, Missus Carron . . . and sir, if you don't mind . . ."

"It's that we got to live here, see?" Meg Larsson put in. "An' that Nancy Halstrop is a stuck-up shrew and a terrible troublemaker . . ."

"Looks down on us like we was dirt," Mrs Mosley added, "and her no better'n us—being one of the Brummells—which she was, afore she married. Everyone knows Halstrop drank their farm away and died falling down a culvert dead drunk and broke 'is neck—even the Crowner made a statement about it and it got into the newspapers. No cedar-getter ever got a Crowner to look into why he died—an' got his name in the newspapers as a drunk!"

"It's all right, Mrs Mosley," Angel Regnier said gently, "we'll not say I was here."

"But we're glad you come—Mrs Green—all of us—we'd rather have you, we don't want Nancy Halstrop near us at birthing times—but we don't want to hurt Amos Murphy's feelings, them being related in a way, through his late wife, Florence, and all. He's a decent man, Amos Murphy," Mrs Mosley pronounced.

"So, if anyone asks yez, Ellie Green gave birth by herself. Though we're grateful to you," she added, nodding to Angel.

Katherine wondered, as they rode away, if Angel would receive any payment from the Green family. Not that she'd want it, but it would undoubtedly be forced upon her. Like the Crolins and the Tallons, the Greens had a reputation for being light-fingered and swift of foot when it came to the occasional sheep or calf, and many the minor piece of equipment from about the various homesteads would betray its presence at a cedar-getter's camp weeks or months later. But the community in the Valley was tolerant; people grumbled, but nothing important had ever disappeared—with positive proof of the culprit. And there was an odd code of honour among the families. They had a horror of debts of any sort, and while regarding items left about in full view as being available to the man quick enough to seize them, they would not, under any circumstances, countenance charity from within the cedar-getting community or more especially from the world of the settlers beyond it.

Angel spoke of the Greens' baby girl, their eighth child, for the first past of the journey, as they walked or rode their horses down the steep, overgrown paths to the Valley floor. Mounted again, they were able to ride three abreast for the rest of the way to Angel's farm, and it was a revelation to Katherine to hear her talking openly with Brendan about her life.

No one in the Valley had ever thought, before, to question the enigmatic Regniers. To have a cultured French gentleman in their midst was odd enough, that he chose to marry an Aboriginal and bring her and their children to the Valley placed Emile Regnier in a world apart. Yet people liked them, and in a period when all but the most enlightened white person regarded black people with, at best, a tolerant sense of moral and intellectual superiority, Angel Regnier was respected in the Valley. With that respect came the feeling that, as with all fellow settlers, it would not to do ask questions; one's past was one's own. Angel, who kept herself and her family well-dressed and neatly groomed, who spoke French at home with her husband, and, with his help, had taught the children to read and write in both languages, had a place of almost mythical consequence in the Valley. One did not question her any more than an Englishman would question the presence of the Tower of London, or a Frenchman the Palace of Versailles. That it was there was enough.

And Brendan, who was too new, too curious, too full of Irish charm and genuine interest in others, asked Angel all about herself and her husband during the miles they travelled down the Valley. And Angel, to Katherine's astonishment, did not seem in the least put out, in fact answered him willingly, with her usual honesty and humour.

"I come from northern Queensland—I don't know who my parents were. My earliest memories are of living in a dormitory with other girls, and all of us down on our knees scrubbing a floor . . . I believe it was a kind of school—there were lessons, too, and I was taught to read while I was there. Emile says there are many places like it. The missionaries take the children from the parents, to help them learn the ways of civilization." Her broad grin came around to Katherine. "And I learnt that, I suppose, though what I most remember is the soapy bubbles in the buckets as I scrubbed floors—odd, isn't it? I wasn't even unhappy . . ."

"But your parents . . " Brendan was concerned.

"I might have come from an island, I'm not sure. I never saw my parents because I was sent from the school to stay with a white couple on a farm near the coast. I worked in the house there. Again, I can't say that I was ill-treated. We—the other servants and myself— were paid no wages, had no free days—and yet it was a life that I grew up to accept.

"The master and mistress had no children, and they—and several of the servants and farm workers—died of typhoid in 1840. I know the year because that's when Mr Regnier came to the property. He had bought it, you see, and was the new owner."

"How old were you then?" the unremitting Brendan asked.

"Sixteen."

"Ah. And he fell in love with you?" he asked, his alert face on Angel's. Katherine thought, "*Do* be quiet, Brendan," with some embarrassment. How could he ask such things?

But, "Yes," Angel was laughing. "He was thirty-six, and very handsome—a man who had travelled the world many times, and had come to Queensland from years in Noumea. He liked brown-skinned people," she said simply, "he saw no inferiority in us— just a difference, he used to say, in that we seemed to enjoy life more than Europeans. And he said he had never met anyone like me in his life. And I had certainly never met anyone like him. So we were married—because we fascinated each other!

"I used to ask him questions constantly—he knew so much. And he let me read his books. I read them all. I liked best the books on medicine, they made clear a great deal of the folklore I'd been taught by the older black women. It was all very interesting to me, as I already helped nurse the sick and deliver babies to the house staff and the farm workers' wives."

She smiled at them both. "We came here because Emile said he was missing the cold weather as he grew older. Can you imagine such a thing? He wanted a climate more like his homeland, but secluded, where he and I could live without too many people being shocked. So we came here."

They had reached the neat gateway to the whitewashed Regnier homestead. Brendan dismounted and lowered the sliprails for Angel. She thanked him as she rode through, and as Brendan replaced the poles, she called back for her remembrances to be given to the Prescotts, especially Suzanna.

"Just think," Katherine scowled wonderingly, "if someone had thought to ask Angel all those years ago, she probably would have told us, just as she told you. All those years of conjecture in the Valley, dispelled by you, you talkative Irishman, with a simple, 'And where do you come from, Mrs Regnier?' "

Brendan grinned, "And now? Will you tell the rest of the Valley and set the questioning minds at rest?"

"No!" She was affronted. "If Angel wants to talk to people, she will, in her own good time." And she rode in silence, thinking of the Aboriginal woman, wondering at her courage and her generosity of spirit. Could I have coped, she wondered, taken from my parents, and treated like a slave till I was sixteen?

The thought brought her mind back to the child, Molly. Yet her answer to the girl's whereabouts, and that of her father's, was very soon forthcoming.

The sound of men shouting, dogs barking, a woman's scream, told of some drama being enacted at Radley's store, even before that questionable establishment came into view. They urged their tired horses into a canter and came around a bend in the road in time to see Frank Crolin come bursting through the door, trip and fall, scramble to his feet and, shouting obscenities and abuse, hurl himself back into the building.

"Quickly—just ride past!" Brendan, scowling, instructed her. But Katherine was curious. As they rode level with the door, she could not help but peer into the dimness of the store's interior. It was then that the fight—for so it had become—erupted out the door once more. The two protagonists, Frank Crolin and none other than the elusive Amos Murphy, hands grappling at each other's throats, snarling unintelligibly, tripping over each other's feet as if involved in some demented dance, lurched and spun about, hit the side of Amos's parked wagon, ricochetted off and fell in the direction of Brendan's horse. It snorted with fright and darted over towards Katherine's mount, Dryad, who spun to face the excitement and backed off a little, her head lowered suspiciously.

It was quite exciting; Katherine had heard of the bloody fights that occurred sometimes at Radley's; she had even seen the results, on cedar-getters and the wild younger sons of some of the settlers—once or twice on her brother, Joe. But this was the first time in her life that she had seen an out-and-out brawl, and when Brendan, tight-lipped, tense, swung himself from his saddle, threw her the reins and said, "Ride on a little, out of sight—wait for me there," she ignored him completely. Dryad backed away a little more to a safer distance, and Katherine led Brendan's big gelding with her, but from there she sat quietly in the saddle and watched developments with interest.

Billy Murphy had been the first out the door after the two men, jumping up and down, waving thin arms in the air and shouting, "Git 'im, Pa, git the blighter! Hit the dirty little cove, Pa! Git 'im! Git 'im!" He sprang up onto the wagon, still loaded with goods from Wollongong, and from his perch exhorted his father to make greater efforts.

Charlie and Davey Crolin slithered out the door, much pressed by the weight of the people behind them, and stood at some little distance, urging their brother on to maim and murder with the same enthusiasm as Billy did his opponent.

There were women there, too; among them Katherine noticed Essie Crolin, all eyes, clutching her shopping basket and as many of her several children as she could gather in her thin arms. Three or four of the Tallon men were there, bigger, more broad-shouldered than the other cedar-getters, pink of cheek and sandy-haired and almost as mean-natured as the Crolins. They seemed to cheer each combatant indiscriminately, enjoying the spectacle rather than supporting either side of the mysterious debate.

Brendan had noticed that Katherine had not moved, and turned back towards her grimly. As he did so, Amos Murphy managed to pull free of Frank's grip and, stepping back, brought his fist about in a forceful arc that knocked Crolin back against the wagon once more.

"That's it, Murphy, give it to him!"

The voice was Mikey Brody's. In the few seconds' amazement while Katherine stared at the old man hoisting up his trousers, hopping about with bloody-minded glee, she missed seeing Frank Crolin, leaning back against the wagon, pull out a knife, did not realize, until the spectators had inhaled sharply, and Brendan had turned . . .

But Frank had already seen that he had gone too far. He held the knife in his hand, gazing about him at the faces, the looks of fear and revulsion—even Amos had fallen back a few steps, warily. Only Mikey's voice was heard, the coarse giggle, and "Stick 'im, Crolin—stick the silly bastard . . . !"

Frank was looking around, wild with rage, unwilling to back down, to sheathe the weapon—and his gaze fell on the large bags of flour, as yet unloaded, stacked with the other goods in the back of the wagon. With one hand he had gripped a coarse calico bag, brought the other hand up with the knife and ripped down the length of the sack. Even as Amos, blind with fury, gave a roar and attacked, Frank threw the flour sack at him.

It struck Amos full across the face and chest, the bag splitting and the contents exploding on contact with Amos and erupting all over the road. His mouth and eyes filled with the white stuff, the wiry Amos threw it back, away from him, his aim and his anger deadly enough for the missile to have an even more dramatic effect on Frank, who was caught totally unawares. Coughing, wheezing, half-blinded, Frank stumbled backwards but neither far enough nor fast enough—Amos had cleared his vision enough to see his opponent and had launched himself forward again. The two, covered in white flour, rolled round and about the roadway like two giant pieces of pastry, and when Billy, himself spattered with the stuff, started to giggle, one by one the audience began to laugh, until even the two fighters had to pause, look up, and scowl at the roaring crowd, all leaning on each other's shoulders in their enjoyment.

Brendan stepped in then and hauled Amos to his feet, at the same time as Davey and Charlie Crolin, the latter still with his arm in a sling, each took their brother by one arm and hoisted him upright.

Bert Radley had appeared sometime during the fight and was standing nearby with a slops bucket, obviously keeping it ready to throw on the two gladiators when he felt the contest had lost its amusement value.

"Ah, leave 'em alone," Mikey snarled, "let 'em finish what they started! Let the lads alone!"

"C'mon, Frank," Davey was urging his older brother, who was still gazing balefully at Amos Murphy. "Let's go home now—we proved our point . . ."

His words only seemed to rekindle Frank's rage. "You think so much of them blacks, you should sign over that little patch of dirt you're farmin'! Let them have it! They walk all over the rest of the Valley, come and go where they bloody like! Why don't you give 'em your land an' go off an' join 'em! You're just as brainless and as big a mongrel as any of them murderin' blacks . . . !"

"They ain't murdered anyone!" This came not from Amos Murphy but Mikey Brody. "The Woddi are peaceful—don't cause no harm. If they take a sheep or two when they're hungry it's no skin off your nose, Crolin—never raised a sheep—never raised nuthin' in your life, except kids! All you do is take—an' not just timber, either!"

For a moment it looked as if all three Crolins would murder the old man; they stepped forward like a well-rehearsed front line, and only paused when Brendan shouted, "There are women and children here—now stop it! All of you!"

Mikey peered at Brendan. "Don't pay no mind to strangers, we don't. Keep out of this, young man."

"Just as a matter of interest, Mr Brody," Brendan asked, "whose side are you on?"

The scowl faltered, then the grizzled cheeks creased into a grin and he gave a phlegmy rattle of a laugh. "I don't feel no loyalty to any of 'em—just like to see 'em make fools of 'emselves—and they've done that alright!" He almost choked on his mirth, bent over with the strength of it, showing worn yellow stumps of teeth.

The old man's spite had a calming effect on those around. Suddenly no one wanted to contribute to his amusement.

"Yairs," Frank snarled at the old man, "making sly comments about them murders bein' done by cedar-getters—when everyone knows that them blacks is behind it all . . ."

"You ain't got no proof of that . . ." Even Bert Radley was stirred to rumble out a defence of the Woddi Woddi.

"What proof do you need? Blacks are always treacherous. Can't let your women near 'em, the animals . . ."

"I dunno what you're talking about, Crolin," Amos gazed at Frank with contempt. "No Woddi Woddi man's ever come near any white woman that I ever heered of. Can't say the same for some white men, and what they do to the black women . . ."

"You shut up talkin' like that in front of my wife . . . !" Frank launched himself forward but was promptly dragged back by his brothers.

"Yairs, Murphy." This was Charlie, whose small and glittering black eyes told Amos he had forgotten nothing of their own battle here, some weeks ago. "You defend them blacks, but you don't speak up when old Brody here tries to blame them murders on cedar-getters—and you one of us, though you'd like to forget it . . ."

"Ma once told us we're even related to you somewhere back, you dog!" And Frank, still held firmly, spat on the ground in Amos' direction.

Brendan placed his hands on the man's shoulders, but Amos did not move, he merely looked at Frank, then at Charlie and Davey, with utter contempt. Only Brendan heard him murmur, "Set a watch, O Lord, before my mouth, keep the door of my lips . . ."

Davey, the youngest Crolin, would have been a handsome, if slight-looking boy, were his features not marred by the eyes being set too close together, and his top lip too short, so it gave the brown, fine-boned face a sneering look. This was compounded by the actual snarl that he turned now upon Amos Murphy. "If your parents hadn't died in that bushfire and that settler hadn't taken you in, you'd be up here in them hills along with us, riskin' your neck to bring that timber out. Yairs—think you're too good for us all now. A bit of schoolin' down in Berry and you think you're so smart . . ."

"Turned against the faith of your parents . . ." Mikey Brody lamented.

"You shut up, old man!" This, at least, elicited a response from Amos. "You haven't been to Mass for fifty years—you ain't a paragon of the Catholic Church, to go preaching at me!"

Brendan had withdrawn a little, gazed from one camp to the other and, obviously deciding that this was the last sputter of the fireworks, he turned towards the horses, shaking his head, a faint smile on his lips until he saw Katherine, who had not moved their mounts any further away. He took the reins of his horse from her with a telling scowl and mounted. The gathering by the entrance to the store seemed to consider itself at this, and people began to make a move to depart. Essie and Annie Crolin gathered their respective families, calling to their husbands, Frank and Charlie. They went, casting insults over their shoulder at Mikey Brody and Amos Murphy alike, while Amos walked tiredly over to the wagon and began unloading supplies, an occupation in which he had obviously been engaged when the fight had erupted.

A woman with harsh, straw-coloured hair under a rather youthful-looking green bonnet hung back a little from the group of Crolins. Katherine had not noticed her before; this was obviously Nancy Halstrop. She had watchful pale eyes in a face that, several years before, would have been very pretty. It was more than time that had marred her; the lines in her face bespoke a grimness and an impatience that would have scarred her from the inside out.

Katherine ignored Brendan's muttered suggestion that they leave. She waited, and a few seconds later, Amos reappeared from inside the store. By now the crowd had all but dispersed. The cedar-getters were heading for their horses or wagons, and Mikey Brody could be heard within the bar, ordering drinks for those that remained, the laughter still in his voice. Only Billy was close enough to hear the conversation as Katherine rode her horse over to Amos, but even as she spoke, she became aware that Mrs Halstrop had edged closer.

"Mr Murphy?"

Amos turned, paused, scowling up at her. Usually he was terse but well-mannered; perhaps, embarrassed at his floury state, he was, just then, merely tense.

"Yairs?"

"I was just wondering how Molly was. I hadn't seen her for some weeks . . ."

"She's gone." It was Mrs Halstrop who spoke, coming forward to stand beside Amos. Amos glanced frowning at her, and began pulling more barrels of molasses from the wagon. Nancy Halstrop continued, with a glance at Amos that was all proprietary interest, "She went to stay with her mother's sister in Berry. She won't be back for some time, she's helping her aunt to look after the kids."

"I see. What was her aunt's name? I might write to Molly . . ."

"She don't read." Amos said, his back to them. "No reason to write . . ."

Katherine was prepared to do battle, and perhaps the astute Nancy Halstrop saw this. Also, her gaze had flickered over Katherine's riding dress, the black silk hat and veil, paused to study even the silver fox's head on her riding crop. And she smiled up into Katherine's face. "I'm sure she'd like to hear from you—Mrs Carron, isn't it? I'm Nancy Halstrop . . ."

"How do you do?"

"Yes, well, of course, you write to Molly. Just care of Mrs Bewley, Berry. There's only one family of Bewleys—it'll get to her."

"Thank you, Mrs. Halstrop . . . Mr Murphy . . . Good afternoon."

"Arr," from Amos as he turned back into the store, and a murmured simper from Mrs Halstrop as Katherine turned her horse and rode back to Brendan, and on down the road towards home.

"Such a pity," Brendan said, when they'd ridden a few hundred yards. "Such an attractive woman—a lovely smile, did you notice?"

"If you mean Mrs Halstrop, I noticed only that she looked to have a bad temper."

"Of course," he said. "That's what I meant by saying it was a pity—to see a woman who could have remained beautiful well into middle age, ruin her looks with her own flawed temperament. And if she has plans to connect herself with Amos Murphy, and it seems she does, then she undoubtedly did all she could to remove Molly from the homestead."

Katherine was worried. "Why didn't Molly come to tell me she was leaving? Surely she would have waited to find out what I'd arranged. I'm sure she would rather have come to Barrengarry than to her aunt's. She mentioned that she had an aunt—her mother died while staying with her some months ago. I thought, when Molly told me about her, that the aunt in Berry mustn't be very sympathetic, or she'd have gone to her instead of me for help."

She made up her mind to write to this Mrs Bewley in Berry, anyway. It would do no harm to tell Molly that there was a position for her at Barrengarry—but perhaps the girl had simply forgotten about the request—she was young enough to be thoughtless and, if so, Katherine should reconsider writing to her. It was ill-mannered of the girl not to inform her that she was leaving.

And Molly was pushed to the back of her mind, where she would stay for some time. Katherine and Brendan were both disturbed by the fight they had witnessed, at how the suspicion had so divided people, and how strong the resentment against the Woddi Woddi had become amongst the cedar-getters; both groups living off the land, competing for the wild game that was becoming so scarce in the Valley and surrounding hills. "I'm glad," Katherine thought, "that the Woddi are leaving soon for the spring walkabout to the sea . . ."

But would matters have improved, once they returned?

Suddenly she wished her father was at home, waiting at Barrengarry; it would help her to speak of these things to her father. But what could one man do?

I'm leaning on Father, just like everyone else, she thought suddenly and crossly. And he can't help us. At the moment I don't know if he's capable of helping even himself, alone in that great house in Balmain.

Twenty

Katherine had had great plans for the spring. She had seen herself organizing all those activities that brought Barrengarry to life; but it had been Brendan who had handled everything, hired the men, organized and supervised the ploughing, the planting, the shearing, and the collecting of the rents from Marcus's tenant farmers in the Valley.

Katherine was left the homestead garden as her domain; that and with the girls, the running of the house and the preparation of the various entertainments usually arranged at that time of year. The

Huckstables. the Cummings, the Murchisons and the Prescotts would all take turns to hold dinners and dances at the various homesteads; and the Brodys also, although, of course, the Prescotts were never invited.

As the weeks progressed, it became apparent, not only to Katherine and the others at Barrengarry, but also to the rest of the Valley, that old Mikey Brody had become a distinct embarrassment to the rest of his family. Marcus, Katherine thought, would be delighted; and for that reason she did not mention the old man's deterioration in her letters.

Laura reported, however, that Stephen's parents had tried unsuccessfully to convince the old man to forgo his drinking and fraternizing with the lower strata of Valley society at Radley's store, but had given up the cause as lost. Mikey would tell them that they were stuck-up and useless, that he and his father had made Cambewarra what it was, and all his children and grandchildren could do was to spend the profits and to criticize him. It seemed to have slipped the old man's mind completely that it had been to better the family's prospects that he had worked so hard; he could see no reason for them to be ashamed of him, and so it was that the old patriarch and his family looked at each other with the same accusation of unreasonableness.

As far as Katherine knew, there was no further trouble at Radley's store; at least, no more than the occasional Saturday night brawl amongst the locals. Kept busy about the homestead, she had no further time to think on the incident she had witnessed at the Valley shebeen, and, with the gradual disappearance of the Woddi Woddi from the Valley to their spring fishing grounds, the spite and accusations aimed against them by the Crolins surfaced in her mind only occasionally, late at night, when she could not sleep; one worry among many, her parents being foremost in her thoughts.

Her mother's letters were always sent from the Balmain address; only Katherine sensed that the address was a lie, that her mother and father had come to some polite arrangement that would, as they had promised, protect the younger girls from the embarrassment and hurt of discovering the truth. Still, her days were full, and, with her renewed interest in painting and drawing and the burgeoning scrub to contribute to her studies in botany, not to mention the evenings playing unwilling duenna to Laura and Edwina, the weeks passed without the depression or the sense of time dragging that she had half-dreaded.

She could not avoid Brendan Kelehan and indeed, as the season progressed and a routine was established, she did not try. He made no mention of his reason for coming to the Valley, nor did he propose a time for his departure. Katherine found herself settling down as she had done in Dublin, to a comfortable acceptance of his presence, and the uncomplicated friendship and support he offered her.

The weather became increasingly warmer; this was the Australia she remembered, and, after several unusually hot days and nights when the temperature seemed never to change, she bowed to pressure from Laura and Edwina, and they ordered several bolts of pastel muslin through a mail order catalogue from a large Sydney store. From the scandalous purchase they made themselves five light summer dresses and again, made no mention of this in the letters to Marcus and Suzanna. After all, Edwina pointed out, their dear departed ones would not want them to suffer in stiff black silks, and there were no people in the Valley that they cared to impress, except Rafe Huckstable and Stephen Brody, and there was little chance that they would object to the girls being seen once more in pretty, feminine colours.

One morning in late October, when Katherine was painting, in water colours, the riot of scarlet japonica blossoms against the lattice of the old summer house, a voice spoke up behind her, so sudden, so rough, that she almost lost her balance on the little stool on which she sat.

She sprang to her feet and found herself facing Frank Crolin.

He had removed his hat and held it in his hand in a gesture of respect made a mockery by the detailed and impertinent perusal he made of her figure, from the flowers on her sunhat to the blue shoes she wore on her feet.

She felt the colour and the anger rise in her, and he sensed it, lowered his eyes, and turned the hat round about in his hands. "Missus Carron, 'scuse me for coming on you like this, but I got something important to ask your father, and I was wondering when he was coming home." The voice, at least, as polite.

Katherine did not know what to say, for her father did not mention, in any of his letters, anything about a return to the Valley. She said, "It will be some months, yet, I feel. Is there something I can help you with, Mr Crolin?"

"Well, yairs, you might. It's about a fence, up around the Bengalee Creek area."

He paused. "Yes?" Katherine encouraged, though she could not remember, among all her father's scattered properties in the Valley, any so far to the southeast.

"It's a right-of-way I'm after, see? Could you maybe let us have that, as it'd make it easier on us, like, to get the timber down to the creek?" He waited.

"Well, this is something my father would know more about . . ." Of course, Brendan was the overseer, she should, by rights, be telling Crolin to see Brendan on the matter . . .

"Yairs—I'd like to discuss it with your father—it wouldn't be inconveniencing no one to let us have a right-o'-way, 'cause there ain't no stock in that area—it's all uncleared." He paused, moved a little from one foot to the other, scowled at his hat. "I suppose I should have gone to that new overseer of yours—but he don't really know the Valley—wouldn't know where I was talking about."

"Mr Kelehan is very capable," she pointed out, "he has property of his own in Ireland."

"Yairs, well . . . that ain't Kangaroo Valley, is it? But I suppose you're right, Missus. I just thought you'd be the best person to speak to, knowing the Valley as you do. But I'll go to the overseer." He turned away.

"Just a minute."

No. She dared not say that he had the right-of-way he wished; she did not know where he meant, and Brendan, whom Marcus had taken all over the Valley, probably did. But it rankled that she was to be thought less in control than the Irishman who was, as Crolin suggested, a stranger. "This is really my father's business—I think he should be the one that you approach." And she was tearing a piece from her precious supply of art paper, and, in brushstrokes of unadulterated vermilion, she wrote Marcus's Balmain address.

Crolin was scowling at the piece of paper. "This might take a while," he muttered.

"I'm afraid that's all I can do. I think you realize that it's the kind of thing in which my father likes to involve himself personally."

"Yairs . . ." But one could see that he was not happy.

He left rather reluctantly, scowling as he said his abrupt farewell, and she could see him, heading down the drive, looking at the piece of paper and shaking his head, muttering to himself as he went.

She went riding after luncheon, bothered by the interview with Frank Crolin, bothered still more by her inability to bring herself to say to Brendan at the table, "By the way, Frank Crolin called in this morning . . ."

She was keeping things from the man. She knew she should not, but the rankling resentment within her would not allow her to pass responsibility to someone she felt had no right to be here, let alone making decisions for her beloved Barrengarry.

Yet her action made her feel defensive, and prevented her from settling to any one pastime in the afternoon. So it was that she rode out on Dryad, her drawing equipment in the saddlebags, but she had no plans even for her painting. The sun beat down from a clear sky, that brilliant clear, deep blue that she had seen nowhere but in Australia. Her head felt hot, constricted, in her broad-brimmed hat with the heavy netting, but to throw it back meant being bothered by the sticky little bush flies that even now were making Dryad snort occasionally, and throw her head about with a jangling of the bit.

She patted the sweating neck. "Are you hot too, girl? We'll get you a drink . . ."

She had not visited this spot since her return, and it held many childhood memories for her. All the Prescott children had swum here; it was the summer meeting place on Barrengarry, close to the Woddi Woddi camp, and boys who had now grown to be warriors, girls who had grown to be mothers, had played here with the white family, diving from the fallen blackbutt log, swinging on the rope, now rotted through, that hung from an ancient willow planted by Katherine's paternal grandmother. Joe had climbed up and fixed the rope—twenty years ago, it must have been, she thought with amazement, as she drew rein by the water's edge, and dismounted to let the mare drink.

The stream that fed the pool had other tributaries, Katherine felt, for even after heavy rain in the hills above, the volume of water in the rock basin seldom varied. It was a steady, dependable stream that cascaded down the mossy rocks and into the pool, falling with a conversational murmur of welcome as it entered, and leaving with a regretful whisper amongst the ferns at its furthest end, to disappear, between tangled banks of rainforest, on its way to Barrengarry Creek.

She did not realize how long she had been standing there, gazing at the barely stirring surface of dark water, lit with green reflections, filled with the ghosts of the children they had once been, until Dryad gave a yank on the reins and almost pulled her over. The mare had had her fill of water and wanted to graze on the sweet grass that grew nearby; Katherine, deciding suddenly, tied the reins to a low branch so that the horse could crop the grass, and began to take off first her hat, then her dress, her petticoat, and, finally, her shoes and stockings.

Madness, perhaps, but this was Barrengarry land . . . She waded into the water, laughing a little, as it was very cold . . .

And there was an echo. More laughter, off to her left, and it made her freeze, one foot still half out of the water.

It had been a low chuckle, and for an instant she had thought it was a man, but there came to her ears the soft barely audible sound of water disturbed, quite close, beneath the shadowy branches of trees that overhung the stream. The very fact that she could see nothing made her relax.

"Who's there?" she asked calmly.

Silence for a long moment, then a husky voice. "What you wear them funny clothes for? Clothes on clothes on clothes, like it winter all the time. You white people, all time shy."

Katherine laughed, and the invisible stranger echoed her laughter. Their voices rang pleasantly, alto and treble, about the rocky cliffs above them.

"Tigoora?" Katherine hazarded, and the faint splashing of water came closer still, until a dark, laughing face appeared over the few, thin reeds, and, "Nah—she still with her man, 'longa Illawarra. We come back sooner. Man things—secret things," she said solemnly.

Katherine nodded. She knew that the men of the tribe had certain sacred tasks to perform, in their proper order, at the correct time of year. That Myeela could tell her little was not surprising; the rites were, indeed, secret, taking place at various sacred places in the Highlands, all hidden from the eyes of women and strangers, black and white alike.

"How many came back with you?" Katherine asked.

Myeela held up both hands, fingers spread wide, closed and opened them again. Twenty. "Babies, too," she added, and pointed upstream, like a dark Lady of the Lake. "New camp—my man says no fences. Gurral come back, we go to old camp." She grimaced wryly. So Myeela's husband had taken them further up the valley, away from much of the civilization. And Gurral, older, steeped in tradition, would take them back to Barrengarry Creek, for the tribe had always camped there, and would continue to camp there, fences or no fences.

"And where are your babies?"

"Camp." A jerk of the dark head in the direction already indicated, the short-cropped ringlets, cut regularly for weaving rope and baskets, glowed like black glass. "Came for reeds—not too many, too early, but came anyway." She grinned. "Older girl look after babies— I done work-work all day—too much work altogether." She studied Katherine and giggled, her hand over her mouth, looking like the girl that she had been all those years ago. "Miss Katey, you look silly—dinkum you do!"

Katherine looked down at herself, the white lawn chemise and knee-length pantaloons. "Well, it's all very well for you," she retorted. "Black women look well with no clothes on. You remember you used to say we looked like frogs. And now I'm grown up," she added, "I undoubtedly look like a fat frog. With knock knees," she added.

"What that—knock knees?"

"Knees . . ." Katherine lifted one of her own and then waddled a little, to pantomime what she meant. "They turn in and bump each other . . ."

Myeela squealed with laughter. "You don't—but as I see small ones, white children, they do! Short dresses, legs fly out—yes! Ah! and they grow up to be ladies—wear long skirts—yes!—because knees go knock-knock-knock!"

She went off into peals of laughter, and Katherine was worried now that this news would travel on the bush telegraph all over New South Wales and enter black legend—all white women have deformed knees—no gammon!

"Not all women have knock knees . . ." she began, but Myeela had disappeared, diving beneath the water to reappear further out into the pool, still laughing.

Katherine considered. It was very hot. This was a corner of Barrengarry where Brendan and the farmhands would not be working, as there were no stock nor crops nearby. The only people who might, perhaps, see her would be the Woddi—and she knew enough of their ways to know that they would be much less embarrassed than she.

"Myeela—if I take off my clothes and someone comes, you must tell me. All right?"

"Yes. I hear anyone coming."

Katherine glanced around at the quiet of the surrounding bush, then, laughing herself, defiantly pulled off her two remaining garments, folding them with the others, and waded quickly into the covering of the dark water.

She was surprised that she remembered the paddling, awkward strokes with which she used to swim as a child, and soon came across the very deep centre of the pool to Myeela, standing under a small, natural waterfall, shaking her head and grinning.

"So shy . . ." she said. "Why you white people all time cover-up? Not cold—hot long time, now—still cover-up. Why that?"

Katherine tried to explain, as they bobbed and swam about, the social reasons behind long skirts, finding, to her own surprise, that the more she spoke the sillier she sounded. Myeela thought so, too.

"Men look at you—no matter. All women look same. Men try to *take* you—white men do that, sometime—you man kill him. You tribe—*you* know . . ." she searched for the right word, "you husband, you father, you mother's—brother . . . all same, kill him."

"But . . . killing is against the law—you know that."

"No killing is law—but taking women—that law, too."

Katherine felt herself losing ground. "But if we cover up, men won't be so likely to . . . to take us . . ."

"Why?" remorselessly. "They know what under skirts. Want it anyway. Maybe want it more, think woman better than she is. Maybe not know knees knock-knock-knock . . ." grinning.

The blunt logic of this appealed to Katherine despite herself. "Yes, but . . ."

"Sh!" One hand held up, the other to her lips, Myeela paused, her dark eyes alert. "Someone come . . ."

And Dryad, over on the opposite bank, had thrown up her head, split the air with a shrill whinny, and begun to dance, sniffing another horse on the air, gazing off towards the southern end of the pool.

"Where? Who is it?" Katherine whispered.

But Myeela obviously felt that she had kept her promise. Katherine felt the water disturbed, that was all; a strong eddy against her legs and body, and when she turned, Myeela, who had been treading water beside her only a second before, had gone, only the outspreading ripples marked where she had been.

"Myeela?" A panicked whisper as she turned about, searching; but though she waited long seconds, no dark head of curls broke the surface, no dusky laughter floated to her, where she half-swam in the centre of the silent pool.

Katherine paddled to the nearest reeds, ducked down until her nostrils were barely above the water, and waited.

Someone was coming. Clearly, perhaps because she was so low and the sound carried across the water, she could hear the soft pad and swoosh of horse's hooves through the grass. She willed them to move on, prayed that they would move on. But they slowed, hesitated, it seemed to her, and then stopped.

She could see nothing, the reeds hid the further bank from her gaze.

Her horse would be there. And the tidy pile of her clothing—with—hell's outhouse!—her pantaloons neatly folded on top.

And the stranger was there, on his horse, gazing at her belongings, and looking around at the pool . . .

The horse's hooves moved closer.

Katherine began to rally her courage. It was not the murderer. It could not be. This was Barrengarry, she was safe. The murderer was miles from here. He could not be a Valley man . . .

She swallowed, willing the panic down. It was a farmworker, one of the Irish lads from Burrawang who came regularly to work for Marcus Prescott after their own crops were planted. And she was Katherine Prescott. Albeit in an embarrassing situation. She was safe; this was her father's land, and she was his heir now, and she was safe. Whoever it was would be so frightened by her rage that he would think twice about talking of this, she would threaten to . . .

A slight sound, off in the bush to her far right; a dark shadow, blending immediately with the other shadows. Myeela had left her.

And it was this, oddly, that made her fear redouble.

How did she know the murderer was not a Valley man? How did she know he was not someone she knew, someone she saw quite frequently, and trusted?

Crickets sounded in the silence. She grew aware, suddenly, that it was late afternoon. And then a horse stamped and she looked up—for it had not been Dryad, it was too far to the left to be Dryad . . .

She was very thankful for the reeds between them, for the fact that she had come no closer to the shore. There must have been a small sandy promontory here, for she could plainly see the chestnut gelding from the chest up, and all of the mounted Brendan Kelehan except for the feet of his boots.

Neither Brendan nor Katherine spoke. She edged slightly to her right, until she could see Dryad, traitorous little head outstretched towards Brendan's mount. Her clothes lay forty feet from where she stood, up to her chin, clasping her arms across her breasts beneath the water.

The seconds passed and she became aware that she should say something, anything, to explain this strange conduct of hers—but no, damn him! Ladies in Dublin and Boston might not go swimming in the altogether, but this was Australia, and Barrengarry, and it was hers, and "What are you doing here?" she demanded, relieved to hear that her voice sounded so authoritative.

Brendan seemed unperturbed. He shifted his weight more comfortably in the saddle and did not appear in any hurry to answer. Finally, however, "Laura told me the general direction you'd taken. I thought I'd meet you and ride home with you. It is getting rather late, is it not?"

"Yes." She floundered about in her mind for a moment, then, "Perhaps you could oblige me by riding off some little way. I would like some privacy in which to dress."

He did not move. He did not so much as blink. She wondered if he had even heard.

"I said, I wonder if you . . ."

"I heard you."

He dismounted from his horse, leisurely, and she watched, growing more and more perturbed, as he led the big chestnut over by Dryad and tied the reins to a branch. Horse and rider had had a long day, for, after a cursory greeting, the gelding, by far the taller, dropped his head over Dryad's neck and appeared to doze happily.

Brendan had left the horses, had wandered off to stand by the pile of her neatly folded clothing. She felt herself flushing despite herself, watching him standing there so calmly, "almost *studying* my undergarments," she thought furiously. It was an infringement, a violation.

"Mr Kelehan! I would be obliged to you if you would remove yourself into the bushes with your back turned so that I may dress!" Her voice broke on this last phrase, and she was furious with herself. He was too silent, and it was harder and harder to remember that she was in control of the situation.

"I'm sure that you would like to dress . . . Mrs Carron." He seemed to talk directly to her camisole and pantaloons and petticoat and . . . "but I'm coming more and more to the mind that this is an excellent time for us to have a short discussion." He had sauntered to the water's edge and was looking directly at her.

Katherine's arms tightened around herself, not so much from embarrassment, for the water was dark now that the cliff was in shadow and she felt sure that her body could not be seen, but there was a sudden sense of cold, coming as much from his words as the steadily falling temperature.

"D . . . discussion?"

"Mm." He had moved off, came back dragging a short, curved stump, and sat down near the water's edge. Sat down as if he were about to sit there for some time and wished to be comfortable. "For a start, let's discuss what you did with the two thousand pounds of Irish Fenian money. What *did* you do with that two thousand pounds?"

"How *dare* you . . . !"

"I'd appreciate an answer."

She glared at him across the patch of reeds, made an effort to remain cool, patient. "I told you the evening you arrived. I left it in the bank deposit box, and gave the key to Daniel Hutton's sister. Do you still doubt my word, when we've known each other so many years?"

"I've known some people longer than I have you—a few of them are dreadful liars."

"But I'm not one of them!" she flared.

"No," he said carefully, leaning back and crossing one booted foot across the other. "You are a very competent liar. And very consistent."

"Brendan . . . !" His name a suppressed shriek of exasperation. "How many times do you want to hear it! I tell you I put the money in . . ."

"I know where the money is."

She blinked. "You do? Then why are you torturing me like this? It's cold in this water, Brendan, and I'll catch a chill . . ."

"Tell me what you've done with the money."

"I don't have it! You said you know where it is . . . !"

"I do. You stole it. You have it. Somewhere. Tell me where, Katherine, and save us both a lot of unpleasantness."

She was silent, tried to calm her breathing and the sudden, frightened pumping of her heart. He didn't believe her. He meant it, every word. If he had been angry she would have felt safer, but it was this calm, detached voice that made her afraid.

"What are you going to do?" she asked, her voice husky with her nervousness.

"I beg your pardon?" He turned his head a little, the better to hear her voice.

"I said, what are you going to do?" crossly.

He considered. "Stay here, I think. For several hours." He looked about. "It's a lovely evening. Clear, not a trace of cloud. It'll become colder as it gets darker. I'll probably light a fire. I shall be quite warm and comfortable, don't worry."

"And me? What about me?"

"You . . ." He seemed to consider further, "Despite the freezing temperature of that pond, you'll probably stay in the water for a long time. You'll lose your temper with me, you'll shout for help, you'll cry—a little, for you don't like anyone to see you cry, I know that—and then you'll become really angry. You'll become so angry— in about an hour's time, I estimate—that you'll come marching out of that water despite your considerable and commendable sense of womanly modesty."

Katherine stared at him, horrified, the full extent of her predicament confronting her. But he was not finished.

"You'll come out of that pond—isn't it a billabong you call it here?—and you'll not surprisingly want your clothes. I know, if I was in your position, stark naked up to my neck in an icy mountain stream, I would like my clothes, very much . . ."

"Then why . . ."

"Because I am remorselessly determined to extract a certain amount of information from you. Because, contrary to what you must be thinking now, in your discomfort, I truly care about your wellbeing. I don't want some pair of thick-necked, ham-fisted Irish-Australians coming down here from Sydney because they think they'll succeed where I failed. I don't intend to fail. You'll tell me the truth, Kate . . ."

"But I *have* . . ." She was close to tears. *Why* wouldn't he believe her? How had he become so cold-bloodedly, so ruthlessly single-minded? She had the feeling that if Bridey Hutton suddenly appeared before them on the bank of the creek and extricated two thousand pounds from her apron pocket before handing it to him, he would claim that it was the wrong two thousand pounds.

"I don't know what I can do to convince you," she said quietly, hurt more and more by the defection of his respect and fondness, made all the worse by the long weeks of pretence when he had, it seemed, believed her.

"Are you crying?" A calm voice from the bank. It was becoming harder and harder to see him in the gathering dusk.

"No!"

"I thought you sounded as though you were. It's becoming difficult to see details in this light. But . . ." rather quickly, as if he sensed her about to move, "it won't get much darker than this—the moon's full. And just to make sure . . ." He went to the pale blur that was her clothing and picked it up, bringing it back to the stump and using it, folded, as a cushion. "That's better," he sighed. "I feel safer now, too. You won't bother trying to clamber out a different way and sneak around me. So unless you want to run through the forest like a naiad, you and I will have to come to some agreement."

She was silent, trying to think. Frogs were beginning to tune their voices along the water's edge. Katherine imagined them bumping into her in the dark water. Frogs—or other things. She shivered, lifted her bare feet, one by one, hating to put them down again in the muddy ooze.

"Please, Brendan, let me come out, and we'll talk."

"No. You're too clever for me. Sitting here, fully clothed, neat as a pin, you'll overwhelm me with your logic and your presence. Then I'll become cross and use the only advantage I have. I'll use my superior physical strength, and I'll beat you. So, you see, you're probably a lot safer where you are."

"Brendan, you've never lifted a finger against me in your life—and you won't."

"Those who come after me . . ."

"Bother them—I'm talking about you . . . Why have you been so quiet about this nonsense for more than a month, can you tell me that?"

"I thought, fool that I was, that you'd remember that I was your friend and that you could trust me. For the past two weeks I've been waiting to find you alone to tell you just what I'm telling you now—I've run out of patience, Kate." And the voice had lost its bantering tone.

She said stiffly, "I've told you all that happened, and now I'm telling you this, Brendan Kelehan—when you find out the truth and beg my pardon for this—I'm never going to forgive you!"

Brendan sighed. The sound blurred with the chirruping of crickets, the tenor and bass of the frogs' chorus, and the sighing of the chill wind in the branches overhead.

The minutes passed agonizingly slowly, but her anger kept her there, not willing to allow his prophesied description of her behaviour to be fulfilled. She did not cry nor, having considered, did she shout for help. The family would presume Brendan was with her, and it would be some hours before they would think to come searching for them. Why, she thought, they're all delighted, undoubtedly, that he and I are off together, riding in the moonlight . . .

Every now and then, Brendan would drawl, "Tell me where the money is, Kate."

And, "I took the key of the box to Daniel Hutton's sister," she would reply, truthfully, tiredly.

Once, "My skin is wrinkling. I'll probably catch pneumonia and die."

Silence.

"Brendan, it's been hours . . ."

"No, not at all, but it is time I lit a fire."

And he did. She watched the small twigs catch alight and swam about a little, jumped up and down to keep her circulation moving, and all the time watched jealously as the flames grew with each piece of wood he placed on the blaze.

"I can show you papers from my bank in Ireland," she said suddenly.

"I had less than four hundred pounds when I left Ireland."

He was down on one knee, adjusting the firewood. He raised his face to her slowly, squinting through the firelight, then came to stand, silhouetted against the flames, feet slightly apart, gazing towards her. It was a pity she could not see the expression on his face, but his very stance told her that he was suddenly tense, waiting.

"You left Ireland to live in Italy with Christopher with only four hundred pounds?"

"And . . . and some jewellery. Jewellery Oliver had given me. You've seen most of the pieces . . . s . . . some fine . . . p . . . pieces . . ." Her teeth kept chattering with the cold.

"Yes," carefully, "Oliver loved buying you jewellery. I daresay you had enough to keep you for a while . . ."

"Yes, that's . . ."

"But not indefinitely." He spoke almost sharply. And still he did not move, and this stance of his, arms folded, legs apart, a considering, yet aggressive pose, was worse than his negligent and possessive seat upon her belongings.

"They were my j . . . jewels," she said. "Don't think what you're thinking."

"What am I thinking?"

"That I s . . . spent the two thousand pounds to b . . . buy myself jewellery."

A pause. Then, "I know you didn't, Kate." And there was something, a gentleness, a kind of caring in his tone, that almost unnerved her, more than all his veiled threats.

"I've . . ." she may as well tell him this, at least, "I've given s . . . some of my jewellery to my grandfather—he . . . sold it for me, and I've bought some land. As a s . . . speculation only. Brendan, can I come out, *please*? Will you please turn around and let . . ."

"It was for Christopher, wasn't it?" The voice was soft, still gentle, and somehow it cut across her own words.

"What? No. I . . ."

"Oliver was dead, and Chris was very ill. You had a few pieces of jewellery that Oliver had given you. You took the family jewels to Oliver's sister—I know that from our sources in Dublin. And I suspect you're telling the truth—you took the key to the safety deposit box to Bridey Hutton . . ."

"Yes!" Her body wracked with dry sobs of exhaustion, "I took the key to her . . . !" She could no longer feel her feet, her hands, and the cold made it hard even to speak clearly.

"But she was gone." His voice, calm, relentless, carried across the water to her. "She married around that time—and her new husband was only a social sort of Fenian—he liked the talk, and the few jars with the lads—but he grew afraid at the political climate—and soon after the trials, he took Bridey to Glasgow. When you took the key to her—she wasn't there."

"No!"

"So you took the money to Italy with you."

"*No!*"

"Christopher was ill. Very ill. He should have been taken to a warmer climate a lot sooner, years sooner, but Oliver wouldn't listen to us, would he, Kate?" His tone was heavy with his own grief, his own regret. "Oliver's dream was for the revolution, and you listened to him, and I . . ." A breath of laughter, all bitterness, "I didn't press you too much to leave without him because . . . I wanted you to go without him."

"I don't understand . . . What . . . ?"

"It would have been wrong. Odd, wasn't it? I was actually trying to do the right thing and keep you both together. I think those years used up every bit of honour that I possess," he said drily. "I was close—so close—to asking you to take Christopher and run off with me . . ."

"Brendan, let me come out of the water . . ."

"Be quiet, Kate." The ludicrous situation did not seem to matter to him. He went on fiercely, "You waited too long, Kate. For Oliver's dream—and then for Oliver. You wouldn't go to Italy while Oliver was in prison . . ."

"He was my husband . . . !"

"I know . . . I understand. But when Oliver died and you had recovered yourself, and realized that Christopher *must leave*—there was precious little money left. About four hundred pounds, as you say. And that wouldn't keep you both forever. There would be doctors' bills . . ."

"Stop it, Brendan . . ."

"And the two thousand pounds were there. Sent by wealthy Americans who'd just spent four years trying to kill off each other, who now, looking for further amusement, you thought, had turned their attention to Ireland's troubles. The Fenian Brotherhood had been born in America. Its plans had frightened the British government into coming down brutally hard upon Irish nationalist sympathizers, military and civilian alike. It had been the cause, albeit indirectly, of Christopher's illness, Oliver's death. The Brotherhood could afford to lose two thousand pounds, and you needed it to save Christopher's life. You didn't, unfortunately, need to use much of it. I wish, my darling, it had been otherwise. But now, where is it, Kate?"

Her voice was low and harsh, unrecognizable even to her own ears. "It *was* a diamond necklace. It was safer to carry as jewellery. I bought it in Rome, but sold it here, for a slight profit. *Now* . . . now it's several hundred acres of land at Moss Vale. So what are you going to do, Brendan? You can't put *that* in your back pocket and take it back to Dublin with you."

He sighed. His stance relaxed, or seemed to. He placed his hands on his hips and studied her. Then he turned his back, walking to the other side of the fire, well away from her clothes.

"Come out of the water, Kate," he said over his shoulder.

Twenty One

He kept himself aloof, back turned, while she dried her dripping, shivering body with her petticoat, and dressed in the rest of her clothes, looking at him warily, all the time, studying the way the firelight played on the thick silver hair that fell over his collar, and wishing she could hit the spot, hard, with some heavy piece of timber.

It would serve him right. She sat on the log and held her now-damp petticoat to the flames to dry it a little.

"May I turn around now?"

"No."

Really, if he had been truly her friend he would have understood, made some excuse to those men eager for the return of the Fenian funds. Everyone in Dublin knew how thousands upon thousands— no one could know just how much—of American dollars, meant for arms purchases, disappeared into English—or even unpatriotic Irish—pockets. Brendan knew the Dublin Fenian Movement—knew all the people concerned, and the way they worked. In such confused times, with the leaders arrested and the Movement gone underground, it would have been easy for Brendan to find some completely plausible reason for the money's disappearance. If he had bothered to try.

"Kate, you must have finished dressing . . ."

"I haven't."

It had been the diamond necklace that had made the money seem hers. She had kept the cash as a kind of safeguard, in case anything had gone wrong and her own money and small cache of jewels had proved inadequate. But buying the necklace in Rome had changed the crisp, new English notes into something not only more portable, but feminine, personal, and when she had worn it to dinner in their hotel, it had become . . . hers.

A memory came to her of Christopher, in his best dark suit, seated on a cushion on his dining chair, his dark eyes, huge in the small, pale face, sparkling into hers. "You're pretty, Mama—you're the prettiest lady in the room—in the whole world!" She smiled into the fire. No compliment given her by a man would ever mean as much to her, or would be spoken with greater sincerity.

A hand on her shoulder, and she started, whirling, to find Brendan standing above her. He did not move his hand, but looked down at her back.

"Your fastenings are crooked," he stated.

"Oh. I . . . it was hard . . ."

His hands were at her back, adjusting the many small buttons. He had to unfasten several in order to refasten them correctly, and the feel of his hands, capable, confident, unbuttoning her clothes— even for the gentlemanly service of refastening them correctly— had her blushing, her heart hammering, and the hands that held the voluminous petticoat were becoming damp. And it was a pleasurable feeling, the only fear coming from the totally unexpected response of her own body to his touch.

The wood that he had placed on the fire had caught with a vengeance now, and she was thankful for the excuse of the blazing heat when he finished with the fastenings and came to sit beside her on the log. Her hands held the petticoat on her lap, draped over her knees like a travelling rug. It was not fair. Who would have thought, after the years of stumbling, unsatisfactory, sometimes resentful attempts at union with Oliver, that she could actually find herself stirred in that way; she recognized the feelings within her, knew that his nearness had enkindled these emotions since the night they had been reunited, at Dovewood.

Now here he was, seated beside her, and his arm came up and around her shoulders, remaining there comfortably, almost negligently, as two friends might sit, sharing old memories.

But there were no memories for Katherine and Brendan, nothing that she, at least, could remember without heartache.

But Brendan was speaking of the future. "What were you planning to do with it? The land you bought. Had you decided to become a farmer?"

She turned and looked at him sharply, but his gaze held no mockery. Indeed, the grey eyes studied her face seriously and at such close quarters that she looked away, afraid of betraying herself.

"No," she replied, and told him, then, of her scheme, how the first of her advertisements had appeared in the Sydney newspapers, and that, thanks to her grandfather's prestige and enthusiasm in describing the delights of possessing a residence in that part of the country, one of the five-acre blocks had already been sold, and the buyer had commissioned the firm who had built Dovewood to design a house of even greater luxury. "I truly think," she added, unable to keep the amazement from her voice, "that people believe anything they read in the newspapers. I wrote the advertisements—which were more like travelogues, really—extolling the beauty of the Southern Highlands, the salubriousness of the air for invalids, the potential of Moss Vale to become a metropolis by the twentieth century—*and* mentioned that the land was *very* expensive because only the upper echelons of society had yet discovered the place . . ." She took a deep breath, excited to be able to tell someone, at last, what she had been doing, "and Brendan, we've been inundated with inquiries. Grandpapa says he doesn't recognize half the names—and the other half are all *nouveax riches*—but it seems people will buy their land at my price, and grandfather is actually enjoying himself, dabbling in trade, so it's working very well."

He was gazing at her, unmoving. And the seconds passed, and still he did not move.

She said, finally, "I'll pay you back the money. It's tied up now, of course. But if I can sell only a few more blocks, I'll have made the two thousand pounds, and you can have it to take back with you." She looked at him, almost fiercely. "I *did* try to find Bridie Hutton—and when I couldn't, there was no one else left in Dublin that I could trust. I always planned to give the money back."

"Did you?" The deep voice made no comment in its tone, but she imagined she heard scepticism, and went on with some awkwardness.

"I didn't ever think of myself as having *taken* anything. Certainly I never saw myself as a thief." She hesitated over the word even then. "When you used the word at Dovewood, I must have seemed the epitome of innocence. In a way I was. Always telling myself that I was custodian of the money, that I was merely borrowing it to use as capital . . . your accusations struck me with as much force—as being unfair, undeserved—as if I truly had managed to give the key to Bridie Hutton."

He did not speak and, for something to do, she busied her hands in turning the damp petticoat about on her knees. "I did it for Christopher," she said. "And . . . I'm *thinking* about it now, as I speak, because I never wanted to think too hard about it before . . . After Chris died, I . . . I did it for myself.

"Not just the necklace! Though I came to love it, you know— terrible, isn't it? I wonder if a heavy collar of diamonds has that effect on all women? It did on me. I only wore it once, in public, but I loved to look at it. Perhaps because I knew I couldn't keep it. But . . ." she scowled thoughtfully, "if you hadn't come back, perhaps . . . perhaps I wouldn't have been strong enough to give that money back." She looked up into his still face and away again. "I'd kept it because of my devotion to Chris—when he was gone . . . I think I realized that I had nothing—nothing but myself. I became a little devoted to myself. I still am." Defiantly.

"I gave a great deal to the Fenian cause. I gave my husband and, as you said, quite truthfully, in my procrastination about taking Christopher to Italy, I sacrificed my son, too." As Brendan made as if to move, to speak, "No! You were right. But in taking them, the cause took my happiness—for all my life, Brendan. My husband is dead, my son is dead, and I have nothing to show for five years of my life. Somehow, with Chris, all feelings of duty, of loyalty, ended. From the time of his death I thought only of myself. Oliver taught me that—watching him going his own way, despite my feelings, or anyone else's. Don't tell me I'm bitter . . ."

"I wasn't about to."

"You were thinking it. And you'd be right," she relented, studying the hands in her lap. "I don't know who I am—if I ever knew— but I'm very much afraid that I've become a woman that I don't much like. I don't think I'd have given that money back," she mused. "I think I'd have kept it. I'd convinced myself that the Fenian Brotherhood owes it to me. So it's just as well you did chase me halfway round the world. Maybe God sent you, to drag me back from the brink—though it's very Old Testament of him."

"Kate?"

"Yes?"

"Be quiet. You know very well why I came here. And if I've tormented you, it's because I was tormented myself, for a very long time."

"But I never meant to . . ."

His hands—he had large hands, long-fingered, sensitive—held her face between them, firmly enough to stop her words, prevent her turning from him. She waited, thinking that he wished to speak, but his face came down to meet hers, his lips were upon hers, and she forgot whose turn it was to speak, or even what it was they were speaking about. When he released her at last, it was all she could do not to lean once more towards him in an unforgivably immodest manner.

"I wish I knew how to speak to you," he said, with an earnest kind of intensity, "but whichever way I try—and I've had months to find a way—I still sound, to my own ears, like an immature, blind fool. If I told you the extent of my foolishness, my selfishness— I'm afraid you'd come to despise me as much as I do myself. There!" He laughed a little, "I can't even tell you why I'm not telling you, without sounding like a whining cad."

"Perhaps you shouldn't tell me," she said. She could see that his distress was genuine, had never known him like this before; even the physical pain, the enormous pressures he had been under in Dublin, at the last, had not broken the man's reserves of strength as this discussion seemed to.

She was speaking the truth; her curiosity was in no way aroused; she had a grim conviction that whatever dangerous game he had been playing on the night he had been shot, he had, since leaving her, been up to more mischief of the same dubious kind. She cared for him, she realized, looking at the strong, stubborn face, the steel of the straight hair that fell forward onto his forehead, now scarlet in the light of the fire. She cared for him more deeply than she had ever before dared to admit to herself. He had trusted her; she could do as much for him.

"Perhaps we're two of a kind," she said gently. "I don't know what it is you've been up to, but I believe it was circumstance that led you there. You're not a wicked man.

"You wanted time, you said a few weeks ago. I think it's a good thing, the time being spent here, away from whatever pressures you have back in America and Ireland. If . . . If you're trying to break free of something, you need to see yourself clearly, what it is you want, what you hope for . . ."

"I know what I want. I know what I hope for."

How could she have not known, she wondered, all those years ago when, at a dinner party at Oliver's apartment, he had dragged the tall, broad-shouldered young man towards her; intense grey eyes, and hair silvering at the temples. "Katherine! Look who's just this minute arrived from County Wicklow—I'm so glad that you could get here for the wedding, Brendan! Katherine's been told all about you, haven't you, dear? This is my dearest friend, Brendan Kelehan— my fiancée, Miss Katherine Prescott."

There had been a look of surprise between them, and a strange form of, almost, recognition. And it had hardened, almost immediately, for both of them, into a wariness and a suspicion. For what they had felt had been instant, undeniable, and abiding. It was also, in Oliver's best friend, in Oliver's future wife, *wrong*.

She had been wildly, totally in love with the quicksilver mind and tongue of the handsome Oliver. The elopement had been scheduled for two days later. They had known each other for exactly twelve days.

Brendan's plotting to upset the plans, their escape, the forged papers, the lies, the excitement and the madness—all would have done justice to a Restoration comedy. But it had not, in the end, been amusing at all, nor happy, as fairytales should be.

How could she now make demands of him? What right did she have to expect explanations, promises? After five years and twelve thousand miles, they sat together in shared warmth, the fire of their spirits, like their rebelliousness, subsided into a manageable complacency but none the less pleasurable for that.

He smiled at her. "I have a further confession to make."

She placed a hand to his lips. "No. We have a lot of time. I need to heal too, you know. Tell me when you really wish to."

"But this is something I really wish to tell you. I don't want you worrying about the Fenians coming to get you. I sent a letter to my Uncle Vincent in Boston while I was in Italy. I told him that the money had been left safely in a bank in Dublin. To save trouble, you had signed it over to me, and I asked him to draw on my own account in Boston and reimburse the Brotherhood." He had the grace to look sheepish at the end of this speech.

"But you . . . ! I was thinking all the time that . . . ! And you let me . . . !"

"Kate . . ."

"You lied to me!"

"As you said, my love, we're two of a kind."

This stroke of logic robbed her of a reply, and then she was laughing and in his arms, and they were holding each other tightly, her head on his shoulder, breathing the scent of him, this beloved, infuriating man who was, despite all that had come between them, claiming her, it seemed, as his own, at last.

"We must go home," he reminded her. "What possible excuse can we give for being so late?"

She imagined the glee with which Edwina and Laura would watch them enter the house, Katherine dishevelled, hair still damp.

"I don't think we need worry," she said, "I think they've been expecting something like this for some time."

But their excuse was even then moving quietly forward through the scrub to their left; muffled laughter, slurring of branches, a child's gurgle—and first, like so many Cheshire cats, the smiles and the wide eyes appeared, and then the faces as the Woddi approached softly to stand, grinning and laughing, about the fire.

Myeela kept glancing between Katherine and Brendan, laughing and making comments which, fortunately, Brendan could not understand, and Katherine merely some of them.

A freshly killed possum was placed on the fire and a young boy newly initiated into manhood, to judge from his gap-toothed grin, proudly showed a red-bellied snake before lowering it onto the fire and heaping it with coals.

Brendan was delighted with the visit, but in the middle of the laughter and chatter he leaned over to Katherine and said, "We do have to eat it, don't we?" More of a resigned statement than a question.

"Only a little. It would be rude to do otherwise," she replied. "Snake isn't too bad—a little like chicken."

Brendan nodded queasily.

But in the end they were rescued before dinner was ready. One of the men was singing a song he had just composed concerning the young hunter of the red-bellied snake, and they were joining in the chorus, on three notes, repeated over and over, when Carl and Laura and two of the farmhands rode into the firelight.

Goodbyes were said and Katherine took advantage of the confusion to slip away to Dryad and shove the rolled-up petticoat into the saddlebag with her unused painting supplies. She smiled as she refastened the leather straps. One could not tell, one simply could not tell, how a day would end.

The small tribe stood and waved them all off, and before the firelight had faded between the trees she could hear the voices once again. Myeele had translated it for her:

Banjee is a brave hunter,
He caught a big snake,
He caught it with his bare hands,
In the half-light as the sun was setting.
In the half-light as the sun was setting . . .
Was setting, was setting . . .
In the half-light as the sun was setting . . .

Katherine had been correct in her supposition. No one, not even the crusty Carl, queried the fact that she had been missing for several hours, or that the man who had gone searching for her had been missing for half that time.

Laura smiled her sweet smile and said nothing and, back at the homestead, Edwina looked as if she would burst with her secret mirth as they all sat to the table for a late supper.

There would come a time, Katherine thought, when she would have to explain something; there was an indefinable difference now, in the way she and Brendan spoke to each other, even in the way they looked at each other. But she would avoid any mention of what lay between them for as long as possible; it was too new, almost too frightening in the way it would turn both their lives upside down. They did not know themselves what they would do, and the last thing that Katherine wanted was to be pressured by Laura and Edwina who, in their innocence, could see no practical difficulties in the way of any two people who loved each other.

The following day Brendan was to drive to Moss Vale for supplies, and as Katherine wished to talk with her grandfather about the Moss Vale land, and because Brendan asked her to accompany him with such an affectionate presumption that she would accept, there was no question of her doing otherwise.

She had expected that they would call in to Dovewood on the way, but Brendan, with a faint scowl, asked that they ride directly to Moss Vale and call in only on the return journey.

"I thought you liked my grandparents," Katherine said teasingly.

"I do," he turned to face her, earnestly, as if worried that she could doubt it. But then he hesitated. "It's hard to explain . . ."

"Try," she said lightly.

He looked at her with that same scowl. "It concerns Miss Barton."

She hoped she looked sufficiently non-committal. "Oh?"

"I can tell you this, I know you to be discreet. The girl disturbs me, Katherine—and take that look of villainy off your face this minute! I'm serious—it's a serious business."

"I thought for a moment that Miss Barton was going to be one of the many to lose her heart to you—I became quite soggy in Dublin, having young ladies crying on my shoulder over your imperviousness."

"That's an exaggeration . . ."

"You were a dreadful flirt, sir." But she stopped her bantering tone then, for he threw her such a look, a glance that said as plainly as if his voice had formed the words, *You know why they were merely flirtations.*

"Tell me about Miss Barton. Why does she worry you?" she asked, chastened.

"She's been . . . This is going to sound very bad, in view of your accusations just now—but she's been writing to me, Kate. Letters that . . . well, they're at once immature, and yet at the same time . . . provocative—in a way that no lady's writings should be." He looked very uncomfortable, and glanced at her as if dreading a further burst of her levity.

But Katherine, too, was serious now. "Letters that were . . . *bold,* as we'd say back in Ireland?"

He nodded. "And I swear, Kate, I've given her no encouragement to think . . . anything. I've been polite to her on the few occasions we've met—I *did* dance with her at the ball, but only out of pity for her shyness, and because I wanted a quiet partner while I brooded over you and that saturninely handsome Rafe Huckstable."

Now she did laugh, but though Brendan smiled she could tell that the subject of Fleur's schoolgirl-like passion was one that concerned him.

"Then you must speak with her," Katherine advised, "and as soon as possible."

"I intend to—but I'd rather visit Dovewood only once, if you don't mind. To visit now, on the way to town, I'd feel I must tell her—and then to call in on the way home as well . . . Do you see? I'd like her to be told, and then not to see me for some time."

Katherine nodded, but could not help saying, "I see your point. One must be cruel to be kind, as they say. Dear me, the weighty responsibilities attached to being a handsome and eligible bachelor! You and Rafe have more in common than you supposed."

He tried to look cross but could not, and they both laughed. It was one of the things she loved most in him, that he took others' problems so seriously. He was a man always ready to laugh at himself, yet she knew, perhaps as no other woman did, how deep he buried his hurts, how, with that memory inherent in his Irish blood, he forgot nothing.

The rest of the journey, over the pass much improved by drier weather and the beginnings, at last, of government roadworks, was made discussing Barrengarry and the progress of the crops of oats and barley, the number and health of the spring lambs, and Valley business generally.

They were discussing the problems involved in setting up a school when they arrived in Moss Vale.

"Look there," Katherine pointed out a family of six or seven children, all strung out behind their mother like so many chicks. "We have about twenty families of that size in the valley—what's to become of them? Their parents are so busy making ends meet that there's precious little time left over for lessons—that's when one or either of the parents have any education."

"Something must be done . . ." Brendan murmured, turning to study the crocodile as it passed him. One of the younger boys held back, gazing at a display of hoops, balls and wooden toys in a shop window. "Freddy!" crossly from his mama, and he trotted off smartly to join the little cavalcade as it paused before crossing the street. Katherine and Brendan smiled after him.

She tried not to wonder, to hope. She told herself, as they shopped at the hardware, feed and general stores, that he was heir to Avonwood, that his family had lived in County Wicklow for hundreds of years; she could not, despite the fact that he seemed to be happy in the Valley, accepted by the often suspicious Valley dwellers, expect him to give up his inheritance. And when the time came, a voice persistently asked her, could she give up hers?

It had rained in the area the night before, and the main road— Brendan laughed when Katherine told him it was called Bong Bong Street, after the Aboriginal name for a nearby, failed pioneer settlement—was still soft mud. It was made worse by a sudden shower while they were buying foodstuffs in the general store, and Katherine had to lift her skirts to wade through three inches of mud to cross the street. Brendan took her arm, and she thought, I want him here, I want him here beside me—come what may.

The wagon was loaded, and all the items on the shopping list were ticked neatly in Brendan's orderly manner. "Lunch?" Katherine suggested, for it was two o'clock, and it would be best to eat now rather than cause an inconvenience to Angela and the Dovewood kitchens.

They were crossing the road again to the one respectable restaurant in the fledgling township, when they passed the same family they had seen earlier, the mother dragging the smallest child by the hand, concerned about the heavy traffic of wagons and coaches and lone riders. Katherine happened to be watching as the second youngest— the mother had called him Freddy, as she remembered—turned and looked over his shoulder as the tall form of Brendan passed him on the roadway.

Katherine smiled; yes, Brendan would be the sort of man to awe small boys. When they were older they would try to emulate him. There was something in the large-boned frame, the set of the neck on broad shoulders and the straight, thick silver hair beneath the black, soft-brimmed hat that must look heroic to young eyes. She was gazing at the square shoulders of the man by her side, still smiling, when she heard a sudden wail from behind them.

Freddy, his gaze doubtlessly still upon Brendan, had fallen without a sound into the thick ooze of the roadway. The cry of rage and fright and discomfort that he gave had half the street turning, startled, for it seemed far too powerful a sound to issue from the small frame now propped up on his hands in the mud.

Brendan was the first to reach him, lifing him up and setting him on his feet. Freddy had taken a deep breath and was ready for another stentorian scream when he found himself looking up into the face of the fascinating tall man in the black hat. The wail faded away as abruptly as if someone had turned off a siren. It dropped an octave and a half in seconds and finished on a hiccup.

"Oh, Freddy . . ." the weary mother returned, bringing the other children with her.

"Watch out, mama!" one of them called, and the whole gathering moved slightly to the right as an overloaded wagon pulled by a team of six rumbled past.

"Come out of the road . . ." she herded her children along, then, safely on the wooden footpath, she turned to Brendan, "Sir—thank you so much . . . Freddy, don't dare start crying again . . . ! Good afternoon, sir . . . Miss . . ." and she began shooing and dragging the meandering group along the walkway. "Just *look* at your good suit, Freddy—what will I do with you . . . ?"

She took both the smaller boys by the hands as she hurried off, Freddy, recovering from his shock to a realization that he was wet and uncomfortable, beginning to protest loudly once more.

Katherine and Brendan gazed at each other. "Just look at your hands," Katherine scolded him in a low mimicry of the woman's voice. "What am I going to do with you?"

Brendan grinned deprecatingly, gazing down at his hands, covered with mud from contact with the prone Freddy. "Perhaps there's a bathroom available at the restaurant . . ."

She was glad of the few minutes alone, seated comfortably at a table where the sun, freshly out from behind the clouds, slanted along the verandah onto a flower box filled with gold and purple pansies. She could see the town traffic go back and forth, the mail coach, at the depot opposite, set off, loaded with passengers and top-heavy with boxes and trunks, for towns and villages to the south.

She was filled once more with a sense of warmth when she thought of Brendan. It was good to have him in her life, good to be seated here waiting for him. She thought of the way he had helped the small child; from her seat by the window she could just see the family, crowding into a store doorway.

That could be herself, she speculated, surrounded by young ones, the exasperations and the joys of watching over them, seeing their stumbling progress to adulthood . . .

The waitress who had seated them had returned with the glass of lemonade Katherine had ordered. She looked up with a smile to see—not the waitress, but a dark-suited young woman, very pale, with intense blue eyes. She was quite tall, and had surely the most slender and elegant figure that Katherine had ever seen.

"I . . . I saw you from the other side of the street. That was Brendan Kelehan accompanying you, wasn't it?"

"Yes . . . Are you a friend of his, Miss . . . ?" For she was only a girl, Katherine realized, and a very frightened, disturbed one at that.

"May I sit down?" And she did, before Katherine assented. She sat with her back very straight, regarding Katherine fixedly. She spoke very clearly, "I daresay . . ." and it was only with this word that Katherine caught the accent for the first time, the faint leaning on the *r*, "that Brendan has mentioned me, though it will come as a surprise for him that I'm here. I'm Mary Rose Kelehan. I'm Brendan's wife."

There were so many emotions there in the lovely face; tiredness, determination, a defiant challenge and a pride in the title that she almost flung at Katherine, as though she knew the effect that her words would cause.

But not the extent of it. Katherine thought, afterwards, that the girl would not have been disappointed. She felt herself pale, felt her features stiffen, knew she was staring at the girl in shock and disbelief. It lasted only a few seconds, but Mary Rose Kelehan had seen it, and it confirmed her suspicions even as it added a touch of triumph to the complex emotions that warred upon the lovely face.

"No," Katherine found herself saying, "No, Mr Kelehan has never mentioned your existence. How very strange, and how upsetting for you. Never mind, we will take him to task for being so very remiss. My name is Katherine Carron, Mrs Kelehan. I've known your husband for many years."

"I know who you are." And there was naked hatred in the blue eyes.

"Really? I'm flattered that he thought to mention me to you. My late husband, Oliver, was one of Brendan's dearest friends. I was delighted when business matters brought your husband to Australia. He has investments here in Moss Vale, did he mention them to you? No? How odd . . . Well, you may scold him now, if you like, for here he is."

Mary Rose's eyes grew huge and she whirled on her chair to face the man who approached behind her. Katherine, like an observer who watched from a great distance, detached by time and place, saw the sudden check the man gave, the grey incredulity in his face as he saw the girl.

He does not love her.

It was a wordless, intuitive acknowledgement. But, all the same, Katherine turned from the sight of the man and the invisible string that drew him closer, like one of the walking dead, towards the table. What did it matter whether he loved her or not?

She gazed out the window. The late October sunlight still fell with bright intensity upon the bed of pansies, deep gold and dark, lustrous purple. Some of the petals had raindrops clinging to them. They reflected the light, like scattered diamonds if she moved her head even a little. She found herself staring hard into the velvety centre of one large, regal flower, felt herself drawn down into the rich soft blackness of its core. It was an escape, a few seconds allowed her, and that was all. When she turned back to them she would be in control, interested, kindly, dispassionate. It shouldn't be hard . . .

Brendan spoke her name gently; as she raised her eyes and turned, in those few brief seconds she saw Freddy's straggling little family proceed from the store and thread its way through the passersby, vanishing in the distance.

Katherine smiled at Brendan. It wasn't hard. All had changed, somehow, and it was too soon to tell what would happen. She only knew that nothing would ever be the same again.

Twenty Two

She had no idea what it was Brendan wished to say. The grey tinge still clung to his features, shadowed in the new lines from nose to mouth, the sudden hollows beneath his eyes. She looked at him and found pity mixed with her rage.

She smiled and stood, shook her head when he went to take her hand, stepping back and around him. "Please . . ." her voice was calm, well-modulated, her smile fell benevolently upon them both. "You have so much to discuss, I'm sure. I shall wait for you at Mrs Richard's shop—I need some trimmings. My dear," she offered in the face of Mary Rose's hostile and icy gaze, "I'm sure you have luggage with you . . ."

"Yes, I . . . I was on the way to the hotel . . ." Her eyes were on her husband, "I saw you both from the depot as I got off the stage . . ."

"How fortunate! Brendan—do see that your wife's luggage is loaded into the wagon . . ."

"Oh," she said stiffly, "I'll be staying at . . ."

"Nonsense, Mrs Kelehan. Your place is at Barrengarry with your husband. Take as long as you like . . ." Hell's outhouse, there was even a note of gaiety in her voice.

And she left them there.

At first, the only thing she wanted was a quiet place to go so that she might be sick. But that passed, thankfully, as she was appalled enough at her reactions without hysterical illness . . .

She walked along, greeting people she knew. And all the time she thought, it's almost, *almost* like it was when Christopher died. The numb disbelief that the world was still going on, and going on *unchanged*. That this did not matter to anyone else.

She entered the dim coolness of Mrs Richards' haberdashery with relief. Here were rows and rows of buttons, fastenings, laces and ribbons. She could spend hours here, studying each one, buying a year's supply, keeping her mind blessedly occupied. She smiled at the approaching Mrs Richards, negated the need for any service just yet and, as the proprietress withdrew, walked slowly, very slowly, along the displays of merchandise, reaching out occasionally to touch the trimmings, allow them to run through numb fingers.

Why hadn't he told her? How could he keep something like this from her? What had he been planning to do?

So all her introspection, all her soul-searching had been for nothing then. The decision was out of her hands, out of *his*. She half-smiled at the irony. Weeks spent agonizing over whether to accept him when he had nothing to offer her—he had given his name to this beautiful innocent-looking girl. And he had not told her.

The waitress at the restaurant had a suspicion that something was wrong at the window table, but she did not know what it was. Infuriatingly, every time she came near the table the man and woman—*not* the woman he had entered with—dropped their voices or ceased talking altogether.

If she had heard their conversation she would have known little more.

It was hard, Mary Rose thought, harder than she had thought possible, to find the right words. All her anger and frustration had boiled up within her on the long sea voyage, had been rehearsed into fine, stinging rhetoric that would reduce Brendan to heartfelt apologies, whereupon she would forgive him . . . All these practised speeches had fled at the sight of her husband with his hand under the arm of that red-haired woman. Why, she had looked to be about thirty; her eyes sharp, her mouth a commanding line and her whole dress and bearing one of an experienced, sophisticated, wealthy woman. She had trapped him, assuredly.

But she could not forget the sight of them helping the fallen child, the way they had stood close together on the footpath, laughing over Brendan's muddied hands. The look of . . . companionship, and closeness that passed, with their humour, between them.

So far, she and Brendan had talked only of her voyage, due mostly to his questions, for she had found herself feeling stiff, unwilling to communicate anything of herself to him; and all the time the rage and grief were welling within her, and she had to remind herself what Myra Gorham had warned: any scenes of hysteria and her cause would be lost. Keeping rein on the emotions that boiled within her took nearly all her energy, however, and she found it difficult to speak in anything but monosyllables. It was hard, when she had wanted nothing more than to attack that woman, claw her face and scream at her exactly what kind of a woman she was—and tell Brendan what a sorry excuse for a man *he* was—to bite her tongue and let the woman walk away. And now Brendan sat talking to her in such a cool, detached tone, and so calmly, as if he had done nothing wrong whatever, and she was expected to forget about it.

Yes, she had come alone—no, she had not told Uncle Vincent and Aunt Rose, for they would never have permitted it—but she had written to them at each major port along the journey. Yes, they were all well when she had last seen them, they knew where she was going, as she had left a note, telling them of the man, Marcus Prescott, the business associate that Brendan had met in Dublin, who was now home in Australia. Mary Rose had left to follow Brendan on the very day that his own letter to her had arrived. The ship, a speedy American clipper, had docked in Sydney only two days before.

Brendan gazed over her shoulder, frowning a little. Mary Rose had to stifle a sob, clench her hands into fists against the rising scream that was building up within her. He was like a stranger. She wondered about the story concerning Marcus Prescott. He had gone on a trip to the Far East, she had been told at the offices of Prescott, Mitchell and Co. His partner, a florid old gentleman with a worried, agitated manner, who did not look well himself, had nevertheless insisted on driving her to the train and had written out clear instructions for finding the Prescotts' country estate. Mary Rose, accustomed to the neat farms and woods of Illinois and Massachusetts, felt her terror rising with every mile that the train, then the jouncing coach, had burrowed through the grey, unyielding bush. And at the end of it all, this cold-eyed man whom she had dragged away from . . . from his mistress, it seemed.

He was gazing at the tablecloth now. His hand, brown, smooth, with a few curled hairs on the back of the palm, moved a little, his fingers, long, tapering to rounded tips, shifted the silver fork an inch to the left, an inch to the right, an inch to the left . . .

He was saying, "I was coming back to Boston in two months' time. It's a pity you didn't wait for me, for I can see that this trip has been very hard for you . . ."

"I had to come. I left as soon as I knew where you'd gone."

He looked up at her. The grey eyes under the thick brows were watchful, studying her, but gave no hint of pity and none of warmth. "Why, Mary Rose?" he asked, his voice soft, the tone flat.

"I was afraid you wouldn't come back. I know who Mrs Carron is. You've forgotten, but you told me about her before we were married. When I received your letter, telling me that you were going on to Australia from Italy, I *knew* she was involved . . ." He had turned away abruptly, and she took the gesture to be one of impatience. "I couldn't let you go. Not like that, without talking to you, without knowing the truth. Now I don't care what the truth is. I'm here— and I'm your wife. When we go back to Boston, we can go back together."

Brendan looked at her for a long moment, and said nothing. But in his very silence, she could see that he had no argument, no point at which to disagree. Her spirit rose a little. In his silence she knew that when she returned to America, her husband would be with her. She knew she had won.

They did not call in at Dovewood, but drove straight home to the Valley, Brendan driving, Mary Rose beside him and Katherine seated beside Mary Rose, pointing out landmarks, asking solicitous and interested questions, doing her best to relieve the tension, and pretending not to see the barely tolerant manner in which her guest replied and the suppressed hatred that burnt in the blue eyes whenever she was caught off guard.

Mary Rose tried, whenever possible, to leave Katherine out of the conversation entirely. She directed all her remarks to her husband, and thus Katherine learnt of Uncle Vincent's purchase of a Rubens, Aunt Rose was spending the entire summer with "the boys" on Cape Cod, and Damian and Nicholas—these, she presumed, were "the boys", were growing quickly and missed Brendan a great deal.

A whole life, Katherine thought bemusedly. A whole life, there on the other side of the world, that he had built for himself and told her nothing about. She grew to feel more and more estranged from him as the miles progressed. It made Mary Rose's jealousy and resentment almost amusing.

Does she think I could love him now? Does the little fool think I would want him now?

Katherine breezed into the house ahead of Brendan and Mary Rose. Carl had met them at the barn, but Katherine had made no introductions—let Peggy tell the old man. No one should hear before the immediate family, and she had planned this, all the way home.

"Just look, Katey," Edwina ran to her as they entered the parlour, a letter in her hand, "Father wrote two days ago, saying he was leaving for a business trip to China and . . ." Edwina stopped, and Laura, who had risen from her chair, came to stand beside her. And it was then, with, she hoped, just the right amount of pleasure and lingering surprise, she introduced her sisters to Brendan's wife.

They behaved wonderfully—only a faint, blank look at the beautiful interloper, a scowl at the stiffly erect form of Brendan, a glance of amazement at Katherine, hoping, it was clear, that this was a joke—then they had recovered, and murmuring their pleasure and delight they each, in turn, took Mary Rose's cold, pale little hand.

In bed that night, Katherine lay staring at the ceiling, imagining the reunion in the guest room down the hall. Would he stay for the remaining four and a half months of his agreement? She hoped he would not; the sooner they were gone, the better. And only last night she had retired to bed with a feeling of happiness that she had not known for years—perhaps never known to that extent, in her life. *Well,* she thought wryly, remembering her words to herself at the pool the previous evening, *you never know how the day will end.*

She went back to the pool the following morning, early. The water was blue, reflecting the clear sky above, and she was cross that it did not look more suitably attuned to the mood she was in. It was a sunny, happy place; a dragonfly, with blue, iridescent wings hovered over the water, and a kookaburra, high up in the trees on the escarpment, cackled his joy in the morning. She sat down on the log before the remains of the fire, and stared from the water to the ashes and back again.

It was there that Brendan found her, an hour later.

"Go away," she said, before he had dismounted.

He ignored her; she heard the saddle leather creak as he climbed down from his horse's back, and there was a pause as if he were tying the reins . . . then he was seated beside her.

They gazed at the blue water before them, watched the dragonfly, and did not look at each other even when he said, "I tried to tell you. Don't you remember? We were seated just as we are now, and you said that you sensed that I was trying to free myself of something . . . You said that I needn't tell you until I was ready."

"I thought you'd murdered someone," she snapped. "I didn't think you'd married another woman!"

His look of stunned amazement made her realize what she had said, and she floundered about a little, trying to regain some measure of her dignity. "What I mean, is . . . You must admit that . . . You were just the same in Dublin, and I thought . . ."

"It's all right. I know what you thought." He gazed at her, and she flushed wretchedly under his scrutiny.

"I even love your faults, do you know that?" he said, mildly. "I couldn't imagine accepting a statement such as that from anyone else, let alone finding it endearing."

"I don't care what you feel. You have a lovely wife, Brendan; I thought to myself last night, seeing her relax and make friends with Edwina and Laura, that you made an excellent choice. Now go back to her, please, and don't make yourself more despicable in my eyes than you already are."

He did not move. She had spoken without looking at him, and when she did, sorry already for her words, it was to find him staring at her as though she had slapped him.

"I've . . ." she could barely speak, "I've known too much pain, Brendan. I don't want any more . . ."

"We have to talk," he said firmly. "I didn't spend the night in the guest room last night—I want you to know that. I went back to my old room, when everyone was asleep. Mary Rose . . . was angry. I honestly don't know why she came . . ."

"I don't want to know . . ."

"Did you mean anything that you said?"

"Yes! Everything!" She faced him. "But *you* meant it as nothing. For six weeks you've been lying to me . . ."

She stopped, realizing that she, too, had been guilty. She, too, had lied. She hung her head a little, tired, perplexed.

Into the silence, Brendan said quietly, "Do you really know what you want, Kate?"

She sighed. "No. But I was beginning to think I did."

He waited, and she continued without raising her head, "I'd decided I wanted you. Foolish in view of events, wasn't it?"

"It was your letter," he said, and she looked up, puzzled, for a moment not seeing the connection. "You wrote to me that you felt you and Oliver would have a new beginning. You were going to Italy, as soon as he was free . . . It was such a happy letter. I had to let you go, Kate." And his suffering was there on his face, and she believed him. "I had to let you go. I'd done enough . . . enough damage, perhaps."

"*Damage?* You gave us nothing but kindness and affection! All those years, I could never have coped without . . ."

"Neither could Oliver," he said, with just the faintest trace of bitterness. "If I hadn't been there he may have woken up to his responsibilities a lot sooner."

Abruptly, he stood and walked forward to the water's edge. She watched every beloved line of his body and felt a loss that was like a physical pain within her. Then his voice came to her, firm, decisive.

"It's still not too late."

She stared at him. He turned to her, his face grim. "I must take her back to America; I'll begin divorce proceedings, and then you can join me." He walked back, took her shoulders and pulled her to her feet. "We were meant to be together, Kate. It's taken you all these years to realize it—I've always known it. We belong together."

"Yes . . ."

He took her face in both his hands and raised it to his. First the grey eyes claimed her, then he was swooping like a grey hawk, and she was pinned, his mouth on her mouth. This was the one man, she knew, who could claim her, who could fill her life, her mind, her soul, for all of her days; she knew this, and knew, in the half-second afterwards, that they could never be together.

If he had not married Mary Rose . . .

But he *had* married Mary Rose.

The girl's face rose up before her, imprinted itself upon her eyelids; Mary Rose as Katherine had seen her this morning, as she descended the stairs. Then the look had puzzled Katherine; now, knowing the girl had spent the night alone, without her husband, she understood; it had been the hapless, hopeless look of one who sees her enemy become her victor.

Katherine had stiffened in Brendan's arms and, aware immediately, he pulled her back from him to scrutinize her face. He knew her too well; her gaze was fixed on the second top button of his shirt, unable to meet his gaze, but he knew.

"No, Kate."

"We can't, Brendan. It's too late."

"No. Kate!"

"Brendan, listen to me." There was such a weight of unshed grief within her that she found it difficult to speak. "There was a moment, some months ago—no, more than a moment, days at least, no matter how much you may deny it now—when you believed that you and Mary Rose could be happy together. I know you, Brendan. You wouldn't have stood there in a Catholic church and married a woman unless you believed you loved her."

"There are different kinds of love, Kate. I was very fond of Mary Rose, I felt protective towards her—but mostly, I was driven by the thought that I could never have you! I thought . . . Dammit, I don't know what I thought. I felt as though my world had come to an end—foolish, but that's how it seemed. I knew there'd be no revolution; Irish independence had sunk under the weight of inertia and betrayal. My friends were imprisoned, I couldn't return to

Ireland—perhaps forever. And worst of all, I'd lost you. I married Mary Rose because I thought she could make me forget. I was coping, living from day to day, having no belief or hope in the future— and then, at a Fenian meeting, I heard someone speak your name— I heard some stranger telling me of Oliver's death . . . Through my grief for him, came the thought of you and Chris—somewhere out there, alone . . . There was just no choice—no way of doing otherwise! I knew in that moment that there was no boundary, no law, no proscription of the Church that could stop me from searching for you. And I've found you—and I'm not going to let you go, Kate."

"Mary Rose . . ."

"I'll take her back to Boston—I'll see that she wants for nothing . . ."

"She wants *you* . . ."

"She's young, and bright and resilient. More than that, she's very beautiful. I have no doubt that she'll marry again. She's not a devout Catholic—but even if she was, she can apply for an annulment."

"And your feelings for the Church . . . ?"

"They don't count. Not in this, not now. All that matters is my feeling for you. I never reached for you, never stepped across the boundaries of chivalrous good manners all the years of your marriage. If I had, you'd be mine, now."

"Don't presume . . . !" she began, but he held her tightly and she stopped, and knew that he was right. Had his arms come about her, in those long, desperately lonely nights in Dublin, she would have been lost. It was a discomfiting thought, to know that one's chastity lay only in the fact that one had not been asked to give it up.

His face pressed close against hers, his arms holding her close to him, he said, "I paid the price for my sense of honour, Kate. I'm not about to make the same mistake twice. I'm not letting you go."

She tried to follow where his words beckoned her, towards a future for them that she could believe in; but she could see only the enormity of the decision he was making, a decision that would alienate him from his family, his faith, and—knowing Brendan as she did—perhaps, inevitably, from himself.

"No, Brendan." Her voice was firm. Part of her mind was amazed that she could sound so calm as she slammed and locked the door in the face of her own happiness. "If you come to regret it . . . My love, I'll never *know*, I'll never be able to be sure that you don't regret it!" She broke free of him, the better to clear her thoughts. "It could poison even the feelings we have for each other, and I couldn't bear that, Brendan. I couldn't!

"And you don't *know* that Mary Rose will adapt to her situation. It's a terrible thing that you're planning to do to an innocent young girl who's had no chance, no time, to learn how strong she may be. Perhaps she'll never recover from this—not just the hideousness of a public scandal and divorce. But from the rejection of her by the man she loves. She does love you, Brendan. She's come halfway across the word to find you. She loves you very much."

He shook his head in the face of this argument from such an unlikely advocate. Yet he sensed her enormous inner strength, and knew that she meant all she said. He could only repeat stubbornly, "I won't let you go, Kate. Don't think that I'll forget you, for I won't. I won't let you talk yourself into saying goodbye. It *won't work*."

"Yes, it will. Being what we are, there's nothing else we can do. I know you'll never let me go," and she studied his face with great tenderness, "and I shall never let you go, either. But you must place me in a small corner of your heart, my darling—and give the rest to your wife, and the children you'll have together."

Who could have thought that this would be the cause of her losing her facade of cool logic? For with that one sentence she was suddenly choking on the memories and vanished hopes that came flooding with it. When he stepped to her and held her in his arms, once more she clung to him. She was right, she knew she was right. But it was hard, so very hard, to let him go, let the warmth and the strength and the living force of him out of her arms.

"Brendan . . ." Her own voice, small, trembling a little, saying— Oh, my God, what was she saying . . . ? "It's . . . It's safe, for me . . . just now. I . . . Can we stay here? A little longer. *Together*. Forgive me, but . . . I want to be with you . . . *once*, just *once*. And then . . ."

And his voice dropped like ice, "And then I go back to Mary Rose."

It was only as she shifted, just a little, in his embrace, that she realized that he held his body rigid; she looked up from where her cheek had rested against his shoulder to see, first of all, the taut sinews in his cheek and neck; he did not even move to look down at her until his fingers had moved to her forearms and she was whipped to his arms' length with a force that jolted her head back and forth upon her neck.

"I am not going to join you in turning what we have into a tawdry little affair. I don't want you for my mistress, you stupid . . . stupid little bitch! Have I loved you for nearly six years for you not to realize *that*?"

"I only wanted to hold you . . ."

"I'll hold you! I'll strangle you! Mother of God, Katherine, what do you think I'm made of! Do you think I could make love to you and walk away from you, back to that mewling, selfish, hysterical child? *Do you*?"

He shook her, and her head rolled back and forth like that of a cloth doll. "It's b . . . better than n . . . nothing!" she managed. Only when the words were out did she realize the immodesty of the words, of her behaviour.

Brendan had let her go. He took a step backwards. And in that one movement she saw, even before he spoke, that the distance between them was not one step, but a world away. The silence went on, and she could find no words to bridge it. Then she heard him say, almost consideringly, "I never realized . . . No, I never realized how little I mean to you."

He had to be cruel. She knew that. He had to come to hate her, or he would never leave her. Yet these, his words . . . a knife-blow must feel like this; cold and sharp and sudden and breath-stealing, slicing inward cleanly, and the pain coming only later . . .

Later, when he had mounted his horse and ridden off, and she was left, standing there in the brightness of the morning, with the stream murmuring to itself, and the kookaburra's mockery, rising and falling, invisible, high up in the hills above her.

Twenty Three

She started awake, her heart thudding, staring in terror at the whispering, dark shapes that circled her . . .

"Katey—are you asleep *already*?"

"She has no nerves . . ."

"She has no *ears*."

"Katey, it's *us*. Are you awake?"

She stared up at the vague shapes of her sisters, on either side of her bed. "Teddi—Laura—what are you . . . ?"

"*Sssh!*" from both of them.

". . . What are you doing?" in a whisper matched to theirs, "creeping into my room and frightening me half to death? What time is it?"

"Only half-past eleven." Edwina's voice. In the moonlight that slanted through the windows she could see that her sisters had not yet changed their dress, both wore the black silks she had seen them in at dinner. They sat down on the foot of her bed with a rustling of taffeta petticoats and a twang of protesting bed wire.

"I was in Laura's room, talking to her for a while," Edwina continued, "and then I went back to my own room, but I couldn't sleep . . ."

"You know my room is next to *theirs* . . ." from Laura.

"And mine is only across the hall and down a little . . . I went back to Laura, and we decided to come to you."

"Why?" Katherine had spent the day riding about the Valley, visiting the O'Mara family, the Cummings', and Emile and Angel Regnier. She had returned only at dusk, in time to change for dinner, and afterwards, on retiring, had fallen asleep immediately despite her emotional turmoil. She was still befuddled with sleep, and could not follow her sisters' conversation.

"For heaven's sake, Katey, can't you *hear*? Listen."

Yes, she could hear. And her brain now registered the fact that the voices had been speaking for some time.

But speaking was not the right word. A man and a woman were quarrelling, the man angry, the woman hysterical.

"No," she breathed.

Edwina said, "And to think we were worried that it might be dull, being left behind while Mama and Father went to Sydney . . ."

"Be quiet, Teddi. This is terrible." She drew up her knees beneath the covers, rested her elbows on them.

What would her mother do in a case like this? Nothing; a lady did not register knowledge of other people's domestic problems . . .

"It was the same last night." Laura's sober little voice.

"*What*?"

"Not as bad, but they did quarrel. Then Brendan went back to his old room—I heard the doors open and shut, and the floorboards creak—you know how the hall floorboards creak. And he was up very early this morning, ahead of everyone, so no one would know."

Edwina shifted on the bed. "Katey, you've been avoiding us ever since that girl entered the house—we demand to know. When did he marry her?"

Katherine sighed. "About six months ago."

"Before Oliver died?"

"About that time. He . . . he didn't know Oliver had died . . ."

"I told you so." Edwina turned to Laura.

"What are you talking about, Teddi?" Katherine frowned.

"Well, it's obvious that he married *her* because he thought he couldn't have *you*. How could he do it? I've never met such an ill-matched pair . . ."

"I feel rather sorry for her," Laura said softly. "She's very young to have to go through such an ordeal."

"She's the same age as me," Edwina pronounced, "and it serves her right for being silly enough to marry him. I believe she trapped him—she's pretty enough to turn any man's head. Luke Murchison called in today and stayed the afternoon—his round little eyes nearly fell out when he saw her. He kept forgetting to drink his tea, just sat there with it balanced on his great knee and *stared*. I felt quite piqued."

Under any other circumstances Katherine would have smiled at Edwina smarting over her admirer's defection, but the voices along the corridor were unrelenting. She found herself straining to hear words, though she knew she should not.

"What are you going to *do*?" Laura demanded.

And Edwina sighed, theatrically. "How could you have borne it, when she suddenly appeared in Moss Vale? If Rafe had a wife that just popped up unexpectedly like that, I'd have died! I'd have fainted away, and then *died*!"

"He can't stay now, Katey, you must see that," Laura announced.

"We must all pretend nicely, of course, but it's just *despicable*. You must write to Father—Oh, bother him going to China . . . write to Mama, then . . ."

"What are you both talking about?" It was easy to laugh at them; all semblance of good manners gone, they perched on the foot of her bed like ruffled ravens, crowing for revenge.

They stared at her. Then,

"You *meant* it?" Laura managed. "All the things you've said about being delighted she's here and how she must stay, and how pleased Mama and Father will be to meet her . . ."

"Katey, don't pretend with us. We know how awful it must have been for you . . ."

"Teddi," patiently, "for how many weeks now have I been telling this family that I feel only friendship for Mr Kelehan? I warned you that he had a fiancée somewhere—I thought it was Ireland—but she's American, of Irish descent."

Another pause. The two glanced at each other. Edwina said, "Yes, but . . . we thought you were . . . *you* know. You always keep things to yourself, Katey—we *never* know what you're thinking or what you're planning. We half-expected, over the past few weeks, to find a note from you, saying you and Brendan had eloped to Sydney."

"Nonsense," she smiled and lied, "I meant what I said."

And they had to be content with this. She said a firm "Goodnight", but Laura shook her head as she went to kiss Katherine's cheek, muttering, "I don't know what Father would say to all this . . ."

She stopped speaking when a door, elsewhere in the house, opened and shut abruptly, almost concurrently with a howl—of pain or rage—that rose in pitch and decibels until the erstwhile peaceful Barrengarry seemed to rock on its complacent old foundations.

The door, somewhere down the hall, opened again and the scream was louder still, shrill, unearthly, and there were suddenly words, "I hate you! I hate you! I hope you'll rot in hell . . . !" And running footsteps and Brendan's low murmur before Mary Rose's voice rose once more.

Both Laura and Edwina had moved suddenly, but Katherine threw herself to her knees and caught their sleeves as they were about to rush to the bedroom door. "Leave them," she hissed. "They'll go into his room or back into their own—we will *not* interfere."

But Edwina broke free.

"Teddi . . . !" A hoarse whisper.

Mary Rose was screaming, "And I'm carrying your child! Your child! Do you hear? Yes, that stopped you, didn't it? Does it mean

anything to you? Go on, walk away from me now! Turn your back
on me now! It shouldn't make any difference . . . It . . . Oh, God,
I hate you! I wish I was dead! I wish I was dead! *I wish I was dead!*"
The words gathered to a shriek, were lost in the jarring clamour,
and accompanied as they were by mysterious thumps and bumpings,
it was impossible to understand, to separate them. It was the gibbering,
howling abandon of a woman totally out of control.

Edwina was at the door. Katherine found herself unable to call
her back, stayed where she was, kneeling on the coverlet, one hand
clutching the foot of the bed, the other still holding the cuff of
the equally stunned and immobile Laura. Even Edwina did not move,
remained in the half-opened doorway.

The screams were diminishing, ebbing away into loud sobs; and
now they could hear Brendan's voice, murmuring Mary Rose's name,
speaking calmly, in a gentle, controlled manner, as a doctor would
speak to a sick child.

The voices grew fainter. It seemed to take a long time, and yet
the whole incident could not have lasted more than a few minutes.
The sobs were more and more infrequent, Brendan's voice barely
audible—and a door shut.

After a few seconds, Edwina seemed able to move, and came back
stiffly towards the other two, her face, even in the meagre moonlight
and the lamplight from the hall, wide-eyed, shocked.

"She . . . she said she's having his baby. And . . . and then she
flung herself at his feet . . . At his *feet*! It was terrible—the look
on his face. D . . . don't worry, he didn't see me—she was . . .
clawing at him, and kicking and hitting her fists and her head on
the floor—Oh, it was *horrible* . . . And he stood there, looking down
at her as if . . . Oh, as if he was looking into an abyss, or . . .
something black and terrible. And he knelt to her, when she had
calmed a little, and . . . and he picked her up in his arms, and carried
her back to their room—and he didn't see me—he walked as if he
couldn't see *anything*—and he carried her like that, as if she was
a child, sobbing on his shoulder, back into their room."

Twenty Four

Peggy was not surprised when Mary Rose did not appear at breakfast, and Brendan asked her to take up a meal to her on a tray. The bemused housekeeper had decided to take her husband Carl's advice, "If they act like crazies is their affair—I do my job—vot they do is vot they want. Chust keep busy!" So Peggy kept busy—Katherine had never seen her so energetic—and she felt sorry for the plump little woman, who hardly dared these days to let herself look too long or hard at any of her charges, in case her worry was apparent on her face. Bad enough that Mr and Mrs Prescott were under a cloud, and had left the Valley for heaven knew how long; but now Miss Laura was seeing Mister Brody regularly, and Miss Edwina was seeing Rafe Huckstable and both these young gentlemen called openly upon their young ladies with only Miss Katherine as chaperone—and she was usually busy with her garden or her painting or the thick books on flowers with long Latin names and only seemed to notice the young men with a vague smile as she passed through on her own affairs.

And Mr Kelehan—such a nice man—who could think he would marry such a strange young woman—no matter how lovely she was? And there was almost something suspicious about someone *so* beautiful—Mrs Kelehan looked as if she had stepped from the fashion pages of the *Illustrated Sydney News*. Just as pale and thin and consumptive-looking, as was ridiculously fashionable just now. All very deceptive, for the sounds of the Kelehans' domestic crisis had floated out across the yard to the rooms she shared with Carl and Peggy had lain trembling beneath the sheets with her fingers in her ears.

Now Miss Laura and Miss Edwina were staying late in their rooms—doubtless to avoid any unpleasantness, and the only two people to face the morning square-on were Miss Katherine and Mr Kelehan, who saw his duty to Barrengarry, at least.

Peggy bustled off to the kitchen to make three breakfast trays, and to tell Carl of the fourth disruption to the household's routine.

Katherine and Brendan had small appetites. The food remained on their plates, though they pushed it about a great deal as they spoke, more to give themselves something to do with their hands, and some excuse for staying, facing each other across the table.

"You slept well?" he asked.

"No. Of course not. Did you?"

He sighed, gazed down at his congealing eggs and bacon. "You heard?"

"We all heard. Brendan . . . what are you going to do?"

"As I told you yesterday. Take Mary Rose home . . ."

"I think that would be a mistake. There's her health to consider; when will the child be born?"

"February, about the twentieth." Brendan's voice, his face, was unreadable; she sensed, rather than saw his inner turmoil. "She . . . couldn't have known, it . . . must have happened just before I left for Italy in May. She didn't know until she was halfway to Australia."

"You can't possibly risk the dangers of another long sea voyage— why not stay until after the baby is born? We can have Doctor Lang attend the birth, and you couldn't find a better midwife than Angel Regnier."

Brendan looked thoughtful, then raised his eyes to her. She wondered if she was wrong, sensing, when he gazed at her, what his heart was saying. That there was love there, love unchanged even by the surprising news of his impending fatherhood, she had no doubt—and no, she could not be mistaken in reading there, within the direct and tender gaze, his gratitude, his admiration, his regrets.

A lifetime of regrets . . . She hated the phrase, but it had surfaced in her mind and remained, stubbornly transfixed there. "Try to convince Mary Rose to stay. A long sea voyage would not be good for her at all. I . . . I shall probably go to Sydney . . ." she began.

"When?" quickly, with a scowl.

"Not immediately. In a month or so, perhaps. Father is visiting the firm's Asian interests, as you know, and I worry about Mama being alone at Balmain."

She was worried that he might ask her why Suzanna did not come home in Marcus's absence, but he did not. Perhaps he knew a great deal more than she suspected, for he nodded with understanding, and said merely, "I don't want you to leave the Valley. If it's difficult for you, I can take Mary Rose to Moss Vale, or even to Sydney . . ."

"But you've made friends here. Luke Murchison would miss you, and Stephen . . ." She did not add Rafe's name, for the coolness between that gentleman and Brendan had not thawed, despite the six weeks since they had first met and the frequency, these days, with which Rafe was a caller at Barrengarry.

"I shall miss you too much, and you know it," he said, and more quickly as she looked distressed, "I know! And we'll speak no more of it after this conversation. I know where my duty lies and I'll abide by it—more because to do otherwise would be to lose your respect than for any other reason. But tell me, just once, so I can remember it when I find myself in moments of despair—tell me that this is really what you want me to do. And swear it!"

It was cruel of him. She held his gaze for a long moment, almost resenting him; but he would not, it seemed, allow either of them the temporary comfort of avoiding the truth, the future.

"I swear . . ." she said, "that I believe your place is with the girl you married, that your loyalty belongs to her and to your child, in the same way mine did to Oliver and my son. I swear that I want above all things in this world for you to be happy—and that my belief is that your only chance of happiness lies in following the dictates of your conscience."

In the pause he smiled a little, almost unwillingly. "You should have been the lawyer, Kate. You have a way of leaving no loopholes. You spent some time last night mulling over words very similar, I take it?"

"Yes. Of course. What choice is there?"

He murmured, "Indeed," very softly, his gaze on the table. He had left his plate of food completely and turned his attention to the silver salt cellar, which he now moved round and about on the white linen tablecloth.

"That's settled then," he continued, looking up at her at last. "But it doesn't change the fact that I want you with me—as a friend only—but I need to know that you're close."

"As I said, I'll stay for a few months. But it's going to be hard, Brendan."

"I know."

"Do you?" Again their gazes locked, and she read in his gaze the steely reminder of the past five and a half years.

"Yes," she sighed, discomfited at her own insensitivity. "Yes, I suppose you do."

"One more thing—you see, I, too, lay awake last night, forming speeches to you," he said. "I'll eventually take Mary Rose and the child back to Boston—we'll have to remain there until it's safe for me to return to Ireland, whereupon I'll take them to Avonwood. I will try to be a good husband and father. But I can't forget that I married Mary Rose under false pretences, and I can't forget that I love you. I will try—for years. I can't tell you how many. But if, after a long time—and it will be a long time, I promise you—

you still fill my heart as you do now, then I'll make due arrangements for my family's welfare, and I'll come for you. I can't do otherwise."

She had slowly inhaled during this and now said, meeting his gaze and making her own unwavering, "I wouldn't, if I were you. I may have remarried by then, and you'll . . ."

"Don't lie to me. As I told you, when this confrontation ends, we'll not speak of the matter again. So don't despoil it by telling me lies, Kate. You won't remarry. I say this from more than the arrogance of knowing that you belong to me. I say it from the knowledge of your character. I'll gain some slight pleasure, you know, over the following years, in imagining you in your independence. Running Barrengarry, visiting at Dovewood, painting in that absurd straw hat that pulls at my heart when I see you scowling up from beneath its brim. Travelling, perhaps, to meet some of your botanist friends whom you correspond with—but if you come to America, or England, or anywhere within a few hundred miles of me—don't tell me. Because I'll leave everything and come to you!"

"Brendan . . . You must stop this. It will tear us to pieces . . . Try to love her—she's a beautiful, frightened child, and she needs you desperately. Don't withdraw from her—even when these bouts of hysteria come upon her . . ."

"I know how to handle Mary Rose." His tone was icy.

"*Don't withdraw into yourself.* Fight her, if you have to—she'd almost prefer you to beat her, I think, but you can't ignore her. She's not strong enough yet to stand on her own."

"Perhaps she won't be, ever. Perhaps she's been manipulating people around her far too long." He shook his head. "I shall do my best, Kate, I've already promised you that. But in the meantime . . ."

"We must stop this . . ."

"We will—we have. But I must tell you—I want to stay on at Barrengarry while your father is away. Will it be too hard on you, having us both here?"

"No. I'll miss you too much if you leave." She smiled at him sadly. "And for the future of your relationship with Mary Rose, it would be beneficial for her to see that I pose no threat to her."

She stood up, not able to bear this cool dissection of their feelings, their plans, any longer.

Brendan, too, stood up, walked briskly around the table to hold her chair and replace it, and went to the door with her.

He did not open it immediately, but paused with his hand on the knob. Her eyes came up to his, and they paused, telling each other goodbye without words. But their bodies had wills of their own, had their own message and were drawn together, a long and tender embrace, the kiss they exchanged one of compassionate longing, holding within it all the years of their love, and all the future years of loneliness that stretched before them.

They pulled back from each other, and with one last look Brendan opened the door and they left the room and each other murmuring a "good morning"—Katherine to go upstairs to rouse her sisters, Brendan to saddle his horse and ride out to the fields of Barrengarry.

It was after a subdued lunch that Katherine, on her knees on an old cushion weeding young dock plants from about the daffodils and scented freesias, heard footsteps approach along the path and looked up to find Mary Rose standing there, watching her. "They smell delightful . . ." she said, nodding at the sweet-smelling freesias, "they remind me of home." Katherine stood, smiled at the girl, who said with some hesitation, "Will you walk with me, Mrs Carron? I wish to speak with you, if I may.

"My husband has told me he thinks it best that we remain here until the child is born." The blue eyes looked across at Katherine, a sideways glance, as she said, "He tells me you're his friend. Only his friend. I would like to hear it from you, Mrs Carron. Just what are your feelings for my husband?"

Courageous, Katherine thought, and honest. What a strange mixture the girl was. She should have no need of hysterics and tempers if she could only face the world with this same stubborn defiance.

"Your husband was right, Mrs Kelehan. I'm very fond of him, I have every reason to be grateful to him for he was a dear and close friend of my husband, Oliver."

"Brendan told me," Mary Rose said, almost unwillingly, not liking the thought nor the taste of the words upon her tongue, "that when he was in trouble in Dublin, before he came to me, you helped him. He told me he was involved in rebel activities—and that was how he received the gunshot wound in his shoulder. You nursed him, he said; you took him in and looked after him, despite the fact that your little boy was ill, and your husband had been arrested . . ."

Damn Brendan, she thought, how dare he better his own case by betraying my confidences. Mary Rose sensed her stiffness, her displeasure. "He told me this only last night, in order, I think, that I see that he owes you a great deal. His life, he says, and I must agree with him; it was very brave of you to accompany him to the station—across Dublin, when all the police were out searching for him . . . You're a very brave woman, Mrs Carron."

What could she say to that?

"Thank you," she said, "but they were difficult times—I'd have done the same for any man of Brendan's character. I'm sure you'd have done the same. I would to God some woman had been able to help Oliver in that way."

The blue eyes—such lovely eyes, with the thickest lashes Katherine had ever seen—were looking at her with open scrutiny and interest. Katherine further volunteered, "I loved my husband a great deal, Mrs Kelehan. I remained loyal to him in life—and I shall not remarry now he is dead." She looked up, swept an arm at the view of bright green fields and dark scrubby hills. "This is my life now. I'm very grateful to your husband for helping us in my father's absence, for it's giving me a chance to learn at my leisure how Barrengarry is managed. This place owns me, you see. The Aborigines say that the land abides forever," she smiled, "and they are custodians of it. I feel the same. I shall live here, make Barrengarry prosper, and I shall die here." She looked directly at Mary Rose. "I would never leave this Valley, not for anything, or anyone."

Every word she had spoken was the truth. Much was held back— but that was necessary, for she saw the path ahead of her, accepted it—and to pause simply in order to hurt this girl with petty, unnecessary revelations would be pointless and cruel. So she spoke only the bare truth, and hoped it would be enough.

Mary Rose seemed to drink in every word, every expression on her face. Then she nodded slowly. She said, "I didn't want to stay here. I thought if I found Brendan I could convince him to take me home to Boston immediately. I was foolish. Sometimes I don't think!" The eyes were lowered. "I'm very sensitive, you see. I have very fragile nerves. They make me react, sometimes, in a way that I shouldn't."

Katherine almost smiled, but managed to frown consideringly instead. "We're all guilty of that."

Mary Rose nodded and they turned back, then, towards the house. Katherine was pleased. The conversation had been a step towards a peace that would be vital, if they were all to live together in reasonable amity during the next few months.

At the verandah steps, Mary Rose paused, looked back over the garden and pine trees, and the spring-green meadows beyond. "I don't know," she sighed.

Katherine was right in that some of the strain and suspicion seemed to leave Mary Rose after that talk in the garden. She stiffened, still, when finding Brendan speaking to Katherine, but it was instantaneous, and her fears were soon dispelled by realizing that she had interrupted a conversation on crops, or finances or other aspects of the management of a large property.

For Katherine it was strange, and something of a relief, to find that the five years of friendship between herself and Brendan stood them in good stead; they returned to the cordial, fond courtesy of those years almost automatically; for the rest, it was a matter of keeping busy, working late, rising early, filling their days, not allowing themselves to think.

Laura and Edwina helped immensely. Being closer in age to Mary Rose—Edwina was delighted to find there was only three months difference between them, Mary Rose only just being the elder—they felt it was up to them to help her adjust, and to feel at home.

The thought of the baby filled them with excitement; they scrambled up to the attic in the days following, dragged down a cradle and an ancient push-chair, polished them and refurbished them; pored over the catalogues from the various Sydney stores, and ordered more goods than Mary Rose could have used had she been expecting triplets.

"One thing concerns me," Laura said as she drove Katherine and herself to tend the family plot in the little graveyard, two weeks after Mary Rose arrived at Barrengarry, "you told me—and Brendan speaks sometimes—of his eventual return to Ireland . . ."

"So?"

"So Mary Rose, I'm afraid, is thinking differently. She . . . she's very sweet, you know, and I've become very fond of her—but she does like to talk about *things*—I mean, personal belongings. It's as if what she owns is very important, the most important thing about one."

"She's quite wealthy, I believe . . ."

"Yes, but we've known some very wealthy people—as a matter of fact," she laughed, "*we're* supposed to be very wealthy—and we don't . . ." she paused.

"What?"

"Nothing—I shouldn't have said anything, I'm being unkind."

"You're being irritating. How dare you begin a subject so interesting, only to become suddenly moral? Tell me at once!"

"Well, we were seated on the verandah last evening before supper, and Mary Rose was telling me about their house in Boston—and how it was furnished—it *did* sound lovely, I wish we had some of it here . . . Anyway, I said to her, was she going to take all her furniture to Ireland with her?

"She turned to me with . . . well, Teddi calls it her mechanical doll look. She stiffens and then turns that lovely head and looks straight through one. If she didn't look so beautiful it would be frightening—as it is, it's very disconcerting. And she murmured, 'Take my furniture to Ireland? But that would be foolish. We'll visit Ireland, certainly, but Brendan and I will be living in Boston.'

"I was so surprised I couldn't think of anything to say. Teddi started to chatter some rejoinder, but I managed to step on her toe—she was sitting directly by me—and she shut up.

"Katey . . . Brendan lives for returning to his home—you know how he used to tell us all about Avonwood . . ."

"It's a lovely place." Katherine smiled. "Very ancient, very damp, but lovely."

"Mary Rose has no intention of returning there with him."

Katherine's heart was heavy. She had been afraid of this.

"Well?" Laura persisted, "isn't that terrible? How awful for Brendan."

"Laura, they won't be returning to Ireland for a long time, and much can happen—if it came to a battle of wills, with Mary Rose tugging one way and Brendan another, I know who I'd wager upon."

"Yes, but . . ."

"Don't worry, Laura. It doesn't concern us. Whether Brendan decides to stay in Boston or return to Avonwood, I'm sure he'll make the right decision for his family."

Laura turned to scan Katherine's face. Then she said, "Something's happened to you in these past few years, Katey. It worries me. Doesn't anything *ever* bother you now? You've been so marvellous about Mary Rose that Teddi and I are almost agog. We say, at least once a day, that we don't know how you cope. You've . . . you've turned into a paragon, you know. You always seem to do and say the right thing—you never allow yourself the least touch of weakness—how can you be so self-possessed?"

"I'm not at all. It's just that I've made so many mistakes in my life that I can understand other people floundering about, making the wrong decisions, the wrong choices. Don't think that I don't care about Brendan and Mary Rose, for I do, but they'll be gone from the Valley in another four or five months, and then things will be back to normal."

And she laughed then, for she saw why Teddi and Laura could imagine her to be so much stronger than she was. *I have a habit,*

Katherine considered wonderingly, *of making cheerful, positive statements—and sounding as if I believe them.*

"It's Mr Crolin to see you." Carl's suspicion and dislike was written into every dour groove on his face as he added, "Mr Frank Crolin."

She was careful to keep any note of surprise out of her voice, aware that the man might be standing just out of her sight in the hall, and said merely, "Send him in, Carl—thank you."

She waited, stiff-backed, standing by her chair, thinking, oddly, "This is what Father should be doing. Not me, certainly not Brendan, but Father." She found herself already expecting trouble, unpleasantness, and the look on Crolin's narrow, swarthy face as he entered the room did nothing to allay her expectations.

"G'd evening, Missus." He bobbed his head, turning his hat round about in his hands, at the same time darting glances this way and that, his narrow black eyes checking the room as a ferret checks his path to a waterhole.

"Good evening, Mr Crolin. Would you like to sit down?"

He eyed the armchair to which she pointed, as if it were booby-trapped. "No, Missus, I'm all right standing, I reckon. What I got to say won't take long."

Oh dear. "Then I shall sit, if you don't mind." She did so, looked up at him with polite interest. "Now, how can I help you?"

"It's them fences," Frank began without preamble. "I done like you told me last time we spoke and I got Charlie's Essie—she's got some learnin'—to write a letter to your father. No letter's come back. I seen that overseer of yours, too, twice, an' he said it's up to Mister Prescott and he'll mention it in his report—whatever that is.

"Fact is, Missus—it's got real hard to find timber on that side of the Valley, and me an' Charlie an' Davey—we found some bonzer stands, just waitin' f' us to cut it. We can cut it all right—but there's a good two miles we gotta go to geddit *out*—unless we get that right of way."

"Mr Crolin, my father's property is grazing property, and if we take down fences . . ."

"But that's just *it*!" he cried. "It ain't no grazing land—maybe he run a few bush cattle once, but that was years ago. The land in that hill section ain't never bin cleared, Missus—never! You can ride up there an' see f' y'self. Ain't never bin cleared—just raw bush—an' a line o' post 'n' rails runnin' through it.

"All we want," he leaned over his circling hat with nervous intensity, "is two rail widths, that's all—just enough f'r our teams to get through. We won't touch no timber o' yours—you see if we do, we ain't stoopid. But we gotta get that timber out, Missus, or next winter'll be even worse for us than the last."

He shifted from one foot to the other. "Essie an' my Annie—they're jackin' up on us—sayin' they want to settle, have proper houses like other wimmin. An' I can see their point, though Charlie don't. Davey's sorta struck on one o' the McMahon girls an' he knows he don't stand a chance while he's a cedar-getter.

"Fact is, time's come when we gotta think about what's happenin'. Timber's gettin' scarcer all the time—kids gettin' sick, dyin'—and it's harder on the wimmin, grant you that. Charlie says we've always bin up in them hills—an' our father was—an' *his* father . . . But I told 'im, an' Essie has too, I reckon, that there was timber enough f'r everyone in them days—we all made a good livin'. But it ain't so any more—only a few more years left, I reckon—and it's take our swags somewhere else or get a selection here and buildin' a farm. Reckon we'd rather stay—most of us, anyway. But we need a stake, and that won't come unless we get that timber out." He paused for breath. "That's it, Missus. We bin waitin' months on this yes or no—would've had more money for food and medicine and our kids wouldn't have been so sick this winter, I reckon, if we'd got money f' that timber. Sale's still good at the yards—it's just gettin' the timber there . . ."

He trailed off hopefully.

Katherine scowled at the carpet near the man's feet, racking her brains to try to remember more of the country in question. It was true that it lay unused—had done so since before the death of her grandfather, Josiah Prescott. There was no stock in those rugged, scrub-covered hills. No reason at all why her father would refuse a right of way.

Probably he hadn't, she decided. Perhaps he never received the letter—Essie might not have addressed it correctly, or it might have been left unopened when Marcus left for the Orient. If he had received it, surely he would have written a reply?

And now? Marcus had displayed his complete lack of concern for Barrengarry in particular and the Valley in general. Brendan obviously did not feel capable of making a decision.

"What distance is the track to be?"

"Just across one corner—a hundred yards, that's all."

The scrub would grow back, she knew how fast. "As long as

the timber isn't touched," she said finally, "nor anything else on our property, I can't see that my father would object to a right of way."

The narrow face with the watchful black eyes looked unsure, then split into a grin. "That's . . . that's dinkum, then? We can start tomorrow?"

"As long as you're being 'dinkum' with me, Mr Crolin. If what you've been telling me proves to be untrue—*in any way*—this agreement is null and void. I must make that very clear!"

"O' course. But you won't have to worry. We don't want no trouble—never have. Like to keep to ourselves, as you know. You an' your dad won't have no trouble over this. An' when we're through we'll put up the fences—good as new."

"Very well."

"I'll be goin' . . ." and he was, already backing towards the door. "Thanks for your time. Missus. You ain't made a mistake, never fear . . ."

But that night she had great difficulty in falling asleep. Had she taken too much upon herself? Yet she must learn—she must. There was no one, really, to take the reins at Barrengarry. Her father too uninterested, Joe gone from them forever, and Brendan—a stranger, with his own responsibilities, who as soon as he was able, would be on his way back to Boston and then to Ireland.

She decided to speak of the matter to Brendan the following day, but when she visited the small secondary parlour that Brendan had taken over as his own office, he was not there. Peggy told her that he had had an early breakfast that morning and ridden about his various duties.

She was disappointed, spent a little time in the office looking at the papers on the desk, the firm, very even handwriting on the farm's correspondence. She touched the back of the leather chair in which he sat—then caught herself up and swore a little at her unconscious self-indulgence.

She was about to leave the room when she noticed the wastepaper basket. A letter, quite obviously unopened, lay within it. The envelope had been crumpled but such was the thickness of the paper within that it had easily straightened itself. Even the handwriting, as Katherine picked it up, was familiar. A slight, spidery hand, the letters slanting sometimes backhand, sometimes forehand, and of uneven size. She had seen the handwriting before . . .

Fleur Barton.

Her good manners warred with her curiosity for some seconds, then she tucked the letter into her apron pocket and carried the wastepaper basket into the kitchen and gave its contents to Peggy to feed to the kitchen stove. She then trotted up the stairs and into her room, sat down at her own desk before her window, and opened the letter.

So much for the paragon of virtue that her two sisters thought her to be . . . yet Brendan did not want the letter, she told herself, and she wanted to know what sort of woman had ingratiated herself into Angela's house. Surely Brendan couldn't be correct in his beliefs about her.

After reading only a page, she wished she had not. She put the letter down on the desktop and stared at the paper itself, trying to distance herself from the feeling of disgust that filled her before scanning quickly the rest of the pages.

Brendan had spared her feelings when he told her of the letters; Katherine understood quite clearly now how he could come to believe that there was something rather strange about Fleur.

The letter begged, pleaded, for a reply. It threatened, promised, suggested . . . the woman's mind allowed itself full licence here, and the suggestions and descriptions of what she and Brendan might do ran to four pages of progressively more erotic and erratic prose.

Yet it did not ring true. If Laura or Edwina had read it they would have seen it as the ravings of a morally depraved mind— but to Katherine, to anyone who had any sexual experience, the subject matter read more like a penny-dreadful romance, coupled with as much knowledge as one could gain without ever having had the actual experience.

This somehow made it worse.

And then, at the bottom of the page—

You say that it is foolish to become fond of you because you belong to another. By this you must mean Katherine. It is due to Katherine no doubt, that I haven't heard from you since you wrote that one, cold letter to me. I knew when you rode off together what you would be doing together, how you would be whispering about me and laughing about me.

Well, if you do not want me, there is someone who does. Rafe Huckstable has called in three times to visit and he looks at me as if he truly desires me, but I wait, as always, to hear from you.

More endearments and pleadings followed, then, abruptly—

If you are Katherine's lover—and everyone talked about the two of you on the night of the ball, you were so devious going onto the terrace together—then I wish you joy of her. She is cold and selfish and incapable of thinking of anyone but herself. I have found out all about her and

it should be of interest to you. I will tell you when you come to me.
More pleadings . . .

I grow so lonely in this great house by myself. If I don't hear from you soon I shall do something desperate. Sometimes I get so angry at the world for being so unfair that I feel like killing myself and everyone near me.

I will do something desperate if you don't come to me.

I cry myself to sleep every night for you and think of nothing but you all the day.

Come to me soon, my darling.

Fleur

The kitchen was empty when she went downstairs. The great black dragon of a stove wheezed and puffed in the chimney corner, and accepted the offering of Fleur's letter with a roar of delight.

Eavesdroppers hear no good of themselves, the saying went. And people who read other people's mail were just as likely to be faced with unwelcome truths about themselves.

Katherine stared into the flames of the kitchen range and wondered how dangerous Fleur Barton might be. But no, the letter—or letters— how many more had poor Brendan received, that he no longer read?— were simply the ravings of a lonely, obsessed woman.

She went upstairs and washed her hands very thoroughly, as if by this action she could as easily remove the words from her mind.

I feel like killing myself and everyone near me . . .

Katherine stopped, frozen, drying her hands on the embroidered huckaback towel, and wondered with a sinking feeling in her heart how Fleur would take the news that Brendan Kelehan had a wife.

It seemed providential for Katherine's prickling conscience that the Reverend David Dodds should visit the Valley that week. An Anglican service was arranged at the Cummings' low sprawling homestead at Yarranga Creek and that Sunday she was able to kneel with the rest of the Protestant population of the Valley in the large feedshed where a makeshift altar had been set up, and offer up her contrition for her sins—prying being foremost among them on that occasion.

Afterwards, many of the families stayed for a picnic on the homestead lawns, and all Katherine seemed to hear was talk of the sudden appearance of Mary Rose Kelehan. People were kind but very interested and, moving from group to group, she found it hard to be forced to hear the same questions over and over.

The Cummings girls, tall, tow-haired and angular—all women now, but unmarried, still carrying that soubriquet—gathered round and fixed her with their pale eyes like so many hungry birds. What was the young Mrs Kelehan like? How did it feel to find out she had arrived? When would it be convenient to call to meet her? How did it feel to have a guest of such obvious sophistication in the house? And was it true that there would be a little addition to the family? Wouldn't that be a burden, caring for a young mother and child? How did it feel . . .?

She came home tired and disgruntled, realizing, from the concern of neighbours, something she had not completely thought through herself. Would Mary Rose be better in Sydney? It was a first confinement, women's specialists were there . . . And perhaps, she thought with a heavy heart, it would be best for all concerned if Brendan and his wife should leave the Valley.

She let Laura, Edwina and Peggy chatter on about the service and the day's activities and rode home, sitting in the barouche as silently as Carl on the driver's seat.

Mary Rose was seated on the verandah when they arrived, crocheting—for she was quite expert with all manner of needlework— a delicate child's bonnet of silk thread.

The two girls settled down beside her immediately, but her gaze was only for Katherine—she called her over to her with some urgency, and lowered her voice to say, "My husband would like to speak with you—in his office. He says it's very important. I don't think," she added, "that he's in a very good mood."

There was a slight chagrin there, at obviously not being included in the matter, but being messenger was some consolation, there was a hint of some kind of triumph in Mary Rose's face that she could not quite disguise, despite her best efforts.

Edwina and Laura, who could not help but overhear the stage-whispered summons, looked at each other and Katherine in silence, but before they could speak, Mary Rose took each of them by the hand. "Now, tell me about your day . . . !"

And leaving them talking over one another, Katherine entered the house and walked along the hall to knock at the door of Brendan's office.

"Come in!" he called, and she entered, standing in the doorway for a second, sniffing at the mood of the man—and his bent head, the hand moving briskly, firmly, dragging his pen in thick strokes across a page of writing paper, did nothing to quell her feelings of uneasiness.

He looked up, stood with barely an effort at good manners and sat down again. Abruptly, "Come in and shut the door, Katherine. Sit down." He immediately continued to write.

No, this was not good.

She looked unhappily around the little office. The furniture had been rearranged to make room for the large desk that had been Joe's, and the single armchairs had been removed from the little parlour to the main sitting-room at the front of the house. The only place for Katherine to sit was on a large settee that had come with Suzanna on her marriage. Unlike the rest of the furniture at Barrengarry, this piece, with its glossy satin brocade, looked as new as when it had been purchased, being so uncomfortable that no one in the family sat on it unless they had to, so it had very soon been relegated to the back parlour and virtual disuse.

Katherine sat on one end of it now, gingerly, feeling like a schoolgirl in disgrace called before the headmaster. The thought should have made her smile, but it did not.

Brendan leaned back in his chair and fixed her coldly with the grey eyes. "Do I, or do I not, run Barrengarry?" he asked.

"Why—of course you do. In Father's absence . . ."

"I ask in order to have a certain question of accountability settled. Are the decisions concerning the management of this property to rest finally with me, or yourself?"

"With . . . you." And she did not like to say it. For even as she loved him, it was *her* Barrengarry . . .

"Then why didn't you tell me that Frank Crolin came to see you five days ago? And why did you give him permission to take down twenty yards of fences?"

"Twenty . . . ? Why would he need to take down twenty yards of . . ." She stopped. He was still waiting for an answer to his question, and it was disconcerting to find him gazing at her with unaccustomed impatience and displeasure. "He . . . he said he'd approached you, and you said you'd ask Father . . ."

"Yes?"

"And you'd received no reply. So I . . ."

"Didn't you consider, for a minute, that I should be consulted in this matter? I did write to your father—and I received a reply—he did not want the fences removed."

"Oh . . . !" The flushes began at her chest and moved with alacrity to the top of her head. He had lied. Frank Crolin had lied . . .

"But . . . he told me you hadn't received a reply, and knowing Father to be so preoccupied . . ."

"Knowing that, you should have referred the matter directly back to me. I had no idea you knew anything of the matter, until this afternoon, when I confronted the Crolins. I won't go into details, Kate, but there were a few minutes up there on that mountain when I thought I was going to be dragged off my horse, despatched with their idea of bush justice and my remains thrown into some ravine. There's no one so protective of his honesty as a villain, and to accuse the Crolins of taking down a fence without permission—*yours*—was enough to have them pointing their rifles at my head with all the affronted dignity they could muster. It was quite enough to make me wish I'd stayed here doing the accounts. They finally persuaded me to come to you and ask you—" he shook his head, "and right up until you admitted it, I held the illusion that you could not— possibly—be so irresponsible and stupid."

"You have no right . . . !"

"I have every right!" He spoke louder than she and sprang to his feet as he did so, and the voice and the movement silenced her. "I rode homewards and crossed the creek and found more than a dozen Woddi gathered there—I rode over to greet them and they were angry, Katherine. I have no knowledge of their language, but Myeela and Tigoora were there and between them they translated for me. Above the gully, where they took the fences down, is a tribal area—it's sacred to them—your father knew it, and it was obviously one of the reasons he had the area fenced off—though he didn't mention it in his letter to me . . ."

Katherine had turned to the door.

"Where are you going?" his voice like a whip at her back.

She faced him, furious. "I'm riding up to that boundary fence— I want to see this for myself."

"You'll do nothing of the kind. I've told them I'm having the fence replaced, and I'll take three or four of the lads—armed—and we'll see to it tomorrow. But the Crolins aren't in any mood to be trifled with, Kate, and I don't think . . . *Kate!*"

It was difficult to keep walking, but she did, making no acknowledgement that she had heard him bark her name so peremptorily, so loudly.

Loud enough for the girls on the verandah to hear. Mary Rose trotted down the hall, as Brendan caught up with Katherine at the door to the kitchen hallway and grasped her forearm. "I forbid you to go up there . . . !"

"What's happening?" Innocently, from Mary Rose. Laura and Edwina hung back a little, more circumspect. Not so Mary Rose.

Katherine broke free from Brendan's grasp. "Don't *ever* tell me what to do!" she hissed.

"You don't know what part the Crolins had to play in Barton's death, or . . ."

"Nonsense! Get out of my way—I'll clear this up . . ."

"What's wrong? Is something wrong?"

"It's nothing, Mary Rose," Katherine turned to her briefly. 'A problem with the estate . . ."

"Come back to the office . . ." Brendan said firmly.

"No! I told you I'm going—get out of my way, Brendan."

"Katey," delicately from a worried Laura, "you can't go riding off in that dress . . ."

And she felt very foolish, caught the sudden amusement in Brendan's gaze at the same time as she remembered that she was wearing one of her best silk and taffeta dresses and a plumed, fashionable little hat; the entire costume, though suitable for church and Valley picnics, ridiculous for scrambling on horseback up perpendicular mountains.

"Excuse me . . ." she pushed past them all, and headed for the stairs.

As she ascended she could hear Mary Rose's voice.

"What's happened? What's wrong? Why are you angry, dear? Brendan? You're not going out today, are you? It *is* Sunday . . ."

No answer from Brendan reached Katherine. She closed the door of her room behind her, paused, leaning against it for half a minute, trying to collect herself, control her anger.

It was a rage directed as much at herself as at Brendan. She had known the sharp-eyed, narrow-shouldered Crolin brothers since they were children, remembered them robbing birds' nests, smashing the eggs on stumps, in their rough scientific curiosity about the developing stages of the birds within. She remembered Carl chasing the youngest, Davey, across the eastern paddock, touching his behind with an eight-foot stock whip, after the dogs had discovered Davey in the hen house. She had had no reason to trust them as small boys—why did she think they had changed?

He looked me in the eyes and he lied to me.

The dismantled fences on the slopes above Paradise Gully were not the only objective of her expedition. She would not in the least mind finding herself face to face with Frank Crolin.

She dressed as quickly as possible in her riding habit, fingers fumbling with the buttons and fastenings in her impatience.

Coming down the stairs, she did not call into the parlour, where she could hear a murmur of female voices, nor did she turn into Brendan's office, the door of which was sulkily shut.

The dogs pranced along beside her as she crossed the stable yard—then surprised her by running forward into the building. She stopped in the doorway, attempting to accustom her eyes to the sudden dimness, aware of movement there in the shadows. No, damn him!

"Brendan?" and her voice made the word more a statement than a question.

Silence. The creak of leather and a stirring of metal-shod hoofs on the cobbles. The shapes of two horses moved towards her and she stood her ground, glaring at the shadowy features of the man who led them. The dogs romped out into the sunshine, paused, front legs flat to the ground, tails in the air, barking a summons. But Brendan stopped in the doorway, holding Katherine's gaze, before handing her Dryad's reins. His own chestnut was saddled also, and Katherine scowled at it and back to Brendan.

"You needn't come," she said, "I'll be careful . . ."

He ignored her statement, led his horse past her, turned it, and gazed at her, his head tilted enquiringly. "Well? Would you like me to help you mount?"

From the wide windows of the parlour, Mary Rose watched Katherine, a dark-clad figure mounted on the chestnut mare, speed past down the drive, the reins controlled, body bent forward. If not for the trailing skirts and the side-saddle, one could think her a jockey involved in a race, such was the intent in that small, slim figure. Two of the farm dogs, long-legged dark gold creatures that looked part greyhound, streaked after her—and then Brendan appeared.

She caught her breath as a feeling like grief struck her, found her hand to her breast as the big chestnut gelding thundered around the house and down the drive; and the fine breeding of the animal, the thoroughbred blood that showed in the length of the shoulder, the powerful long legs would, she judged, mean that by the time they were onto the main road, the chestnuts would be racing neck to neck, side by side. And Brendan would slow his mount then, for the object after all, was not to pass Katherine, but to draw level, to accompany her, *for he wanted to be with her.*

She moved forward a little, half-uttered a cry—but even as he vanished around the curve in the drive, she knew he could not hear her, even had she screamed.

The scream was close, its silent clamouring within her brain pressed against her eyelids, burned in her throat. She half turned into the room—Edwina and Laura—oh, they were kind, they were her friends, she could tell by the concern and pity written on their faces . . .

"He's gone . . ." she managed to speak through trembling lips, "he rode off—after your sister, and he . . . he didn't once look back . . ." The sob rose from deep within her, and broke the shell of her calm. For it was too much to be borne, she rejected all she had seen with every scream she uttered; she beat off the reality and expended her hate and her pain at one and the same time in this wild, timeless place, her refuge, her defence . . .

He was not here to see, but she heard the flutterings about her, caught sight from where she lay on the floor of the little slippers and the trailing skirts going back and forth in terrified agitation. Above her own shrieks, she could hear someone calling for Peggy, for sal volatile, for damp cloths . . .

Once more she was at home, and Mama and Papa were there, and holding her, cradling her and telling her that it was all right, it was all right, she was their little love, their little princess, and she could have whatever she wished for, they would see to it, they would look after her . . .

The floor was dusty, the aged pile of the carpet rough against her face. Brendan . . . He didn't look at me . . .

But her grievance was not strong enough for her to block out the fact that the room was silent.

She lay sobbing loudly, but time passed and she was tiring; her face lay in the crook of her arm, her nose was unpleasantly close to the floor. It could not be hygienic . . . And yet no one had approached her; not a word, not a touch from Laura nor Edwina.

Sniffling, she raised her head.

The room was empty.

Impossible. She sat up, hiccupping, drawing shuddering breaths into her lungs, more miserable than ever at this defection. She was alone—completely alone in a foreign country, with no one to care for her, no one to love her.

She burst into fresh tears, drumming her heels on the floor, wishing with all her heart that she was back in the grand old house in Chestnut Street. Never in all her entire nineteen years had anyone treated her so callously.

She sat on the faded carpet, her knees drawn up and arms about them, sobbing until she was too exhausted to do more than whimper.

She would kill herself, that would serve them right. They would understand once she was dead what they had done to her . . .

The child stirred within her. She had forgotten it, felt a rush of guilty compassion, pressed her hands lightly to her stomach and felt the little form turning round about, stronger and more energetic than it had ever moved before. She had been delighted and a little frightened when, just over a month ago, the first flutterings of life began within her, but this, this seemed as if the little creature knew, understood her very thoughts.

What about me? it said, *I'm here, part of you* . . . The little limbs seemed to be beating a message to remind her. Her life was no longer her own—and . . . she was not alone. Why, all this time she had been upset, crying in this empty room, she was not alone. She was here with her child. My son and I . . . My daughter and I . . . We were here. We are here. My child and I, *we're here*.

"Mrs Kelehan?"

Mary Rose looked up towards the door, startled, but relaxed when she saw the comfortable form of Peggy entering the room, carrying a tray on which tea things rested.

"I thought you'd like a cup of tea—you must be exhausted." The tone was kindly, sympathetic. She added, as she set the small table, "I sent Miss Edwina and Miss Laura off outside, ma'am. I know you wouldn't like them to stay and be upset—they wanted to stay, mind you—but I wouldn't have it. Can I help you up, ma'am— you'll be much happier in your chair . . . there . . ."

Mary Rose found herself in a soft armchair, a cushion placed at her back.

Peggy was pouring tea, her pink, scrubbed face lowered, the blue eyes on the stream of tea as she said quietly, "Mr Kelehan explained a little about your nervous problem a few days ago. I agreed with him that it's just a passing phase you'll grow out of—and he told me what to do. My little sister, Maggie, used to have tantrums like yours, but she grew out of it by the time she was sixteen, and now she's all growed up with a family of her own, and as sane a women as you could find, bless her! Your trouble is, you've been too protected, poor dear—never had the knocks and bruises my lot here have had. But you'll be fine. When you feel it coming on you, we'll all leave you alone, and you can holler as much as you like, we'll understand. And afterwards, I'll make you a nice cup of tea."

She looked up. "Shall I call the misses in, now, ma'am? They'll surely want to know you're not hurt or nothing. Is the lemon cake all right, do you think—we got some seed cake, too, if you'd prefer I got that for you?"

Twenty Five

Katherine wished she could remain angry longer than she did. But the sobering fact was that by the time they had reached the head of Paradise Gully and began to edge their way up the slope of Brown's Mountain, she was thinking mostly of the Woddi; of old Gurral, his despair and anger that yet one more violation had been perpetrated. The fence would have been bad enough, Katherine thought, as Dryad picked her way amongst the ferns and fallen timber and leaf-litter. But he would have seen the reason behind it, Marcus would have explained it—and the fence would not bother the Woddi, they were regarded as a strange aberration of the greedy white men, and merely nuisances to have to clamber through on their walkabouts.

She found she wanted to know more; what had Tigoora and Myeela to say about the sacred place? And had the Crolins actually threatened Brendan? Now that she was no longer on the defensive, she began to worry. They were violent men, and they had long memories and a capacity for resentment. What if Brendan, riding alone about the Valley on his duties should be shot by some unknown assailant? The Crolins moved in the bush like shadows. It would be difficult to prove any such crime was connected with the Crolins' maledictions when Brendan informed them that the fence would be replaced.

The thought of a shooting, however, made her remember that Amos Murphy had shot Charlie Crolin in a brawl at Radley's some two months before—and so far there had been no retaliatory measures. Perhaps they were simply waiting their opportunity, but in view of the fight between Amos and yet another of the Crolin brothers a few weeks later, it would seem that the bad blood between Murphy and the family required only brief but regular letting to keep honour satisfied.

She hoped the threats against Brendan were more verbal posturings rather than any serious promise. And something else bothered her.

"You think I'm a fool, I know," turning to him to break the silence of several miles, "but there's another matter that I didn't approach with Crolin. Do they have a lease for the timber they're taking? It hadn't occurred to me before that they might not, but after what you've told me, I wouldn't be surprised if they were taking that cedar illegally."

Brendan was riding slightly ahead of her, there was no path here, and the horses ranged where they could, in picking their way upwards.

Brendan scowled back at her, considering, obviously, whether he wished to speak to her at all, but finally relented.

"I don't know if they have a lease. They said they did, but it was back at their camp—it doesn't matter too much if they were lying because it's Crown land according to the map, and doesn't affect your father except in the matter of this right of way. It was worth a little blackmail value, however, and I used it as a lever to try to convince them to leave off logging in the area. I don't *want* to turn them in to Sergeant Lloyd unless I have to—they have wives and children, most of them, and Her Majesty won't miss the two acres or so that they've cleared."

Two acres . . .

"The Tallons were working there with them, they said, but it was only the Crolins there today—they saw me riding up here and followed."

"Why did you ride up here?" curiously, and then she wished she had not asked. He was so often busy, it had not passed her attention that he seemed to be avoiding Mary Rose. There were few reasons why a man would ride several miles up a desolate mountain on a Sunday, merely to ride down again immediately afterwards.

"Stephen Brody told me yesterday that he thought he'd heard axes up this way—and this was the only free time I had to check." He was rather defensive, his errand being performed on the Sabbath, for he said, "I came from curiosity, merely. It wasn't *work* as such."

"I understand," she said, and she did; understanding also that he seemed to be filling in every hour of his days.

There was little else to say, and they climbed without further dialogue, dismounting to lead their horses where the ground was too steep, too dangerous.

Katherine disliked the strained and guarded silence between them. Yet uncomfortable as it was, she was still too angry with him to apologize. Yes, she has done wrong in not reporting Crolin's two visits, but neither should he have treated her like an errant child. She had acted in good faith, was it her fault that Frank Crolin was a lying little cad?

"Here it is . . ."

After the peace of the climb through virgin bushland, she was shocked to suddenly come across fallen posts and wire, and a broad passage slashed through the forest, raw earth turned over, trees newly-felled hauled to one side, leaves stiff and bleaching in death. She looked about, appalled, distressed.

"But . . . this is Barrengarry land . . ."

"That's right."

"He cut a road through our land? He cut *our trees*?"

"They couldn't weave in and out between them, not draught horses pulling cedar logs behind them. Didn't you realise that they'd take down the trees in their way?" His voice mild, his glance mere enquiry.

She looked away. Dryad lifted her feet carefully over the wire lying on the ground. The cedar logs had dragged great grooves in the soil, with the next rains there would be great pools of water in a roadway of deep mud.

Katherine rode on. The road through the trees did traverse the western corner of Marcus's property, as Frank had said, and here beyond the second stretch of fence they had taken down, the Crown land began, and with it, the Crolins' decimation.

It took a long time for her to drag her eyes away from the man-made clearing, stumps jutting up from amid young, broken and bruised trees, casualties of the cedar-getters' attempts to haul the large fallen logs from the area.

When she did chance to look up at the surrounding hills and skyline, wondering where the Woddi's sacred place might be, she inhaled so sharply, sat so still in the saddle that Brendan, riding beside her, paused to study her features before saying quietly, "Kate? What is it?"

"I remember . . ." she murmured, eyes still on the curves of scrub-covered hills. "Joe and I came here—we were very small. Nine or ten, no older. I know where the sacred site is." She turned to Brendan, but her gaze had already clouded with her memories, and she dismounted from her horse, led the mare over to a large fallen branch in the shade and seated herself, her gaze hardly leaving those brooding hills.

Brendan dismounted and stood watching her. She said, "There's a cave, up there—" she pointed, "or . . . not really a cave—a deep recess in the rock face—and two large—oh, huge—rocks standing sentinel to either side. Joe and I rode our ponies up here—and played bushrangers round about the rocks . . . we'd seen other cave paintings before, so the drawings on this particular rock didn't instil much interest in us . . . I can't even remember details of them—except there was a snake, and men and women . . . Tigoora has since told me that there is a being called the Rainbow Snake—you can see how a rainbow might appear that way to them—and he was responsible for the entire world as they know it. Well, the snake was there, and other drawings, but Joe and I were ignoring them, running round and about the two rocks shooting at each other—" she pointed two fingers horizontally at Brendan, "Bang—pow! We were having a wonderful time, then the next minute we were surrounded by Aborigines—only the men—they were covered with clay and feathers in patches on their cheeks and body. They grabbed us quite roughly and dragged us off to where four or five old men stood. We were trembling in our boots, too afraid to cry, standing there while they talked about us—and what made it worse than that—we knew enough of the language and could judge from their actions just what they were thinking—and it wasn't pleasant. On any other day it *might* have been all right—but this was special, we'd never seen the Woddi Woddi in such intricate regalia. This was obviously a very sacred day. We shouldn't have been there—Joe an uninitiated boy, and as for me—a female! That upset them the most. I knew the word for 'girl' and they kept repeating it—the oldest man—even older than Gurral in those days—saying it over and over that I meant bad luck, bad magic, very bad things.

"Gurral took our part. His words were harder to understand because he spoke calmly—the other old man kept shaking his spear, stamping his feet. Gurral could have been arguing for him to kill us after dinner, not before.

"It was Gurral, finally, who came to stand in front of us, took our faces in his hands and gazed at us—I don't think I've ever been so frightened in my life—that broad black face, those huge brown bloodshot eyes, above the nose with its five inches of bone perforating the skin near the lip . . . eyes like no man I'd ever seen— *peering* at me—than at Joe. Pulling us together, one hand under each chin, the easier to study us together. I don't know what he saw, two small pale faces, alike in a way, with our freckles and our green eyes—and my thin red pigtails, and Joe's white-blonde mop of silk fringe. We might have looked as foreign and threatening to him as he did to us.

"When he turned to the other elder, he said something about—one son—or an only son—and I was mentioned, too, but he kept saying that one phrase that I understood, while four or five of the older men argued and shouted over each other, and the oldest kept up his claim that we were bad luck, bad magic. One middle-aged warrior even grabbed hold of me—and he had a nulla nulla in his other hand—a club," she explained, seeing Brendan's puzzled frown, "but Gurral took the man's wrist—and Joe grabbed hold of me and shouted at them—he was very brave, 'leave my sister alone—you leave my sister alone!' and with Joe pulling on me, and my own terror, I broke away from the man with the nulla nulla and huddled against Joe."

So long ago—lost, almost, in her memory. She had never tried to find the place again, "lost it" to herself, as a kind of self-protection. If she did not know the way, she could not then return there.

Yet here she was.

"How did you manage to escape?" Brendan asked.

"Gurral talked them down. I don't know what it was—he talked and talked—and he kept mentioning my father—my grandfather, Josiah Prescott, was one of the first white men ever to settle here. They sensed he was a kind of leader, heard the stockmen and farmworkers calling him 'Boss' and did likewise—they saw him as an elder in his 'tribe'. When he died, they passed the title to my father. It annoys some of the other Valley people—especially old Mikey Brody. But the fact is, Father speaks the Woddi language, listens to their problems, does his best to help them. I think the only reason Joe and I weren't killed that day was because of the respect in which the Woddi held my father. Gurral told them that Joe was his only son, and I think—" carefully, for she was considering that far-off afternoon through twenty years and a terror that had almost obliterated the events, "I think he stared so close in order to tell them that he saw no harm in us."

And Gurral, respected for his magic, his wisdom, had either been mistaken, or had seen the danger and lied to save the Boss's grief. And there was another reason. Knowing well the white community's speed and over-zealousness in exacting revenge he had acted to save his own people.

She sighed, feeling a heavy sadness within her, for nearly twenty years had passed and the old men had been right. The white girl child had brought bad magic.

"What's the matter? Why did you sigh like that?" Brendan's voice, gentle, unobtrusive as always. And it was fairly easy to find words for the complex emotion that had just possessed her.

"It's strange—when you're a child you long to be free of the constrictions, the limitations that the adult world places upon you. And yet you find when you are grown up that problems are now less easy to solve, indeed some are more puzzling than they were when you were a child. Sometimes they're worse—for one can see further, can see more pitfalls, see more reasons to be afraid." She said suddenly, "Why did you do that?"

"Do what?"

"I saw you move slightly while I was speaking. Am I boring you?"

He smiled, rather wryly, "No, I . . . I suddenly felt an overwhelming desire to put my arms around you, to comfort you perhaps. And then I thought immediately how foolish that would be. I knew you would push me away."

She stared at him for some seconds. Then, "I think I would like your arms around me, very much."

It was difficult, their horses' reins still over their arms, for the horses were tired and eager to be home and nipped at each other in a fretting sort of way, and nudged and nibbled at Katherine and Brendan's backs while they embraced. They began to laugh, and as she looked up into his face and he down at her, the familiarity and warmth between them gratefully returned after the intensity of their quarrel, made them pause, struck silent with that rare oneness between a man and a woman, when one wonders not only at the perfection of the beloved but at the wondrousness of the gift, that both could feel the same.

And slowly, slowly, it ebbed away, leaving the cold grey realization that they had no right to feel this.

Both were startled by a noise off towards the edge of the scrub, bushes and branches trampled, muffled shouts, hoarse cries, "Davey! Come back!"

A figure, slim, not tall, leapt a fallen tree trunk and came towards them—the hat came off the head and bounced on the cord that held it under the chin. The figure laughed as it ran, and the laughter was not a pleasant sound, not did it promise amusement to anyone but its executant.

"Got yez! Just look at yez!"

"Davey!" More figures from the bush, more Crolins, carrying guns.

Davey, the youngest, was dancing up to Brendan and Katherine, jerkily, warily, delighted with himself. "Busy boy, today, ain't you, Kelehan? Was complaining that it's a bit crowded up here, and yet you come by with yer little lady friend for a quiet bit of . . ."

Brendan lunged forward savagely—Davey stumbled back, frightened—and once, twice, the sound of rifles being cocked, and Katherine and Brendan both looked up, to find Frank and Charlie regarding them from along the barrels of their hunting pieces.

Davey had a few seconds to recover while the others studied the situation. He was not easily crushed, and began jiggling about the captives once more, secure in the fact that his brothers controlled the situation.

"Got yez, all right," he half-muttered, half-sung, with all his unconstrained energy keeping him moving. "Old man Prescott'd like to have seen what we saw. Pity we don't have one of them camera things—hey, Charlie? Hey, Frank?" He whirled like a dervish to face his brothers and back again without a check, "An' your pretty little wife back in Barrengarry—she'd have somethin' to say, eh, Kelehan? Eh?"

"You're a dumb little arse'ole, Davey!" Frank lowered his gun for a minute to scowl at his brother. "Why d'you think we was calling you back? If you'd waited a couple of minutes more we might've caught them doing something *really* interesting. Why'd you have to stop 'em before they got properly started?"

"Yairs," a grumble from Charlie.

Davey's humour fell away from him, his thin, almost handsome face collapsed in disappointment. The possibilities streaked through his head in all their potential and were gone. He grabbed his hat, and flung it on the ground. "*Shit!*"

Brendan still held her by one elbow—the pressure was now so telling that it hurt. "I'll help you to mount, Katherine . . ."

"Now that's an idea . . ." Before they could move, Davey's face came up brightly. He turned to his brothers. "Well?"

They gazed at him blankly.

"Well? She's here, ain't she? An' she was goin' to do it with *him*. You know the ol' saying about not missing a slice off of a cut loaf . . ."

Frank's gun came down again; he seemed to consider. He placed the safety catch back on, held the rifle easily in two hands, walked forward and, bringing it up suddenly, bashed the butt with all his weight into the middle of Davey's face.

Katherine recoiled a pace towards Brendan. Despite her fright and disgust she found her nose prickling, her eyes watering in unconscious sympathy with Davey Crolin. He rolled about on his back, crying like a child, both hands clasped to his shattered face, the blood oozing between his fingers onto the leaf litter.

Charlie, slightly taller though more slender than Frank, came to stand beside his brother. He looked down. "You broke his nose, I bet."

Frank sighed. "Yairs," heavily. He looked up at Katherine almost shamefacedly, "He always was a dirty-minded little devil. He ain't like the rest of us."

Charlie shook his head, half-bent to Davey, then changed his mind and straightened. "Dunno if you should have hit 'im so hard. Didn't have to break his nose."

Frank was still gazing morosely at the sobbing Davey. "I wanted him to remember it," he said.

Charlie scowled across at Brendan. "You, too," he said. "You take a good look. We can do that to our own brother, think what we can do to you, without losin' no sleep at all."

"Don't threaten me," said Brendan mildly.

"We ain't threatening," Frank rejoined, obviously at one with his brother. "We're just giving you fair warning. Leave us alone to do our jobs, and we'll leave you alone."

"Now get on your horses and get out of here, 'cause I'm gettin' angrier by the minute, that Frank had to hit Davey. Not that he didn't do right," as Frank's eyes came around to him, black and deadly, "but there wouldn't have been no cause if you'd stayed home, missus, where you should be—and not up here with your overseer— and him a married man!"

"Yairs," from Frank.

"If you think . . ." she was furious; heaven only knew what she would have done had Brendan not placed an arm about her, catching her off-guard as she stepped forward, so her own impetus helped swing her completely around him, until his body was between herself and the Crolins.

"Say nothing," he told her softly, "don't lower yourself to justify . . ."

"Let go! And you two—" past Brendan's shoulders, as he edged her towards her horse, "you'd better find that lease you have for this land, for I've had enough of your lies—and I mean you, Frank Crolin!"

"*Kate!*" A deadly whisper.

"*Stop pushing me!* I don't believe for a minute that you've got a lease to take this timber—so don't threaten us—you're the ones who'll be in trouble if I find one more tree cut down! Do you hear?"

Brendan practically threw her onto the horse's back, causing her to bump hard against the leaping head, bruising her right thigh before she could lift it over the pommel into position. She found the stirrup, settled her left leg up against the leaping head and arranged her skirts, glaring all the while between Brendan and a strangely silent pair of Crolin brothers. The only sound came from Davey, sitting up now, still clutching his nose and whimpering quietly.

"Missus. You should have left while you was ahead." Frank spoke quietly and it was worse, somehow, this deliberate, deadly tone.

"Katherine, go!" Brendan had whirled to her, stepping aside, slapping Dryad on the neck—and at the same time, the Crolins rushed for him.

Dryad leapt beneath her as she called Brendan's name in belated warning and in fear for him. But the panicking horse, as frightened by the raised rifles, as of the slap she had received, had lunged across the clearing towards home.

"Stop right there—we've got guns . . ."

She had no idea where the new voice came from, had all her energies expended in controlling the frightened Dryad, in turning her about, for there was no way that she would leave Brendan . . .

Dryad was still plunging and dancing as she managed to guide her back, and Katherine saw at a glance the tableau before her: Brendan on the ground, not far from Davey, blood pouring down his face, raising himself on one elbow slowly, dazedly. The voice had halted Frank and Charlie where they stood, the former still bent over Brendan, his hand gripping the fallen man's collar, the latter with his rifle butt raised once more, arrested before the blow was struck.

For three riders stood at a little distance, and never had Katherine been more glad to see the faces of Stephen Brody, Rafe Huckstable and Luke Murchison.

"You all right, Kelehan?" Luke spoke, not taking his eyes from the Crolins.

Brendan seemed to have difficulty in focussing for a few seconds. "Yes . . ." he rose to his feet carefully, using the log Katherine had been seated on as a kind of lever.

"Can you mount?"

"Yes, I . . ." His horse had escaped but was standing nearby, patiently.

Katherine rode to it, scooped up the reins and led it to Brendan, ignoring the Crolins, even Davey, who scrambled back out of her way like a crab, muttering curses in a black and nasal tone that was fortunately unintelligible.

Brendan took his horse's reins, smiled up at her with something like his old debonair manner, spoilt only by the blood that insisted on running down into his left eye. He mounted his horse, and then took out a clean handkerchief, dabbing it at the cut, before holding it there and scowling one-eyed and piratical, at Frank, Charlie and Davey.

"I think it's time you considered the benefits of searching for cedar out of Kangaroo Valley. Unless you can show me that government lease when I bring my men here tomorrow, I don't want to see even one of you here again!"

He spoke quietly, but they understood well enough. The narrow faces kept turning from Brendan to the three mounted figures with their rifles. The darting black eyes registered, along with their malevolent and brooding resentment, the knowledge that members of three prominent Valley families had witnessed the attack—not to mention Prescott's daughter. The aim had been to frighten her and Kelehan into silence, but even that had been a rash move and they knew it, and regretted it.

No one moved, and it was Charlie who, judging this to be the moment for discretion, hauled the still mewling Davey to his feet and turned with an attempt at a careless kind of saunter down the hill, avoiding the broad pathway cut through the Prescott land. Davey and Frank, with final murderous looks at the riders, slithered after their brother, down the scrubby slope and into the shadows of the gully.

Brendan watched them out of sight, then turned his big chestnut and rode to the three men, shaking each, in turn, solemnly by the hand.

Rafe, who seemed very amused by the incident ("the most exciting time I've had since I tried to arm-wrestle Bert Radley for fifty guineas"), told Katherine and Brendan how they came to play the part of rescuers, as they rode home.

"We called in at Barrengarry this afternoon, not together, though we do look like the Three Musketeers, don't we? No, we arrived one at a time . . . Mrs Kelehan, Laura and Edwina were having tea, and we were, both of us, invited to share it—then *this* fellow arrived," he looked darkly over at Stephen, "and when he was told where you two had gone, he suggested that we forgo our cucumber sandwiches and lemon cake, and go look for you."

Luke was the eldest of the men, big, bearded, with curly dark hair which a few years ago to his horror, had started to recede from the broad, good-natured brow.

"He's not one to panic, young Stephen, so we thought we'd best follow his suspicions, just in case—too much violence in this Valley lately—can't take chances."

Katherine looked over at him gratefully. Edwina spoke disparagingly of his clumsiness, of his round face and small eyes—

yes, next to Rafe, poor Luke paled by comparison. But such was Rafe's good fortune in the lottery of genetic makeup that nearly any man suffered the same fate. Alongside Rafe, Stephen looked a trifle soft and boyish, Brendan's strong features looked long and gravely hawklike, and poor Luke did indeed look round-faced and homely. But the small eyes, bright green and merry, were intelligent and kindly, the mouth, within the black beard, firm and generous. He was a man about whom there was nothing small, mean or petty, a man of big actions and, Katherine thought, were it not for the fact that I never loved him, I could have done a great deal worse than follow Father's advice and set my cap for Luke Murchison.

"I know what the Crolins are like," Stephen said, taking off his hat to brush the damp blonde fringe back from his forehead. "That's why I was worried when I heard axes up there—I told you," he turned to Brendan, "and did suggest, then, that you shouldn't go up there alone." He looked at Katherine. "I'm so glad we were there."

She hoped no one noticed the intensity with which the words were spoken. Too often, when no one could see, that same intensity had crept into Stephen's face. *Hell's outhouse* . . . Katherine smiled graciously, and turned to study the terrain before her as though Dryad actually needed help to find the way home.

Rafe trotted his horse up to draw level with her. "Mr Kelehan is doing a very competent job of running Barrengarry," he said, with a gracious nod towards the blood-spattered Brendan, "but he doesn't know the Valley ways. Perhaps, if you need to ride further afield in future, you could call on one of us to accompany you— we all carry rifles on our saddles now, and as you saw, one never knows when a gun may be needed." Another look at Brendan, then to Katherine, "There isn't much to be done at Bendeela just now, so if you need me . . ."

Katherine smiled politely, glanced at Brendan, expecting the reply to come from him, but he was riding with one hand only on the reins, the other pressing his handkerchief to his forehead and the one eye that she could see was fixed in its gaze on his horse's ears and he seemed to be lost in some thoughts that he found fairly amusing, for a smile played around the edges of the broad mouth.

Stephen had ridden closer also and echoed Rafe's offer. Only the voice of reason, from Luke, put in, "But they have several stockmen on Barrengarry at the moment."

"Yes," Brendan seemed to come to life with this, "we will be more careful from now on—and I shall borrow that fine Henry rifle

of Mr Prescott's—it'll bring back memories, as I have one identical
to it back in Ireland. And as Luke here has suggested, we have the
Clancy boys, and the Wests and Gillespies from Burrawang—they're
all strong, tough lads and just spoiling for a fight, I'm sure. Though
I'm grateful for your offer," and Brendan inclined his head towards
the two with a grace equal to Rafe's, despite his gory aspect. "I'm
sure Miss Laura and Miss Edwina wouldn't thank me for endangering
their champions a second time."

There was a pause.

Luke murmured, "I wonder if we'll get a second chance at that
lemon cake?"

Peggy pounced upon Brendan the minute he came through the door,
not, unfortunately, before Mary Rose caught sight of him. So it was
up to Katherine to serve more tea and lemon cake to the three rescuers
while the husband was having his head dressed in the kitchen and
the wife was being treated with cold compresses and sal volatile
in her bedroom upstairs.

It was only later, when the three men had, regretfully as always,
left to ride to their various farms, and Brendan, his head swathed
in a clean white bandage by the tenderly ministering Peggy, had
visited Mary Rose in the darkened room, that he came downstairs
and found Katherine waiting in his office.

He did not have a chance to seat himself before she stood, lowering
the book on farm management that she had been leafing through,
and announced with cool composure that she would be leaving for
Sydney the following day.

She was calm, smiling, and betrayed no sign of her inner turmoil,
remaining visibly unmoved even in the face of Brendan's obvious
unwillingness that she should go.

How could she explain what she had felt up on that mountainside?
When she had thought he would be killed, she had felt a wild
recklessness, a grief close to madness. Only in nearly losing him
had she realized that he was more precious to her than life itself.

With the knowledge that he would soon be taking his wife and
child and leaving the Valley forever, came the determination that
he would not take her heart, her soul, into that new life in America.

She would go to Sydney; she would find some happiness, some
courage, something to hold to in the empty years without him.

Twenty Six

There was no way of avoiding Dovewood; Katherine would have to call in there, tell her grandparents that she was going to Sydney for some time, ask for messages or packages that they wished to send on to Suzanna. Though heavens knows where she is, Katherine thought.

It was Fleur who came to meet her on entering the big house. Katherine had seen the woman only twice since the decision was made for Fleur to remain at Dovewood, and on the occasion of both visits to Barrengarry Fleur had been her quiet, demure self. Now however there was a change; the dimpling, smiling Fleur who took Katherine's hand in such a fond, familiar way, this Fleur in a beautifully cut lavender gown that would have done justice to a wealthy heiress, bore no resemblance at all to the meek little woman Katherine had first seen in second-hand mourning in the parlour at Barrengarry.

Her dark hair was dressed in the very latest style, her cheeks were bright and the grey eyes shone with humour.

Why, she looks truly lovely, the bemused Katherine had to admit, and she found herself feeling pleased and relieved, for she had not known what to expect from Fleur Barton and forgot, in her study of this transformation, to be resentful of the place of obvious respect in which Fleur seemed to be held at Dovewood. Fleur ordered the servants about and spoke of Edwina and Angela with easy familiarity, lacking even the respectful awe that Katherine, trained strictly in the school that children should be visible but inaudible, had never been able to shake, despite the fondness and affection that existed between the Gordons and all their grandchildren.

Katherine pushed aside the thought of the letters sent to Brendan Kelehan—they had been written while the young woman was still overcoming her shock at her father's death and the sudden change in her own fortunes. It would take some time for her to recover; perhaps she had already begun, perhaps something had happened to bring this open vivacity to Fleur and that last letter, the one that Katherine had read—and she cringed, inwardly, remembering—had been the last aberration of a disturbed mind before finding herself once more.

Even so . . .

"Brendan Kelehan is married, Grandmama," she told Angela when they were walking alone in the garden that first evening. "He had married a young American lady, Mary Rose O'Boyle, and a few weeks ago she came to join him here in Australia. They'll be staying at Barrengarry until the birth of her child in February."

"A child in February? And she came all the way from America by herself?" Angela looked astonished but almost admiring. "A gallant young woman—but Americans are, aren't they? Such a pretty name, too—Mary Rose. We must have them to visit soon."

Katherine had been watching Angela closely. No, there had been no consternation on her face, no hint that she knew of any infatuation for Brendan on the part of her young companion.

"If you don't mind, I'd like you to tell Fleur," Katherine said.

"I? Tell her what—that Mr Kelehan has a wife and a baby on the way?" Angela, no fool, was, to Katherine's discomfort, regarding her warily. "Are you saying it should *matter* to Fleur?"

"They . . . well, they were friends, and—sometimes, you know— it can come as quite a shock. I know it did to me." Angela was still gazing at her steadily. "I think," Katherine finished, "that it may be a bit of a shock to Fleur also."

"You, perhaps, I can understand," Angela said gravely, "for you were close, platonic friends for many years and a marriage, even in those circumstances, can distance people from each other. But Fleur . . . My dear, she's only met the man three times—could this news really upset her? Has she confided in you?"

"A little," Katherine admitted unwillingly. "Really, Grandmama, it's not my place to talk about this." I've interfered enough, she thought. "I simply feel that the news should come from someone she is fond of, whom she trusts."

"Nonsense, girl, she likes you, she trusts you. You're closer to her age than I am . . ."

"It's perhaps for this reason that I'm *not* the best person to tell her. In Fleur's eyes, I have been very fortunate in knowing Brendan for so long and in being with him, as far as she can see, at Barrengarry. I don't know how to explain it . . . In this matter, Fleur is not as dispassionate, nor as stable, as we might think. She was such a plain little thing for so long—I believe she came to fix on Brendan for no other reason than he was the first man to show her any kindness. And in a nature as passionate as Fleur's, I don't believe he will be forgotten easily."

Angela walked in silence for a few minutes, bent to pluck some lemon grass and rubbed at it. The fragrance lifted even to Katherine's nose, but Angela, the lovely face so concerned that Katherine felt doubly sorry she had spoken in such depth, seemed not to notice the perfumed herb she held.

"A great deal of what you say makes sense, now I think about it. Yes, my dear, of course I'll tell her—but only to think that I'd come to suspect she had developed a *tendresse* for that rascal, Rafe Huckstable. He's called in a few times on his way to and from Moss Vale, and he flirts outrageously with every woman in the house—even myself. I had noticed, however, that his gallantries seemed to impress Fleur, perhaps more than they should a young woman of her age."

"I'll leave it to you then." Katherine handed over the burden of Fleur and Brendan gratefully. "I'll be leaving first thing in the morning, anyway. If Fleur is upset . . ."

"Why should I be upset?"

Fleur stood on the lawn, a little to their left. She had appeared from behind a thickly flowering specimen of white oleander very old and quite large; it was impossible to tell how long she had been there.

"Oh, Fleur." Quickly, quickly. "I may be leaving before you come down to breakfast in the morning—you won't think ill of me, I trust . . ."

"Of course not." The new, confident Fleur smiled warmly, and fell into step beside Angela. She said, "I hope to visit Barrengarry again soon, Edwin and Angela worry about the girls, don't you, Angela? How are they, Katherine? And how is Mr Kelehan?"

The face was open, the eyes ingenuous. And Katherine could not tell if it was natural or feigned. Again, as in the library at Dovewood, when Fleur had claimed she would marry Brendan Kelehan no matter what lay in the way, Katherine felt uneasy, a sense of being in the presence of an adversary, without knowing what the contest was nor why it meant so much. It seemed personal, deadly, beyond the competition—if that was what it was—of two women in love with the same man. The feelings of hostility made Katherine wish she could step back a little, to recoil almost; and the contents of the letter came back to her mind and she knew that Fleur had not changed at all.

"How is Mr Kelehan?" Fleur repeated softly.

But it was Angela who replied. "Fleur, dear, Katherine has just told me the most wonderful news. Mr Kelehan's wife, Mary Rose, has just arrived in Australia from America. I was just saying that we must have them . . ."

"Wife?"

It was frightening, the sudden pallor, the tone of voice, hoarse, harsh, as if constricted in her throat. Even Angela stared before, being the woman she was, she took Fleur's arm companionably. "And they're to have a little addition to the family in February. We must write and tell them how pleased we will be to have them visit." Angela's eyes claimed Fleur, willed her strength, her poise, into the younger woman.

Fleur held the gaze, then turned to Katherine. "His wife?" she said once more, and Katherine was worried. Was anything penetrating?

"Yes," she answered, gently but firmly, "he's been married for some eight months. She's a lovely girl—only nineteen, but . . ."

"Nineteen . . ." The word fell as forlornly as a pebble bouncing down the walls of an empty well.

On the whole, Katherine thought, Fleur had taken the news extremely well. And it was only then, watching Fleur rally, her training and good manners asserting themselves as Katherine's own had done, that Katherine realized how much she had been dreading this errand. She wondered about Rafe Huckstable; hoped that Fleur's reaction, the lack of sullenness or indignation, did not mean she had already begun to transfer her affections from Brendan to Rafe.

Still, it was not her concern, and perhaps now Fleur herself might be free to form some other, more worthwhile alliance. Certainly there were enough visitors to Dovewood for her to meet any number of eligible young men.

She was grateful to put the problem of Fleur and her sensibilities from her, and after dinner her grandfather drew her into his study and delivered news that made her forget, momentarily, all the problems waiting back at Barrengarry. Seven of the blocks of land in Moss Vale had been sold, at the prices she had asked. Katherine leaned back in the deep leather chair, hugging herself with delight, gazing bright-eyed at her grandfather, sharing conspirators' laughter with him, knowing—and this was her private triumph—that she would now be able to pay Brendan Kelehan all she owed him, and have a small sum left over, even now, for herself. By the time she had returned to Barrengarry in a few weeks time, the deeds should be ready for her to sign, and she would receive her money.

She went to bed that night feeling more happy, more content than she had felt for months, sat at the dressing table and wondered at her own daring and at the gullibility of people who read newspaper advertisements. What a gamble it had been! Now, for the rest of her life, she would wonder if that stretch of country road, ninety miles from Sydney, with its jewelled gardens and stylish mansions were truly part of the burgeoning gentility of the Moss Vale region, or if she had forced the matter ahead. Within twenty years the governor would have a summer residence at Sutton Forest and few of the Sydney *ton* were not possessed of houses of lesser or equal splendour within carriage distance.

She had been expecting Grace, her grandmother's maid, to help her undress and take down her hair, so did not look up when there was a knock at the door but called "Come in," while still lost in wonderment at how her fortunes were changing. It was in the oval mirror over the dressing table that Katherine saw that her visitor was not the matronly Grace, but Fleur Barton.

"I hope you don't mind my coming to talk to you. Am I too late? Am I keeping you from your rest?"

"No, not at all." And this, of course, was a polite lie, as the trip from Barrengarry was long and arduous, and Katherine was naturally very tired.

Fleur, oblivious to this, wilfully or otherwise, seated herself in the little satin-covered bedroom chair, spreading her fashionably flounced skirts about her, and looked up at Katherine with a smile.

"I'm still so surprised," she said, "to hear your news about Brendan Kelehan."

"Oh?" Katherine raised her eyebrows inquiringly.

"Why, yes," said Fleur, "you see, Brendan had been writing to me, and we spent a lot of time together on the two occasions I visited at Barrengarry. He gave me, as I think I told you after the first time we met, an unmistakable impression that I meant a great deal to him."

Her look seemed to expect some reaction from Katherine, who merely stared at her, wondering where the conversation was leading, what was to be demanded of her. *And I wanted this time to myself,* she thought, aggrievedly, jealous of these moments of optimism that Edwin's news had brought to her.

"Didn't you know?" Fleur asked. "Didn't he speak of me to you?"

"No," Katherine said instinctively, and was immediately sorry, seeing the scowl upon Fleur's face.

"Do you mean to say that he gave no special message to you to give to me? No letter?" Her scowl deepened.

"No," Katherine repeated, "though he did give his best wishes to you, and my grandmother and grand . . ."

"That's not what I mean." Briskly from Fleur. She paused, her eyes taking in Katherine where she sat at the dressing table, studying her from head to foot, then, "Katherine, are you telling me the complete truth?"

Into the silence, for Katherine was too amazed to answer immediately, there came a knock at the door. Before she could move, Fleur had crossed the room, greeted the round features of the lady's maid and said, "Mrs Carron won't be needing you for a few more minutes, Grace; she'll ring when you're required." And as the woman bobbed a curtsey and withdrew, Fleur shut the door.

Katherine had risen, finding Fleur's action presumptuous, and irritated by it. "If I wish the servants to be dismissed, Fleur, I shall do it myself."

"I'm so sorry." Empty words, her smile held no dismay, certainly no penitence. "Is it true—about his having a wife—and a child on the way? How can it possibly be?"

"He was very remiss in not mentioning it, but I assure you it's the truth. He was married in early April; he and his wife didn't know, when he left America, that she had just conceived—that was in May, and the child is due to be born in February next year . . ."

"He never told me! We're very close, and he never told me!"

Katherine could sense the rising tension in the younger woman, checked her own annoyance, forced her voice to be calm as she said, "Fleur, do sit down . . ."

"No! I want to know, and I want to know now! Is it the truth, or are you lying to me?"

"Fleur, why on earth would I want to lie about something like this?"

"You know very well why! You love him. Don't try to deny it—everyone knows about it—your sisters spoke of it, and your grandmother, the very day after the ball, when he arrived. And now you've had two months with him at Barrengarry to try to make him forget me, and you know you've failed—so you've come here, before him, to try to make me believe he's committed to someone else—and you can't say it's you, can you?"

"Fleur, this is madness . . . !"

"Do you deny you love him? Do you? Look me in the face and tell me that you don't love Brendan Kelehan!"

The vehemence of the demand for a statement that would be a lie, caught her up, silenced her for a second too long.

Fleur's face was spiteful, triumphant. "You can't. You can't deny you love him!"

"What I feel is no concern of yours. And what Brendan Kelehan feels is no concern of yours. I swear to you, he's married, his wife's name's Mary Rose—if you don't believe me, you may write to Edwina and Laura . . ."

"You've undoubtedly poisoned them against me also. You've done your best to turn everyone against me ever since you found me at Barrengarry, for you knew when you saw me that I was a danger to you, that I fitted into your world, and with better grace than you. If Marcus had been my father, I'd never have disobeyed him! If I had had your family, I'd have loved them and treated them with respect. You had responsibilities to them, yet you denied them and ran off like a stupid girl—and I wouldn't have! I'd have treasured every moment in that house, with those people, yet you—you threw it away! And you hate me, for you can see that I deserve it more, and when you saw Brendan and I look at each other at the ball that night, saw that he recognized that I was a better woman for him . . . You've done everything you can, ever since, to take him away from me!"

Katherine moved towards the door. "Fleur, I think you'd better leave—I can't believe you could be so . . ."

But Fleur had moved in front of her, blocking the way. Her face was white, only her eyes were alive, lit with vindictiveness and a deadly kind of malice. "No. Wait. I haven't finished . . ."

"Oh, yes you have . . ."

"There's something else I have to tell you."

Katherine backed off from her, sturdily enough, to face her firmly. "Fleur, you have nothing else to say that would interest me . . ."

"Oh, but you're wrong, you are very wrong, Katherine."

She did not begin immediately and Katherine, not having anticipated the abrupt calm that seemed to have descended on Fleur, found herself unprepared for the woman to turn and smile, unprepared for her next words.

"Where were you born, Katherine?" she asked.

Katherine, mystified, could only scowl. "Why do you want to know?"

Fleur smirked, her chin moved a little, tilted in a way, Katherine realized, that it often did when she felt rather satisfied with herself. Katherine decided not to wait, not to banter words, her dislike for the younger woman was so strong she could taste it on her tongue. She turned to the door once more.

"Don't go, yet." Quickly from Fleur. "I have something to tell you. Something of great interest—I'm sure I would want to know, if I were you."

Katherine looked back, regarded her with distaste. "But you're not, Fleur."

Yes, she thought, in the months and years that followed. That was the time to leave. Even with Fleur's voice pursuing her along the hall, it would have been best to leave at that moment, with those words. But, though she had turned to the door she had not taken more than two steps when Fleur's voice came to her ears and she stopped.

"I'd want to know," the woman said softly, "if I was illegitimate."

So the little spider had her, possessed her attention for all her purposes. Katherine could only stare like a petrified moth caught in the tangles of a web as the light, silky voice spun on and on and Katherine could not, now, break away, though with all her heart she wished she could.

"I read everything." Fleur smiled, beginning conversationally. "Magazines, books, old letters in attics . . . But no, the letter I mean wasn't in the attic—but it *was* at the back of that very tall wardrobe in your grandmother's room. She actually told me to look there— can you imagine it? Old people do tend to forget, and she knows I like reading romantic novels, and she keeps all her old books there, because Edwin doesn't like them lying about for the servants or guests to know her taste runs to such stuff.

"But there was much more than books there. Hat boxes, Katherine, filled with old papers. Your family's history, in old hatboxes! It took me several weeks to sift through it all, and I found a great deal of interesting information. The best thing—by far the best—was a letter from your mother to Angela written from Melbourne. 'Dear Mama,' it begins—I almost know it by heart—'Dear Mama, we have found our darling baby girl. Marcus and I can only thank God for the providence that has led us here. They called her Daisy, but we will call her Katherine . . .' "

"Stop it! Stop your damnable lies, you bitch!"

"Oh, now you show your true colours! Where is the lady now? But you're not a lady, are you—just named after Suzanna's sister in an effort to give the illusion that you belong to the family."

"You're lying!" It was a lie, of course it was a lie—it had to be . . .

"There's only one way to find out, isn't there? Ask them. Ask your parents. They'll undoubtedly tell you what they told your grandmother in the letter. How dirty and sick you were when they brought you home, but how you would pass for Suzanna's daughter, because of your red hair . . ."

The anger was so great it was congealing within Katherine, setting, almost, into an icy calm. There was nothing else to be done but control herself for she realized, with part of her bruised mind, that any reaction she gave to Fleur fed the woman's hate, brought her the twisted gratification that she craved.

"Why are you bothering with all this, Fleur?" she managed. "Do you really need enemies? For right or wrong, with this tale of yours, you're making an enemy of me—and I can be a very dangerous enemy, Fleur."

"Don't try to frighten me. After the life I've lived, and all I've been through, nothing you could do would bring me anything but a yawn. You might have begun life in the gutter, Katherine, but you don't remember enough of it to benefit you. You're as spoilt and soft . . ."

"You stupid girl. You stupid, stupid girl . . ." From the door that had opened quietly without either of them seeing, Angela Gordon's voice sounded more sad and pitying than angry, and her face, strong, still beautiful, held that same look of regretful contempt.

And Fleur's face betrayed her, the sudden fear, shame, anger and anxiety that fled across her features showed Katherine clearly that the woman must be unbalanced. She had not wanted Angela to discover this side of her personality. She stood like marble, white and unmoving, unable to cope with this eventuality. It was impossible to believe, but somehow she had not thought beyond the moment of her triumph; for all her cunning, her greed for the victory of the moment had defeated her.

"Angela, I . . ." At first, her friend's name was all that she could manage while she struggled to find some way out of the iron trap in which she had placed herself. "I . . . I feel ashamed. I went too far—I was angry, and hurt. Katherine said things, cruel things . . ." Her eyes filled with tears, they spilled silently down the pale cheeks, but then she smiled bravely. "These things happen, though, when two friends quarrel over the regard of a gentleman. I'm sorry, Katherine."

Katherine was silent, her blood turned to ice, still unmoving, unbelieving. And Angela's look of composed disparagement had not altered.

Fleur looked from one to the other with growing dismay. "Of course," she muttered, "I was speaking nonsense—it's the sort of thing one says when one is terribly upset. If you'll . . . if you'll only forgive me, we'll never mention this again."

It was almost a standard plea of someone who had transgressed too far—and yet, perhaps because the words came from Fleur, Katherine felt she could sense the hidden threat. "*If* you'll only forgive me," she had said, and though she had cleverly placed no emphasis on the word, it was there.

Katherine turned to Angela, the natural action of a confused and frightened child turning to a loved, omnipotent adult. Yet this was foolishness, she had discovered before now, discovered further on retreating to the Highlands from Italy, that the world was treacherous. Even those closest to her could not provide her with any answers, any help.

But Angela, daughter of a settler who had made his fortune driving two thousand head of cattle from south of Wollongong, fifteen hundred miles to Adelaide, South Australia, was made of stronger stuff. Born by a campfire without a midwife, Angela still held within her all the fibre of the women who carved a place in this unknown continent, and she did not fail Katherine now.

"Fleur, my dear, I am afraid you will not be forgiven. It grieves me to say this but you will pack your bags tonight, my dear, and late though the hour is, you will be driven into Moss Vale, to the inn, and tomorrow you may decide what you wish to do and where you wish to go. I strongly advise you to go home to Campbelltown, for I'm afraid, Fleur, that you have a nature that only your mother could possibly understand, let alone love. You are right about one thing, though. We will not mention this again. For if I ever hear it whispered—indeed, if I ever hear it breathed, this entire colony will not be big enough for you to hide yourself. I will find you out, and I will see that you are ruined. And I think you know that I'm capable of doing it."

Angela sailed to the door and held it open. "Now, you'd best begin as soon as possible—you may call Grace to help you. Goodbye, my dear, and I sincerely wish you to be better treated than you yourself treat those who've loved you."

Only on this last did Angela seem to falter, but Fleur did not hear. She had fled, out the door and along the hall, and the sound of her weeping was clearly audible as she ran.

Angela ordered tea from the kitchen and the two women sat in silence, waiting first for the tea, then for the sounds of departure. Grace came to check if it was right that Miss Barton should be leaving at this late hour, and the housekeeper, bemused at this upheaval, came to check if it was correct, what Grace had said, how the carriage should be ordered to drive Miss Barton to Moss Vale . . .

And there were voices and footsteps and bumping of trunks down the hall, and the stir of wheels and horses' hooves on the gravel of the drive, then the sounds faded and the house seemed to rest, uneasily.

Into the haunted silence, over tea that had gone cold in the cup that she held to warm her frozen hands, Katherine at last raised her eyes to Angela.

"It is true? Marcus and Suzanna . . ." she made herself use their Christian names, "they . . . *found* me, in Melbourne?"

Angela's expressive eyes were lowered, and she sighed. "I'll regret until the end of my days that I allowed that girl into this house . . ."

"It's true, isn't it?"

She looked up. "Yes. They found you in Melbourne, but Fleur didn't know the whole story . . ."

It had been true. All the poisonous things she had said. She, Katherine, had been a dirty child of the slums, adopted by a childless couple—and only then did they have a child of their own. Joe. Joe, who had been wanted; Joe, the cherished dream that had finally come true for broken-hearted people who thought they would never have a child of their own. And Laura had followed, and then Edwina.

All her life, she had been led to believe her birthplace to be Balmain, though she had always said she had been born in the Valley. That had been her home, she liked to say she was born and bred in the Valley—she loved it more than Joe or Laura or Edwina did, and was not to be blamed because Suzanna and Marcus had remained in Balmain for eighteen months after her birth. But they had not—for her first eighteen months were undoubtedly spent in Melbourne . . .

"Katherine, are you listening?"

"Yes, Grandmama . . ." *But she is not my grandmama . . .*

Angela had been speaking of how families keep secrets from each other for reasons of love, so as not to cause undue worry and hurt. She had said that a child who was chosen, wanted, was held in as much love—sometimes more—as those children who were issues of one's body . . .

But it was all a pretence. She had no right in that family, no rights to Barrengarry. She was an interloper, there on sufferance, not needed really, once Joe had arrived . . .

Angela had stood, had left the room abruptly. Katherine stared after her. She had offended the older woman—she must have—she could not collect her thoughts, must have seemed as if she was careless or disinterested in Angela's words, and this was not so . . .

Her grandmother's footsteps, to Katherine's relief, were heard returning along the hall, and she entered the room with her usual positive glide and pulled a small flask from the reticule that she carried with her.

"I went to fetch this . . . drink it down—*and*, I may add, this is one family secret that we *do* keep!"

She poured a generous amount of liquid into Katherine's tea cup. It was brandy and tasted even worse with cold tea than on its own, but she sipped it obediently.

"Now, young woman, no self-pity, no wilting looks—you just listen to me.

"Don't think that you were the first to consider eloping in this family; my eldest daughter, Katherine, for whom you are named, eloped with a young man when she was barely sixteen. She was a beautiful, wilful, flighty girl, too much, I'm grieved to admit, even for her young man to control her, for once they were away from parental guidance, Katherine could see no reason at all why they should marry. I think she wanted to avoid the unpleasantness of someone finding she was under age, perhaps, and reporting her whereabouts to us . . . for whatever reason, she lived for some months with this kindly, foolish, besotted boy of eighteen. But when the money ran out and he had to find a job—in a printing firm, I think it was—and came home to their single room tired, cross and dirty, married life seemed to lose a great deal of its excitement for our Katherine."

The deep voice was sad. "She left him, as she'd found another, older, wealthy man to look after her, and they travelled to Melbourne . . ."

Katherine sat up slowly, stiffened, gazing at her grandmother's face. It was grim, resigned.

"Ah, yes—I have your attention now, I see . . ."

"We knew nothing more of Katherine's whereabouts until news came that she . . . she had died, in a pauper's hospital in Melbourne. The cause of death was a pregnancy that had ruptured the fallopian tube—strange, that I've never spoken that phrase, yet the doctor's words have stayed with me; for of course, Edwin and I went to Melbourne to bring our girl home. She must have been frightened, must have known something might go wrong, for she had given our names as the next of kin. And she had told the hospital something else—she had had a baby girl, had left her with a family some miles out of the city, to be looked after until she could provide for her. The young man—I will call him Katherine's fiancé, as he would have married her even then, despite everything, if she had not been taken from us . . . He came to Melbourne with us, and helped us search for Katherine's daughter. We never found her, and after six weeks of extensive searching, advertising, contacting police, orphanages, hospitals, we had to give up and come home.

"The young man came back to Dovewood with us for, though it might seem hard to believe, we knew him to be a good man—and when it was obvious that our youngest daughter was in love with him, we gave our blessing for them to be married. They had no honeymoon. They returned to Melbourne to search for Katherine's baby girl . . .

"Oh, my dear, knowing this, can you now think that you were not wanted, that you are not loved?"

Twenty Seven

Barrengarry
Kangaroo Valley
Via Moss Vale
New South Wales
3rd December, 1866.

Dearest Katey,

Why, oh, why did you have to go off to Sydney? I *told* you how miserable we'd all be without you and I was *right*.

Brendan is hardly ever at home, and when he is, perforce, he is locked in his office, leaving poor little Mary Rose wandering the corridors like a wraith, wringing her hands and lamenting.

She *has* been very good, though. Since that time when she saw you and Brendan ride off to check that boundary fence together and had her fit of hysteria she has somehow calmed down quite a lot and when crossed becomes merely very tense and then quite soulful and melancholy. This is much better for her as, truly, I have never seen a woman that dolefulness more suited, for in repose one can see how truly beautiful she is—like the statues of the Madonna we saw when in Italy.

We are all pleased that she seemed to be settling in at last and is even quite cheery most of the time, though she has begun to attempt to *organize* us, which you can imagine can be trying at times. Peggy knows just how to run Barrengarry, as you know, and it cannot be easy for her to have Mary Rose following her about, peering into pots and pans, counting the linen and sniffing about the pantry, all the while telling Peggy that things are done on a much more efficient scale back in Boston, and drawing up little lists of hints for Peggy to follow.

Yesterday, however, I feel things came to a head as Peggy does not take kindly to anyone telling her how to cook a roast—and we have never heard of cranberries, anyway. Well, Peggy turned on poor Mary Rose and said that while she is most flattered that Missus Kelehan is taking all this bother to Improve her, she really doesn't need Improving, as things what suit Boston don't necessarily suit New South Wales, and she, Peggy, for one, would truly be appalled if she really thought that a genteel young lady like Missus Kelehan really knew so much about what went on below stairs.

This was an undeniable and pitiless reproof and Mary Rose retired to her room for the rest of the day. This morning she is very quiet and has spent her time turning hems in the parlour.

I myself am quite saddened, at the moment, as I have not seen as much of Rafe as I would like, though I suppose it is not ladylike to admit too much eagerness to see a particular gentleman, but there it is. His father had been building shops in Moss Vale, near where the railway station will be, and Rafe is in the township a great deal, overseeing the building etc. I do miss him, Cummings had a picnic last week and he was not there, and they had dancing and I had to dance with Luke all the time and he is so sweet but just not Rafe, but then no man is, he dances so divinely. Dancing with Luke is rather like waltzing with a large brown bear—but that sounds cruel and I know you won't approve. I don't know why you don't marry Luke, you always defend him.

I am a little worried about our Laura, too, as she has been far too withdrawn since you left. She had a small quarrel with Stephen on the Monday, but he came to offer repentance on Tuesday, but then she has seen very little of him since and I think it is upsetting her. Of course, it may be that she misses you and Mama and Father. I know I do. It is hard to write to Father—the last letter came from some strange place in Borneo. But you can talk Mama into coming home, and I wish you would.

Do write soon,

Your Affectionate Sister,
Edwina

Barrengarry
Kangaroo Valley
Via Moss Vale
New South Wales
26th December, 1866.

Dearest Katey,

I am replying to your letter straight away, as it has disturbed me a great deal. Now you are not here, I am, as eldest after you, responsible in a way, and with the best interests of everyone here at heart, I hope you will reconsider and come back soon. You have, after all, been away more than a month, now. Teddi is very upset— we all are—that you did not come home for Christmas—we missed you terribly, Katey. I can understand that Mama feels she must stay to look after her ill friend (I keep asking if I know her, and you always neglect to tell me her name), but there is no such tie upon you, surely, and we miss you so much.

We are all well, however. Mary Rose is becoming a trifle disgruntled with her condition, poor dear, and is beginning to find Valley life a little boring. She took an interest in the running of the house for a while, but seemed to lose interest after a few weeks. She has now begun to attack Edwina's and my wardrobes, hacking away at dresses and coats and bonnets, with a copy of one of her American or Paris fashion magazines in the other hand. I must admit we found it a trifle disconcerting to discover that we were so old-fashioned—Teddi even mutinied and said she didn't *want* to look like a Parisian fashion plate; but keeping us both—and herself—*à la mode* is making Mary Rose more cheerful and quite fills her days, so we have decided to bear with the expense of all the trimmings and patterns that seem to arrive daily in the mail (or rather, poor Father will), and live with the fact that we are being made over into the incarnation of the *dernier cri*.

Brendan is looking very tired, as he works such long hours, and

we all worry about him. But I must say, Barrengarry is thriving
and our tenant farmers like and respect him; everyone Edwina and
I meet tells us how they like him and hope he will stay on, if not
on Barrengarry, then on his own selection. Teddi mentioned this
once, lightly, to Mary Rose, and she went *white*. Needless to say,
no more was said. Barrengarry will be greatly at a loss when he
goes, and I will even miss little Mary Rose—the house is never dull
since she came, and she does try so very hard. (I shouldn't call her
"little" Mary Rose, should I, as she towers over me! Still, I worry
about her as much as I do about our Teddi—perhaps more.)

Carl has caused us some worries as he was ill with a bad chill
last week, and it became worse, and I sent for Angel Regnier. It
was a very dark and stormy night, and Mary Rose answered the
door, and almost fainted with fright when she saw Angel, whom
she had never seen close to before. Angel was wearing a large black
oilskin cape with a hood, and I must admit she frightened me, also,
when I heard Mary Rose scream and came to the door to her aid.

It sounds rather funny now, as I write this, and Teddi and I laughed
about it also, but the unfortunate thing is that Mary Rose has decided
that she does not like Angel, and is barely polite to her. I think
it's more because she was made to feel foolish than anything else;
she says her family knew many black people in Boston. But Angel,
she says, makes her feel on edge, and then she talks as she used
to when she first came to us, about her delicate nervous structure,
and I truly want to slap her. She does not like the Woddi either,
and does not want to meet Myeela or Tigoora, and they are fascinated
with her, having seen her from a distance. She tells me she finds
Australian black people to be extremely ugly. This sent Edwina into
one of her rare and terrible rages, and the house was most unquiet
for a few days, until Mary Rose apologized to her and said that
she probably looked most unattractive to them, and peace was made.
But she still will not go to meet them.

Another thing is bothering me, and I cannot talk of it with
anyone here, not even Brendan, who doesn't much like Rafe
Huckstable and may feel that he has to confront him, and I don't
wish that.

I went with Brendan and Peggy to Moss Vale for supplies, and
separated from them for a short while, in order to purchase some
trimmings from Mrs Richards' Haberdashery. As I was crossing the
street to return to them, a very smart new carriage passed me, and
seated within it were Rafe Huckstable and, of all people, Fleur Barton.

Grandmama had written to me and, of course, you mentioned

in your first letter that Fleur had decided to go home to Campbelltown, but I don't see how that could be. The carriage is brand new, Katey, and it doesn't belong to the Huckstables, or we'd surely know, as this incident occurred more than a week ago.

Katey, Fleur and Rafe appeared to be very *intimate*, their heads were close together and they were chatting like friends of long standing. I did not like it at all and, of course, I have not been able to share my worries with anyone. It would break Teddi's heart if she knew.

To make matters worse, the day that you left for Sydney, Rafe had words with Stephen, though I don't know why, and it made Stephen so testy that he quarrelled with me.

You and I have talked about Rafe before—I had thought he had reformed—even Father had decided to trust that he was becoming a mature man—but now I am very worried. He still comes to call, and to see the devotion that Teddi showers upon him makes me— quite honestly, Katey, it makes my nervous structure quite as fragile as Mary Rose's!

I hope this letter does not worry you too greatly. Carl is mending slowly, but you may like to write to him directly. I think he feels rather lost at the moment, having only part of the family at Barrengarry. Before, we were either here or at Balmain, but we were always *together*.

You might also ask Mama for me to write more of what she is doing, as she says so little about herself and only comments on our news. Do tell me who her sick friend is—do we know her? Perhaps we could send her some books, or a few of Mary Rose's Paris fashion magazines.

Do come home soon to us, you and Mama,

    Your Fond Sister,

      Laura

P.S. I hope it isn't Mary Rose that is keeping you from us—she mentions you quite often, and has stopped being jealous, I think. She has learnt so much and is truly very sweet when one becomes used to her. Whatever, the house is alive and interesting all the time, whereas you must find the Balmain house to be a bit lonely most of the time, surely.

Do tell us when you are coming back to us. A merry and blessed Christmas, dear Katey and Mama.

      L.

Laura was right, the house in Balmain was a lonely place, more so even than she knew, for the only occupants were Katherine, Libby and Tobias.

Libby trusted Katherine and had explained on the first day, having instructions from Suzanna, the complicated duplicity that had been practised in the house for some months.

Suzanna was living in the Blue Mountains, a village called Springwood, Libby volunteered, with her rather flat features lowered as if afraid even her unremittingly impassive eyes would give something away.

Katherine knew little of Springwood other than it had been founded about fifty years previously, when Cox has built the road over the mountains—the enormous feat, given the rugged terrain, of one hundred miles in only six months. The road had reached Bathurst, on the furthest, western side of the Blue Mountains, in 1815 and that same year, on the eastern side, Springwood had been established, a high, scrub-surrounded resting place for travellers and settlers headed west. Katherine had never been there, this little information she gleaned from Libby, but there was no need to ask the housekeeper who Suzanna was staying with; there was no mention of any gentleman's name between them.

Suzanna's letters for her daughters came to the Balmain house, in a large envelope addressed to Libby. Libby posted them in Balmain, for they were already stamped, and addressed to one or the other of the girls in Suzanna's handwriting. When a reply came, Libby placed it in a larger envelope, marked it *Crest Cottage, Springwood, via Penrith, N.S.W.*, and, affixing a stamp from a special supply left with her, sent the letters from the Prescott girls or from Edwin and Angela Gordon on to Suzanna's new home.

Katherine had bought Christmas gifts for the girls, bought a smart cravat and a novel in German for Carl, bought gifts for Peggy, Brendan, Mary Rose and the coming baby, and answered letters from both the Kangaroo Valley and the Springwood camps, never mentioning Robin Mitchell's name, partly from respect for Suzanna's reserve on the matter and partly from her own unwillingness to face the fact that her mother was involved in a liaison that, if it were known, would ostracize her from all society.

The old house and the gardens that ran down to the harbour gave their own kind of comfort and healing; there were so many happy memories within these walls and without, in the peaceful and colourful garden, resplendent now in summer. Yet there remained the sense of displacement, of aloneness that had come with Fleur Barton's words at Dovewood. Katherine felt she could not return to Barrengarry, yet the silence of the house in Balmain, though it had been a place of respite for some weeks, could not be a home with her family scattered at such distances from each other.

She found an anger within her, a resentment, not only towards the selfish child who had been her natural mother but towards Marcus and Suzanna as well. The lengths they had gone to, the lies they had told—for her sake, Angela had insisted—did little to lift the dark sullenness from her mind. How did she come to have a birth certificate, she had challenged her grandmother, saying that she had been born at the house in Balmain, on the correct date, 11th of October, 1835?

The answer came that when no Melbourne birth certificate could be found, no record at all of the birth other than what the young mother had told the doctors at the hospital and the baby-minder, they had brought the child back to Balmain and applied for a registration of the birth in New South Wales. Even Libby was implicated, for she, too, lied to the Justice of the Peace when they filled out the declaration, and on the form in the records office Libby was down for all posterity as officiating midwife. The only problem had been the year of the birth. No one had asked to see the child, and they simply made her a year younger than she was, before going travelling, Marcus, Suzanna and their young daughter, on a visit to New Zealand for over a year. No one had queried nor questioned their bonny, bright little girl when they had, eventually, returned to Kangaroo Valley, just after Joe's birth at Balmain.

It was bad enough, Katherine thought bitterly, for a woman to find out that she was thirty, instead of twenty-nine, but to know they had deceived her for so long, would have gone on deceiving her, had not Angela been unable to throw away that first, joyous letter of Suzanna's, saying that their search had ended, and they had found the child.

Through her bitterness, her sense of helplessness, her sense of having been a small and unknowing pawn in the game they had all played, came the knowledge sometimes that they must have loved her a great deal to do this thing. They would not be the first relatives to alter family records, and no doubt they would not be the last. Yet it rankled, the years of deception, and the way that the truth had been spewed from the mouth of the pernicious Fleur.

She ran speeches through her head, where she confronted her parents with her knowledge of the truth, but her father was still overseas, and Suzanna had enough heartache without the added burden of this.

Yet she wanted to see her parents, to look upon them, see them with the sense of distance and detachment that she now found within her.

And then the letter from Barrengarry arrived.

Dearest Katey (Laura wrote),

I know I only wrote a few days ago but something has happened.

As far as Brendan and our stockmen can ascertain, no further timber has been taken from the area above Paradise Gully, but there was a quarrel in that region yesterday, between the Woddi, Charlie Crolin and Walt and Elias Tallon (they are the two tallest of the Tallon boys—unidentical twins, I believe, but alike in their ways, which are not very generous nor civilized).

Brendan has called in Sergeant Lloyd, as the Tallons are threatening to take matters into their own hands.

It seems four of the Woddi Woddi men were hunting in the area, and they crossed the paths of the Tallons and Charlie Crolin. The Woddi had wounded a wallaby, but Walt Tallon brought it down with his rifle, and claimed it. This is how the quarrel began, but it culminated in Timalong, Myeela's husband, spearing Walt Tallon in the leg. Charlie Crolin then shot at Timalong, but does not know if he was hit—the Woddi just vanished, as you know they can.

Tom Lloyd has been up at the cedar-getters' camps, telling them that this must go no further, for it seems the Crolins and Tallons are furious and say that there just is not enough game to go around, and the law is protecting the blacks at the expense of the whites—and so it should, as hunting and gathering is all the Woddi Woddi know, and the Tallons have been taking trees and animals for so long that they think they have a right. It makes me think of what Father used to say about their attitude; "If it moves, shoot it, if it stands still, cut it down."

I am glad that, if this incident had to occur, it happened up in the hills, and not in the Valley—people here are very upset about it, and if the Crolins had not decided to move on—did I tell you?—they have gone to a new camp above Budgong Vale. I hope the Tallons will be gone soon, too.

No one can find the Woddi to talk about what happened, but everyone knows the terrible things the Crolins have been saying for some time, and the consensus of opinion is that the Tallons and Crolins were waiting for an excuse to fire on the Woddi.

The letter went on to ask Katherine, once more, when she and Suzanna would be coming home; it was obvious this breach in the cordiality between the Woddi and the white community had upset Laura and, it seemed, the whole household. Katherine held the letter in her hands, and felt a stirring of unease. She considered returning to the Valley immediately, hating to think of the feelings of betrayal and distrust that the incident would cause in the Woddi camp—

and it was made worse by the fact that the altercation had taken place close to a sacred site. How much of that had contributed to Timalong's anger?

But what could she do? And the Crolins would surely not come back into the area now, and perhaps the Tallons might have received enough of a fright to move also, as Laura suggested. Yes, reason must prevail; there was no point in her rushing back to Barrengarry when she could not do anything to help, to go back to the house where all the same problems remained, just as she had left them, except now she felt a stranger to the Valley herself, she who had been taken in out of pity and a sense of family pride and proprietorship.

But she was filled with a sense of restlessness and knew she could stay at Balmain no longer.

In after years she would wonder at her own dark melancholy, her self-indulgence. For she should have returned to Kangaroo Valley, to Barrengarry. Instead, she realized, as she packed her clothes into her valise, "This is how Father must have felt. I know where I should be. But I can't face it; no, not yet." It was the first insight of understanding into the man she had accused of running away.

Twenty Eight

The railway went as far as the neat little township of Penrith, and from there it was a matter of another bumpy, lurching ride in a public coach, across the bridge over the Nepean River and up the scrubby foothills into the low series of plateaux that made up that section of the Great Dividing Range called the Blue Mountains. From the station at Penrith they had looked gentle, azure-tinted hills, but the journey seemed, in parts, too similar to the ascents from Kangaroo Valley for Katherine to feel comfortable. It was worse, somehow, their vehicle now being a top-heavy mail coach, which, even when the passengers clambered out to walk up part of the dusty roads, seemed in imminent danger of rolling back into a steep gully, boxes, trunks, horses, driver, Her Majesty's Royal Mail and all.

Why hadn't Mama taken Robin to the Highlands? Katherine wondered. Why, there was a natural spa at Mittagong, and the countryside was much prettier . . . Springwood seemed to be a huddle of lovely sandstone cottages set in a few fields hard-won from the surrounding scrub. But when she had asked for the residence of Mrs Mitchell, and hired a buggy to transport herself and her luggage to the house, she understood some of the appeal of the place.

CREST COTTAGE read the name on the plaque by the door and it was an eminently suitable description. For the little house, its square, Georgian style ornamented by a verandah on three sides, sat perched on the top edge of a sloping green field. Two horses and three goats grazed peacefully on the rich grass, and beyond the field . . . Beyond the field the land sloped down into a gully, the following hill not so high, and the foothills—for the back of the cottage and the field faced the east—could not be seen. The land dropped away down, down, it seemed, and there below she could see the flat scrub and patchwork fields and meadows that stretched on and on, back towards Sydney and the sea, lost in haze, more than thirty miles away.

The driver of the cab helped her down with the luggage; she paid him and stood, looking past the cottage at the view, as the carriage rolled away, back towards the village.

How high they must be, Katherine marvelled. It felt as if the little house sat balanced at the edge of the world . . . And the words, though meant in admiration, sobered her suddenly. It was quiet here, except for the faint notes of a bellbird, as melodious as a tiny silver chime.

Yes, they were right to come here, she thought, as she carried her valises up the little path between neat flowerbeds of wallflowers and petunias. No one would know them here, as someone would have recognized her mother, had they taken a house in the Highlands. And this view, that seemed to stretch as far as forever, would gratify the heart of one who was ill and imprisoned, by the weakness of his own body, to the confines of a single room.

She lifted her hand and knocked on the door, realizing, as she waited, that the feeling of slight apprehension that Peggy called "butterflies in yer stomach" were beating within her with wings made of steel. She took a deep breath in an effort to dispel them; this was silly, it was Suzanna inside this house . . .

The door opened. In the pause, Katherine thought, I shouldn't be shocked, I should have known how it would be—but her senses reeled as she stood there on the little verandah, Suzanna at last before her. Her pale face was wan with fatigue above the demure dark house-frock, the white apron—and above everything, permeating the fresh air and drowning even the scent of the many flowers in the garden, was the smell of the sickroom, the medicines and salves and that indefinably dark odour of a house where death hovered close by.

"Katey? Oh, my dear . . . !"

And Katherine had stepped forward into her mother's embrace.

My mother . . . My mother . . . For there was no doubting that; within her terror at the unmistakable atmosphere of the cottage, bringing back those final weeks of the heartbreaking struggle for Christopher's life, Katherine knew that she would have come, even if she had known the seriousness of the situation. Her mother needed her—and, rocked in Suzanna's arms, she knew that the woman *was* her mother, that the foolish, tragic figure of the girl who had died in Melbourne was a dream, a shadow. She would never speak to Suzanna of the fact that she knew. Suzanna had given so much, had suffered so much, Katherine could not burden her with this.

Instead, she pulled back in her mother's arms and smiled. "I've missed you—and I've been worried about Robin. I'm here to stay for as long as you'll have me. I want to help you both."

Suzanna at first looked disbelieving, then, her gaze almost sightless, she leaned forward against Katherine's shoulder, and remained pressed there, without speaking. Katherine was concerned, was about to speak—but Suzanna's thin shoulders trembled, then heaved rhythmically, silently, with deep, broken sobs of exhaustion and relief.

Robin did not recognize Katherine at first. He moved in and out of consciousness, but seemed to rally, two days after her arrival at Crest Cottage, awoke, and asked, in a faint, bleak voice, for broth and more pillows, and smiled in what seemed like genuine pleasure to see Katherine there.

After he had eaten, he asked for a further helping, and when Suzanna left the room to fetch it, the luminous, dark blue eyes followed her to the door, before coming back to Katherine, and his hand gave a weakened but undisputed summons for her to move her chair closer.

"Can't tell you . . . so happy, so glad to have you here. Difficult for you, of course—I'm a terrible burden on your mother, but . . ."

"No, Robin, you aren't—you mustn't talk like that . . ."

"Katherine, listen-listen-listen . . ." shaking his head and speaking through her words in his soft, tired, halting voice. "We must reach an understanding now—*right now*—if you are to stay. I am not going to get well—Oh, hush, my dear, *please*. I'm a sensible man, and I have excellent hearing and I assure you I would disregard the times I've heard the doctor tell Suzanna I'm sinking, if I didn't have my own body telling me even more forcibly." His smile was genuine, without self-pity. "What I'm trying to say . . . is that I don't have much time . . . and I don't want to waste my words. It's my last vanity, that I want to be listened to. I shall speak the truth always— and I want you to accept it—and help *her* to accept it."

He paused, and lay quiet for a moment, only his eyes, alive, eloquent, kept speaking to her.

"I . . . understand," Katherine said. And her heart ached with the sudden memory of Oliver, for Robin was so like Oliver, at the end; the same courage, decisiveness, the unremitting self-honesty.

"There's no need," Robin continued, pausing every few words to draw breath with difficulty, "for me to ask you . . . take care of Suzanna. I know you will. Don't know . . ." A worried frown creased his forehead, pale as marble, "Don't know if I've done the right thing for Suzanna . . . I love her. Love her deeply . . . and she loves me . . . you see that, don't you?"

"Yes," she said, with honesty.

"No excuse, I suppose . . . flaunting society . . . and all I could give her, in the end . . . was a few months—and this." The blue eyes left her face to take in the sickroom, the bedside cabinet with its surface crowded with medicines.

"She has no regrets," Katherine murmured, amazed, still, that she found she could defend them—and defend them to the very man responsible for her mother's indiscretion.

"Love . . ." The young man smiled with a trace of irony. "Does love excuse everything, Katherine? When the world turns against one, and one's conscience keens in the dark of the night—is love enough? And if it is—what when it has gone? Is the *memory* of love enough?"

She felt helpless. "Oh, Robin . . ."

"Can't do it to her. Shouldn't have. Totally selfish of me. Loved her . . . so much. Would have faced them all—had to. Father won't see me . . ."

"Your father . . . ?" Katherine had not contacted Laurence Mitchell while in Sydney, presuming the family either knew nothing of the circumstances—or knew everything, and accepted unwillingly.

Whatever, she knew her questions could cause nothing but further damage, so had kept to herself.

"Not just . . . Father. Whole family—refuses to see me. They don't know . . . how bad it's become—I had to make Suzanna promise—not to tell them. They'll feel badly when it's all over . . . but I've written letters to them . . . they'll feel better, reading the letters. I had to choose, you see . . ." The eyes were burning, it seemed to mean so much to him that she understood. "Had to choose—Suzanna . . . or *their* respect, *their* regard." He shook his head restlessly. "No choice—no, not even now, if I'm honest. Only Suzanna mattered."

Again he lay silent, and she listened, as Robin must listen day in and day out, to the short rattling breaths that connected him tenuously to the world. She longed to tell him not to talk, not to tire himself, but knew he would have none of it. Something had to be said.

"You must see that Suzanna goes home, after . . . *this*." His voice was a whisper. His eyes went to the door and back to Katherine. His hand, white, with long, tapered fingers, took her own, squeezed, willed her to understand and obey. "Must get her back to Marcus—he loves her, and I think he knows it now. Tell him anything—lie to him if you have to. She'll need him, you see. She's not like you . . . can't cope. Not the same strength."

"You'd . . . let her go back? As his wife—as if . . . nothing had happened?"

"Yes."

But she saw what pain that *yes* cost him. And she realized, then, the extent of the love Robin Mitchell had for Suzanna. "She wouldn't go—and . . . and I honestly don't know if he'd have her back."

"You can persuade him. You must."

"Robin . . . I'm not so strong. Father is a proud, obstinate man, and he's been hurt . . ."

"I know—do you think I don't know? But he was foolish . . . for years . . . took her for granted. Now—he's run off to the Orient—wouldn't stay, fight for her. But he might have learnt . . . the most important thing. He's not a fool—he must have learnt. Where . . . would he ever find . . . another like her?"

And such was their gaze upon each other, a look of mutual warmth and understanding, that Suzanna paused, on entering the room with the tray, and stood, smiling.

Robin said, "Telling Katherine . . . how special you are."

Suzanna sat on the edge of the bed and Robin ate his second bowl of broth obediently. But he refused to rest, became testy when Suzanna tried to leave the room with Katherine. "No! Stop mothering me! Must tell you . . ." He turned to Katherine. "In the drawer—desk drawer—in the parlour. Business papers, records—Prescott, Mitchell affairs. Copies to study. Read them—learn *everything*. When you go home, talk to my father—all the clerks . . . learn *everything* . . ."

"But . . ."

"Only you, now . . . have to keep Marcus in check . . ."

"Robin, I can't run that company . . . !"

"No, no . . ." impatiently, moving the dark head of hair on the pillows. "Learn everything, ask questions—talk to my father—always liked you . . . he worried, when Joe died—but knew you . . . had good sense. Father respects . . . a woman on her own, making decisions. Keep up with what's happening—*make Marcus aware that you know*—someone has to. Remember—" warningly, "all I said to you at Balmain."

He had not forgotten. It had not been idle chatter. He had spoken to her then out of his concern for the family, as he spoke, now.

"Robin . . ." Suzanna begged, seeing the crimson spots beneath his cheekbones, the too-bright eyes, "Robin, please rest, now."

He smiled up at her, took her hand—and Katherine felt that isolating feeling of being excluded, a witness to that most powerful personal rapport that exists between two people in love.

It was good that Robin was able to experience the beauty of that summer at Crest Cottage, to see its bounty, the gardens blossoming in flowers of every hue beneath the clear, cloudless sky. He would lie propped up on his pillows during the brief times he was strong enough, and would gaze out at the flower beds and the orchard of half-a-dozen plum and apple trees, the leaves bright green against the blue distance that beckoned into infinity outside his window, and murmur, "Hasn't the weather been kind?"

His gentle gratitude reached within also, to the two women, and he accepted each caring gesture with humour and a touching appreciation.

Katherine moved through her days with an aching heart and tried not to think of tomorrow or the day after. Each morning, sun-filled and glorious, was enough in itself. And Suzanna, she knew, must feel the same.

"It's so wonderful to have you here, to know that I'm not alone, that . . . that someone—besides myself—truly cares." Suzanna shook her head slowly, wonderingly.

The doctor was with Robin, and it was one of the few moments that mother and daughter shared, one of them always being on duty in the sickroom. Now, they sipped tea in the little parlour, a brief respite from their vigil, and Suzanna smiled at her daughter.

"I've always been proud of my children, all of them. But it's a special gift of God that you have such understanding, Katey. Understanding and strength—enough for me to lean on you. Thank you, my darling."

"Mama, I love you—nothing's changed that. Even Laura and Teddi would come—no, really, they would, if you wrote to them and explained . . ."

"Explained . . . Robin?" Suzanna smiled sadly. "Oh, I'm sure they'd try; they're darling girls and they have the kindest hearts. But no, Katey. They don't have your maturity—to know that Marcus and I are estranged is bad enough. To find that there was another man in my life would frighten them, threaten them. Life will hold enough disappointments and heartaches for my girls without inflicting my mistakes upon them."

"Mistakes?"

"No, that's not right, not true," almost fiercely. "Robin isn't a mistake—if anything it was my infatuation for Marcus all those years ago . . . But no. No, I can't have regrets. I don't know, Katey . . . I'm not thinking clearly . . ."

"If there was a mistake, Mama, then it lies between you and Father. And not in the dim past. He should have seen how unhappy you were. If he had made you love him, you would never have turned to Robin . . ."

"Darling, there's no point in going over all this." She looked at Katherine fondly. "And I won't say there was a mistake at the very beginning. I can't say that Marcus and I should never have married. You children have given us so much joy that there should be friendship, at least, between us despite everything. One can't wipe away all those happy, early years. Marcus thinks, just now, that he can. And I pity him. I hold those years very close to me, very dear, even as I hold dear all that Robin has given me. And I'm the richer for it."

"Oh, Mama . . ." Katherine crossed the room and reached for her mother. For a moment they held each other close. Katherine murmured, "I tried to be like you, you know. As a mother. I think I succeeded. How does one tell? Four years and four months . . . such a little life."

"There'll be other children, Katey."

"No, Mama. That's another character trait I've inherited from you." Katherine touched her mother's hair, smiling, and moved back to her chair. "I know how to adapt, how to bow to the inevitable."

"But I don't want you to do that! Katey, you mustn't let your disappointment in Brendan make you embittered . . ."

Katherine laughed delightedly. "I'll admit something to you, Mama—I did come to the decision that I loved Brendan. And I would have married him, had Mary Rose not appeared with a prior claim upon him. But until Brendan arrived in the Highlands, I was quite prepared to settle for the life of a wealthy widow. It had many attractions, all refreshingly selfish. And once over my disappointment, as you call it, I'm seeing those attractions luring me once more. Just think if I *had* married Brendan—you'd have lost me to Ireland yet again! This way I shall be here to take care of you in your old age!"

"Nonsense! I could slap you when you talk like that! Find a nice young man, Katey. Someone like Luke Murchison . . ."

"And breed heavy-footed young farmers. Mama, we're both exhausted," she bounced to her feet. "I suggest we postpone this conversation, for we'll never agree."

Suzanna sighed. "You're so independent, so self-reliant. It must be a great chore to you, I think sometimes, having people worry about you when you are *so* determined on going your own way."

"That's it exactly, Mama. You've summed up my prickly character quite perfectly."

But her mother was not to be diverted with flippancy. "You're not prickly, Katey," she said seriously. "You've simply been unhappy for some time. And you've learnt something that no one, man or woman, should have to learn."

"And what's that?"

"That ultimately one can trust only oneself."

There was something in the tone of voice, a bleak wistfulness, that worried Katherine. She rallied. "But Mama—basically, everyone knows that—*you* know it—or you couldn't have made the kind of decisions you've made."

Suzanna shook her head, smiled at her daughter as she stood and began to gather the tea things. "I have no need to live out that knowledge like a creed, my dear. For some reason, you do. Somewhere in those five years away from us, you lost the ability to *trust*, Katey. That's what makes my heart ache for you. If love found you again, I'm afraid it would hammer on closed doors."

Katherine said stiffly, "But you see, I don't see anything really wrong with that."

Suzanna paused in the doorway, nodded slowly. "That's what I mean," she said.

Barrengarry,
3rd January, 1867

Dearest Mama and Katey (Laura wrote),

I will write this one letter to you both as the news is the same. Timalong has been found and had been shot in the shoulder, but it is a flesh wound apparently, and is already healing. We are all relieved, as the days went on and on, and there was no sign of him, and those Woddi Woddi that could be found all claimed not to have seen Timalong for a long time. They were worried that he would be in trouble with the white man's law, I think.

Sergeant Lloyd has made a report but is pleased that his superiors agree that he is not to take the matter further.

The Crolins have moved out of the Valley at last, in the vicinity of Illaroo to the south. I feel very sorry for Essie, as she had almost made a home at the other camp, they were there for three years. She still does embroidery for us—the work is so beautiful, I do not know how she does it.

Mary Rose has taken to trying to Improve the cedar-getters and delivers lectures to poor Essie on how she is failing her children by not settling in a proper community. Essie can write a little, as you know, but she is not a strong woman, and when her children refuse to learn, and run off to the bush, as she says, What is a Woman to Do?

This is not good enough for Mary Rose; she simply cannot grasp that Essie and the other women cannot *make* their husbands give up logging and take to farming. She has even been to visit the Tallons. We didn't know she had gone, but she finally came home—she harnessed the sulky *herself*—declaring the visit a great success. She had almost convinced Mrs Tallon and Mrs Green to move their husbands and families closer to a town—and made them Seriously Consider not having quite so many children as it was injurious to the health.

Do not read this aloud, and burn it afterwards, but I was very forward. I could not resist myself, for babies simply *come*, as you know, and I asked her how she had suggested to them that they stopped the babies, and she replied, "Self-restraint," very archly.

Carl is mending nicely, and he and Peggy wish to be remembered to you and they . . .

Forgive me, but I cannot now remember what it was I was about to write.

Mama, you simply must come home, or at the very least you must write a stern letter to Edwina. Katey will tell you—I haven't until now because I did not wish to worry you—that Rafe has been cooling considerably towards poor Teddi. He had told her that it would be best if they saw each other less often, in case of gossip. But this is ridiculous, coming from a man who never cared the slightest about how he compromised a woman, nor about causing scandal, let alone mere gossip, which is an insult to those acting as chaperone; to me, as Teddi's older sister, and to Mary Rose, who is a respectable married woman. Gossip indeed!

In view of what I told you in one of my letters last month, Katey, I fear that Rafe's attentions have drifted elsewhere. I have heard from Stephen, who has a married sister in Moss Vale, that Fleur Barton has taken a house there. It is a proper establishment, with housekeeper, maid and coachman, but there is no sign of her Mama. I had liked Fleur so much, as I know you both did, too. I *still* cannot bring myself to tell Teddi what are, after all, only my suspicions.

But someone will have to do something soon, as I found her, just now, very guiltily trying to hide a letter to Rafe, and her tear-stained face makes me think that what she is writing is not really very restrained.

Dear ones, the summer is half over, and still you are not home. I have already told you what a sad Christmas it was for us, not having you all here—and I won't whimper about that now. But the New Year is here and still you cannot tell us when you will be coming home. I must ask you yet again—is it merely Mama's friend being ill, or is there something else wrong?

Have you heard from Father?

Please write soon, or better still, come yourselves.

A very happy New Year to you both,

Your loving Daughter and Sister,

Laura

Katherine had begun a reply to her sister but had fallen asleep on the settee. There had been days of long vigils by Robin's bedside, and neither she nor her mother could remember when they had slept more than three hours at a stretch.

But now Katherine had. She awoke with a start to find the kindly face of Doctor Jago, Robin's physician, hovering above her. "I let myself in," he said in his quiet tone, "there was no reply to my knocking."

Katherine, crumpled, flustered, scrambled to her feet. "I've slept for hours . . ." She blinked dazedly at the sunshine that sliced in bars of brilliance between the heavy, drawn drapes. "I was supposed to relieve Mama at seven!"

"It's ten, now." Doctor Jago turned towards the sickroom. "Never mind, my dear, you'll be all the more refreshed for the extra rest, and your mama can sleep for a longer time. I wish she'd let me bring in a hired nurse—but . . ." He shook his head, as if Suzanna's stubborn devotion needed no further explaining.

He was at the door, and Katherine was about to follow him in, but he paused and she almost bumped into his back.

He made room for her silently.

It was obvious to both of them at once, seeing that still, handsome mask, that Robin had some time in the night, given up his tenacious struggle. The features were calm and looked very young, despite the pallor of death; one of the long, sensitive hands lay outside the coverlet. On it Suzanna had lain her face, and in an exhaustion of silent grieving, had fallen asleep. Her hair was loose, and cascaded over the coverlet and down her back.

"She should have woken me . . ." Katherine murmured.

The doctor shook his head. "There wasn't time."

He turned to Katherine, sighed, placed a hand on her shoulder in a fatherly fashion. "Come, you had best be the one to speak to her. Softly, my dear."

He walked with her to the bed, but it was Katherine who had to wake her mother to the morning, and the grey reality of the rest of her life without the man she loved.

Twenty Nine

Katherine expected bitterness, recriminations from the Mitchell family, but whatever Robin had written in his letters to his mother, father and sister produced the effect he must have desired. They came to the little Springwood chapel where his coffin lay, and their son's remains were brought back to the family plot at Rookwood.

Laurence Mitchell himself, grey, more aged than Katherine had ever seen him, the skin hanging in folds from the once broad, hearty face and big-boned frame, came to visit the women at Crest Cottage. He was courteous, subdued; accepted Suzanna's offer of a tour of the neat little house and gardens, and when he left, declining tea or other refreshment, he took Katherine, then Suzanna by the hand, wordlessly, before turning away.

When the carriage drove off, a bemused Suzanna looked over to her daughter. "He stayed a long time in Robin's room, gazing at the bed, at the view from the window. He finally went to stand by the window and said quietly, as if to himself, 'Yes, I can understand why this is a good place.' " Suzanna's eyes were questioning.

"Something Robin must have said in his letters," Katherine offered.

"Yes," Suzanna murmured, her gaze on the vanishing coach.

"Mama, are you very upset? About not going to the funeral?"

Suzanna shook her head, smiled sadly. "No, I wouldn't go, even if it were possible. As Marcus's wife I could attend, but I didn't want to make Mrs Mitchell and her daughter unhappy. Robin belongs to them now. I have my memories."

They turned back towards the house. The brightness of the summer blooms, without a softening of shadow anywhere, seemed to pulse against Katherine's retinas; the thought of entering the cottage oppressed her. She realized she did not want to stay much longer, and that Suzanna should not.

"Mama?" She stopped on the path, touched her mother's arm. "Let's go home."

"Home?" a dead tone, it seemed to have no meaning for Suzanna. Her gaze was empty.

"Back to the Highlands, to Grandmama and Grandfather—to Dovewood."

A light seemed kindled suddenly in the green eyes. "Dovewood . . ." and tears, the first Suzanna had shed, for her grief for Robin had stunned her; she had walked about, working dutifully but unbelieving, since that terrible morning. Now the tears came. "*Home to Dovewood . . .*"

Angela Gordon sat down on the stone garden seat, facing Katherine with something of the inscrutability of the marble Artemis in the nearby fernery. "Your mother has told me," she said.

Katherine stared. "Told you?" They had been at Dovewood only twenty-four hours, and for most of that time Suzanna had kept to her room. Now, however, in the pleasant cool of the summer evening, Edwin had coerced his daughter into playing croquet with him. Angela and Katherine had declined, and left the other two on the emerald carpet of the lawn and wandered off along the paths within the rose garden. Katherine waited for her grandmother to speak and when she did not, repeated, "Mama told you what?"

"Everything. Well, enough. I know where you've been, both of you, and who it was you nursed until the end—poor boy . . ." The grey eyes were shadowed a moment, then lifted to Katherine with all their old directness. "And I know how it came about that it was Suzanna who nursed him."

She did indeed know everything. Katherine was at first cross with her mother, then relented. It was natural that she would turn to her own mother for understanding. Questions would be asked. And Suzanna needed support, knew she could rely on Angela's compassion and strength.

"He . . . he was a very special person, Robin." Katherine felt moved to defend the young man.

"I only met him once, at a ball at the Balmain house. A pale, handsome young man. As to his character, I will take your word for it, you're a discerning young woman—you'd not stay in a house under those circumstances unless you felt respect and sympathy for the boy." Her eyes, keen, astute, swept over Katherine from head to foot and back again. "I'm sorry that you had to go through it, however. If I'd been Suzanna, I'd have served you tea and scones, and sent you packing. But I'm not Suzanna," she sighed, "for I would not be in that situation in the first place."

"You mustn't blame Mama . . ."

"Of course I blame Mama," Angela mimicked irritably. "The girl has no sense, never did. A loving, feeling, kindly saint of a girl—

totally unable to manage on her own. My mother was the same—
Laura's another one, but she has a streak of the Puritan in her, Laura.
That, if nothing else, will keep her emotions under control. No,"
she scowled at Katherine, "I knew when you both returned, that
something was dreadfully wrong—at first I thought it was over That
Matter—the one Fleur raised, the little witch—but ten minutes alone
with Suzanna and I realized that she didn't know, her heart's too
full of grief for her young man—that's why you didn't tell her,
isn't it?"

"Yes—and because she *is* my mother. There's no doubts, no
questions or hidden resentments. I can accept—and forget. Fleur hasn't
hurt me."

The grey eyes seemed to drink this in, then she stood and moved
off down the path slowly, her hands clasped behind her, the straight-
backed figure all concentration. Katherine followed. "I'd hoped you'd
marry again," Angela said, and turned as Katherine involuntarily
laughed. "Yes, you may well giggle now—even I can be amused;
for I see something in you now that was not there before you left
for Sydney, and it's changed you, my dear."

"Something? You mean I've hardened?"

"No, it's not as simple as that . . . When you came back to Australia
you were coming *home*. To a sense of security, of stability that has,
poor darling, proved an illusion. Nothing is the same as when you
left, Katherine, is it?" she asked soberly. "No, it never is. But you
thought to escape from the memory of your husband's long illness,
his tragic death, and then, worse, the loss of your darling Christopher.
And you came back to find Joe gone from us—and everyone—bar
your grandfather and myself—totally involved with their own
problems, and so far removed from all you'd gone through that you
were not only left to cope greatly by yourself, but found yourself
drawn into your family's problems."

"I can cope with that. As a family, we're supposed to help one
another . . ."

"You've had no peace, child. I hadn't realized, until you left,
how miserable the younger girls were over their beaux—and it seems
you were party to your parents' problems for some months. I wish
I'd known, I'd have brought you back here . . ." She sobered, "But
I had Fleur here. You must have disliked her from the start—you
should have told me your misgivings, Katherine. How's one to grow
old gracefully unless one can trust one's descendants to protect one
from foolish decisions? But there—even I add burdens to you, even
in jest."

"Grandmama, they aren't burdens . . ."

"You should have had peaceful, contented surroundings—months of it—a year or more of it. Instead, you go to Springwood. Knowing what awaits you there, you go. You'd come home to escape the memory of illness and death, and for Suzanna you step right back into that nightmare. You did it willingly," Angela said gently, "and you've emerged stronger for it—not *harder*, my dear, no. But like your father, I had liked that nice Luke Murchison, and I had liked your Brendan Kelehan—till he found himself otherwise engaged . . . but I feel now, somehow, an independence and a strength in you that . . . that precludes your leaning prettily on a husband for advice and support—and as for bending your will to his . . ." the wistful words ended in a sigh.

Katherine smiled. Her grandmother was very astute. Katherine had had much opportunity to observe the loving interdependence between Suzanna and Robin in those last weeks, but while she was impressed, affected deeply, she was not envious. She thought, "There is only one man to whom I would wish to give up myself—all of myself—one man whom I trust to take care of my feelings, my life— and I can't have him." But she did not say this aloud to her grandmother.

During her stay at Dovewood, she signed the contracts for the blocks of land, and visited the bank to deposit her money and draw a cheque for the amount of two thousand pounds.

Brendan stared at the piece of paper in his hand.

"You needn't have done this."

"But I wanted to." She seated herself on the slippery brocade sofa and watched him happily as he stood in the centre of his office, holding the cheque with no real degree of delight, or even relief.

"You'll need it," he said, looking down at her, "and I have enough . . ."

"Perhaps. But it means a great deal to me to repay you. And indirectly cancel my debt, what I did in taking the money in the first place. In fact, I feel worse, owing the money to you—I could, perhaps, have lived with the fact that the Fenian Brotherhood was out of pocket. Please, Brendan," she smiled at him, keeping her tone light, while she longed to stand, to go to him, touch his face, smooth the faint frown from his forehead. Any hope she had held of feeling detached, indifferent to him, had vanished when she had met him in the hall on her return. His face had lit with a smile and they had run a few paces towards each other, to stop—and shake hands. Her heart had ached then, it ached now. Whatever she had learned at Springwood—if her grandmother had been right, and she *had* learned something—it had not helped her to cease loving Brendan Kelehan.

She said, and the words twisted within her, hurt her, "You'll be going home in a few months, with Mary Rose and a young baby. There'll be more expenses than you thought possible, now you're a family man. Make me happy—let me do the right thing, and accept it."

He sighed, agreed unwillingly, seeing that she meant her words, and tucked the cheque into his pocket.

Katherine smiled, and rose to leave; it seemed, suddenly, as if she had not been away, there was this urge to leave his presence as soon as any business was discussed; for only in absence could she think clearly, avoid the longing to be closer to him than across a table, across a room.

"I haven't seen the girls," she said, turning brightly to him in the doorway. "Are they out?"

"Visiting the Cummings, I believe Laura told me as she left. Stephen was with them."

But this was not quite the truth. Katherine was in her room bathing in the hip tub after the long journey, when the door was flung open. Laura practically leapt through the door, and shut it behind her.

"Oh! Oh, Katey! Please excuse me! Oh, Katey dear, I'm so glad you're home!" Laura kissed her sister's soapy forehead, reached for the towel and handed it to her. "Please get dressed, you must help us! Brendan is still in his office, isn't he?"

"He was when I left him half an hour ago. Laura . . . ."

"*Please* hurry. What dress do you want—no, your riding habit—the blue one? The black? The green? Which?" Laura was flinging open wardrobe doors. "*Do* hurry, Katey!"

"The green! Laura, I'll hurry if you tell me what's happened. And if it's serious, Brendan should be informed." She rose, dripping and reluctant, from the warm comfort of her tub and began towelling herself briskly.

"I think Mary Rose has run away."

"What?"

"She's taken the wagon, and lots of supplies—tea, sugar, flour—she's practically emptied the pantry—and she's been ordering mysterious packages from the Sydney catalogues for weeks now. She left quite early this morning—Stephen met her on the road and she seemed very agitated, told him she was delivering parcels to Mrs Crolin, who'd been ill . . ."

"The Crolins are over near Cambewarra Mountain now—"

"Yes, so obviously she's taking that road over the mountains. Stephen couldn't accost her, so he rode to tell us. Today is Brendan's day to do accounts, thank goodness, so he doesn't know. He found Edwina, Stephen and me sneaking out, but we told him we were going to visit the Cummings. Poor man, he believed us, nodded vaguely, with that silver hair all fallen over his forehead, and went back to his desk. It *was* close! It would break his heart if he knew."

"But . . . have you found her?" She pulled on pantaloons and camisole, stockings and boots.

"No! There's no sign of her. Poor Teddi and Stephen must be halfway to Kiama by now . . . I came back to tell Brendan. We must tell Brendan now, don't you think?"

Katherine chewed her lip. "No. No, not yet. You go on downstairs, tell Peggy and Carl to say *nothing*. Can you start to saddle Dryad for me? And you'd better find a fresh horse for yourself . . ."

By the time Katherine was dressed and running across the stable yard to Laura and the waiting horses, Katherine had a plan, but Laura was the first to speak.

"Carl said Brendan saddled his horse and rode out just after speaking with you . . ."

"Where did he go?" Katherine asked, "why would he leave the accounts?"

"Carl and Peggy don't know!—He simply rode off without telling them where he was going, or how long he would be . . ."

"He might not be heading towards Cambewarra . . ."

"No—and he might just stay away long enough for us to bring Mary Rose home and put everything back where it belongs. Oh, Katey—the baby is due in only three weeks! Do you think her pregnancy has . . . well, *unhinged* her? I believe ladies in a delicate condition will do the strangest things. Stephen's sister said she used to chew bits of coal—"

"Laura—will you mount this horse, please? We're wasting time!"

Laura came to herself, allowed Katherine to give her a leg up into the side-saddle and waited until she scrambled onto Dryad.

They did not press the horses, but trotted down the drive and broke into an easy canter that took them within a mile of the foot of the escarpment, then dropped back to a walk to rest them before the climb.

It was then that Katherine said, "What if Mary Rose was telling the truth?"

Laura looked over at her, amazement on her face, "In what she told Stephen? That she was taking parcels to the Crolins? Really, Katey!"

"No, truly." Katherine persisted. "Isn't it just the sort of thing that Mary Rose would do? She is so desperate to help those around her, Laura . . ."

"Yes, but everyone knows what the cedar-getters are like! Why, I was insulted and abused by Charlie Crolin last year, for bringing medicines and poultices for the children when they had influenza. They won't take help of any kind—and as for charitable packages . . ."

"Does Mary Rose know that?"

"Of course she must! Why . . . she'd have . . . I'm certain we've mentioned . . . she would have heard . . ." The features beneath the heavy blonde hair and veiled hat looked stricken. "Oh, Katey—what if you're right? Their new hut isn't far off the track, either—she might be able to take the wagon to them . . ."

"I think it's possible—do you know what sort of thing she was ordering from Sydney?"

"Well, baby's things—children's clothes . . ." her eyes widened, "yes—clothes for children of three and four—Edwina had peered over her shoulder and told me later. We thought she was simply being a little eccentric—overplanning for the baby, you know. But Mrs Crolin has small children . . ."

"I'll ride up there—you go on to find Edwina and Stephen—I think you'll meet them returning by now, as there are inns along the way and Mary Rose would be very memorable if she was seen passing."

"And if we come across Brendan?"

Katherine sighed. "I suppose we'll have to tell him—he'll wonder why Mary Rose isn't with you."

They came to a fork in the road, and Katherine waved before turning Dryad down the right-hand fork towards where the road began to rise, up into the hills and the area known as Budgong Vale.

Katherine prayed she was right, and that Mary Rose's misguided philanthropy had led her to attempt to alleviate the cedar-getters' poverty. There were several families living up this way now. Frank and Annie and family, Charlie and Essie and family—and Davey Crolin, still single, lived with one or the other of his brothers. The two Tallon twins, Walt and Elias, lived in the area also, with their numerous broods of large-boned, sandy-haired children, as bold and swaggering as their fathers.

And it made Katherine change her mind; perhaps Mary Rose might be safer on the open road, headed for Wollongong and Sydney and a boat home to America, than up in these hills with men as impudent and violent as Davey Crolin . . . She was making herself nervous. Perhaps she should have brought Laura . . . But if trouble ensued, it could involve them both . . . But there would be no trouble, nothing could happen . . .

A bitter Davey Crolin, his nose smashed and crooked, the tiny jet eyes watching malevolently from the bushes, seeing her alone, remembering . . .

When she heard the sounds from before her, around a bend in the track that coiled up the hill, she almost pulled Dryad to a halt, such was her nervousness. But no, she scolded herself and rode on.

She recognized the horses as soon as they came into sight—and seated on the wagon was Mary Rose, hunched over, miserable, but safe. The truly odd thing was that she was not driving; holding the reins was Frank Crolin, hat down about his ears, narrow mouth set grimly. His expression did not change, though he must have seen Katherine by now. As she approached he reined in the horses.

It was then that Katherine saw that Mary Rose was crying, or sobbing rather; great sobs that shook her body.

"Mary Rose . . ." she began.

"You're her kin, ain't you?" Frank said without preamble.

"Well, I'm . . ."

"I gotta get back—come away without my dinner to get her home— an' all *this*!" He jerked his head towards the wagon, but Katherine had no eyes for the parcels in the back; she was fearful for Mary Rose. The girl looked ill, her face swollen, red-eyed and dirty where dust had clung to her cheeks and the tears had made tracks in them.

Frank was jumping down from the wagon, paused to glare balefully between Mary Rose and Katherine before saying, "We might be poor—we *know* we *are*—but we don't need no charity. We take care of our own, and I can provide for my wife and kids. Tell her to stay home . . ." *Her* being indicated by a dismissive jerk of the head as meaning Mary Rose. "Tell her to see to her own house before tellin' other people how to run their homes." And he almost snarled at Mary Rose, "Don't you come near our place nor my woman again, you hear?"

There was a physical threat there—Katherine felt her stomach contract, even as Mary Rose gave her protesting little scream and buried her head in her hands to block out the sight of the vicious little man.

"You've made your point, Mr Crolin—you may leave now if you like."

Katherine did not meet his eyes as he turned to her, but dismounted and led Dryad around behind the wagon to tie the reins firmly to the vehicle. Dryad was curious but unprotesting; only she watched, with one ear twitching, the narrow frame of the cedar-getter turn with an oath and trot off, back along the road in the direction he had come.

Mary Rose did not look at Katherine as she scrambled up beside her. Katherine studied her for a moment, then turned to check the contents of the wagon. Flour, sugar, tea, blankets and linen, and the brown paper parcels that had come from Sydney.

"Are they clothes in those parcels," she asked gently, "for the children?"

No answer.

"Mary Rose . . . ?"

A sob, a hiccup, "Yes."

Katherine made no further attempt at questioning, but untied the reins and chirrupped to the horses.

Her silence as they trotted along seemed, finally, to disturb Mary Rose sufficiently for her to glance up once or twice, before saying, her eyes to the front as she fumbled for the lace handkerchief in her sleeve, "You find this very amusing, I have no doubt."

"No."

"No?"

"You were trying to help them. Annie Crolin and the children."

"N . . . not just Annie—her sister-in-law, Essie, and Mrs Larsson. No one would take anything though. Except Mrs Halstrop—she accepted the bolts of cloth I brought them—she was very gracious," Mary Rose sniffed, "which is more than I can say for that . . . *horrible* man. And . . . and even Essie Crolin wasn't friendly. When she saw all the gifts I'd brought she grew pale, Katherine, and seemed to cool towards me—she wasn't grateful or pleased at all."

"Mary Rose, they're proud people . . ."

"Proud and hungry, Katherine! You can't eat pride!"

"Then they'll starve. That's the way they are."

"Foolishness!"

"Yes, perhaps—for I can't help but think of the children. But you must respect their ways . . ."

"In Boston, Aunt Rose and I used to take packages to poor people, and . . ."

"Mary Rose—*you are no longer in Boston.*"

"I wish I was! I wish I was a thousand—a *million* miles away from this God-forsaken valley! I wish I'd never come here! I wish I'd never married Brendan!"

Katherine half turned towards the girl, exasperated but still sympathetic—she put out her hand to touch Mary Rose on the shoulder—but froze, for running along the dusty bush track towards them was Banjee, the young Woddi boy who had caught the black snake by the creek. Hero of the song they had all sung, he was wearing the Woddis' usual summer garb of a waistband of plaited fibre with a very inadequate fringe at the front.

All humour had gone from the strong dark face, he was shouting incoherently in the Woddi tongue, waving an arm back the way he had come, and a second later, using the other to beckon them on.

Katherine slapped the reins on the horses' rumps, and they broke into a shuffling trot, coming alongside Banjee who fearlessly leapt up beside Mary Rose, gibbering all the time, his eyes round with concern, the bone through his nose bobbing up and down before Mary Rose's terrified face.

"Get him away! Get that savage away from me!"

For a few yards they rattled along, the almost naked Banjee shaking Mary Rose by the arm, urging her in Woddi, to come, see!—and Katherine struggling to free herself from the hysterical Mary Rose, who screamed and shrieked that she was being attacked, raped, murdered, and crying out for the husband she had repudiated only a matter of seconds before.

Mary Rose clung like a burr, shrieked the louder when Katherine tried to leave her with the wagon, to follow Banjee when he leapt down and raced off through the scrub.

"Don't leave me! Don't leave me here!"

"Mary Rose, he's gone! You don't want to go with him, do you?"

"No, I want to go home—he tried to kill me . . ."

"Stop it! Now stop it before I slap you!" She raised her hand threateningly. Mary Rose stopped.

"This is terrible—think of your baby—what he'll think, hearing you shouting, feeling your heart racing—he's going to be born in three weeks—are you going to frighten him into coming early?"

"He won't! I wouldn't! He can't—can he?" her eyes were wide.

"Stay calm, Mary Rose. Take deep breaths—I have to see what

Banjee wanted—something has happened . . ." She climbed down from the wagon.

"He could kill you, and then they'll kill me . . ." Her voice was rising.

"Mary Rose, do you want to have that baby now, in that wagon?"

Mary Rose gulped, took a deep, shuddering breath. "Come back soo-oon," she whimpered. And Katherine, torn with agitation, yet also with a despairing fondness for the girl, touched the tear-stained cheek before turning to follow Banjee, as quickly as trailing skirts would allow, down the slope into the closely growing scrub.

The five Woddi hunters were standing in a semi-circle, watching her approach, yet still carrying on their own conversation—to a stranger, it would seem that they were quarrelling, but they were energetic talkers in their own language, and each man was desirous of putting forth his own ideas now. Timalong, Myeela's husband, was there—turned slightly from Katherine she could see the puckering scar on the fleshy part of his shoulder. He and two of the other men were standing at rest—one leg bent and braced against the knee-cap of the other—they looked like garrulous black birds, watching somewhat warily something that lay on the ground before them.

Katherine stopped, feeling ill. But Banjee had run forward to her, had taken her arm, urged her on; and now the men urged her to come also, pointing downwards at the man who lay on his face in the summer grass.

Brown boots, brown trousers—*Brendan* . . .

No. She came closer, and the figure was grey-haired but older than Brendan—the blood-stained shirt made of a coarse cloth and slightly worn, the brown moleskin trousers, too, had seen much wear . . .

Timalong was shaking his head, "No dead, no dead whitefeller, Missus, no dead!"

She must go to him, bend to him—the face was turned away from her, she leaned over even as the man gave a deep and painful groan through lips stiff with dried blood.

It was Amos Murphy.

Thirty

M ary Rose, seated nervously in the wagon, found herself being approached by five chattering, all-but-naked black warriors—and this was terrifying enough, but they carried between them the bloodied body of a dead man, and it was enough to have her clinging to the sides of the wagon, paralysed with fear.

Katherine followed close behind them, overseeing that they lay the man gently in the back of the vehicle. Their eyes lit up at the sight of the tea, sugar and flour bags, and they stroked them admiringly, looking at the Boss's daughter and telling her in Woddi that she was very rich, very fortunate.

Katherine hesitated only a moment, then began handing out the supplies to the men, with a look at the stunned Mary Rose that said clearly that the goods should go to those who appreciated them.

When the wagon set off down the road, moving more easily for the lighter load, it was accompanied for a few hundred yards, by the Woddi, very pleased with the consequences of their charitable deed, each man loaded down with sacks and barrels and bolts of cloth, under their arms or balanced on their heads, as much as they could carry.

Mary Rose had relaxed only a little on hearing that Amos Murphy was not dead at all, for she felt she had more to fear from the Woddi than the unconscious Amos. She managed to remain still, however, when Timalong trotted alongside the wagon, reached up and touched Mary Rose's hair, chattering to Katherine in the Woddi tongue. It was only when the men had called their farewells and had loped off down into one of the gullies that Mary Rose asked in a small, shaken voice, "What d . . . did he say—when he touched my hair?"

"He said your husband was very fortunate."

"Oh?" A tentative smile. "Did he?"

"Yes." The horror of their discovery had made Katherine feel light-headed. Timalong's words, which she had only just managed to understand, now made her laugh, unable to resist telling Mary Rose the entire truth. "He said, if only you were a Woddi Woddi, you would be highly prized—your hair would make a handsome waistbelt for a great leader."

Mary Rose's jaw dropped, then shut with a pop, and she sniffed, looking before her, patently unimpressed.

Katherine, too, sobered quickly. She kept turning around to gaze at the silent, unmoving form of Amos Murphy. Mary Rose, who did not recognize him, asked who he was, and Katherine told her the little she knew of Amos's background.

Arriving back at Barrengarry, she sent one of the farmworkers to ride for Doctor Lang and Sergeant Lloyd. Brendan was still absent, and Katherine, Peggy, and another of the farmworkers who had been mending a fence close to the homestead, managed to carry the man up the stairs to one of the spare bedrooms.

When Brendan finally arrived home, after an afternoon spent checking stock in the western end of the Valley, the wagon had been unharnessed, the remaining goods hidden in the pantry, Stephen, Laura and Edwina had returned, and no one, Katherine hoped, would know the purpose of the original pilgrimage.

Will O'Mahony, another of the stockmen from Burrawang, had been dispatched to notify Molly, away in Berry, of her father's accident and another lad was sent to Murphy's farm to fetch Billy, Amos's young son. The boy stayed by his father's bedside for three hours, but in the end was led by a sympathetic Carl out to a bunk with the young farmworkers, for it was clear that Amos would not regain consciousness that night.

Doctor Lang said the same thing, when he arrived just after dusk. There was nothing that could be done; keep the patient warm and quiet, and wait. He looked tired and pale—stayed for a meal with the family, then insisted on riding back to Moss Vale immediately, as there was much need of his services; with the hot summer, the diphtheria was rife in the town. He did not stand too close to Mary Rose, and told them no details of the illness that was sweeping Moss Vale families, but it was clear, to Katherine at least, that he was worried that even he might spread the contagion elsewhere.

Katherine could not sleep that night. The house was silent, and she and Peggy and Laura were sharing the watches over the injured man, but knowing that she had only six hours before she would take her turn did nothing to relax her mind for rest.

She rose and tiptoed down the hall, opened the door and found Peggy reading by a shaded lamp beside the bed. Amos, his grizzled beard still marked by the cuts and abrasions, his head swathed in bandages, lay still and barely breathing, on the pillows. There were no broken bones, Doctor Lang had said, other than the crack in the skull, and this was serious enough as the blows had been severe.

"No change, Miss Katey." Peggy's pink, chubby face was raised to her, the bright eyes blinked over her round spectacles. "Do go back to bed, like a good girl—soon enough I'll be knocking on your door. Now do as I say—and go straight to sleep."

Katherine smiled. "Yes, Peggy." And she left the room as obediently as she had as a nine-year-old, when Carl had brought Peggy to Barrengarry to become his wife and the centre of the homestead.

Katherine closed her own bedroom door behind her—and gasped in fright at the white apparition hovering over her dressing table . . . Then she relaxed against the door, realizing that the hazy spectre was the mirror's reflection of Mary Rose.

She stood by the tall foot of Katherine's walnut bed, gripping it nervously, her usually slender figure now ballooning beneath the white, lace-trimmed nightdress. Yet she still looked child-like, retained a touching innocence in the wide-set blue eyes.

"I . . . I couldn't sleep. I wanted to say I was sorry, for all I did. I . . . Everything I try to do is so . . . so *stupid*! I realized it, finally, today—and I'm ashamed, Katherine . . ." Her eyes filled with tears.

"Mary Rose," gently, "it's forgotten. We, none of us, will mention it again. And besides," she smiled, "the Woddi Woddi are very happy tonight, and you've learnt a great deal about the dubious sense of honour amongst cedar-getters."

"I was trying to help, truly I was! I was brought up to help other people—my father used to say that it was our responsibility— we had wealth, so we must, as Christians, share it with those less fortunate. I . . . I used to resent that—all the time spent visiting the sick, making packages for the poor, helping with church bazaars for the missions . . . And then, Mama and Papa were gone . . . and since I've been here I've tried to do what Mama would have wanted me to do. I miss her so much, Katherine. When the girls would read your letters, telling of how you and your mama would work in the garden, or do the housework together—even nursing your sick friend together, until the end . . . I envied you . . ."

"Oh, Mary Rose . . ."

"No, don't look at me as if you pity me! You've been too kind already, when to think . . ." She was sobbing, deep, heaving sobs that Katherine could not but believe must be injurious to her, "I thought you were trying to take Brendan away from me— Yes, I did! I'm . . . ashamed of so much—I'm s . . . *stupid*, Katherine— and . . . and . . . I'm afraid! I'm so afraid . . . !"

Katherine moved to her, placed an arm about the trembling

shoulders, hunched with misery. "Mary Rose, why? What's making you afraid?"

"You were right—about the baby. I was silly and hysterical, and I should have thought about my baby." Her hand moved to her stomach, rested there protectively. "I shouldn't have been in that wagon in the first place—but I was trying to help! I wanted to do something *useful.*" She raised terrified eyes to Katherine. "What if I die, Katherine? Women die in childbirth all the time. What if I die—and I've been so wicked and selfish and so cold towards Brendan—I've been a bad wife, and if I die I'll spend a century in Purgatory, at the very least."

"Mary Rose, you must stop upsetting yourself . . ."

"I won't get hysterical and foolish again—I promise I won't," she gulped. "I only came to tell you that, and to ask you where Doctor Lang has gone."

Katherine stared at her. She felt her blood leave her face in a cold rush of dread. "He went back to Moss Vale," she said calmly. "Remember, he said at dinner that several children were ill with the diphtheria. You're not . . . having pains, are you, Mary Rose?"

"Oh, no. I . . . I just wondered where he was."

Katherine managed to disguise her sense of relief. She steered the girl towards the door. "Go back to bed now. You need your rest."

But Mary Rose paused in the doorway, lowered her voice and looked a little embarrassed. "I *had* wanted to ask the doctor something. It . . . it's very embarrassing. But . . . you've had a baby—you could tell me. I . . . I had to get changed before I came to see you. I was in bed, and I felt . . . something . . . *give way.* And then I was very *wet.* I barely got out of bed in time. Brendan is still asleep. I'll clean the carpet in the morning—but it frightened me, you see. Does that happen often when one is in my condition? Katherine?"

Katherine would smile to herself, running backwards and forwards between Amos' room and her own where, because it was closest to the stairs and therefore the kitchen, Mary Rose was made comfortable, in fresh linen and with pillows at her back, to await the birth. Angela had said Katherine should have peace and a quiet existence—what would her grandmother say to this madness?

A message was sent to Doctor Lang, in a sealed envelope: *Mrs Kelehan's water has broken, please come urgently. Mrs Carron.* But Katherine was afraid, though she did not show it in front of the others. The diphtheria epidemic was serious, he had dragged himself away from some very sick children because of the urgency of Amos Murphy's case. Would he return, less than twenty-four hours afterwards, to attend a childbed? He had said himself, when leaving, that he might be monopolized by the extent of the epidemic, that the Valley was fortunate in having Angel Regnier.

"No!"

"The doctor may not arrive until tomorrow, Mary Rose . . ."

"I don't care! I won't have that woman! I don't like her!"

"Mary Rose, don't you see that you'll need help?" Katherine did not wish to frighten the girl any further, but she sat down on the edge of the bed and faced Mary Rose squarely, knowing that safety of mother and baby depended on this very vital matter. "They call it labour," she said firmly, "and that's just what it is. Hard, exhausting work, Mary Rose, and you need someone knowledgeable to tell you when to push . . ."

"You've had a baby. You know all about it. You can help me." The blue eyes looked desperately, helplessly up into Katherine's own.

Gazing into the fearful young face, even in her exasperation with the girl, Katherine was moved by the obvious, though misplaced, trust. She thought, despite everything—no, for to tell the truth, despite Brendan—we have found our way to a fondness, a friendship. It was a tiny miracle, and Katherine was affected. She took Mary Rose by the hand. "My dear, I'll stay with you, and do all that I can. But the birth of a baby requires a midwife—someone with experience . . ."

"Mrs Halstrop. Call Nancy Halstrop."

Katherine stared, aghast. "No, Mary Rose," she managed finally, still not quite believing the girl could be serious. "I know nothing about the woman, except that the cedar-getters won't have her— close as their loyalties lie, they call for Angel Regnier when they have their babies. Doesn't that tell you anything?"

"I know why they don't have her! She told me when I visited her a few weeks ago—they resent her because she married a settler and moved away. And she's tried to educate herself, and gain some refinement, and the other women are jealous. That makes sense, doesn't it?—Oh . . . !"

Mary Rose gripped Katherine's hand hard, as a spasm of pain swept through her. When it had passed, the eyes looked up at Katherine in terror. "Is it going to hurt like this? No one told me it would be like this. It's . . . it's like monthly pain, isn't it? Only a hundred times worse. I can't take pain, Katherine—I'm not brave, you know I'm not!"

"I think you are," Katherine said emphatically. "You've had a protected life, and then a great tragedy in losing your parents. But the girl you were *then* is *not* the woman you are now. Don't you *feel* different, Mary Rose? When you see your Aunt and Uncle Kelehan in Boston once more, won't they be meeting someone they've never met before? You've learnt so much here, and it's made you stronger than you know. Don't think back to what you were—think of what you are. You're Brendan Kelehan's wife—and soon you'll be a mother. And mothers are strong people, Mary Rose, the strongest in the world."

The girl seemed to drink in her words and calmed a little. Katherine herself relaxed; from her own experience with Christopher's birth, the fear itself had been the worst thing. She had, towards the end of her pregnancy, borrowed books from Oliver's friends who were medical students, questioned the doctor and the midwife who would be present, and was, finally, as ready as she thought anyone could be, sailing out on untravelled, unknown waters. But the pain had taken her by surprise, so strong, towards the end, that she had felt possessed totally, merely an instrument, caught up and used by a malignant fate, all autonomy gone. She had almost panicked once or twice, but reminded herself of the technicality of what was happening. It *would* end, she knew it would end . . . She listened to the doctor and midwife, and talked with them between contractions. And she was fortunate that the specialist was a good man—Brendan had recommended him as the doctor who had delivered many of his numerous nieces and nephews—and he was knowledgeable and respectful of her desire to understand the workings of her own body. She told Mary Rose this and finished, "Doctor Lang would be the same—and Angel Regnier—I doubt if you could find a more capable midwife in the country—she knows more than many doctors—perhaps more than most."

"I . . . want . . . Mrs Halstrop. I . . . don't want . . . that woman."

Katherine felt helpless to break through the illogical fear and superstition, though she tried, speaking calmly, gently, for a further hour.

They were both tiring; Katherine decided to leave Mary Rose to sleep for as long as she could, but just as she was rising to go, another contraction made Mary Rose stiffen, her face convulse.

Katherine glanced at the bedside clock. An hour and a quarter between the pains . . .

She held the girl's hand until the spasm ebbed, soothing her, telling her to relax. When it had passed, she left Mary Rose dozing lightly to check on Amos, the confident smile she had worn for Mary Rose's sake falling from her face the moment the door was shut. It would be close. Perhaps the child would be born before Doctor Lang arrived . . . And who would be here, who would deliver the baby? Katherine remembered Mary Rose's long, fine-boned arms and shoulders, remembered her narrow frame, the tiny waist and small hips, slender as a boy's, in those few months before the baby altered her figure. But the slender bone-structure remained the same. Katherine felt a stab of fear.

She herself was two or three inches shorter than Mary Rose, but her hips were broader, they had made a comfortable cradle for Christopher for the first nine months of his existence, and had released him to the world with the minimum of fuss and discomfort. The twenty-eight-hour labour—interminable to Katherine at the time— had been, according to doctor and midwife, an orderly, incident-free, copybook birth. And if that was the best she could hope for Mary Rose, she thought soberly, then she wanted the best medical help possible.

There was no change in Amos Murphy's condition. Ignoring Peggy's admonitions to go to bed, to get some rest, Katherine hovered briefly by the man's bedside, wondering at the terrible wounds he had received and praying that he would recover.

"It's scary, ain't it, Miss Katey?" Peggy whispered from her chair by the bed, "him being beaten about the head and left to die in the bush—just like those other poor unfortunate men. Praise God that Mr Murphy has survived—he might be able to tell us who's doing these terrible things. Miss Katey, there's nothing you can do— you look dead on your feet—It's past midnight . . ."

"Peggy, don't tell me to go to bed . . ."

Peggy sighed. "I suppose you're too worried to rest properly, anyhow. I think I will be, too. I'd feel a lot better, Miss Katey, if we could send for Mrs Regnier now."

Katherine was inclined to agree, but hesitated. Then, "No, we'll wait until morning—Mrs Regnier is only fifteen minutes' ride from here, and the pains are only . . ." She stopped, having forgotten that Peggy had never had a child herself. Her round little eyes now blinked owlishly at Katherine, braced for something unpleasant. When Edwina was born, Katherine remembered, a year after Peggy had arrived at Barrengarry, she had hidden in the kitchen, sobbing for poor Mrs Prescott, and the most the doctor and Angela could make her do was to boil the water and fetch clean cloths and sheets. Any description of Mary Rose's condition was just as likely to bring on a similar nervous paralysis, so Katherine concluded merely by saying, "I think we'll wait for morning."

She dozed in the chair beside Mary Rose's bed, waking every hour or so when a contraction would rouse the girl from her sleep, to soothe and speak with her.

"Brendan . . . I want Brendan . . ." Mary Rose murmured once, and Katherine had to explain that the baby might not come until later in the day, that Brendan would actually be more worried than they because there was nothing for him to do but wait, and wasn't it kinder to let him sleep for these few hours?

And the girl agreed sleepily, saying, "Poor Brendan . . . He'll be frightened for me, won't he, Katherine? He doesn't know how brave I can be. Poor Brendan, like Papa, when Damian and Nicholas were born . . ." and with a yawn, she drifted off to sleep once more.

At six there was a faint tapping at the door and a clean-shaven and fully-dressed Brendan came into the room, his worried scowl alleviated somewhat by the sight of Mary Rose peacefully resting, lying on her side, one hand cradling her face like a child.

"You should have woken me," he said to Katherine, touching her hair as he passed close to her to stand by the bed. "You look exhausted. I'll watch with her for a while, go and have some breakfast and a few hours' sleep."

"Brendan, we don't know how long it will be . . ."

But he had grinned, taking her hands and pulled her gently to her feet. "I'm the eldest of eight children—I've picked up enough knowledge to tell that nothing will happen in the next hour—go and eat, before Peggy comes looking for you. She's organizing the house very well, refused to let me come in here until I was 'half-way decent-looking'—in case I frightened Mary Rose, I take it." He led her to the door, the gesture of a fond brother. "If she calls for you, I'll come and fetch you."

Katherine was grateful to go, and finding Peggy had roused a wide-eyed Laura and Edwina, she left both her sisters seated in Amos's room while she and Peggy ate a breakfast of porridge and eggs and drank some reviving cups of hot coffee.

It was during this meal that the young stockman who had been sent to fetch Doctor Lang knocked on the back door and was invited into the kitchen. While Peggy prepared a meal for the exhausted young man, Katherine read the short letter he handed to her, almost apologetically.

Dear Mrs Carron,

I know you will understand my dilemma when I tell you that a little girl of five has died of the diphtheria only today, a few hours after I arrived back in Moss Vale. Six other little ones are seriously ill. I go from house to house with no pause and cannot see how I dare leave my small patients again so soon, even for the birth of Mrs Kelehan's child. You have, after all, the expert services of Mrs Regnier, of which I am sure you have already availed yourself.

I will come, of course, as soon as I possibly can, but you are a woman of great sense and will understand, I am sure, the decision I must make, difficult as it is.

I remain, with respect,
        Your dutiful servant and friend,
        Doctor Robert Lang

She sat staring at the piece of paper for some time. It was not really a surprise, she thought numbly; she had expected something would delay him. A child of five . . . A year older than Christopher . . . Somewhere in Moss Vale, some woman was grieving, as she had grieved, all those thousands of miles away . . .

She shook her head. There was no time for such thoughts.

She rose from the table, informed the already uneasy Peggy that Doctor Lang would not be able to attend for a day or so, and headed through the house to the stairs before Peggy could bleat her questions about what were they going to do now . . .

It was only as she had her hand on the newel post, about to turn and climb the stairs, that she glanced up towards the front door, seeing a shadow move across the glass panels. Then she was running forward, flinging open the door gratefully, before Angel Regnier had time to knock.

"How did you know?" Katherine gasped, conscious of the fact that there was a slight note of hysteria in her tone. "How did you know? I was about to send for you . . ." She drew Angel into the hall, took her cloak, but the black woman's smile was grave.

"Sometimes I know—it's an intuition, I suppose, though Emile says I worry about my patients so much I'm in sympathy with them. What's happened? Is it Mrs Kelehan?"

And Katherine told her of Amos Murphy, and the effect that his discovery had had upon Mary Rose.

"I must scrub my hands," Angel stated, "but I'll see her before Mr Murphy, as he needs rest more than anything I could do for him, just now."

After Angel had washed her hands carefully in the upstairs bathroom, Katherine had to pause at the bedroom door and warn

Angel, awkwardly, with embarrassment, of the girl's insistence on seeing Nancy Halstrop.

The dark eyes regarded Katherine seriously at the end of this. "I'm worried, Katherine. If she's afraid of me, I could do more harm than good."

"Nonsense! You couldn't possibly . . ."

"There is no logic here, as you and I know it. The young lady is fragile—in her body and in her mind—you know it as well as I do. I sensed her suspicion of me the first time I met her . . ." And, as Katherine began to speak, "I know it's because I'm foreign to her—I think she connects me with the Woddi Woddi—to her, I'm a savage, masquerading in an Englishwoman's dress. But . . ." she sighed, a sigh of determination as much as resignation. "We will try. You go into the room, please, and announce that I'm here. For me to walk in with you would be presumptuous, and might frighten her more."

So Katherine knocked and entered the room alone.

Mary Rose, between contractions, was sitting up, smiling brightly, obviously enjoying the visit from the tender and solicitous Brendan.

Both now turned to her expectantly. She shut the door quietly behind her.

"Have you heard from Doctor Lang?" Somehow Mary Rose knew that something had happened.

"Yes." Katherine handed the piece of paper, folded tightly in her hand all this time, to Brendan. He looked at her inquiringly and, faced with her steady gaze, he read the note aloud.

Mary Rose permitted him to finish, but her eyes were already on Katherine's face. "I don't care what Doctor Lang advises. I want Nancy Halstrop. She's kind, and genteel and very experienced . . ."

"Mary Rose, what proof have you that . . ."

"You said you cared about me, that you'd stay with me and look after me!" There were genuine tears in the girl's eyes, tears of fright and helplessness. "Yet you try to force me to have that woman near me when I hate her! She frightens me! I don't like her, and I don't like you, for being so cruel, Katherine!" She turned to her husband, took both his hands, "Make her understand, Brendan," she pleaded. "It's *my* body, *my* baby! Make her do as I want! I want Mrs Halstrop!"

Brendan was no fool, and the look he threw Katherine told her that he was aware, as she was, of the danger of Mary Rose's whims. He turned back to his young wife—but Mary Rose's womb had begun to close on itself, pulling and straining the abdominal muscles, its function to expel the little guest within it, with no compunction about the pain that raced along the body's nerve ends, registering with gasping effect. Mary Rose doubled over with a muffled sob that both witnesses knew to be unfeigned, involuntary. "*Please, Brendan . . . !*"

Brendan turned to Katherine. "Send for Mrs Halstrop."

"Brendan, Angel is . . ."

"Do as he says!" Mary Rose raised a mottled, agonized face to the woman by the bed. "He's my husband—do as he says!"

Katherine left the room, shut the door behind her, and faced Angel Regnier, standing at a politic distance along the hall. Still, she must have heard at least some of the girl's outburst.

"I'm sorry, I couldn't . . ."

"I heard. Please, don't worry. I stopped in to check on Mr Murphy— as I said, there's little I can do just now. Come downstairs . . ."

Katherine followed Angel, and, as she helped her on with her cape, the black woman said, "I shall fetch Mrs Halstrop."

"You? But—no, you shouldn't have to . . ."

The dark eyes met Katherine's. "Ah, but I want to. Nancy Halstrop doesn't like me, but she respects me. I'll drive her here, and talk with her. If there are any complications—and there may not be— hopefully she'll tell you to send for me. If Mrs Kelehan has a difficult labour for two or three days she herself will raise no objection to my presence, I assure you."

The big, elegant woman climbed into her carriage and drove off, and so moved was Katherine that it was only after the sturdy sulky and the cobby carriage horse had disappeared down the drive that she realized she had not properly thanked Angel, nor said goodbye. The woman's strength amazed her; to be filled with empathy and compassion for a foolish girl, even when rejected cruelly, unjustly, for one's facial features and the colour of one's skin . . . Yet, for Mary Rose, Angel was setting out to fetch a woman she despised, who would undoubtedly crow over her in a smug, simpering way, all the distance from her bush-surrounded hut.

Katherine closed the front door, and winced as she realized, too late, that she had almost slammed it.

Mary Rose sent Brendan away, after he had fed her some broth that Peggy had brought up on a tray.

"I'll be in my office," he told Katherine, at Mary Rose's door, and she felt for him, white-faced, anxious, for he was helpless to do anything now but worry if his decision had been the correct one—and Katherine could say nothing to relieve his fears.

She was with Mary Rose when she heard the sound of the horse and sulky returning. She had been waiting for it, sitting by the bed, talking to Mary Rose, bathing her forehead, and fretting inwardly all the while. She left the room calmly enough, but almost ran down the stairs, finding Laura just opening the front door to Nancy Halstrop. Outside, she could see the straight-backed figure in the sulky, heading away once more down the drive. She had to consciously control her anger and frustration before she could turn to face Nancy Halstrop.

The face beneath the rather ostentatious bonnet looked flushed and triumphant, the narrowed eyes flickered all over the hall, resting avariciously on each piece of bric-a-brac, before settling on Katherine with a semblance of polite humour and an underlying current of malice. Katherine took her cloak and the horrendous hat, after the formality of greetings was observed, then, "Laura," she said gently, "would you take Mrs Halstrop to the bathroom—show her the soap and the nailbrush and a clean towel, please?"

"I know all about hygiene, Mrs Carron." The thin voice skated over her impatience and dislike. "Young Mrs Kelehan is in the best hands possible."

Katherine took in the food stains on the front of the fashionably-trimmed dress and though Nancy closed her hands quickly, she was not quick enough for Katherine to miss the black crescents beneath the fingernails. "I will hope for the best hands, Mrs Halstrop. I will insist on the cleanest."

"Katherine! Katherine . . . !" The voice, lost, despairing, pain-filled, had her turning and running back up the stairs and into the room where Mary Rose lay. "I can't bear it! I can't bear it!"

But there was no choice; there could be no going back, no escape. The door was shut after the aproned and freshly-scrubbed Nancy Halstrop entered, and the world contracted to three women, the pain, and the unseen, demanding presence of the child who was struggling to be born.

Katherine changed sheets, gave sips of water to Mary Rose, fed her a few mouthfuls of broth now and then, mopped perspiration from her face, opened the door to call for more linen, jugs of cool water, and, in between, held Mary Rose by the hand, learnt of Crystal Lake, Illinois, of Patrick and Bernadette O'Boyle, of how Mary Rose wanted to make her mother proud. She *would* be brave. She *would* . . .

Katherine let Nancy Halstrop rest, bathed Mary Rose, rubbed the narrow back, brushed the long, pale hair, and felt her own heart contract with each spasm that yet brought nothing, no sign of the child.

And Mary Rose was brave. That she sometimes screamed that she would be brave brought tears to Katherine's eyes, and she found herself screaming with her, "Yes, you are, yes, you are, my dear!" as the pains came closer and closer upon each other, faster, stronger, and Nancy Halstrop said, "Push!" at last. For time had ceased to have any meaning—and Mary Rose pushed—for hours, it seemed, bearing down to force this weight, this obstruction, this thing that tore at her, out, out, out . . .

"Who's that! What's that . . . ! What's that . . . !" Mary Rose gasped, for it was not over, but the child came forth bellowing, and Katherine, laughing, lifted the girl's shoulders a little so that Mary Rose saw the already squalling form of her son come forth from her body, ungrateful, protesting, smeared with blood and vernix, slender, strong, and perfect.

Mary Rose, crying and laughing by turns, seemed to forget the long hours of discomfort immediately. "My son . . . ! My son . . . !" she kept saying, telling Katherine over and over again, her face alight. When the baby, bathed and neatly dressed, wrapped in the lovingly-made shawls, was placed to the small breast, the afterbirth came away quickly, and the bleeding, "Thank God . . ." Nancy Halstrop was heard to mutter, was no greater than it should be. Sponged, padded, dressed in her prettiest nightgown, Mary Rose received the homage of her husband, and Katherine and Nancy Halstrop made their way downstairs, both almost tripping in their exhaustion. The labour had lasted forty-three hours. Katherine had been awake for fifty-eight.

She had no memory until she was roused from a chair in the parlour to say goodbye to Mrs Halstrop. It was dusk—or was it morning? Brendan was there, shaking the woman's hand at the door, and Edwina was there, and Laura, and Peggy and Carl.

Katherine felt a strange sort of bond with the midwife. She imagined prisoners—even those with little personal sympathy, must feel like this—when condemned and forced to share a last cell together. Yet they had brought the mother and the child through; please God they would now be safe . . . She took Nancy's hand in gratitude—and stopped.

Why hadn't she checked? Why? Mary Rose had been so demanding, there was little time . . .

"Katherine . . . ?" It was a slight warning tone in Brendan's voice. His hand came to her forearm.

For her own hand held Nancy Halstrop by the wrist, and she gazed from the clean white hand with its black-rimmed nails to the pinched face, the fearful eyes, the two patches of pink appearing on the cheeks.

Nancy said, "It's . . . it's dried blood, that's what it is. Dried blood does that."

She pulled loose from Katherine's grasp. Outside, one of the farmworkers waited in the buggy to drive her home.

Katherine whirled to face Laura. "Did you see her scrub her hands? *Did you?*"

"I . . . I showed her the bathroom, like you said . . ." Laura looked wretched, her face white. "I'm sorry, Katey . . ."

"It's dried blood, I tell you . . ."

"Dried blood is red, not black . . ." Her lips felt stiff, she felt dizzy, turned towards where she thought Nancy Halstrop should be, but the hand with which she lashed out connected at the woman's face only lightly, with the fingertips, enough to frighten but not to hurt. And Katherine wanted to hurt.

"You're too fussy, you are! You hadn't ought to tell me my job! I don't take orders from you—Mister Kelehan paid me, not you . . . !"

"Dried blood is red, not black . . . !" The woman shrank back in terror, and then she was gone, and there was only Brendan's face above her, Brendan's hands on her shoulders. There was a sensation of weakness, maddening, frightening, and Brendan's face was pale, concerned—he spoke her name, but he was speaking into the darkness.

Thirty One

K atherine slept for fourteen hours, waking on a Tuesday afternoon with a feeling of having dreamed the past three days or more. Her fears, before she had fainted into Brendan's arms in the hallway, seemed foolish to the point where she felt uneasily ashamed; Mary Rose was well after all, having slept almost as long as Katherine. And beside her bed, in the cradle that had rocked all the Prescott children ("except myself," Katherine thought with philosophical detachment), slept James Patrick Brendan Kelehan, named after both grandfathers and his proud papa.

Katherine thought, I am beginning to understand love. For with the pang that this wonderful child was not hers and Brendan's, was the knowledge that Brendan took great joy in him, and looked with gratitude and tenderness upon Mary Rose. The jealousy that had dripped poison into Katherine's veins all these months, that had driven her from the Valley, the jealousy that she had struggled against with all her logic and all her humanity, was easing at last. To see him happy, to know that his marriage might yet bring him comfort and joy as he grew older was a compensation of very real aspect. She wrote with truth to her mother at Dovewood that she felt hopeful the fair-haired son they had created might be the means by which Mary Rose and Brendan might find a strengthening bond between them.

Yet, for all that, it was difficult not to feel her own loss keenly as she saw the young mother cradling the loved child, and she thought of Christopher and grieved. She knew, much as she would miss Brendan, that the return of the family to America or Ireland would in some ways be a relief. In the meantime she kept busy, subjugated her own feelings of loss by caring for the unfortunate Amos who, three days after they had found him, still had not regained consciousness.

The house seemed full of people and very busy. The Cummings girls, in their fondant-coloured laces and muslins, wafted up the stairs to view the baby and offer little parcels wrapped prettily in tissue and ribbon to the glowing Mary Rose. Emilia Huckstable and her mother called, both, Mary Rose told Katherine afterwards, regaling her with advice on her son's upbringing and education.

Billy Murphy stayed with the stockmen and rouseabouts in the men's quarters, going each day to his own farm to tend the animals and returning in the evening to sit with his silent father, who showed no signs of waking. Sharing his vigil for much of the time were the other house guests: Sergeant Lloyd, accompanied this time by a young constable. Tom waited almost as anxiously as Billy for the man to wake, and had hopes that Amos could supply him with the identity of his assailant.

"Was he carrying any money on him?" Tom had asked Billy the night he arrived at Barrengarry.

"P . . . Pa never had much money—but he'd gone to Wollongong two days before, with the colt he'd bred from our mare, Bracken— I think he must have been jumped on the way back, 'cause his own horse came home, but the colt didn't."

Billy had found Amos's horse, saddled, reins dragging, waiting patiently at the Murphy farm gates the day before. There was no money in the saddle bags, nor any money in Amos Murphy's wallet, found in the pocket of his blood-spattered jacket.

The neighbours who came to visit the mother and baby stayed to question and be questioned about Amos Murphy, but no one, not the Cummings nor Murchisons nor Huckstables had seen nor heard of Amos's movements that day. Increasingly disgruntled, Tom and the young constable, Jemmy Crowe, took turns, one to stay by the sick man's bed, the other to ride out, carrying the investigation further afield.

The influenza kept many families from calling on Mary Rose, as Carl had not been the only one to catch the stubborn strain, and any family with a relative affected naturally kept clear of the new-born child.

Laura and Edwina, after the first tender and joyous fondling of the baby, had then to forgo any further contact with him or his mother, as, four days after the birth, Myeela came to the homestead, scratching with her fingernails on the glass and, when Laura looked up from her book, beckoned to her. Four of the small ones were ill—the tribe had been south, near Lake Wollumboolla, but had brought the children back to the Valley. Now some of the adults were ill also, but not as bad as the children. Would the misses come?

Katherine was unable to go, having Amos and Mary Rose to care for, and worried about the girls and the mysterious illness. She prayed it was not the diphtheria, but that night when the girls came home, bathed, and changed their clothes to seat themselves, exhausted, at the dinner table, they were able to tell Katherine that it seemed to be the same influenza that was affecting the white community. In Burrawang, an elderly aunt of Stephen Brody's had died of it only a week before.

The news of the Woddi Woddi being affected sobered all of them at the dinner table; there were few enough of the tribe in the Valley now; when Josiah Prescott had first come here to settle, there had been groups of a hundred and eighty or two hundred people camped on the banks of the Barrengarry Creek. The white man's diseases, unknown to them, were enemies against which there was no protection, no real means of battle.

That night, in Amos Murphy's room, Tom Lloyd sat with Katherine, and he asked her about her family's history in the district. She found him easy to talk to, had always liked the man, and they found themselves, as the hours wore on, exchanging their family backgrounds in hushed voices, while the pale form of Amos slept on, frighteningly still.

Tom told her of his family coming to Moss Vale from the Canterbury district outside Sydney; of his younger brothers and sisters, and his parents, who had fifty acres of orchard near the township. "Of course, living so close to Moss Vale, I see a lot of Miss Barton these days," Tom said with a smile, and Katherine did not know how the conversation had led to this point, except that their various stories had turned, at last, to the present—and Fleur Barton seemed to be a definite part of Tom Lloyd's present.

Katherine said carefully, "I believe she has her own establishment, now, in Moss Vale. Is her mama with her?"

"Oh, no. Didn't you know? I felt sure she would have written to you. Her mother passed away some months ago—I reckon she simply fretted away over Mr Barton—you know how it is with some couples who've been married for many years. My grandparents were the same—my grandmother died, and my grandfather survived her by only two months . . ."

"Was Fleur with her at the time?"

"No, she'd made so many friends in Moss Vale, she said, that she couldn't bear to return to Campbelltown. She wrote to her mother, begging her to come and live with her, but the old lady wanted to stay in the same house she'd always had, with all her familiar things around her . . ." The frank, open face looked puzzled. "It's so strange that Fleur didn't write to tell you. She speaks so highly of you—of all your family. She's always asking me about you— asks all her friends for news . . ."

Katherine felt an icy wave of anger sweep over her. So Fleur

was still prying, still spinning her little webs of intrigue, even in
Moss Vale. And she had stayed there, rather than go home to be
with her mother, who would not, Katherine knew, have suffered
her loneliness in silence. Had Fleur ever issued even one invitation
for her talkative little mother to join her? Katherine wondered. And
finally, in her aloneness, the foolish, harmless little woman had died.
Katherine turned away a little, so that Tom might not see the look
of disapproval that must surely be written on her face—her eyes
slid over Amos Murphy's face—and returned. The deep-set blue eyes
were gazing at her; the mind behind them was conscious at last.

"Mr Murphy . . . ?" Katherine leaned forward.

Tom Lloyd had almost forgotten the man and started a little, then
groped for the bedside table where his notebook and pencil lay.

"Mr Murphy, I'm Sergeant Lloyd—do you remember me?—Mr
Murphy?"

The gaze was dull, the face immobile, but first the eyes, then
the head moved slightly towards the sound of the policeman's voice.
There was a faint sound, which might, or might not, be an attempt
at speech.

"Mr Murphy, can you remember who hurt you? Someone beat
you up pretty bad—you'll be all right, you're at Barrengarry—but
we must know who did this to you. Can you hear me? Do you
understand?"

The eyes remained fixed glazedly on Tom Lloyd's face. The
policeman glanced over at Katherine, puzzled, worried.

Billy Murphy was sent for, and the young boy sat by the bed and
gently tried to draw forth some response from his father. Feeling
alone, unguided, apprehensive, Billy gave way to a few embarrassed
tears when Amos closed his eyes once more and seemed to sleep,
without showing any sign of recognizing his son.

Brendan had joined them in the sickroom, and now placed a hand
on Billy's shoulder. "It may take time," he said. And Billy looked
up at him gratefully.

"He's a hard man, Mr Kelehan, an' rough. But he is my
Pa, an' . . . an' . . ."

Katherine held the door open, reached out a hand towards the
boy. "Come downstairs and have some supper, Billy."

In the kitchen they found Will O'Mahony, who had been sent
to Berry to contact Molly Murphy and tell her of her father's accident.
Will stood, seeing Katherine and Billy enter the room, dusting crumbs

from his mouth and hands; he, too, was having a late supper, and appeared, from his fatigued young face and the faint line around his brow where his hat had rubbed a mark from dust and sweat, to have only just now stepped from the saddle into Peggy's warm and accommodating kitchen.

And this was true. "I got a letter here, Missus—from the girl's aunt." It seemed as if he would say more, but hesitated, and merely pushed the letter into Katherine's hands. She told him to continue eating and, as Will and Billy both began to eat reheated lamb stew, tore open the crumpled envelope and began to read the laborious, ill-written letter.

Dear Mrs Carron,

It is with much regret I got to tell you that Margaret Murphy that they call Molly ant with us no longer. She has gon to try her luck in Sydeny. We gave her a good home and yet this was not good enaugh for her. I dont suppose she told her father either what she has gon and done. She sez she has gon to look for work in the clothing trade. We told her these was bad enaugh times for imployment, but she woud not listan. Tell her father we done right by her. Wich is more than she done by us. A girl with her moral caracture will not ammount to much anywheres and is sure to come to greif but tell her father and my dear friend Mrs Halstrop we done our best.

I remain,

Your obedient freind,

Mrs Alfred Dinsmore Bewley

Katherine, mindful of the presence of the thirteen-year-old Billy, did not read the letter aloud. Instead, she told him only that his sister had gone to Sydney to seek employment. Even this was enough to worry Billy, who was not so ingenuous that he was unaware of the dangers in a young girl being alone and unprotected in the city.

"What'll we do?" His eyes startled, his round, Irish face suddenly pale beneath its covering of freckles. "Molly don't know nuffink about the city! Pa'll kill her if he finds out! Maybe I could go . . ."

The adults rounded on him firmly. He was needed here to help tend the family farm in his father's absence—and his father, too, would recover much sooner if he saw a familiar, loved face near him when he woke.

They convinced him there was little he could do, and Katherine, seeing his crestfallen young face, found herself declaring that she would see if she could trace Molly's whereabouts—Mr Prescott had many contacts in the world of industry. She would write letters and when she was next in Sydney . . .

The idea began to emerge even as she spoke. Her father's last letter had said that he would soon be returning home—that had been written some two months previously, so he might be arriving back in Sydney any day . . .

I am escaping again.

Billy went off to his bed in the men's quarters; he had already made friends among the young rouseabouts, who were—some of them—only a year or two older than himself. Katherine waited until he had gone before turning to Will O'Mahony.

"Do you know anything more of Molly other than what's in the letter, Will?"

"Em . . . I dunno what she wrote, Missus." Will's broad brow clouded with uncertainty. "I'd spent a couple of days looking for their farm, and she seemed to feel sorry for me—gave me a good meal, and talked a lot, both before writing the letter and afterwards, 'til I could get away from her. She's a fierce good woman, Missus. I mean, she was so godly she was rigid with the extent of it, Ma'am, if you're knowing what I mean."

He glanced over towards the back door, out of which Billy had vanished, over at the silent Peggy on the other side of the table, and Carl, dozing by the chimney corner with his gnarled brown hands linked on his stomach. Lowering his voice, he said, "She starts off polite enough about the girl, and says only that she cried a lot, during the time she was with them, but did her work well enough . . . but the more she talked, telling me all the time that she could see I was a good Catholic boy and wouldn't be led easily into the way of sin meself . . . Well, Ma'am, me mammy and daddy might have other ideas on that, but Mrs Bewley seemed fierce determined that I was as holy as she was, and that was considerable indeed.

"And 'twas then she began telling me of the girl being forward and bold—and I thought she meant impudent, you know, Ma'am— but that wasn't it at all—and finally, thinking me a rare innocent, she tells me that the girl was trying to lead her Daniel into sin, and that she was a sly, lying hussy and hadn't she—Mrs Bewley, I mean—found the two of them together in the barn when the girl was supposed to be milking the cows?

"And . . . and the few times I've ever seen the Murphy girl, Missus, 'twas at Mass here in the Valley, at Cambewarra, the Brody's place, when Father Farrell came through—and a more quiet little thing I've never seen. And I was thinking this, Missus—and if you'll forgive me—" He glanced once more between Katherine and the rapt Peggy,

"I was thinking, too, that finding two people alone might not mean it was the girl making the suggestions, necessarily, begging your pardon.

"And it was then—being the meal time—that all the other Bewleys came in from the fields, but Mrs Bewley introduced them and kept right on talking, and I saw Daniel's face—Arra, Missus, a more sly, close-eyed, slithery sort of a lad you've never seen—and blushed like a girl he did when he saw where the conversation was headed, and for all his mother throwing him 'Didn't she, Daniel?'s and 'Wasn't she, Daniel?'s, he'd duck his head and croak a bit and divil else he'd say.

"So, on leaving, I took meself down to the meadow where he'd been working, and I waited and called him aside when he came down from dinner and threatened to bring the girl's father and all her uncles—sure, I don't know if she has any, but I painted 'em big and mean and thirsty for the truth of it—and got it out of him, Ma'am, that he'd always liked young Molly and 'twas his idea to become more than friendly in the barn—though he swore he didn't lie to his mam, but let her think what she would. So I boxed his ears and put my fist into his eye lightly, Ma'am, on behalf of young Catholic girls like Molly who oughtn't to have their names besmirched, and came away home with the letter as his mam had bid me.

"Oh—I have one more thing to add. Being suddenly taken with the idea of helping me, he'd told me he'd seen Molly studying an advertisement that was in a Sydney newspaper—for workers in a clothing factory—and he remembered the name. Nettlefield's, it was. I remember it, because that was my last sight of young Daniel, Ma'am, sitting in a goodly patch of the stuff."

Katherine woke sometime before dawn, her heart still pounding, realizing that her old nightmare had claimed her once more. The chilling cold, the dark, the fear and the longing to escape . . .

The night was warm, but she shivered with the memory, rubbed her upper arms as if to stir her frozen blood.

It was no use pretending to herself. She was growing more and more tense and unhappy. She had been too close for too long to Brendan and all his affairs—if he was going to leave, she must begin to distance herself. And besides, though she had decided to protect her mother and not tell her of her knowledge of her own birth, she had no such hesitation about telling her father. There were too many questions unanswered, and Marcus held the key.

In the morning she went about her duties, beginning with the filling of all the lamps in the house, the replacement of burnt-down candles in the bedrooms and dining room; and she sat for an hour or so with Amos Murphy. He smiled at her, seemed to listen when she read the newspaper to him. As she was leaving he murmured something, and when she bent over the bed to hear, she was sure the words he repeated were "Thank you." She smiled, and patted his hand before going off to the kitchen to tell Peggy of what she felt sure was progress in the man's condition.

Mary Rose was the first person she told that she had decided to leave for a short visit to Sydney, and the girl seemed genuinely disappointed. "You won't be long, will you? Not months and months like you were at Christmas time?"

"No," she promised, "I won't be long away. But my father is due home soon—he may be back already, and I must see him about some business affairs."

Mary Rose's fair head turned towards the window, and her voice was as wistful as the view of green hills, hung with cobweb traces of low cloud. "We'll be leaving ourselves in only a month or so," she said.

Katherine was surprised, as much by the tone of regret as by the words themselves. "We'll miss you," she said, and despite her pain each time she saw Brendan, she knew, at last, that it was the truth. She had seen Mary Rose blossom painfully into an adult, had seen the selfish child become a woman, not due to pregnancy and parturition alone, but from confronting the difficulties, the stumbling blocks, the shaming refusals of a stubborn community that represented faithfully, sometimes disagreeably, a world that would not bend to her whims. She had come to trust Brendan and saw him as her friend and her refuge, and her baby's dependence, coming as it did on the heels of her own stumbling discoveries of her own weaknesses and strengths, seemed to give her an added security, an anchor in time and place.

The lovely face which had regained its healthy cream and roses tints, the eyes which in her new fulfilment had lost none of the child's sparkle in the blue depths, glanced once at Katherine before returning to the landscape outside. "I never believed I'd get used to this place," she murmured with quiet gravity. "I was so very unhappy at the beginning . . . but when we leave," and her eyes came directly to Katherine's face and remained there, "there's so much I'll miss; Edwina and Laura and Peggy and Carl—and I shall miss you. I couldn't have come through James's birth if it hadn't been for you . . ."

"Of course you would, Mary Rose. I merely held your hand . . ."

"Yes," the girl agreed quite readily, "and I don't think you'll ever know how much difference it made, particularly your words to me, earlier, when the pains had just begun—'mothers are the strongest people in the world'. I know that now; I've had time to think, lying here all these days, of my own mother, the sacrifices she made for me—and other women I've known, other mothers. Having James, I understand so much more than I did before." She seemed to hesitate for a moment, then, "I understand you a lot more now, too. What losing your Christopher must have done to you. And . . . despite everything, how you've managed to carry on, to survive. I think you're the strongest person I've ever known, Katherine. I wish I had your strength, but I don't."

She smiled, seeing the first warning of impatience in Katherine's gaze. "But I'm finding my strength," she added quickly. "In the meantime I'm glad, so glad to have known you. I'm glad you're my friend."

Katherine, moved between fondness and her knowledge of her own uncharitable and envious thoughts, could say nothing to this, but took the girl's hand and gave it some understanding pressure.

Mary Rose smiled brightly, "Do you know—it's foolish, perhaps— but I've been thinking . . ." she stopped.

"Yes?" Katherine prompted.

Again there was a hesitation. "Well . . . No," she sighed ruefully, "I shouldn't have said anything. I will tell you," she added, "but later. I have to do more of my thinking first. Do you mind?" She looked rather anxiously up at Katherine.

"No, dear, of course I don't mind." She had a small suspicion, however, that Mary Rose had been about to say that she would like to stay in the Valley a little longer. But she was learning self-restraint; it was a question that must, obviously, be discussed first with Brendan.

Katherine drove that afternoon to visit Angel Regnier, and told her, as she had each day since the birth, of the progress of Mary Rose and baby James.

"It seems that she'll be fine," Angel smiled. "I know the worry that you must have had over Nancy Halstrop and her slovenly ways— dirty hands—even dirty fingernails—have killed more mothers with puerperal fever than we'll ever know about. But Peggy was told how to sterilize the towels and sheets . . . ?"

"Yes—I showed her myself—we placed them so close to the kitchen fire that many of them scorched . . ."

"Scorching is a small price to pay—I don't know what it is, but I've found that heat is the best method for killing any chance of infection. If Mrs Kelehan can survive the actual birthing without any infection from that Sairey Gamp of an excuse for a midwife, then she'll come to no harm in Peggy's hands. Has Doctor Lang called yet?"

"No, but everyone who calls has some tale to tell of how badly the diphtheria is affecting Moss Vale and Bowral. I sent a message to Doctor Lang, the day after the birth, for I knew he'd want to know that mother and baby were recovering well, but with the situation as it is for him there, I can't see how he could dare to leave—and if he did, he'd risk bringing the diphtheria to Mary Rose and the baby."

Angel nodded, seated in the large leather armchair in her comfortable, book-lined parlour, as majestic as a queen. Katherine continued, "I worry about Amos, however. Would you come to see him? He's awake a great deal of the time now, but he's so lethargic, and doesn't seem to recognize anyone. He's barely spoken a word, and Tom Lloyd is becoming frantic—he's sure that if Amos could only speak, we'd have the name of the killer."

Angel drove back to Barrengarry with Katherine, but there was little she could do for Amos. Cool poultices, rest, nourishing broth, she suggested, and gradually, she felt, when he was ready, he would speak. She offered to come every day to help Peggy nurse the man, and Peggy, who, now that baby James had made his entrance into the world and was soft and pink and, for the most part, clean and sweet-smelling, was quite happy to devote her time to the care of Mary Rose and her son.

The Woddi children seemed to be recovering from the influenza, though it was a pity, Laura said, that they would not have Angel Regnier to the camp. It began with the Woddi menfolk, she believed, their awe and suspicion of a woman who was as tall as any of them, and almost as strong. Whose skin was as black as theirs, and who had yet adopted all the white man's ways. Perhaps they feared her influence upon their own womenfolk, for at the mention of Angel's name, Myeela, Tigoora and the other women would look away, shake their heads and say, "That one—she have no Dreaming. Bring bad things."

Katherine, herself a little in awe of Angel Regnier, never presumed to ask her if the Aborigines' suspicions hurt her, for she sensed that if she could help them, Angel would—it was not in her to allow any suffering to go unaided. But it seemed an infringement to ask her feelings on the matter, and Katherine could only guess, from the fact that Angel never mentioned the black people, but would look after them sometimes, in a gentle sorrow, that their evasive resentment hurt the woman, and hurt her deeply.

Katherine was tired, she slept so little of late, her mind still revolving with events of the day, worry for those under her roof, and worry, too, for her mother, leading a half-life at Dovewood, refusing to come to Barrengarry, even to be with her beloved daughters. For Mary Rose's new-found fulfilment and the friendship the girl offered, Katherine was grateful; but it only made her feelings for Brendan more of a torture. They spoke at mealtimes, when the business of the property necessitated it, and for the rest they avoided each other; only when alone did the silent torment that each was suffering make them come to themselves, having been gazing into each other's face with a glance that contained all their frustrated longing, their bafflement and heartbreak and the love that had not died no matter what their logic and their faiths demanded of them.

Five days after Mary Rose gave birth to her son, Katherine, without informing Brendan, who had left the homestead early, had Will O'Mahony drive her to Moss Vale and, the following day, on to the train at Picton.

She looked back once as they topped the escarpment. There was mist clinging, still, about the treetops; it swirled like gossamer across the void and only once, as the buggy headed off along the crest, through the trees, did the mists clear, enabling just one brief view of the patchwork fields and winding river below. It was her last glance at Kangaroo Valley, as she had known it, and it would never be the same again.

Thirty Two

The dour face beneath the starched white cap broke into a smile. "Welcome home, Miss Katherine! Did you get your father's telegram already? He sent it off this morning . . ."

"No, Libby—I was on the train myself, coming here. You mean, my father's home?" She swept into the hall, looking up the stairs, into the parlour and turning excitedly back to Libby.

"Why, no, Miss—not at the minute. He said he'd be back for dinner . . ."

"He *is* home! Libby, you silly old goose, I meant home from the Orient!" Katherine strode into the parlour, Libby following.

"Oh, that he is, Miss." Her voice was disgruntled. "And you can tell by all these artifacts and the ungodly, heathen smell of the place!"

And so Katherine could. Sandalwood and incense were in the air, and there were three screens of black lacquered timber with embroidered silk panels, four large chests, heavily carved and with brass locks and hinges gleaming, all crowding the parlour.

"Haven't unpacked the half of it—his study is filled with more crates—he told me and Tobias not to put nothing nowheres until he's told us, and he arrived back yesterday morning and hasn't been home more'n to change his clothes. How's the missus, is she well?"

This last was spoken with tender compunction, close on the heels of the other thoughts, as if ready to push all aside. The large, rawboned face, with the jaw and cheekbones so sharply delineated that they seemed to have been sculptured roughly and draped with one layer of skin, was nevertheless alight with worried intensity.

"Yes, my mother is with my grandparents at Dovewood. It's the best place for her at the moment, Libby. She's eating well once more, and being spoilt and cosseted by her own adoring mama and papa—and wandering in the gardens, and playing the piano, and she's taken up her sketching again, and has even brought the harp down from the attic—and she hasn't played that, they tell me, since she was a girl."

She was laughing, and the faithful Libby laughed too until the moisture in her eyes proved too much and then the fine line of emotion, as yet unseen in the woman by Katherine, was crossed, and she held her apron to her nose and excused herself, going off to put on tea and declaring, all along the hall, that she was so happy, so very happy . . .

Katherine gazed after her, glad within herself that she could place the worries at rest within that staunchly loyal, briskly starched breast.

Katherine sighed, seated herself on a chair, listening to the traffic rolling up the street, the grating rumble of the city sounds, distant voices, metal wheels on cobblestones.

It had been wonderful, finding her mother healing within the loving surrounds of Dovewood, the smile on the beautiful face sad with her sense of loss, but a smile, nevertheless. When Katherine had left her that morning, Suzanna's last words had been, "Don't worry for me. Oddly enough, I'm content. I've lived all my life for my children and two men, Katherine—Marcus, then Robin. I'm suddenly realizing that there's no man who needs me. It's a frightening and . . . and a kind of *liberating* thought. For I'm not lonely. What Robin gave me will be with me always, and this is more than many women know in a lifetime. As for the rest, I have Mama and Papa and my girls; I'm surrounded with love."

Sighing again contentedly, warmed by the memory, Katherine looked around the beloved parlour, and her gaze came to rest on the portrait above the fireplace, her father, her mother, herself and Joe, and the little black and tan terrier, Charmian . . .

Katherine, on the low stool, leaning her head towards Suzanna—a likeness there, for the artist, at least. Joe looked a serious, wise baby, characteristics that owed more to the artist's ideal than to Joe, for Katherine remembered her mother saying that he had laughed and gurgled and bounced about upon her lap, and it had been very difficult to keep him still. Marcus . . .

Marcus stood behind Suzanna's chair, a little aloof, in a dark suit, gazing towards the artist with a look of severity. One would think, if one were a stranger, that he was not a happy man . . .

She stared at the painting for a long and unquiet moment, then abruptly rose and went in search of the housekeeper.

"Libby? Did Father leave the house wearing his business suit, or his best dark suit?"

Libby thought, placing biscuits on a doily-covered plate, paused to consider. "His best black, Miss Katherine. I presumed it was somewhere important, but then he often wears it out some days . . . Miss Katherine, where are you going?"

Katherine called back along the hall for Libby to fetch Tobias and to share the tea and biscuits. She, too, would be back in time for dinner . . .

The sexton knew the grave, knew Marcus also, he informed her, limping ahead of her through the park-like grounds, past the neat crosses, plain rectangular stones, ornate vases, urns and winged angels that guarded Sydney's dead. "Been coming here for years—every week, regular as clockwork when he's in the city. Goes off to the country though, don't he? But when he comes back, there he'll be, carrying his flowers, same as always. Now—over there, Miss—see 'im, near the poplars there . . . I'll leave you then, Miss . . ."

But he waited and, her eyes on her father's sloped shoulders, it took her a second or two to realize the sexton was still hovering hopefully.

"God bless you, Miss," his dirt-ingrained, gnarled little hand closed around the coin she gave him, and he turned and made his way back to his cottage.

Sydney weather was warmer than the Highlands and the leaves of the poplar trees, though turned, most of them, to bright sunny yellow, were still thick upon the trees and fell only occasionally, spinning down, caught in a zephyr breeze, to whirl about Marcus where he stood, his hat in his hand, above a white marble slab that read: *Katherine Ann Gordon.*

She did not want to approach too closely in case she startled him in her black travelling suit and the hat with its heavy veil.

She felt awkward, changed the bouquet of white chrysanthemums from hand to hand. Part of her mind admitted unwillingly, *I shouldn't be here at all. I am intruding.*

For he stood staring at the headstone and the green turf that it marked, at the sturdy vase in which his offering, a half dozen pink roses, stood, just before the inscription. From where she stood Katherine could not read it, doubted that her father even saw it, his communion with the lost spirit seemed to have taken him many miles from Rookwood.

"Father?"

The shoulders stiffened, the head came up.

"Father?"

He turned slowly to face her. When they were looking directly at each other, she saw that he did not look shocked, nor displeased.

"Katherine?" quietly enough. "How strange to find you here. I . . . I was visiting the grave of your aunt. I was on my way to pay my respects to a business associate . . ." There must have been something written there on her face, for he stopped, then began again on a different tack, gesturing to the neat little grave before him. "I don't know if you've ever visited the Gordons' family plot . . . all their children—your aunts and uncles, had they lived . . ."

"And Katherine." She moved forward. She had nearly said *and my mother*, but had changed the words at the last moment, for it would have been too brutal.

She stood beside her father, and now she could read the inscription.

Katherine Ann Gordon
who departed this life 14th July 1837
Beloved daughter of
Edwin and Angela Gordon

She stood gazing at the inscription for a long moment, while the scent of the full-blown roses filled the air, and the small yellow leaves fell silently around them, to litter the grass like gold coins.

Marcus's voice was heavy, "Why are you here, Katey?"

She could not look at him. "I know. About you—and . . . and Katherine . . ."

"Your mother told you." Sharply.

"No! No, Father. It happened while you were overseas. Fleur Barton told me."

"Fleur . . . !" it was a harsh whisper of disbelief.

"She found Mama's letter to Grandmama—the one in which she notified them that you had found me . . ." Katherine gulped, finding the by-now strange taste of tears in her throat.

Her father had stepped to her, she felt the rough wool of his jacket against her face as she was held to him gently, heard the rumble of the voice in the broad chest, "The poisonous little witch— *why*? In God's name what could she have hoped to gain?"

"It was all caused by jealousy, I think. Over Brendan, initially, and then—seeing Dovewood and Barrengarry . . . the sort of childhood I had, the love, the acceptance . . . and the material comforts. Fleur had none of these."

"No excuse," Marcus Prescott stated. "Suzanna's grandparents, my grandparents—they started with nothing and worked their way to riches—while still retaining their integrity. My God—did she tell your mother? Did you?" He held her at arms' length, the hazel eyes searched her face.

"No, Papa. How could I? She'll never know. She's been through enough."

Marcus's face was grave, intent. "I've had no contact with her—

I haven't asked Libby—the woman knows too much of this family's business already. How is is your mother?"

"She's well," Katherine said, and a spark glimmered within her as she gazed into her father's haunted face. Truly, he looked more ill, more unhappy than Suzanna. He still cared, she thought, and hugged this small hope to herself.

"The girls' letters spoke of her being at Balmain with you, for some time." He stopped, waited.

"No," she said gently, "Mama was at Springwood, in the mountains. I stayed with her. She nursed Robin until the end. He died early in January."

It was difficult to watch the warring responses that possessed her father; he turned away, walked from her, kept his face averted. Katherine waited, understanding his need to cope alone, to grasp the sudden change in fortune, to stifle the unworthy thoughts that, to any man with all at stake that Marcus had, must rise with that knowledge of a hatred rival thus removed.

He said, emotion thick in his voice, "I knew he was ill . . . I didn't truly realize—*January*! Such a short time! So young . . . and I . . . my God, the hatred I've nursed . . . the injuries I've counted and gloated over all these months—right up to now! Even last night, lying in our bed . . ." his feelings were so strong they choked in his throat; he lowered his head, his strong masculine figure so dejected, so lost, that Katherine moved towards him.

"Mama is at Dovewood, Father. I . . . I know you have your grievances and perhaps you will never be friends again because of all that has happened—but you will, for Laura and Edwina's sake, you will try to forgive each other, won't you? And find some semblance of courtesy between you . . ."

"Courtesy . . . Is that all there is to be left for us?" Marcus turned to her, regarded her morosely. "I've had nearly five months alone, Katey. Five months in crowded cities or crowded ships, surrounded by strangers. I've had no one to commune with but myself and my thoughts—and with the long nights, I've found myself confronting the past. I can't blame your mother—and I'm glad you call her that, glad too, that you've had the kindness and the good manners to keep your knowledge of the truth from her. I can't blame her, Katey, for what happened, for turning from me. I did blame young Mitchell. I hated him, saw him in the repository for all my grievances and bitterness—and now he's gone—twenty-nine years old, dear God! Undeserving of that! Undeserving of all I'd thought against him. And I'm lost, Katey. I've no one to fix my resentment against but myself . . . yes, where in truth it belongs. I see years of neglect and ill-treatment of your mother, leading to the day she finally lost her love for me. And she did love me, more than I knew—more than I deserved."

Katherine was appalled, her heart aching so within her that she could not move, could not speak.

"And . . . coming here. Every week, when we've been in Sydney. For nearly thirty years I've kept it from you children, but Suzanna knew. It must have hurt her deeply. But . . ." his eyes on the grave, "I never thought of it from her point of view. I was so young when we married, my only thought was to find you. Suzanna . . ." He looked up at Katherine as if in wonderment at his own selfishness. "I married Suzanna because she loved me. Because she was a good and gentle girl, because she was Katherine's sister, and as close to Katherine as I was ever to be again. And because . . . because I wanted to find you, our child—and you would need a mother."

"Oh, Father . . ." The reproach came heavily, without volition, from her throat.

"And it seemed so right at the time. Joe came, and the girls— and Suzanna was busy—but she wasn't Katherine. Katherine haunted me all those years. I kept blaming myself for what happened, thinking of the things I could have done to stop . . ."

"Nothing could have stopped her," Katherine broke in sharply. "I don't believe anything could have stopped her doing what she pleased, Father. She chose her own ways, she was honest to herself— but she was strong-willed and nothing could have saved her from the life she chose."

Marcus's gaze was wondering, he shook his head as he stared at his daughter. "Yes. I know, I suppose, that that's the truth. She could have called for us at any time—but she never did—she never wanted to come home. But . . ." his eyes narrowed, "how do you know all this? Who were you talking to?"

"Grandmama."

"Angela," softly. "Of course. Yes. A strong and wise woman. She adored Katherine, but she saw her clearly. And you," his eyes reflective, "you understand her in the part of yourself that *is* her. No, don't deny it, Katey. We all see Katherine in you— the wilfulness, the determination on independence, the way you guard your most precious thoughts. Do you see why it almost killed me that you ran off so secretively to marry Oliver? You looked at me, afterwards, with just that same cold defiance that your mother used when I last saw her." And this time, Katherine knew he meant that first, tragic Katherine, when he inadvertently said "your mother".

They sat on a low stone wall, near a wooden-latticed pergola used for services when the weather was bad. The sun shone brightly but the wind, faintly chill with the first hint of the winter that was to come, blew the leaves from the poplars down like showers about them.

"The family that Katherine left you with was called Newman— a struggling farmer and his wife and four young sons. The reason we couldn't find them—firstly Edwin, Angela and I, then Suzanna and myself after we married and came searching for you—was that Newman himself had died when a horse he was breaking had fallen on him, and his wife and children had to sell the farm and move to the city. They tried to find Katherine, but no letters were answered. By then she'd been abandoned by the . . . rogue . . . she had taken up with, and had no money to send for your board and keep.

"We were so determined, Suzanna and I, we placed bigger advertisements in the newspapers than Edwin and Angela had, and we doubled the money offered for information. Still, we were on the point of giving up, when Mrs Newman finally contacted us from where she was living in Fitzroy. She had remarried and was doing fairly well—she didn't want any money, simply to set matters straight. She'd left you in an orphanage, twenty miles from the farm—they, in turn, had placed you with a family who were farming in the foothills of the Dandenong Ranges. The mother of this family had died six months later, and the father brought his widowed sister to care for himself and his family.

"The man was a drunkard—what humanity he might have had was gone long before. We finally traced you to the house. It was in a state of indescribable squalor. Suzanna and I went through the rooms, I was pushing the man and woman out of our way bodily, as they screeched and harangued us. They'd admitted they had you, but tried to bargain for you, at least the woman did—I've never forgotten—the man is a shadowy blur in my memory, but the woman . . . a narrow face and greasy pale, pale hair like an albino ferret—and pale bloodless hands that she kept kneading together, as she talked of letting us have you for two hundred pounds . . .

"There were children everywhere, naked or half-naked, filthy, pathetic little creatures, with stick-like limbs and swollen bodies—

dark-haired boys, fair-haired girls, dark-haired girls . . . The rooms were rat-infested, overflowing buckets of excreta lay in corners. Cockroaches crawled ahead of us as we walked.

"We couldn't find you. Suzanna was weeping, holding on to my arm and weeping—she was seventeen years old, I remember. And I—I was as rash a nineteen-year-old as you could find, and I wanted my daughter. I whirled on the man, who until then had been presuming on our youth and our gullibility to shower filthy and insulting threats at us, and I attacked him. The woman finally screamed for me to let him go, to stop hurting him and she'd show me the child. I hadn't realized what I was doing, had no idea that Suzanna, too, was begging me to stop. I had been holding the man by the hair, bashing his skull against the door lintel. There was blood down his face, all over my hands . . .

"He was still alive, and we left him there and followed the woman to the kitchen. We'd checked there already, but behind a door that couldn't be seen for a drying rack, on which soiled clothes were strung, were steps leading down into a kind of cellar. The woman lit a candle, and we followed her down the steps.

"It wasn't a true cellar, one that's excavated under a house. Rather it was a kind of lean-to affair, built much lower than the rest of the house, as the land sloped down sharply at the rear.

"There seemed to be a thousand empty grog bottles stacked against the walls and rolling about the floor. Suzanna stumbled, and we heard rats go scampering away into the darkness. Other than the bottles, there were only three things in the room, a low, rotting bed and mattress, reeking of stale urine, a child, and a dog.

"You wore a dress that must have belonged to one of the older children, the sleeves rolled up. The dog was curled up asleep, and your tiny arm was wrapped about it, your head resting against its body.

"Even there, in that hideous squalor, your hair barely discernible as the red which we knew it to be, you looked an angel. In the candlelight, we stood looking at you, as the tears rolled down our faces. You were eighteen months old, and so weak you could not have stood—but they had you attached to the bed by a rope around your waist—so you wouldn't fall off, I suppose, and the baby napkin that you wore would not have been changed for a week . . .

"We took the clothes from you, and we wrapped you in Suzanna's shawl. She carried you—for you were her child from the moment she saw you—and I . . . I carried the dog, for you looked for it and cried for it, but I would have brought it anyway, for I know

you would have died without the wretched creature—it would have
kept the rats from you, and it kept you warm."

"Charmian . . ." she said, and so moved was she, so eerie was
it to find that the little terrier had been so intrinsic a part of her
life that her skin prickled, her eyes welled dangerously with tears.

"Yes," Marcus said readily. "Although you'd never know from
the painting the state the little animal was in when we found her.
We carried both of you out of the house, and I flung twenty guineas
at the woman, with threats of bringing the police to her. Still she
screamed abuse as we drove away, that we stole her child and stole
her dog—she seemed as much grieved over one as over the other.
Of course, we reported the family to the authorities. We could do
nothing else—the other children were treated little better than you
yourself."

"Charmian . . ." Katherine repeated, trying to recall the little
dog clearly, but it was hard—one day she had simply not been there,
and Katherine had fretted for a long time . . . "What happened
to Charmian?"

"I think she was already quite an old dog when we found her.
Perhaps she had been with the family when the mother had been
alive, for she had a gentle nature."

"She slept on my bed . . ."

"Yes, washed and perfumed and brushed. We couldn't part the
two of you. One day, when you were five, Suzanna came into your
room and found Charmian curled up on the coverlet beside you.
She had died in her sleep. Just like her namesake, Cleopatra's
handmaiden, who chose to face death with her mistress rather than
be parted from her. She never deserted her charge, even to the end.
We were glad she was included in the portrait—Suzanna and I always
believed that we owe your life to that little dog."

The wind, stronger now, rustled through the graveyard, and
Katherine shivered, it brought her dream to her. The dark, the cold,
the feeling of restraint, of being helpless and unable to move, and
reaching, crying for something, someone warm . . . the faithful
Charmian.

Katherine still held her own bouquet of chrysanthemums. When
she and her father stood, she walked with him to Katherine's grave
and kneeling down, arranged her own white flowers amongst the
fragrance of her father's roses.

She stood then, gazing down at the final resting place of the girl
who had borne her. *Mother?* she asked the question for the first time,
Did you love me? Did you want me?

There were no answers. And was there need for any? That young and foolish Katherine, driven by her own reckless desires, had cared enough to mention her to the hospital staff where she lay dying. She had thought of her daughter then, at the end, and all had come to good, after all. One could ask no more than that. Except a blessing on the spirit of the girl who had died, alone and friendless, so far from Dovewood and home.

They were silent for the most part, seated in the comfortable rail carriage on the trip back to the city. It was only in the hired cab, passing several factories in the Chippendale district, spilling their content of workers, men, women and children out onto the footpaths, that Katherine turned to her father and told him of Molly Murphy.

Her father listened, gazing out the window then frowning thoughtfully for some minutes. Katherine was worried that he was still preoccupied with his memories, with his marriage, but he said finally, "Nettlefield's . . . Yes, I know the company—not a large concern, and there's something unsavoury about the name, but for the moment I can't think of what it is. I shall ask Laurence at the office tomorrow."

Katherine wondered at the future of Prescott, Mitchell and Co. Not that there were not other assets in the family name, real estate, railway shares, and stocks and bonds of a safe if unadventurous description. But the importing and exporting firm of Prescott and Mitchell had always seemed as inviolable as Barrengarry itself. How would Laurence feel about the Prescotts now?

She had reckoned, however, without that particular bond between men; friendship, once sworn by Laurence Mitchell and Marcus Prescott, could bear the strain of this scandal. At the office the following day—and Katherine, remembering Robin's advice, insisted on accompanying her father—it seemed to her that Laurence Mitchell treated Marcus with a restrained warmth and empathy.

Why, he pities Father, Katherine, thought, watching the two men. Laurence has lost his son, but Father has a runaway wife. Of the two, the rectitudinous Laurence Mitchell would be hard put, Katherine decided, to choose which was the greater grief. Perhaps he even feels guilty that it was his son who seduced Marcus's wife.

Laurence was delighted with the results of the overseas business trip and Katherine, seated in a chair by the window with a view over George Street and its clattering, rolling, shouting, swearing traffic, kept her eyes on that view, and her ears tuned to hear and remember all that was discussed. Later she would study the papers her father brought home—with his permission or without, she thought grimly. From Edwin Gordon and Robin Mitchell she had learned a great deal since returning to Australia; the family fortunes were her concern, now Joe would not be there to take the reins in future years. No one would welcome her, nor make her task any easier; indeed she had no doubt but that she would meet discouragement at every turn, from Laurence Mitchell and her own father down to the lowliest spotty little clerk in the forwarding department. She was a woman, and a woman had no place in business. Unless she made herself a place, Katherine decided grimly.

It was at the end of the meeting, when they were ready to leave, that Marcus mentioned their quest for the Murphy girl and the company of Nettlefield's. Laurence thought for a while, then said, "I remember—two women maimed in an accident with machinery— the Benevolent Society had to step in to help pay for the medical expenses, the company refused to donate anything—not that they have to, with no laws of compensation." This last for Katherine's benefit, as Laurence knew Marcus would be all too familiar with the difficulties of the lives of the factory workers.

"It's not such a bad life as it seems," Marcus said thoughtfully on the way home in the buggy. "Remember, before factories, what course was open to girls and women who had no man to support them? There was domestic service, or the streets. Some servants live terrible lives of virtual slavery, low wages, only Sunday free, and the rest of the time it's drudgery in another's house, and no future until some man carries you off to begin a family of your own.

"Conditions in some of the factories are very bad, as there are no legal checks—an employer has no compunction about making his workers slave in hot airless rooms for twelve hours a day. But after the twelve hours, the workers are free to spend their evenings as they wish. And there are no legal checks, I might add, on the wealthy, to make sure that their house staff work in kitchens that are properly ventilated, or that the sleeping quarters have windows, and are dry in winter and cool in summer.

"And what of the widow or the deserted wife—and there are thousands in this city since the gold rushes—who have children to support? One can't get a housekeeper's job with eight children— or even two. Thus the factories, with their better wages and shorter hours, have such appeal to women and girls, and that's why you hear our friends moan constantly about the servant problem. Given a choice, I'd rather sew seams in a sweat shop than work as a lady's maid."

She grinned at the scowling, vital man beside her. "Why, Father, I think you would look very well in a little white cap with black ribbons."

"This is a serious subject—none of your frivolity, miss. If Molly were older I'd say let her go, she's bright and she'll make her way in the world. But she's friendless, and she's young and impressionable. And I doubt if she's running *to* something rather than away— anywhere—from her life back in Berry. But we have to face a possibility." He looked at Katherine steadily, but his unease showed nevertheless. "We might find the innocent country lass has taken on some unwelcome sophistication, and finds the idea of a return to Kangaroo Valley, even to Barrengarry, a very tedious fate indeed. She may very well laugh in our faces."

The chief clerk of R. B. Nettlefield's, Clothing Manufacturers, nibbled his rather pendulous lower lip, and surveyed the two people standing before him.

Both were clad soberly, the woman in black, a veil of tulle attempting and not quite succeeding in dimming the luxuriance of auburn hair in heavy rolls at the nape of her neck. The man was of average height, with that aura of success and power that came, not merely from his well-tailored clothes and silver-tipped cane, but from his attitude—when he spoke, he expected to be listened to; when he asked, he was accustomed to being obeyed.

The man had asked for the owner, but Mr Nettlefield was in Melbourne; he then asked for the manager, but Mr Watcombe was having a late lunch round at the Native Rose Hotel—though "He's away on business, too," was the safest answer to give. "Can I help you?" For it would look very well if he himself could introduce some new business into the firm.

It was the woman who spoke. A trifle forward of her, he thought. "We're looking for a young friend of ours who we believe might have sought employment with your firm just before Christmas. Her name is Margaret Murphy, but she's mostly known by the name of Molly."

So. No new business. And there on his desk was work that had been piling up there for days—and work, for that matter, that Mister Watcombe should be doing, but hell would freeze over before he could expect aid from that quarter. Long lunches at the Native Rose and talking in corners with every new girl who came through the building were more his style. No, these two with their stupid questions—and what friend of theirs would be working in a factory, tell me?—they would involve him in a fruitless search for which he'd get no credit, and only his valuable time wasted.

"I'm afraid no one of that name works here." He did not like them, their expensive clothes and their ability to walk out of this factory and never have to come back, day in, day out, year after year . . .

"Can you be sure?" He noted with pleasure that the woman looked anxious. It was oddly pleasing that he had the capability to make her look anxious.

The man spoke then. "How many women work here?" The words less a question than a demand.

"About two hundred," readily, from his habit of responding to an order, though in this case he cursed himself half a second later.

"And you know them all by name?" politely enough.

"Yes. No. That is, I'd remember if . . ."

"Molly Murphy isn't a name that would stand out amongst others," the man considered. "Perhaps we should visit the workroom—we may see her."

And he had taken the woman's arm, and they had marched through the door that led to the main body of the factory before it was possible to gallop around the long and cumbersome front bench and go after them. They were walking up the room, between the rows of tables and machines, the man asking questions here and there of various women, his companion seeming to be in awe of her surroundings.

"Mr Galvin?" The foreman had sidled up to him, was gazing at the visitors. "Who're they, then? New customers?"

Galvin was still gazing at them, taking in the horror and disgust on the woman's face as she looked around the building. "No—they've no right to be here—help me to get them out." For he would need the foreman's help, perhaps. He himself was not tall, nor strong, and the stranger, though well into his middle years, was both—and he carried a stick.

"Hadn't we better find out what . . ." the foreman began.

But Galvin had already reached the couple. Work had stopped, he saw in the periphery of his vision; all along the rows, at the cutting tables, the sewing machines, the pressing boards, heads that should have been lowered busily were raised, women were half-standing from their seats, turning to speak to each other.

"You'll have to leave," Galvin stated, but found it difficult to meet the hazel eyes of the man, cool as agate. "You've got no business here, Mr Preston . . ."

"Prescott. I have told you my business here." And the infernal man raised his voice, "I am trying to find Molly Murphy, who came here from Kangaroo Valley last December."

"Stop it!" Galvin said promptly, and almost had the temerity to place a hand on the man's arm but thought better of it. "I've told you, we've got no one of that name here."

"Wait a minute . . . we did have." It was the foreman who spoke. He did not like Galvin, knew that the customers did not like his insolent officiousness—but he was excellent with accounts and bookkeeping, and Mr Nettlefield would never find anyone else who would do the job as well on the low wages he paid to Galvin. Still, there was no need to create trouble—even if the man and woman were not customers, they might know Nettlefield or some of the more important customers. Galvin never thought of repercussions, never saw much of the world beyond his small narrow nose, and the world he saw was small and narrow also.

"Sir,—I remember a lass called Molly Murphy, up from the country. She . . ."

And with a rush of blood to his head, he remembered. He looked wildly at Galvin, but there was no help to be had there. Indeed, it was not even triumph on Galvin's face—it was blank. Galvin wouldn't remember. "She's gone," the foreman finished. "She left—about three weeks ago."

"Do you know where she went?" the woman asked. "Her father is ill. She'd want to see him."

The foreman felt helpless. There was only one person who'd know where the girl might be . . .

"I know Molly Murphy."

The foreman felt as if he were on a rack, as all eyes turned in the direction of the speaker. There, in her neat pale grey frock, Bridget Murray stood in the centre of the passageway, her firm Irish face with its deep blue eyes going from himself to the lady, the gentleman and back again. She ignored Galvin, as they all tried to do.

"I share lodgings with Molly," the girl said. "You'll find her at home. She's doing piece work. Not," she emphasized, "for this factory. She's not been well. Not lately, that is."

Bridget gave an address in Surry Hills, and Galvin and the foreman watched as the man wrote it in a notebook. He then looked up at the girl. "Thank you, Miss—?" his voice finishing in a query.

"Bridget Murray." She dimpled with genuine pleasure at his unfeigned courtesy.

"Thank you, Miss Murray. We'll call to see Molly straight away. Good day, gentleman," and with a bow, he left them. The woman with him looked pale. She paused in the doorway to look back at Bridget Murray and the two hundred or more women and children— some were as young as nine or ten—crammed into the tin-walled, tin-roofed room, the rusted walls unlined and cobwebbed, the meagre light from half a dozen small dirty windows showing that multitude of pale faces raised to her, incuriously. In the heated, airless gloom, she had an odd sensation. It was as if she looked into strategically placed mirrors and saw her own reflection, repeated time and again; the faces of the women and children that looked back at her were her own.

"How long are they there, did you say?" she muttered to her father when they were in the buggy once more, and Tobias had touched the whip to the horse's rump.

"Twelve hours a day, if they're lucky—sometimes fourteen or fifteen. We have hopes that we might be able to have legislation passed to limit it to twelve hours a day."

Katherine leaned back in her seat. "Twelve . . ." she murmured. "They begin at six in the morning?"

"Yes."

"And finish at six at night, at the very least."

"I wonder what happened to Molly?" mused her father. "Did you notice the look on the foreman's face? Culpability of some sort. I hope the girl hasn't come to any harm . . ."

"Where do they eat? What about retiring rooms?"

"They'd bring their own midday meal. Sandwiches, mostly. There'd be a small area at the back of the building—a separate room if they're lucky, in order to eat. Retiring rooms—there'd be toilets out the back—primitive, filthy . . ."

"You've never been there . . ."

"My dear—I've visited a thousand factories like it. There's precious little difference between them. There are a few factory owners who care about their employees, but the majority are only after profits—I don't need to tell you all this—have you been deaf to my haranguing at the dinner table all these years? Have you not known the purpose of all the committees I serve on? Did you not realize the extent of the problem until today?"

"No," promptly and honestly. "The charitable work, from what we, the family, could see, has been mostly fund raising—I saw the luncheons and the musical soirées, and the afternoon teas and the bazaars. I knew you went into rough, dangerous places to check on conditions and to talk to people, but you never expounded on the descriptions at the dinner table, you know you didn't. I have been very protected."

Her gaze was fixed before her, and she saw a vision of her life in Dublin, the poor she had seen—and Dublin had more poor than did Sydney—and the helplessness she had felt. The cure, Oliver and all their friends had said, would only come with self-government. But it was more than that. All over the world, the tyranny was localized, personalized. That tin shed back there was Mr Nettlefield's realm, a dictatorship where he could, having financial power over those women, keep his prisoners working under the barest minimum of safe and humane conditions, under the negligent eye of a disinterested government.

They drove directly to the address Bridget Murray had given them, one of many identical workman's cottages, grey, dispirited, crouched together in terraces as if in a hopeless effort at unity against the poverty of the street.

Children, ragged, curious, impudent, ran across the road, out of the tiny yards and narrow doorways, to stare with open wet mouths at the well-dressed strangers.

Tobias sat muttering in the driver's seat as Marcus jumped down and helped his daughter to alight, before knocking on the cracked and peeling paintwork of the front door.

"Yes?"

It was an unfortunate face; broad and pale, nature seemed to have pushed it together, so that the chin curled up to meet the nose, and the forehead and nose were lowered to meet the chin. The fact that there were only three blackened teeth in the mouth that lay between did not help matters. But the hair was neatly brushed into a severe roll, and the patched dress was clean enough. "What might you be wanting?"

"We're friends of Molly Murphy's family. My name is Marcus Prescott, this is my daughter, Mrs Carron. Bridget Murray told us that she and Molly lived here."

"Oh, yes. So they do. Good girls, quiet . . ." The woman stood back to let them into a hall that smelled of stale food and old, smoky walls. The smell of bad drainage that pervaded the street was only slightly lessened once the door was shut behind them. Their hostess ambled off down a corridor of sagging, protesting floorboards. "Aye, good girls—reg'lar with their rent, clean in their habits, and not a gentleman to be seen sniffin' about them, not that they couldn't have 'em, I imagine, particularly that Bridget—the little one's peaked, a bit frail . . ."

They were climbing narrow stairs to a little attic. The woman knocked on the door and bellowed, so suddenly and so loudly that Katherine started, "Molly, love! Visitors to see yer!" She turned to smile toothlessly at the strangers, and waddled off down the stairs.

There was no answer from within the room. Katherine, disturbed as she was to hear that Molly was "peaked", was nevertheless uneasily relieved. Surely the girl was not with child, if the obviously watchful landlady could be so sympathetic. Molly, at fourteen, taken advantage of by some unscrupulous man at the factory . . . this had occurred to her.

Why didn't she come to us, when she had to leave Berry? she asked herself, glancing at her father's concerned scowl as he stared at the closed door. Why did she come here, when she could have come to us?

Marcus knocked on the door—still no answer.

"Molly? It's Marcus Prescott and Mrs Carron."

Silence.

"Father, I'm worried . . ." Katherine placed a hand on his arm.

Marcus muttered, "Yes . . ." and tried the door. It swung open.

It was a small room, all four walls sloped upwards, following the roofline. There were shadows of two settle beds, a small dresser and wardrobe. The light from the one window, flush with the sloping walls, shone on a table pulled as close as possible to catch each strained beam, and on its surface lay a rainbow array of coloured silk sleeves, blue and violet, crimson and rosy pink, wine-colour and royal blue, primrose yellow and magenta . . . and seated on a chair pulled to the table, her back to the window so that the light fell on her work, Molly Murphy sat slumped forward, her face fallen onto one thin arm, pillowed in the myriad colours of her silks.

Thirty Three

It took them some minutes to rouse the girl. Marcus carried her to the bed, propped her up on pillows and left Katherine slapping the girl's wrists, calling her name urgently, while he ran down the narrow stairs, two at a time, to tell Tobias to go find a doctor and bring him back to the house immediately.

When Marcus returned, closely followed by the anxious landlady, Molly was just opening her eyes. She stared at Katherine, on her knees on the rag rug on the floor, and smiled a tremulous smile. "Oh . . ." she said, in a small, happy voice. "I fell asleep . . ."

"Molly, how long have you been ill?"

"No . . . No, Mrs Carron, it's just a chill—just a summer chill . . . and I was working late last night . . . I worked *all* night," she corrected, wonderingly. "But it's daytime now, isn't it? Where's Bridget? Is it still morning?"

"Poor lass . . ." The landlady wrung her hands. "I never thought it was so bad, sir. She had the doctor twice last month, but I thought she was better. I expect you'll be taking her with you? She needs looking after, poor child, and there's no one to do it, here . . ."

The sight of a sovereign appearing in Marcus's hand cut short her talk. She was a plump woman, not one, Marcus judged, who would go without her food. "Here—Make some broth—nourishing, mind, not just hot water. And bring it here for the girl."

"That I can do—that I can do, sir." And she was off down the stairs with surprising nimbleness.

Molly had closed her eyes once more and appeared to be sleeping. It frightened Katherine further—the child was affected by something more than mere exhaustion.

The doctor—and Tobias had taken good care to find a reputable practitioner—agreed. Molly had managed to sip a little of the broth before he came, and Marcus and Tobias waited outside the door with the perturbed landlady while he examined the girl. He called them in, finally, to announce that Molly was suffering from pneumonia and malnutrition.

Katherine, present throughout the examination and not really surprised at the diagnosis, was suggesting to her father that they waste no delay in conveying Molly to the house in Balmain, when

Bridget Murray came flying up the stairs. She took one look around at the faces, then walked over to the bed, dropped to her knees by the pale form of the girl, and took her hand. "Molly . . . ?"

Molly opened her eyes. "Are you home, then? I feel a bit poorly, Bridget. Can you take my work in for me tomorrow?"

"Of course, on my way to work. And see, your friends are here—they'll look after you—you don't have to worry, now . . ."

"My friends . . ." Molly's gaze came up and around to Marcus and Katherine, and it was only then that she seemed to question their presence, here in the poky little room, when they should be a hundred miles away in Kangaroo Valley. She burst into sudden, exhausted tears, and Bridget and Katherine tried to comfort her until the doctor and Marcus stepped forward, and Marcus picked up the girl in his arms and carried her downstairs to the carriage.

Katherine stayed back for a few minutes, speaking to Bridget.

" 'Twas the manager, old Watcombe. Not that he's all that old, sure—about thirty-five. But he's such a lecherer, Miss. We've all had to put him down firmly—though some have succumbed to his charm, sure, and lived to regret it. Molly—*well*—she didn't give him a chance. He took her out back one day, into the storage room on some pretext, and when he tried to . . ." She paused delicately, "Well, Molly screamed blue murder, Miss. Screamed and screamed and hit him and called him a beast and Lord knows what else. Mother of Mary, she brought everyone in the factory running, and then, of course, an issue being made, it was his word against hers—and things being as they are, Miss, Mr Watcombe told her to leave, and she did.

"She got sick after walking 'round in that rainy spell we had some weeks back. When she finally found work, she was too ill to continue for long, but her finishing work is first class, Miss . . ." She ran to the table to show Katherine the patterned ruching and beading on the sleeves. "And they let her take work away. She gets five pence for each sleeve she finishes—it's good money, but it's difficult, close work, as you see—and it takes so long . . . I suppose . . ." reflectively, "it *isn't* good money when you think how long it takes to do each one . . . But she's had no choice. This room costs eighteen shillings a week. It'd cost the same if we were men—but a man in a factory makes thirty-five shillings a week, Miss. I'm a woman, and a qualified tailoress, working the same hours as a man—I make fourteen shillings a week. Molly, though she's so clever at her work, is still a junior—even doing outwork they pay her half what they'd pay a grown woman. We don't have any money left over—and then Molly had to have the doctor twice last month, and a gurrier he was—not like the gentleman you found for her—this gombeen last month, he demanded his money straight away . . . She paid him, too, soon as she could—proud, she is, Miss, and honest—it's fierce fond of her I am." The pretty young face looked distressed.

"How old are you, Bridget?"

"Seventeen, Miss. I'm the middle of eighteen children, and I truly feel older than that, so I usually say I'm eighteen. My parents have a farm out Windsor way—I'm one mouth less to feed, being here, but I miss them. Still, I'll be seeing them soon enough."

"You're going home to visit?"

She looked reluctant, then said, "I'll be going home for good, Miss. Mr Watcombe came back from lunch—at four o'clock—and that weasel Galvin in the front office, didn't he tell him of your visit. Watcombe called me into his office and threatened me to say nothing to you—I think he thought your father was some sort of inspector, Miss. And he made himself so disagreeable, and said such snide . . . *grubby* things about Molly and me that I told him he was a low-living slimey gombeen and that I'd not work there a minute longer. Don't tell Molly though, Miss. I'll go home to Windsor for a while, and perhaps try to find work there, or in Parramatta."

"Bridget," Katherine warned gently, "there are thousands looking for work in Sydney, and I don't think the situation will be any better in the country towns. There's never been such unemployment in the colony."

Bridget held Katherine's gaze fearlessly. "Could *you* stay working at Nettlefield's, Miss, in them circumstances?"

"No," Katherine sighed. "Bridget, have you thought of domestic service? Fourteen shillings plus keep in a rather remote country house with gardens—until, of course, some young farmer proposes to you, which I have no doubt will happen in a year or two?"

"With Molly, Miss?" The dark blue eyes danced into life.

"With Molly, when she's well. If she wants to come home."

"Miss, she's talked of nothing but Kangaroo Valley for months. Take her home to the Valley, and she'll be well in no time at all!"

Marcus, bemused at finding himself leading an expedition of three women home to the Southern Highlands, nevertheless made all the arrangements, and carried the child Molly from the buggy to the train while Katherine and Bridget, in her new dark costume and bonnet, oversaw the loading of the luggage.

Marcus found a room at the inn at Moss Vale for himself, for nothing Katherine could say would make him consider going on with her and the two girls to Dovewood.

They were not expected at the big house, but rooms were quickly prepared for them, Bridget in the servants' quarters and Molly in one of the guest rooms. The elder girl had already taken on the position of nurse to the young invalid, who was improving rapidly in the atmosphere of trust and security, and Katherine was free to seek out her mother and speak with her alone.

"He's staying at the inn?" Suzanna, cutting roses in the garden beds that lined the drive, paused to look up at her daughter in mild surprise. "But he knows he's perfectly welcome here—Mama and Papa will be puzzled and upset that he's not staying here."

"Really, Mama. Sometimes I think your head is filled with fluff."

"Katherine!"

"I'm sorry. I am, truly. But you don't seem to understand the situation in the least."

"You mean he's still angry and hurt—and you're taking his side once more. I might have a head full of fluff, Katey, but you swing about like a pendulum—spend a day or two with your father and you change loyalties, forgetting everything we went through together."

"I'll never forget that," she said gravely. "But you're doing Father an injustice. It seems to me that you're rather enjoying the life of a single woman—perhaps you'll find that you never need a man in your life again—and I can't criticize you for that—you've given most of your life to looking after people, so perhaps you're right in thinking only of yourself now. You deserve to.

"But, you see, Father hasn't reached that state of dispassionate interest, with which you seem to regard him. In fact, quite the opposite. He's had many long months in which to think of his life, and he actually blames himself for everything that's happened. He said—and I don't think he'd like me to betray his confidence, so don't tell him I have—that he'd been very selfish, and was only now seeing how you must have felt all these years. He said that you were a woman in a million, and he was too young when he met you to realize what he had—and he doesn't expect you ever to forgive him, and that's why he's staying in Moss Vale."

There was a pause, and Katherine turned to look over at the house. "I'll go and check on Molly now. Grandmama said the child should stay here until she's fully recovered—it's very kind of her. Bridget

will stay too, of course. I'll be riding home to Barrengarry tomorrow
with Father.''

"So soon?" Suzanna looked up. "Must you leave tomorrow . . . ?
You don't think you'd like to stay for a few days?"

"No, Mama. We're running short of supplies, and Carl will have
to be taking the wagon to Wollongong—if Peggy wants to go with
him it will leave only Teddi and Laura to look after Amos and Mary
Rose. I shouldn't really have gone to Sydney—but I'm glad I did.
It was wonderful to see Father again—and of course, if I hadn't
gone, who knows what might have happened to poor Molly? Are
you coming into the house?"

"No . . . No, I'd like to cut some more flowers . . ."

So Katherine left her mother there, standing beside her basket
of roses, the scissors still in her hands, forgotten, her face frozen
in the same expression of bewildered surprise she had displayed at
Katherine's first mention of Marcus's feelings.

Suzanna was preoccupied at dinner, and Katherine half-expected
and hoped that she would order the carriage for a trip to the
township—but no such order came. Instead, she retired early, as
thoughtfully distracted as she had been all afternoon.

The following day, Katherine borrowed a sturdy bay gelding from
the stables, bade goodbye to the family and the two girls, and rode
into Moss Vale. Since Molly and Bridget would be coming on to
the Valley in a few weeks, their small amount of luggage could
wait and travel with them. So, with nothing further to delay them,
Marcus hired a horse from the blacksmith's and, after an early lunch
at the Rose and Garters, father and daughter rode home to the Valley.

"I saw Tom Lloyd this morning," Marcus scowled. "I didn't want
to tell you over breakfast, it's not a pleasant topic to be reminded
of, but Amos Murphy still hasn't been able to identify who tried
to kill him."

"He's no better then?"

"Well, yes, he has improved. He asked for you," Marcus looked
over at his daughter, half-amused. "It seems you've won a heart
with your tender ministrations, Katey."

"Really, Father . . ." She was in no mood for teasing.

"Tom was sorry you weren't there—perhaps Amos might have
said something to you—but after being told that you were in Sydney,
he muttered that he wanted to go home, and he kept that up, no
matter what Tom could do to try to have him remember the incident.
In the end, Tom and Brendan decided to drive him back to his farm—
Billy will be there with him and apparently, to Billy's disgust, Nancy

Halstrop has been visiting the farm every day to take care of the house, and insists that she'll nurse Amos. He seemed happier on arriving, but still won't speak. And this was three days ago."

"Father?" A thought occurred to her. "Don't you think there's a possibility that Amos *does* remember—but doesn't want to tell?"

Marcus threw her an incisive glance. "It occurred to me—to Tom also. That would be bad, wouldn't it? Amos is a tough man—it would take a lot to make him afraid. But still, it could be the concussion—Doctor Lang visited Barrengarry the day after you left, and he said for Tom not to expect too much, too soon."

"How long ago was that?" Katherine considered. "Why, eight days! So much has happened—and I've only been away eight days! And did Doctor Lang see Mary Rose? Is she all right?"

"I asked Tom, but he didn't know much detail. Mary Rose was very tired and resting, so he wasn't able to see her. But she, too, may take a while to recover, Katey. She's a frail little thing," he added reflectively. "I hope Brendan isn't planning on burdening her with too many children."

The conversation was moving onto indelicate ground, but Katherine had to murmur an agreement. She could not see how Mary Rose could cope with a life of almost perpetual childbearing.

"The thing that bothers me most is that until Amos speaks, Jim O'Mara is still under suspicion. It seems he's bought some new cattle and can't give any real reason where the money came from. Despite that, I can't believe what the gossips say of him. Whoever is committing these murders and robberies is a devious and a cruel man—perhaps a little insane. I can't believe that of Jim O'Mara."

Katherine thought of the big, sandy-haired farmer, his open face lined by years of hardship, and agreed. But with children to support . . . hadn't many an honest man gone mad with despair in trying to keep his family alive? Still, her father was right—Jim O'Mara—even should his mind break—could never kill, calmly, cold-bloodedly.

"Tom's very hopeful that there'll be an end to the business soon, though. He'll be returning to the Valley himself tomorrow—he's had Constable Crowe oversee the job of putting strong bolts on the door of Bert Radley's cool room—you know the old sandstone annex to the pub? He keeps supplies in there, but there are heavy bars on the windows, and Tom thinks it'll make a strong makeshift gaol, should he be able to bring in the culprit and need to hold him in the Valley. Disturbing, isn't it?" Marcus said drily, "that the community gets a gaol, before a church or a school or even a police station?"

"It's not a gaol, Father." She spoke to alleviate some of the traces of bitterness in her father's voice. He was obviously much more affected by the shame brought down upon his beloved Valley than even she had realized.

Please, God, let it be over soon, she prayed, as they came down the last of the slopes onto the Valley floor. Let life return to normal for us. If Amos would only speak of who had done this thing . . . It was disturbing that he could, or would not, tell. Had the man's brain been damaged permanently? Or . . . and this was almost as chilling a possibility—had what he'd suffered, what he'd seen so disturbed him that he could not face the reality, and had blotted it out of existence?

But the tension was beginning to leave her, despite the grimness of their conversation, for there before them were Barrengarry's gates, and the little bridge, and the curving drive. There was the house, looking mellow in the last light, as the shadows of the western escarpment marched across the Valley floor towards it. It was a golden evening, one of those rare sunsets that touch the world so infrequently and seem to linger in a last intense glow, as if aware of the value of the gift bestowed. Katherine smiled, controlling the gelding's extended trot, in order to prolong the moment with its view of her home, touched with light as delicately as if highlighted by a master's hand.

"Katey! Father . . . !"

They heard the sounds before they saw any sign of life.

"Father . . . ! Father . . . !"

Katherine's smile had faded, for there was a note of hysteria and despair in the voice, made more evident as the front door was flung open and Edwina came stumbling down the front steps towards them.

Katherine struck the astonished gelding with her crop, bent over his neck as he sprang forward, and she and Marcus covered the last of the distance to the house at a gallop, reining in and dropping to the ground by Edwina without consciously realizing they had dismounted.

Edwina fell sobbing into Marcus's arms; at first it seemed as if she were ill or hurt, for the small face was ghostly pale, the eyes black-shadowed and hollow, the lids swollen. She was muttering, so quickly, so unintelligibly through her tears that it was some seconds before Marcus or Katherine could understand what had happened. "Laura . . . she's worsened—I couldn't leave! And we *can't* find Mrs Regnier—I was with Laura for so long—too long, she's delirious, you see—and Mary Rose . . . Oh, Katey!" The huge eyes came around with something like terror to Katherine, "She's so still—I'm so afraid . . . ! We *couldn't* find Mrs Regnier—we didn't know where she was . . ."

His arm around his youngest daughter, Marcus turned her towards the house. Katherine gathered the horses' reins, tied them to the rail and hurried up the stairs after her father and sister, throwing her hat and riding crop on the hall table beside Marcus's dark top hat and gloves. She stood pulling off her own gloves in the doorway, her heart thudding with fear, as she watched Marcus pushing Edwina down upon the settee, fetching a half-tumbler of brandy from the sideboard.

"Drink this, Teddi, then tell me what's happened . . ."

"I don't want . . ."

"Drink it!"

Edwina obediently took a gulp of the liquid, sat panting for a few seconds, then looked up at her father, and over to Katherine as she walked into the room. "The . . . They're both sick! B . . . both of them, and calling for their mamas, and . . . and Mary Rose went rigid, like th . . . this . . ." She did a grisly imitation of a convulsion "—and these past two hours she's been asleep and she *won't wake up*, Katey!" the voice rose in hysteria. "She won't wake up, and I think she's dying . . . !"

"Where's Brendan? Where's Peggy . . . ?"

"Carl and Peggy went to Wollongong—everything was all right, it seemed then. And . . . and that night both Laura and Mary Rose had fevers, and Brendan rode for the doctor in Moss Vale—I thought he'd be back by now . . . Will O'Mahony has been searching for Mrs Regnier—her husband said she was up at a delivery at a cedar-getter's camp, but he didn't know which one—Oh, Father—Katey—it's been horrible—the girls have just become worse and worse . . . I think Laura has the influenza, but I don't know what's wrong with Mary Rose—I think it's some sort of complication after the baby—she's had bad pains in the stomach, but she wouldn't complain—she didn't want to make a fuss . . . I should have spent more time with her—but I was nursing Laura . . . It's my fault—it's all my fault . . . !"

Katherine touched the head of dark, tousled curls, and headed for the hall. Behind her, Marcus lifted Edwina's feet up onto the settee and commanded, "Drink the rest of the brandy and then lie down and rest, Teddi . . ."

"But, Father . . ."

"Drink it, never mind that you don't like the taste! Then lie down and close your eyes—do as I say, or I'll come back downstairs and box your ears!" His voice softened. "You've been a brave girl—but Katey and I can handle things now. Just rest, Teddi. Everything will be alright."

Marcus's deep, clear voice carried to the top of the stairs, and Katherine prayed that her father was correct.

Father and daughter checked on both girls, Mary Rose, now back in the large guest room she shared with her husband, and Laura in her own little room at the end of the passage. Marcus and Katherine stood gazing at each other and in that brief pause, Katherine was always to remember that time seemed to stand still, the only sound was of the full-blown climbing roses tapping at the closed windows of Laura's room, as if trying to awaken the girl from her restive sleep.

They went to work without consciously deciding what must be done, scrubbing their hands in the bathroom, Marcus returning to sit by Laura, to bathe her face with the flannel that lay beside the basin of cool water, to speak her name soothingly. There was no response to his presence, only an intermittent muttering of Joe's name, of Stephen Brody's, but mostly a low whimpering of "Mama . . . Mama . . ." that made Marcus's hand tremble, his voice break on Laura's name.

With Will searching for Angel Regnier and Brendan riding about the Moss Vale district, looking for Doctor Lang amongst all the families inflicted with the diphtheria, there was no point in either she or Marcus leaving the house to go for help. But standing once more by Mary Rose's bed, Katherine felt a helpless terror growing. What could she do? Was there anything to be done?

For Mary Rose lay very still, and at first sight it would seem as if the girl was asleep. But no calling of her name roused her and when the baby in its cradle made a weak and whimpering attempt to cry, still the pale lids remained closed.

"Mary Rose . . . ? Oh, Mary Rose, wake up . . ."

Katherine, seated on the edge of the bed, took the girl's hand in hers. Though both hands had been lying beneath the coverlet, the long, slender fingers were cold to the touch, the narrow chest rose fitfully in shallow breaths as if the air entered the lungs reluctantly, drawn in with effort.

What did it mean—what did it mean . . . ? Could Mary Rose have caught the influenza virus from Laura, despite their precautions, through the well-meaning Edwina tending both the girls? Had the crisis already passed for Mary Rose, and was this the deep, safe sleep of total exhaustion, or . . .

Her mind reeled back from other possibilities. Twelve days . . . Twelve days since the child's birth . . .

"Oh, Mary Rose—wake up . . . ! My dear, wake up . . ."

The only sound in the room was the child's faint protests, and Katherine finally left the room, running down the stairs, heading for the kitchen to warm some weak milk, for the baby—despite Edwina's best intentions—might have been neglected in the nursing of the adults . . .

"Oh, God, don't let anything happen to them . . . God, look after Laura and Mary Rose and baby James, and I'll give you anything— I'll never think of Brendan again, I swear it—only let them all be safe, let them get well . . ."

The hall was suddenly dark as a shadow loomed on the glass panels, blotting out the last of the afternoon light.

It was almost an answer to her prayer, and she flew down the last steps, flung the door wide to be confronted with Angel Regnier.

"I've been with Mrs Larsson's eldest girl—only fourteen—some man had taken advantage of the girl . . . the child was stillborn. Will met me on my way down from the camp—dead on his feet with fatigue. I sent him to his quarters. The bathroom is through here, isn't it?" Katherine trotted beside the woman as she headed for pump and soap and scrubbed her hands carefully. All the while, Katherine told her of the few symptoms she could determine in both patients.

"I was worried in case the young American lady still would not see me . . ." Angel frowned as she dried her hands.

"Mrs Regnier, she's too ill to recognize even the cry of her baby."

Angel looked at her gravely but did not answer, and her very silence made Katherine afraid as both women headed for the stairs.

In Mary Rose's room, Angel Regnier seemed to pause, just for an instant, and Katherine, walking close behind her, could not fail to notice. It was as if something in that still form on the bed was speaking to the woman, though she covered it immediately and was even now bending over the girl.

But something was different. Even in the short time she had been away, Katherine saw that there was a change. There was a translucence to Mary Rose's skin, a stillness that was even more frightening than before. If she had not begun to breathe more strongly, Katherine would have been terrified. As it was, she watched, from the foot of the bed, as Angel gently examined Mary Rose, checking the flow from her body, gently palpating the abdomen . . .

"This is no influenza, Mrs Carron." The capable hands were

readjusting the nightdress and bedclothes, and only then the black eyes were lifted to Katherine's face.

"Is she sleeping? Is she all right? If you like, I'll sit with her, or would you rather nurse her while I see how my sister is . . ."

"There's no time, Mrs Carron. It's hard for you, but you know the signs." Angel held out her hand, and there were tears in the dark eyes. "Come, Katherine, say goodbye to your friend."

"No . . ." Katherine breathed. 'No, you're wrong, you must be wrong . . ." She was across the room, down on her knees by the bed, had taken one, both, cold hands in hers.

"Don't, Mary Rose. Don't leave us. Mary Rose, you mustn't. Your baby—James needs you! Brendan needs you. Mary Rose . . ." Her voice broke. "You mustn't leave us, Mary Rose! You mustn't go . . ."

Angel, behind her, placed a large, warm hand upon her shoulder, and while she was grateful for the pressure, for the friendship and support it represented, still its message chilled her, she felt the dry sob rise in her throat. For upon the bed lay what was now, she knew, a beautiful and lifeless doll. Mary Rose had gone from them.

It couldn't happen like this. It couldn't. There was some mistake . . .

But Katherine looked up into Angel Regnier's face, saw the sadness, the ancient wisdom in the eyes that seemed to will some strength into Katherine, despite the unashamed tears that ran down the dark cheeks.

"It should not have happened. We'll say it once, between us, and then we must forget it, and accept it. Do you understand?"

"No! No, I can't understand! I'll never understand!"

"We have responsibilities to the living, Mrs Carron. Your sister will need us both—and the child . . ." She glanced over at the cradle. "Do you have goats on the property?"

Katherine was staring at Mary Rose, the perfect features carved in marble, the fair hair curled in long tendrils over the pillow. *Brendan will never forgive me. I will never forgive myself.*

"Mrs Carron! Do you have goats on Barrengarry?"

She looked up at the black woman, almost unseeingly. "No . . ."

"We have a nanny goat who's a good milker, I shall have one of my boys bring her here tomorrow."

Katherine, still on her knees by the bed, was aware that Angel was fumbling for her handkerchief, had blown the flat, blunt nose, and was now moving, with that graceful silence of hers, over to

the corner of the room. All Katherine could think of was the girl
who lay so still upon the bed, like a carving of a sleeping angel.
If only one could go back—an hour—even half an hour . . . could
things be different? How could this happen, it can't have been meant
to happen . . . God would not be so cruel . . . Brendan . . . the
child . . . God would not let them suffer this loss . . .

"Take him, Mrs Carron." Firm but gentle came Angel's voice
to her dulled brain, and firmly but gently the soft bundle that was
Mary Rose's son was placed in her arms.

"No . . ." A plea from her heart, for it was a terrible, terrible
punishment, to look upon the face of that child that she had longed
for, yet avoided, ever since the day she had helped him into the
world. But he was there, moving small fists, and she gazed down
at the fair head of hair, the small, pink face, puckered crossly, chewing
hungrily on a tiny clenched fist that he obviously found inadequate.
He turned his face towards the warmth of her body, and her heart
ached. "Please—you take him . . ."

"I have work to do." The deep voice, sorrowful. "Go downstairs
with him, Mrs Carron. Here—some napkins for him . . ." They were
tucked into the blanket surrounding the child, and then the strong
black arms were pulling her to her feet, pushing her towards the
door.

"I . . . I can't . . ."

"You can. He needs you. Take care of him. Warm milk weakened
with water—no cream. Boil it, of course. Change his behind, and
cuddle him—he's been ignored for hours, poor lamb. Oh—give him
some tepid boiled water first—he'll be thirsty. Go. I shall be busy
here for a while, then I'll go to your sister. And Mrs Carron!"
Katherine paused. "Don't let anyone in here, unless it's the doctor."

She nodded numbly, and turned for one last look at Mary Rose.
Angel was bending to light the lamp and its friendly glow only made
the picture more unreal, like a bad dream from which there was
no waking.

Katherine said, "There was so much I could have said to her.
Something . . . I've heard that a person can come back—even from
the brink . . ."

Angel shook her head slowly. "She was in God's arms already,
Mrs Carron. Do not mourn for her."

"But . . . I didn't know what to say! There were so many things
I could have said . . . !"

"You said you would miss her, that you loved her very much.
Isn't that what a friend should hear, at the last?"

"I . . . I didn't say that. I didn't hear myself say that . . ."

Angel smiled gently. "*She* heard you, Mrs Carron."

Thirty Four

Katherine stood outside in the hall, the door having been softly but firmly shut behind her. There was no reality here either, and she came to herself only when the child gave a sudden, lusty cry, as if he felt he had been patient with her long enough. Katherine held him to her with one arm, and made her way along the hall and down the stairs, slowly and carefully, frightened of stumbling in a world that threatened to shift beneath her feet, and grasping the banister tightly with the other hand.

The hall was deserted. She carried her small burden through the house to the spacious kitchen. It was cool here, unusually cool, as there were very few days when she could not remember the large stove being unlit. It was cold now, brooding in a pile of ashes fallen from its mouth like charred crumbs from a dragon's jaws.

Katherine muttered Angel's commands to herself as she went about the physical motions of carrying them out. A place for the child was the first problem—there was a large, shallow baking dish hung on the wall, and James found himself lying safely in this on the scrubbed kitchen table, while "Tepid boiled water . . ." Katherine murmured, going to the black urn on the back of the stove, turning the brass tap and finding the water just that temperature.

James had no experience nor liking for a cup, but with the instinct for self-preservation of the young, he slurped and gulped the tiny drops of warm water fed to him and later, his clothing changed and warm and dry once more, he made a meal of the diluted cow's milk with the minimum of protest at the indignity and the disruption to his routine.

Angel came to check on them, nodded approvingly at the scene of the sleeping babe, rocked on Katherine's lap, the fire lit and the urn bubbling with fresh hot water.

Katherine could find no words within her, and sat dully, holding the sleeping child; she was only just aware of Angel moving about the room, fetching a tray and doily and cups and saucers.

"I'll take this up to your father—I've made some barley broth for Miss Prescott."

"Laura . . ." Katherine thought suddenly, with growing horror that she could have so forgotten her sister.

"She'll be all right—I called in to see her before I came downstairs. She's conscious, and having her Papa there, holding her hand, is the best medicine for her. I had to call your father outside to tell him the news of Mrs Kelehan. He agrees with me that your sister must not know, for a few days at least."

Katherine's voice sounded harsh even to her own ears. "Why did Mary Rose die? It was an infection, wasn't it?"

Katherine was sure that if she could, Angel would have kept the grim condemnation from her voice, but she, too, was too involved, and she could not. Her "Yes," should have told Katherine all she needed to know, but now it was in the open she had to hear all the truth.

"Her dressings would have been changed constantly—all the linen heated before the fire, just as I told you—Peggy is scrupulous, and Edwina, I know, wouldn't have been careless of Mary Rose's health. Edwina said she'd first developed the fever three days ago, just after Peggy and Carl left; but that she admitted to having pains in the stomach and feeling ill before that. She . . . she was trying to be brave . . . *Oh, God* . . ."

"*Mrs Carron*, you must stop this. There's no point in blaming yourself . . ."

"It was that woman, wasn't it? And if it was her, then it was my fault equally as much. She . . . she didn't scrub her hands, Mrs Regnier—she didn't scrub her hands because she resented me telling her what to do . . . !"

"Child, are you going to blame yourself for that? For telling that woman to do something that it should have been second nature for her to do? You are right—it was probably her lack of hygiene that caused the sepsis—but all this will not bring the girl back to us. Until there are schools for midwives, until they can have rules that stop any woman setting herself up as an expert, taking the lives of mothers and babies into ignorant or inexperienced hands, then we'll always have the Nancy Halstrops with us."

"I should have made Mary Rose have you here—I should have convinced Brendan . . . Dear God, we gave way to that silly child on this—*this*—and she's dead because we didn't see that she made the right decision!"

"No, Mrs Carron," firmly. "She would have her way. I heard her. There was nothing any of us could do. We could not break through her fear." She pushed a cup and saucer, that Katherine had not even noticed, towards her across the table. "Come, drink the tea I've made for you."

Angel took up the tray of tea things and carried it from the room. Katherine replaced the sleeping baby in the baking dish, which she had padded with several clean tea towels into quite a soft little bed, and sat gazing unseeingly at him as she drank the hot tea, scalding her tongue and barely noticing. Her hands kept shaking; she had to hold the cup in both hands, and even then it trembled.

Outside the window, a sleepy magpie called. The callous normality of the world went on, beyond the walls of Barrengarry, and somewhere out there Brendan was desperately searching for a doctor for his young wife. Katherine, too shocked for tears as yet, thought of his return with mounting terror. Better if she were miles away, better she were dead than to look him in the face and see his hurt and despair and the knowledge that she, Katherine, had failed Mary Rose.

I shouldn't have allowed that woman near her . . . I should have gone with her to the bathroom, stood over her as she scrubbed her hands . . . I shouldn't have gone to Sydney . . . I should have told Carl and Peggy not to leave the property until I returned . . .

The front door opened. She heard it, and the sound brought her to her feet with a lurching of her heart. She ran as far as the door to the hall—but stopped. No. She could not face him. Not now.

But he would go upstairs, to the room he shared with Mary Rose and the child . . . What if Angel was with Laura and Father? What if he entered the room and found Mary Rose . . . ?

She was running along the hall, hearing the sound of footsteps on the thin carpet of the stairs to the first floor . . .

"Brendan . . . !"

The footsteps stopped, and there was a murmur of voices. It was only then that she realized there was not one man, but two, and as she rounded the newel post she found herself gazing up at the surprised faces of Brendan and Doctor Lang.

"Thank heavens . . ." The words came from her unbidden, with a sudden rush of relief—and this was madness. What could the man do? For it was too late. He could not work miracles. She stared at the thin, brown face of Robert Lang as both men came down the stairs to her. Fatigue was written on their features, and concern.

She wished she could turn away, but Brendan had reached her. "Kate? Mary Rose, and Laura . . ." He had taken her arms, pulled her closer to face him, but she would not, could not, meet his eyes.

"Angel Regnier is here . . . She's with Laura . . ." she managed.

"Kate." His hands were on either side of her face, brought it up forcibly to meet his gaze and she would have gladly faced death in that moment, for she knew that the truth must be written there, they were too close for him not to see into her soul and read the truth there.

Robert Lang had already turned towards the stairs but then paused, suspecting something terribly wrong in the second that Brendan knew.

Doctor Lang had to step back, up against the wall as Brendan pushed past him, ran up the stairs, uttering one, unintelligible cry from his heart. Katherine stood holding the newel post with both hands, her forehead resting on them, wishing she could block her ears to that sound that she knew would echo through her dreams until the end of her days.

"Katherine?" Lang queried gently, "The girl is dead?"

She nodded, feeling her head jerk, up and down, as if by its own volition.

"Will you be all right, my dear, if I go to her?"

"Yes," she breathed, and to show him she was in control, she walked quietly into the parlour, stood just inside the door, gazing at the sleeping Edwina, curled like a little girl upon the settee, and listened as the tired tread of Robert Lang faded on the staircase above her head.

She must go back to the baby . . .

Always find something to do, she thought. One task at a time, and perhaps madness could be kept at bay. It could gibber behind each drape, drool and snarl behind one's reflection in a mirror, or hunger outside a window, scratching at the glass, but it could not touch one.

She must go back to the baby . . .

"I want to cry for Mary Rose . . ." She was shocked to hear that she had spoken the words aloud. But still no tears came; heavy as her heart was, much as she longed for the release of the grief within her, nothing, no loss had broken that wall she had built about her. She was beyond tears now, knew it had been so, ever since that long night she had watched by Christopher's bedside, when her tears of worry had gradually ceased with the knowledge that the impossible was happening and her son was dying. She remained, now, standing leaning in the doorway of the parlour, sobbing drily, wishing for oblivion. *It should have been me. Mary Rose had everything to live for. It should have been me.*

She started violently when a rapping on the front door, sharp and sudden in the stillness, brought her back to reality.

She turned, stepped into the hall, and halted. The face of a demon peered at her through the glass of the door—but no. It had been the remnants of her haunted mind. This face was human.

Katherine moved past the hall table to the door and, opening it, stood regarding Nancy Halstrop.

The knowing eyes flickered past Katherine into the hall and, seeing the action, Katherine stepped aside to allow the woman to sidle in. She took in the door to the parlour, the empty hallway and the stairs before turning startled eyes to the front door, which Katherine had shut firmly.

"What do you want?"

Nancy Halstrop narrowed her eyes. "You got no cause to use that tone to me. I came here from the best of intentions, to see Mrs Kelehan. If it pleases you, Mrs Carron, I'll go upstairs . . ."

She took a step, but Katherine's voice made her halt. "Why do you want to see Mrs Kelehan?"

The finely-chiselled little chin came up. "If you must know, I heard she was sick. That Regnier woman was up in the hills delivering one of the Larssons, and I only knew about it because I visited her afterwards and one of the brats told me. While I was there, young O'Mahony comes tearing up, horse all asweat, looking for that interfering black . . ." She stopped. "He wouldn't tell me what was wrong, but I guessed it was Mrs Kelehan. I delivered her child, and I should have been consulted, if anything else was to be done. I don't want that Regnier woman saying I did wrong by Mrs Kelehan, spreading false rumours . . ."

"Why should you think she'd do that? You took all precautions, didn't you?" Her voice was icy. She felt detached, as if she watched herself speaking to the woman, but felt no connection to the scene.

"Of course I did. I won't have anyone saying otherwise. I'm a widow that has to make her own way in the world, and all I've got is my good name—and that black bitch has been spreading rumours about me, to the point where even Larsson's little tart of an eldest girl lied through her teeth, rather than admit that she was too afraid to have me at her birthing. That black bitch has made me look bad time and again . . ."

"Because your patients die, Mrs Halstrop? Why did you leave the district where you lived for so long with your late husband? Would it, by chance, be because too many of your patients died with puerperal fever?"

"I never lost a patient! I never lost a patient yet! And if you go saying that around this Valley, then stuck up Prescott or not, I'll sue you!"

"Leave my house, Mrs Halstrop."

"It ain't your house! Though you'd like to make out you own the whole bloody Valley! Daring to lift your hand to me—I bet it was you who sent O'Mahony looking for that Regnier woman tonight, wasn't it? It was!" The eyes were bright with malignant triumph. "You called *her* in, because you bin saying that I don't clean my hands properly!"

"You didn't. Your nails . . ."

"A bit of colour under the nails don't make no bloody difference!" Her uneasy, nasal vowels were slipping, her grammar and good manners thrown to the wind. "How was I to dig out every bit of black from under my nails when I was needed upstairs? How do you think them filthy blacks get on, having their babies in the dirt? Don't try to tell me I ain't proper, just because I don't measure up to what *you* . . ."

"Mrs Carron . . . ?"

Angel Regnier stood halfway down the stairs, but Katherine was never to know what she was about to say. Nancy Halstrop's face drained of colour, and she turned to Katherine with a hiss. "*She's here.* You let that . . . that *gin* touch that girl after I did all the work? If she's sick now, and she dies, don't you go looking around for someone to blame—it'll be *her* handiwork!" A stubby finger was thrust like a spear in Angel's direction.

Katherine had taken a step towards the woman, but it was Angel Regnier, perhaps attempting to diffuse the moment, who said, "Mrs Halstrop—it would be best if you went home now. This is a house of bereave . . ."

"Don't you dare tell me to go! Poisoning everyone's minds against me! *You* get away from my patient! You've no right to be here! I was her midwife, not you! *You* go! You ain't a midwife, anyway! You're just a black whore! Some old Frenchman's black whore!"

Katherine's riding crop still lay on the hall table, and it was gratifying, so gratifying, that first blow that she struck across the vicious, sallow face.

"*You* killed her . . . *You* did it . . . ! She trusted you—and she's *dead*! Because of *you*!" And her words were addressed more to herself than Nancy Halstrop. "She trusted you . . . and you *killed* her . . . !"

She had the odd sensation of having lived through this moment before . . . Brendan's hand had jerked the riding crop from her stiff fingers and pulled her away. As she turned, she had a brief glimpse of Angel's face, pained, concerned, her father edging past her on the stairs, calling Katherine's name, and then only Brendan's face above her, just that agony-filled, haunted face that she had so wanted to avoid seeing. She had been here before—the day the child was born, Brendan had had to pull her back from the woman who now crouched, screeching, against the wall, her hands and arms covering her face . . . Katherine had fainted that day, exhausted and overcome by the thought of what might happen . . . And here was the reality, and even that oblivion was now denied her. Her mind remained clear, cruelly clear, as Brendan led her away, back towards the kitchen, and she could hear behind her Nancy Halstrop's shrill threats, and Edwina sleepily demanding, "Father? What's happened? Is everything all right? Father? What's happened?"

Thirty Five

Katherine refused the idea of a holiday at Dovewood, though her mother, in her letters, pleaded with her, Brendan and Marcus ordered her, and Edwina and Laura, recovered sufficiently to travel, begged her to accompany them with a fondness and light-heartedness that almost concealed their worry for her.

She paused sometimes, passing a mirror, shocked at the change in herself, and thought, wonderingly, that perhaps they were right in their concern. If Laura or Edwina had suddenly become a gaunt shadow like this, she would undoubtedly behave exactly as the rest of her family did towards her. But she knew there was no benefit to be had from a mere change of scenery; this was something that no distance could alleviate.

"The last time I spoke to Mary Rose," Laura said one morning when Katherine was seated beside her sister's bed, reading to her, "she told me that she wanted to stay in the Valley. I was very surprised, but pleased for Brendan, as he seems to like it here. Mary Rose said she felt like a different person here—and she said she'd miss us all so much if she had to return to America. Her son was an Australian, she said, and she seemed proud of that, and she told me she'd like him to grow up in Australia. It was very strange to hear her talk like that and I thought it may be only a whim, you know how she would get these sudden enthusiasms." Laura's face, still pale with the effects of her illness, nevertheless lit up with humour at her memories; but the glow faded, as abruptly as it had appeared. She finished soberly, "But she said she'd been thinking about it for some time, had half-mentioned it to you, Katey, but wanted to wait until she was absolutely sure."

Katherine, her book held forgotten on her lap, remembered Mary Rose, sitting up in bed. *I have something to tell you . . .*

So that had been the secret. The grief closed like a fist on her heart, a grief that was never far from her as she went about her mechanical tasks day by day. The irony made it worse; the priest had come from St Xavier's in Berrima, the solemnities had been observed, and Barrengarry, only briefly brightened by Mary Rose's lively enthusiasms, was as it had been in those dark days after Joe's death, a house that seemed expectant, waiting, poised for a presence, a quick footstep, a laugh that never came. And Mary Rose slept in the lacy shadows of a eucalypt, part of the country to which she had tried so hard to adapt, a country that had taken with one hand, yet given bountifully with the other, a country she had wished, at the last, to call her own. And this, at least, would be granted. She would sleep amongst those people she had come to call her friends.

Laura recovered from the influenza, serious though it had been, with no after-effects except a slight and persistent cough; this did not deter her from wishing to travel to Dovewood. Both she and Edwina were longing to see their mother, and to put them behind them, for a while at least, the sadness that clung about Barrengarry.

And there was another reason why the two girls were eager for the change. Stephen Brody and Rafe Huckstable were not often at the homestead these days. Stephen had kept aloof since the mysterious quarrel with Laura while Katherine had been staying at Balmain, and Rafe—Rafe had seemingly followed his old pattern and had withdrawn himself from the environs when it seemed—as it had appeared to all of them who saw him with Teddi—that he had decided at last to commit his heart to someone other than himself. Katherine was cross with both men, wished they had the loyalty of the sturdy Luke Murchison, whose patient courting of Edwina and kindness to Laura and Katherine, did much to cheer them in the weeks after the funeral.

Peggy and Carl had returned to the Valley two days after Mary Rose's death with supplies from Wollongong. Katherine and Marcus could not blame them for choosing to make the journey when they did; it had seemed so safe a time for them to take a welcome break from the responsibilities of the homestead and to stay with Peggy's relatives in Wollongong for three days while they bought the necessary supplies. When they had left the Valley, everything had seemed secure; Miss Laura and Miss Edwina were well, Amos had gone home to his farm to be nursed by Billy and Nancy Halstrop, Mr Kelehan was firmly in charge of the property and there were several young stockmen and farmworkers on the place. They were not to know that Laura was only just beginning to sicken with the influenza virus, that Mary Rose had been hiding her discomfort from Peggy for some days, or that, most tragic of all, a difficult confinement would take Angel Regnier away from her home hurriedly and that the preoccupied Emile had mislaid her note, could not, despite his anxious efforts, remember the name of her patient. So Peggy and Carl had come home, rested and content, to find the dark wreath upon the door, the house hushed, and the narrow little coffin amidst its blaze of candles in the parlour.

No one in the house was immune from his or her own feelings of culpability. Each person had a silent litany that threaded through the days, "If only . . ."

One bright moment in that grim time at Barrengarry came with the sudden arrival of Edwin Gordon's ancient brougham, driven by Charles, the almost equally ancient coachman, the luggage tray loaded with Marcus and Katherine's trunks from the Sydney visit. Seated within the vehicle, spared because of the plentiful servants at Dovewood, who would also be caring for young Molly, and the knowledge that Katherine would have only Peggy to help run the house and look after baby James, was Bridget Murray.

She settled in well, liking Peggy immediately, and declaring herself much more at home in the rambling, informal comfort of Barrengarry than in the rather overpowering opulence of Dovewood. The first day that Bridget helped with the washing, Peggy informed Katherine with a grim smile that young Patrick O'Mara, Jim O'Mara's eldest boy, was dangling his elbows over the fence, talking to her for an hour or more. "She's a good girl and she's fond of us, Miss Katey, but we'll have lost her to be somebody's wife before the year is out, you mark my words."

Bridget, thankfully, kept her head, and seemed to enjoy the attentions of the young farmers of the Valley without allowing them to take her mind from her duties, and for this Katherine was grateful. Bridget did most of the cleaning, Peggy looked after the baby, and Katherine helped her father or Brendan or the two servants, as the need arose.

She avoided taking charge of the child herself, though her breast ached when she heard him cry and she longed to be the one to lift him up, to soothe him—but she dared not. There was a fierce pride that pre-empted the mother's longing within her. She would not have Brendan think that she was using the child to draw some bond between them. He had been too bruised, too tormented by fate for her to intrude her own needs upon him. Though more than ever aware of her desire to comfort him, to be comforted by him, she felt she must keep this uneasy distance between them, so they went through their days in much the same way as they had done before the tragedy. What sort of a woman would she be—what sort of woman would he think her, if she ran to his arms now? So she grew more strict with herself in her loneliness, held herself aloof from any but the most unavoidable conversations with him. And all the while it was as if she were separated from the other half of herself.

Laura and Edwina were to leave in the brougham with Edwin to return to Dovewood, but a wheel was noticed to be loose after the severe jolting of the descent into the Valley, and the girls' departure was delayed a further two days while a farmworker, experienced as a wheelwright, mended the wheel and re-affixed it sturdily.

Stephen Brody had come to bid a farewell to the two sisters a few days before, a rather uneasy visit with the parlour seeming to echo with all the words that remained unsaid. Laura had retired to her room immediately after he had left, and Marcus, whose glaring presence had not helped put Stephen at his ease, declared to her as she went upstairs that it was just as well the young brat was showing his true colours.

Katherine was cross with her father, but Laura reappeared in an hour or so, seemingly recovered in spirits, so she felt no need to approach her sister on the matter.

She was to wish she had when, two days later, seated on the front verandah hemming towelling squares for the baby's constant needs, she was startled to look up and see Stephen riding up the drive.

Laura had gone walking with Edwina, over the back paddocks to the creek, and she was about to tell Stephen this, as he left his horse tied to the front fence and came smiling up the path to her. But—

"I can't believe I've been so fortunate. I've found you alone, haven't I?"

She was puzzled, then suddenly wary. "Why, no—Bridget and Peggy are in the kitchen, and . . ."

"You know what I mean. We can talk."

"About what, Stephen?"

It was the only thing to do, of course. She seated herself once more in the one comfortable old wicker chair and gestured, with a polite smile, for Stephen to take another. He stood there for some seconds, the tanned, handsome face showing the fleeting dismay of being wilfully misunderstood.

"You know why." He shook his head a little, puzzled; one hand brushed the fair hair from his forehead, a gesture of exasperation he used to make, even as a child.

She took pity on him. "Stephen, I think you should know—Laura is . . ."

"I can't go on, Katherine. I simply can't. I . . . I know this really isn't the time, so soon after Mrs Kelehan's death, when you must be grieving . . . but . . . Katherine, it's been seven months since you came home . . ."

"Stephen, I don't think we should . . ."

". . . Seven months when I've been alive only when I've been able to be with you. I've . . ."

It was her nerves, that's what it was, this sudden, mad desire to laugh—she covered her mouth with her hands, for it was terrible, this scene, and serious, and she must not think how comic he looked, how insane this moment was . . . "Stephen, you must stop," she said, managing to speak firmly, standing and moving towards the front door. "I wouldn't have thought you could be so foolish . . ."

"Foolish! No, don't go running back into the house! I'm here now, where I've wanted to be for six *years*, Katherine, and I'm not about to be sent away like an errant schoolboy!"

"But that's exactly how you're behaving. We decided that there was only friendship between us six years ago . . ."

"*You* decided, Katherine. I had no choice in the matter. Friendship—after all we shared before you went off and made that dreadful marriage . . ."

"*Dreadful marriage*? Stephen, how dare you . . . !"

He looked stricken, miserable. "I . . . I didn't mean that—but he *was* a foreigner, even if he was Irish—he wasn't one of your own people. I couldn't believe you could so such a thing. When your family came back and told me the news, I . . . I wanted to die. And that's not idle rhetoric . . ." He jumped up onto the low verandah, stood over her with the memory of his pain upon his face, the force of his thwarted desire a kind of threat to her. The scene had long ceased to be amusing.

"Stephen, I think you'd better go . . ."

"Oh, *damn*—I can't get through to you, can I?" He turned away to the view of the garden, then whirled about to face her. "I spent years—*years*, trying to cope with the loss of you. I began to get over it only when Laura told me of the birth of your son."

"Stop it, Stephen!"

"It made it real, somehow, the birth of your boy. Your marriage had seemed simply a kind of betrayal until then. With the birth of the child you were suddenly a mother—the mother of *his* child." There was a kind of gentle wonder to his face which might have moved her, were it not for the pain he was causing her, stirring these memories. "And I could *see* you then, in my mind's eye, going about your chores, making a comfortable life for the three of you. I saw you as *his*, not mine. And I began to forget you then. I made myself forget. I worked hard, I've made myself successful with the farms, and the other businesses are finding their feet. And I began to notice Laura. She was so sweet, so like you—and I probably would have asked her to marry me, months ago, but when I heard that you were . . . were a widow, and might be coming home . . . I was so glad—so glad I'd waited!"

"You'd have been happy with Laura, Stephen, you know it . . ."

He shook his head. "It doesn't matter. There's no point in thinking about all that. Because I love you. If I was told tomorrow that you'd bring me three times the heartache I've already suffered because of you, I'd still choose to love you. There isn't life without you, Katherine."

Katherine sank slowly into her chair, staring in front of her. Had she done all this? Caused all this agony, these years of suffering, without even realizing it?

"Stephen, my dear . . . this is terrible. I . . . What is it you want of me? No!" As he began to speak hotly, ardently. "Don't say my love, for you don't have that, you can't have that. I . . . I never felt that way about you, Stephen. You were . . ."

"It's Rafe, isn't it? I suspected, years ago—Oh, not from anything you've said. It's him—all the time he's been courting Edwina it's been obvious that he comes alive only when you're in the room . . ."

"Stephen you're wrong! I'm pleased that the friendship between Edwina and Rafe is over, of course I am—you would be, too, if she were your sister. But I do *not* have my cap set for Rafe or any other man." She stopped, studied his face warily. "Stephen, have you spoken to Laura about me? Good grief, Stephen, you haven't told Laura that you're in love with me?"

"No, of course not—I'd do anything to avoid hurting Laura. I think the world of her."

"You know that she hasn't yet gone . . ."

". . . But I can't go on letting her believe I care for her when it's you I love. Have you any idea of the tortures I've been through these past months? I was even jealous of Brendan, until his wife arrived—and even then I was jealous, because you and Brendan were so friendly, so at ease with each other. To have known you all those years in Dublin—to live in the same house with you here at Barrengarry, to see you each morning at breakfast—I like the man enormously, but sometimes I've hated him, for being able to be close to you when I couldn't."

"Stephen . . ." she begged, "please try to understand. I've always been fond of you—before I left to go overseas all those years ago I knew we were close. But in my mind it was the closeness of friends. Oh, Stephen, I never meant to hurt you—you've kept your feelings so well-hidden until now . . ."

"I knew what you'd been through, losing your friend Mrs Kelehan— and it's only been a year since your husband died. I've waited until now because I didn't want to rush you, I wanted to give you time . . ."

"And in the meantime, you used Laura," she reminded him. "You led her on, Stephen—how could you!"

"I . . . I had to—how could I have called so often if I didn't have an excuse . . ."

"That's despicable . . . !"

"All right, I'm despicable! I'm a cad of the worst order—but you led me on, also, all those years ago. It may have been only friendship on your part," he said bitterly, "but you must have seen that it was more than friendship that I felt for you. We'd walk by the creek, and you'd allow me to put my arm about your waist, remember?"

"Yes . . ." softly, unwillingly.

"And we'd hold hands at every opportunity, and several times you let me kiss you . . ."

"Three times, not several. Three, and it was totally unexpected each time. I didn't lure you on . . ."

"No," he admitted, grudgingly, "I kissed you without your sanction, I admit it—but you were so sweet and generous afterwards, even though you pretended to be cross . . . Oh, it's all a game to you, isn't it? It seems it's a game to everyone—it's so hard to tell what's sincere! Are you telling me now that . . . that I've loved you for six years, and you thought of me as a *friend*—that is, when you did think of me at all? *Did* you ever think of me?"

Be kind? Or be honest? And which, in the long term, would be the kindest?

"No, Stephen. I was busy looking after my husband and my son. I rarely thought of you. You belonged to a world I'd left far behind me, that I never expected to see again. I'm sorry— I *am* sorry . . . I had no idea you thought so fondly of me . . . And you're right—I was thoughtless, and didn't consider your feelings—I should have."

"It's late for that now, isn't it? You flirted with me, and it meant nothing to you . . ."

"No," heavily. "It meant that I enjoyed your company—and I enjoyed your arm about my waist, if you must know. But nothing more serious than that. And it was so long ago, Stephen . . ."

"Not to me."

"But . . . what did I give you, my dear, that you could base your loyalty and affection on? I've known you all my life, and we've talked and laughed together—but I never, *never* gave you any hint that I saw a future for us . . ."

She paused, for to see his hurt, hurt her, also. While his devotion was a wonderful compliment, it was also a burden, and she was sensible enough to realize, even now, in the midst of this confrontation, that the Katherine he had mourned for all these years bore no resemblance to the woman now before him.

"I don't believe you." The fair head of curls was lowered, he glared at her from beneath his brows, like a young bull prepared to stand his ground. "It's my fault—obviously I've approached you at the wrong moment . . ."

"No, Stephen. It's as well you chose this moment. I can't bear to think of Laura being hurt any more than she has been. Stephen, if what you love in me is gentleness and amiability and affection, then you're declaring yourself to the wrong woman. I'm wilful and independent and impatient . . ."

"You never were with me, before you left for Europe."

"Stephen, haven't you noticed that it's actually easier to be kind to someone you don't truly love? When one is in love, the merest slight is agony; whereas for a friend one can bear all sorts of aggravations with tolerance. I never cared for you, Stephen, to the extent where my emotions made me forget my good manners. I . . . I never loved you, Stephen."

This was the bitterest blow. She saw in his face the pain of watching his tenderly nursed dreams shatter and collapse around him. Yet, foolish man, how could he allow them to have arisen in the first place?

He had always been a dreamer, a good-natured, lackadaisical, handsome boy, who had grown into manhood equally as handsome, with his clear brown skin and blue eyes untroubled by matters outside the Valley, spoilt by doting parents and a grim but fond grandfather who, though demanding and hard upon the rest of the world, had nevertheless found excuses in his heart for Stephen's small vanities. A lack of self-knowledge, of curiosity about the outside world was not really regarded as a handicap in the Valley; indeed, they would, perhaps, have led to dissatisfaction and rebellion. Stephen's complacency had not bothered Katherine—he was her friend. But she had demanded more of the men she had loved; the depth, the sparkle of intellect, the aura of danger that Oliver and Brendan—and even Rafe—had possessed. She gazed steadily at Stephen, knowing, with a feeling of helplessness, that anything further she would say would be wrong. But no. There was one more thing . . .

"Stephen, all those characteristics I said I lacked—Laura has them. More than that, she'd love you, if you gave her the chance. And the love of someone like Laura is surely worthwhile . . ."

"Don't bring Laura into this . . . !"

"Laura is involved in this. *You've* involved her in this—and she deserves better. Laura is the best . . ."

"Don't tell me what Laura is!" Stephen's face was white with his rage and disappointment. And he had had, so far, so little disappointment in his life. He was handling this rejection very badly. "Laura is the best? Yes, I do believe she is. You've changed, Katherine. Whatever's happened to you in these past six years or so has made you hard and cold—it's taken the life from you. I don't believe there's enough left to be called a real woman."

He's right, she thought, so amazed at his perspicacity that she forgot to be hurt at his words. *He's right. He's right.*

Stephen had leapt down the verandah steps and vaulted over the front gate. He was on his horse and had turned it away down the drive at a fast canter before Katherine realized she was still seated there, had been seated there all along, with a square of white towelling and the needle and thread still held in her hands.

The afternoon was mild, the sun still shone brightly in a clear and limpid sky, but its strength was diminished, the rays had lost their summer ferocity, and now, in early autumn, were warming and kindly.

Katherine remained seated in her chair, and tried to regain some of the peace that the fragrant, somnolent garden had given her until Stephen's sudden appearance; but it was difficult now; his outburst had disturbed her, and would make her days unquiet, she reflected, for some time.

Behind her, from within, someone came walking briskly from the kitchen, along the hall towards the front of the house. The tread was heavier, faster, than Laura's—Edwina's impatient stride. Katherine was glad the girls had returned, was about to call to them that she was out here, on the verandah . . .

But Edwina was not preceding Laura. She was searching for her. "Laura . . . ?" she called, and then the footsteps paused. The doorway to the parlour. "Oh, there you are. Why don't you pull aside the curtains? It's dark in here . . . Laura?"

No. Katherine's heart sank. How could Laura have returned to the house, all the way along the hall to the parlour, a wall away, without Katherine hearing her?

Laura walks like Mama, a soft, gliding step. If she didn't wish to be heard, she would not.

"Laura?" Edwina's voice persisted. "Laura, what's the matter?" Edwina was becoming anxious, so of course Laura had to speak, knowing, as she did so, that she would be betraying her presence in the parlour to her sister, seated just outside the windows on the verandah.

"I . . . I had a slight headache. I thought I'd lie here in the quiet and the dark for a while."

"Shall I fetch you a cool drink, or a cup of tea?"

"No . . . no, thank you, Teddi—I'll be all right."

"I *will* get you a cup of tea—you sound quite wilted. I'll just go upstairs and change first—I shouldn't have gone after those wildflowers—my boots are all muddy . . ."

The voice faded with the *tap-tap* of her firm little footsteps, back along the parqueted floor and up the carpeted stairs.

In the silence, Katherine sighed, drawing air painfully into her lungs, realizing that she had forgotten to breathe. Her heart heavy, she stood and dropped her sewing onto her chair.

When she entered the parlour she could not, at first, see anything but shadows in the room; the drapes had been left closed to avoid the morning sun slanting in to further fade the furnishings, and no one, on this particular day, had been into the room and bothered to adjust the curtains. Certainly Laura had not. She lay face down on the comfortable old velvet settee, her head turned sideways, resting on a cushion. She did not move, but must, if her eyes were open, see Katherine poised in the doorway. Still she made no move, and Katherine walked into the room and seated herself in a nearby chair.

She said gently, "How long were you listening, Laura?"

A pause, and a sigh like a breeze through a lonely landscape. "Since Stephen began to sound loudly passionate. I was walking up the hall, heading towards the stairs, as Teddi had stopped to play with the baby in the kitchen. I heard voices, and I started out towards the verandah—and then I realized it was Stephen . . . and I heard him accusing you of preferring Rafe to *him*—and . . . I couldn't leave, couldn't stop my ears. I had to come in here, to sit down—I thought I was going to faint . . . but I could hear just as clearly as I could in the hall." Her voice faded a little; the whole speech had come in a dispassionate, lost tone that seemed to have no wish to be connected with human feelings. Katherine understood it only too well.

"He doesn't mean it, Laura."

A silence, and when Laura spoke it was clear that her mind was following its own course, she undoubtedly had not even heard her sister. "I had no idea, you know. I believed him, when he said he couldn't live with the strain of our families disapproving of our seeing each other. That made sense; he's very fond of his parents and respects their wishes, even if he is old enough to make his own decisions.

"To hear . . . all that he said to you . . . it was so *calculated*. And suddenly, all the love I'd had for him was meaningless. He's demeaned it. You said it yourself."

"No, Laura . . . !" in desperation.

"I heard you, Katey," still in that dull, expressionless voice. "You said, 'You used Laura, you led her on.' And he said, 'I had to.' "

Laura sat up on the settee, adjusted her hair calmly. Now Katherine's eyes had become accustomed to the gloom, she could see that Laura was dry-eyed, but her hands shook a little as she removed a loose comb from her hair and replaced it neatly. Only then Laura said, "I don't blame you, Katey—but it will take me a long time to forget this. You should have told me. You should have warned me earlier, and I might not feel such a fool."

"Laura, I didn't know until he marched up the garden path and began declaring himself like a . . . a . . ."

"Like an impetuous man very much in love."

The calm, firm voice, so mature in its sentiments, seemed to belong to a strange woman, it seemed impossible that it was her little sister who spoke thus. "Laura . . ."

Laura stood. She came over to Katherine and kissed her cheek. "I'm upset now. I don't blame you, Katey, truly. It's hard, though, for me to think clearly—I'm so filled with ungenerous thoughts about the world that I must seem ungenerous. I don't mean to be. You've always looked after me, protected me, and helped me have my way with things when Father would feel he had to be strict or stubborn. But this time, Father was right, Katey. I'd . . . I'd appreciate it a great deal, though, if you didn't tell him."

"Of course . . ."

"I . . . I've been thinking, here by myself, that I won't stay at Dovewood for long. Libby and Tobias are still at Balmain, I'll go there for a while, stay right away from the Valley and . . . and everything, for a year perhaps."

"What will you do?" Katherine wondered what her parents would say to this rather independent idea.

"The same things you did when you were there. I have my friends, and there's charity work to become involved in, Father has asked me often enough to consider it. He'll be returning to Sydney himself soon, I should imagine, so I won't be unchaperoned for long. I know how he's always felt about Stephen, though he's tried to hide it lately, which is good of him; I can't imagine that Father would object to my going to Sydney if it would mean I was planning on setting about forgetting Stephen Brody." She looked determined. "If he asks, I shall tell him it was a mutual parting, for I had enough pride to let Stephen think I agreed with him . . ."

For the first time, with her final words, the tears threatened and, as Katherine rose to speak her name, Laura precluded further speech by murmuring, "I have to go upstairs—I still haven't finished packing. At least I shall be dressed in the latest fashion, Katey," she paused to say in the doorway. "We have Mary Rose to thank for that, Teddi and I. She made us over completely . . ."

The sentence was left hanging in the air, in all its poignant ambiguity, and it was too much for the sensitive Laura. Katherine sat in the dimness of the parlour and listened as the light footsteps ran up the stairs and faded on the upper storey.

The land had not been cleared here; it was a high, sweeping timbered slope where the cattle that had been breeding wild over the past thirty years or more grew strong and untamed and dangerous. The spring muster had culled the herd, if the shy renegade cattle could be called that, but there had been one or two stories of settlers on the lower slopes being confronted, and even chased, by rangy, red-eyed young bulls; and it seemed as if the fences—sturdily enough built by Marcus's father in the early days of settlement—were at last beginning to prove inadequate.

Brendan had ridden up here alone, as each day he used the slightest pretext to work without others about him. He did not understand the workings of his own mind any longer; always a thoughtful man, he now felt confronted by the black depths of an abyss whenever he attempted to gain some order, some insight into what had happened, what he could do. No answers came, only his own heartache, his sense of failure, and a culpability that haunted him as surely as the beautiful face with its cloud of gold hair haunted his dreams and his every waking moment.

And the one person he wished to turn to, who could, with a word, even a silent touch, offer him some kind of comfort, some healing, walked about her home, in the days since the tragedy, with a pale mask that made her seem a stranger to him. The green eyes that turned to him—when she did turn to him—were icy with what seemed to him her disappointment, even her contempt.

And there was nothing to be done. No words, no action, that could break down the barrier between them. He looked at Katherine, and he read in her eyes that he had failed Mary Rose, that though the incompetent midwife might live at liberty, it was Brendan's choice,

Brendan's decision, in the face of Katherine's disapproval, that had ultimately cost Mary Rose her life. And seeing all that, what would she say, should he approach her, take her in his arms . . . The thought of her scorn, her further contempt, chilled him.

But . . . perhaps they could forget in time—perhaps, in time, they could speak of it, and he could tell her . . . What? How many years, he wondered, could make her forget his treatment of Mary Rose? His coolness, his impatience towards her, all born of the fact that it was Katherine whom he loved—it was a poor excuse, and not an offering that any woman of feeling and sensibility could ever accept.

He heard the child crying before he heard the woman's voice. Small, dark-skinned, about two years old, he came stumbling out from a clump of honeyflower shrubs—a naked boy of the Woddi Woddi, obviously lost and bewailing the fact loudly, small fat fists knuckling at his eyes, the face blotched and stained with dirt and tears.

Brendan rose in his stirrups, checking the surrounding scrub; Katherine had told him once that a Woddi child was rarely lost and seldom panicked, the bush being its natural habitat and the devotion of the mother such that she would never be far away.

The child had pulled back a little on seeing him, fright robbing him of sound for a moment, and it was in those few seconds of silence that Brendan heard the shouting, the muffled screams.

He was down from his horse, had scooped up the youngster and was running towards the sound before he had time to consider; only on seeing the two struggling creatures on the creek bank did he drop the child and plunge forward alone.

Davey Crolin was at a disadvantage, his trousers being about his knees and his mind totally occupied with trying to hold down the fighting, spitting fury of the woman beneath him. By the time he saw Brendan rushing down upon him, pulled back and prepared to stand, it was too late. One hand at his shirt to lift him a little, Brendan brought his other fist about with deadly accuracy, striking Davey full on the jaw and sending him sprawling backwards to fall half-in and half-out of the water.

Brendan pulled the woman to her feet, noticing her cut lip, swollen eye. He glanced over towards the child, and seeing him padding towards his mother, pushed her gently in his direction. "Go! Quickly—go!"

One frightened glance at him, another back at the already stirring Crolin, and the younger woman—Brendan did not know her name, but had seen her with Myeela and Tigoora on several occasions—had fled. She bent with two fluid movements to pick up first her single grass-woven garment, then the boy, before vanishing silently, totally, into the scrub.

"What'd you do that for? Someone'd think she was your woman, the way you go on!"

Brendan stepped towards him but Davey, propped up on his elbows, scrambled back, like a mud crab, along the bank. "You know what they did! *They* killed Penman an' Barton . . . planted the stuff on my brother . . . !"

"What?" Brendan paused.

"S'true! Lying ol' Amos Murphy—nigger lover that 'e is—he told the police that Charlie beat 'im up! Everyone knows it's them murderin' blacks!"

"Your brother, Charlie . . ."

"Our Charlie never done nuthin'! But now Lloyd has locked 'im up in that rotten little cell at the back of Radley's store—and he's callin' in the magistrate! An' them rotten blacks done it!"

He was not yet game to rise, struggled to pull up his trousers in his prone position, but could not manage it. He climbed warily to his feet, began pulling them up, and whined. "Why'd y' have to stop me—she was calming down—I'd have let you have a go after . . ."

Later, he told himself he needn't have beaten the man as severely as he did. But suddenly, there on the bank, seeing Davey Crolin hoisting at his trousers, wiping the mud from his eyes and offering a share in the violent taking of an innocent woman, the thin barrier of Brendan's rage gave way to a violence that, later, frightened even himself. He remembered that he waited for Davey to pull up his trousers and climb out of the mud. He remembered that with each blow he struck to the narrow face and body that he repeated "You *won't* do that *again* . . ." as if he could as easily impress the thought upon that narrow mind.

Davey was no fighter, and no match in build nor ability for Brendan, but he carried his own methods of equalizing matters.

It was when he had stumbled backwards slightly, and Brendan, unthinking, had followed, that Davey pulled the hunting knife from its scabbard at his belt, whirled with it in his hand, and sliced upwards at Brendan's chest. The older man leapt back, saving his own life by less than the length of the short and deadly blade. The pain registered, but Brendan was beyond feeling. He found Davey's wrist within his grasp and bent it down and out, ignored the howl of agony, and when the knife fell, he pushed Davey in one direction while he bent and hurled the knife away into the bushes the opposite way. Davey heard it land, but did not see the arc it made, did not see where it fell, and his second howl, one of frustration and sheer terror, was worse than the first. "She was only a gin . . ." he whimpered, "only a gin—who cares about her . . . ?"

Brendan stopped himself from killing the man only when he realized that Davey had been unconscious from the blows for some time. He left him there then, spreadeagled on the ground and breathing sonorously through a nose broken for the second time, and made his way back to his horse.

He met only one vehicle on the road back to Barrengarry, but the occupants of the smart new buggy could not help but notice and, later, comment on the state of his clothes, his pale, angry, preoccupied frown and the terseness of his greeting. They—and particularly the woman—noted the blood that had sprayed, quite heavily, the front of his pale blue shirt.

"I'm visiting Bendeela, at the invitation of Miss Emilia and her parents." The pretty little face with its perfect skin dimpled at him from the speckled shadows of an expensive lace parasol. "Perhaps you and your employers, the Misses Prescott, would like to visit—could they, Rafe?"

Rafe had been scowling at the silent and dangerous apparition of the horseman before them. "Yes," he drawled, still preoccupied, "tell Mrs Carron and her sisters that they're welcome at Bendeela at any time, and that Miss Barton will be staying with us for a week."

"I'll do that. Good afternoon . . ." He lifted his hat a little to each of them, with a brief but graceful bow from the saddle of the impatient chestnut, before riding on.

He heard words, sounding like a command, from the vehicle behind him, but they were not addressed to him and he was too far to hear them clearly.

Rafe Huckstable, clearly annoyed, had brought the whip down upon the horses and snapped, "For God's sake, Fleur—don't stare after the man like that!"

Thirty Six

When Brendan returned to Barrengarry he made no mention of the incident by the creek, nor, for the moment, of meeting Fleur Barton and Rafe Huckstable. All three Prescott sisters were entertaining Luke Murchison in the parlour, listening avidly to the tale of how the murderer had been apprehended at last.

"Amos was finally persuaded to talk—it seems that he was afraid of the Crolins seeking revenge on him if he told the truth—for it seems as if it's only Charlie that's implicated. Well, Tom Lloyd and Constable Crowe went up to Charlie's hut—they searched the place and found nearly three hundred pounds buried in a hole in the earth floor of the hut. Charlie had moved the bed over it, but the earth was still freshly turned. The money was wrapped in a piece of calico, and with it was the wallet belonging to poor Penman, and a gold watch with Gilbert Barton's initials on it.

"His wife, Essie, is almost hysterical, claims she doesn't know who planted the money there. Davey and Frank, of course, say they don't know where he is, and that they don't know anything about it . . ."

They all looked up then, seeing Brendan in the shadowed doorway. He smiled apologetically, declined their invitation to join them, and went upstairs to change his clothes. The girls, accustomed both to the silence of his grief and to the often muddy state of his clothes when he came in from a day in the saddle, asked no questions about his appearance and thought no more of it.

"I'm really rather sorry that crinoline hoops are becoming smaller," Edwina sighed, stowing the last of the metal-banded petticoats on top of the clothes in the huge square trunk. "I suppose we'll have cage crinolines with us for a while yet, but it's only a matter of time before it's back to ordinary petticoats and the hoops go altogether. It's such a pity—having one's skirts held so far away from the body is *so* much cooler in this climate."

She looked up, across her bedroom to where Katherine was placing the last of Edwina's little bonnets in the hat box, gazing at her reflectively as she did so. "I'm glad that you're looking forward to the visit," Katherine smiled. "Mama is missing you both so much, I know."

Edwina, satisfied, went prattling on about the fashion for drawing all the fullness of one's skirts towards the back of dresses. "Don't the designers realize how big our behinds will look? Or is that the idea?"

Katherine was silent, lost in her own thoughts, and Teddi chattered on regardless.

Brendan had told Katherine about seeing Fleur on her way to Bendeela with Rafe and about the invitation to visit, at which Katherine had laughed with genuine amusement. "The Kangaroo River will flow backwards before that day comes," she remarked, and Brendan looked closely at her, not knowing, of course, the extent of her bitterness towards Fleur.

He had gone off to Marcus's office soon after, and Katherine found him to be quite subdued at dinner. Something seemed to be brooding behind the grey eyes, and Katherine found herself wondering, as she did so often, if he was close to declaring a day when he would take his son and leave for America. He had always said he would go, and now he had the chance, small comfort as it was, to begin again and leave much of his heartache behind him.

And she, Katherine, was part of it. How would he be able to forget that she had played a part in his greatest tragedy? When he remembered her, it would surely be with uneasy fondness, overshadowed by the loss of a beautiful wife who would remain forever young and progressively idealized, even more than if he had truly loved her, for there would be guilt there, and regrets for the missed opportunities, the moments unseized, the words unspoken. He could spend the rest of his days, she thought, holding internal dialogues on what-might-have-been. Brendan belonged more completely to Mary Rose now than he ever had.

Marcus, for reasons that he did not discuss with the family, was returning to Moss Vale with the girls and Edwin in the coach, and Katherine was glad that they would have the extra protection of their father on the trip. For, despite the detailed combing of the surrounding hills, no sign had been found of Charlie Crolin and now Davey had gone missing, Jim O'Mara informed Marcus, when passing on his way to Wollongong for supplies. With men like the Crolins wanted by the police—and she had had experience enough of their potential for violence that day on Brown's Mountain—it was best not to travel alone on the tracks leading in or out of the Valley.

Even Jim O'Mara was meeting up with Andrew Cummings and they were sharing the Cummings's wagon on the trip to Wollongong. Marcus came back from chatting with the man at the gate, smiling to himself, and was able, at last, to tell Katherine the reason behind Jim's new-found and—to Tom Lloyd—suspicious wealth.

"A still up in the mountains beyond his place—he told me because he knows I stood up for him during the time when suspicion was fairly rife. He said he's put aside a couple of bottles for me."

"Father—and will you accept it? It's illegal . . ."

"It's his father's recipe—I used to drink it with my own father when I was a lad. I might try a bottle or two—just to see if the quality is as good as it was . . ." And Marcus sauntered off to his office.

The trip to Dovewood had been delayed two days, but there was still much to do in helping the girls with their last minute packing. Even when the carriageful of waving, beloved people had disappeared down the drive, there was no time for Katherine to miss them. Bridget had the afternoon off and had been invited by the elder O'Mara girls, and exhorted by Patrick, to visit their farm. Katherine helped Peggy to look after the baby, washed the many napkins that James required and as quickly filled, and found time to write to her mother, pleading with her to see Marcus, to at least consider the thought of a reconciliation, for something within her told her that the events of the past year had evolved some changes in Marcus and changes that were, on the whole, for the better.

She would have liked to have visited poor Amos Murphy who, it seemed, was only slowly recovering from his shocking beating, but the ubiquitous Nancy Halstrop was now, a resentful Billy told Tom Lloyd, living at the homestead. So Katherine sent a note of good wishes to him instead, with a cooked chicken from Peggy's oven, asking Tom to deliver it to the Murphys' selection when he returned to the high country to the south in the search for Charlie Crolin.

It was two days after Marcus, Edwin and the girls returned to Dovewood that she was called from her father's office by Bridget. Katherine had been studying all that Barrengarry held of the reports, correspondence and history of her family's business concerns, while the first of autumn's drenching rains fell steadily, unrelentingly, outside the window.

She was beginning to understand Robin Mitchell's concern—in

the letters unwritten, the cheques uncashed, the bills unpaid, it was patently clear that whatever Marcus Prescott felt for the trials of the world at large, his attitude towards his business responsibilities was careless indeed. The clerks at Prescott, Mitchell and Co. must have been organizing his bookwork for years—and how much of the running of the company had been left to the capable Laurence, and then Robin himself? Barrengarry was running extremely well; that it did so must, on the study of poor past records, be because Brendan Kelehan was so alert and so thorough in his management.

Bridget's summons startled her, but she felt no sense of guilt in having been caught reading so carefully through her father's files. Her surprise came from the fact that her visitor, now waiting in the parlour, was Emilia Huckstable.

"Are you certain we won't be disturbed here? The maid—she won't eavesdrop, will she?"

Katherine had no time even to seat herself before Emilia marched back to the door and opened it. Bridget was, of course, nowhere to be seen, having been summarily dismissed—not by Katherine, but by Emilia. No, she did not want tea. No, Mrs Carron did not want tea, either . . .

The arrogance was not, as one would have supposed, typical of Emilia's behaviour—at least, in someone else's house. Though she valued her own opinion, she valued society's more, and she had been strictly raised to observe those niceties of good manners. Within their boundaries she pressed her vantage as far as she dared, but obvious rudeness was not her style. Now, with this plea for seclusion and secrecy, Katherine stared at her, bemused.

Emilia shut the door and sailed back into the room, pulling nervously at the cuffs of her sedate grey costume and looking, on the whole, more agitated and ill-at-ease that Katherine had ever known her in her life. She decided to wait. Emilia was a woman who preferred to set her own pace—and that of others, too, Katherine thought wickedly, where it was possible to do so.

"I don't know if I should have come. But I can't take the risk that I may be right. And if I am, and my father finds out, then Rafe will be in serious trouble." She faced Katherine, in whose head all warning bells were jangling wildly. "You and I have no personal sympathy, but in your father's absence I had to come to you. I daresay you'll know what steps to take. Do you want to sit down?"

"No, thank you."

"Nor do I." Emilia hesitated, then, "You know Miss Barton, I believe. I mean—of course you do—she stayed here, she and her late mama, when her father was killed. I . . . I have been grieved, of late, to realize that my brother has formed an attachment for Miss Barton. It's particularly upsetting for my parents, who are so fond of your sister Edwina. Though she is young, we thought that she had a strength of character that might, in time, curb Rafe's recklessness. We were all disappointed when it seemed that Rafe was not, after all, serious in his attentions. What grieves me most is that young Edwina was so deeply hurt by his abandonment."

"Really, Emilia, you presume a great deal. Edwina is more circumspect than you give her credit for; she's a strong-willed young woman who nevertheless . . ."

"Strong-willed—exactly. I'm coming to that. Forgive me, but I know that you have had tragedy in this house—the past few weeks have been very difficult for you, and I must presume to tell you that you haven't paid as close attention to Edwina as you might. She has called to see Rafe three times in the past three weeks. Twice, he refused to see her. It was pitiable . . . the poor child—please!" as Katherine began to speak, "don't interrupt me with a defence of your sister. Our servants at Bendeela are as discreet as it is possible for servants to be—and when Edwina broke down and cried, only I was in the room to see.

"I found Rafe's behaviour reprehensible, particularly since I knew he was seeing Miss Barton whenever he visited Moss Vale. I had liked the woman on first acquaintance, but she is one of those creatures whom poverty alone, it seems, keeps within the boundaries of modesty and good taste. Since coming into her father's fortune she has blossomed into a flower of most gaudy aspect, and it's quite clear that she had Rafe picked out from the start as a most suitable husband."

No, Katherine thought grimly, *she first picked out Brendan Kelehan.*

"When Rafe told us he was bringing Miss Barton home to stay at Bendeela, we were braced to the possibility that he was planning to announce his engagement."

"*What?*" Even with Brendan's news of Fleur's visit to Bendeela, Katherine had never considered that the relationship would go so far as matrimony. Rafe had never come closer to that state in his life than he had with Edwina. But *Fleur* . . .

Emilia, in her very wide, unfashionable crinoline, glided across to the fireplace aimlessly, as if she needed an excuse for movement, action of any sort. She continued, "When she arrived three days ago, however, it was quite clear that Rafe was withdrawn, preoccupied. He was not in the least as you would imagine a man on the eve of an engagement to be. Fleur, however, was a picture of happiness, so good-humoured and delighted with Bendeela that it seemed she was positively oblivious to Rafe's gloom.

"His mood did not improve. And only the day following their arrival, that is, two days ago, they quarrelled." She paused. "This will distress you, but they quarrelled because Edwina came—it was her third visit—to see Rafe. And he spoke with her, in the study, for some time. It was very early on Tuesday morning—Edwina left Barrengarry later that day, did she not?"

Katherine felt herself grow cold, with shock, with anger, and with apprehension. Edwina had, on the morning of the day the family had left, crept out of the house very early, returning when the family was at breakfast. She had been pink-cheeked, contented with herself and the world, declaring that the early ride she had taken through the mist-hung morning had been the most beautiful she had ever known. And something had happened, obviously, for her to feel so at ease with herself when, until then, she had looked forward to Dovewood as a kind of panacea for her hurt and disappointment over Rafe. Katherine had helped her pack, and Teddi had continued to be elated; and Katherine realized that she had not thought to question further, to look for reasons for the abrupt change of mood.

"Edwina was at Bendeela . . . speaking to Rafe. Not . . . pleading with him?" Surely not—Oh, Teddi, have some pride, some restraint . . .

"I don't know," Emilia said bluntly, promptly. "I only know that she left the house smiling, and Rafe was more withdrawn than ever. He walked with Miss Barton in the garden after breakfast and she came back to the house alone, demanding that my maid help her pack. Within an hour she was on her way back to Moss Vale, one of our farmhands driving her carriage."

Katherine found that she wished to sit down, after all, and sank into a chair. After a pause Emilia, too, subsided amidst a creaking of stays and a thunder of taffeta, to sit bolt upright, gazing at Katherine.

"I followed my brother into his study and confronted him. We have always been close, and I knew he'd tell me things he'd keep back from our parents. At first he refused to discuss anything, but I persisted." Emilia hesitated once more. She had a normally sallow complexion but now an unattractive flush mottled her cheeks. Katherine, gazing at her, forgot the slights, the acerbic disapproval over the years and felt, of a sudden, only pity for the woman. Rafe was her life, and whatever misconduct Rafe had committed, must now, it seemed, be brought to Katherine's ears. For Emilia, it was a double torture.

"He . . . he admitted to me that Miss Barton had loaned him money—to pay some outstanding debts. He was fond of her, but she was . . . using his indebtedness to further inveigle him.

"Rafe . . . is not a strong man, in some ways. He has great physical courage, but . . . in his ability to face moral dilemmas . . . he takes the line of least resistance. Many men do. It is a matter in which, I'm proud to say, I think we women are their superior. In this . . . relationship . . . with Miss Barton, he had allowed it to . . . to drift along, further than he should have. I believe it was his embarrassed financial situation that made him feel that he couldn't ask Edwina to marry him."

Katherine found her voice. Unable to prevent herself, she said coolly, "Edwina is a wealthy young woman—Father would settle an ample sum upon her on her marriage. Rafe would have realized that. The truth is, Emilia, he became bored with my sister, as he's become bored with Fleur Barton."

"No!"

"It's the truth. He's incapable of sustaining any relationship. Rafe's affections begin to falter somewhere between himself and his reflection in a mirror."

"He loved you. For years. Have you forgotten that?"

Katherine became aware that she had been staring at Emilia for some time.

The woman stood up, impatiently. "Oh, I'm not going to discuss this—you don't deserve to have that boy's hurts trotted out for you to gloat over. Do you think I didn't know about the secret trysts between you and my brother, the year before you left for Europe? I tell you, he tells me everything. He'd begun to think you'd never notice him, then he met you in Sydney and for several weeks you had him dangling after you. You toyed with him, treated him contemptibly, breaking off the relationship without a reason—and then refusing to see him or speak with him. You came back to the Valley and immediately began to amuse yourself with poor Stephen Brody . . ."

"I didn't! Stephen was—is—my friend! And as for Rafe, how was I to know that I was any different to any other girl he'd conducted a flirtation with?"

"You knew! Of course you knew—a woman does know when a man cares for her. But you didn't care! I tried to warn him before he went to Sydney, not to try to see you, to risk having himself hurt, but he wouldn't listen—and it happened just as I foresaw it would. You were the most arrogant girl in the Southern Highlands, Katherine Prescott—you never cared for *one* of the young men who came courting you, pretending to be too busy with your painting and your interest in botany—an affectation! Just an attempt to point out how you never belonged with the rest of us in the Valley— no wonder you married in Ireland—you'd have jumped at any chance to climb socially—to be the wife of a farmer like Rafe just wouldn't be good enough for you. But don't sit there and tell me that you didn't know what you did to him. You were always a sly, self-interested, cold-blooded woman—but even you couldn't be that blind."

There was nothing Katherine could say. She wondered, briefly, if Rafe had thought up this interesting little melodrama in order to feed Emilia's empty, hungry little heart and thirsty imagination.

No, that was petty and unkind, and she was using ridicule to avoid facing the truth. It had never occurred to her that Rafe might have genuinely been in love with her, during those weeks in Balmain all those years ago. She had no doubt that the affection would not have been strong, nor as lasting as Emilia imagined it to be—but the woman was right, she had not considered Rafe's feelings, however lightly engaged, at all. And even now, as with Stephen's outburst, she found an impatience growing. She wanted simply to push all these complicated emotions out of the way, not to think about them, for there were far more important matters to discuss.

Emilia was saying bitterly, "I wish to heaven your father or mother were here—I'd go to them. I even considered going to Mr Kelehan, as he seems a man of sensitivity and integrity. But he's had enough to contend with, losing his lovely wife, poor man, and now, with a baby son to raise . . ."

"Emilia, come to the point. What's happened?"

Tight-lipped, Emilia said, "Rafe told me he still wished to marry Edwina—he had not told Miss Barton, but he had made it quite clear that their friendship would not end in matrimony. I was very relieved, even though I was sorry Miss Barton felt that she had to rush away back to Moss Vale; it was not a very dignified thing to do.

"Then, this morning, I found that Rafe had left the house early. I went to check his room—normally, I wouldn't do this, but there had been something in his attitude, his bearing, since Edwina's visit that made me suspicious. I know him so well, you see—and I know when he's holding something back . . .

"Two of his travelling trunks were gone. Not large ones, but impossible to carry on horseback. I checked the stable, and the buggy was gone. Rafe never drove, he always rode—and there were other things missing—his best suits, the portfolio from his desk that contains his private papers . . .

"I . . . I have a ring, left to me by my grandmother, and I always said Rafe might have it as a wedding ring for his wife. He reminded me about my promise, jokingly, the morning that he said he had decided for Edwina once more. I was afraid . . .

"I went to my father's safe where the ring is kept. It was gone. I believe, Katherine, that my brother and your sister have eloped."

Thirty Seven

It had been a dry summer, and the grain and the hay had been harvested early. Nevertheless, even on a day such as this, when heavy raincloud hung weeping over the Valley and surrounding escarpment, and any sane man would choose to answer his correspondence or attend to accounts, Brendan was not to be found in the homestead. So, after seeing Emilia off in her carriage, Katherine rode out in search of him.

She found him with Will O'Mahony and two other stockmen, standing or kneeling over a labouring cow, prone amongst its damp and careless companions in an open field. When Katherine called to him he left the animal and made his way through the grazing herd, pausing to wipe bloodied hands on the saturated yellow grass.

From the other side of the fence he stood looking up at her from beneath the brim of his dripping hat, but his smile was warm and she forgot the rain, the smell of Dryad's wet coat and the slipperiness of the reins between her fingers, forgot even the seriousness of her errand in the sudden power of his welcome gaze upon her.

"It was twins—quite a difficult delivery—excuse my hands . . . What are you doing out here in this weather?" He took in the fact that she wore one of her father's oilskin cloaks and a broad-brimmed hat, the veiling she had draped around the brim the only concession to femininity.

"Can you leave? Will you ride to Dovewood with me? I shouldn't panic, perhaps, but the news came from Rafe's sister, Emilia Huckstable, and unless she truly believed he was about to disgrace himself totally, she'd never confide in me." She took a deep breath, aware that he was looking most concerned already. "She believes Rafe has driven to Dovewood, is planning on meeting Edwina, and eloping with her . . ."

"Surely not. The little idiot . . . !"

"Edwina is infatuated to the point where she's quite capable of such recklessness—I can't think what we can do except ride after her . . ."

She stopped. The grey eyes were raised to her with a deep and telling regard.

Had he said words like this—perhaps the very same words, to Marcus Prescott, in Dublin all those years ago? The blush crept up her cheeks, and she could not pull her gaze from those kind and knowing eyes that, while they spoke no condemnation, were, nevertheless, a reminder of her own pride, her own foolishness.

Dryad stirred restlessly beneath her, shaking her head and spraying fine drops of rain from the deep gold mane. Katherine wished, suddenly, that she had ridden to Dovewood alone. Even silent, the man made her feel a fool; gazing at him, the man she should have been wise enough to trust years before, she knew she *was* a fool.

When he spoke she expected a reproach, however lightly spoken, but no—he said, "I'll come, of course." And turned back for a moment, to tell Will and the others that he was leaving.

Dovewood was in a state of agitation, and Katherine knew that her fears had been justified. The concerned Angela, Suzanna and Laura sat nervously waiting for news in the warm parlour, while all the men, including Marcus, fetched from his rooms in Moss Vale, rode or drove out in the drenching rain to search for the runaways.

"She left a note, thank goodness," Suzanna handed it to Katherine, who read it aloud to Brendan.

Dearest Mama,
Please do not think badly of me, but I have followed my heart and have
eloped with Rafe. We will be married in Sydney. You will not be reading
this until the morning, and we have several hours' start, so please *don't worry*
Father by asking him to come after us. I have known for the past year or
more—as you have all known—that Rafe and I belong together. Please think
of my own happiness and don't try to stop us.

Katherine looked around at her mother, grandmother and sister.
"Foolish girl, it's her happiness that concerns us . . ." But by then
her gaze reached Brendan, and she went on hurriedly, aware of
the faint smile about his lips. "Have all the roads been checked,
Mama?"

"Your father and two trusted servants have ridden towards
Wollongong," Suzanna answered, "in case they've taken the coast
road, and your grandfather and Charles, in the brougham, have driven
to Moss Vale and through Bowral and Mittagong, in case they were
planning on taking the train from Picton."

"What about the road to Glenquarry?" Katherine asked.

"No, dear," Angela said, promptly, "they wouldn't go that way.
You know how difficult that area is in bad weather—and it's been
raining relentlessly for two days."

Laura spoke up. "Perhaps that's why they would take that road,
Grandmama. It's low-lying and very swampy," she added for
Brendan's benefit. "It runs close by the Wingecarribee Marsh."

"And it joins the South Road—they could drive all the way to
Yanderra and avoid the main road and the railway works."

"I'll start at once." Brendan stood, but Katherine had risen from
her chair at the same time.

"I'm going, too. Grandmama, can we borrow two of your horses,
please? Ours are exhausted."

"Of course, but don't you think, Katey . . ."

Brendan also was protesting at the idea of her accompanying him,
but she silenced them both. "Brendan doesn't know this area the
way I do. I'll borrow Grandmama's Ranee, if I may—she's sixteen-
two hands and absolutely tireless. I won't delay you, Brendan—and
I may just save you from becoming lost. So—shall we start?"

Glenquarry was a pleasant, open farming district with views of strange
volcanic structures that humped like dozing monsters in the hilly
ranges towards the east. The roads that led from Dovewood, north
towards Glenquarry, were normally easy; broad tracks through low-

lying, sparsely-wooded country, but now, after two days of persistent rain, the face of the area had changed. The Wingecarribee River, which flowed into the Marsh, rose and rose, and the marsh spread its boundaries out, covering a vast tract of forest country with water.

When Brendan and Katherine passed through, mounted on two tall, hardy horses, the road were not yet impassable, but for all that it was an ominous landscape. The trees grew some ten feet apart and there was little undergrowth, so one could see some distance into the forest on either side of the road to more grey trunks and still more receding into the distance. Facing north as they rode, they could see no mountain high enough to rear itself over the treetops and their scant feathering of leaves. The trunks of the trees, slender, not without their individual grace of shape, were the dominant sight, and made more eerie, more striking, by the shallow, sluggish floodwater.

For the road had been drowned in water; it was a rippling canal between the slim trunks of the trees, and grey sky was reflected on grey water, and the pale, lissome eucalypts had doubled their lengths in haunting reflections in the faintly stippled floodwater, new silver on old silver, between lowering sky and the mirror image of lowering sky. It was a landscape that one's dreams alone could paint, an earthly kingdom with no sign of earth anywhere, mile on mile.

Katherine said, "It's beautiful," but she could also have said, "It's terrible." "Yes," Brendan replied and would have replied so to either observation. Their horses splashed on, along that road of metallic grey, between metallic trees, and the accord that still existed between Brendan and Katherine drew them together in awed silence as they moved cautiously, inexorably forward.

Once Brendan, allowing his horse to stray too close to the left, found himself almost unseated as it fell forward into a drowned culvert, but it struggled and wallowed its way out, and they were careful then to ride very close to the centre of the avenue of water.

A mile or more was travelled thus, and then the road must have dipped even lower for the water, which had, until then, been halfway up the horses' forelegs, now covered their knees. Brendan was about to tell Katherine that this was foolishness, they would have to turn back, when he caught sight of a dark speck between the trees.

They kept on, for Katherine, too, had seen it. The road curved to the left and there, as they waded along it, was the buggy, a very wet and bedraggled Rafe and Edwina standing in the sluggish water, attempting, with what seemed like the last of their strength, to push the buggy free, while the equally exhausted horses lunged and reared helplessly, becoming, at the same time, more hampered by the ooze their hoofs were stirring and more frightened by the sensation.

Rafe was the first to see them. He looked up, froze, then slowly straightened, standing away from the wheels to watch the riders approach, his whole bearing one of detached calm.

"Katey?" Edwina, crying with exhaustion, had seen them, had left Rafe and had taken three stumbling steps towards them through water that swirled about her knees. Rafe shot one ironic glance at her, and though she could not have seen it, she pulled up short as if by an invisible string attached to him. She remembered her loyalties, albeit unwillingly, and stood, wretched, sobbing, at the end of her emotional and physical strength.

Katherine rode up to her. "Oh, Teddi . . ." It was all she could manage, but the hurt reproach, the patient condemnation were there in her voice, and Edwina lowered her face into her hands and sobbed the louder, her shoulders hunched with shame and misery.

Katherine started to dismount. "Stay there, Kate," Brendan ordered, himself jumping down into the floodwater. "There's no point in your getting wet."

She shook her head. "You'll need all our strengths combined—besides, I'm drenched already." Still, the cold of the water came as a shock as she dropped from her saddle, and the slow filling of her riding boots was a horrid sensation; she wished she had thought to take them off and tie them somehow to the saddle.

There was no time for outbursts of anger, recriminations or even questions. Edwina was sent to stand at the horses' heads to calm and encourage them, and Brendan went to find a strong branch with which to attempt to dislodge one wheel from the mud, while Rafe, similarly armed, worked on the other.

Pushing, heaving, Katherine between the two men, the buggy at last moved forward, and so fast, with the carriage horses' relief, that Katherine lost her grip on the back of the vehicle and fell headlong into the water. She scrambled to her feet, the muddy, unpleasant taste of the floodwater in her mouth, before either man had realized she had fallen, and came up laughing at the shocked concern on their faces.

Perhaps, she thought afterwards, it was just as well it happened. It created a diversion and made the already wretched and embarrassed Rafe feel even more culpable. Where he would, perhaps, have insisted that he and Edwina be allowed to continue their adventure, he was discomposed sufficiently by Katherine's bedraggled appearance and shivering form not to argue when Brendan said firmly, "We'll go back then, shall we? Miss Edwina, would you care to ride your grandmother's horse? Your sister would be best seated in the carriage, with the rug about her, I think." He looked steadily at Rafe. "Dovewood, firstly, to see the ladies settled, Mr Huckstable."

Rafe looked as if he had words ready, heated and unpleasant, but he bit them back and turned to help Katherine into the carriage, before climbing in himself and taking the reins, his face white, his lips set.

Edwina allowed Brendan to lift her up into the side-saddle, and she whispered, barely audibly, to him, "Thank you. I . . . I'm glad you came . . ."

It was enough for Brendan. Taking responsibility himself, he halted, when they arrived at the gates of Dovewood, and sent Katherine and Edwina on, mounted on the two horses. Then he paused by the buggy, looking up at Rafe coldly. "Mr Prescott will undoubtedly see you in the near future, if you wish to speak with him, but until then I think you would be much safer to return to the Valley alone."

Rafe applied the whip to the tired horses and drove off without a word, but the look he threw Brendan had much within it to make a lesser man aware that he had made a dangerous enemy.

It seemed that Rafe and Edwina had quarrelled almost from the time he had driven the buggy past Dovewood's gates, at a prearranged hour in the dark, early morning, to find Edwina waiting for him with her few, carefully packed belongings.

He had been furious with her for leaving a note, and she, being worried for her mother and grandmother particularly, and never a girl to accept an unmerited rebuke, had defended herself, at first sweetly, and then vehemently, as Rafe grew crosser with the miles and his tone grew cooler. Explaining her concern for her family, attempting to convince him how worried they would be, had gone a long way to making Edwina realize the extent of the love and security she was leaving behind. Rafe, with his temper, was pushing her inexorably towards changing her mind about eloping.

"I hadn't really thought things through," she admitted to Katherine the day after her return. She had had a stormy scene with Marcus and Suzanna, united in their grief and worry over their youngest daughter, and had then retired to her room, where she had spent more than twenty-four hours alternately pummelling her pillow and weeping copiously into it.

"I haven't told Mama and Father this," she said, sitting on the window seat beside her sister, "but I became quite frightened out there on the road with Rafe. I'd been so excited and happy when I saw him at Bendeela and found that he still loved me—despite his flirtation with Fleur Barton. Oh, I know the rumours, but she's such a *forward* creature that I couldn't blame him for being unable to avoid her snare altogether. I was so *relieved* to hear him say he still loved me . . ."

The lovely eyes clouded a little, and she turned to gaze wistfully out over the damp, dripping, gold-leafed gardens. "I was happy right up until the time I had to sneak out of Dovewood— and I kept thinking of all the people in the house whom I loved, and who loved me. And I remembered how hurt we all were when you eloped—I'm sorry, Katey!—and then I began to question Rafe's sudden change of heart, and I remembered how aloof he'd been for months, and how I'd . . ." She looked at Katherine, thoroughly wretched. "I'd told him that Father would come around, once we were married, and that he needn't worry about how he would support us because Father would give him a job at Prescott and Mitchell, and we didn't *need* Mr Huckstable's money.

"Katey, it all made perfect sense at the time, to make him feel better about a problem that had bothered him for months. It . . . It was only when I was waiting by the gates, in the rain, at four o'clock in the morning, that I began to think that it would have been so comforting to have the gentleman pursue *me*, to have him tell *me* that there was nothing to worry about, that he could solve the problems and look after us.

"I forgot these things when I saw him driving towards me, and when I was lifted up beside him and we started off, on our way to a new life, his arm about my shoulders, feeling the warmth of him beside me . . . I felt so trusting, so *safe*, that I admitted to him that I'd done something that he'd asked me particularly not to, which was to leave a note.

"And our relationship began to sour from that moment," she finished soberly, "for all my fears by the gate in the dark and rain came back to me, and as we drove further and further away from Dovewood I became more and more convinced I'd made a terrible mistake."

Her eyes filled with tears. "I was so happy to see you and Brendan riding through the rain towards us! I was never so happy to see anyone in my life!"

Laura, in telling her parents about her decision to put the thought of Stephen Brody behind her, did not have the difficulty she had expected in persuading her parents to allow her to go to Sydney, especially since the much-chastened Edwina now wished to accompany her.

The only shadow over those following days of preparation was Angela hearing from a friend in Moss Vale that Fleur Barton was spreading rumours of a foiled elopement between Edwina Prescott and Raphael Huckstable. Angela announced this to the family after dinner, when they were seated about the parlour, Katherine beginning to strum a piece on the piano. The news stilled her fingers on the keys.

Angela looked around at each face and concluded, "So it's as well Teddi is going to Sydney." She looked at her granddaughter kindly. "I tell you this, my dear, because someone may speak of it to you, even in the city. I don't know how the woman heard of it, but she's malicious enough to do her best to damage any or all of us. If you're prepared, you can laugh at it, deny it as ridiculous. It will be your word against hers—there's no proof at all."

Edwina sat very still, the appealing, heart-shaped face sombre. She looked, of a sudden, much more mature than her twenty years, and addressed herself first to her grandmother, speaking carefully and thoughtfully.

"There may be no proof, but there is rumour and conjecture. And I know how Fleur Barton came to hear of it, Grandmama. I understand Rafe, I understand his weaknesses. I think he went to Fleur because his pride had been bruised, and he wasn't ready to go back to the Valley and face his parents. I believe he told Fleur of the elopement himself, in case she heard of it from someone else."

She turned to Marcus. "If it's all right with you, Father, Laura could go on to Sydney alone—Libby and Tobias will look after her, and we have many friends—you wouldn't mind, would you, Laura? And you'll not be away from Sydney much longer yourself, will you, Father? You see, I don't want to go away knowing that everyone is talking about me. I'd rather stay here, and in a few weeks, go back to Barrengarry as if nothing at all is amiss. If I go to Sydney now, the Southern Highlands will snigger and titter and say that the rumours must have been true and that I'm running away because

I'm ashamed. I'd rather stay—even if . . . if it will be unpleasant—and make people doubt Fleur's story. Anyway, I've got nothing to be ashamed of. I've been silly, but not wicked—I can still hold my head up in society, and I plan to do so."

The room was silent; Brendan and Katherine, Edwin and Angela, Suzanna and Laura all gazed at this self-possessed young woman as if they were seeing a new Edwina, as indeed they were. Only Marcus moved. He crossed the room with a stern frown, took her hands and pulled her to her feet. He gazed down at her for an unquiet moment, then he smiled slowly and embraced his youngest daughter. "You surpass my hopes for you, Teddi," he said gruffly.

Molly was improving daily and looking forward, she told Katherine, to returning to the Valley and to Barrengarry. "Though I don't know, to tell the truth, if I'm looking forward to meeting Pa again. I'm real glad he's well and recovering—but he's a hard man, Mrs Carron, and he's strict when it comes to duty. He won't forgive me easily for running off from Mrs Bewley."

"If he doesn't understand when you tell him the truth, Molly, then I shall speak to him. But I'm sure you'll find him more sympathetic than you imagine. He's been very ill and convalescing for a long time, and in those cases one has plenty of time to consider matters; I believe you'll find that he's simply very pleased to have you back safely and in a good position at Barrengarry."

"Hope so, Missus Carron."

And Katherine left her with the knowledge that the girl was still not utterly convinced of a warm and forgiving welcome. *If her forebodings prove correct*, Katherine mused, *how much of the ill-will will be due to Nancy Halstrop?*

The family gathered on the front drive of Dovewood to bid goodbye to Katherine and Brendan. Edwina would return in the carriage in another week or so, bringing Molly with her. Katherine, looking at the smiling, bright-eyed vision of Suzanna, knowing that since the unfortunate elopement Marcus had been staying in one of the guest rooms at Dovewood, nursed a secret hope that when Edwina and Molly returned, she would find the carriage occupied by Suzanna also. Marcus had declared, that night Suzanna had told him of Robin and that she was going to him, that she was never to set foot in the Balmain house or at Barrengarry again, and Suzanna had accepted that; it was impossible to expect otherwise.

But now Edwina's reckless adventure had brought Marcus and

Suzanna together again, and though there was an understandable tension between them, it was as if they, too, had noted the change in each of them, as Katherine had. There was, at the moment, no warmth between them, but there was a kind of shy, courteous solicitude, and Katherine had heard no mention of her father leaving Dovewood to return to his rooms in Moss Vale. The three sisters did not mention this new accord, even between themselves; it was too fragile a thing to be spoken about; all conjectures took place within the daughters' hopeful minds.

Edwin had had a visit from a friend who was resident in Sydney, a man prominent in politics, and he, Edwin and Marcus had been closeted together in the gun room for much of the morning.

Edwina ran to fetch them in order for them to say goodbye to Brendan and Katherine, already mounted on their two chestnuts.

The political gentleman shook their hands, and Edwin and Marcus took turns to embrace Katherine. It was while Edwin was still speaking to Katherine that Marcus came to Brendan, stood by the horse's withers and placed his back to the rest of the gathering.

"I've had some news, from our Honourable Member here. It will be in all the local newspapers soon enough, but it was only announced in the *Herald* yesterday. You know an Irishman by the name of Colonel Kelly?"

Brendan was immediately wary. "I've met him once or twice."

Marcus nodded. "Somehow I thought you might. On the fifth of this month, Mr Kelehan, your friend Colonel Kelly led a rebellion in Ireland."

Marcus did not miss the sudden triumph and hope on the younger man's features, yet he could not allow them to remain long. "It failed. There are still scattered skirmishes, in Cork and other country areas, but the police were ready and the main force, out of Dublin, was crushed within twenty-four hours. Colonel Kelly has fled to England. Her Majesty's government is preparing for a further series of political trials. The charge will be high treason, Mr Kelehan."

Thirty Eight

Katherine waited until they were a good two miles from Dovewood before she spoke, realizing that whatever her father had said to Brendan, it had affected him deeply, and he would not speak of his own accord. "What's wrong, Brendan?"

He told her then, the little that Marcus had confided to him, finishing, "I think your father wished me to draw a moral lesson from the failure. That I was better off being here than involving myself in foolish, doomed patriotic enterprises."

She was quiet a moment, then, "And you don't think so."

It was hardly a question and he made no comment, but glanced at her in a preoccupied fashion and turned to watch the road before them, stretched taut through the autumn patchwork of fields, and she was left to surmise his feelings.

It was not difficult. All their youth, Brendan's, Oliver's, Daniel Hutton's, Pat McNally's, Tim Gleason's, and the others of their circle, had been given to the dream of self-government for Ireland. That England would not willingly release its hold on land that had been overrun by English forces, whose revenue helped swell English coffers, had them agreeing with the Young Irelanders of '48, and the followers of Wolfe Tone in 1792, that open rebellion was the only answer.

It could not be surprising that this rebellion failed, when both Katherine and Brendan knew that most of the able leaders had already been imprisoned for their writings, or their voiced sympathies, or their perilous attachment to the Fenian Brotherhood. What they did not know was that the call to rise had been made at a time of snow and blizzards, that the leaderless population was confused and ill-armed, and that the fervour, so strong in 1865 and even 1866, had been gradually fading with the daily arrests, the losses of the regiments loyal to Ireland's cause, the split in the American movement, so that now, in March, 1867, the cause was lost almost before the few scattered battles had begun.

But none of that mattered, Katherine reflected. Even doomed to failure, she knew that the man who rode beside her, gazing obdurately forward as if staring down a future he wished no part in, was longing, at that moment, to be standing at some barricade in an Irish street, shoulder-to-shoulder with other Irishmen, their grievances declared and defended and worth dying for.

She wanted to say, "You did all you could." But she knew that to him, at this moment, it was not enough. She wondered how long his mood would persist, for the bad news could not have found Brendan at a worse time, at a deeper emotional trough of his life.

Seeing Constable Crowe outside Radley's store that afternoon, gave her hope that there might be some news, something to take Brendan's mind from the events unfolding half a world away.

Constable Crowe was just leading his horse into the road, preparing to mount and return to his billet at the Cummings homestead. His boyish face grinned a welcome to them and, tired themselves, Katherine and Brendan dismounted for a few minutes to talk with him.

"A great deal has happened." The young constable looked concerned, but rather satisfied. "The sergeant hasn't made it common knowledge yet, but he did call at Barrengarry this afternoon—found no one but the servants there."

"We've been in Moss Vale—Mr Prescott will return in a few days' time," Brendan said. "Have you found . . . anything?"

The faint hesitation, almost a stumbling over words, was so unusual in the articulate Brendan that Katherine glanced at him. He was gazing at Crowe, who noticed nothing amiss but swelled a little with the importance of his news.

"We've found Davey Crolin, up on the side of Brown's Mountain—dead, I'm afraid—about two days, the sergeant reckons. Terrible, isn't it?" For he was gratified by the reaction of his audience. Katherine had murmured, "Oh, no . . ." and Brendan had paled, stared at the young constable with disbelieving horror.

Jemmy Crowe had a round, pleasant countenance and very soft, very dark eyes that would remain gentle even in later years, when the experiences of his vocation had vulcanized his character and carved obdurate lines upon his face. He had the long top lip and rather blunt nose that made people immediately presume he was of Irish stock and this annoyed him, the more so since he was born of a Kerrywoman and a farmer from Donegal and couldn't deny it. The assumptions were added irritatingly to the belief in his family of many brothers and sisters, that you could read Jemmy's thoughts on his face as easily as you could tot the years of a tree by counting the rings on the stump. It was a grievous matter to the young man that he had no sense of mystery, never seemed able to surprise people. He was not yet old enough, nor wise enough, to realize that the fondness people had for him, their pleasure in his unchanging good humour and attention to duty, was more valuable than any aloof persona that hinted of dark and terrible experiences.

But he had an audience now, and was himself the relater of grim tidings that obviously shocked the man and woman. He finished delicately, "Seems like he fell victim like the others, bashed to death. Wouldn't think that Charlie would turn on his own brother, would you? Oh—you did know we caught Charlie?"

Both shook their heads a little, not speaking.

"Got him out the back, in the 'gaol'—notice I use the term loosely—still looks like a storeroom to me . . ."

"You think Charlie killed Davey? His own brother?" Brendan Kelehan asked. He looked ill, very shocked at this terrible supposition.

"Well, we only captured Charlie on Monday night. Davey Crolin could have been killed that afternoon, or even earlier.

"I have a theory," he warmed to his subject, "that all three of the Crolins were in on this business. That they quarrelled over the spoils—the sergeant worked out that the three rent collectors alone carried more than eighteen hundred pounds between them—and Charlie killed Davey.

"I'd wondered, myself, if Frank Crolin wasn't in on it, too. He's the most intelligent of the three—but vindictive—you wouldn't want to cross 'im. Charlie is a bit slow-witted—and Davey was the firebrand of the three. Still, there's no proof to link Frank with any of this—and while I'd like to see him caught and charged if he's guilty—I still think of all those children—Charlie and Essie have six, and Frank and his wife have seven. If Frank is taken too, what would become of their families?"

"Has Charlie spoken?" Katherine asked. "Has he been questioned about the murders?"

"Oh, yes, hour after hour Sergeant Lloyd and I have been with him. But he won't speak, just sits there dully, though he was game enough up above Budgong, firing shots at us until he ran out of ammunition and we were able to rush him. You know what cedar-getters are like—an independent lot. When we first put him in that cell—and it's much bigger than the ones at Berrima, he screamed like a demon, all day, all night. Bert Radley fixed him, finally, by telling him that he'd be sent to Berrima straight away if he kept that up, and he quietened down after that."

"But . . . Davey could have been beaten days earlier—could have lain out there—Where is Sergeant Lloyd? I want to see him." Brendan seemed agitated, had half-turned away towards the horses.

"He's up in the hills questioning Frank Crolin. When he comes back, I'll tell him to call by Barrengarry, if you like. Or is there something I . . ." Jemmy Crowe had sensed, at last, that something was wrong, his professionalism had noted and decided to act upon Brendan's sudden, suspiciously unnerved behaviour. He took a step after the Irishman, was about to lay a hand on his arm.

"Jemmy! *Jemmy* . . .!"

It was hard to tell at first where the terrified yell issued from, then the young constable had left them, was racing hard, around the timber shebeen, towards the stone storeroom at the rear, and Brendan followed.

When Katherine caught up with them, Jemmy was already gripping an hysterical Bert Radley, his big face white above the black beard, dark eyes red-rimmed and protruding, gibbering, "It weren't my fault!—*You* told 'im! I said I didn't think he done it! You and that sergeant—I said he wouldn't have done it!" His wild eyes found Katherine's, almost unseeingly, fixing on her as a possible sympathetic face. "Unless it was guilt . . . Could have been guilt . . . !"

The door to the makeshift cell was wide open, Jemmy stepped in and gave a shout, "Kelehan! Oh, God! Come and help me, Kelehan, for God's sake!"

"No, Missus . . ." At the door Bert Radley, trembling, put out a beefy arm to prevent Katherine from following Jemmy and Brendan into the dark, confining space.

But she saw it, briefly, before Radley had pulled her away. Flour sacks had been torn open, ripped into broad strips—some lay knotted and entwined on the floor, amid the trampled white stuff. A cord of it still hung down beside the body of Charlie Crolin as it turned, slowly, hanging limp from the roof beam by its calico rope.

Thirty Nine

Numbed, Katherine allowed Bert Radley to lead her into the store, and she sat on a roughly hewn bench, finding herself shaking, disbelieving what she had just seen.

She refused the offer of a brandy from Radley's casks, remembering what Joe had said about that gentleman's dubious brews, and was thankful when Brendan and Constable Crowe appeared in the doorway. She looked up at them, expectantly, but both men shook their heads, obviously unnerved themselves by the horror of the incident.

Brendan did not wait for long, but helped Katherine to her feet and guided her outside, towards their horses. She had been feeling ill, more than she realized, sitting in the stale atmosphere of cheap liquor and smoke, and she gulped in the fresh evening air.

"Are you all right? Can you ride home?" Brendan asked, concerned for her.

"Yes," she smiled, "of course—we're so close . . ."

Home. She suddenly longed to be back at Barrengarry.

But they were only a mile onwards from Radley's store when Stephen Brody passed them on the road, heading homewards from a visit to Luke Murchison. The young man chattered to them for a few minutes, oblivious to the grimly bemused silence of Brendan and Katherine. Then, "Shocking things happening, lately—terrible!" Stephen shook his head, scowling. "To think that someone we knew was doing those murders . . . I'll be pleased when Sergeant Lloyd takes Charlie Crolin to Berrima gaol—it's shed a pall over the Valley, this business . . ."

And Stephen stopped, having seen the short, almost unconscious glance that Katherine and Brendan exchanged. "What's the matter? It's not . . . Has something happened? Have they found . . ." He was so agitated, so concerned, that Katherine reached out and laid a hand on his arm.

"Charlie is dead, Stephen. The whole terrible business is at an end. They found Davey Crolin dead, only this afternoon—it's a wonder you hadn't heard. And when Charlie was told that Davey's body had been found, he . . . he killed himself in his cell."

"Charlie . . . killed himself? How? *Hanged* himself?"

Katherine nodded, feeling ill at the memory.

Stephen looked, if possible, more sickened than Katherine. He was white about the mouth, and the blue eyes looked between the man and woman uncomprehendingly. "Davey . . . He . . . Who killed Davey? Do the police know?"

"I think they suspect he and Charlie quarrelled over the dividing of the money they'd stolen—that's what I surmised, anyway." She glanced at Brendan for corroboration, but he was not looking at her, and she realized then that so far he had taken no part whatsoever in the conversation.

Stephen rode on then, much subdued by the news, and Katherine rode beside a silent Brendan who, despite her attempts at conversation, remained withdrawn all the way home to Barrengarry.

Peggy, Carl and Bridget were disturbed to hear the news. They told the three servants what had happened directly they entered the hall; Peggy murmured, "Poor Essie Crolin . . . and the children!" Katherine felt more heavy of heart than ever, for there had not been time, in her shock and in her concern for the brooding Brendan, for her to realize that Essie was now a widow, her six children fatherless. *And no land*, she thought, no home of her own but the tent on the timber grounds.

Neither Katherine nor Brendan had much of an appetite for dinner, and that little was eaten in silence. Afterwards they retired to the parlour, and they talked of Ireland and Irish politics in tired voices, in the manner of people speaking to each other at the funeral of a dear friend.

Bridget gave them a few moments' pleasure when she knocked on the door and presented Brendan with James, newly bathed and scented. He and Katherine took turns holding him, talking to him, while the five-weeks-old James chewed his fist and watched their faces and the firelight with bright, intelligent grey eyes.

When Bridget called, half an hour later, to carry the infant off to bed, the little spirit seemed to take some of the warmth of the room with him when he went. Katherine watched the smile that his son's presence had given him gradually fade from Brendan's face, and the lines appeared to deepen from nose to mouth as he gazed into the fire.

Katherine felt helpless. At the end of an hour of silence, broken only by occasional, desultory conversation, she said anxiously, "Brendan, I know you wish yourself back in Ireland, helping the effort—but my dear, there's so little you could do. When James Stephens was leader, he should have raised the Brotherhood to arms in '65, you know that as well as I. All you could give to Ireland now is your life, and you have James to think of—you have to live, for James."

She had called him "my dear", without forethought, and the rest of her speech had been hurried and accompanied by a blush that she hoped he would ascribe to the warmth of the fire.

But Brendan seemed unaware of everything. "James . . ." he murmured. "Yes, of course. James."

Katherine stared at him. He stood leaning against the mantelpiece, tapping his chin lightly, thoughtfully, with the thumb of his clenched fist. He did not look at her. "It's an interesting problem, Kate. Does one live for one's child, on the assumption that any father is better than a dead father, or does one do the right thing and accept a death that is honourable?—Not to the world, perhaps, but to oneself and to God, and that's what matters, after all." He looked over at her then, coolly, dispassionately, and she knew he was still gazing within himself. "I wonder which decision James, when he becomes a man, would wish for me to make?"

"You don't have to make a decision," she said brutally. "It's made for you. You're twelve thousand miles from Ireland. There's nothing you can do. And if you go back there now, to sacrifice yourself when that child needs you, I . . . I don't think I shall ever forgive you. I don't think I will ever feel the same way about you again."

Now he saw her. After that outburst he was looking directly at her. She stumbled a little in adding, "There's one other priority to be considered even before one's country. And that's one's family. You must do what *you* feel is right, not what a society demands of you."

There was an unquiet silence that went on and on, and his grey eyes were fixed on her face as she sat, straight-backed, in her chair, her hands clasped tightly together in her lap.

Brendan nodded slowly, and then, to her surprise, he had turned away towards the door.

"Brendan?"

She reached him in the hall, heading past the stairs for what she instinctively knew was the back door, the stables, and his horse.

"Brendan, don't shut me out." Her arms were around him, her face raised to his.

"Kate . . ." And his tone was heavy with a kind of helpless sorrow. "I can't explain to you. It means something to me not to disillusion you utterly—and I will if I stay, if I speak any further to you."

"You can't disillusion me. How could you, after all we've been through? You know I . . . I love you."

He gazed down at her, the haunted grey eyes softened for a moment. "I love you, too," fondly, without passion. "I'm sorry . . . that I've failed you so badly. Kate, if anything happened to me . . . would you look after James?"

"Stop it, Brendan!" Her balled fist struck his chest, impulsively. "I won't have you speak like this! I won't!"

"Kate, *listen!*" His gaze was intense as he held both her wrists in his grasp. "What if I told you that I did something wrong, very wrong, in Ireland, something for which the law would be justified in taking my life as punishment? What if I escaped and went unpunished, yet carried that stain on my conscience—and then committed, albeit unwittingly, a crime similar to the first? Could I walk away *twice*? You said I have to do what *I* think is right, not what I feel is demanded of me. You meant the words to keep me safe, for the child's sake. But I couldn't raise my son, teach him right from wrong, if I had no sense of integrity myself . . ."

She was blindly, helplessly furious. "Damn you," she hissed. "Damn your patriotism, your desire for martyrdom, your Catholicism, your sense of guilt! Men have ruled kingdoms and guided whole continents, men have raised families and headed benevolent institutions—men with more blood on their hands than we could ever guess at! I don't know what sins you're talking about, and I don't want to know—but I won't have you riding away from here with your damnable pride and your warped sense of honour. Who *are* you trying to prove yourself to? Not to God, for he knows your place is with your son. Are you trying to exonerate yourself to Mary Rose? To Oliver? To all our friends in prison in Fremantle, or fighting or hiding in the Irish countryside? What are you running for, Brendan?"

The hands that held her wrists were trembling; he let them go, carefully, as if, in his inner rage, he could have as easily snapped them, and said in a restrained voice, "I'm going to find Sergeant Lloyd."

He was striding towards the back door of the house, Katherine running to keep up with him, about to question him once more—and there was a heavy hammering on the front door.

Both Brendan and Katherine froze. It was so late—at least eleven o'clock. They looked at each other. Whoever it was, was impatient, the hammering was repeated.

They turned back wordlessly along the hall, and it was Brendan who opened the door.

They had not realized that a light, misty rain had been falling. It clung to the shoulders of Sergeant Lloyd's overcoat, to the hat that he now, seeing Katherine, removed and held in his hand.

"Tom? Come in . . ." Katherine said, smiling. "It's a very late time for you to be riding about—is . . . is everything all right?"

Foolish words, she cursed their inanity. But matters were not right, for Tom Lloyd, after the door was shut, leaned back against it. The blue eyes looked quite dark and solemn in the lamplight, and they gazed steadily at Brendan.

"Mr Kelehan may, I hope, help me—I have a few questions for you, sir. Do you know anything about the murder of David Crolin?"

Katherine stared at Tom, turned to gaze questioningly at Brendan, waited, expecting a denial . . .

"Yes."

No. What was he doing, what was he saying? He couldn't mean it . . .

A heavy, impatient sigh from Tom Lloyd; the glass in the door panels rattled as he shifted his weight forward then leaned back, scowling blackly at the man before him. "Dammit," he said. "Dammit, Brendan, you fool."

She made an offer to leave them, feeling ambivalent even as the words left her mouth, part of herself longing to discover the mystery of Brendan's behaviour, part of herself longing to be away, far away, where she could not hear him condemn himself—and she knew, as surely as she knew the depth of her love for him, that that was what he was about to do.

But, "I want you to stay," he said, and walked ahead of them into the parlour. He seemed changed with Tom Lloyd's arrival. The passionate agitation that had marked his behaviour all evening had been replaced with a steady calm. "Sit down, Kate," he said, gently enough, and Katherine sat in a chair to the left of the fire, and the room belonged, suddenly, to the two men. They were of a height, though differing some seven years in age; one with straight, silver hair, the other with a tousled head of rain-damp curls; but both faces were strong, firm, the eyes, as they gazed at each other, betraying their opposition and, at the same time, their respect for each other.

"Did you kill him?" Tom asked.

"No. At least, I don't think so. He was still alive when I left him, but unconscious."

"He could have died of his injuries . . ." It was half-statement, half-question.

"Yes," Brendan scowled. "It's possible. But he was alive when I left—it was by the creek, near the eastern boundary of Huckstable's Cambewarra. I believe, according to Constable Crowe, that Davey Crolin was found on Brown's Mountain."

"He could have stumbled there, and died."

"Yes." Heavily.

"You're making this very easy for me." Tom Lloyd's face was unreadable. "Why did you beat him?"

Katherine could not contain herself. "Brendan, stop answering these questions—you're a lawyer, you must know that you don't have to tell all these . . ."

"Incriminating details?" Brendan half-smiled. "Remember our talk, Kate?"

"Yes—but I don't agree with this." She turned to the sergeant. "Why did you come to Brendan? What made you think that he could do such a thing?"

Tom looked between the two of them. "I had a message delivered to me, from Miss Barton in Moss Vale, saying she had information. I rode there to question her—then came back here—that's why I'm so late . . ."

"Fleur *Barton*? But she's most unreliable! Why, for months she's had an inf . . ." She stopped, remembering suddenly that Tom Lloyd had long had an infatuation himself, and for the very same woman. "She's resented my family since my grandmother asked her to leave Dovewood . . ."

"Why?" Tom pounced. "Why was she asked to leave?"

Katherine looked at him, and felt a kind of pity for him. It was not the police officer who asked the question, but a man in love, hungry for any detail, good or bad, about the object of his affection.

"Private reasons," she said tersely, "between my grandmother and Miss Barton."

Tom looked dissatisfied, but decided not to press the question at this stage. He turned to Brendan. "Miss Barton claims that she and Rafe Huckstable met you on the road, coming from the direction of Cambewarra *and* Brown's Mountain. She said your shirt was spattered with blood, your coat and trousers muddy, and your knuckles were gashed. May I see your hands, Mr Kelehan?"

Brendan held them out, stoically. Tom approached, turned them one by one towards the lamp light, noted the healing grazes across the knuckles of both hands, the right betraying more damage than the left.

Tom raised his eyes to Brendan. "Why?" he said.

Brendan looked at Katherine, her face pale, her eyes betraying her unwillingness to believe this, any of it, and he addressed his answer as much to her as to the sergeant.

He told of his feelings after Mary Rose's death, of his desire to be alone, away from the sympathy, the kind respectfulness of the stockmen and their occasional, forgetful good humour. He told them of riding out to check fences by himself, of seeing the young Woddi child, and of hearing its mother's cries. Of finding Davey Crolin attempting to rape her.

"I dragged him away from her, and I beat him. He tried to defend himself—pulled a knife and sliced at me . . ."

"Did he cut you?"

"Only slightly . . ."

"Show me, please."

Brendan turned to Katherine, one eyebrow raised.

"I shall turn away." She smiled despite herself, and turned to face the fire, but Brendan said, "Mrs Carron, you nursed me when I was ill, in Dublin—you have seen me without my shirt." He removed his jacket, then his shirt, and Tom Lloyd forgot the thought of Crolin's knife when he saw the ugly, unmistakable, puckered hole in the man's shoulder.

"How did you come by that?" Lloyd's tone was businesslike.

"Does that have any bearing on this matter?"

"No—but answer me. How did that happen?"

"A friend shot me in the shoulder. Accidentally."

"An Irish friend."

"Yes."

Lloyd scowled, dragged his eyes from the bullet wound to meet Brendan's gaze, and there was a subtle change in the young policeman, a new wariness.

"The cut is here," Brendan said mildly, his hand to the narrow scarlet line across his ribs. It was healing well, and was not deep—but deep enough, Tom considered, to have caused the man discomfort.

"What happened to the knife?" Tom asked, handing Brendan his shirt.

"I threw it away into the bushes. I didn't look for it afterwards. I was insanely angry with the man. I didn't stop hitting Crolin until I realized he was unconscious. Why? Did you find the knife on him? If you did, it would mean that he regained consciousness and made his own way to Brown's Mountain . . ."

"The knife wasn't found on him," Tom said grimly. "It's quite possible that he was so badly hurt that he was confused, and didn't think to look for his knife. He was dazed, wandered some miles from where you fought with him, and died—even twenty-four hours later. Do you agree that that's possible?"

"Brendan . . ." Katherine warned.

"Mrs Carron, you must stop interrupting or I'll have to ask you to leave the room." Tom looked over at her sternly.

Katherine bit her tongue, held herself silent with great difficulty.

"Answer me," Tom demanded of Brendan. "You left him unconscious, and you came away and made no effort to find help for him, or let anyone know where he was. Am I right?"

Brendan held the cool gaze equally coolly. "Yes," he said, and finished buttoning his shirt.

Tom Lloyd frowned, seemed about to speak, but turned away. He walked amongst the polished, well-loved pieces of furniture, stared at the paintings on the walls, and addressed Brendan over his shoulder. "Fleur said Rafe Huckstable would also be a witness—he commented to her on the state of your clothes after you parted on the road that day."

Brendan said "Yes," carefully. "I expect Rafe Huckstable will give evidence to that effect."

"And I mean evidence, Mr Kelehan. In Berrima courthouse!" Tom burst out angrily, whirling on Brendan.

Brendan looked at him, gave a bemused smile. "I presumed you meant at a legitimate trial."

"Of all the . . . !" Tom brought his hand down on the back of the armchair near where he was standing, and turned to march to the other end of the room. "Can't you think of *anything*? Anything that might stand in your favour? I don't want to do this, Kelehan, do you understand? This could be dangerous. Even if you *didn't* kill him, people like to stop looking for culprits when some poor man is in the gaol—and with you admitting all this to me there's a good chance I'll be under pressure to close the investigation. And it's a distinct possibility that a jury will convict you—at least of manslaughter. You're looking at possibly twenty years in gaol, man, if they don't hang you!"

Brendan looked at the sergeant tiredly. He picked up his jacket and shrugged into it, pausing to look with some compassion upon the young policeman. "Tom, what do you want of me? I've told you the truth."

"Yes, well . . . as far as the four walls of this room are concerned, I wish you hadn't. Davey Crolin was a crawling, slimy thing that someone should have stepped on years ago. Since I started searching for Charlie I've had a lot of people talk to me about the Crolins. All of them agreed that Davey was the meanest of the lot. It was well-known amongst the cedar-getters that he took ad . . . ad . . ." He glanced apologetically at Katherine, but was already committed, "He took advantage of some of the black women—and there's been a few cases of attempted rape—at the least—in the white community as well. It's hard to tell the extent of the claims—both the Woddi and the cedar-getters are fairly close-mouthed—but there wasn't a cedar-getter I spoke to who didn't say that Davey was a lower form of life. So don't think that I'm upset that someone like Davey Crolin is dead. I just wish that with Charlie's death there could be an end to this."

His gaze met Brendan's steadily, and in a different voice, he said, "I wouldn't be here if Fleur hadn't sent for me. I . . . I saw a different Fleur tonight. I thought—all this time—I thought I knew her. But I realize I don't know the real Fleur at all. She's in love with you, Kelehan, isn't she?"

Brendan was silent for a moment, then shook his head. "I don't pretend to understand Miss Barton either, Tom. But you have my word on this—I've never given her any encouragement."

Tom nodded slowly, looked over at Katherine, then retreated before the sympathetic look upon her face. "I thought, for a while, tonight that I was seeing something new . . . but later, on that long ride to the Valley through the dark, I realized that what I saw tonight had been there all along, and I'd just blinded myself on purpose. She set her cap at you first, didn't she? And now . . . it's Rafe Huckstable. She'd never have . . . She's ambitious, Fleur—a policeman . . . just wouldn't have been good enough," he finished morosely.

Brendan said, "She only told you the truth tonight. I did meet Fleur and Rafe, just after I had the fight with Crolin . . ."

"Very well! Will you *stop* yabbering so much about what you did! Dammit, Kelehan, I'm going to have to take you in, do you realize that? The whole Highlands is upset about these murders—and to let you go free on your own cognizance, when Charlie was gaoled . . . the inspector won't like it. He'll be coming down from Moss Vale tomorrow for the inquest into the two deaths. Charlie hanging himself while in custody is bad enough. I can't tell him that I let you walk around loose when you've admitted to beating Davey Crolin into insensibility and leaving him there, to be found dead later."

"It's obvious what's happened! Someone killed Davey *after* Brendan left him."

Both men turned to Katherine. "Yes," Tom said warily, 'I'm hoping that's what happened. Your friend here has burbled such a damning statement of his own volition that I think if he *had* killed Davey, he'd have said so." He glared at Brendan, then turned back to Katherine. "In some ways, his injuries were similar to all the other murder victims—massive head injuries. His skull was bashed in—here." He indicated a place to the left and about four inches above the base of the skull.

"I didn't do that," Brendan said readily. "I struck him with my fists—the ground was soft, and he didn't fall on anything hard or sharp . . ."

"You didn't hit him from behind with a blunt object, like a rock, or a piece of wood?"

"No." Icily.

"Yet a man as outraged as you were then, might not remember what he did. You already told me earlier that you were grieving for your wife, that the sight of Crolin taking advantage of the woman made you—what was your phrase?—'insanely angry' . . . A man insanely angry might do more damage than he expected to, or wanted to."

The two men watched each other guardedly, yet each, at the same time, calculated the other's measure. Then, "I've only my intuition that tells me you're innocent," Tom said gravely. "I have to see matters in the way I've been trained, in the way my superiors would see it. I have to take you to the only gaol we have . . ."

"No!" Katherine stood up, driven by her sense of horror. "Tom, you can't mean to place Brendan in that cell—not when Charlie Crolin . . ."

"The body's in the barn, with Davey's. The storeroom's been cleaned—and I have no choice, Mrs Carron.

"Brendan Kelehan," his voice heavy, gritty with his dislike of his own words, "I'm arresting you for the murder of David Crolin."

Forty

Katherine had followed the two men out of the room and along the hall, bemused, unthinking. It was in the kitchen, at the back door, that Brendan turned to her, held her shoulders and kissed her forehead before saying, "Go back, Kate. Go to bed. Come and visit me in the morning—and bring me some of Peggy's lemon cake."

His smile, the light, loving tone of his voice, tore at her heart. She reached for him, and suddenly he had pulled her to him—his arms were warm and close about her, his lips were pressed against her hair.

It was all over too soon, and he was holding her, straight-shouldered, as if willing her to have courage, at arms' length from him; had stepped back, whirled and left the house. Katherine had a brief glimpse of Tom Lloyd's look of apologetic regret, before the door shut behind them both.

Upstairs in her room, she waited at the window and watched the two horses canter down the drive, Brendan's solid chestnut, after only a few hours' rest, pulling in front of Tom Lloyd's tired bay.

It's as if he's eager to get there, Katherine thought bitterly, blaming Brendan, not the chestnut gelding. It's as if he can't wait to begin his punishment, the expiation of whatever sin he imagines he's committed.

She undressed slowly, preoccupied with her thoughts, and lay in bed staring into the darkness above her. It was many hours before she fell asleep, and then her dreams were confused nightmares in which Mary Rose pleaded to her for help, Fleur laughed as she told Katherine that Brendan was to hang that very day—and then she was pushing through the crowd outside the Berrima gaol, crying Brendan's name and that she loved him, but the jostling spectators would not let her through . . .

She awoke at half past five and lay trembling with relief that it had been a dream, it had not—thank God—come to that . . . She bathed and dressed, taking her time, knowing it was far too early to ride to the makeshift gaol cell. She felt alone, and more frightened than she would have thought possible only twenty-four hours earlier. She missed her family, longed for her parents or even young Laura or Edwina, someone close to confide in.

Peggy was awake when Katherine came downstairs to the kitchen, preparing a bottle of warm goat's milk for the baby. James was crying lustily in his daytime cradle in the corner, and Katherine lifted him up, held him to her.

"You can give him his breakfast if you like, Miss Katey." Peggy smiled, held out a chair by the kitchen fire, and handed Katherine the feeding bottle as she seated herself with the baby.

"Miss Katey . . ." Peggy's face was concerned as she seated herself on a chair at the other side of the table, "the two horses that left last night . . . has something happened?"

"Mr Kelehan has gone with Sergeant Lloyd to answer some questions . . . about Davey Crolin's death. Brendan saw him, before he died." She added this last just before Peggy was about to erupt with questions, and it silenced her for several minutes on the subject.

"I'll get you some tea, and some porridge . . ." And she rose and set about the task, leaving Katherine feeling relieved.

She looked down at the baby. Motherless, and with an honourable fool for a father—what would become of the child? *Oh, lamb . . .* she lowered her cheek to lie against the fine down of his head, *how I would love you if I dared!*

Two large slabs of lemon cake in her saddle bag, her hair coiffured carefully beneath her most fetching green hat and in her best bottle-green riding habit, she set out at seven o'clock. Bother what people may say of her appearance; Brendan, in a prison cell, and one with so recent and so grisly a connection, should be entitled to see her at her best.

But she did not ride to Radley's directly. Instead, she turned off and steered Dryad down the scrubby track towards the neat, whitewashed gates of Emile Regnier's selection.

She went to the back door, as was the custom with most of the country houses where there were no servants to free the ladies to sojourn in the front parlours. She knocked, and Emile came to the door, welcoming her warmly, inviting her in. Katherine obeyed, finding great appeal in the large, almost European room with its white-painted stucco walls and gay curtains at the window. The smell of herbs, drying in rows on the walls or hanging from the ceiling beams, was fragrant and comforting. She saw that the family was still eating breakfast, and she handed Angel one of the slabs of lemon cake. "I . . . I came for a visit . . ."

The warmth, the atmosphere of a room that was the heart of a family household knit with love, had Katherine suddenly, inexplicably close to tears. She knew she must look strange, could tell by the consternation on Angel Regnier's face, the way Emile exchanged a glance with his wife and was suddenly, heartily ushering the two women into the parlour, setting a match to the neatly stacked logs and tinder. No, he said, Angel was not to worry, he would finish feeding the children and would set them to work at their lessons—he would bring tea to the ladies in a short while. Before the door to the kitchen was closed, Katherine could hear his voice, firmly addressing the handsome, brown-skinned children at the table. "Jacques, do not eat with your mouth open . . . Jean-Paul, keep your elbows off the table . . ."

Then the two women were alone in the room.

Before Katherine could speak, Angel said as she seated herself, "I was going to come to see you as soon as breakfast was over. I'm disturbed—but I see you are, too. Tell me what's happened."

Katherine told her, beginning with the news of the failed Irish rebellion, for it struck at her core that all Oliver had worked for, all they had both sacrificed, had been for nothing. And she spoke of Brendan's withdrawn silence, his talk—when he finally did speak— of self-tortured doubt and guilt. And finally, she spoke of the knock at the door that had brought Tom Lloyd and an accusation of murder that Brendan could not completely deny.

It was a comfortable, welcoming room; Katherine had time to look about at the books that lined all four walls, the fresh flowers in the vases on the table tops, as, when she had finished speaking, Angel walked amongst her well-loved and well-cared for possessions to the window. A small, brightly-coloured finch chirruped in a cage nearby, and Angel seemed to study it unseeingly. The large oak clock ticked away in the corner.

"I hope you don't mind my coming here like this," Katherine found herself adding. "I don't really have many women friends here in the Valley. And I never knew it until last night, when I wanted to run to someone, to talk to someone. I've never needed to do that very much. I've always had my mother and grandmother and my sisters—I suppose I never felt the need for friends outside the family."

Except Brendan. Brendan, who gave and gave of himself, and I accepted everything, and didn't question, didn't consider his feelings, for all those years . . .

"Sometimes your family can't help," Angel was saying. "Even when you know they love you." She turned from the window.

"Something is happening, Mrs Carron. I had sensed it—it's been worrying me for some days—and your telling me of these Crolin men only makes me more afraid."

She came to Katherine, sat down in a chair opposite her. "One of the Woddi women came to me yesterday, just on dusk. I was working late in the garden, gathering the dry flower heads, and I didn't hear her approach, but I knew she was there. Her name is Tigoora . . ."

"I know her . . . !"

"She's very frightened, Mrs Carron. As I'd always suspected, the elders had forbidden her to come near me, but she and the other women are so afraid that they're desperate. They have their own female powers, their own rites, and some magic; they considered, at a meeting, and decided that I might be powerful enough to help them. Gurral, their leader, has died . . ."

"Gurral . . . killed?" Katherine felt herself pale, she did not understand it but she felt, suddenly, very afraid.

"Not killed. He . . . I don't quite understand it, but it almost seems as if he gave up his life willingly. He stopped eating, went to a sacred place—she didn't say where this was—and two days later, he was dead. The elders told the rest of the tribe only that he had gone to speak with the spirits, to ask them for advice. I've never heard of this happening before. In part of my heart I wonder if the old man saw the future too clearly, saw what lay ahead for his people, and simply could not bear it. The other part of me sees the sense in the elders' words—perhaps he did 'sing himself' to sleep, in order to act as a kind of mediator. Whatever it is, the Woddi Woddi are already intent on a course of action; they'll be following Bugong Creek down towards the Shoalhaven River, and moving further south—Tigoora couldn't tell me more.

"What frightens me is that men—white men on horses—have been searching for them. That's why you wouldn't have seen any of the Woddi Woddi for some days."

Katherine felt ashamed. She had not, even before the chase to Dovewood after Edwina and Rafe, thought often of the Woddi, and had not visited Myeela or Tigoora for some time. That they had been hunted, slipping away into gullies, hiding in fern-covered caves to escape their hunters chilled her. Who would be doing this?

"We must tell Sergeant Lloyd . . ."

Angel nodded. "You know him, that's why I was coming to you. I've heard—Emile told me—that the Crolins and other cedar-getters are often at odds with the Woddi over the little wild game that's left in the area. There was a spearing, too, some months ago—remember? And . . . and what if the Woddi were watching Mr Kelehan beat Davey Crolin, but thought his punishment was not great enough? If a Woddi warrior extracted tribal revenge against Crolin for the rape of his woman, and somehow the other cedar-getters came to know about it—that would be all the excuse they need, Mrs Carron. I've seen it happen too often—these men don't want to wait to find one guilty man. Their resentment is against an entire race. It's not just murder they want—it's the destruction of an entire people."

Katherine left immediately and rode Dryad hard along the muddy valley roads towards Bert Radley's store.

Two wagons stood outside, and several rough, ungroomed horses switched their tails at the few hardy flies that were surviving the autumn weather. Voices were raised within the store and Katherine did not register the words until she was in the doorway, where she froze.

"They done it, I tell yez. Them black bastards done it! That boy in the gaol out back might have had a grudge against Davey Crolin—which one of us didn't? Thieving little mongrel once pinched three of me best laying hens when I was laid up with me gout and couldn't catch 'im. But that Kelehan bloke didn't *kill* Crolin. He ain't the type—is he, eh?"

Murmurs from about the room, mostly positive ruminations on the subject of Brendan's innocence.

Someone saw her silhouette in the doorway, and the noise slowly ceased. Katherine's eyes gradually accustomed themselves to the dimness, though her nostrils tried to reject the smell of pipe smoke and dried sweat that hovered in the crowded room, along with the usual odours of stale alcohol, damp and mould—and, since last night had obviously been a busy one, the smell of urine that came from the area all around the pub, where the clientele had been too drunk or too confused to go any further to relieve themselves.

The man who had been speaking when she entered was Mikey Brody. Katherine searched the faces along the bar that had turned towards her. Members of the Greens, Larssons, Mosleys. It was ominous that Frank Crolin was not here, drowning his grief and uttering lugubrious threats. Nor was there any sign of the tall, heavy-shouldered Tallon twins, with their pale, dangerously flat gaze, nor other Tallons and Greens who were closely related to the Crolins by ties of blood and bloody-mindedness.

"Is Sergeant Lloyd here?"

"He's off in Moss Vale. Should be back soon with some bigwigs from Berrima courthouse." Bert Radley had been standing against the wall, close to the door, and Katherine almost started at the deep voice behind her. She nodded, and left the building. Yes, it was just as well Sergeant Lloyd was bringing back some higher representatives of the law. The magistrate for the inquest, she supposed, and probably the police inspector Tom had mentioned.

She went to her saddlebag, took out the paper parcel of Peggy's lemon cake, and headed around the building towards the cell.

It filled her with horror to see it, the mossy, sandstone slabs, the heavy wooden door with its iron grille-work, all just as it had been when they had found . . .

"Brendan!" For his face had appeared at the aperture, and her heart rose in relief and gladness.

"You look surprised," he said mildly, as she ran to the door, then added ruefully, "you didn't think I wouldn't keep our appointment, did you?"

They laughed together, and it was as if they were back in Dublin, or at Avonwood—back to the early days, playing croquet on the lawn, watching Christopher toddle after Oliver through the throng of guests, hearing the hum of Irish voices beneath the mild blessing of an Irish summer sky.

She was drawn to him, as if the heavy door did not exist, for it was suddenly less of a barrier than the grief and the pride that had kept them from each other for so long. She moved close to the grille-work and stood on tiptoe. They kissed, feeling the cold iron on their faces, their fingers locked around the grille-work, holding to each other. When they pulled back at last, he gazed at her warmly. "And is there a file in the lemon cake?" he teased. "I didn't think I needed to remind you how these things were done."

She had dropped the parcel in her desire to reach him, reading on his face the same hunger that she felt to be close to him. "Oh . . ." She bent and retrieved it, handed it to him through the bars, though it became a trifle squashed in its passage. "I'm afraid there's no file—I don't have a head for these sorts of adventures, obviously."

"What's the good of you? And I suppose you've forgotten the dynamite—have you no initiative, Katherine Carron?" He had unwrapped the parcel, and now broke off a piece of cake, biting into it cheerfully.

She swallowed tears that threatened to close her throat. His humour, his patient self-possession were undoing her.

"Brendan, I've news from Angel Regnier . . . it isn't good . . ."

She stopped, glancing up towards the road on hearing a noise. An expensive and handsome buggy was progressing briskly towards the inn; the driver, Constable Crowe, drew the team of matched greys to a halt. Beside the vehicle rode Stephen Brody and Tom Lloyd.

"Brendan, I must go . . ." She fled towards the newcomers, leaving Brendan spluttering through his cake, "What—Kate, come back! What are you doing . . . ?"

"Sergeant Lloyd . . ." she began as she approached him, but Tom was looking very grim and moved past her purposefully, following the occupants of the carriage, a police inspector and an elderly gentleman in black suit and top hat, into the building. "Just a moment, Mrs Carron—forgive me, but this is very important . . ."

She went in after them, stood near the door, unnoticed.

"That Kelehan boy should be let loose—the law ain't got no right, locking up an innocent citizen when them murdering blacks can get clean away with . . ."

"Granddad, stop it!" Stephen had marched to his grandfather, laid a hand on his arm.

Mikey turned, stared at his grandson soddenly, as if barely recognizing him through a heavy fog, and then, slowly, his gaze wandered to the sharp contrast of white shirt and black serge suit that was the magistrate and, flanking him, the stern, upright form of the Inspector and a grim-faced Tom Lloyd.

"Leggo, son—who're these gen'l'men?"

It was the magistrate who spoke. "I'm Frederick Lawrence, of Berrima; this is Inspector Morris. Your grandson met us on the way from Moss Vale, Mr Brody. He was very concerned with the fact that a Mr Brendan Kelehan had been arrested for the murder of David Crolin . . ."

"Stephen . . . you went for the police?" The old man's features seemed to crumple; trembling, he looked up with pitiable red eyes at his beloved grandson. "Stephen . . ." he murmured, "you didn't."

"Come here, granddad—it'll be more comfortable and private at Cambewarra; these gentlemen will come with us, and . . ."

Once more, Mikey shook off the hand of his grandson. "You went to *them*—an' told 'em what I told you. In private—our secret! You told 'em . . ."

Stephen glanced wretchedly around the rapt audience of cedar-getters, settlers and policemen. "Please, Granddad—don't say anymore. You'll be all right. I told them what happened—you can't be blamed. But you must let them release Kelehan . . ."

"Don't tell me it'll be all right! Was it all right when the rotten bloody police dragged my father off in chains to this country—for stealing a calf in County Meath—you can't trust a policeman—ain't I always told you that . . . ? Leggo of me arm, y' little turncoat bastard!"

"It's different here, Granddad, it's not the same as it was in Ireland! You like Sergeant Lloyd, don't you? Please, come with us to Cambewarra, Granddad—don't make a scene . . . *please* . . ."

Mikey looked belligerently at Stephen and around at the faces in the bar, one by one. He sighed, dragged a hand beneath a damp nose, sighed again, glanced upwards at Stephen and muttered, "Yair . . . I reckon."

They turned to the door and Katherine backed out, raced around the building and up to the grille where Brendan was waiting.

"Something's happened! Mikey Brody has been in there, spreading vicious lies about the Woddi Woddi killing Davey Crolin, and now Stephen and Tom and a magistrate and an inspector are here, and they're taking Mikey back to Cambewarra for questioning. He obviously knows something about Davey's death—and they're going to let you go—I'm sure of it!"

He gazed at her with dazed hope, then grinned and burst out, "Well, don't just stand there, woman, get back there! Find out what's happened and tell Tom to get me out of here!"

"Oh . . . Oh, yes!" She half-turned, came back to the grille-work and their lips met once more, briefly but joyfully, before she sped off once more, half-tripping on her hampering skirts.

Mikey was being helped into his sulky by Stephen, and they set off, followed by the brougham containing Morris and Lawrence.

Tom Lloyd was standing by, receiving some last minute instruction from Inspector Morris. He nodded, as the carriage moved off and headed, not for his mount, but towards the cell—and Katherine stood in his path.

He grinned at her. "I'll be taking Brendan to Cambewarra, Mrs Carron, and I think, after questioning, he'll be allowed to return to Barrengarry. I've already spoken to the magistrate, and I think he's going to see things our way."

"What way? What happened?"

"Let's release Brendan, shall we? Then ride with us a little of the way, and I'll tell you both the story."

Crumpled, unshaven, but none the worse for his ten hours in the Radley storehouse, Brendan fetched his horse from the paddock, saddled and mounted it, and rode with Katherine and the Sergeant through the crowd of curious drinkers who had congregated on the narrow verandah to see him off.

Stephen Brody had been riding from the Valley in search of him, Tom said, when he found him escorting the carriage and its officials, just out of Moss Vale. Stephen had returned with them, telling his story as they rode.

He had been afraid for his grandfather, the young man had said; he was old and unwell, and Stephen did not think the old man would survive any amount of time—however brief—spent in a prison should Mikey be blamed for Davey's death. So, though Mikey, shaken, had admitted what had happened, his grandson had advised him to stay silent—until early that morning, when news had reached Stephen that Brendan had been arrested. He had ridden first to the ancient hut, the original Brody homestead, where Mikey still made his home, and demanded that his grandfather tell the truth—but Mikey had been adamant that he knew a better way. He would tell everyone that the Woddi Woddi had killed Crolin. No one would know *which* Woddi, Mikey argued, and though the law might question and perhaps threaten, the tribe would be left alone. Stephen had been horrified by this reasoning, had tried to argue with the old man—but he had already been drinking for some days, ever since the accident, and Stephen could get no sense from him; that was when he had decided to find Tom and tell the truth.

Brendan, Tom admitted, had been correct in everything he had said in his statement, for if Stephen was to be believed—and it seemed he would be, though it would be better if Mikey confessed—Davey Crolin had recovered and, forgetting to search for his knife, had stumbled out of the scrub onto the roadway.

It was on the roadway that Mikey Brody had overtaken him with his wagon. Mikey was a little the worse for drink, having just come from spending the day—as he spent nearly all his days—at Radley's store. Mikey had offered to drive Crolin home, seeing him with smashed nose and bruised face, but Davey did not wish to return home—not just yet. He was beginning to recover his wits and told Mikey that Kelehan had beaten him up, without warning or provocation, and he wanted to get even with Kelehan.

Mikey had refused to turn the wagon around, and the two men had struggled for control of the reins; for even Mikey realized that

Kelehan would not beat Crolin without just cause, and that Crolin was angry enough to be very dangerous.

Crolin had finally reached for his knife—and began cursing that he remembered now—Kelehan, the dog, had stolen it. That was when he had looked around and had seen the rifle that Mikey always travelled with. He tried to grab it, and they struggled—the match more even than it would normally have been because Davey was at the last of his strength, and Mikey was furious at this commandeering of his possessions. The horses were confused and panicking—they broke into a canter coming down one of the hills. Mikey, unable to hold the horses and keep control of the gun, struck Davey with it. He had meant only to stun him, then to get him out of the wagon and let him walk home for his pains. But Davey fell off the wagon before Mikey could gain control of the horses, and rolled off the edge of the road, down a very steep slope, and struck his head against a tree.

The rain would have washed most of the blood away—and Mikey tried also to pull the man up to the wagon again—but when he saw that Crolin was dead, he left him where he lay. "We'll go back this afternoon," Tom finished, "and look more closely for blood on the tree—but if Mikey tells the truth—and I can't see why Stephen would go to all this trouble if it wasn't the truth—then all you'll be faced with is a charge of assault—and given the circumstances you may get off with a fine and a warning."

"And Mikey?" Katherine asked.

"It's hard to tell. It depends on whether the magistrate believes him. Those lies he was telling as we came into the inn won't make him appear in a very good light—the old troublemaker."

Katherine spoke up then, and told the two men about Tigoora's visit to Angel Regnier—and how she herself noted that Frank Crolin and the Tallons and the more hot-headed members of the Green clan were ominously absent from the gathering that morning in the shebeen.

She could tell, at the end of her speech, that both Tom and Brendan were worried.

"There's nothing we can do at the moment," Tom frowned. "Mr Laurence and the Inspector will want the matter of Davey Crolin settled. Then we have to go back to Radley's, have the place closed, and hold the inquest." He wrinkled his nose. "The sooner we get some suitable public buildings in this valley the better."

Katherine left them, rather reluctantly, at Sawyer's Creek; there was one last, long look from Brendan, then they had each turned away, and Katherine forced herself not to look back, to gaze at him as he rode away.

All that afternoon at Barrengarry she waited in a chair by the parlour windows, a book unread upon her lap, thinking of Brendan, praying that nothing would go wrong, that the matter of Davey's death and Charlie's suicide could be settled, that the forces of the law could turn their attention to preventing more violence. And she prayed for Brendan to come home to her—soon, soon. And she would speak with him, she decided, she would tell him of the depth of her love for him, of her need of him, and propriety could go hang, she thought fiercely; they had spent the past six years ignoring their feelings for each other, placing their sense of honour and duty ahead of all else. Not any more. No. This time nothing would come between them.

The waiting seemed interminable, and when the clatter of buggy wheels was heard on the bridge, she did not stop to wonder at why the magistrate's carriage would be calling at Barrengarry, but ran out onto the verandah, her only wish to see Brendan astride the large-boned, handsome chestnut, cantering up the drive safe—and safe ever afterwards.

But the carriage was not that belonging to the Berrima magistrate, it was Edwin Gordon's solid and stately brougham, and seated in the carriage was young Molly Murphy, Edwina, Marcus Prescott— and Katherine gave an involuntary cry and ran down the steps to the drive—for seated by her husband, and holding her arms out towards her eldest daughter was Suzanna.

Molly, almost well now, was settled in a warm room next to Bridget's, and while the elder girl looked after her friend and unpacked her things, an overjoyed and beaming Peggy made tea and served it to the family in the parlour.

Tom Lloyd had called by Dovewood very early that morning and told them of Brendan's arrest. Tom was worried, he had told Marcus, about Katherine being left alone at this time, with only the servants, and Marcus had agreed that they should all return immediately. Katherine, unable to take her eyes from her parents—together, *together* and at home again—told them of the newer developments at Radley's store, and about the visit to Cambewarra, and the inquest.

Marcus, intrigued and concerned at the turn of events, worried, mostly, for the Woddi Woddi, announced that he would ride out and find Brendan and the police contingent, refusing to allow

Katherine even to complete her voiced desire to accompany him. She sat in the parlour with her mother and Edwina, bristling with helpless resentment, as her father rode off.

Edwina, into a silence, asked in a small voice if Rafe had called at the homestead and Katherine, more crossly than she had meant, answered in the negative, and hadn't Edwina had enough of Rafe Huckstable's shenanigans to last her all her life?

Edwina looked upset and Suzanna declared gently that it *would* have been only honourable of the young man to call at Dovewood or at Barrengarry to ask an apology of the family, to which Katherine, her eyes on the clock, her mind with Brendan, with the Woddi Woddi, with the hours that were slipping towards dusk, snapped, "If Rafe Huckstable had an ounce of honour he wouldn't have attempted to disgrace Teddi in the first place."

Edwina gave an involuntary sob and left the room very hurriedly to run up the stairs. Suzanna sighed, cast a reproachful look at her eldest daughter, and followed Edwina to offer comfort.

Katherine sat stiffly, silently in her chair, listening to the ticking of the old clock, finding that she was tapping her foot in time to the measured beats of the passing seconds--until she could stand it no longer. She rose and ran softly, swiftly, out of the house to the stables and saddled Dryad.

Was she being foolish to leave now? Already the sun was resting itself on the top of the western escarpment, the slopes in black shadow, the sun's rays slanting through the tree trunks, turning them to striations of salmon pink and rose and deep purple-brown in the shade. The dry stubble of the hay fields glowed like molten gold with the sun behind it, and the leaves of the eucalypts moved like a black lace mantilla stirring in the chill breeze. It was a moment of glory that began to ebb away even as Katherine gazed; one of those brief—all too brief—Australian dusks that compensates in an intensity of beauty for its regrettable transience.

Radley's store was all but empty. It was strange—why had she not met her father and Brendan on their way home?

Bert Radley shook his head. "Inquest?—Tomorrow, maybe. They never come back from Cambewarra. One of the Larssons met 'em on the road and told 'em there was trouble—he didn't want no part of it, but Frank Crolin and the Tallon boys and a few of the Greens have taken guns and gone after the blacks for what they did to Davey Crolin."

"But . . . they didn't! He died by accident!"

"Yair—I figured old man Brody had something to do with it,

the way he was going on this morning. Frank Crolin and the Tallons never came in here—but Mikey's probably been spouting his poison for days, trying to cover himself. All those Tallons wanted was an excuse to get the blacks—and Frank is so crazy, a few of the men told me, that he'd attack anyone or anything. And the Tallons'd follow Frank into hell, if he asked 'em. Where're you going, Missus? There's nothing you can do . . . !''

"Where's Sergeant Lloyd and the others?"

"Gone to see what they can do to stop it, according to Larsson—the Woddi were last seen headed south—they could be a hundred miles away by now. Them cedar-getters—they should stay outa the Valley, up in the mountains where they belong. I bin here twenty years and none of the settlers have had any complaints about the blacks—we all got along real well."

And even the face of the usually-suspect Bert Radley was creased with a genuine frown of affronted civic pride.

Katherine stumbled out into the last light of the day. The sun, a sliver of scarlet, fled behind the mountain, and the march of darkness across the Valley was complete.

Forty One

There was nothing Katherine could do; overcome with her sense of helplessness, she rode homewards to Barrengarry, almost oblivious to anything around her. Dryad, sensible to the fact that her mistress was not truly in control, dared to take the initiative and trotted quite briskly, but good-humouredly, along the roads, heading for her stable and the warm chaff and bran that she felt confident would await her.

It was when they were half a mile from the track that turned off towards Regniers' selection that the rider, coming hard from the other direction, overtook them.

The first warning was the rider's horse, whinnying a shrill greeting to Dryad, who danced sideways, agitated, but even with this edging across the road, the two horses almost collided. Dryad half-reared, lashed out first with her heels then with her teeth, and spun to face the strange animal. Katherine, startled, had only the impression of a tall, slim figure sitting well in the saddle of a big horse, and the smell of sweat, human and equine, that meant they had been riding hard for some time. The light was very poor, it was only by the shifting of dark outlines and the voice, low and mocking, that made Katherine recognize the rider.

"Ill met by moonlight, proud Titania," Rafe Huckstable mocked, and she could just discern that he bowed from his seat in the saddle. Then, "I have just come from your house—but no matter. I shall escort you home. You shouldn't be out on the roads so late at night." He moved his horse level with hers, manoeuvred it close so that the shoulder of the larger animal pushed the smaller Dryad. The Galloway mare walked on but snapped viciously and effectively at the horse's neck as she did so. She would not be pushed, and Rafe's mount, for all his urging, kept a wary distance as they walked.

"I know the way to Barrengarry, Rafe—thank you, but there's no need to delay yourself . . ."

"Oh, but it's no bother at all—quite the correct thing to do, in the circumstances. Offering protection to a helpless woman."

Had he been drinking? It was always so hard to tell with Rafe. Perhaps she should say "thank you"—but she was still wary, and more, she found that she had very few civil words to say to the man.

Rafe, too, was now silent. His breathing was heavy, and that and the horses' hoofs on the damp, soft ground, were the only noise apart from the frogs on either side of them, and these fell silent as they approached, beginning their steady, pulsing songs once more only after the riders had passed.

Katherine wished Rafe were gone, wished him a thousand miles away. He was not coming into the homestead, that was for certain. She had a feeling that his visit there had been neither long nor pleasant, and there was a gathering, stormy resentment within him even now. It oppressed her with every yard they travelled, until she began to feel . . . threatened. And this was ridiculous, for she had known him all her life . . .

"You know," he began, "I found it very difficult to forgive you for what you did in taking Edwina from me."

So it had not been her imagination; there was a resentment there, and it had been building all this while into a dark thing, a wholly malevolent thing . . .

"Rafe," she said firmly, "Edwina made her own choice. My father doesn't have *that* much control over her, let alone myself."

"Edwina is young, and easily led." His voice sounded calm, at least. "She's at an age where she was ripe for a love affair. And of course, with a naive young thing such as she, who had spent far too much time in her own company, no doubt reading romantic novels . . ."

And she thought, *he's right, he knows Teddi well in that, at least.*

". . . she'd have fallen for any man she was pushed at . . ."

Katherine, stung, lashed back, "Or any man who pushed himself at her?"

He turned to look at her, and the venom of his glance was obvious even in the scant starlight. It came at her in waves. "You used every ounce of your not-inconsiderable influence to convince her that I was unworthy of her. And no doubt you'll continue to use that influence to convince her that she'll be happy with a boring, boorish ox of a farmer with more bank balance than brains . . ."

"She's too young to marry yet—but when she does choose, I hope she chooses a man with maturity and stability and moral strength, for that's what counts, Rafe, in the long term . . ."

"Don't lecture me. Edwina will be married within the next twelve months—perhaps within the next six, if that ponderous Luke Murchison has lost none of his tenacity. But even he may object to soiled goods."

The silence throbbed loudly. She shouldn't ask, she shouldn't— he wanted her to ask, so she shouldn't.

"Just what do you mean by that?" flatly.

"Only that I could have made sure I held her loyalty. I have, though doubtless you won't believe me, more self-control than Edwina. But perhaps Luke won't even bother to question, but simply be rather distant from now on."

"Don't be presumptuous. And Edwina wouldn't have . . ."

"Oh, wake up, Katey! Edwina was ripe for it. Like many stupid young girls she thought that a physical relationship means that the man feels some kind of commitment. But don't worry—as I said, I was in control. So when Edwina finally marries in orange blossom and a white gown, you can thank me for her unsullied virtue."

"Are you drunk, Rafe? Even if you are, this is unforgivable . . ."

"I'm not drunk. And what hurts you, fond sister that you are, is that what I'm saying is the truth. She's such a passionate thing, little Edwina. You've been married, Katey, you know about passion— you displayed enough of it in Drummoyne all those years ago. Yet you were coy, at the eleventh hour, unlike Edwina, during our trysts by the creek . . ."

She had had enough; having forgotten her foolishness of those years ago, it was now dragged up before her and worse, her sister's love for the man besmirched and turned into something facile and dirty in that sly, smirking mouth. Her only desire was to shut it, silence it—the whip in her right hand came up and cracked across his face with stinging force. Before his cry of pain and surprise had faded, she had applied her heel and the same whip to the startled Dryad, and bending low over the mare's neck, she was carried forward, away from him, and that was all that mattered.

She did not turn around to glance behind her, kept her eyes on the road before her and hoped that Dryad would keep her balance and her sense of direction. It was madness, madness to ride like this on such a night, but there could be no stopping—after all that had happened in the past few days, all that may be happening yet, in the dark, untravelled hills to the south. Barrengarry represented her only sanctuary, her only safety . . .

And she heard him then, behind her, with a sense of some surprise first, for surely he would have given up, ridden home to Bendeela. After the surprise came the fear, for the hoofs pounded crazily after her own mount, pounded louder and louder until they were competing with Dryad's, a confused drumming that felt as if it would burst her eardrums, split her head with the sound and her terror . . .

The pain was in her arm, and she could not understand it. It was dark, and her arm hurt, and it was very very quiet.

Dangerous, this quiet, and she knew it, but did not in her confusion, know why, and cried out incoherently and moved—

The hand was tight upon her mouth, the pain was tight upon her arm—both feelings of constriction bringing a fear—physical terror—that Katherine had never experienced before.

"Stop squealing. You fell, you silly little fool." Rafe's voice—and memory returned. The voice was as cool as ever, mellifluous, even in its venom. "You damn' near brought my horse down on top of yours. You cause trouble, Katherine, wherever you go, do you realize that?"

She was lying on the ground. It was damp and cold, and Rafe leaned above her, his face quite close, blotting out the stars. He took his hand from her mouth when it was clear that she was not going to struggle. "Are you hurt?" he asked.

"Yes. My arm . . . The right one . . ."

He began to feel along its length. She flinched at his touch, then moaned a little at the tearing pain that claimed her.

"Yes, it's broken." The detached voice above her in the darkness.

Katherine murmured, "Take me home . . ." And the words sounded like a plea, but she did not care. "Take me home, Rafe, please."

He sat back on his heel and looked around him, appearing not to have heard her. The silence went on and on, and still Rafe did not speak but looked about him, his attitude considering, withdrawn.

Katherine rolled onto her side and with difficulty pushed herself to her knees, then, unsteadily, began to rise, but he was kneeling before her in the dirt and his hands were on her shoulders, making her face him.

What does he want? Her mind tried to cope with the sudden, purposeful gentleness of his touch, the way his hands moved lightly on her shoulders, as if he were making up his mind . . . for what?

"Well . . ." Her voice was bright and brave. "I . . . I think I'm all right. My mother will be worried, though—Father isn't home at the moment, but he and Brendan will be along here any minute. I'd hate them to find me like this—will you fetch my horse for me, Rafe?"

"In a minute. Let me hold you . . . let me look at you—as much as I can. It will be the last time. I . . . I had rather a scene with your mother and Edwina at Barrengarry—made a fool of myself, I'm afraid. I was too sure of Edwina's feelings. Should have known that you can't trust any woman—especially a Prescott."

"Rafe . . ."

"And none of this would have happened, if it wasn't for you. We'd be married by now—perhaps for five years or more, and you'd be a tame Kate, a conformable, household Kate, as Shakespeare would have it. We'd have four or five children and I'd keep you so busy, my darling, that you'd not have the time nor the energy for your wilful ways.

"But instead you married some mewling Dublin poet, and you've come back even more defiant than when you left. You're still looking, aren't you? You've never found it—not in all the years since you ran from me, that rainy night in my town house. You grew afraid then, and you ran, and you've been running ever since."

"I don't know what you're talking about—what am I running from, what am I looking for?"

"A real man. The kind of man who knows what you want, and how to treat you."

"You're mad . . ." His hand had moved down to the collar of her riding habit, had found the swell of her breast. "Rafe, *no* . . . !"

She was pulled forward into his embrace, and there was the long-forgotten feel of him, the smell of him, even the same trace of the cologne he had worn, in that mad, wild time in the buried past. His lips were the same, the demand upon her was the same . . .

And her heart remained cold. His strength was a greed, a forceful, deceiving masculinity that had all to do with his drive to possess her and nothing to do with what it meant to be a man, whole, complete, fearless, with an inner core of honour, without which there could be no respect, not from the world nor, she knew, from herself.

He sensed it, not just her coldness, but the withdrawal of her mind from him and it made him furious. He barely controlled his voice. "It's too late, isn't it? I should have realized it years ago— there were ways of persuading you that we were right for each other. But I was a fool, and I withdrew to lick my wounds, and let you go. If I hadn't been so foolish, it would all be different, now . . ."

"No, Rafe . . ."

"It would!" And there was a kind of desperation in his voice. "I . . . Don't you see how different it would have been? How different *I* would have been? I needed your fire, your strength, Katey. I wanted more than anything for you to be proud of me. For you I'd have settled down, found some kind of belief in the future, worked for that future. When you left me, that night in Drummoyne—Dear God, I couldn't believe it was over, that it could end so quickly, without a word, without a single regret!—When you left that night, all my hope left with you. You despise me now—don't deny it, I've seen it on your face—but I've become a creature of your making. You took the life from me—I haven't cared, ever since, what might happen to me. It just doesn't matter."

She inhaled slowly, deeply, realizing that for some seconds she had forgotten to breathe. "Rafe, I couldn't, *couldn't* have that much power over your life . . ."

"You did. You never knew . . ."

"I couldn't . . . !"

"I loved you! Only you! All my life . . . !"

"*Your* life! It was your life, Rafe, not mine! How dare you try to lay the blame for your failures upon my shoulders!"

"You could have saved me . . . !"

"You should have saved yourself!"

"If you'd married me . . ."

"You'd have dragged me down with you!"

They were terrible words. That they were the truth, or, at least, that Rafe himself saw them as truth, was borne out in the long pause that followed.

His voice was low, self-mocking. "And you don't even know the depths to which I've descended, do you? I don't know whether to tell you and destroy the last illusion you have about me . . . or show you."

"Rafe, help me to my horse this instant. I will not stand for this! Behave like the gentleman you've always claimed to be, and bring me my horse!"

And the command, her tone of complete confidence, almost worked. She felt him to be startled, then unsure; but it was only for a second. One of his hands moved up to her neck, and he laughed softly. "You almost had me springing to obey you, you know. Such is the legacy of a lifetime lived under the shadow of the Prescott empire. All my life spent bending and scraping to your family. And all the while we were never—any of us in this Valley—allowed to forget for an instant that the Prescotts could crush us—any time they chose."

"Rafe, that's not so . . . Your family were our friends . . . !"

"People like you don't have any friends!" He pulled her to her feet, so roughly that she cried out in pain despite herself. Rafe said, in a lower voice, "You have sycophants, not friends! My father had to fight your grandfather Josiah for years to stop him from buying up the entire Valley! Your family might have dependants, and tenants, and servants—but you—*you*, Katey, never had a friend in this Valley outside your own equally self-indulgent family!"

She was shaking with suppressed rage. She looked about her. Rafe's horse was about six yards away and Dryad, she could just discern, was a few yards beyond that, grazing unperturbed and apparently unhurt.

"Ah!" he said sharply, his hand coming about her neck to take her chin and force her face towards him. "You're not going to leave. You do understand that, don't you? I've already talked too much . . ."

The truth came to her dulled mind slowly, too slowly for her to act quickly enough. He had taken her sound arm and was yanking her off to the scrub at the side of the road—even with the pain in her left arm, she managed to claw at his hand as she screamed, screamed and screamed and prayed that someone was close enough to hear.

The air was knocked from her lungs as he fell upon her, and all power left her body momentarily as his weight pinned her, her broken arm across her body and trapped—the pain an explosion that seemed to take the world with it.

What had Rafe meant? Why was he going to silence her? Had he meant to kill her? She rose up from unconsciousness already grappling with the same thought she had taken into the darkness with her, as if she swam to the surface, half-drowned, hampered by a burden. Rafe . . .

She had no idea how long she had fainted—a few seconds, half a minute . . . She knew instinctively that Rafe was there, one of those two dark shapes that were struggling on the roadway, cursing and struggling in the darkness. She backed away, afraid still, confused, not knowing who the assailant was . . .

But it must be a friend—it was someone who had cared to rescue her . . . Run, or stay? And what could she do to help? There might be timber in the scrub with which she could attack Rafe—but which man, whirling, grappling there, was Rafe?

And it was over—two sharp punches to the other man's stomach— Katherine could hear the agonized exhalation that must, must, have meant broken ribs—and one, two, three battering punches to the head—the neck jerked backwards and the man toppled, unconscious, Katherine knew, before his body had hit the ground.

Her heart pumped hard with terror as the standing figure raised his head and stared at her. He took three steps towards her, Katherine shrinking back slightly, ready to run, then, "Mrs Carron? You all right?"

And she had rushed forward, was sobbing into the wiry arms, while Amos Murphy, taken by surprise, patted her shoulder awkwardly, murmuring almost bemusedly, "There, there. He won't hurt you no more. Don't cry . . . there, there . . ."

There were no tears, there never were. It seemed that nothing could tap that well of emotion that lay pent within her. "I'm all right, Mr Murphy. Can you help me to my horse?"

"Your horse has gone, girl. Frightened off, I reckon."

She looked around in consternation, to find that it was true. Her own screaming, the shouting of the two combatants had proved too much for Rafe's flighty thoroughbred, and the usually placid Dryad had followed it.

"Can't have gone far . . ." she murmured. Her head felt light. She placed a hand to her head, which had been throbbing, she realized, ever since her fall. The swelling over her right temple felt enormous beneath her fingers. "I don't think I'm very well . . ."

"Here, I'll get up on my horse, and help you up behind me."

"I've got a broken arm . . ."

"You'll be right . . ."

The saddlebags were full and bulging—they made it difficult for her to keep her legs forward, away from the horse's flank. He was off on a journey, Amos told her as they rode off, leaving Rafe where he lay sprawled on the muddy roadway. "Lucky I was riding through this way, heard you yelling. Young mongrel—if he ain't dead, he deserves to be."

She dozed with her head on Amos' back, found herself speaking, almost despite herself, of the Woddi, of her worry for them.

You can't do anything. Whatever's happened, nothing you can do can change anything.

I can try. I don't know what I can do, but I must try.

You don't know these men, you don't know what they're truly like. They're capable of any godless act. Leave their punishment to God . . .

I don't want to punish them—I want to know what's happened to the Woddi Woddi. I must know . . .

Best leave these men alone. Crolin, the Tallons, they're men that God has forgotten.

I must try to help the Woddi Woddi. I must do something.

It's a risk. There's danger.

I must try. I must try.

"Alright now, you have your way."

She started, dazed, uncomprehending. A hand was beneath her head and the cold rim of a mug struck her teeth before cool water flowed into her mouth. She swallowed, gratefully. Everything was all right . . . But she felt concerned when some of the liquid spilled down her chin, and opened her eyes . . .

She was not at home. She was not safe. The firelight flickered over the hollow cheekbones and eyesockets of Amos Murphy, glowed amber on the grey hair and whiskers and made the man seem like a demon from hell. She sat up, staring about her. There were bush noises all about them; they were in the bush and it was night, and from somewhere behind Amos Murphy Katherine could hear the gurgle of a stream, the chuckling rush of a moderate-sized creek in flood. She gazed from Amos' face to the small fire before which she lay.

"This is their fire," Amos said. "It was still smouldering."

She looked at him blankly. He gestured at the blazing twigs and small branches. "The Woddi. They were here, when it happened. You said you wanted to know. So I brought you here. It wasn't on my way, but you kept arguing, you had to see." He looked about him, and there was a kind of fear upon the tough features. "Eerie, though. I came too late, see. Heard the noise, the shooting, and came—even though I'd have been crazy to . . . There were no bodies. I don't know why, but there ain't. Them Tallons and that bastard Frank, they wouldn't have hung around . . . who hid the bodies? 'Cos they're gone, every last one of 'em, almost."

"No," she said. "No, that can't be right. That can't be . . ."

"We can't stay here too long. Just until you're a bit rested. It's rough country here, and we've got a long way to go."

She felt nauseous, swallowed on the bile that rose into her mouth. The pain in her head was almost blinding, but she gazed around her, avoiding Amos' eyes, the watchful, wild look in them made her almost as afraid as of Rafe . . .

She rolled onto her side and struggled to her feet, thankful that he did not try to hinder her. What had he said? *They were here.* The Woddi Woddi. No, they couldn't have been. Amos was as confused as she was—perhaps Rafe's blows had concussed him, perhaps they were both wandering about in the bush, dazed and lost and ill . . .

Where was this place? A creek to her right, scrub to her left. The fire was lit on the rocky beach that edged the creek.

"Where are they?" she asked, "the Woddi. You said they were here. Where are they now?"

Amos stared at her, then looked away, chewed at a corner of his moustache that drooped near his mouth. "Shouldn't have listened to you—you're not yourself just now. I tell you, it was too late when I got here. You gotta understand that. Frank Crolin, and the Tallons and their mates—I heard the shooting. I was . . . busy . . . collecting things—but I come up here to see.

"If you want to look, you'll see the blood. But it was a good two hours before I got here—and the bodies were gone. All except . . ." He hesitated, then, "There's a child back there—behind a fallen log." He went on more quickly, "I don't think that Crolin had them buried— I think the tribe came back—what was left of them. They missed the child, it was hidden. If you like, I'll bury it now. I didn't have time before. I was . . . I was scared, see. Troopers everywhere, and settlers, lookin' for Frank and his mates. Not that they'll ever find 'em—they're almost as good as the blacks at vanishing in the bush when they want to."

Katherine stood, swaying slightly, looking about her. Yes. There were dark stains on the large, elliptical pebbles. She did not want to believe Amos. Yet she did. "Oh, God . . ."

"Sit down now. Rest. We got a long way to go." He lowered her to sit beside the small fire.

"How far away from Barrengarry are we? I must get home soon, my mother will worry that . . ."

"About time you stopped worrying what your mama would think, I reckon, don't you? You're a woman—got to go your own way."

She blinked at him, confused. "But . . . we must tell the police— if we ride fast, we might catch up to them . . ."

"Dunno where they are. Could be anywhere in these hills. Anyway, I told you. I don't want to go anywhere near the police. Keep them out of it."

"But they have to know . . . what happened here."

"Let 'em find out for themselves, I say."

His tone was becoming testy. Katherine struggled to follow his wayward reasoning; it was the blow to her head, that was it. Amos must be making sense; it was she who was obtuse . . .

"I must go home," she repeated. That was the truth, that was real, the thought of Barrengarry and safety. She must go home to Barrengarry . . .

"I'll buy you a new horse when we get to Berry."

Katherine stared at Amos, who seemed oblivious to the effect of his statement. He was stirring the fire with a green twig, his face turned from her a little, thoughtful, confident. "God's will, I reckon, finding you on the road like that. I was headed Moss Vale way, knowing that Frank and his mates would be looking for me to ride out the way I'm used to. Fooled 'em, I thought—but then you talked so much about the Woddi . . . I reckoned I should set your mind at rest, even if it upsets you a bit."

The confused arguments that had drifted through her mind while riding behind Amos, believing he was taking her home . . . how much were her own thoughts, and how much had she said aloud and been answered by Amos? *Crolin, the Tallons—they're men that God has forgotten.* She had always believed that no man was beyond the memory nor the forgiveness of God. The words had been Amos's.

He was looking directly at her, quietly. Then, "Always liked you. A good girl, grown to a good woman. You nursed me when I was sick. First thing I saw, after that little bastard Charlie Crolin struck me down was your face. Couldn't speak to you—helpless as a child, I was—and you nursed me. Ain't gonna forget that. Nancy—she tried to tell me it was pity, but I knew better. A lady like you don't bother with a bloke like me unless there's something deeper. You never made me feel I wasn't good enough for you. An' you cooked me that chook, too, and sent it to me—I'd have come to thank you for it myself, but I was still feeling crook, and that Nancy Halstrop kept tellin' me that you'd laugh in my face. Then when I got better, all this business with the Crolins started. I couldn't be sure who Charlie might have blabbed to—so I had to play it real careful for a while."

It was worse, this time, the fear rushing back, down upon her mind; worse for the brief time of safety and relief she had known. No, staring at the man, she felt that there were no reserves of strength left within her with which to cope with this new revelation.

"Mr Murphy, you must take me home. My father and Mr Kelehan and the stockmen will be out searching for me . . ."

He had been crouched beside the fire, but he stood now, slowly. She was disturbed to realize that he was a great deal taller than she remembered and even after the weeks of his illness, he was a strong man, all corded, wiry muscle, only just past his middle years.

"You talk like a spoilt child. You are spoilt, I reckon, but you're not ruint. I got plenty of money to keep you, don't you worry about that."

And she knew, beyond the haze of her physical pain and weariness, her terror for Myeela, Timalong, Tigoora and the Woddi, that she herself was in danger.

"Mr Murphy, I don't know what you're talking about. We can discuss it back at Barrengarry . . ." Somehow she climbed to her feet, holding her right arm close to her body. But he stood before her, legs spread a little, unmoving. "Now, don't say you didn't know. You wouldn't have looked after my Molly like you have—been kindness itself to my family . . . My Billy worships the ground you walk on—you wouldn't help the family of a man unless you saw them kids as your own. And I got nearly all the money—Crolin didn't know the half of it—I never planted it all in one . . ."

"Stop it! It's horrible! I don't want to know!"

Her hands were over her ears; in panic and exhaustion she refused to hear him; it was her one mistake, and it was a deadly mistake.

Amos stared at her. He looked away, a puzzled frown on his face, then turned back to Katherine, and the firelight, or his madness, played along the slope of his cheek and jaw. The face appeared to be working, but as he moved closer to her, she saw that his eyes alone were alight with life. The grim face was set.

"You don't know, do you? You never worked it out. Lloyd never did—nor any of the troopers—but I thought you knew. I . . . I liked to think that we understood each other. That's why it was breaking my heart today to leave the Valley without you. And when I'd collected everything and was crossing the Valley—I heard a scream, and followed it and found that Huckstable bloke trying to hurt . . . *you*. I'd thought you . . . Then you weren't. You didn't come looking for me." The bruised hurt in his voice. When she didn't answer, "*Were* you?" he barked.

"No, I . . . was going home, I'd been looking for my father . . ."

He gave a short laugh. "By now your father and all them troopers are probably looking for *me*. Nancy—she followed me when I went to collect everything . . . Don't know what it is but I always have people sniffing round my heels. It's the money, I reckon. Money draws people like manure draws flies, don't it? First Charlie Crolin, then Nancy Halstrop."

Katherine swallowed painfully on her fear. "Charlie Crolin followed you . . . because he suspected you were the man who . . ."

"Must have been watching me for weeks—lucky I'm so careful. He only managed to clean out two caches after he jumped me—and then took them home with him, the fool. I thought long and hard about that—was almost certain he'd do that. And since he didn't know where I'd hidden the rest of the money it would have been useless for him to name me . . ."

"But he didn't . . ." Katherine murmured.

"No. He was real stupid, Charlie. Thick as two bricks. And then they threw 'im in that cell and he went a bit strange in the head, I reckon—just gave up, never said nothing. So much good it all done him in the end. And when that fool of a Constable Crowe told 'im that Davey was dead—well, that finished 'im. He wasn't too bright, Charlie, and he thought he'd get the blame for Davey's death. Charlie never was any use without Frank telling him what to do. Frank's the clever one—the only really dangerous one. It's lucky for me that Charlie was so scared by that prison cell that he didn't even tell Frank what the real story was—or maybe he was so scared of Frank that he didn't want him to know what he'd been up to. It was all lucky for me, but. Even Charlie jumping me, knocking me down from behind like the dog he was. 'Cos when I woke up, you were there . . ."

"The caches . . . it was money, and valuables . . . from Gilbert Barton . . ."

"And Harcourt and Penman—and a few others. I buried a few of the bodies, when I had the time. I never set out to do it in cold blood—the killings, I mean. I had just cause. Harcourt—he was the first—the bloke they found at Burrawang. You want to know why I killed him?" His lips moved as he bent forward to her. Katherine thought it was a snarl, but then realized he was smiling at her.

"Why did you kill him?" she asked, her voice thin even to her own ears.

"Harcourt was partners with a gutless, hypocritical dingo of a rent collector called Richard Barnes. When my family was killed in the bushfires when I was a boy, this Barnes offered to take me in like his own son—he didn't have any children of his own. None of the other cedar-getters offered to look after me—they were all worried about one more mouth to feed, though they accepted my two little sisters—they both died before they were five—and there were times, living with Barnes, when I wished I'd died, too. I was treated like a slave, like a boot-licking lackey in that man's house, with his wife who hated me. At least I was useful to *him*—ran his messages, wrote his letters, filed his receipts . . . He kept on saying, 'When I die, this business will be yours and you gotta know how to run it.'

"That was real funny, in the end, because you know what happened? The old bastard had a fit of apoplexy one day, screaming at that vicious little shrew of a wife of his, and he keels over and dies—without leaving any will. None they could find, anyway—but knowing the old man, there probably wasn't one. He was smart in business, all right—real organized—but he never believed he'd die.

"Since Barnes had no children, his half of the business went to his wife—and the partner, Harcourt, he bought the old girl out. And he presumed—he *presumed* that I'd still work for him. I asked him for my share, for back wages that I never got, and told him that I should have some part of what the old man had left . . . But he laughed at me. He didn't even bother to say no. He just laughed at me.

"I waited. I moved back to the Valley, and married, and worked my father-in-law's place, inherited it when the old man died. One day, when I was down in Wollongong, I paid a visit to Harcourt's offices, late at night. I still had the key, after all those years. I emptied the safe, and made it look like a break-in. I got quite a lot out of it. But I wasn't finished with him. The police never tracked me—and I waited for the right time to get Harcourt, waited years, asking questions, getting a pattern of his movements. Sixteen years after he'd laughed me out of that office, I caught up with him on a quiet road in Burrawang. I let him know who I was, and what I was doing. I let him make his peace with the Almighty . . . And I took my revenge for all them years I suffered.

"There was much more money in his saddlebags than I'd expected, and it got me thinking about rent collectors generally—and I knew most of 'em, back in Wollongong. They were all the same. A bloke has to be scum to be a rent collector. No one'd miss one less in the world. O'Mara—him with all those kids—he was always complaining about Edgar Penman—always said he had a feeling the man had more money than he pretended to have. And he was right. I was sorry O'Mara was under suspicion for a while—but any fool should know that he wasn't capable of putting even a wretch like Edgar Penman out of his misery. But O'Mara was scared of the police all the same, couldn't tell them how he had a bit more money than he should—he was making ends meet by distilling a few bottles up there in the hills, and selling it to Bert Radley. He couldn't cough *that* up as a reason."

"Did . . . did Mr O'Mara know that you . . ."

"No, no one did. You didn't—and I thought you knew me. Thought you understood everything. You seemed to, when you looked at me."

The sky—was it lighter? She looked around her and yes, there was a faint pale haze off to her left. So that was east—she knew that now. It would help her get home, if she could get away.

"What are you looking for?" There was an edge to his voice.

"I . . . I can see the sun coming up."

Amos was gazing at her thoughtfully. "You worry me," he said.

She tried to smile, to keep her tone light. 'Why?" she asked.

"You're not how I thought you'd be."

If this side of the creek was east, she must follow it upstream. And better to cross it. Perhaps Amos couldn't swim . . . But could she, hampered by her broken arm and her heavy skirts? The creek was not broad, perhaps thirty feet wide, but it seemed to flow very swiftly—the current might carry her further downstream . . . But she could always double back—the main thing was to get away, away from this man and his madness . . .

"I don't know what you mean," she said politely. "I realize that you've suffered a great deal at the hands of mercenary, selfish men, and . . . and I appreciate you feeling that you can trust me with your story . . ."

"But will you stay with me? That's what I got to ask myself."

She studied his face, tried to find an answer that would satisfy him, but she was not sure, not certain, how his mind worked, could not follow it down its dark and tortuous ways.

"Promise me you'll stay with me. I don't trust you, see, because you're different to what I'd thought you'd be. More . . . cold. I used to dream that you'd be . . . but no matter. You're a lady, though, and I reckon you'll keep your word. Say, 'I promise I'll stay with you forever and never leave you.' Go on."

It was a simple lie, made under duress. Why, then, was it so difficult to make her tongue and lips form those words? Her fear and revulsion, was that it? They possessed her almost totally. "I . . . I promise . . . that I'll . . . stay with you forever . . . and never . . ."

He leaned forward to her suddenly and she stopped, almost recoiling. No, not even to save her life could she continue, and he looked into her face and knew it.

He pulled back, studied her quietly, and his voice was low, reflective. "I might've known. You can't have everything. Nancy told me about you—I talked in my sleep and said your name, so she knew, and then she never let up, the vicious little tart. She wasn't *in* my bed, you gotta understand that—It was when I was ill, godless, brazen woman she was—she tried . . . as if I'd have her. But she heard me say your name, and from then on she never let me forget it—laughed at me, told me I was an old fool, that you was a Prescott and you'd never look at the likes of me. She said you only looked after me and Molly out of pity, and . . ." his voice was morose, "and it's true, isn't it?"

"No, I liked you. We were friends . . ."

"We was never friends! No, the more I think of it, we was never friends. I was never invited to the big house, like Luke Murchison and Stephen Brody and that Rafe Huckstable. I never set foot in the place until I got beat up . . ."

He was becoming angry. She searched around in her mind for something to divert him. "I . . . I don't understand—you say you killed Gilbert Barton, and yet we found him on the road, you and the children and myself, the day I returned to the Valley . . ." But the answer came to her with sickening clarity, even as she spoke.

He had thought he had killed Gilbert Barton. And then, two days later, the spectre of the man he thought he'd murdered had lurched like an avenging ghost up the road towards him. No wonder he had paled, Katherine thought, remembering that she had had to speak his name, so mesmerized was he by the horror before him . . .

And he had sent the children off to fetch help, and sent her back to the wagon for brandy. And when she had come back to him, Gilbert Barton was unconscious—and never opened his eyes again.

For while Amos Murphy was alone with him, in those few seconds when Katherine was searching through supplies in the back of the wagon, he had made sure that Gilbert Barton would not, when his confusion left him, recognize his assailant.

Something shattered within her, the horror was too great even for the fortifications, the emotional bulwarks she had erected about herself over the past twelve months. She rose to her feet suddenly, her hand to her face with a "*No . . . !*" that was a refusal to hear, to see any more, a denial of the terror she was living through.

He caught her before she had stumbled back more than a few steps, and she was knocked sideways with the force of their meeting, down upon her knees, painfully, on the rocky creek bank.

"I got no time to play games!" His breath upon her face, one hand gripping her shoulder, the other in her hair. "Don't you realize, it ain't just the police I've got to worry about? Nancy told me what she'd heard through the other cedar-getters' wives—I was a marked man, because I informed on Charlie to the police—it was only a matter of time before Frank'd want his revenge. He couldn't move before now—too suspicious—but Frank and the others wanted to even the score with the blacks, and when Nancy told me that Frank and the Tallons had packed up and shot through, I knew they were after the blacks—and me—before they were finished with this place."

"They . . . want to kill you?"

"Bloody right, if they can. Now get up—I got no time to waste talking no more. You understand it all now, why we gotta get to Wollongong—even Nowra, and then we might be safe . . ."

Her weight rested on one hand, propping herself upon the rocky surface; holding it behind her, her hand closed around one large stone, held it tightly.

"Very well," she murmured, "we'd better go, before they double back and find you . . ."

"This fire was a dead giveaway, but I done it for you. Let's just hope . . ."

He was right-handed, as she had hoped. He let her go for an instant, and groped with his right hand to take her left, to pull her up, hesitated, remembering that her left arm was broken—and in that instant she came to her feet, leaned forward towards him, using the force of her own weight to drive her arm with the stone held in her fingers, hard into his left temple.

That he cried out was bad, for it meant he was conscious to feel the blow, she thought, as she ran for the creek, lifting her skirts to run as far as she could into the water, then to dive forward, praying he could not swim . . .

He caught her in midstream, the trailing long skirts of her riding costume still floating, providing a handful of cloth for him to grasp, even while he spluttered and gulped, half-drowning, almost out of his depth. She felt herself being drawn back, inexorably back, towards a terror that almost froze her mind and heart with fear. She screamed, though water filled her mouth and choked her—his hard hand, both his hard hands were upon her ankle, around her knee, pulling her back to him, and he held her by the waist, pulling her inwards to him, and she clawed his face, screaming, fighting away from those burning, sunken eyes—screamed and did not stop screaming until the hard hands had closed about her throat and shut off the sound with pain.

Waist-deep in water, head bent backwards, helpless to do anything but tear with breaking nails at the hands that held her neck—she heard his voice, saw his face against the paling sky, the darker trees that bent over them.

"Wanted you ever since I saw you in Wollongong on the day you come home—all lost-looking in your widow's weeds—a real lady. And my Florence passed on only a few months earlier—knew you were the only one to take her place . . ." His voice broke a little, the hands tightened. "But you're as bad as Nancy—all women are the same—liars, cheats . . ." The world was turning red, starred with myriad floating shapes, and only his voice held any reality; it rang in her head like the voices of a chorus of demons, of devils in a pit that seemed to open before her with his words. "She's gone to hell where she belongs, has Nancy—tried to threaten me, tried to blackmail me. And you—you're worse, because I loved you and you betrayed me . . ."

And the water was about her, and it did not matter, for she was floating already . . .

And he let her go. Pulled her up out of the water and let her go, so that her mouth, open and gasping, filled with water that ran down her throat and threatened to finish what his hands had begun . . .

She stumbled, fell, and the water closed about her once more, but she was conscious now, and she fought, held her breath as best she could, and found the rocky bottom of the creek and stood— to hear the final echoes of the shotgun blast, still echoing amongst the hills all about her.

Only then did it make sense, looking about, seeing Amos Murphy being carried away downstream by the current. His sightless eyes seemed to be upon her until his body rolled over in the water to float face down, hiding mercifully, in the dark of the mountain stream, the scarlet stain that covered his entire chest.

Katherine stumbled, fell, half-swam out of the terrifying, polluted stream. She paused on the stony shingle, waiting, without emotion, beyond emotion, for the shot that would kill her. For they had returned, Frank, Walt, Elias . . . she could not see them, but she knew that they were there, deadly but silent now, as the weapons they carried.

She shifted her weight, lost her footing, lurched sideways a little, finding her balance with difficulty for the yards of woollen cloth were saturated and pinned her to the spot by their dragging, leaden weight.

The shot did not come. She teetered forward, fell to her knees and to one hand, and now, in the light of dawn that brightened by the second, she could see the bloodstains on the rocks, her hand touched one dark patch, and there were more, on the stones, on the grass . . . Four . . . five . . . six . . . seven . . . She was crying, her tears fell on the iniquitous stains, and she did not care if the shot came, almost wished that it would come.

But the scrub lay silent, and then a distant magpie warbled, and, closer, some native finches squabbled in a tree. The bush was waking and gathering its courage. The faint, hesitant bird-calls increased, and still Katherine was alive.

She stood and dragged the heavy encumbrance of her skirts to the edge of the scrub, making for a fallen log . . .

A fallen log.

The child lay where he had said it would be found. Mamoa, Tigoora's son, the child she had seen born . . .

His body lay where it had been thrown, and the features were calm, the eyes closed. There was no blood here—but the back of the little head was swollen . . .

She cradled the naked little body in her arms, crouched on the ground, the loneliness of the bush all around her, and wept, the bonds of rigid control breaking at last. She wept tears of grief and helplessness, against the injustice, the ugliness of it all. She wept for Myeela, Tigoora, Timalong and old Gurral, who had foreseen, in his wisdom, the horror that was to come. She wept now for Christopher, as she had never been able to weep for her son, and she wept for Oliver and for Mary Rose.

Tigoora was dead—she knew her friend was dead, for she would never have left her child, were she alive. The cry that Katherine gave, the long, agonized cry of grief that woke a thousand echoes in the cliffs and folds of mountains around her, was the cry that Tigoora could not give for her son; it was a cry for all women, for all times, for all mothers whose children lay dead of a violence born of men's greed. She cried, and the thousand, thousand voices cried with her.

Down, down . . . It was a blessed, warm darkness of forgetfulness. Katherine was lying unconscious against the fallen tree, the child in her arms, when Marcus, Brendan and Tom Lloyd found her, three hours later.

Forty Two

Dovewood in the winter of 1867. Quiet days spent watching the trees shed their leaves, seeing them bend before sleeting storms, through the rain streaming across the glass. And always, reflected in the panes, the gold lamplit warmth of the rooms, the hum of voices, a piano, recitations of Byron and Wordsworth, the gentle comfort of safety that always seemed to embrace her whenever she came to her grandparents' home.

On the cold clear days when the low-hanging winter sun threw its warming rays across the gardens, she went walking with Angela or with Edwin, with the ageing beagle, Cassie, trotting at her heels.

More pleasant yet were the days when Marcus or Brendan would drive Edwina and Suzanna for visits. These were never long visits, and she missed them when they returned to Barrengarry, but she knew why her parents had suggested she stay at Dovewood for some months, and she knew, in her heart, that they were right. She needed this time, the quiet time that, as Angela had said, that until now had been denied her. Though the horror of the autumn was still with her, would, undoubtedly, always be with her, yet she found herself healing, slowly, as the months passed and spring began to wake, equally slowly, in the dark folds of the mountains and the sloping farmlands of the Highlands.

She was seated on the little verandah of the playhouse reading Charles Harpur's *A Poet's Home* early one afternoon in September, when she heard footsteps approaching through the new bright grass. From the orchard, whose gnarled branches and white and pink blossoms she could see through the silver trunks of the birch trees, Brendan came walking towards her. He had not yet seen her, and her heart contracted with something like fright, to realize that they would be alone, here, for the first time in months. Her heart thudded painfully and she looked away, not comprehending the fierce conflicting emotion that ordered her—despite her knowledge of him, the familiarity of the tall figure with the easy walk, his jacket flung over one shoulder—to run, to hide. It was too soon, too soon . . .

But he had seen her, had seen too the confusion on her face. He had stopped walking, was standing fairly close, watching her with a look that could have been love, pity, fond exasperation, or a combination of all three.

"Hello," she said.

"Good afternoon. Your grandmother told me you might be here." He looked at the little building, walked a short way around it on either side. "There's roses growing over the roof out the back," he said.

"Yes," she smiled at him, "they're in bud, aren't they? They'll bloom soon, and last right through the spring into . . . summer."

He had disappeared, but was suddenly at her side, having circumnavigated the playhouse, and in his hand, held out to her, was one of the creamy-gold roses, the first to flower, its petals open, curled, perfect.

"Thank you . . ." Their hands touched as she took the flower, and suddenly he had taken her hand, held it as he seated himself on the verandah beside her.

"An old trick, I'm afraid," he lamented with a smile. "No, don't try to pull free. We've held hands often—we're friends, are we not?"

"Yes . . ."

But they had not held hands since Mary Rose came to them, a year ago.

Katherine tried to relax, not understanding why she should be so disturbed by his nearness, his touch. For suddenly there was a demand, it was as blatant as if he had voiced it, and it had happened too quickly, his appearance and this sudden change in him, so different from the self-contained, withdrawn man of the past seven months, since Mary Rose had died.

"Who has come with you?" she asked cordially, "Mama and Father . . . ?"

"No, I rode here alone today. I wanted . . ."

"And how are things in the Valley? Is everyone well at Barrengarry?"

"Yes," he said patiently. "Your sending your father a hundred pounds from the money you made from the land sale has touched his conscience. He's given the land next to Cummings' place, about ten acres, for the school. Since then, we've all been rattling tin cups all over the Valley—we have the two hundred pounds needed for the building—and they've started work already."

"Already!" She squeezed his hand in her excitement, and then, seeing the light suddenly kindled in the depths of the grey eyes she said confusedly, "That's wonderful . . . and Mary Rose would be so pleased, it was a dream of hers, too, you know . . ."

He did not take his hand from hers, but there was a lessening of pressure and his gaze faltered; it was as if a ghost had passed across his mind—and so it had.

Katherine said gently, "And Mama and Father are well? And Edwina?"

He grinned at the thought of Edwina, for her courtship by Luke Murchison, instead of coming to an end with Teddi deciding to retire to the quiet of Barrengarry, was progressing by leaps and bounds. Luke knew about Rafe, had offered sympathy and understanding as a friend, and the susceptible Edwina had wept upon that broad shoulder all one long afternoon. After that, she was dignified and friendly and glad to see him whenever he called—and he had called more and more frequently.

Brendan said now, "Luke is still mooning about the homestead, and Edwina is still flirting with him, the minx. She dresses each day with the utmost care, and practically waits by the window for the sound of Luke's horse's hoofs on the bridge, whereupon she rushes to seat herself at the piano or in a decorative pose in an armchair, or out in the back garden with a parasol, ready to look up . . ."

"And say, 'Mr Murchison, what a pleasant surprise!' "

"I see you've played these games yourself," his eyes speculative and merry.

"A long time ago. It was wonderful fun, as I remember. And anything else? Have . . . have the Woddi come back?"

The pain passed fleetingly over his face, for she had asked this question each day for months, and no one could give her a positive answer, and they had worried over her, she knew it, and yet she could not have helped herself. Gradually, she had ceased pestering each visitor from the Valley and she knew they, the ones who loved her, had been relieved, had hoped she had begun to forget.

But she had not. She was merely silent.

For how could one forget that the Woddi had fled from the one place that had meant safety for them, that they had left the Valley only to disappear in the rugged mountain country to the south? Was she to forget standing by while the police buried Mamoa? Was she to forget riding home to Barrengarry behind Brendan on his big chestnut, afraid to turn around, for she would have seen the oilskin-wrapped body of Amos Murphy across the saddle of the horse that had carried herself and now bore the murderer and his terrible, ill-gained fortune? Forget the voices of the men—hushed by Brendan—when they spoke of Nancy Halstrop, found dead in Murphy's house early that morning by a visiting Molly? Molly, who had run like a crazed thing to where the troopers and settlers were searching for Katherine and, the link occurring to all of them, telling them as much as she knew—of those hills to the south, amongst which her father used to vanish time and again in previous months. Forget that the Woddi seemed to have vanished, and so had Frank Crolin and Walt and Elias Tallon?

"Katherine . . ." Brendan was holding her and she leaned against his shoulder, felt a weakness that threatened to turn once more to tears, and she had cried enough, surely she had cried enough . . . "I came to see you because I want you to leave with me. I've heard of a ship sailing for America in five days' time—a new steamship, good cabins, very comfortable—James is weaned now, but we can even take some stock, a cow and a goat if we have to. I've asked Molly to come, she's wonderful with the baby, but not possessive, and I think the travel will be good for her. If I call for you tomorrow morning—or would you want to come back to Barrengarry first . . . ?"

"Stop—Brendan. Please, stop!"

She stared at him, unable to comprehend all he was asking of her. "What are you saying? Leave Australia? To go where?"

"Boston, first," he said, smiling patiently, "and I've had a letter from Dublin that tells me that public opinion is divided about these treason trials. The Fenians have more sympathy than even we had hoped for. In a few years—less, perhaps, we'll be able to return to Avonwood."

She did not speak.

"I don't blame you for hesitating," he said ruefully. "But I promise you, my days as a rebel are behind me. I want to farm Avonwood, and watch James grow, and . . . and look up to find you standing beside me." Still she said nothing. Concerned now, "Do you know what I'm asking you, Kate?"

It was difficult to speak. "Yes," she said carefully, "and the answer is no, Brendan. It has to be no."

There was a chattering in the trees above them; three rosellas, scarlet and blue against the new green foliage of the birch trees, hung upside down, turning somersaults in the branches, screeching, gabbling to each other. Katherine looked up at them, cognizant of their beauty, but when her gaze returned to Brendan, it was to see that he had not moved, his eyes had not left her face.

"Tell me why." His voice flat, deadly.

She looked away, shifted a little where she sat, legs curled up beneath her skirts on the dry verandah boards.

He must have thought she was about to rise, for his hand, which had held hers gently, now closed upon her wrist quite hard.

"No—don't go! Look me in the face and tell me why."

"I wasn't going to leave," she said, her tone more heated than she had meant in the chaos of her emotions. She had not been thinking all these months; she had thought he was grieving for Mary Rose, that in his despair and his feelings of culpability he would never reach for her again . . .

And she had never thought clearly of the practicalities if he should. Now he had not simply reached for her, he held her wrists tightly, and leaned towards her with all the threat of the long years of their denial, and she could not gather her wits, knew only one thing, the one thing of which they had never spoken.

"Brendan, I can't leave the Valley."

The words were spoken, but he gazed at her as if he hadn't heard.

"I can't . . . leave . . . the Valley," she repeated. "I came *home*, when I came back from Italy. Despite everything that's happened—and it didn't happen *in* the Valley—the people I care about weren't a part of all . . ."

"It was close enough." His tone was brutal. "For Heaven's sake, Kate—it's one thing to hold land in a place but it's another to give your life for it—Good Lord," he said wonderingly, "I sound English—I sound like an Anglo-Irish landlord . . ."

"Exactly," she hissed. "And you show as little understanding. My people have been in this country for three generations. I belong here.

I tried to give it up in Dublin—you know how I mourned for it. I missed them all—even mad old Mikey Brody who can't see that times have changed and this isn't the outback any longer. I want to stay, to see the school built, and a post office . . . I want to go back and find the Woddi . . . they are there! Somewhere! It's their home, part of their Dreaming. Angel will help me, I've written to her—we're going to try to find them . . ."

"And me? Where do I fit into this?" coolly.

She gazed down into her lap where the rose lay on her closed book. She touched the petals, murmured, "I think it's too soon, Brendan. You must think of Mary Rose . . ."

He let her go, moved away a little, restlessly. "Do you have any idea of what I feel whenever I think of Mary Rose? I married a young girl I was infatuated with—the infatuation lasted a few weeks—and she loved me, despite this. She bore my child, despite this. And now she's dead. At nineteen years old, she's dead, buried thousands of miles from her friends and family, because of my selfishness, and my unrelenting obsession with you!"

She was shaking a little, managed to say, "Then you can see I'm right. Neither of us is ready, Brendan. Mary Rose would always be between us, and I don't want that."

Quietly he asked, "What do you want, Kate?"

She smiled sadly, "You asked me that by the pool near Barrengarry a year ago. Do you remember? I answered 'You' and I still mean it." She looked at him pleadingly.

"I remember." His eyes were cold, unreadable. "You felt safe saying it, because there was Mary Rose between us. Now she's gone, God help me—and still you use the girl."

"Brendan, don't talk like that! I tell you, I'm confused. I hadn't thought you would come to me like this . . ."

"*How long must I wait for you*?" His face was pale, dangerous. "You tell me, Kate—when will the time be right?"

He had walked to the edge of the verandah, stood over her where she sat leaning against the wall of the little building. "In . . . a few months, we could talk about it . . ."

"But you've given your answer. You won't leave Barrengarry."

"I . . ."

"Why do you want the 'few months', Kate? For me to change my mind and stay in Australia?"

He was too close to her, it was too hard to lie to him with him so close that their bodies almost touched. She cursed herself for allowing the warmth, the safety of Dovewood to lull her senses—

the real world was out there, beyond the gates. Even her little sanctuary here, with the ghosts of the three children who had attended her childhood, seemed a clinging to the past, to things immature and nebulous.

She almost reached out to him but changed her mind, said instead, carefully, "You seemed happy at Barrengarry. Everyone in the Valley thinks so highly of you—it isn't often that a stranger is so easily accepted there. I hoped . . . *I didn't consider*, Brendan—but yes, in my very soul I hoped that you'd come to love the place, that we could make our home there. Was that so very foolish? A new life for us, away from Ireland and her troubles . . ." her voice faltered, she looked away from his gaze, for no flicker of understanding or warmth was to be found there.

"You were right," he said readily enough. "I do love it here. The country, the weather—the vitality of the place—you feel all you have to do is throw seed on the soil and you'd have a crop . . . But it takes more than sunshine and good soil to make one feel at home, Kate. I've left responsibilities behind me, and I have to go back."

"Yes, but . . ."

"There can't be any buts. I have to go, and I have to go soon."

She stared at him, then spoke her thoughts as they formed in her mind. "What are you running away from, Brendan? Is it your guilt over Mary Rose's death? You may leave her grave behind, my love, but she'll still be with you, always. Better to make your peace now. Until you do, there can't be any life for us together."

"You're using her as an excuse . . ."

"You're running away from yourself and trying to use *me* . . ."

"If you loved me, Kate, you'd come with me . . ."

"It's because I love you, Brendan, that I have to say no."

And it ended there. He turned on his heel and walked away through the birch trees.

"Brendan!"

She caught up to him in the orchard, amid the unpruned rioting blossoms of the ancient apple trees. "Please wait. Three months— even one month . . ."

He held her tightly, at arms' length from him. "No," he said calmly, studying her face as if he wished to remember it, "I'd thought, with part of my mind, that you'd say no. I think you always would have said no, Kate. First there was Oliver, then Chris, then your desire to run home to Australia, then Mary Rose, now what you see as my unstable emotional state. Never in all these years have you reached for me. Dear God, if you'd told me what you knew of Oliver and Daniel—do you think I'd have let you stay in a house with a man like that? I'd have taken you and Chris to England or America, or back to Australia—Chris would probably be alive *if you'd only been honest with me . . .*"

"Stop it!" She tried to cover her ears.

"You needn't have said you loved me—just trusted me to take you out of that life of deceit and betrayal—Kate, I'd have killed Oliver with my bare hands if I'd known he was coming to you after being with . . ."

"Brendan, please, *please . . . !*"

He realized he had gone too far and stopped, calmed himself before saying, "I'll always care for you, Kate. Always. But something's changed now. You do see, don't you? I'm faced with the knowledge that you never really loved me . . ."

"I did—and I do! You mustn't say that!"

"Perhaps you do. Yes, I have no right to judge you in that— it's just a matter of degree, isn't it? You never loved me enough to change your life for me. You never deviated an inch from what you wanted for yourself . . ."

"You're wrong—oh, you're wrong! I was too proud to admit to you that I'd made mistakes! Too proud to come running to you . . . How can you say you're in love with me if you can leave me so easily to go half a world away?"

"Didn't you do just that? And yes, something's changed. It must. I'll stop loving you—I must! Unless I wish to go mad."

"Brendan, please . . ."

But he did not wait to hear, had let her go, was not looking at her, and she stopped. They stood in silence, for his whole bearing was of one who wished he could move away, was kept there only by good manners and a reluctance to say the final goodbye.

In the end, they did not say goodbye. She knew that all that could be said had been said, and it was she who turned and walked away, slowly, beneath the tangled, gnarled branches that met overhead, loud with bees about the crowns of white blossom. When she paused at the playhouse verandah to pick up the book and the rose, and to look back—he had gone.

"Only look, Katey—it's the *Moss Vale Gazette*—who'd have thought!"

Angela, seated in the parlour with Edwin, stood up and snatched the paper from her husband, ignoring his protests as she riffled through the pages. "Edwin was just reading it to me . . . Dear, I wish you'd you'd have kept the place . . . ! Here it is!" Her face was alight with triumphant mischief.

" 'The engagement is announced of Miss Fleur Ethelreda Barton—*Ethelreda!*—'of Moss Vale, to Mr Rafe Winton Huckstable of Kangaroo Valley and Drummoyne.' "

"Why, how . . ." Katherine was, for the moment, lost for words. "How . . . suitable," she murmured finally.

Edwin snorted delightedly.

Angela plumped down in a chair. "I never thought she'd do it, you know," she sighed. "How unfortunate. With her money and his position, we'll be running into them all the time. And it so tires one, cutting people dead."

"Then don't, Grandmama." Katherine had to laugh.

"Of course we will. Although," she added hopefully, "knowing Fleur, they may spend all their time in Sydney—there are too many people out here in the country to stir unpleasant memories for her. I know I shall remind her. Constantly."

She looked up at Katherine, caught the withdrawn look on her face. "My dear, the news—it surely hasn't truly upset you . . . ?"

"Oh, no, no, Grandmama . . ."

"What's the matter with you, Angela?" Edwin said gruffly from around the stem of his pipe. "*Brendan*, my dear."

"Of course . . ." Angela looked again at Katherine, more consideringly. "That silly announcement put his visit out of my head. Where is he?"

"He . . . didn't call in at the house? Then he's returned to the Valley, I should imagine."

"But he only just got here! I've ordered an extra place for dinner . . . Oh, my dear . . ." Angela had stood, came across to Katherine. "He did propose, didn't he? What happened? Sit down here with me. Tell me."

Katherine laughed ruefully, feeling more and more like a child, allowed herself to be pulled down beside Angela on the settee, and Edwin, all attention even though Angela had dropped his newspaper back in his lap, watched them from his bright and knowing eyes.

"He wanted me to leave with him, in five days' time, for America. I said I wouldn't go."

"Go to America? Why, of course you can't. What's the matter with that boy? After all you've been through, he wants to drag you off to America!" She sobered. "So that's why he rode away without saying goodbye. Most unlike him."

"He received a shock, I expect," Edwin put in. "He didn't consider that Katey'd refuse."

"Yes," Katherine tried to smile, for her grandparents' sake. They were very fond of Brendan. "He seemed to expect me to agree and leave at once."

Edwin and Angela exchanged a look. "Yes . . ." Angela murmured, "this is most unlike him. Yet it was far too soon after poor little Mary Rose . . ." She left the sentence unfinished. "What could the boy have been thinking of? Did you expect this declaration, my dear?"

"No! At least, not now, not so soon . . ."

"Quite right," Edwin pronounced firmly, "the boy's not thinking straight. He's lonely down there in the Valley, and he's missing the sophistication of Dublin and Boston. A good thing if he goes back there for a year or so. Then he can come back to you if he wants to live here, or you can join him in America."

Katherine was laughing, "Grandpapa, you make it sound so simple . . ."

"It is," stated Edwin. "If he loves you, he'll come back, if he doesn't, good riddance!"

"Really, Edwin—have you lost all your romantic sensibilities?" Angela turned to Katherine kindly. "My dear, we wanted to tell you something, in view of all that has happened, and now, according to Suzanna's letters, Edwina is on the point of becoming engaged to Luke Murchison . . . tell her, Edwin."

Edwin cleared his throat, "It's no wonderful thing, just a millstone around your neck probably. But I'm impressed by the way you've handled the sale of your land here in Moss Vale, and the questions you've been demanding of your father have made him take severe stock of his business life. In short, we want you to have all our assets when we go."

"Grandpapa . . . !"

"Dovewood, the stocks and lands, the lot. The Murchison property adjoins Barrengarry, so that's one point in favour of Luke and Edwina staying on in the Valley once they're married. I don't know what Laura will do—she seems, by her letters, to spend all her time at parties and the theatre with her friends. I daresay she'll marry soon, and your father will see her well settled. But you, my dear, should be closer to Sydney than the Valley . . ."

"But I love the Valley, Grandpapa, that's why, when Brendan . . ."

"We've already talked about it. I don't personally think you've seen the last of young Kelehan, but even if you have, he's not the sort of man who could bury himself in the country all the time."

Katherine agreed silently. Brendan had always spent more time in Dublin than at Avonwood. But . . .

"I don't know what to say to you both . . . thank you—and I hope the day you speak of never comes!" She embraced them both, tears of love in her eyes.

"And don't worry about Brendan," Angela said. "He's been singing the praises of this country for a year or more—even if he goes home to Ireland, he'll be back."

Katherine knew she could not let Brendan leave without saying goodbye, and in his present mood it was quite possible that he would forego seeing her again. So it was that the following day, Edwin and Angela accompanied her back to the Valley, their coachman driving them in the solid old brougham. The sky was clear bright blue, and the view of the Valley as they descended, the emerald green of the fields, the toy-like homesteads in their surrounds of dwarfed and blossoming fruit trees, stirred her heart as she gazed down upon them, spread before her.

It was wonderful to cross the bridge and see the house appear around the bend in the drive, the azaleas, pink, white, scarlet, peach-coloured, glowing amongst the garden hedges, to see Bridget run out the door only to disappear again immediately, running up and down the stairs to rouse the old house for a welcoming.

Brendan did not appear until that evening and having stabled his chestnut first, he knew by the gleaming black brougham in the barn that Katherine must be home.

That evening after dinner everyone seemed in high spirits; Suzanna played the piano, Marcus sang two songs by Tom Moore that made Katherine weep openly, Edwina and Angela played a duet on the piano—and even Luke was prevailed upon to growl and mumble his way through a bass aria of Mozart's, to Teddi's accompaniment.

There was no time to speak to Brendan before he announced that he had to be up early and must now retire. He took her hand with all cordiality, like a fond friend, and left; the warm crowded room seemed immediately colder without his presence.

And the next morning he was away early about his duties and Katherine spent the morning with her mother and grandmother and baby James, his joyous crowing laugh and the wide grey eyes reminding her of all she was losing, so soon, before she had come to know him. I was right, she tried to tell herself, yet her heart ached already, with regrets. I was right, not to allow myself to love him . . .

Yet she loved the child, for all that.

The little marble headstone held only the words, *Mary Rose Kelehan*, and the dates of her brief life. Katherine laid the small posy of violets on the green mound and stood for a moment, lost in her thoughts; it was more than a sadness, it was a kind of dark bewilderment that still possessed her.

She felt that she should explain, somehow, to Mary Rose—but surely this was foolishness. Her faith told her that Mary Rose now had a perfect understanding of all that had happened—and, after all, had Katherine and Brendan done anything so very wrong?

I gave him up, she told Mary Rose silently, *I gave him up, though it tore the heart from us both to leave each other. But we found the strength, in our sense of what was right, and because we cared for your happiness. And now you're gone—and we're both lost.*

There was no reply. Mary Rose's turbulent little spirit was at rest. Somewhere, Katherine thought, it cared about all of them, struggling on here, but it gave her no answers, no comfort.

She turned away with one last glance, and went to stand by Joe's grave. She placed a second bouquet there, and remained a moment in prayer for the soul of her vital, reckless young brother. Then she turned away to her horse, closing the crooked little picket gate behind her.

When the black woman stepped out onto the road before her, her heart nearly stopped. But no—this was no ghost. It was Myeela, thinner than Katherine remembered her, her short-cropped curls now grown past her shoulders. A hair belt hung beneath a stomach that swelled with new life and a short, possum-skin coat covered her shoulders, for though the sun shone, a keen wind was blowing from the snow to the south.

Katherine dropped down from the saddle and walked slowly towards her. The dark eyes watched her, impassive.

"Thank God . . . Where were you? Thank God, you're safe!"

Myeela looked nonplussed, concerned at the tears, then submitted with a dawning smile to the embrace that Katherine gave her.

"Myeela, what happened? Did they . . . The tribe . . ." She could not finish. "Tigoora . . ." she managed.

"Tigoora . . . gone."

"And . . . Timalong, your husband . . . ?"

"Him gone." The face carved from onyx, only the eyes carrying the shadow of the terror, the grief.

"I . . . I found Mamoa by the fallen tree. He was buried there."

Myeela, suddenly interested, nodded. Katherine had a feeling that the little body of Mamoa would soon be taken up, hidden away with that of his mother, according to the ways of the Woddi.

"Your children, Myeela . . ."

"One boy left. The rest . . . gone."

Katherine felt helpless, the rage and anguish mounting within her. "The police have been looking for the men who did this. My father has offered big money to know where they've gone. They'll be caught and punished!" And she watched the haunted, unreadable expressions on the face of her childhood friend and wondered if she believed what Katherine herself wanted so desperately to believe.

There was a soft slurring of bare feet through the grass to the side of the road; a boy, about fifteen years old, stepped out. Katherine thought at first, with a rising heart, that it was Banjee—but no. This boy was shorter, thicker set, and he had a scowling, suspicious face. He gazed at Katherine with uneasy curiosity, then glanced at Myeela and gestured for her to come.

He disappeared into the bush, and Myeela turned to follow him.

"Myeela?" Katherine asked. "I've not seen that boy before . . ."

"That one—him my husband now. Timalong gone. I first wife 'longa that one." Her hand came to rest on her stomach. "His child."

"You've been given to a man from another tribe?"

"Him Woddi Woddi—'longa big water—him Gurral's brother's son's . . ." she tried to find the English words and failed, but pointed instead towards Brown's Mountain. "All same sacred place, all same Dreaming."

Katherine understood. The boy was undoubtedly Woddi Woddi, but not of the branch of the tribe that came often to the Valley. The scattered remnants of the tribe had met together, somewhere in the south, and this boy was being trained, by whichever of the elders were left, to be among those who would return to the sacred places, to perform whatever rites must be observed.

And what will happen, she thought despairingly, when there were no longer any old men to train the younger ones, when the young men no longer knew or cared about the old ways? If she asked Myeela this, the answer would be simple. *We lose our Dreaming.* This would mean more than "we lost our traditions"—it would mean "we lose our souls."

She felt cold, and it was more than the wind, chill off the Southern Alps. She watched the black woman walk away through the scrub; she wondered if she would see her again, and prayed that she would.

Myeela seemed to sense her distress for she hesitated a moment, and then she turned back to Katherine. Her head came up and she spoke, sharing a last secret with the white woman who had shared her childhood. It was a terrifying trust, and Katherine held the secret until the day she died.

"Them bad ones," Myeela said, the dark eyes meeting Katherine's with calm defiance, "them that kill Timalong, Tigoora, all belonga me, belonga Woddi Woddi—them bad ones—*they gone.*"

Stephen Brody called to see Katherine that afternoon. Puzzled, she agreed to walk with him in the garden.

He began without preamble, "I owe you such an apology. I've been a fool, Katherine. I've spent a wretched seven months trying to see what can be saved of my life, and I had to come to you for advice."

"Stephen," she smiled. "Such passionate remorse! Of course I accept your apology. But what advice can I possible give you?"

"Tell me . . . You'll laugh at me!" The man did look wretched, blushed a little, the handsome face thinner, more intense than Katherine had ever seen it, except for the unfortunate declaration of several months before. "Tell me if you think I stand a chance of winning Laura back. I wanted to write to her," he went on hurriedly, "months ago—but I'm too ashamed. I wouldn't blame her if she never spoke to me again."

"Neither would I," Katherine murmured mildly, and told the unhappy Stephen how Laura had heard almost every word of their last conversation on the verandah at Barrengarry.

If Stephen was pink before, he was scarlet now. They passed a small garden seat, and he sank down upon it and put his head in his hands. "That's it, then, isn't it? I can never face her again."

"Stephen, you're a fool. At least she knows the problem, and she knows that you tried to save her pain. I don't think your cause is lost, not if you really love Laura." She sat down on the other end of the seat and watched him.

He lifted his face hopefully, and doubt, elation, and doubt once more, all raced across his features in quick succession. "I . . . I'd give anything to believe that! I've had so long to think, you see—and standing up there in Berrima courthouse, pleading guilty to withholding evidence . . . I know I was very lucky to get off with just a warning—Granddad and I were both very fortunate—but the whole seamy incident made me question my life, where I was going. In the days before the trial and afterwards, I used to lie awake thinking how Laura would have been able to calm my fears—sometimes without saying a word—just her presence used to make me feel braver, more at peace with myself . . .

"And I thought back to all those years when I longed for you, and strolled about all the time with Laura, never considering how important a part of my life she was. I'd be thinking, 'If only I was with Katherine', 'What a perfect day this would be if I were only with Katherine'—and to look back on those days now, is to see they were perfect, just as they were. All the years of my happiness, Katherine—all wasted because I was too blind to see the truth. You were right, you see—everything you said was right. Can you ever forgive me? Can *she*?"

Katherine was silent for a moment, thinking hard, then, "Do you have relatives in Sydney, Stephen?"

"Yes. In Strathfield and Balmain and Elizabeth Bay . . ."

"Balmain will do nicely. If the farm can spare you, go to Sydney. For a month or more, if need be. Ask to see Laura at our Balmain house, tell her all you've told me."

"She won't believe me! She won't forgive me—not like that."

"Not at first. I should be very cross with her if she did. But with flowers and persistence and humour and self-castigation and a firm proposal of marriage and a promise to cherish her forever—*provided you mean it*—then Laura could, in six months, or a week, be persuaded to capitulate, I think.

"No, Stephen, don't kiss my hand. I'm sending you off to months of agonized waiting and plotting and more waiting. But I'm relying on one important factor—for I believe that Laura still loves you, very much."

That night after dinner, just as she was about to ask to speak to him alone, Brendan announced quietly to the family that he would be leaving early the following morning.

The room was silent for a long moment. They had expected this, but from the glances that came around to Katherine, briefly, puzzled, there had been a possibility in each of their minds that this journey would not happen.

But Molly was packed and ready, had been for days; and James's belongings, like Brendan's, were neatly folded into trunks and valises, ready for the long sea voyage.

Katherine smiled sadly, as all the family did; but she was the only one who did not join almost in unison to ask that he postpone his leavetaking, that he stay with them.

What had she expected of this trip to Barrengarry? she thought, lying awake in her bed that night. And the answer was there before her already. *He should have changed his mind. I've come home, and it's made no difference. Seeing me again, here in the place we both love, has made no difference. I might just as well have stayed at Dovewood.*

And could the reason that kept them apart really be so simple? That they were two people who could not agree to live on the same side of the world?

No, there was something more. She wanted his love as she had once had his love and been unable to grasp for it. It had been offered then wholly, utterly her own. Now, he carried the ghost of Mary Rose in his heart, and he could not be wholly hers again, they could not face the future together with the shadow of his imagined guilt between them. *If he could hear Mary Rose's name without wincing,* she thought, *I'd . . . I'd even follow him to County Wicklow. We'd raise a thundering brood of little boys . . .*

And they'd grow up, and in another twenty or thirty years they'll be plotting patriotic insurrections in Dublin's dark little bars, and laying down their lives before English guns . . . No. NO.

Here was where the future lay for both of them. Why couldn't he see that one cannot go back, that the past cannot be recaptured, that nothing about Dublin and Irish politics would ever be the same, when the best, the bravest, were confined in prison cells in Fremantle? But Brendan could not see. His grief for Mary Rose blinded him. It would take time for him to realize that he would be happier in this new country where he had already made a place for himself. It would take time for his grief and his guilt to fade and leave him free. And time was the one thing he would not allow her.

She would not, could not, clutch at him, have him under just any circumstances. They had had more than that, even in Dublin; a mutual respect, each knowing that the other was in command of his or her own life. Now Brendan was not; he was running blindly, as blindly as she had run home to Barrengarry, and while she felt for him, she could not save him.

Falling asleep just after dawn, she awoke late to find a strangely silent house. She dressed hurriedly and raced to the kitchen, startling Peggy, and was relieved to find that good woman walking about with baby James, crooning to him, patting him on the back.

"Gone? Of course he hasn't gone, Miss Katey. But there's a big 'do' on over where they're building the new schoolhouse, don't you remember? Mr Brendan insisted everyone went, as planned, they all said their goodbyes to him earlier. He's in his office if you want to say goodbye."

And even the normally circumspect Peggy was caught out, just as Katherine turned away, in giving her a look of regret—and, yes, of pity.

She knocked on the office door.

"Come in!"

This is the last time, she realized. The last time I shall enter this room and find him here . . .

He was standing by his desk sorting out papers, when she entered and shut the door behind her. He looked up at her and paused, the papers in his hand. No smile. He had not forgiven her. Only the naked love and pain were on his face, betraying him even at the last.

"I don't . . . want it to end badly between us. I mean . . ." swiftly, cursing her choice of words. "I don't want you to go away thinking regretfully of all that's happened. My feelings haven't changed, Brendan. I want more than anything for you to stay, and . . ."

He smiled gently and she stopped, waited, praying that he understood.

"My feelings haven't changed either," he said, and sighed and looked about the office. "I don't want this goodbye to be an unhappy one—but I've too many years with you at the centre of my life to leave you without pain. I'm sorry if it shows. I shouldn't have come to Australia, to Kangaroo Valley—I came with unreasonable expectations. I suppose . . . I've always had unreasonable expectations—about everything. And life caught up with me here."

"Life catches up with us wherever we are."

"That's my Kate," he laughed, "and you're right, of course."

"Brendan . . ."

"I still find it strange, though, to think of us now, as we are. So diametrically opposed." His gaze was sombre. "I never thought I'd see that . . ."

"We're not diametrically opposed." She felt stung to reply, but looked at him, caught the steady gaze from the grey eyes, and conceded, "Yes. Yes, I suppose we are. But it's not my fault."

"Nor mine."

"I only want you to wait . . ."

"My darling, I've waited too long. Far too long."

And she had no answer for him. She looked away, found the settee and seated herself slowly. He was right. He had waited far too long. And that *was* her fault . . .

"Perhaps it's just as well." His smile was strained, it pulled at the corners of his mouth, creased the tanned cheeks, almost against his will. "Perhaps there's something dangerous, something not quite of this world about love such as I had for you. God is right, sometimes, in not indulging people in their whims."

"Is that all I was to you? A whim?"

"You know you weren't." And there was pain in the grey eyes that had seen too much pain. He turned away a little, and she realized the victory in seeing the effect of her words was no victory at all, for he was withdrawing from that hurt, withdrawing from her.

She did not know how to beg. That was the trouble. This was the time to plead, to promise, to *touch*.

What prevented her? What kept her on the polished perfection of the brocade settee, while he—he stood over by the desk, still picking up papers, letters, and studying them, discarding them or packing them neatly.

He had a great deal of paperwork already in the depths of the bag. Amazing, she thought bemusedly, how much he had accumulated in one short year. There, with the slim, leather-bound journals and personal receipts, would be almost a day-to-day record of his life in the Valley. And the account books; they would be staying. She would be able to look at them, in months, years hence, and see how he had organized Barrengarry, the lives of all of them . . .

Click.

He had shut the bag, and Katherine almost started. So soon? He was ready so soon? Brendan was turned from her, emptying his rejected papers into the capacious wastepaper basket. She stared almost hungrily at his back, felt her hands clench with the overwhelming feeling of helplessness.

What could she say, what could she say?

She seemed numb, to be thinking of inconsequential details, unable to gather her wits for the most important task—the words to make him stay, the words to make him take her in his arms . . .

Carl knocked at the door and entered on Brendan's bidding. Katherine found herself watching the old man almost with hatred, stared at his mouth forming words that told of the carriage being ready and waiting at the door, that young Master James and Molly were already seated, the luggage strapped down. But when he turned to go, she was willing him to come back, to prolong the moment, any moment, between now and . . .

Brendan sighed, picked up the bag. He gazed at her. "Will you come to say goodbye at the carriage, Kate?"

And she murmured, "Of course," through stiff lips, stood, and led the way out the door.

She was conscious of every step she took in her soft, blue leather shoes, of the way her petticoats rustled the weight of her crinolette, and the heavy drapes of skirt that swung as she walked, a march of dignity that had little in common with the lurching pace of her heart.

She could hear his footsteps behind her; the last walk they would make together. It would be thirty paces perhaps, no more—and then she would pause, and he would draw level and pause also, and with a few fond gallantries, he would leave her forever. Thirty paces . . . less, now, in which she could turn and *know* she would see him there, would look into his face, her eyes meeting his. He was there, close behind her, watching her, no doubt as he had, now she thought about it, all these years.

Twenty paces . . . Ten . . .

There was the door, the verandah, the steps; there was Peggy, sniffling into her handkerchief; and in the carriage, Molly, dwarfed in her smart black coat and bonnet, the chubby bundle of soft white wool in her arms the invisible and sleeping James.

Here was Carl, holding the carriage door, dressed in his best suit, touching his hat to her . . .

The wind was icy against her cheeks; she was cold without her shawl, and she shivered slightly. This, an unconscious gesture of her frailty, made Brendan cross the boundary between his fondness and his decision to distance himself from her. For his arms were about her suddenly, holding her tightly, his head bent to lay his cheek upon her hair.

"Goodbye, Kate."

She barely heard the words. And when he let her go it was to turn immediately and run lightly down the steps towards the waiting carriage.

Molly was smiling through tears as she called goodbye, waving with one freckled hand, above the little burden of the child in her lap. Peggy was calling farewell and good luck from where she stood on the gravelled path.

Brendan's eyes met Katherine's as the carriage turned. He lifted one hand, almost stiffly, in farewell, and it was then, gazing into his eyes as the distance between them increased, that Katherine realized that whatever his reasons for leaving he had not, as he had claimed, ceased loving her. It was written there on his face, in his eyes, that he loved her and would never cease loving her.

The carriage had gone, she had heard the wheels fade into the sounds of a bush morning, and Peggy was saying, solicitously, "Are you all right, Miss Katey?" And only then did she realize that she had not once lifted her hand, had not spoken one word of farewell.

Thirty-three paces it had been; she counted them on her way back to the silent office, counted them for something to do with the seconds, minutes, that seemed to stretch before her, time that had no right to *be*, as if all her life, all the world, had ceased with his leaving.

She stood still in the centre of the office. It would soon become a parlour again. How many weeks, or even days, before the household ceased saying, "Brendan's office"? The room was at once empty, silent, and yet still throbbed with his words, his presence.

She moved, still with that careful, measured tread, over to the settee and seated herself exactly as she had been, a few minutes before. She fixed her gaze upon the carpet just a few feet before her, as she had while he was there, and it was as if, not lifting her eyes, she could believe he stood there still, between herself and the window, sifting through papers, rustling through the past, keeping the important, the valued—and for the rest . . .

There were carriage wheels crossing the little bridge.

She froze, listening, straining her ears to hear any further sound— and yes, the drumming of horses' hoofs, the clatter and whirr of carriage wheels, coming closer . . .

It could not be him. He would not come back.

But she could not move, wanted to run to the window, fling the casements open, or rush to the door, run those thirty-three steps— and at the end of them . . . But the horses and carriage were still— he was here. The heavy front door burst open and his footsteps . . .

No.

She knew now. Knew that brisk, heavy, purposeful tread even before the door to the office was swung wide.

She could not look up. There was an indefinable ache in her chest— a heaviness and yet an emptiness that could not be called physical pain, and yet robbed her of any volition to speak, to move.

After a moment's pause, the door was closed and the footsteps, barely audible in the deep pile of the carpet, moved towards the desk.

She felt a resentment growing within her. It was better to be alone; she desperately wanted to stay here, to absorb what remained of the atmosphere of those last moments.

Now, if she raised her eyes, her father would be standing silhouetted against the window. He was waiting, she could sense it, and the power of his personality was such that, even still as he was, her beloved ghosts were withdrawing, fading. So, finally, she was able to look up. And she sighed. There was only her father and herself, in a very ordinary room.

"I passed the carriage. Molly was so excited it's a wonder she hasn't squashed that baby. Brendan . . ." Her father leaned back against the desk and studied the ceiling, "Brendan looked as ill a man as ever I've seen."

She found her voice. "The sea voyage will do him good. And I think he'll be happier, once he's back in Ireland."

"Do you think so? I doubt it, somehow. He's closer to his Irish friends being here—most of them are in gaol in Fremantle—and you're here. There's not much of his old life left to him, he'll discover."

"Avonwood . . ."

"Ah, yes, of course—the old family home. Hasn't lived in it for . . . how many years—six? But I daresay he'll get used to it. A year or so in a quiet, damp environment is probably what he needs right now."

She wished he would go away. The stirrings of fragile hope that came with Marcus's mocking words only hurt her more.

"Get your coat, Katey—I want you to come back to the school with me."

She considered arguing with him, telling him she would prefer to be alone. But she sensed already that he would tolerate no excuses; he understood too well how she felt, what she was doing, and to him it was self-indulgence.

And perhaps he was right. Without another word she rose and walked once more into the hall. Marcus helped her on with her cloak. Out in the drive, Tobias was holding the horses' reins; Katherine descended the steps accompanied by her father, tying her bonnet strings with fumbling, numb fingers as she did so.

They drove without speaking, along the bush tracks, and although Marcus smiled and waved to folk who called to them, Katherine rode in withdrawn silence, feeling, still, the same ache within her, a paralysis that made her feel as if she would break, simply shatter, if she moved, spoke suddenly.

And yet the thought came to her, of its own volition, *I will survive this*.

For she had thought her life had ended when Oliver died, and again, when Christopher was taken from her. But she survived.

And I'll survive this, she thought. I'll build something here for myself—for Mama—and even for Father, though he'll die before he admits that I'm of any use to him. I'll help him organize the school and raise the money for the church . . .

Her eyes found the high escarpment to the south and she thought of the Woddi Woddi, scattered, making their way as best they could in a world that was demonstrating heartlessly, and even viciously, that there was no place for the old ways, the timeless traditions and strong sense of place that lay at the very heart of the people.

But they must come back, Katherine thought. Father will find them, and I'll help him; we'll do all we can to convince them to return. For they belonged here and she feared for them, set apart from the sacred places, torn from the soil that gave them strength and purpose.

She could not speak for the world and its injustices, but she could devote her life to seeing that here, at least, people could live together in peace.

It was an outsized dream, perhaps too big for her. But if she started . . . if she achieved only a little . . .

A sudden clamour of human voices startled the bush, a flurry of magpies, bronze-wings and lorikeets from the trees above them made Katherine look up, realize with something of a start how far they had come.

There, to their right as they approached, was the schoolhouse clearing—and a building stood within it. Only the skeleton—one could see through the framework to the bush, recoiled and brooding, on the other side of the few acres. But there were four walls, and one could see an inner partition or two—a cloakroom for small, wet boots and coats, and, at the other end, a cubicle of office space. Katherine smiled, gazing up at the men, still laughing, whooping, and the crowd below who, seeing the last rafter hammered into place, were giving three cheers . . .

And it was then that those on the roof saw the buggy coming, and one of them—it might have been Jim O'Mara, bellowed, "Three cheers for Mister Prescott!"

Through the laughter and the roar of voices cheering, Katherine smiled at neighbours and friends who gathered around the buggy and the high-stepping matched bays. Here was Edwina with Luke and his sisters, Mikey Brody with his sons and their wives and children; Bridget Murray, Jemmy Crowe and Will O'Mahony, the Cummings girls and their parents, Doctor Lang and at least two priests or ministers; all the O'Mara children, Rupert and Martha Huckstable with Emilia, and Angel and Emile Regnier, their children dancing about them. And at a distance, together and not quite a part of the settlers' group, Essie Crolin, Mrs Mosley and Mrs Green. All had brought their children, there were children everywhere, excited by the contagious good spirits of the adults, though yet uncomprehending of the great change that was manifest in the little building taking shape before them.

Katherine saw, beyond the crowd, the tables set in the shade of the trees, caught, on the breeze, above the fresh tang of the raw timber, the smell of roasting pork. Suzanna was there, and Angela, and Edwin . . .

The men were climbing down from the skeletal rooftop; a milestone had been reached, somehow, with the roof timbers being set in place. The men went to join their families, to eat and drink and probably celebrate for the rest of the day. Tomorrow they would set to work again.

Marcus had reined in the horses, and Katherine found she had been gazing upwards at the roof and that her father, also, had not moved from his seat in the buggy.

She did not know what she was expecting, something like her own thoughts, perhaps, but she had never heard Marcus speak in this manner before. It was as if he looked at himself, at all of them gathered here, and felt a kind of bitterness, though his eyes did not stray from the schoolhouse and he spoke so softly that Katherine wondered, indeed, if he even meant for her to hear: "To be a pioneer in this country is to share a kind of glory and a kind of shame," her father said. "For to build all we have built, we've also destroyed much. That's one sin we have to bear. The other, and it would be a worse one, would be to forget it."

Katherine said, "I won't."

He looked at her. "I know you won't, Katey," gently. "I wasn't addressing you. I suppose I was waxing poetical, addressing all those growing minds that will be passing through this schoolhouse and a thousand like it, generations of children who'll accept what the history books say, and never think to look beyond them. It's not often that a man has a feeling of his place in space and time," Marcus smiled. "I did, just then, and it went to my head."

Most of their friends had now moved off towards the tables, but Marcus remained still in the driver's seat, his gaze once more on the raw timbers of the little roof.

"I was thinking of someone else, too, who won't forget—though he'd like to." His sharp glance caught the intensity of interest in her face, though she looked away, scowling, immediately.

"Father . . ." she began.

"No, don't interrupt me. Don't tell me you don't want to hear, for it wouldn't be the truth. While I'm in a reflective mood, I'll give you my reflections on this matter.

"He'll be back," Marcus said. "When he's forgiven you, when he's forgiven himself. When the grey boredom of his days begin to make him remember this place, and the summers . . . When he's looked long enough into that misty northern twilight, and realized nothing new is before him. He won't miss all this for a while, mind you—he needs to heal, and Ireland is a good place for that."

He looked at her, a gentle, considering look, before turning back to address the pointed timbers, his eyes squinting beneath the brim of his hat. "No, he'll be back. I've seen many men pining away for their homelands in Europe—most of those who return come back in a year or so. And they were men who never fell under Australia's spell, as he did. He'll miss the sun, the depth and height of the sky, the colours, the space. He'll miss the challenge, and the pain— this country *costs*, and he's a man who needs to pit himself against the odds."

Once more he turned to her, this time almost coolly. "And he'll miss you. You cost, too—you're part of the pain. But he's a man of habit, and he's loved you for too long to stop now. When he stops hating you, the love will still be there. I may be wrong . . ." he scowled.

She linked her arm through his. "No, I think you're right," she said.

He almost laughed. "I believe that's the only time in your life you've ever agreed with my judgement."

"It's a very good subject with which to begin," she smiled. "You must deliver the same judgement whenever I begin mooning about Barrengarry in the following months."

"I'll deliver more than that if you think you're going to indulge yourself by languishing away," he threatened, as he lifted her down from the carriage.

But there would be little chance of that. As they saw Suzanna, near the tables, waving to them, and they walked towards her, Katherine's heart was already singing a kind of litany. Her father's logic had told her only what she already knew. He would be back.

THE END